Tales of Enchantment
and Disenchantment
A History of Faerie

Tales of Enchantment
and Disenchantment
A History of Faerie
with an exemplary anthology of tales

by
Brian Stableford

A Black Coat Press Book

Visit our website at www.blackcoatpress.com

ISBN 978-1-61227-838-4. First Printing. March 2019. Published by Black Coat Press, an imprint of Hollywood Comics.com, LLC, P.O. Box 17270, Encino, CA 91416.
Printed in the United States of America.

TABLE OF CONTENTS

Brian Stableford: A HISTORY OF FAERIE

Introduction

Writing a history of the literary genre of *contes de fées* [tales of fays] is not easy, for several reasons. There are problems involved in defining the field, complicated by problems of translation arising from the frequent habit of translating *fées* into English as "fairies," and acute problems in tracking the development of the genre from its invention through its initial development and its various metamorphoses. Almost all of its key works were originally published anonymously, and some of the attributions made by bibliographers remain dubious to various degrees. Most problematic of all, after a brief period when a few such stories were able to obtain the royal privileges required for licit publication in pre-Revolutionary France—the years 1697 and 1698, with a slight overlap to either side—such licenses became exceedingly hard to obtain, to the extent that the genre was effectively situated outside the law, not only requiring texts to be published anonymously, but compelling many authors to conceal their authorship rigorously, and never to declare in print what they might have known about the authorship of other works in the genre, at least until the authors in question were dead.

Because of those circumstances, much of the history of *contes de fées* went unrecorded at the time; many of the key actions determining that peculiar pattern of publication were covert, and can only be the subject of inference and speculation. That void of information was colonized, over time, by a number of myths and misunderstandings, further blurring the picture. By 1734, when the first attempt was made to compile a tentative bibliography of the genre, many of the data were already uncertain and mysterious. When Charles-Joseph Mayer attempted to compile a definitive collection of generic items in 1786, *Le Cabinet des fées, ou Collection choisie des contes des fées et autres contes merveilleux* [The Showcase of Fays: A Select Collection of Tales of Fays and Other Marvelous Tales]—without the benefit of a royal privilege—which initially ran to thirty-seven volumes, subsequently expanded to forty-one as newly-recovered material was added, he found the task of locating copies of many of the relevant materials, and identifying their authors, exceedingly difficult.

Without Mayer's heroic preservative endeavors it would now be impracticable for anyone to attempt to piece together the jigsaw of generic items sufficiently to glimpse the narrative linking them, but even with his invaluable aid the task would have been enormous, had anyone wanted to attempt it after the 1789 Revolution. In fact, no one did. The extirpation of the genre attempted by the royal censors in the eighteenth century was only partially successful, because a number of writers were still interested in producing *contes de fées*, and were prepared to publish them even at the risk of prosecution and punishment, also defying the naked contempt of many commentators who thought the genre inherently worthless, at best fit for children; what the censors failed to achieve, however, negligence eventually accomplished. As soon as *fées* became legal they became so scarce in contemporary French fiction that they almost disappeared for a century, and when they made a tentative comeback, they were no longer the same, having been comprehensively severed from their roots.

By the time anyone thought it worthwhile to attempt to produce a scholarly account of *contes de fées*, the task was impossible in practical terms. In 1883 Adolphe de Lescure published a book not unlike this one, *Le Monde enchanté, précédé d'une histoire des fées et de la littérature féerique en France* [The Enchanted World, preceded by a History of Fays and the Literature of Faerie in France], in which he tried to define exactly what the word *fée* meant before its appropriation in the 1690s by writers of *contes de fées* and how that usage changes its meaning, and then to offer a critical commentary on the work of those early writers, illustrated by an exemplary anthology. By that time, howeverer the history in question had been so thoroughly mythologized that Lescure was looking at it through an extremely murky lens; the second part of his account is very thin, and highly questionable in its assessments. In all probability, no one else could have done any better at the time, however, because the labor involved in getting access to the original materials, gathering them, reading them, collating and comparing them would have been far too difficult, even with a set of the 1786 *Cabinet des fées* to hand and access to a library that allowed some of the supplementary references listed in the bibliographical supplement in volume 37 of the collection to be followed up.

That situation did not change throughout the twentieth century, but it was dramatically transformed in the early twenty-first by the advent of *gallica*, the Bibliothèque Nationale website, which began posting scans of all the primary material that was still recoverable, making it available for simultaneous consultation and comparison. That facilitated a sudden increase in academic interest in *contes de fées* and paved the way for an increase in the quality of commentary. Much of the interest manifest so far, inevitably, has focused on individual authors, that being an understandable and necessary characteristic of academic endeavor, which always tends toward greater specialization. However, the enormous treasure-trove of data opened by *gallica* also makes it feasible—to the extent that it ever will be feasible—to form a broad overview of the origin and evolution of the genre, and that is what the present essay attempts to do.

The narrative that the exercise in question attempts to recover is a strange one, and includes numerous puzzles that are beyond the scope of solution, but that only serves to make it more fascinating. Fifty years ago it would have been regarded as a matter of little relevance to contemporary literature, from which the legacy of *contes de fées* had been virtually eliminated, its produce either fossilized or only preserved in a drastically distorted form. Since the 1970s, however, there has been a spectacular increase in the production and popularity of a kind of generic "fantasy" that has revivified many of the imaginative materials previously recycled in *contes de fées*, and which can be compared and contrasted with that genre in several interesting ways. *Contes de fées* and modern generic fantasy can now be seen as two key links in a strand of imaginative literature that extends forwards from Classical literature and Medieval Romance all the way to a significant sector of contemporary literary production, and its extensions into visual media, connected not merely by the complex transference of imagery but by the underlying psychology of composition and consumption.

In order to understand modern generic fantasy fully, it is necessary to understand its roots in previous literary genres, and one of the most important of those previous genres is that of *contes de fées*; it is also the most widely and deeply misunderstood of those previous genres. There are, of course, many people today, as there were at the end of the seventeenth century, who would consider that understanding essentially worthless, because they consider that kind of fiction inherently despicable. *Plus ça change, plus c'est la même chose*, as Alphonse Karr—a dabbler in fantastic fiction himself—once remarked. That contempt is itself a problematic part of the history, a kind of intellectual allergy that invites more accurate analysis, however impracticable it might be to offer such a diagnosis with any degree of confidence. However, the task attempted in these pages is one that can now be attempted, for the first time, and it is surely sufficiently interesting to be worth attempting. The present essay can only be a preliminary sketch, but it is a start.

When Charles-Joseph Mayer set out to collate the genre, ninety years after its inception and brief heyday, he already found it confused, and felt compelled to add the appendix *et autres contest merveilleux* [other marvelous tales] to his title. The other tales that he thought it necessary to include, because their history was entangled with that of *contes de fees* by 1786, were oriental fantasies of a kind pioneered by the spectacular success of Antoine Galland's *Les Mille et une nuits* [The Thousand and One Nights], usually known in English as *The Arabian Nights*, which appeared in twelve volumes between 1704 and 1717. That new genre seemed to many readers and commentators to be filling a partial void left by the virtual suppression of *contes de fées*, providing an alternative lexicon of fantastic motifs. Some of those new motifs were appropriated by the writers of the "contraband renaissance" of *contes de fées* published without the benefit of royal licenses, which began to gather momentum in the 1730s, functioning either as an alternative to the fictional milieu of *contes de fées*, or something that could be hybridized with it.

Although Mayer's move was entirely understandable and justifiable, the present essay will not conflate the two genres, and will only interest itself in Gallandesque fantasy insofar as material therefrom filtered into later *contes de fées*. For the purposes of the present investigation, *contes de fées* will be defined simply as tales that contain *fées*, which I translate as "fays" because the word "fairies," previously employed as a translation, already had a considerable literary history in England in 1697, which routinely referred to imaginary entities quite different from French *fées*, in spite of a certain amount of overlap. That overlap did permit a filtration of imagery into the French genre, which eventually led, if not to an authentic fusion, at least to a considerable confusion, but in a slow fashion that is of sufficient interest not to be skipped or excessively blurred.

That confusion became pernicious because, when early English translators of works by Marie-Catherine Le Jumel de Barneville, Baronne d'Aulnoy (1651-1705) and Charles Perrault (1628-1703) translated the word *fées* as "fairies" and *contes de fées* as "fairy tales" they imported a whole set of conceptual prejudices into the notion of the genre as it was perceived in the English-speaking world. Fairy poetry was a thriving genre in England in the Elizabethan and Stuart eras, in which "fairies" were generally conceived as supernatural beings akin to such mischievous spirits as Irish leprechauns, Scottish brownies, Cornish pixies and the English Robin Goodfellow, or Puck.

English literary fairies were subjected to innovative transformations and given a particular *gravitas* by William Shakespeare in *A Midsummer Night's Dream* (c.1595) and Edmund Spenser, in *The Faerie Queene* (1590-96), although the kind of fairies featured in the former play have nothing in common with the land of Faerie featured in the latter epic poem, thus adding a substantial measure of obfuscation to the terminology. Fairies of the kinds featured in most Elizabethan lyric poetry and drama are based on images derived from popular folklore, although that imagery were drastically transformed when they were adapted for literary purposes, even prior to Shakespeare's modifications. *The Faerie Queene*, by contrast, takes its imagery from chivalric Romance, most directly from Ariosto's *Orlando Furioso* (1516-32), an elaborate Italian pastiche of French romances featuring knights associated with the court of Charlemagne. It is heavy with allegory and also with flattery, the eponymous figurehead being a manifest transfiguration of Queen Elizabeth.

The paradox has frequently been pointed out that although Spenser's epic is set in Faerie [the Land of Enchantment], fairies do not actually figure therein; indeed, the fairies of folklore and lyric poetry would have been radically out of place there. The poem was, however, translated into French in 1590-96 as *La Reine des fées*, and that would have been one of the employments of the word *fées* most familiar to French writers a century later. That importation was peripherally relevant to the conceptualization of *contes de fées* by the writers who defined and shaped that genre in the 1690s, not simply because of its conceptualization of a land of Faerie and its linkage of that notion with the fictional milieu of French Medieval romance, but also, and more especially, because the central obsession of Spenser's epic is the conceptualization and illustration of the idea of Virtue, which is also one of the central obsessions of French *contes de fées*.

Lescure, in the introduction to *Le Monde enchanté*, makes scrupulous attempts to clarify what was by then a direly confused history of usages of the word *fée,* already clouded by various misunderstandings and scholarly fantasies. He identifies its ultimate origins in the Latin *fata* [fate] and points out more recent usages in the Breton language, where it had entered folklore with reference to supernatural beings akin to nature spirits, but he identifies the particular adaptation employed by the writers of the 1690s quite differently and distinctively, as a derivative of Medieval romance, specifically Arthurian romance. He offers a crucial characterization taken from a romance that he titles *Lancelot du Lac*, part of a sequence of thirteenth- and fourteenth-century romances nowadays known as the Vulgate or Lancelot/Graal Cycle:

"All women are called fays who know enchantments and charms, and who know the power of certain words, and the virtue of stones and herbs; it is the fays who give wealth, beauty and youth."

It is in Arthurian romance that the two key models of *fées* as they were imagined by the female writers of the 1690s can be found, the more important being an enchantress who crops up in numerous romances with a name rendered variously as Mourgue, Morgue and Morgaine. She plays a significant and central role in the fourteenth-century romance *Ogier le Danois* (tr. as *Ogier the Dane*), where she is called Mourgue la Faye. Her name was eventually standardized in English by Thomas Malory's *Le Morte d'Arthur* (1485)—one of the crucial paradigms of English prose printed by William Caxton—as Morgan le Fay, thus helping to license my preferred translation of *fée* as "fay." The other important Arthurian model for the *fées* of the 1690s is the enchanter Merlin's protégée, seductress and ultimate captor, Viviane, marginalized by Malory—who called her Nimue—but considered more important and iconic by aficionados of the French romances.

In the works of the writers who initiated the French genre of *contes de fées*, therefore, fays are human enchantresses rather than supernatural beings, and certainly not mischievous spirits like Shakespeare's Puck or Ariel—but the matter is not entirely clear-cut, partly because the characters in Arthurian romance had implicit prehistories of their own that gave them a certain ambiguity, which the writers of romance felt free to vary as much as they liked. The character of Mourgue/Morgan is very variable; she is often a human *magicienne* routinely credited with a blood relationship to Arthur, but she also features in some romances as "the lady of the lake" and the ruler of the magical land of Avalon (a role transferred to Nimue by Malory); her name is derived from Breton and Welsh folklore, in which a *morgen* is a kind of water-spirit closely allied with

Greek sirens. On the other hand, Viviane is identified in some romances as a daughter of the Roman goddess Diana, thus being akin to the nymphs of Graeco-Roman mythology.

The latter connection is maintained in the metaphysical context into which the salon writers fitted their fays, where there is almost no trace of the Judeao-Christian God or religion, but where Amour is ever-present and various other entities from the Graeco-Roman pantheon, including nymphs and Zephyr, are routinely present, often supplemented by the four classes of "elemental spirits" described in *Liber de nymphis, sylphis, pygmaes et salamandris, et de caeteris spiritibus* (1566, falsely attributed to Paracelsus): undines, sylphs, gnomes and salamanders. That supernatural schema had been recently popularized in Parisian literary culture by the anonymous *Comte de Gabalis* (1670), a supposed guide-book to the magical invocation of spirits, probably written by one of Louis XIV's courtiers as a satire of occult science, but taken seriously by many of its readers. In many *contes de fées*, elemental sprits, nymphs and sirens are represented as subsidiary entities at the beck and call of human enchantresses, but the distinction is not always absolute, and, like Mourgue la Faye, the fays of the French tales often have a hint of the supernatural about their identity as well as their science.

Similarly, the word *faerie*, although it is usually employed in *contes de fées* as common noun meaning "enchantment," is also used in a Spenserian sense, as a proper noun, sometimes only with reference to the polity of the fays, but sometimes also with reference to the land where they live. The location of the fictitious world in which *contes de fées* are set was infected by ambiguities from the outset. *Contes de fées* are replete with references to "the time of the fays," implying that the stories are displaced from the reader's world temporally, set in Europe, but in a remote past that has some analogies with the world in which Medieval romances are typically set, roughly equivalent to a period between the fifth century A.D. and the ninth, albeit with many anachronisms, but that temporal location came to seem increasingly problematic as the genre evolved, and many stories offered "solutions" to the problems in question, the inevitable net effect of which was further confusion. Although the standard practice in the *contes de fées* was to feature fays living in the lands ruled by human kings and queens—albeit in magically-constructed palaces, often sighted in locations remote from cities—there are also numerous stories in which a distinct land of the fays is problematically situated, sometimes tacitly or explicitly removed into a magical "parallel world," inaccessible without magical permission.

Given that these kinds of confusions and ambiguities were inherent from the outset in what the original inventors of *contes de fées* wanted to do, it is hardly surprising that more ambiguities and embellishments proliferated as soon as other writers began to adapt *contes de fées* to their own literary agendas, especially as those other writers were often familiar with the English tradition of fairy literature as well as that of French Medieval romance.

While such ambiguities might seem pernicious to a scrupulous rationalist, in literature, unlike logic, ambiguity can be a good and useful thing, inherent in such narrative strategies as allegory and symbolism, and such genres as parable and fable. *Contes de fées* participate in all of those things simultaneously, and their apparent simplicity—in philosophical as well as narrative terms—is inherently ambiguous itself, being a deliberately paradoxical kind of complexity. The world of Faerie, however it is conceptualized, is a world in which one cannot say axiomatically, with Aristotle, that "A is A" and "A is not B", or, with Gertrude Stein, that "a rose is a rose is a rose," because the roses in *contes de fées* are generally so replete with overt and covert symbolism that beyond appearances they are anything but roses, and A is not only often not really A, but is ever-ready to metamorphose into B.

In the final story included in the exemplary anthology appended to this history, penned by Anatole France in the early years of the twentieth century, the author, a historian of ideas as well as a litterateur, attempted to produce a kind of requiem for *contes de fées*, and in passing he offered a list of the famous fays of literary mythology who had, he proposed in a tongue-in-cheek fashion, provided imagistic foundation-stones for the genre:

"There were still fays in those times, and those who were titled came to court. Seven of them were asked to be godmothers: Queen Titania; Queen Mab; the sage Viviane, educated by Merlin in the art of enchantments; Melusine, whose story Jean d'Arras wrote and who became a snake every Saturday—but the baptism was held on a Sunday; Urgèle; the white Anna de Bretagne; and Mourgue, who brought Ogier the Dane into the land of Avalon.

Of the seven, Mourgue and Viviane have already been identified as crucial, and Mab and Titania are borrowed from the English tradition, the former widely dispersed in fairy poetry and the latter made famous by Shakespeare. Urgèle was a recent addition, familiar in Anatole France's day via the oft-revived comic opera *La Fée Urgèle* (1765), with music by Egidio Duni and a libretto by Charles-Simon Favart, although the fay in question had been mentioned in passing a year earlier in Voltaire's narrative poem "Ce qui plait aux dames" and was also cited in the nineteenth century by Honoré de Balzac. The reference to Anna de Bretagne is enigmatic, but probably refers to a legendary apparition of a white-clad lady in the Breton village of Ker-Anna, which is usually associated with the legend of Saint Anne. Melusine, however, was by far the most significant addition to the register of the seventeenth-century *fées*, in which she was incorporated, albeit anomalously, from the very outset, and where she became the most influential individual inclusion, her story being recycled several times over, and contributing a highly significant motif to the characterization of fays in general.

The notion that *contes de fées* are based on popular folklore is a drastic distortion; they are entirely based on literary models; although those literary models did occasionally draw upon folkloristic notions and motifs, they usually did so remotely, and with enormous transfigurations. The bare bones of the story of Melusine, greatly elaborated in Jean d'Arras' *Roman de Melusine* (1393), had been drawn from a collection of tales allegedly originating from the oral culture of spinners—stories told to one another by women working with distaffs and spindles, or with spinning-wheels. That particular circumstance probably assisted the technological apparatus of spinning to assume a curious iconic significance in *contes de fées* and representations of *contes de fées*, and their more general representation as "old wives' tales" reflects that association.

Insofar as "tales" are contained and transmitted in oral culture they tend, of necessity, to be brief anecdotes relatable in a matter of minutes. If such tales are converted into written narratives, however, they necessarily undergo dramatic transfigurations of length, complexity and coherence. Literary tales cannot be straightforward representations of folktales, but they can, with an admirable paradoxicality, give rise to new folklore by feeding their partial substance back into oral culture. That is what happened to a few of the seventeenth-century *contes de fées*; whether or not they had been based on previous folkloristic imagery, they certainly gave rise to some, although they were generally subjected to a further transfiguration in so doing.

One of the most striking examples of the creation of new folklore by a *conte de fées* can be seen in the anthology appended to this history in Charles Perrault's "La Belle au bois dormant," usually known in English as "The Sleeping Beauty." Everyone is familiar nowadays with the popularized version of the story, although many people might be surprised by how little the familiar version resembles Perrault's text. Modern recycled versions only salvage the first half of the story, and they routinely transform it by introducing motifs—most significantly the kiss with which the prince is often alleged to wake the sleeper—that are not in Perrault's story.

Something similar had already happened with the legend of Melusine before she was added to the cast of exemplary fées. Basically, it is the story of a knight who marries a beautiful woman on condition that he will never attempt to see her while she is bathing; inevitably, he peeks, and sees that the lower part of her body has been transformed into a serpentine form; having violated the taboo he loses her forever. The story already existed in numerous versions before the invention of *contes de fées*, and one of the most elaborate, François Nodot's *Histoire de Melusine, Princesse de Lusignan*, was published in 1698, while the vogue for *contes de fées* was at its brief height, although it is not usually considered to belong to the genre, being regarded as a straightforward reformulation of the *Roman de Melusine*.

The importance of the recruitment of Melusine to the Faerie of the late seventeenth-century writers is that it not only lent impetus to an inherently supernatural variety of fay, but imported into the standard mythology of *contes de fées* the notion that fays are periodically required to turn into snakes—or, more generally, into some kind of animal. Although she was not usually labeled as a *fée* prior to the seventeenth century, once that label was applied, Melusine became and remained the most famous fay of all, in spite of the fact that she did not fit the archetype of the fay described in the definition quoted above by Lescure.

In fact, the importance of the idea of metamorphosis within *contes de fées* extends far beyond the specific kind of metamorphosis sometimes required of fays by analogy with Melusine. The imaginary milieu in which *contes de fées* are typically set hybridizes the fictitious world of French Medieval romance with that of Graeco-Roman mythology, and one text that was far more important than any other in defining and shaping the Graeco-Roman element of that fusion was Ovid's *Metamorphoses*, the favorite Classical text of the *éminence grise* of the female salon writers of the seventeenth century, Mademoiselle de Scudéry, and hence of many of her followers.

In Ovid's poem, various episodes in the supposed history of the world from its creation to the present day are linked by the theme of metamorphosis, often inflicted violently on a victim by a god, for reasons associated with amorous pursuit or vengeance. Metamorphosis became an important theme in *contes de fées* in a similar context, as a standard aspect of the repertoire of faerie, and it became increasingly important as the genre developed rapidly in the late 1690s, central to the "climactic" tales written by Madame d'Aulnoy and the Comtesse de Murat before the progress of the genre was abruptly cut off. Melusine's importance within the genre is thus archetypal as well as anomalous, however paradoxical that might seem.

The notion of what was or could be meant by the term "*fées*" in the phrase "*contes de fées*" is, therefore, complicated in various interesting, if confusing, ways. By comparison, the interpretation of the term *conte* [tale] might seem much simpler, but that matter too is not unproblematic. At its simplest, the word *conte* refers to a short work of fiction modeled on an oral narration, but the writers who featured *fées* in their work were unclear from the outset as to whether that was the most appropriate label for what they were doing, and some of them struggled conscientiously with the matter of terminology: the question of what ought to distinguish a *conte* from a *nouvelle* or an *histoire*. The substance of the dispute is remarkably difficult to translate into English, where the relevant terminological confusions do not mirror the French ones precisely.

The principal popularizer of the term *conte de fées*, because she used it as a title (we no longer know exactly when, for reasons that will be detailed shortly) was Madame d'Aulnoy, and it was because of translations of her work, as well as Charles Perrault's, that the term "fairy tales" was popularized in English. Many of her *contes* were, however, initially designed for presentation to the public within frame narratives, in which they are represented as stories told by characters in the frame-story, and those characters do not refer to the stories as "*contes*." Instead, they usually refer to them as "*romances*"—a word that was then used in French almost exclusively in a musical content, to refer to what in English would be called "ballads." With reference to printed texts, the word *roman* had already become commonplace, but although its meaning had become very blurred, it was normally used to refer to long texts, and in seeking an alternative, Madame d'Aulnoy was attempting to find an intermediate term for stories that were longer than *contes* but shorter than *romans*—a problem that afflicted English terminology too, eventually responsible for such neologisms as "novelette" and "novella." D'Aulnoy was not the only writer to make such an attempt; Mademoiselle L'Héritier had already debated the question, toying with such improvised terms as "*historiette*," which similarly failed to catch on.

Because of the enormous and enduring popularity of his work, the popular notion of what a *contes de fées* ought to look like was largely established by Perrault, and he has often been represented by literary historians—including Alphonse de Lescure—as the originator of the genre, whom the other writers involved were merely copying, but that is a gross distortion, which will be explored further in due course. One of its effects, however, has been that it has partially concealed the fact that Perrault's work differs very sharply from that done by the actual inventors of the term and designers of the genre. Perrault's *contes* are, indeed, short, designed for reading in a single session from beginning to end, within a timespan of less than half an hour—approximately 3,000-4,000 words at the longest. Very few of the tales written by the female inventors of the genre fit that pattern; only a handful of them are shorter than 8,000 words, and the more ambitious ones extend further than 20,000 words. When they were read aloud in salons, therefore, they must have been presented as "serials" read in installments—and, indeed, consideration of their narrative construction endorses the supposition that they were written in sections, made up as the authors went along, probably with the aid of ongoing critical input from their immediate audience.

In the 1690s, the standard length of a printer's volume was between 30,000 and 40,000 words, and "novels" of that approximate length were still being produced in France long afterwards, although it was a standard tactic of the seventeenth and eighteenth centuries to extend works over four, seven or even ten volumes, sometimes over a number of years, so that they were initially offered to the public as serials. No one active during the first wave of *contes de fées* produced works of that sort, even filling a single volume, but they were coming close before the ax fell, and the last work of the first wave to receive a belated royal privilege—*Florine*, in 1713—was a single-volume work, albeit a rather short one. When the genre was revived in the 1730s, however several single-volume works appeared in rapid succession, still routinely described as *contes* even though that appellation stretched the definition of that term to absurd limits, some of the key works exceeding 30,000 words in length.

Such terminological arguments might seem to be mere quibbles, but the use and preservation of the term *conte* cast a long misleading shadow over the genre in France, and even more so over its English equivalent, which has blurred recognition of the fact that the typical and dominant forms of the genre were what English-language terminology would nowadays be more likely to call "novelettes" or "novellas," while short stories were a rare exception, not confined entirely to the work of Perrault, but nevertheless peripheral to its core and its greatest literary achievements. The exemplary anthology hopefully illustrates that, in spite of the fact that the nature of the exercise compels a certain prejudice in favor of shorter works and requires the virtual exclusion of the longest ones.

The Culture of Literary Salons

It is impossible to obtain a proper understanding of the origin and development of *contes de fées* without an understanding of the cultural environment in which they were born and nurtured, and the particular influence on the development of French literary salons of Mademoiselle de Scudéry.

Madeleine de Scudéry (1607-1701) was orphaned at the age of six and was raised, along with her brother Georges, by her uncle, a clergyman. She and her brother settled permanently in Paris in 1640, having already become members of the *salon* [in the sense of a periodic social gathering] that was hosted at the Hôtel de Rambouillet by Catherine de Vivonne, Marquise de Rambouillet (1588-1665) from 1608 until her death. The Hôtel de Rambouillet was a significant place of rendezvous for members of the French court, and it hosted all kinds of social events, but it was the literary salon invented and initially guided by the Marquise—anagrammatically nicknamed "the incomparable Arthénice"—and dominated by its female members that made it notorious even in its own day. It was the cradle of a primitive feminism that was transferred to Scudéry's own salon, launched in 1652, which became the heart of the movement in question for nearly half a century, formally inherited toward the end of her life by her friend and protégée, Marie-Jeanne L'Héritier de Villandon (1664-1734)

The literary and feminist aspirations of the movement were parodied by Molière, initially in the brief farce "Les Précieuses ridicules" [The Ridiculous Affected Women] (1659)—as a result of which the most prominent salon members became commonly known as the *précieuses*—and more elaborately in the five-act comedy, "Les Femmes savantes" [The Savant Women] (1672). The subject-matter of the 1659 farce is the supposed effect on its young female protagonists of reading the works of Mademoiselle de Scudéry, who was then by far and away the most popular writer in France, although her works were initially published under her brother's name. The books that obtained the unprecedented popularity in question are no longer read, partly because of their enormous length; they reached their peak of achievement and celebrity in the prodigious ten-volume *Artamène, ou le Grand Cyrus* [Artamenes; or, Cyrus the Great] (1649-1653) and the ten-volume *Clélie, histoire romaine* [Clélie; a Story of the Roman Empire] (1654-1660). The latter endeavors were, in effect, potentially-interminable serials, ancestral in their narrative techniques and concerns to modern TV soap operas, and their intense concern with the psychology and morality of their characters helped to give birth to the modern novel.

The primary subject matter of Scudéry's serial novels is her idea of Virtue, especially as manifest within the context of an idealized version of Amour, and although she did not invent that idealization, which had long had prolific literary representation in lyric poetry, she certainly provided it with a new narrative context, a new rhetorical strategy and a new analytical depth, in what she labeled, by analogy with Medieval romances, *romans*. There is a direct line of descent from the mythology of virtuous amour promoted in Scudéry's works to the mythology of amour still central to what are now known in English-language culture as "genre romances": formularized love stories extolling passion within a context of exclusivity and fidelity.

The success of Scudéry's works was very important in terms of the literary marketplace of her era; indeed, it was a crucial factor in the subsequent reorientation of that marketplace toward prose fiction, and the consequent changes in its financial reorganization that occurred over the next three centuries. Although seventeenth-century printers did occasionally pay authors for the privilege of printing and selling their works, it was still far more common for authors to have to pay printers, or to persuade patrons to pay on their behalf, for the distinction of publication. Whether Madeleine or Georges de Scudéry made any money out of the voluminous sales of her works it is difficult to tell, but the printers certainly made lots of it, and probably more than they had ever made out of printing poetry, plays or works of philosophy, in spite of the prestige attached to the latter genres. In a just world, that success might have raised the prestige of prose fiction to equal that of poetry, but no one can be in the least surprised by the fact that did not happen in the 1650s, because we are still living amid the residue of the backlash of contempt that not only inspired Molière but thousands of other hostile assaults.

In the context of her salon, Mademoiselle de Scudéry routinely referred to herself as "Sapho" (the French spelling of Sappho), an appellation derived—with explicit acknowledgement—from an account of the poet contained in Ovid's *Métamorphoses*; exactly what she meant to imply by it is not entirely clear, because she only wrote about herself in decorously masked terms, nor can we be sure exactly what inference her contemporaries took from it, but many of them presumably supposed, rightly or wrongly, that it referred to her sexuality as well as her poetic talents. The vast majority of those who took that inference, however, could not have had any idea whether, or how, that sexuality might have been translated in terms of practice, and the person who was in the best position to know, her principal protégée—Mademoiselle de L'Héritier, who similarly never married—never gave any explicit indication.

That self-appellation is probably not irrelevant to the fact that Mademoiselle de Scudéry's concept of virtue sees heterosexual intercourse as an aspect of marital duty, not as something to be sought for pleasure, and something to be avoided at all costs outside the limits of marriage. The particular idealization of amour developed by Scudéry and embraced wholeheartedly by Mademoiselle de L'Héritier put an immense emphasis on the cult of virginity. That conceptualization of amorous virtue remained central to the genre of *contes de fées*, although it was not unquestioned therein even at the outset. A conscientious veil was, however, drawn over certain gray areas in the definition of virginity, as it usually was in life, as well as literature, at the time.

In addition to her fiction and her poetry, Scudéry was a prolific writer of non-fiction, a great deal of which was devoted to the art of conversation, and the application of classical analyses of rhetoric and eloquence to contemporary oral and written discourse. She not only inherited from the incomparable Arthénice the idea that the principal focal point of female salon conversation and the principal endeavor of female intelligence should be literature, but she attempted to dictate how that conversation and endeavor should be organized and conducted; she made her salon into a literary workshop, in which she sought to define what the works produced by its members ought to be attempting to contrive, and she strove to establish tacit and explicit rules for their discussion and evaluation. As with the modern literary mythology of "romance," a direct line of descent connects Scudéry's endeavors with modern writing workshops, and she played a crucial role in the development of countless cauldrons of subsequent literary inspiration.

The importance of the latter point, in respect of the invention and development of *contes de fées* in Parisian literary salons is that the process was entirely conscious, strategically contrived in the context of a particular literary theory. Mademoiselle de L'Héritier's "Les Enchantements de l'éloquence, ou Les Effets de la douceur" (tr. as "The Enchantments of Eloquence; or, The Effects of Mildness"), which gives every appearance of being the source text of two of Charles Perrault's most famous stories, "Cendrillon" (tr. as "Cinderella") and "Les Fées" (tr. as "Diamonds and Toads"), attempts, among other things to illustrate and develop an argument about the essential moral purpose of fiction and the rhetorical role that ought to be played in fulfilling that purpose by "eloquence." That story was probably one of the earliest exemplars of a *conte de fées* to be produced; it was certainly consciously intended to be, and actually became, a highly significant exemplar for the salon writers who invented and defined the genre.

The Invention of Contes de Fées

There is no way to know exactly when, where and by whom the writing of *contes* de fées was initiated, but some clues can be gleaned from two works of fiction published in the relevant period.

In a historical novel by Madame d'Aulnoy set in Tudor England, *Histoire d'Hypolite, comte de Duglas* [The Story of Hippolyte, Earl of Douglas] (1690), one of the characters relates an allegorical *conte*, "L'Île de felicité" [The Isle of Felicity]. The tale is set against the fictitious backcloth of Classical mythology, but its narrator says by way of introduction that it is a "*conte approchant ceux de fées*" [a tale similar to those of fays]. Whether or not that implies that the notion of *contes de fées* had already been introduced to Parisian literary salons as early as 1690 is perhaps open to question, but it does demonstrate that the idea of a *conte de fées* was already present in d'Aulnoy's mind at that time.

Whenever the idea was first promoted more generally, it was almost certainly introduced into a salon as a kind of calculated exercise or game, like one briefly described in a historical novelette set in mid-sixteenth century Spain, *Inès de Cordoue, nouvelle espagnole* (1697; tr. as "Ines de Cordova") by Catherine Bernard (1662-1712). At the beginning of the novelette, the young queen of Spain, Elisabeth de France, while entertaining her lady companions and friends in her apartment, as she does on a regular basis, proposes a storytelling contest. The passage in question is often cited as a representation of the way in which *contes de fées* must have been invented:

"She proposed, in order to create a new amusement for herself, making up gallant tales. The order was received with pleasure by all the ladies who composed the little court; rules were agreed for those sorts of stories, of which the two principal ones were that the adventures should always counter plausibility and the sentiments should always be natural. It was judged that the charm of the tales should only consist of making visible what was happening in the heart, and that there should also be a kind of merit in the marvelous imaginations, which would not be retained by the appearances of verity."

It seems highly probable that some such suggestion must have been made in one of the literary salons in Paris, most likely by Mademoiselle de L'Héritier, who had certainly become an ardent propagandist for the writing of *contes de fees* before 1696, as evidenced by a letters she published in that year, undated but perhaps dating back several years. It is known that in the early 1690s Baronne d'Aulnoy and Catherine Bernard were both members of a literary salon hosted by Anne-Thérèse de Marguenat de Courcelles, Marquise de Lambert (1647-1733), along with the poet Antoinette Deshoulières (1638-1694). The same group were probably regulars at d'Aulnoy's own salon, and that of Made-

21

moiselle de Scudéry and Mademoiselle de L'Héritier. The most prestigious participant in the salons in question appears to have been Marie-Anne de Bourbon, the dowager Princesse de Conti (1666-1739) who attended them in the company of her frequent companion, Charlotte-Rose Caumont de La Force (1654-1724), and subsequently with the latter's cousin, Henriette-Julie de Castelnau, Comtesse de Murat (1668-1716). That group of *femmes savantes* constituted the core of the coterie who initiated the writing of *contes de fées*.

The salons in question were also attended by men, including the tutor to the young Duc de Bourgogne, François Fénelon, Charles Perrault, and perhaps Perrault's friend, Jean de La Fontaine (1621-1695), the author of classic fables in verse derived from ancient sources—Aesop and Bidpai—elegantly and wittily rendered into French verse. Deshoulières and La Fontaine both died before any *contes de fées* reached publication, and Scudéry was very old by then, but their various influences are nevertheless manifest in the genre, in different ways. Perrault's work shows the influence of La Fontaine very markedly, and he probably thought of his own work as following in La Fontaine's footsteps rather than participating in a game that, because it was devised and played by women, he probably felt obliged to regard with studiously patronizing contempt—which did not prevent him plundering its materials wholesale.

Although the dowager Princesse de Conti is not known to have made any published contribution to the genre, she was a highly significant member of the group, and must have been the person who introduced the coterie, along with the game, to the Palace of Versailles. She was the oldest princess of the blood—i.e., legitimated daughter of Louis XIV—and had been married to her cousin, Louis-Armand de Bourbon, Prince de Conti (1661-1685), at the age of thirteen. Widowed at the age of nineteen, she continued to reside at the court, where she was known as the dowager princess because her late husband's heir, his brother François-Louis de Bourbon (1664-1709), married another cousin, Marie-Thérèse de Bourbon (1666-1732). The dowager princess never remarried, apparently turning down several royal proposals, and never had any children; she was enormously influential at Versailles—she was said to be the king's favorite daughter—and her court-within-a-court, of which La Force and Murat were key members, undoubtedly had a huge influence on the fashionability that *contes de fées* seem to have obtained, albeit briefly, within the court.

The importance of Catherine Bernard's representation of a story-telling game in *Inès de Cordoue* is not restricted to the suggested "rules" for the writing of such stories—the idea that they ought to focus on "making visible what was happening in the heart" and the specification that they must contain "marvelous imaginations"—although those certainly became and remained essential aspects of the genre. Also significant is the notion that there was an element of competition in their composition: a competition whose fallout, in her novella, ruins several lives, although we can only speculate as to whether she might have seen something similar brewing in the salons in which she took part.

Some of the writers who dabbled in the genre would surely have said, if anyone had asked, that they were not competing with anyone, but merely dabbling in the genre for amusement, and the pleasure of taking part, but even if they meant it, the fact remains that they were operating within a competitive framework of sorts, constantly comparing their own works with those of others. Some such competition certainly existed in the minds of the writers who joined in the game most ardently, and that element of competition was vital to the rapid evolution and proliferation of the genre.

As this account of its origins makes clear, the genre of *contes de fées* began as a game played by aristocrats, and that is what it remained even during the bulk of the Contraband Renaissance of the mid eighteenth-century, but it is worth observing that there was already another genre of publishing that recycled material from Medieval romances, admittedly in a much more slavish manner, and which had undoubtedly helped to familiarize the raw material on which *contes de fées* drew in the wider audience to which they were introduced by general publication. At the beginning of the seventeenth century a series of cheap pamphlets, known as the *bibliothèque bleue* because they were bound in blue paper covers, was launched in Troyes by Jean and Nicolas Oudot, aimed at poorer readers. Its contents were very various, but it included abridged versions of numerous Medieval romances, those originally written in verse being rendered into prose.

The series continued throughout the seventeenth century and the greater part of eighteenth, and the medium eventually began to reprint *contes de fées*; a few of the original works of the mid-seventeenth century—notably Mademoiselle de Lubert's—were issued in a very similar format. The *bibliothèque bleue* and its analogues probably played a significant role in popularizing *contes de fées* in France in the eighteenth century, but *ipso facto*, they also played a part in enabling the contemptuous attitude to them that became commonplace at the end of that century. The Oudot family retained control of the original line until 1760, but competition was provided by a rival family, the Garniers, one of whose members—Charles Garnier—acquired some significance with regard to the history of *contes de fées* at the end of the eighteenth century when he attempted to move his operation upmarket, popularizing the works of the Comte de Caylus and reprinting other notable works, as will be seen in due course.

The Initial Publication of Contes de Fées

If the salon writers really did start the game of composing *contes de fées* as early as 1690, the stock of such tales had several years to build up before possibilities for publication were suddenly opened wide by the immense success in 1697 of Charles Perrault's *Histoires et contes du temps passé*, better known as *Contes de ma mere l'oye* (often known in translation as *Tales of Mother Goose*). The latter was originally its subtitle but became its title in the reprint editions that followed post-haste—to the authorship of which Perrault rapidly owned up, having initially tried to pass off the first edition, quasi-apologetically, as the work of his youngest son. Mademoiselle de L'Héritier and Catherine Bernard had both inserted *contes de fées* into longer works before the publication of Perrault's volume, but once the success of Perrault's collection became spectacular, the printers of Paris had an obvious incentive to obtain privileges to publish the similar works, of which a considerable treasure-trove was by then awaiting their attention.

That change of fortune was dramatic; it seems highly probably that *contes de fées* had previously been produced with little expectation of publication, although Mademoiselle de L'Héritier had included her two paradigm examples "Les Enchantements de l'éloquence" and "L'Adroite princesse, ou les Aventures de Finette" (tr. as "The Clever Princess; or, The Adventures of Finette") in a 1696 collection of *Oeuvres meslées* [Miscellaneous Works], along with poems, historical fiction, essays and letters. Catherine Bernard had also embedded two *contes* in *Inès de Cordoue*, "Le Prince Rosier" (tr. as "The Rose-Bush Prince") and "Riquet à la houppe" (tr. as "Riquet with the Crest"), although the latter does not actually feature *fées*, the titular character and agent of metamorphoses being the King of the Gnomes.

Charles Perrault had previously produced three items in verse that are relevant to the history of *contes de fées*—although only one actually features *fées*—assembled in a small volume in 1695 before being reprinted in the final version of *Histoires ou contes du temps passé*, which was expanded after its first appearance in subsequent editions. The most substantial of the poems, described as a "*nouvelle en vers*" is "La Marquise de Salusses, ou la Patience de Griselidis" (1691 in the *Mercure Galant*; subsequently retitled "Griselidis"; tr. as "Patient Griseldis"), the others being "Les Souhaits ridicules" (1693; tr. as "The Ridiculous Wishes") and "Peau d'Ane" (tr. as "Donkey-Skin").

One of the prose items in the collection, "La Belle au bois dormant" had also appeared previously in the *Mercure Galant*, in 1696. Seven further prose items were added to 1697 editions, in two stages: "Petit chaperon rouge" (tr. as "Little Red Riding Hood"), "La Barbe-bleue" (tr. as "Bluebeard"), "Le Maistre chat, ou Le Chat botté" (tr. as "Puss-in-Boots"), "Les Fées," "Cendrillon, ou La Petite pantoufle de verre," "Riquet à la houppe" (tr. as "Ricky with the Tuft") and "Le Petit poucet" (tr. as "Hop o'my Thumb").

Four of Perrault's eight prose stories—"Petit chaperon rouge," "La Barbe-Bleue," "Le Maistre chat" and "Le Petit poucet"—make no mention at all of *fées* (the word *fée* is only employed in "La Barbe-Bleue" as an adjective meaning "enchanted," not with reference to a person) and only one of the *contes* in verse, "Peau d'Ane," employs *fées*—the granter of the ridiculous wishes is Jupiter. The expanded *Histoires ou contes du temps passé* is not, therefore, a collection of *contes de fées*, strictly defined, but merely a collection of *contes*, in which approximately half the items include *fées*. Even in "Cendrillon" the word is not explicitly applied to the heroine's helpful godmother, although the inference that she must be a *fée* is very tempting. Perhaps ironically, Perrault's version of "Riquet à la houppe," although clearly based on Catherine Bernard's, introduces *fées* into a story that originally had none, and also changes its ending and inverts its moral.

In shaping his stories, each equipped with a moral in verse—and sometimes more than one—Perrault appears to have had La Fontaine's models very much in mind, and his other published works include numerous brief animal fables. He seems to have considered tales produced in salons as raw material ripe for casual plunder, in much the same way that La Fontaine had appropriated the substance of his fables from Aesop and Bidpai.

Because we have no information as to the order in which the tales told in salons were composed, it is impossible to prove that Perrault appropriated material from the members of the female coterie rather than *vice versa*, but the assumption made by many later commentators that the female writers were copying him has no basis other than unthinking sexism. Alphonse de Lescure's apparent conviction that Perrault was a great literary genius, while the female writers were mediocre practitioners who added unnecessary and undesirable complication to imitations of his work, is utterly absurd; as a writer of prose, Perrault is frankly mediocre, and he cannot hold a candle to Mademoiselle de La Force, let alone to Madame d'Aulnoy and the Comtesse de Murat, the principal power-houses of the genre. The truth is that Perrault routinely produced crude, stripped-down versions of stories that are much better in what were presumably the original versions. The fact that "La Belle au bois dormant" and "Cendrillon" gave rise to items of modern folklore does not detract from the fact that their models are considerably finer literary achievements, and merely reflects the circumstance that Perrault was taking a considerable step in the direction of their vulgarization.

No one could see it at the time, or for some time afterwards, but it is clearly visible now that Madame d'Aulnoy's story "Finette Cendron" is a conscious derivative of both of Mademoiselle de L'Héritier's stories, probably produced in a spirit of competitive elaboration, and that it not only helped to provide the raw material of "Cendrillon" but also of "Le Petit poucet." The opening sequence of "La Belle au bois dormant," in which an evil fay gatecrashes an endowment party and sabotages the benevolence of a group of good fays, closely resembles a scene in d'Aulnoy's "Serpentin vert" (tr. as "Green Worm"), and might have been appropriated therefrom, although there is no way to prove that d'Aulnoy's stories had been read aloud within Perrault's hearing long before they achieved publication. The anthropophagous ogres who feature in the forgotten half of "La Belle au bois dormant" as well as "Le Petit poucet" feature in other early tales by Madame d'Aulnoy as well as in "Finette Cendron."

Whatever debt Perrault might have owed to the female salon writers, however, might be considered to have been repaid in kind by the opportunity that the success of his book opened for other writers of *contes de fées* to get into print. His volume was rapidly followed up late in 1697 and in 1698 by a number of others, including *Les Contes de Contes* [Tales of Tales] signed Mademoiselle de ***, subsequently identified as the work of Mademoiselle de La Force, which contained eight stories; *Contes de fées, dédiez à Son Altesse Sérénissime Madame la Princesse Douairière de Conty, par Mad. la Comtesse de M**** [Tales of Fays dedicated to Her Serene Highness the Dowager Princesse de Conti by the Comtesse de M***] and *Les Nouveaux contes des fées par Madame de M*** [New Tales of Fays by Madame de M**], subsequently identified as the work of the Comtesse de Murat, and each containing three stories; *Contes moins contes que les autres* [Tales less Tale-like than the Others], subsequently identified as the work of Jean de Préchac, containing two stories; and *Les Illustres fées, contes gallants dédiés aux dames* [The Illustrious Fays, Gallant Tales dedicated to the Ladies], belatedly attributed, perhaps unreliably, to the Chevalier de Mailly, containing eleven stories.

That list might be incomplete, and by far the most significant omission therefrom is one of the great mysteries of the boom in the production and publication of *contes de fées*: the original publication of the works of Baronne d'Aulnoy. Countless reference books state that those works were originally published in 1697-98, but none can specify by whom or in what format. The Bibliothèque Nationale does not have copies of any editions of her work published in those years, nor does any other library whose holdings are listed at WorldCat.org. All the accounts of Madame d'Aulnoy's work contained in reference books appear to have been reconstructed by inference from reprints produced after 1717, when Estienne Roger reproduced all the works that d'Aulnoy is now known to have produced in volumes 3-6 of his illicitly produced *Cabinet des Fées*, which were eventually crammed into volumes 2-4 of Charles-Joseph Mayer's similarly illicit 1786 *Cabinet des Fées*. The early English translations of Madame d'Aulnoy's work were definitely made from Roger's *Cabinet*.

Each of Roger's four volumes appears to have combined two volumes of original editions that were probably planned, and perhaps issued, as two pairs, a singleton and a three-volume work entitled *Le Nouveau bourgeois gentilhomme, or fées à la mode* (tr. as "The New Bourgeois Gentleman"; the subtitle translates as "Fashionable Fays"]. In the *Cabinet* versions the second couplet is separately titled *Les Contes de fées*, but no individual titles are attached to the first couplet or the singleton. That title has therefore been speculatively attributed to the first four elements of the assembly, while the rest are sometimes listed as *Nouveaux contes de fées* or as *Fées à la mode*. That is a highly unusual and rather puzzling blur of information, about the possible reasons for which we can only speculate.

The first bibliographer who attempted to compile a definitive list of *contes de fées* was Nicolas Lenglet Du Fresnoy (1674-1755), in the second volume of *De l'usage des romans, où l'on fait voir leur utilité et leur differents caractères, avec une bibliothèque des romans* [On the Usage of Romances, which shows their utility and their different characteristics, with a Library of Romances], illicitly published in 1734, allegedly in Amsterdam, with the by-line "M. le C. Gordon de Percel." In the section on Madame d'Aulnoy, the bibliography records eight relevant volumes under the collective title of *Les Contes de fées*, dated 1698, but there does not appear to be any previous presently-recoverable record of any such volumes.

Lenglet Du Fresnoy also records an edition of Madame d'Aulnoy's *contes de fées* that he dates 1708, allegedly published in Amsterdam, which certainly does exist, although other references suggest that the two-volume edition published in that year by Pierre Mortier only features the contents of the first five hypothetical 1698 volumes, the remainder following in 1711 in a two-volume version of *Le Nouveau bourgeois gentilhomme*.

It might be relevant that Lenglet Du Fresnoy cannot be complimented for his general accuracy in regard to Madame d'Aulnoy; he mistakenly attributes *Histories sublime et allegoriques* (1699; actually by the Comtesse de Murat) and *Les Chevaliers errans* (1710; actual author unknown) to her as well, illustrating the difficulties in determining authorship that existed at that time, and were to continue thereafter. It is not impossible that his sparse listing of a 1698 eight-volume edition of her works is as speculative as some of his attributions, and that he had simply inferred their existence from inspection of the Roger's *Cabinet*. If some such edition did exist, however, it must have been published without the benefit of a royal privilege, in sufficiently small quantities to have disappeared completely before reaching any library capable of preserving copies. At any rate, if it were not for editions published without the benefit of the royal privileges after 1708, Madame d'Aulnoy's contributions to the genre she helped to invent and form would have been obliterated from the historical record.

That circumstance is very peculiar. Of all the authors involved in the invention and production of *contes de fées*, d'Aulnoy was the most solidly-established, in terms of her reputation and popularity. She had obtained privileges for the publication of a dozen books in the early 1690s, including a fictitious *Relation du voyage d'Espagne* [Account of a Journey in Spain], a series of equally fictitious "memoirs" of the Spanish, English and French courts, a couple of *nouvelles espagnoles* [Spanish novellas] and two historical melodramas set in Tudor England, *Histoire d'Hypolite, comte de Duglas* and *Le Comte de Warwick* [The Earl of Warwick]. Given that, and the fact that Mademoiselle de La Force and the Comtesse de Murat seem to have obtained licenses for publication of their *contes de fées* in 1697 and 1698 without any initial difficulty, why should d'Aulnoy have been forced to publish hers illicitly? There certainly cannot have been any lack of printers eager to market them.

It is possible that the question is approaching the problem from the wrong angle, and that it should be asking how La Force and Murat were able to obtain licenses when many authors could not. If so, then the answer presumably lay in the patronage of the dowager Princesse de Conti, one of the most powerful influences in the court. The enigma of the initial fate of Baronne d'Aulnoy's *contes de fées* is, however, compounded by the further enigma of what happened to La Force and Murat, and to the genre as a whole, after 1698. One further volume appears to have been published in 1699: the Comtesse de Murat's *Histoires sublimes et allégoriques par Madame la Comtesse D*** dédiées aux fées modernes* [Sublimes and Allegorical Stories by the Comtesse de D***, dedicated to Modern Fays], containing four stories. After that, however, the stream of licenses dried up.

Only three more volumes of *contes de fées* appear to have been published under royal license between 1699 and the death of Louis XIV in 1715. The first was *La Tyrannie des fées détruite, nouveaux contes, dédiez à Madame la Duchesse de Bourgogne par la Comtesse D.L.* [The Tyranny of the Fays Abolished, new tales dedicated to the Duchessse de Bourgogne by the Comtesse de L.] (1703), whose author is unknown, although many modern bibliographies, including the Bibliothèque Nationale catalogue, attribute it to a fictitious "Comtesse d'Auneuil"; it contains four stories, one incomplete. The second was *Les Chevaliers Errans et le Génie familier par Madame la Comtesse D*** [The Knights Errant and The Familiar Spirit by the Comtesse de **] (1709), apparently by the same author; it contains two portmanteau works, the second incomplete. The third licensed volume was *Florine, ou la Belle Italienne* [Florine; or, The Italian Beauty] (1713), subsequently attributed, perhaps dubiously, to Françoise Le Marchand. The Comtesse de Murat published a portmanteau work containing two *contes de fées* in 1710, *Les Lutins du château de Kernosy* [The Goblins of Kernosy Castle], but without the benefit of a privilege.

Whether or not Madame d'Aulnoy's works were actually published in 1697-98 the last items they contain were certainly written in 1698, and all of her known work in the genre was surely prepared then for publication in eight volumes, even if they were forced to await illicit publication at some later date. The manner of their preparation, however, has some interesting aspects. Their appearance suggests that Madame d'Aulnoy intended at one time to use the same tactic as Catherine Bernard in embedding some of her tales within two *nouvelles espagnoles*, but that packaging presumably came to seem irrelevant, and the two novellas were then wrapped around with a further frame before being recast as the third and fourth of the eight volumes she hoped to publish in 1697-98. The six long *contes de fées* embedded in the three projected volumes of *Le Nouveau bourgeois gentilhomme* were presumably intended to be the selling point for their container rather than *vice versa*.

The latter envelope includes much sly commentary on the sudden fashionability of such tales, and leaves no doubt of the difficulty that *contes de fées* had in being taken seriously, at least in terms of public representation, even by their own writers, because they were regarded with sneering contempt by "serious" people—a contempt presumably increased rather than diminished by the vogue that briefly boosted them to popularity. Further evidence of that hostility is provided, in scathing terms, by a pamphlet produced under privilege, *Entretiens sur les contes de fées et sur quelques autres ouvrages du temps pour servir de préservatif contre le mauvais goût* [Conversations on Tales of Fays and a few other Works of Today, to serve as a Preservative against Bad Taste] (1699; by Pierre Villiers). The Parisian featured in an imaginary conversation with a Provincial argues that it is impossible for a *conte de fées* to have any literary merit, because their inherent absurdity is fatal to any such ambition. It is, however, unlikely that the abortion of the genre by the royal censors was carried out on esthetic grounds, given that most of the "*galant*" fiction [literally, fiction about elegant society, but carrying an implication of slight salacity] they authorized is conspicuously devoid of any literary merit—as Villiers' Parisian also complains.

There is surely an element of disingenuousness in Madame d'Aulnoy's teasing implication in *Le Nouveau bourgeois gentilhomme* that the interpolated stories—the finest of her works—are childish, slapdash and silly, because she certainly poured a great deal of effort into them, and there is a naked determination in the stories in question not to be outshone by Murat, who was a more careful and more polished writer, and equally imaginative, although evidently not as fluent or as rapid in production. Even if d'Aulnoy's earlier stores had been a trifle casual, her later work is certainly not lacking in the application and intensity that Murat brought to hers, and that effort was very effective. If, as seems highly probable, Perrault stole freely from d'Aulnoy's work, as well as from L'Héritier and Bernard, in shaping his much slighter tales, it must surely have caused her immense chagrin to see him achieving astonishing popularity with material ineptly recycled from her superior endeavors, and the refusal of a privilege permitting licit publication of her work added real injury to that insult.

Seen from the distant viewpoint of the present day, the principal beneficiaries of the brief fashionability of *contes de fées* now seem to have the assiduous d'Aulnoy and Murat, no one else managing to issue more than a single volume. Quantitatively, at least, d'Aulnoy won the tacit competition, and held on to the laurels, although in terms of influence on later writers, Murat was probably the more highly esteemed. The most interesting aspect of their competition, however, is the effect that d'Aulnoy's endeavors evidently had on Murat's, and *vice versa*. If they had not been consciously and manifestly in competition, listening attentively to one another reading their works and then trying to outshine them, *contes de fées* would not have undergone the evolution and sophistication that allowed them to serve as significant inspiration in the 1730s and 1740s for the writers of the "contraband renaissance." At the time however, neither of them can have felt like a winner, and even though Murat had achieved a measure of the licit publication that d'Aulnoy had not, they must both have felt that that they had been brutally stopped far short of the finishing line of their private duel, and that their careers had been cruelly assassinated.

The Fall of the Empire of the Fays

The rush to publish *contes de fées* in 1697-98 in the hope of cashing in on Perrault's unexpected success was short-lived; it lasted little more than twelve months, after which the flow of royal privileges permitting licit publication abruptly dried up, slowing to a tiny trickle. The fact that the subsequent privileged publications failed to duplicate Perrault's triumph in terms of sales was probably a factor, but the collections by Mademoiselle de La Force and the Comtesse de Murat were certainly sufficiently popular to warrant reprinting, and to encourage the continuation of the trend purely on commercial grounds. Other factors, however, seem to have come into play very forcefully, and some of their effects were obvious, including the removal from Paris of at least four of the major writers involved in the production of *contes de fées*, and the virtual silencing of almost all the remainder. In effect, in spite of its demonstrated popularity, the genre was suppressed, with the sole exception of the mediocre works of Charles Perrault, which came to seem archetypal partly because the opposition was so comprehensively eliminated.

Exactly why that sharp interruption happened can no longer be determined with any certainty, but it was certainly not spontaneous; the nascent genre was brutally crushed, with a violence that extended to banishment, active persecution and imprisonment. That happened without any great publicity, however, and the reasons for it were never made clear at the time or afterwards; it remains a mystery, in which only a few clear points of evidence stand out within a fog.

The first member of the initiating coterie to suffer manifest suppression was Mademoiselle de La Force, who was banished from Paris even before her own collection appeared in December 1697, sent to a remote nunnery where she was effectively imprisoned for the next sixteen years. Some documentation survives of her protest against that imprisonment, including a letter addressed to the Prince de Conti, which resurfaced in the mid-nineteenth century. Although La Force protests her innocence vigorously in the letter, she does not actually specify what charges had been laid against her, nor does she name the individual responsible for her internment, although the suspicion is inevitably strong that it must have been either her former protectress, the dowager princess, or the Prince de Conti himself.

Madame d'Aulnoy appears to have been the second of the three major writers of *contes de fées* to leave Paris for good, sometime in 1699, but there is no reliable information as to why she left, where she went or what she did thereafter prior to her death in 1705. Much has been made in posthumous commentaries—including the account given by Mayer in volume 37 of the 1786 *Cabinet*—of the allegation that a friend of hers was executed for attempting to murder her abusive husband, occasioning the suggestion that she might have feared implication in the affair, but there is no real evidence to support that hypothesis.

The Comtesse de Murat left the capital shortly after d'Aulnoy, and was resident for a while thereafter with an aunt in Limousin. She was already under investigation by the Lieutenant-General of Police, whose reports survive, and who continued to pursue her after she had left Paris, with the result that she was arrested in Limousin in 1703 and committed to the Château de Loches, then the largest of France's state prisons (without any formal charge or trial), where she spent the next seven years, save for brief transfers to other prisons, only being released when her health had been comprehensively ruined. Why she was under investigation and who instigated the pursuit is unknown, but the Lieutenant-General's reports have survived; they consist entirely of malevolent gossip, with not a shred of solid evidence of any criminal conduct.

At the most, Murat seems to have been suspected of libertinism and lesbianism, but the former is an accusation to which few members of Louis XIV's court could have been immune, and the latter an inevitably vague suspicion. Some such suspicion might also have hung over Mademoiselle de La Force, Mademoiselle de L'Héritier and Catherine Bernard, none of whom ever married, but the "crime" was impossible to specify, let alone to prove, and it is not clear why, even if it were true, anyone should have cared very much. Mademoiselle de Scudéry had been calling herself "Sapho" for nearly fifty years, seemingly without attracting any particular hostility, or even comment. Baronne d'Aulnoy, who had borne six children, would seem to have had a ready-made defense against that particular charge, although the fact that two of her children had been born after her separation from her husband cannot have aided a reputation for virtue. *Hypolite, comte de Duglas* includes a scene in which the heroine, who has attracted the passionate attentions of a marchionesss while disguised as a man, agrees to put on male attire again, briefly, purely for her benefit—a daring narrative move for the time. The frame story of *Le Nouveau bourgeois gentilhomme* includes some sly implications of lesbian lust on the part of Madame du Rouet and Madame de Lure, but they are not suggestive of anything except an awareness of its existence that must have been commonplace at the time.

It is not impossible to imagine scenarios in which the relationships between the dowager Princesse de Conti and her confidantes became difficult and embarrassing, occasioning vengeful action on her part, or on the part of the Prince, fueling a hostility that might have extended to the entire coterie, but it seems improbable that petty scandals of that kind, no matter how well-founded, could have prompted the sweeping suppression that seems to have occurred. La Force, d'Aulnoy and Murat must surely have done something—or have been suspected of something—worse than passionate dalliance with one another, or with a widowed princess of the blood, in order to provoke such reprisals. In any case, if it had been aspects of their personal conduct that were responsible for d'Aulnoy's refusal of licit publication and Murat's imprisonment, that could hardly explain the long-lasting subsequent persecution of the entire genre to which their work belonged.

One possibility is that it was not so much suspicions of lesbianism that attracted stern and concerted hostility to the salon coterie and their work as suspicions of heresy, the latter "crime" having become subject to severe repression since the revocation of the Edict of Nantes in 1685. Catherine Bernard and Mademoiselle de La Force had both converted from Protestantism to Catholicism in consequence of repression, and such converts always remained subject to suspicions of insincerity and possible backsliding, while Madame d'Aulnoy had almost certainly spent time at the Château de Gudanes—where her mother, the Marquise de Gudanes by virtue of a second marriage, was resident—and which had long been the property of a powerful Huguenot family. It might well be significant, in this context, as previously mentioned in passing, that one of the key features of the fictional world in which *contes de fées* are set is that it is devoid of any trace of the Roman Church and its deity—with one significant exception.

In the opening scene of "La Belle au bois dormant," the gatecrashing of the good fays' endowment party by the evil fay, which Perrault probably appropriated from d'Aulnoy, the most significant difference between his account of the incident and d'Aulnoy's is that in Perrault's version the interrupted ceremony is an explicit Christian baptism, whereas in d'Aulnoy's it is not. Similarly, when Perrault's princess eventually recovers from suspended animation, she is married to the prince by the castle almoner, whereas weddings in stories by d'Aulnoy, Murat and La Force are conducted under the aegis of Hymen, administered by fays or, occasionally, by "druids." In spite of the supplementary presence of fays, therefore, Perrault's tale might well have seemed far less offensive to the powerful Churchmen in Louis XIV's court than the similar works of d'Aulnoy, Murat and La Force, the narrative background of which is blatantly pagan, and in which the most important deity by far is Amour, although the temples at which characters occasionally go to worship are sometimes dedicated to the goddess Diana.

Whether or not the "rules" drawn up for the production of *contes de fées* in the context of the salon game actually specified the rigorous elimination of Christianity from the conventionally-adopted background, that certainly became a significant paradigm feature of such tales. Although the principal motivation for the placing of a new and idiosyncratic version of *fées* at the heart of the genre was undoubtedly feminist, permitting the construction of a hypothetical world in which the most powerful agents of virtue and evil alike are women, the necessity of avoiding criticism on religious grounds must have been debated by the designers of the genre. The construction of fays carefully avoided all the ideological baggage associated with the terminology of "witchcraft," even though evil fays are mostly indistinguishable, in their appearance and conduct, from contemporary popular notions of witches.

Witchcraft was still regarded by the Church in 1697 as inherently Satanic, and its role in the Church's violent pursuit of heretics had not yet faded away completely. The seventeenth century might be represented in retrospect as an Age of Reason, but it was still only on the threshold of the Age of Enlightenment, and the Church was still employing fire and the sword to defend its obsolescent dogmas against creeping skepticism and freethinking. The desire of the writers of *contes de fées* to isolate their heroines from any possible suspicion of Satanism probably played a significant role in their conscious decision to remove them into a fictitious world devoid of the entire apparatus of Christian moral terrorism—but that "solution" might have compounded the problem in the eyes of suspicious Churchmen ever alert to heretical wiles.

If a sudden realization on the part of influential Churchmen in Louis XIV's court of the near-complete absence of the Roman Church from *contes de fées* in general was responsible for abrupt clerical hostility to the genre, that might well have been the major factor involved in the enmity that developed at Versailles, suspicions of libertinism and lesbianism on the part of its feminist writers merely supplying a convenient aid to targeting. The royal censors were, of necessity "professionally devout," and given the forceful influence of the Church over the philosophy of censorship in the seventeenth and eighteenth centuries, and the inevitable wariness of the licensing bureaucracy in consequence, the taint of heresy is the likeliest hypothesis that could account for the almost complete removal of *contes de fées* from the protection of privileged publication.

However, religious disapproval might not have been the only factor involved in generating the bad odor into which the genre, and fantastic fiction in general, fell with regard to the officious noses of the royal censors. The expulsion from Paris of La Force, d'Aulnoy and Murat coincided with another, more extravagantly publicized banishment of a writer whose contribution to the specific genre was exceedingly minor, but who was nevertheless a member of the same salons and a writer of fantastic fictions, and might have come to seem to the royal censors and their masters to be tarred with the same brush: François de Salignac de la Mothe-Fénelon (1651-1715).[1]

Fénelon was the last person in the court who could be suspected of heresy; as a priest he had been specifically commissioned to employ his famous eloquence to strive for the conversion of Huguenots to Catholicism, and his ardent preaching in that cause had won him friends and influence in aristocratic circles, leading to his appointment in 1689 as tutor to the eldest son of the Dauphin, the Duc de Bourgogne, then an unruly seven-year-old. In order to aid in the formation of the character of his pupil, who was supposedly destined to inherit the

---

[1] Fénelon's full name suggests a family relationship, albeit probably distant, to Baron d'Aulnoy, but whether that provided any kind of link between him and the Baronne, in reality or in the perception of others, it is impossible to determine.

French throne—which eventually passed to his younger son, whose father, grandfather and elder brother had all pre-deceased Louis XIV—Fénelon made use of his liking for stories, inventing moralistic fables and tales to illustrate and dramatize the principles of virtue, moderation and pacifism that he was attempting to inculcate in him.

Many of the tales that Fénelon invented for that purpose were animal fables similar to those adapted from Aesop and other ancient sources by Jean de La Fontaine. Others used imagery adapted from Classical history and mythology, including a long series of episodes mapping out the supposed adventures of Telemachus, the son of Ulysses, during his search for his absent father. At some stage, however, probably because he and the young Duc attended salons in which the game of *contes de fées* was being played, Fénelon borrowed that imaginative apparatus too, in at least four tales. They must have been devised while he was gradually preparing *Les Aventures de Télémaque* for possible publication, at which stage it had to be submitted to the censors, and was presumably brought to the attention of the king.

Fénelon was still in favor in 1696, when he obtained a royal nomination as Archbishop of Cambrai, but that favor came to an abrupt end in 1697. Whether the king actually read *Télémaque*, or—as is more likely—he was simply told about it by one of his advisors, we do not know, but of the fact that he disapproved of it very strongly there is no doubt. That is not surprising, given that the rhetoric of the novel is severely critical of the principle of absolute monarchy and the abuses facilitated thereby—in effect, preaching radical politics in a work addressed explicitly to the heir to the throne, and tacitly criticizing the present monarch for numerous alleged abuses of power.

Because of his status within the Church, Fénelon could not be persecuted in the same dismissive fashion as La Force or Murat, but he was expelled from Versailles with an effective order never to leave his distant diocese again, and he was not given a privilege to publish *Télémaque*, although some copies were printed in 1699 without that benefit. It was not until Louis XIV and Fénelon were both dead that the author's family reissued *Télémaque*, in 1716, and followed it up in 1718 with a volume of his fables and short stories, including four *contes de fées*, still without the benefit of a royal privilege. *Télémaque* became a best-seller anyway, and was rapidly hailed as a classic; some influential commentators considered it to be one of the most important philosophical works of its era; it was loudly touted as such by Baron de Montesquieu, Jean-Jacques Rousseau and other leading *philosophes*.

Télémaque probably did more than any other single text to demonstrate that the possession of a royal privilege for licit printing might be unnecessary in enabling a book to be widely ready and greatly appreciated, although Madame d'Aulnoy's tales, easily available after 1717 in illicit versions, might have helped. Indeed, *Télémaque* probably played a major role in suggesting that a royal privilege might even be undesirable for an author who wanted to be read sympathetically by the thinking people whose intellect the royal censors had the mission of circumscribing. Before 1716 illicit publications were still a trickle, albeit a significant one, but they soon became a mighty flood, to such an extent that their persecution *en masse* became quite impossible, active suppression having to be concentrated on relatively few titles deemed particularly pernicious— although writers who issued their works outside legal channels inevitably found it politic to remain anonymous, and the printers issuing the books routinely employed false title pages claiming publication in Amsterdam, Brussels, The Hague, Geneva, or anywhere except the actual place of their publication, Paris.

Fénelon might not have been the only writer of *contes de fées* to cause direct offense to the king. *Contes moins contes que les autres* (1698) which contained only two stories, "Sans Parangon" (tr. as "Peerless") and "La Reine des fées" (tr. as "The Queen of the Fays") was eventually identified as the work of the prolific Jean de Préchac (1647-1720), who had been writing historical fiction, plays and poetry for twenty years, mostly in a "gallant" vein. Préchac's two *contes de fées* are quite unlike those produced by the female writers, although both of them start out as if they intend to be, deploying the stock materials of the genre in a conventional fashion. "Sans Parangon" rapidly becomes a transfiguration of the life and career of Louis XIV, represented as a relentless and ultimately hopeless quest to win the favor of Belle-Gloire (Beautiful Glory), here symbolized as an enchanted Chinese princess. The story is clearly intended as an item of egregious flattery, but it might have backfired; although Jean de Préchac lived for another twenty years after its publication, he does not seem ever to have obtained another royal privilege to publish anything at all. Although it is pure speculation, it is possible that when Louis XIV was told about the story— probably by a rival flatterer with more expertise in the art—he reacted violently against the idea that he could be represented symbolically as a lovelorn fool engaged for life in an essentially absurd and hopeless quest to please an imaginary Chinese princess.

Any offense caused by Préchac must have been a very minor issue, certainly incapable of prompting the suppression of an entire genre, but it might have seemed to the king and his advisors to be one more straw on the back of a heavily-loaded camel, and one more confirmation of the fact that the genre was dangerous, potentially if not actually. One way or another, however royal support was comprehensively withdrawn, and never restored, condemning *contes de fées* to be a fugitive genre from 1699 until the 1789 Revolution, save for five intriguing exceptions, which will warrant further comment in due course.

The Work of the Major Writers

It ought to be remembered, in considering the work of the most important pioneering contributors to the genre of *contes de fées* that it was, in every case, only a minor component of their overall literary endeavor. All of them did other work, including poetry, dramatic works and other prose fiction, most of it historical fiction, often in a "gallant" vein, and often shaped as *mémoires* of notable individuals, frequently revealing supposed "secrets" unrecorded by history by virtue of being purely fictitious. With the possible exception of the Comtesse de Murat, all the salon writers appear to have regarded their work in other genres as more important and more prestigious and might well have been offended, as well as surprised, had they been able to anticipate that, three hundred years later, their *contes de fées* would be the only thing for which they are remembered, to the extent that they are remembered at all.

When Joseph de La Porte compiled his mammoth *Histoire littéraire des femmes françoises* (5 volumes, 1769) he included long accounts of all the major female writers of *contes de fées*, but gave far more space and emphasis to their other works, and was generally dismissive of their *contes de fées*, regarding them as essentially trivial. As his work progressed, however, he seems to have become increasingly intrigued by the genre and sympathetic to it. His research eventually proved very useful to Charles Mayer, and by the time his *Histoire* was complete and ready for publication, La Porte had already compiled an anthology of rare items entitled *La Bibliothèque des fées et génies* [The Library of Fays and Genii] (1764-5), of which he advertised himself as the "scientific editor." The Bibliothèque Nationale only has the version incorporated by Mayer into the *Cabinet*, so the first edition was presumably illicit. La Porte probably regarded that interest as a guilty pleasure, however, in much the same way that the writers of the 1690s did—or, at last, felt obliged to pretend that they did, again with the possible exception of Murat. The following account, however, will inevitably focus on the *contes de fées*, only referring to the authors' other works by way of setting them in context.

Mademoiselle de L'Héritier is often said in reference books to be the "niece" of Charles Perrault, although she was actually a more distant relative, and that presumed relationship added a certain suggestive fuel to the supposition that she got the idea of writing such tales from him, although it was almost certainly the other way around. *Oeuvres meslées* includes an ironic note, employed as a preface to one of the "*nouvelles*" reproduced therein, suggesting, with tongue-in-cheek, that he might like to appropriate it. She did know his family well, therefore; she was aware of the collection that Perrault had compiled in his

37

son's name long before it was published, and knew that it contained stolen goods. Prior to the collection of her poetry that fills most of the remainder of the volume, the author also took the trouble to reproduce a brief explanatory essay, in the form of a letter, explaining what *contes de fées* are and why she considers them worthy of attention and emulation, suggesting strongly that she was the prime mover in urging others to dabble in their production.

That letter claims in passing that Mademoiselle de L'Héritier had toned down the story of "L'Adroite princesse, ou les Aventures de Finette"— borrowed from the French translation of Giambattista Basile's *Il Pentamerone* (1634-36; Fr. tr. 1672)—in regard to the immorality of Finette's sisters, who both fall victim to a cunning seducer, although the violent conclusion to her story is certainly not toned down, being garish in its action and its symbolism alike. In her subsequent work L'Héritier was usually very careful to preserve what she called *bienséance* [decorum], and is not without reason that her study of "Les Enchantments de l'éloquence" is alternatively titled "Les Effets de la douceur." She was far less restrained, however, in another fantasy, "Le Parnasse reconnoissant, ou the Triomphe de Madame Des Houlières" (tr. as "Grateful Parnassus"), a flamboyant eulogy to Antoinette Deshoulières, regarded in her heyday, at least by the *femmes savantes*, as the leading lyric poet of her era. The story is interesting not only for its extravagantly fervent feminism, but for its graphic imagery and the sly wit of some of the comments made in passing on the personnel of the Underworld and Parnassus and their attitudes to men and women.

The restraint of *bienséance* might be partially responsible for the fact that L'Héritier does not appear to have published any more *contes de fées*, strictly speaking, after 1696, although some might have been intended to be featured in the unpublished completion of the fragmentary portmanteau work *La Tour ténébreuse et les jours lumineux, contes Anglais* [The Dark Tower and the Luminous Days, English Tales] (1705), the existing text of which was printed illicitly, ostensibly in Amsterdam. Whether or not that is the case, the fervent championship of the genre in her earlier essay suggests that there must have been a more powerful reason for her subsequent discretion. The existing text of *La Tour ténébreuse et les jours lumineux* was reprinted by Mayer in his *Cabinet des fées*, primarily because of the Faustian fantasy "Ricdin-Ricdon," which does not feature fays but subsequently provided the basis for one of the most celebrated "fairy tales" when an abridged version of it was adapted a century later by the Brother Grimm as "Rumpelstiltskin." The other fantasy interpolated within the historical frame narrative is "La Robe de sincérité" (tr. as "The Robe of Sincerity") which is devoid of genuine faerie, although it makes abundant use of charlatanry and hypothetical technologies that substitute for magic in an interesting fashion.

One other collection of stories by the author, *Les Caprices du destin* [The Caprices of Destiny] (1718), is reproduced in *gallica*, as is her translation of *Les*

Épitres héroïque d'Ovide [The Heroic Epistles of Ovid] (1732) but if Mademoiselle de L'Héritier wrote anything involving fays during the later years of her career, it never reached print identifiably, even without the benefit of a privilege: a significant absence on the part of the genre's first and most ardent propagandist. Because she died in 1734, she did not live to see the genre's renaissance in print, but it is not impossible that she was aware of the salons in which that rebirth was gestated, and might actually have participated in them. There would have been a certain propriety in that.

Catherine Bernard's contributions to the genre might seem very slight, especially by comparison with her work in the fields of poetry and drama, where she obtained considerable prestige and still retains a substantial reputation. Her contribution only amounts to two short stories even if the fay-less "Riquet à la houppe" is permitted entry. Given that she was present at the beginning, however, and undoubtedly joined in with the game herself, as well as publicizing its nature, she is fully entitled to be considered one of the originators of *contes de fées*, and her contribution to the genre ought not to be reckoned trivial in spite of the paucity of its wordage. The most interesting aspect of "Le Prince Rosier" and "Riquet à la houppe" in the context of the genre as a whole, however, is their stark refusal of the "happy endings" that were generally considered to be almost obligatory.

That refusal arises partly from the adaptation if the tales to their particular context—the novella in which they are interpolated is a stark tragedy—and they deliberately mirror the rhetoric of the whole, but it is startling nevertheless that they adopt the fundamental strategy of the *conte de fées* in order to flatly deny one of its most fundamental tacit assumptions. They are rebel tales that deliberately subvert not merely the typical narrative strategy of *contes de fées* but the entire mythology of amour on which such tales are based, hence undermining their concept of Virtue. "Le Prince Rosier" remains a fascinating example of a road not taken by the other pioneering writers in the genre—or at least, only taken as a brief experiment in two stories by Madame d'Aulnoy, one by the Comtesse de Murat and one by Catherine Durand, probably all influenced, if not inspired, by Bernard.

The example Bernard provided in *Ines de Cordoue* was probably also influential in prompting Madame d'Aulnoy to embed some of her early short stories—significantly including both of those with downbeat endings—in *nouvelles espagnoles*, and hindsight encourages the suspicion that the Comtesse de Murat's portmanteau *Les lutins du château de Kernosy* was probably planned in parallel with d'Aulnoy's subsequent portmanteau, *Le Nouveau bourgeois gentilhomme*. Given that, it is probably fair to regard Bernard's influence as subtle rather than slight, and it ought not to be discounted as trivial in spite of her omission from the *Cabinet des fées*.

The most famous of Mademoiselle de La Force's tales, from the viewpoint of the present day, is "Persinette," for the ironic reason that a copy of it was translated by Friedrich Schultz, who represented it falsely as a German folktale, having retitled it "Rapunzel" (1790), and it was subsequently collected under that title by the Brothers Grimm. The Grimm version was very widely reprinted, and still gets the credit for subsequent transformations of the story, including the Disney film *Tangled* (2010). However, La Force had appropriated the key elements of the story herself—including the striking motif of the captive princess letting down her hair in order that the prince can climb up to her prison—from "Petrosinella," in Giambattista Basile's *Pentamerone*, although her version is not only considerably elaborated but has a plaintive tone in its later phases markedly different from the easy buoyancy of Basile's story.

Although the author was well-known before the publication of her collection of tales by virtue of her "secret histories," most notably *Histoire secrète de Marie de Bourgogne* [The Secret History of Marie de Bourgogne] (1694; the "Marie de" was dropped in subsequent editions), set in the fifteenth century, her most interesting work, in terms of providing a context for her *contes de fées* might have been written after her exile; it was only discovered when the manuscript was sold with Louis-Philippe's book collection in 1852. *Les Jeux d'esprit, ou la Promenade de la princesse de Conti à Eu* [Intellectual Games; or, The Princesse de Conti's Excursion to Eu], published in 1865, consists of imaginary conversations supposedly taking place in the second decade of the seventeenth century between the then Princesse de Conti and her petty court, not only including accounts of games they play but various fantastic dreams—for which the members of the company attribute speculative psychological interpretations—and improvised commentaries on hypothetical metamorphoses of perceived objects. It casts some light on the psychology of her own tales—which, although they do not refuse happy endings, frequently express reservations about their plausibility—and might contain significant reflections on her uneasy relationship with the present Prince de Conti and the dowager Princesse de Conti, from whose custody the manuscript was presumably handed down to Louis-Philippe.

What distinguishes La Force's tales from those of her most famous contemporaries, in fact, is their evident moral unease, which sometimes extends to outright challenge, particularly in a remarkable rant addressed to Amour in the conclusion of "La Puissance d'Amour" (tr. as "The Power of Amour"), which includes the judgment that "One ought to abhor your fires, never feel them, let alone speak them; they spoil minds and corrupt mores." Although the bare bones of "Persinette" have survived as a children's story, that is only by adaptation of a darker tale, and it is significant that La Force chose to lead off her collection with "Plus Belle que Fée" (tr. as "More Beautiful than a Fay"), which is a significant exemplar, embodying several motifs that were to be frequently recycled and elaborated by Madame d'Aulnoy and the Comtesse de Murat and imitated by several later writers. The story has a particular emotional loading that is subtle and effective, and an element of wry black humor that might seem slightly surprising in a work composed in the 1690s, but is also echoed by d'Aulnoy and Murat, sufficiently to be regarded as a key element of the genre's core.

One of the most celebrated products of Mademoiselle de Scudéry's *précieuses*, popularized by an engraving reproduced in the first volume of *Clélie*, was the allegorical Carte du Tendre [Map of Tenderness], which supposedly charts the reliable path to true love. La Force produced her own allegory of that sort in "Le Pays des délices" (tr. as "The Land of Delights"), as did several of the other collaborators in the game, but a comparison of the imaginary geographies and the journeys that they map out illustrates very clearly that La Force was possessed of a far greater skepticism than her mentor, matched among her contemporaries by Catherine Bernard in the allegorical account of the Isle of Youth in "Le Prince Rosier" and Murat's depiction of the difficult-of-access "L'Île de Magnificence" (tr. as "The Isle of Magnificence").

La Force's skeptical notion of Amour and its supposed routes to happiness is also symbolized and expressed in "Tourbillon," and further elaborated in both "Vert et bleu" (tr. as "Green and Blue") and the emotional roller-coaster plot of "L'Enchanteur" (tr. as "The Enchanter"). All eight of her stories, in fact, provide subtle evidence of the same painful existential wounds that led the author to say of herself, in the self-portrait she included in her pleading letter to the Prince de Conti (found in the same auction lot as *Les Jeux d'esprit*) that "I have always been deceived, and only found in my entire life one good [female] friend; I have had perfidious and false friends in quantity..."

Although less prolific than d'Aulnoy and Murat, and therefore less various in the motifs that she adopted and deployed, La Force's stories are as substantial as their early works. Although by no means lacking in focus, they routinely follow strange narrative trajectories that give them an almost surreal quality, and it is not surprising that one existing tale that she acknowledged when adapting it for her own purposes, in "L'Enchanteur," was the enigmatic English romance of *Sir Gawain and the Green Knight*, which must have appealed to her fondness for the nonsensical in the same way as the roles played by a craving for parsley and exceedingly long hair in Basile's "Petrosinella."

All of the stories in *Les Contes de Contes* must have been composed before the author's banishment, some of them several years before, but the last of them, "La Bonne Femme" (tr. as "The Good Woman") can surely be reckoned an intriguing anticipation of the sentiments associated with her exile. Its deep disenchantment with court life is, once again, something found very forcefully in tales by d'Aulnoy that must have been written afterwards, offering intriguing insights into the developing collective consciousness of the core group of writers. La Force was undoubtedly out-competed by both d'Aulnoy and Murat, both quantitatively and qualitatively, but her contribution to the competition, and hence to the genre, was nevertheless substantial, and perhaps vital to its evolution.

41

Henriette-Julie de Castelnau was the daughter of Marquis Michel de Castelnau, the son of a famous Maréchal de France; Michel de Castelnau had followed his father into a military career, and died of wounds sustained in battle in 1672, while his daughter was still a child. Her marriage to Nicolas de Murat, the colonel of an infantry regiment, in 1691, was arranged, belatedly by the standards of the day, and seemingly reluctant. She fled the marital home shortly after giving birth to her son—a scandalous thing to do in those days—and went to live in Paris, where she was probably taken under the wing of her cousin, Mademoiselle de La Force, and hence under the protection of the Princesse de Conti. At any rate, she was promptly introduced into the salons where the game of *contes de fées* was already under way, and to which she must have taken like the proverbial duck to water

Although she was far less experienced than the other members of the coterie, Murat's initial collection of *contes de fées* was not her first publication; it followed closely on the heels of a two volume work whose first title page bears the title *Mémoires de Madame la Comtesse de M****, although there is a second title page that relegates that description to the subtitle, after the title *La Défense des dames* [The Defense of Ladies]. The latter was probably Murat's chosen title, the other having been given priority by the printer. Many people, perhaps not surprisingly in view of the marketing move made by the printer, seem to have assumed that the book really consisted of memoirs and read it as if it were autobiographical. Indeed, many subsequent accounts of the author's biography borrowed from it freely, even in the knowledge of considerable contradictions between the narrative of the text and actual documentation of the author's life.

In fact, *Mémoires de Madame la Comtesse de M**** is a work of fiction, pure and simple, although its fundamental argument—that it is sometimes entirely justified for wives to leave their husbands—was evidently one in which Murat had good reason to take an intense interest. We can only speculate as to whether Murat realized that her work of fiction would be mistaken by some readers as an account of her own life, and if so, whether she came to regret it, but it surely made a considerable contribution to the scandal that followed her around for the rest of her brief life at court, and long thereafter. Colorful as it is, though, it is considerably less so than the reports on her conduct compiled by the Lieutenant-General of Louis XIV's police, which dutifully repeat scabrous hearsay accusing Murat of persistent libertinage and lesbianism—and those slanders, too, have been incorporated into the accounts of her life compiled by other speculative biographers.

The first volume of Murat's initial collection contains "Le Parfait amour" (tr. as "Perfect Love"), "Anguillette" (tr. as "Anguillette") and "Jeune et belle" (tr. as "Young and Beautiful"), and the second "Le Palais de la vengeance" (tr. as "The Palace of Vengeance), "Le Prince des feuilles" (tr. as "The Prince of Leaves") and "L'Heureuse peine" (tr. as "The Fortunate Penalty"), plus a brief narrative poem. The first of the six stories can be regarded, along with

L'Héritier's "Les Enchantements de l'éloquence" and La Force's "Plus Belle que fée" as one of the archetypal *contes de fées*, one of the primary models that many later writers in the genre followed, and which helped to establish the foundation-stones of its essential mythos; it certainly established the basic thematic template of almost all of Murat's *contes*, and those of the later writers whose inspiration she provided. The "perfect love" to which the title refers is the kind of amour held up by Mademoiselle de Scudéry as a supreme ideal: emotionally and morally absolute, sentimentally all-consuming and indomitably faithful. In Murat's story and its many clones, however, the sentiment and the fidelity are subjected to enormous stress, applied by relatives or jealous rivals intent in breaking the amorous bond between the hero and heroine.

In "Le Parfait amour," as in many of its clones, the heroine is imprisoned from the very beginning by a powerful guardian prepared to move heaven and earth to keep her apart from the hero who loves her, for whom she has plans of her own. The hero is aided in his difficult quest of liberation by a benevolent fay, albeit under conditions that prove awkward of fulfillment. Murat takes the melodrama to an extreme; when the hero and heroine are eventually captured by the evil queen, they undergo ingenious mental and physical torture, intended to break their commitment to one another, which brings them both to death's door; they do not waver, however, and they are rescued in the nick of time by a *deus ex machina* provided by the benevolent fay. All of those features became key moves in the competition between Murat and Baronne d'Aulnoy, as the two writers groped for narrative extremes, and urged one another to push the generic envelope further.

From the very beginning, Murat was intent not only on elaborating that basic schema but also in varying it. The longest of the three stories in her first volume, "Anguillette," is one of very few tragic variants of the basic pattern, ending not with the union of its protagonists but with their deaths, following a plot that has first drawn them apart and then confronted them with one another when both are married to other people, so that their union has become impossible and their unconquerable attraction can only lead to mutual annihilation. It is significant that having done that once, Murat never did it again, accepting that the conventional "happy ending" was an essential and inviolable part of the formula. Nevertheless, presumably recalling that her own marriage—like those of Baronne d'Aulnoy and the dowager Princesse de Conti—had been anything but a happy ending, Murat continued to retain a subversive cynicism that she clearly had difficulty setting aside.

"Jeune et belle" follows the same basic pattern, save for a role-reversal in which is the "hero" is a young fay and her inamorata a hapless but beautiful shepherd abducted by an ugly, old and lustful fay—an archetype who was to crop up in many more tales, unarguably perfected by d'Aulnoy, but not without stern competition. Although the shepherd's release is obtained after the customary ration of tortures, the point is explicitly made in the story's finale that the reunited couple live together long and happily without the intervention of Hymen—i.e., without ever getting married.

Murat never did that again either—at least, not so explicitly—but "Le Palais de vengeance," the first story in the second volume of the initial set, which was nominated as her finest by one of her most enthusiastic fans, the Comte de Caylus, contrives a more ingenious subversion. After the customary routine of pressure and ordeal, the evil enchanter who has tried everything to break down the resolve of the lovers finally throws in the towel and allows them to be together—but he obtains his revenge by imprisoning and isolating them in a glass palace where they have no alternative but to see one another, and only one another, for as long as they live, the suggestion being that the passage of time will inevitably transform the anticipated paradise into a kind of hell, or at least a purgatory. Again, having made that skeptical point once, Murat refused to labor it.

"Le Prince des feuilles" is content to reproduce the basic formula of "Le Parfait amour" in a more elaborate fashion, but the essence of the story lies in the manner of that elaboration. The complication of the plot of "Le Parfait amour" had been obtained by introducing a subsidiary cast of elemental spirits—gnomes, undines, sylphs and salamanders—who are distinct from fays and enchanters but allied with them. That hypothetical schema is reproduced in other stories by Murat and other members of the initial coterie, with a measure of ambiguity that confuses undines with the sirens of Classical mythology and adds other nymphs drawn from that source in building a syncretic supernatural hierarchy. The complication of "Le Prince des feuilles," by contrast, is secured by pure invention: the elaboration of a colorful web of unprecedented supernatural inventions that is admirably exotic in its deliberate symbolism, and which tends in its display to calculated surrealism.

In that regard, the story follows precedents set, a trifle half-heartedly, in "Anguillette," but it does so more scrupulously and more intensively. Murat apparently decided that she had now mapped the way to go in future; that strategy, she did repeat again and again, with ever-increasing complication; and that was what made her, in the view of such enthusiastic successors as Mademoiselle de Lubert and the Comte de Caylus, the principal architect of *contes de fées*, even more important as a model for later endeavor than the more prolific and eventually more famous Baronne d'Aulnoy.

The final story of Murat's initial set, "L'Heureuse peine," is perhaps the weakest of the group, although it is certainly not lacking in innovative supernatural apparatus, and its subversive element is a trifle tokenistic, tacking on to a conventional conclusion a comment suggesting that perhaps the marriage will not be happy after all, for the simple reason that marriages never are. Perhaps she felt obliged to add that observation to a story presumably composed before Perrault changed the nature of the playing field, and her next set of works, evidently written with the likelihood of publication in mind, is content to employ the convention without challenging it in such a straightforward way. She never abandoned the subversive element in her work, but she refined its ironic rhetoric very considerably as her career advanced further.

In 1699 Murat published a portmanteau work, *Le Voyage de campagne* [An Excursion to the Country], in which a group of travelers tell one another stories in the course of a discussion of various matters of interest to them. Most of the stories are allegedly drawn from their personal histories, but they include one item of fantastic fiction, "Le Père et ses quatre fils" (tr. as "A Father and His Four Sons") whose teller represents it explicitly as an experiment of sorts: a *conte* from which fays are deliberately excluded, although the other accumulated apparatus of *contes de fées* is retained. Further interest is added to the experiment by the comments surrounding the tale in the frame narrative, which include brief remarks on the appeal and literary propriety of fantastic fiction. The frame story is not as anodyne as the capsule description might make it seem; it is subtly subversive in both political and religious terms, and the characters have utopian aspirations; it is perhaps surprising that it was granted a privilege, but less surprising that it remained one of the author's most popular works, reprinted several times in the eighteenth century and reproduced in Charles Garnier's multi-volume compendium of *Voyages imaginaires, songes, visions et romans cabalistiques* [Imaginary Voyages, Dreams, Visions and Cabalistic Fiction] (1787-89) along with Mademoiselle de Lubert's edited version of *Les Lutins du château de Kernosy*.

Literary experiments of a far more extravagant kind, however, are featured in Murat's masterpiece, *Histoires sublimes et allégoriques par Madame la Comtesse D*** dédiées aux fées modernes*—a dedication whose textual expansion suggests strongly that what she means by "modern fays" is her fellow writers rather than their characters—published later that same year. It contains four stories: "Le Roy porc" (tr. as "The Swine King"), "L'Isle de Magnificence (tr. as "The Isle of Magnificence"), "Le Sauvage" (tr. as "The Savage") and "Le Turbot" (tr. as "The Turbot"), three of which are extravagant extrapolations of stories in Gianfrancesco Straparola's *La Piacevoli notti* (1553), the first and fourth produced in manifest competition with Baronne d'Aulnoy, who wrought her own extravagantly elaborated versions of "Galeotto," as "Le Prince marcassin" (tr. as "Prince Marcassin"), and "Pietro," as "Le Dauphin" (tr. as "The Dolphin").

Although Mademoiselle de L'Héritier had used the terms *conte, histoire* and *nouvelle* interchangeably, Murat surely had a deliberate distinction in mind in choosing to label the stories in her 1699 collection *histoires* rather than *contes*, the label she invariably used elsewhere, and she surely meant to imply more than the fact that the stories are longer than those in her 1698 collections, Whereas all the stories in the earlier collections are set in "the time of the fays," a remote mythical past, only the first of the four stories in the 1699 collection follows that convention; the other three all contain references establishing that they are set in the year 1697, and that the lands in which fays operate are in the same world as contemporary France—a modification that has inevitable corollary implications regarding the ambiguous nature of their fictitious fays.

The second and fourth stories in *Histoires sublimes et allegoriques* are peculiar novellas, portmanteaux of a less orthodox kind than *Le Voyage de campagne*, in which several narratives are carefully interwoven, in a fashion that later became known as "the Galland method" because of its elaborate use in Galland's *Les Mille et une nuits*. Portmanteau works had been common for a long time before 1699, and such packaging might even be regarded as the principal mode of presentation of prose fiction prior to 1700, but most previous examples of its use had simply inserted stories into a frame like beads on a string, rarely overlapping and entangling them as Murat does very deliberately and intricately in "L'Île de Magnificence" and "Le Turbot." Both stories are remarkable for the imaginative extravagance of some of their subplots—an extravagance also evident in the other two stories in the collection, but which has far more scope in the novellas, and exceeds considerably the inventive adventurousness of "Le Prince des feuilles." The stories d'Aulnoy produced in parallel match Murat's for length, and in the grotesquery of their imagery, but not for intricacy and ingenuity

In both novellas, and also in "Le Sauvage," the deliberate linkage of the stories to the year 1697 relates to a specific event in that year: the marriage of the Duc de Bourgogne, the son of the Dauphin and tutee of François Fénelon, to Princesse Marie-Adelaïde de Savoie, arranged by a clause in an important political treaty. That marriage became the excuse for the most lavish party ever held at Versailles, extending over several days. It was the great social event of the brief heyday of *contes de fées*, not only co-opted by Murat and briefly referenced by d'Aulnoy, but forming the centerpiece for one of the few *contes de fées* to obtain a royal prerogative after 1699, as part of an exceedingly curious aftermath of the genre's abortion, the bizarre and significantly-titled novella *La Tyrannie des fées détruite* (1703; tr. as "The Tyranny of the Fays Abolished")—a matter that I shall take up in due course.

We can, of course, only speculate as to how Murat's literary career might have developed if it had not been for the personal disasters that afflicted her after 1699, but it is a safe assumption that she could have, and probably would have, continued the pattern of elaboration begun in *Histoires sublimes et allégoriques* and produced even more complex and adventurous works of fantastic fiction. In the event, her production was completely disrupted, although some bibliographies credit her with an exceedingly elusive work entitled *Un Dialogue des morts* (1700), which might be a phantom title. When she did begin publishing again she could only do so without the benefit of privileges. *Histoire de la courtesane Rhodope* [The Story of the Courtesan Rhodope] (1708) and *Histoires galantes des habitants de Loches* [Stories of the Gallant Inhabitants of Loches] (1709) presumably belong to the genre of salacious fictitious memoirs, but *Les*

Lutins du château de Kernosy is a fascinating portmanteau novella which provides an interesting context for its two interpolated *contes de fées*, "Peau d'ourse" (tr. as "Bearskin") and "Étoilette" (tr. as "Starlet). The nature and tone of the exercise suggest strongly that its original version must have been planned, and probably written, in parallel and in direct competition with d'Aulnoy's *Le Nouveau bourgeois gentilhomme*.

A few other stories have been belatedly added to Murat's canon; the first of them to be published, in an unsigned illicit 1718 collection entitled *Nouveaux contes de fées*, was "Le Buisson d'épines fleuries [The Flowery Thorn-Bush]; none of the other stories in the collection appear to be hers, but a manuscript version of that story was apparently found among Murat's papers, where it bore the title "La Fée Princesse" [i.e. a fay named Princess] (tr. as "The Fay Princess"). The attribution is surely correct; appearances suggest strongly that the story belongs to the earlier phase of Murat's writing of *contes de fées*.

Like the vast majority of the early *contes de fées*, Murat's stories are, fundamentally, stories written by an aristocrat, for the consumption of a select audience of aristocrats, about an imaginary world that is in large measure a transfiguration of Versailles in its heyday, full of princes and princesses who have absolutely nothing to do but watch "fêtes" and "spectacles" and fall in love with one another, under the ever-lurking threat of ennui. Like their competitors, however, they are stories written by a clear-sighted renegade female aristocrat, for a select audience of female aristocrats, who knew perfectly well that all the fêtes and spectacles in the world cannot hope to keep ennui at bay for long, and that falling in love, no matter with whom, will always let you down, one way or another—and precisely because Murat knew that, she also knew the full value of pretending that it might not be so, within the fictitious world of an absurdly fantastic story. No one handled and embellished the rhetoric of that consciousness better than Murat, and that is why the most determined and most clear-sighted of the writers who attempted to resurrect the genre of *contes de fées* after its deliberate assassination chose her as their primary exemplar.

Very little is known about much of Madame d'Aulnoy's life. Joseph de La Porte devoted abundant space in the third volume of his history to her travelogues and historical novels, but only gave brief and rather dismissive mention of three of her *contes de fées*, and claimed to have been unable to discover anything about her biography other than a (mistaken) birth date and the year of her death. Subsequent researchers ascertained without much difficulty that Marie-Catherine Le Jumel de Barneville had been born into the minor nobility of Normandy, and married off by her family at the age of fifteen to the much older François de La Mothe (or La Motte), Baron d'Aunoi (or d'Aulnoy), but not much else.

It is not surprising that the horrors of forced marriage, especially between teenage girls and middle-aged men, are very widely featured in *contes de fées* as a particular object of disapproval on the part of their female authors, so d'Aulnoy cannot be held individually responsible for the obsession with that motif, but it is easy to understand why she so often waxed lyrical about it. Her own marriage was a disaster. She had four children in rapid succession, two of whom died in infancy, and her marriage effectively ended when the Baron was arrested on a charge of lèse-majesté and was sent to the Bastille on 30 September 1699, on the order of Jean-Baptiste Colbert, one of Louis XIV's principal ministers—whose secretary, for many years before his death in 1685, was Charles Perrault.

Baron d'Aulnoy eventually turned the tables on his denouncers and was released, after claiming vociferously that he had been stitched up by his mother-in-law, with the collaboration of a lover and another accomplice, but he does not seem to have resumed marital relations with his wife. The Baronne was arrested, and might have been briefly imprisoned, but was soon released if so. The truth of the matter is now impossible to ascertain, but the accusation routinely flung around in later commentaries that the Baronne was one of the instigators of the plot to frame her husband is pure speculation; the probability is that if the baron really was framed, the true reasons were political and undisclosed; Colbert is unlikely to have lent his hand to a petty family dispute. At any rate, d'Aulnoy's mother, who became the Marquise de Gudanes by remarriage, fled to Spain. There does not appear to be any reliable information as to where the Baronne was during the 1670s and the early 1680s, but for some of the time, at least, she was probably with her mother. During that period she had two more children, but the identity of their father, or fathers, is unknown.

The widely-published speculation that Baronne d'Aulnoy spent time in Holland and England is devoid of real evidence, and the suggestion that while she was there she worked as a spy for the French government is pure supposition, but, one way or another, she appears to have had some credit at court when she resurfaced in Paris again late in the 1680s, at which time she began to write fairly prolifically. That credit evidently disappeared in 1697, although she presumably assumed that it was still effective when she prepared her *contes de fées* for publication.

In all, d'Aulnoy's known contribution to the genre amounts to twenty-four tales, five of which were initially packaged within *nouvelles espagnoles*, one sandwiched between the two nouvelles in question, and six embedded within *Le Nouveau bourgeois gentilhomme,* the remaining twelve being divided up into three batches of four, five and three respectively. The batch of three and the six contained within *Le Nouveau bourgeois gentilhomme* are considerably longer than their predecessors and more intense, culminating in the two novellas based on Straparola, clearly written in competition with Murat, although it is arguable that the most striking and most original of her works are the three novellas that precede them, particularly "La Princess Belle-Étoile et le prince Chéri" (tr. as "Princess Belle-Etoile and Prince Cheri").

In terms of the feminist component of fay mythology, d'Aulnoy eventually provided some of the most extravagant exponents of female power. In "La Princesse Carpillon" (tr. as Princess Carpillon") the character identified as "la fée Amazone"—which can be construed either as "the Amazon Fay" or "the fay [named] Amazone"—functions in much the same fashion as a twentieth-century superhero, clad in a shiny costume and popping up when required to save the innocent from seemingly certain disaster, slaying monsters and villains with her fiery lance. In "Belle-Belle, ou Le Chevalier Fortuné," (tr. as "Belle-Belle; or, The Cavalier Fortuné"), the heroine, in male disguise, effortlessly outshines her rival knights in the arts of dragon-slaying and seduction, although she does have a team of male sidekicks under her orders, each of them endowed with a particular superhuman talent. Those are late examples, however, and in d'Aulnoy's early work, especially, female heroism had been in much shorter supply.

In the early "Gracieuse et Percinet" (tr. as Gracieuse and Percinet") the agent of benevolent enchantment is male, and in "La Belle aux cheveux d'or" (tr. as "The Golden-Haired Beauty") the male hero is aided entirely by talking animals, without a fay in sight. Although the hero of "Le Prince lutin"—the last story in the first batch of four—makes abundant use of a fay gift, once he has received the gift in question it is left almost entirely to his ingenuity to exploit it, and the "gallant" use he makes of it is not calculated to appeal to feminist readers. In the third story in what was presumably intended to be her first collection, "L'Oiseau bleu" (tr. as "The Blue Bird"), which features the first of the sadistic fays who were to become a key feature of d'Aulnoy's work in the genre (Grognon, the archetypal harridan in "Gracieuse et Percinet," is not a fay), much of the magical opposition to the heroine's evil stepmother, repulsive stepsister and the latter's hagwife godmother, is provided by a frankly misogynistic male enchanter, which leaves the poor heroine a trifle short of female support by comparison with many of her peers, until the conclusion of her taxing ordeals.

Apparently, d'Aulnoy thought better of that attitude, perhaps swayed by her more robustly feminist peers. In the first story of the second batch "La Princesse printanière" (tr. as "Princess Springtime"), which features one of the most striking of her grotesque evil fays, Carabosse, the eponymous heroine is a more active character than the heroines of the first batch, although her naïve and rather foolish efforts are wasted on an utterly worthless male whose good looks and dandyism conceal a selfish and treacherous character. "La Princesse Rozette" (tr. as "Princess Rosette") similarly takes the lead in directing the course of her affairs with similar naivety. In the more elaborate and bizarre "La Branche d'or" (tr. as "The Golden Branch"), the balance of effort and ingenuity is conscientiously even, in a narrative that switches the viewpoint back and forth between hero and heroine. In "L'Oranger et l'abeille" (tr. as "The Orange Tree and the Bee"), a tale that similarly cultivates the esthetics of the absurd, Princess Aimée, clad in a tiger-skin and wielding a stolen wand, takes the lead in organizing her escape, along with a virtuous but slightly hapless prince, from the anthropophagous ogres into whose direly unsafe custody they have fallen. In the last story in the batch "La Bonne petite souris" (tr. as "The Good Little Mouse") the sympathetic characters are all female, and the two male characters are both utterly horrible.

It might well be the case that, although the nine stories in the first two batches are probably presented in the approximate order of their composition, the three stories embedded in the first of the *nouvelles espagnoles*, "Don Gabriel Ponce de Leon," are no later than them. "Le Mouton" (tr. as "The Sheep"), "Finette Cendron" and "Fortunée" all give the impression of being relatively early works, and "Finette Cendron," as previously mentioned, might well have been a direct influence on at least two of Perrault's tales. "Le Nain jaune" (tr. as "The Yellow Dwarf,") which is the first of the two stories embedded in the slighter Spanish novella, "Don Fernand de Toledo," like "Le Mouton," refuses the happy ending otherwise compulsory in d'Aulnoy's tales, and also shares with "Finette Cendron" a particularly ostentatious moralization. All of d'Aulnoy's stories, like Perrault's, carefully append explicit morals in doggerel verse to the narratives, but the supposed morals often appear to be arbitrary, and sometimes feebly inapt; "Finette Cendron" and "Le Nain jaune" are two of the very few stories she wrote that give the appearance of having been planned in advance and designed to extrapolate and illustrate their concluding morals.

Some of d'Aulnoy's other stories give the impression of have started out with the intention of illustrating particular moralistic conclusions, but then becoming distracted and going astray in the wilderness of their own fantastic imagery. In the story sandwiched between the two Spanish novellas, "Babiole," the second story embedded in "Don Fernand de Toledo," "Serpentin Vert," and the second story in the following group of three, "La Grenouille bienfaisante" (tr. as "The Benevolent Frog"), that tendency to get carried away by strange imagery becomes extreme, and freely indulged, to the point that the three stories in question become decidedly surreal. However, probably under the powerful example of Murat, most of d'Aulnoy's later work attempts much more coherent organization and more intricate plotting.

"La Princesse Carpillon" marked a new departure in that regard, and although it employs a deformed male villain closely akin to the one featured in "Le Prince lutin," the story is very distinctive, not merely in its remarkable characterization of the Amazon Fay but in its careful construction of life-stories of its hero and heroine, and the acute problems that arise when they eventually meet from their mistaken ideas of their relative status, which seem to make their relationship impossible in spite of their *amour parfait*—a narrative strategy recapitulated, with further exaggeration, in "Le Pigeon et la colombe," the third of the stories embedded *in Le Nouveau bourgeois gentilhomme*.

The third story in the batch of three, "La Biche au bois" (tr. as "The Woodland Hind") begins with a deliberate recapitulation of the initiating incident of "La Princesse printanière", in which the heroine is condemned by virtue of the curse of an evil fay to be raised from infancy in a subterranean palace, prohibited from seeing sunlight before a deadline in her teenage years. That is a variant of one of the perennial motifs of the genre: princesses isolated from the world in inaccessible places, often high towers, more often in luxury than in abject misery. Although the motif is, to some extent, a reflection of the way in which aristocratic daughters were routinely brought up in seventeenth-century France, carefully isolated from society and maintained in calculated ignorance until they reached the age of marriage (usually construed as fourteen or fifteen), the psychological underpinnings of the image in "La Biche au bois" are more complicated, and murkier than a simple analogy might suggest. In "La Princesse printanière" the emphasis of the story is on the ignorance of the heroine and the catastrophic effects of that ignorance on the naïve awakening of her sexuality, but in "La Biche au bois" the effect is more complicated, and the adventure of the princess, when she is inadvertently led to break the interdiction, far more graphic, involving one of the drastic metamorphoses crucial to the development of many of d'Aulnoy's plots.

The first of the six stories embedded in *Le Nouveau bourgeois gentilhomme*, "La Chatte blanche," also includes deliberate recapitulations of motifs previously employed not only by d'Aulnoy but by her fellow writers, including the disastrous craving in pregnancy employed by La Force in "Persinelle." The story includes a good deal of surreal imagery and calculated extremism, but mingles them with so many typical motifs—three brothers competing in challenging tasks, the desperate attempts of a prince to extract an imprisoned princess from a high tower, etc.—that it became a kind of model *conte de fées*, frequently reprinted in isolation from its original context, although it is arguably the weakest of the batch of six by virtue of its relative disorganization and inconsistency.

"Belle-Belle, ou Le Chevalier Fortuné" also deals in the esthetics of the absurd in its depiction of the heroine's seven "endowed men," each of whom is blessed with a rather absurd special talent, but who make up a team collectively capable of superheroic tasks. The story is, however, more coherently organized than "La Chatte blanche," and remarkable in the depiction of its female villain, a dowager queen driven to vengeful excess by her failure to seduce the knight who is a woman in male disguise, and who is in love—seemingly hopelessly— with the king. Although the starkly clear implicit moral of the story is that hell hath no fury like a woman scorned, that is not the message summarized in the concluding doggerel. It is, of course, impossible to know whether d'Aulnoy had a real model in mind when designing the character, or, if so, who it might have been.

Similar female villains are featured in the next two stories in the final batch; the queen in "Le Pigeon et la colombe" is determined to murder the princess with whom her son has fallen in love, because she is disguised—for good reason—as a shepherdess and thus seems too far beneath him, but that queen's atrocities, nasty as they are, pale in comparison with those of the appalling queen mother in "La Princesse Belle-Étoile et le prince Chéri," who imposes horrible torments upon her innocent daughter-in-law, her three children, and another of her grandchildren, aided by her victim's horrible sister and a vile maidservant, who similarly seem to have no real reason for their actions but sadism and inherent evil. It seems unlikely that either royal character could have been modeled on anyone in Louis XIV's court, but that might not have prevented at least one member of the court suspecting that she might be an intended target of caricature, perhaps making some contribution to d'Aulnoy's abrupt fall from favor.

It is possible that "Le Prince marcassin" and "Le Dauphin" were written before the previous two items, and moved to the end of the queue because they were both derived from Straparola, and were obvious parallel exercises to two of Murat's stories. The comparison between them and Murat's "Le Roi porc" and "Le Turbot" is, in fact, a fascinating study of the different directions the extrapolations imposed by the rival writers took. It is arguable that the narrative moves that Murat made in both cases to free her central characters from the curses imposed upon them, although admirable ingenious and intricate, are less honest than the more straightforward confrontations with adversity featured in d'Aulnoy's narratives, but the variations in their imagery and the contrasting strategies of their plotting provide a graphic illustration of the enormous potential contained in what might seem at first glance to be a rather limited lexicon of images and a relatively narrow set of narrative maneuvers.

Although d'Aulnoy's endeavors in the genre went through a number of distinct phases, certain consistencies remained that expose intrinsic features of the genre as it was conceived by its inventors. At no stage in her career as a writer of *contes de fées* did her absolute commitment to Ovidian and Scudéryesque Virtue waver, and she was always a diehard champion of altruism and forgiveness. One might imagine that a reasonable Churchman would approve of that, but in fact, it is entirely possible that a devout critic would have thought it pernicious, and dangerous, precisely because the tacit argument of the narratives in question—perhaps accidentally, although one cannot help suspecting that d'Aulnoy, along with Murat and La Force, would have stood by it heroically if challenged—is that Christ and the Christian God are utterly irrelevant to virtuous sentiment and action. The world of the fays is a world replete with evil and with appalling actions committed simply for the love of evil, but it is also a world that has no need of assisted redemption, where opposition to evil is provided entirely by instinctive decency and the effects of a very particular, and perhaps peculiar, notion of Amour.

Madame d'Aulnoy can now be seen as the most extreme promoter of that ideology as well as the most prolific, probably because she was consciously engaged in a constant competition in extremism that she wanted to win. None of the leading writers of *contes de fées*, either during the 1698 boom or the mid-seventeenth century revival was afraid of calculated excess when it came to imaginative innovation, but no one else was as flamboyant in that excess as d'Aulnoy; because her work lacked the polish and narrative organization of Murat's, it also lacked her delicacy and discretion, and that might have been the reason why pious observers appear to have thought that d'Aulnoy was the most dangerous of an inherently dangerous bunch: the writer whose works ought to be first in the queue for banning or burning—which might well be why their early editions really do seem either to have been aborted before publication, or burned afterwards, silently but thoroughly.

By 1734, as Lenglet Du Fresnoy observed, d'Aulnoy was being promoted, in the shadow of Perrault, as a writer primarily fit for reading by children, and the entire genre was typically regarded by subsequent commentators in the same light, but in fact, Perrault and Fénelon were the only writers involved in the initial boom who designed their work for the consumption of children, and it is by no means difficult to make out a case for d'Aulnoy's work, in spite of the routine attachment of specific—but highly unconvincing—morals, being blatantly unfit for children. She was not the only writer in the genre to feature sadistic fays who take great delight in torturing their victims extravagantly and ingeniously, but she set the standard for such horrors with such characters as Carabosse in "La Princesse printanière," Magotine in "Serpentin vert," Lionne in "La Grenouille bienfaisante" and Grognette in "Le Dauphin." Nor was she the only writer to deal extensively in unrelentingly vicious and murderous ordinary women—mothers and sisters as well as stepmothers and scorned lovers—but no one else matched the sheer nastiness of Duchesse Grognon in "Gracieuse et Percinet", the king's sister in "Belle-Belle, ou Le Chevalier Fortuné" and the queen mother in "La Princesse Belle-Étoile et Prince Chéri." Nor did any other writer take generic work as far into the esoterically perverse realms of surrealism as d'Aulnoy did in the triptych constituted by "Babiole," "Serpentin vert" and "La Grenouille bienfaisante."

It makes far more sense to regard d'Aulnoy and Murat as significant writers in the development of what would be dubbed stylistically "decadent" fantasy in the late nineteenth century—the idea of which assisted a second, albeit limited renaissance in the production of *contes de fées*—rather than as writers for children, and one is bound to wonder what they might have done had they been allowed to continue with the process of evolution that they had begun and taken forward with such rapidity. Having already moved from the production of novelettes to novellas, it seems highly likely that one or both of them might have progressed to the writing of full-length novels, or even works of more epic length, with plots of a complexity and narrative sophistication to match. Given that both writers had extraordinary imaginative range, it is hard to imagine that they would have run out of inspiration any time soon, even without the spur of their ongoing rivalry, had they not been violently stopped in their tracks. It was not to be, however, and we have to be content to be grateful that they contrived to publish as much as they did during their brief window of opportunity, leaving behind fugitive material that could be recovered once the worst of the tempest of repression had blown over.

Considered separately Madame d'Aulnoy and the Comtesse de Murat were both great writers of imaginative fiction, but seen as the core members of a competitive collective they are surely unique in literary history, and it is as part of that collective endeavor that Madame d'Aulnoy became fully entitled to her classic status, even though her modern reputation is somewhat misrepresentative of her actual ability and achievement. It is routinely overlooked today that her work first reached print as literary contraband, which the censors of the day attempted with the legal might at their disposal to suppress and annihilate, as a dangerous encouragement to freethinking—but it survived, and thrived, in spite of that, and to some extent because of it, and it set a fine example for almost all of the authors who came after her in keeping the flickering flame of the genre alive in the burgeoning Age of Enlightenment.

Fellow Travelers

All of the writers who became peripherally involved in the writing of *contes de fées* during its brief period of fashionability developed the generic materials that they adopted in accordance with their own priorities. Like "Sans parangon," the second of Jean de Préchac's two *Contes moins contes que les autres*, "La Reine des fées" is transformed as the narrative develops into an allegory of French history, albeit one that is odder and more enigmatic—and hence, perhaps, more interesting—than its predecessor.

The other licensed publication that appeared in 1698, *Les Illustres fées*, is more straightforwardly attached to the central mission of the genre, as defined by its inventors, but the stories in it are mostly notable for their routine failure to create much dramatic suspense in contriving their conclusions, which often fade out limply. It is difficult to understand why so many subsequent bibliographers, from Lenglet Du Fresnoy in 1735 to Antoine Barbier in the nineteenth century, were prepared to attribute the collection to Madame d'Aulnoy, although that absurdity was avoided by Charles-Joseph Mayer, who could see the distinction very clearly. The author of *Les Illustres fées* is closer to Perrault in his determination to restrict the length of his stories to what might be read aloud in a single sitting, even though several of them would have benefited from further expansion as well as more dramatic tension.

The stories in the collection are also closer in spirit to "gallant" fiction than most *contes de fées*, especially "Prince Roger," which sets out as an interesting picaresque tale employing magical treasure buried by Melusine, before abruptly changing direction when its initially-libidinous hero abruptly and inexplicably falls prey to amorous exclusivity. In general, the stories featuring robust male heroes, including the son and victim of "Le Roi magicien" (tr. as "The Magician King"), the giant-slaying "Prince Guerini," the excessively fortunate "Le Favori des fées" (tr. as "The Favorite of the Fays") and the unfortunately gullible king in "Bienfaisant, ou Quiribirini" (tr. as "Beneficent; or, Quiribirini") are composed with more verve and conviction than those focused on their heroines, such as "La Reine de l'Ile des fleurs" (tr. as "The Queen of the Isle of Flowers") as "La Princesse couronnée par les fées" (tr. as "The Princess Crowned by the Fays").

That feature of the collection lends strong support to the notion that the author was a man, although its attribution to a prolific author of gallant fiction whose initials were decoded as "Monsieur le Chevalier de Mailly" seems a trifle flimsy, in spite of its eventual acceptance by Mayer and the Bibliothèque Nationale catalogue, and the consequent attribution to Louis de Mailly (1657-1724). Whoever the author was, though, he took the opportunity to imitate

Préchac by casting a blatant exercise in egregious flattery as a *conte de fées* in "L'Île inaccessible" (tr. as "The Inaccessible Isle"). Louis XIV would have discovered far less reason for taking offense at his portrayal therein than he could have found in "Sans parangon," although the story might not have delighted Madame de Maintenon, who is now thought to have been secretly married to the king, by virtue of its depiction of his successful seduction by a phenomenally beautiful queen and their spectacularly happy marriage.

The fourth male author whose dabbling in the production of *contes de fées* prior to 1697 has left detectable evidential traces, Francois Fénelon, did so with the most obvious moralistic and educational agenda, and his stories are the most straightforward in that regard. The longest of them, "Histoire de Rosimond et Braminte" (tr. as "The Story of Rosimond and Braminte") is a cautionary tale recommending discretion to anyone gifted with a ring of invisibility by a fay, but the author apparently felt that he had not made the lesson sufficiently emphatic, and followed it up with the briefer but more dramatic "Histoire du roi Alfaroute et de Clariphile" (tr. as "The Story of King Alfaroute and Clariphile"). In two stories with female protagonists, "Histoire de Florise" (tr. as "Florise") and "Histoire d'une vieille reine et d'une jeune paysanne" (tr. as "The Story of an Old Peasant Woman and a Young Peasant Girl") the characters in question learn by experience that the lot of a simple peasant girl is infinitely preferable to that of a queen—a contention by which the young Duc de Bourgogne might not have been entirely convinced. The stories remained unpublished until they were issued in a collection of *Fables* published in 1718.

Lenglet Du Fresnoy lists one 1698 collection of *Contes* that seems to have vanished completely, by the Breton playwright Pierre de Lesconvel (1650-1722), which he dismisses as trivial, although the sparseness of the data he provides suggests that he not had actually seen it. Charles Mayer makes brief reference to it in his *Cabinet*, but his comment and all listings in subsequent bibliographies seem to be based entirely on Lenglet Du Fresnoy's note. If it is not a mistake on Lenglet Du Fresnoy's part, other texts published in the era might also have vanished, leaving no trace in 1734.

Two works that did achieve illicit anonymous publication were *La Comtesse de Mortane* (1700) and *Les Petits soupers de l'été de l'année 1699, ou Galante aventures, avec L'Origine des fées* [The Little Suppers of Summer 1699; or, Galant Adventures, with "The Origin of the Fays"] (1702) by an author nowadays identified as Catherine Durand Bédacier (1670-1736), although she only seems to have used the surname Durand. The former portmanteau includes the interpolated tale of "La Fée Lubantine" (tr. as "The Fay Lubantine"), a more violently tragic story than Catherine Bernard's atypical couplet, prompting one to wonder whether it is entirely coincidental that Bernard and Durand, the authors of the most spectacularly downbeat *contes de fées* in the original set, were the only two not of aristocratic heritage. "Le Prodige d'amour" (tr. as "The Prodigy of Amour"), the first of two *contes de fées* in the 1702 portmanteau, is a much more orthodox tale, but "L'Origine des fées" breaks the pattern flamboyantly, not only accounting for the origin of the fays, as the offspring of Jupiter and a nymph, but also their apparent disappearance from the world after a period of allegedly-inevitable decadence.

Both of the portmanteaux cited were successful, and were reprinted more than once before being included in a posthumous five-volume collection of *Oeuvres de Madame Durand* produced with the aid of a royal privilege in 1737, which presumably prompted Pierre-François Beauchamps, in his novella *Funestine*, published in that year to afford "Durand" a place of honor in the eponymous heroine's library, alongside d'Aulnoy and Murat, and to take some inspiration from "L'Origine des fées" in his own account of the prehistoric origin and subsequent extinction of fays.

Another work that is presumably by an author who attended the salons in which *contes de fées* were read prior to 1699 is *La Tyrannie des fées détruite, nouveaux contes, dédiez à Madame la Duchesse de Bourgogne par la Comtesse D.L.*, published in Paris by Jean Fournil under royal privilege in 1703 and followed by *Les Chevaliers Errans et le Génie familier par Madame la Comtesse D*** published by Pierre Ribou, similarly under royal privilege, in 1709. At some point in the mid-eighteenth century the name "Madame d'Auneuil" seems to have been suggested as the possible author of the former collection, possibly by someone uncertain as to how "d'Aulnoy" ought to be spelled, but Joseph de La Porte makes no mention in his history of any Madame d'Auneuil, and when Charles Meyer first cited the name in his *Cabinet des fées* it was to express his conviction that no such person had ever existed, although he subsequently changed his mind and identified the person in question as Louise de Bossigny— a designation accepted by the Bibliothèque National catalogue.

Louise de Bossigny is mentioned elsewhere as the wife of Louis-Claude Barjot, Marquis d'Auneuil, who died in 1700—a death date sometimes attributed, to the "Madame d'Auneuil" credited with the two works in question in spite of their dates of publication—and that seems to be the source of the suggestion that Louise de Bossigny might have been responsible for the two volumes published in 1703 and 1709. There never was a Comte of that name, but Louis-Claude Barjot did have a younger brother, Jean Barjot, Seigneur d'Auneuil et de Carville, and his second wife was named Marthe de La Croix, which might provide a better explanation for the L in the signature than the surname Bossigny, although neither could explain the "Comtesse." The attribution of the texts to either of those actual Madame d'Auneuils is, therefore, purely speculative and very dubious.

Given the apparent difficulty of acquiring royal privileges for *contes de fées* in the period in which they appeared, the wonder is, of course, that "Comtesse D.L." managed to obtain two. The first might, to some extent, reflect that the title story of, *La Tyrannie des fées détruite* (tr. as "The Tyranny of the

Fays Abolished") the title of which might have seemed ironically apt to the censors, is an exercise in extravagant flattery. Flattery of the royal family was, of course, extremely commonplace in all the literature produced by Louis XIV's courtiers, but "Comtesse D.L." went to an unprecedented and highly unusual extreme in the novella in question, as the story's dedicatee, the Duchesse de Bourgogne not only features as a character in the story but plays the role of a messianic redeemer, abolishing the seemingly-unassailable tyranny of the evil fays—who have long delighted in afflicting couples of young lovers vindictively by metamorphosing one or both of them into animals—simply by means of her charismatic and majestic presence when she arrives at Versailles.

"Comtesse D.L." was obviously familiar with the Comtesse de Murat's work, and although she was not nearly as polished or as imaginative a writer as Murat, she was certainly trying to take over where she had left off. The title novella of her first collection employs Murat's method of story-construction developing portmanteaux of interconnected tales in a crude and tentative fashion, but "Les Chevalier errans" (tr. as "The Knights Errant")—which is the author's most impressive story, in spite of a certain clumsiness and disorganization—carries it forward very extravagantly.

As previously noted, three of the stories in Murat's 1699 collection refer to the celebrations associated with the wedding at Versailles on 7 December 1697 of the Duc de Bourgogne, then fifteen years old, and his cousin Marie-Adélaïde de Savoie, a result of the Treaty of Turin, by virtue of which Savoy switched sides in the Nine Years War and became France's ally. Neither Murat nor "Comtesse D.L." mentions in their references to the event that the bride was only a couple of days past her twelfth birthday, having been considered too young for marriage when she first arrived in Paris some months previously. Presumably, the young duchesse, who was several years older by the time *La Tyrannie des fées détruite* was published, and must by then have come into contact with *contes de fées*, appreciated the role she played in the story, and the Duc might have been influential in obtaining the privilege for its publication. No one was to know that shortly after her husband became the Dauphin of France, following the death of his father in 1711, the Duchesse would die of measles; the Duc insisted on staying by her bedside throughout, caught the disease, and followed her to the grave within a week, followed in his turn by his eldest son, leaving the younger one to succeed to the throne as Louis XV after the death of Louis XIV in 1715.

Although the presence of the title story of first collection might conceivably be a sufficient explanation of how that volume broke the pattern and obtained a royal license, it cannot help to account for a second license being granted to *Les Chevaliers errans*. The likelihood is, therefore, that the author of the two texts was a person of sufficiently considerable influence in the court to override the tacit interdiction of such works. As to who that might have been we can now only guess, but if one were making a book on it, the favorite would surely be the dowager Princesse de Conti rather than the obscure wife of the obscure Marquis d'Auneuil, whose presence at court seems to be otherwise unrecorded. The mystery, however, remains insoluble.

The subsidiary stories in the 1703 collection are undistinguished, although "Agatie, princesse des Scites" (tr. as Agatie, Princess of the Scyths") is interesting in its attempt to connect "the time of the fays" to actual history and geography, introducing a dose of *realpolitik* into its story-line. "La Princesse Léonice" (tr. as "Princesse Leonice"), the only other completed story in the collection, is more orthodox in its account of the fierce rivalry between two royal sisters, which moves inexorably toward the recruitment of fay magic, imprisonment in a high tower, the reversal of inconvenient metamorphoses and climactic dragon-slaying. The incomplete story, in which a knight provided with a ring of invisibility finds its temptations deadly to his pretentions to chivalric virtue, seems to have been aborted for precisely that reason, and it is perhaps not surprising that when the author continued her literary quest, she elected to do so with the aid of a far more robust model of post-Quixotic knightly perfection. Although one or two of the fellow knights errant he picks up along his way are considerably less perfect, he is careful to tell them to stand back and look after the ladies and the horses when the time comes for his climactic confrontation with the forces of evil, in order that Virtue might triumph in glorious isolation.

The second portmanteau in the latter collection is rudely interrupted, like the final story in the first collection, and summarily aborted; the mock-Oriental frame narrative containing the interpolated stories is simply abandoned, as if forgotten. Nor does "La Princesse Patientine dans la forêt d'Erimente" (tr. as "Princess Patientine in the Forest of Erimente"), the interpolated story that actually concludes the printed text, fit that pseudo-Gallandesque frame, seemingly having been transplanted from an alien fictional world: the allegorical sector of the classical *conte de fées*. It is, however, a striking work in its fashion. The story's representation of contemporary marriage as a matter of innocent young women barely out of childhood falling into the brutal hands of disgusting ogres who abuse them horribly is not unusual, but the conclusion of the tale is, in which Prince Courageous, eager to do battle against the monsters protecting the cave where his beloved princess is being held captive, is sternly told to put away his unnecessary sword, the rescue in question being women's work. When the mission is complete, the prince is graciously permitted to continue adoring the princess from afar, provided that he never lays a finger on her, while she enjoys a perfect bliss with her steadfast female best friend, under the tutelage of their benign protectress, the fay Clementine. The symbolism is not difficult to decode, although the royal censors seem to have turned a blind eye to it.

The story of Patientine might have been written long before its publication, perhaps in the 1690s, because it certainly does not fit the aborted portmanteau into which it was inserted, which must have been of recent composition, and clearly reflects an important shift in the literary landscape of fantastic literature. The Orientalist Antoine Galland (1646-1715), who had been working in the Royal Library for many years, and was certainly acquainted with Charles Perrault and the female writers of *contes de fées*, issued the first two volumes of *Les Mille et une nuits* in 1704; the complete set eventually ran to twelve volumes, the last of them published in 1717.

Supposedly derived from Arabic manuscripts, there is some controversy as to the extent that Galland's compendium really qualifies as a translation of the manuscripts in question rather than a drastic reworking, with interpolations of pure pastiche, allegedly based on tales told to him orally by a Maronite monk from Aleppo, although skeptics inevitably suspect that he simply made up such tales as those of Ali Baba and Aladdin himself. What is not in doubt is that the first two volumes—for which, as an allegedly scholarly work, there was no difficulty obtaining a privilege—achieved an instant popular success, continued by the subsequent volumes, which rapidly gave birth to a host of imitations, all of them claiming to be translations from various exotic languages, almost all of them falsely.

The success of such works was not immediately seen as an extension of or supplement to the genre of *contes de fees*, although Lenglet Du Fresnoy links them in his 1735 bibliography. By 1786, however, the proliferations of the genre of pseudo-Oriental fantasies seemed to Charles Mayer to have been so confused with the contraband renaissance of *contes de fées* that the two genres appeared to him to have become inseparable. Several authors involved in that renaissance dabbled in both kinds of fantasy, and there are several hybrid works. The most significant imagistic overlap between the genres, however, arose as a result of a linguistic confusion.

In translating from Arabic to French Galland rendered the Arabic word *jinni* (whose plural is *jinn*), which refers to powerful, mostly malevolent spiritual beings akin to demons, as *génie*, which usually referred in French, with reference to spiritual beings, to more benign entities. When Galland's work was translated into English, the translators thought rendering it into English as "genius" would be misleading, so they simply transcribed it as genie, thus giving rise to an idiosyncratic class of beings which took on a literary career of their own. *Génies* of a sort already had a minor role in *contes de fées*, in the sense of Roman protective *genii* [still echoed in English in the phrase "the genius of the place"], and when the renaissance of *contes de fées* began in the 1730s several of the writers who made crucial contributions to that renaissance expanded that role vastly, substituting *génies* far more reminiscent of Arabic *jinn* than Roman protective spirits for the male enchanters of the original *contes de fées*, in a reconfigured hierarchy of agents of enchantment. That move had an implicit effect on the way fays were perceived, emphasizing the supernatural component of their presumed identity and taking a step away from their original characterization as human *magiciennes*.

60

Steps of that kind had, of course, been made before, encouraged by the recruitment of Melusine to the ranks of illustrious fays. Catherine Durand's account of the origin of the fays was one such move, and another, even more striking, was made in *Florine* (1713), the last *conte de fées* to obtain a royal privilege while Louis XIV was still alive. As with *La Tyrannie des fées détruite*, the fact that *Florine* received that privilege seems puzzling, as it presumably required some special circumstance to justify it, probably some particular influence at court. The work might, however, provide an interesting link between the first phase of *contes de fées* and their renaissance, because the work is nowadays attributed to a writer who probably played a key role in that renaissance, Françoise Le Marchand (?-1754). If she did write *Florine*, as seems not unlikely, she must have been very young at the time, although her precise birth-date remains unknown, but it does read like the work of a very young author, perhaps a precocious teenager.

Before becoming Madame Le Marchand, the individual in question was Françoise Duché de Vancy; she was the daughter of the playwright and composer Joseph-François Duché de Vancy (1668-1704), a gentleman of Louis XIV's household, who was the king's *valet de chambre* for a time; his musical works—greatly admired by Madame de Maintenon, who obtained a pension for him—were mostly based in Classical and scriptural sources; he was also an antiquarian, elected to the Académie des inscriptions et médailles, who must have known Antoine Galland well. Little is known about Françoise Duché de Vancy's life except that she eventually became the hostess of a notable salon attended by celebrated artists, composers and litterateurs—but that was after her marriage and long after the publication of *Florine*, so it is best left for comment until a later stage in the present narrative.

Although she cannot have had any influence herself over the royal censors, if she was the author of *Florine*, Françoise Duché de Vancy's relative youth might have worked in her favor. If, as seems likely, she had spent part of her childhood at Versailles, as a companion of one of the various royal children, she could well have endeared herself to the maternal sentiments of people very near the throne, including Madame de Maintenon. If she had attended literary salons prior to 1697 it could only have been as a child, but that is by no means impossible, and if she did, it would not be surprising if *contes de fées* she heard read there made a deep impression on her.

Florine differs sharply from the core examples of *contes de fées* in making its fays frankly supernatural beings of a highly idiosyncratic kind, although that is hard to reconcile logically with the fact that their nasty stand-in queen, seemingly alone of her kind, has a mysteriously-sired son—a motif inherited from Mademoiselle de La Force's "Plus belle que fée," on which *Florine*'s plot is obviously based.

In the first part of the relentlessly eccentric allegorical narrative, the heroine, in quest of the "imperial rose without thorns"—which, we are told explicitly, is a symbol of virtue—is warned that in the course of her journey she will meet a series of tempters who will endeavor with various degrees of cunning to draw her away from the true path to virtue and draw her to her doom. She avoids falling prey to the temptation of indolence, refuses even to set foot on the road to the palace of "volupté" [sensual pleasure] and runs away in frank horror at her first glimpse of drunken debauchery, but she only narrowly avoids the last in the sequence of temptations: marriage, perhaps an odd inclusion in a list of things to be avoided at all costs on the road to virtue, all the more so as poor Florine cannot ultimately escape the formularistic ending of all *contes de fees*. It is, however, perhaps not inappropriate that the first wave of *contes de fées* should have concluded, belatedly, with a work written by an innocent that is both paradoxical and puzzling.

The Contraband Renaissance

It is highly likely that numerous *contes de fées* produced for the Parisian salons before 1699, and others produced after that date, which could not reach print at the time, were still around for some time thereafter, and a few of them almost certainly resurfaced in due course. Shortly after Estienne Roger had combined several of the collections published in 1697-98 and *Florine* with Madame d'Aulnoy's works in his *Cabinet des Fées*, thus facilitating the preservation not only of d'Aulnoy's work but some of Murat's, both of Préchac's and the stories in *Les Illustres fées*, an anonymous collection of tales was issued as *Nouveaux contes de fées* (1718). There is considerable reason to believe that the stories it contained where not new at all, and that some, at least, dated back at least twenty years.

When Charles Mayer compiled his version of *Le Cabinet des fées* in the late 1780s he accepted, albeit a trifle belatedly, the attribution of *Les Illustres fees* to the Chevalier de Mailly, and he also attributed *Nouveaux contes de fées* to Mailly. It is not obvious why Mayer made that speculative attribution, but it is possible that he recognized the second item in the collection, "Les Perroquets," as a retitling of "La Princesse couronnée par les fees," which had previously appeared in *Les Illustres fées*, and drew the inference that the other stories in the collection might be by the same author. He could not know, however, that another story in the collection, "La Buisson d'Épines fleuries" would subsequently be attributed to the Comtesse de Murat, on the basis of a manuscript found among her papers, and he presumably had not read Catherine Bernard's *Inès de Cordoue* , thus preventing him from recognizing a third story, "Kadour," as a plagiarism of her version of "Riquet à la houppe," with the names of the gnome king and the princess he victimizes altered in order to disguise the theft.

Had Mayer realized that those other two stories were stolen goods, he would surely have doubted his speculative attribution of the collection to Mailly, and formed the suspicion that the stories in it were all by different hands. It is not impossible that Mailly was the plagiarist, and that some of the other stories in the collection are his, but it seems far more likely that he, Bernard and Murat were all victims of theft by an unknown hand. None of the other stories appear to be plagiarisms of previously-published stories, and they were probably gleanings from the salons where the game was played. The other stories are variable in theme and length, but several are notable, including "La Petite grenouille verte" (tr. as "The Little Green Frog"), which includes an interesting brace of magic mirrors, "Le Prince Perinet, ou L'Origine de Pagodes" (tr. as "Le Prince Perinet; or, The Origin of Pagodas"), which is a boisterous surreal extrapolation of the theme of vengeful metamorphoses, and the transvestite fantasy "Le

Médecin de satin" (tr. as "The Satin Physician"). "Le Prince Arc-en-ciel" (tr. as "The Rainbow Prince"), although derivative of Mademoiselle de La Force, also has some nice surreal touches, although the most surreal and innovative item in the collection is the bizarre "Le Navire Volant" (tr. as "The Flying Ship"), in which the fays retreat from the human world in a fanciful flying machine, but employ exotic means of keeping in touch with human society.

The two novelettes contained in *Le Prince des Aigues-marines et Le Prince Invisible* [The Prince of Aquamarines and The Invisible Prince] (1722) by Louise Cavelier (1703-1745), who became Madame Levêque (or Levesque) a year after its publication when she married one of the king's men-at-arms, was undoubtedly a new work, being the work of a writer not even born during the first wave of *contes de fées*, and still in her teens when she produced them. The book was published anonymously in Paris, with the unusual benefit of a royal privilege, so such privileges were not absolutely impossible to obtain at the time. It might seem unlikely that a teenage commoner from Rouen was able to acquire one, and one can only speculate as to how; she might have encountered her similarly humbly-born husband in entirely innocent circumstances, but it was not unknown for highly placed individuals at the court, including the princes of the blood, to arrange marriages with servants of the court for their mistresses, for the sake of convenience. At any rate, the volume was reprinted posthumously in 1744 when the renaissance was more fully under way and a demand had been clearly demonstrated for such works.

As might be expected of a work by such a young author, the stories are a trifle crude in their narrative construction, and flamboyant in their plotting. The hero of the first novelette is cursed at birth by the fay Noirjabarbe that when he reaches the age of twenty anyone who sees him will instantly drop dead—a circumstance that proves fortunate when he is about to be murdered by bloodthirsty savages at the moment he turns twenty, but causes great difficulties thereafter, especially in his romance with the Princess of the Isle of Night, even though she had been forced to live in a lightless tower for much of her life; the path of true love runs so unsmoothly that she eventually has to submit to a forced marriage to Noirjabarbe's hideous son, from which her liberation is a trifle belated, although—equally surprisingly—it occasions no comment on the part of the eponymous prince. "The Invisible Prince" also has extreme difficulties in wooing his beloved Princess Rosalie, because of the rivalry of a powerful prince of genii.

The author went on to publish several more books of poetry and drama, and two novels, including *Célenie, histoire allégorique* (1738), which is not a *conte de fées*, although the eponymous heroine is temporarily metamorphosed into a dog by the magic of her governess.

It is possible that several of the items contained in *Nouveaux contes de fées allégoriques* (1735), like at least some of the items in the 1718 anthology, are leftovers from the first phase of the genre's evolution, although the longest item, "Boca, ou La Vertu recompensée" (tr. as "Boca; or. Virtue Recompensed") is definitely the work of Françoise Le Marchand, who appears to have collated the collection and paid for its printing. No copy of the collection is presently available for consultation, although "Boca" was reprinted several times and is easily accessible, but the Bibliothèque Nationale catalogue lists the other contributors, anonymous at the time, as "La Présidente Dreuillet, Monsieur de Villeroy and Madame de Caylus," all three of whom were deceased

Elisabeth Dreuillet (1656-1730), author of "Le Phénix," is known to have been a member of the *petit court* maintained by the Duchesse du Maine (Louise-Bénédicte de Bourbon, 1676-1753), at the Château de Sceaux. A contemporary review of the book by Abbé Pierre-François Desfontaines reports that "Le Phénix" is the tale of Prince Discret, metamorphosed into a phoenix by an evil fay, much to the distress of Princess Espérance. After describing "Boca," Desfontaines names the third story in the collection as "Amours de Lysandre et de Carlin" but does not name the fourth, so there is some uncertainty as to which story is attributable to François de Neufville, Duc de Villeroy (1644-1730) and which to the Marquise de Caylus (1673-1729). All three of the authors supplementing Madame Le Marchand's story had been important courtiers in the 1690s and all of them had been closely acquainted with Madame de Maintenon, who had taken responsibility for bringing up the future Marquise de Caylus when she was orphaned.

We can only speculate as to how Madame Le Marchand came by the works she assembled in the anthology, although she might have acquired them while the authors were alive. The presence in the group of Madame de Caylus opens the possibility that they might have reached Le Marchand via her son, Philippe, Comte de Caylus (1692-1765), another member of the Duchesse du Maine's *petit court* and almost certainly a member of Francoise Le Marchand's salon as well, who subsequently became the most prolific contributor to the renaissance of *contes de fées*. However Le Marchand came by the materials, though, the list of names reinforces the hypothesis that she had once had powerful friends at court, who were much older than she was; the Duchesse du Maine—yet another survivor of a disastrous arranged marriage, contracted when she was fifteen— might have been one of them. Although the duchesse was rumored to be on bad terms with her fellow princess of the blood, the dowager Princesse de Conti, it is not at all improbable that she was present in the Princesse de Conti's apartment when *contes de fées* were being read there, and might even have played the game herself.

The Comte de Caylus might have known Françoise Duché de Vancy as a child, and he certainly knew her as an adult; as an antiquarian and an important pioneer of archeology, he would have been interested in her father's work in that vein. In one of his stories there is an apparent reference to a *conte de fées* by the renowned artist and writer Charles-Antoine Coypel (1694-1792), which had not been published at the time and which he could only have heard read aloud in Madame Le Marchand's salon. Some insight into that salon is offered by a footnote added by Mayer to his reprint of Coypel's story in the 1786 *Cabinet*, with reference to Coypel's brief introduction into the story of a character named Thémire, said to be still active in Parisian literary circles. The note includes an excerpt from a letter written by Coypel to an unnamed friend in which the artist waxes lyrical about "Thémire," making it clear that it was a nickname adopted by Le Marchand:

"The moderns say, then, that Thémire is the image of their Deshoulières? For myself I say that, by the grace of God, Thémire only resembles Thémire. Thémire has an imagination so prodigious that it requires nothing less than her prodigious reason to regulate it. Now, Mademoiselle Sapho had a great deal of imagination, but reason…zeft! Madame Deshoulières perhaps had a great deal of reason, but would she have imagined *Boca*? I ask you. You can see that I'm right to tell you that Thémire only resembles Thémire. Besides which, Thémire is incomparable for sentiments. On great occasions Thémire's reason would be capable of loving the persons that her heart detested, and her mind arranges all that so well that the devil, or what is worse, a woman, could not tell whether it is the heart or the reason that loves. Finally, to complete the portrait of Thémire, her character is so mild that in all the petty bickering of society, she makes efforts to persuade herself that the wrong is on her side, and it is always the reason that dominates."

The likening of "Thémire" to "Mademoiselle Sapho" (i.e., Mademoiselle de Scudéry) implies that Le Marchand saw her own salon as a direct descendant of Mademoiselle de Scudéry's, formed in its image. The note also makes it clear that although Le Marchand published very little, she was greatly admired by at least some of the members of her salon. In Coypel's story, "Thémire" is not only credited with the "recently published" *Boca*, but also the "soon-to-be published" *Javotte*—which never actually appeared in print—and numerous other *contes de fées*, some of them written when she was very young, perhaps including *Florine*. Evidently, the author gave up seeking publication after financing the publication of the 1735 collection, content thereafter with the private adulation of a select audience.

The self-selection of Le Marchand's pseudonym is significant. Thémire is the chaste heroine of a prose narrative by the historian and political philosopher Baron de Montesquieu, *Le Temple de Gnide* (1724). Montesquieu's Thémire is a favored devotee of a uniquely delicate cult of Venus in which the kind of amour the goddess favors is opposed to and contrasted with vulgar physical lust (closely akin to the alternative Amour featured in Madame d'Aulnoy's story "Le Pigeon et la colombe"). Montesquieu's work enjoyed a brief heyday of celebrity, which led to Thémire being the subject of numerous songs and other literary

works written in the mid-eighteenth century. Montesquieu would have been interested in Joseph-François Duché de Vancy's work for the same reason as
Caylus, and almost certainly knew his daughter.

"Boca" is a longer novella than any produced during the first wave, beginning as the tale of the eponymous hero, a woodcarver magically lured into an
exacting quest to liberate a petrified process from a long-lasting curse inflicted
by a loathsome prince of genii. The heart of the work is, however, the long account the princess then gives Boca of the manner in which she ended up in her
predicament, after falling in love with a prince disguised as a girl—while protesting all the while that she would also love the female best friend with whom
she had spent many happy hours alone in "the palace of pleasure," for as long as
she might live. Curiously, even though the story is subtitled "virtue rewarded,"
poor Boca does not seem to obtain any reward at all for his trouble except for
that of being allowed to live and die contentedly as a virgin.

Le Marchand's collection was not the only unprivileged collection of pre-
viously-unpublished *contes de fées* to appear in 1735. *Trois nouveaux contes de
fées, avec une préface qui n'est pas moins sérieuse.*[Three New Tales of Fays,
with a preface that is no less serious] was attributed by Mayer when he reprinted
the three stories in his *Cabinet* to Catherine de Lintot, who had been previously
identified as the author of *Histoire de Mademoiselle de Salens* (1740), but he
added to that attribution the remark that the author was now fifty-eight years old.
As that would imply that she had written the stories in collection at the age of
seven, either "fifty-eight" must be a misprint or the attribution is incorrect. That
did not prevent many subsequent sources copying the paradoxical claim, although the Bibliothèque Nationale catalogue puts a dutiful question mark after
the suggested birth date of 1728. Joseph de La Porte had previously included
Madame de Lintot in his *Histoire littéraire des femme françoises* (1769) as the
author of the 1740 novel, but he had not attributed the collection of *contes de
fées* to her and he did not offer a date of birth or any other biographical information. Perhaps significantly, Mayer did not include Lintot in the extensive annotated list of authors of *contes de fées* included in volume 37 of his *Cabinet*.
The attribution must therefore be reckoned dubious.

The three stories, "Timandre et Bleuette" (tr. as "Timandre and Bleuette",
"Le Prince Sincer" (tr. as "Prince Sincere") and "Tendrebrun et Constance" (tr.
as "Tendrebrun and Constance"), constitute a rather limited body of work, but
they are nevertheless rather remarkable. They show a very marked evolution,
each story being more substantial, more complicated and more imaginatively
innovative than its predecessor. They clearly attempt deliberately to take up
where Baronne d'Aulnoy and the Comtesse de Murat had been forced to leave
off, in terms of their imaginative extravagance, their use of metamorphoses and
their quirky employment of allegory, and they do so in a robust manner that is
certainly not merely imitative.

In particular, the stories show a marked development in the direction of the calculatedly absurd and the surreal. Although it is arguable that the multiplicity of those trends make the stories rather untidy and imagistically overloaded, there is more virtue in striving to do too much than settling for barely doing enough; the hectic pace and bizarre imagery of "Le Prince Sincer" and "Tendrebrun et Constance," in particular, give the stories a peculiar charm that might have remained unique had not Pierre-François Beauchamps, Mademoiselle de Lubert and the Comte de Caylus taken up the thread, almost certainly with an awareness of those models.

Fays also feature, albeit marginally, in a longer romance published in 1735, a satirical account of the *Voyage merveilleux du Prince Fan-Férédin dans la Romancie* (tr. as "The Marvelous Voyage of Prince Fan-Férédin in Romancia"), written by the Jesuit Guillaume-Hyacinthe Bougéant in direct and explicit response to Lenglet Du Fresnoy's *De l'usage des romans*. Bougéant's work, reflecting on Lenglet Du Fresnoy's analysis and celebration of romances, provides a striking allegory of the situation of fiction in Paris in 1735, symbolizing the world of publishing as a city in which the various annalists of Romancia each have their own street and shop-signs, according to their particular character, discriminating between *enfileurs* [threaders], *souffleurs* [blowers (of soap-bubbles)], *brodeurs* [embroiderers] and others, including *lanterniers ou faiseurs de lanternes-magiques* [manufacturers of magic lanterns], which last category includes writers of *contes de fées*, the contemporary scarcity of which is noted, but not explained.

Although two fays are featured among the population of Romancia, the protagonist does not actually get to meet them, even in the somewhat cursory fashion in which he encounters centaurs, hippogriffs and all manner of other fantastic creatures and phenomena. The genre is tacitly regarded as something already consigned to the remoter annals—Bougéant obviously had not had an opportunity to see *Trois nouveaux contes de fées* or Le Marchand's volume before writing his own text—and no characters from *contes de fées* obtain the privilege granted in the satire to those in several more recent works, who are permitted to take their creators to task for their ill-treatment before a stern imaginary tribunal. Bougéant observes that Romancie has already been geographically divided into *Haut Romancie* [Higher Romancia] and *Bas Romancie* [Lower Romancia], and that the former is becoming depopulated, reflecting his perception that contemporary writers were showing an ever-greater tendency to eschew the use of the supernatural in their fiction.

Bougéant judged too soon, however; *contes de fées* were not dead, but had merely been consigned to an enchanted torpor, like the Beauty in the Dormant Wood or his Prince Zazaraph. Not only were many works penned in the 1690s still available and still popular, but they were still influential, about to prompt a new generation of writers to take up their literary quest and to attempt to carry forward the evolution that Madame d'Aulnoy and the Comtesse de Murat had begun before being cut off in their prime.

During the six years that separated the publication of "Boca" and the three tales attributed to Madame de Lintot from the publication of the Comte de Caylus' first collection of *contes de fées*, several other significant novellas of a related stripe were published in the same fashion, most notably *Funestine* (1737; tr. as "Funestine") by Pierre-François Godard de Beauchamps (1689-1761), *Tecserion* (1737; tr. as "Tecserion; or, The Prince of Ostriches") by Mademoiselle de Lubert (1702-1785), and "La Belle et la bête" (1740; tr. as "The Beauty and the Beast") by Madame de Villeneuve (1685-1755). There is no way of knowing, now, whether any of those writers attended Madame Le Marchand's salon, but if one or more of them did, they might well have been key participants in an intriguing community of interest.

That community of interest, if it existed, presumably extended to other contemporary salons, presumably including the Duchesse du Maine's *petit court*. The Duchesse not only hosted literary salons at the Château de Sceaux but is said to have obliged courtiers capable of such improvisation to make up stories for her during frequent periods of insomnia. Beauchamps was a member of that court, and it is conceivable that his *conte de fées*, and some of those composed by Caylus, owe their origins to inventions made for that purpose. Beauchamps' principal literary endeavor was a licensed four-volume history of the French theater, *Recherches sur les théâtres de France depuis 1161 jusqu'à présent* (1735), but several illicit publications are also attributed to him, at least speculatively, including contributions to the genre of "libertine fiction" that began to flourish in the 1730s, much to Guillaume-Hyacinthe Bougéant's disapproval.

As well as taking some inspiration from Catherine Durand, who enjoys a privileged position in the eponymous heroine's library along with the Comtesse de Murat and Madame d'Aulnoy, *Funestine* echoes d'Aulnoy's "Serpentin Vert" in following the fortunes of a princess stricken with extreme ugliness by a nastyminded fay, but the novella is a bizarre patchwork, whose narrative trajectory veers in several different directions. The story is occasionally interrupted by the author in order to comment on what he is doing—inconsistently, as he sometimes admits to being the creator of the text and sometimes pretends to be translating from a manuscript in a mixture of foreign languages—and it includes several interpolated anecdotes. In one of the latter, the renegade fay Imagination describes her love affair with Extreme, the brother of Fabulous, and his betrayal of her amour with the flamboyant Chimera, which could be read as a wry representation of the brief fashionability of *contes de fées* in the 1690s, or as a parallel commentary to Bougéant's on the apparent pattern of evolution of contemporary fiction. The climax of the story surely has *La Tyrannie des fées détruite* in mind as well as the sad fate of the 1690s genre, providing a much more violent end to the fays' evil "tyranny."

Like Madame d'Aulnoy in *Le Nouveau bourgeois gentilhomme*, Beauchamps makes narrative moves intended to distance himself from his own endeavor, going so far as to express explicit contempt for himself for stooping so low as to write a *conte de fées*, but he is clearly being deliberately disingenuous. He was not to know when he wrote the story that he was in the forefront of an outlaw renaissance, and does not seem to have been tempted to repeat the adventure, but he might well have been delighted to discover, as time passed, that he had not only been a pioneer of sorts but perhaps an influential one, as the sarcastic tone, deliberately flamboyant manner and casual surrealism of his story was echoed in several other works published during the heyday of the contraband renaissance.

The likelihood is, however, that the development in question was intrinsic to the spirit of the age, reflecting the increasing fashionability of the opposition to the kind of orthodoxy represented by the distributors of royal privileges by the *philosophes*, following the lead of Montesquieu and Voltaire, who soon discovered the utility of fantastic fiction as a means of expression, borrowing motifs eclectically from Oriental fantasies and *contes de fées* as well as innovating ingeniously as the need arose.

The writer of the 1730s renaissance who followed most evidently and more directly in the footsteps of the Comtesse de Murat and Madame d'Aulnoy appears to have been baptized Marie-Madeleine de Lubert, although she was also known as Marguerite de Lubert, an appellation she might have used to distinguish her from her similarly-forenamed mother. She became one of the most prolific writers of eighteenth-century *contes de fées*, publishing several long novellas in the form of booklets, although the precise extent of her work is difficult to ascertain, because of difficulties of attribution, and some of the stories retrospectively credited to her are probably by other hands.

Mademoiselle de Lubert was the daughter of a lawyer attached to the Parlement de Paris, and is known to have exchanged correspondence with Voltaire, who wrote a poem about her in 1732 addressing her as "Muse et Grace." Otherwise, little appears to be known about her life; Joseph La Porte stated that he could not comment on her character, not having the privilege of being acquainted with her, but described her as "retiring et studious" and commented on the fact that she "has preferred liberty to the engagements of marriage."

Tecserion, ou Le Princes des autruches (tr. as "Tecserion") was the first of Lubert's *contes de fées* to be published; it was reprinted in 1743 as *Sec et noir, ou la Princesse des Fleurs et le Prince des Autruches* (the replacement title unpacked the anagram of the earlier one), along with five other novellas in an identical format, all allegedly published in the Hague by an unnamed publisher. The other five novellas are *La Princesse Lionnette et the prince Coquerico*, (tr. as

"Princess Lionnette and Prince Coquerico"), *Le Prince Glacé et la princesse Étincelante* (tr. as "Prince Frozen and Princess Sparkling"), *La Princesse Camion* (tr. as "Princess Camion"), *La Princesse Couleur de rose et le prince Celadon* (tr. as "Princess Roseate and Prince Celadon") and *La Princesse Sensible et le prince Typhon* (tr. as "Princess Sensitive and Prince Typhon"). The last-named, however, is markedly different from the others in length, character and style; it is possible that the publisher simply added a work by another hand into the set.

That possibility seems more plausible because another booklet published in the same format in 1752, also allegedly in the Hague but with the publisher named as "Pierre de Hondt," a satirical *conte philosophique* entitled *Cornichon et Toupette, histoire fée*, was also attributed to Lubert by Charles-Joseph Mayer, although it is very difficult to believe that it is her work, giving every appearance of having been written by a male *philosophe* with an agenda very different from Mademoiselle de Lubert's. On the other hand, writers often do want to vary their work, adopting seemingly different personas in order to follow different agendas, and there is no doubt that Lubert had the intelligence, philosophical acumen and literary ability necessary to have written *La Princesse Sensible et le prince Typhon* and *Cornichon et Toupette* had she had the inclination.

Treated as ephemeral publications, most of the 1743 booklets soon disappeared from view and became scarce—the Bibliothèque Nationale does not have a complete set—but Mayer managed to find copies of *La Princesse Lionnette et the prince Coquerico*, *Le Prince Glacé et la princesse Étincelante* and *La Princesse Camion* to reprint in his *Cabinet* and all five of them are now available for consultation on-line. Although the author might have published a few similar items later in life, it is also possible that, having released her early works in a fashion that seems suspiciously like an unceremonious dumping, she never went back to that kind of activity.

La Princesse Couleur de rose et le prince Celadon ends with a wry acknowledgement of the fact that the author had completely lost control of a plot that had developed too many complications as it evolved, and had felt forced to bring it to a cursory and highly unsatisfactory conclusion—an experience that could have discouraged a sensitive writer. At any rate, most of the subsequent literary work that is definitely Lubert's consisted of editing earlier works for republication, including a four-volume edition of *Amadis de Gaules* (1750), and new editions of *Les Lutins du château de Kernosy* and *La Tyrannie des fées détruite* (she amended the spelling of *Tyrannie*), which helped to preserve both works from oblivion, being the versions subsequently reprinted by Garnier and Mayer.

Tecserion begins with an explanatory "preliminary discourse," but the apology for *contes de fées* provided by the brief essay is a trifle disingenuous, and it would probably be a mistake to regard it as if it were an honest reflection of the author's attitude to the genre. The preface claims that the story is intended purely for the frivolous amusement of readers, and contains no "mystery" or "allegory" warranting further critical analysis or decoding. Given its elaborate description of the strange utopian society of the planet Venus, to which the hero and heroine are removed by fay magic in order to protect them from the amorous pursuits of the eponymous the King of the Ostriches and the coquettish Ranuncule, few readers would be tempted to take that claim entirely seriously. There are certainly aspects of *Tecserion* that are there simply because they are colorful and decorative, delighting in the free play of the imagination for its own sake—and that is arguably the author's greatest literary virtue—but the narrative muscle and momentum of the story is provided by its ironic celebration of and skeptical commentary on the mythology of amour. The other novellas in the 1743 set are similar in their outlook and method, with the exception of *La Princesse Sensible et le prince Typhon*.

Tecserion remained the most ambitious of Lubert works but also the most confused and inconsistent, clearly made up as the author went along, with no certainty as what conclusion she actually wanted to contrive, or how to get there, but that helps to give it a certain fascination. Several of her other stories are more coherent and more competently organized, but the sacrifice of the bizarrerie of *Tecserion* had costs as well as benefits; *La Princesse Camion* probably strikes the best balance between quasi-surreal extravagance and narrative discipline; there is a certain justice in the fact that it remained the best known of Lubert's works, by virtue of its more frequent reprinting. Although *La Princesse Lionnette et le prince Coquerico* is more conventional, the unusual elaboration of the character of the aged fay Cornue and her doomed quest to win the heart of Prince Coquerico, in spite of strong opposition from the naïve Lionnette, gives it an exceptional narrative energy.

Le Prince Glacé et la princesse Étincelante does not make as much use of metamorphosis as a plot lever as its companions in the set, but it is similar in its employment of erotically-motivated fays and enchanters to harass the deliberately-mismatched young lovers whose tribulations provide the substance of the plot, as well as in the remarkable convolution of its story-line and its determination to provide a conclusion distinct from the stereotypical formula. It has particularly close connections with *Tecserion*, carrying forward that story's fascination with the spoliation inflicted on amorous relationships by coquetry and infidelity. *La Princesse Couleur de rose et le prince Celadon* introduces a similar convolution, and is even more scathing in its attack on coquetry and infidelity—to the extent that it becomes frankly unjust in condemning innocent mistakes almost as violently as deliberate perfidies—but, as previously noted, the author is ultimately defeated by her own complications and eventually has to hack through the Gordian knot of her plot with an atypically crude improvisation, with which she was clearly dissatisfied herself, although it does not distract from the fact that the story has a fine flamboyance in its early phases.

Because of the thematic and methodical consistency of the five novellas that are definitely Lubert's, they add up to a whole that is greater than the sum of its parts, and it is a pity that uncertainties regarding the authenticity of other attributions make it difficult to assess exactly how large and how various that whole was. In spite of that uncertainty, however, Lubert was undoubtedly one of the major contributors to the contraband renaissance, and the most faithful of all to the productive pursuit of the mission mapped out in 1698 by the evolution commenced by Murat and d'Aulnoy.

Madame de Villeneuve's "La Belle et la Bête" was first published in 1740 as the longest item in a collection entitled *La Jeune Américaine et les Contes marins* [The Young American Woman and the Marine Tales] signed "Madame de ***" and bearing a title-page alleging that it had been printed in the Hague. The collection was incomplete, only two volumes being printed of what was clearly intended to be a five- or six-volume set. The frame story containing the included tales breaks off abruptly, and most of the stories advertised in the prefatory note are missing.

In 1865, some years after the author's death, the two earlier volumes were reprinted as the first two items in a five-volume collection entitled *Contes de Madame de Villeneuve*, similarly bearing title-pages claiming publication in the Hague, but the three added volumes did not contain the material missing from the earlier collection, being almost completely taken up by a single full-length novel—in excess of ninety thousand words—"Les Nayades" (tr. as "The Naiads"). That collection too is manifestly incomplete, the final page advertising the imminent continuation of the series of tales with "L'Empire du temps et le pouvoir de la patience" [The Empire of Time and the Power of Patience], which never materialized (the 1768 book entitled *Le Temps et la Patience* bearing Villeneuve's signature is simply a reprint of *La Jeune Américaine*.) Presumably, the author had intended to work on that continuation before her death but was unable to do so.

Madame de Villeneuve had begun life as Gabrielle-Suzanne Barbot, born in Paris to Protestant parents. In 1706 she was married to Jean-Baptiste Gallon de Villeneuve, a lieutenant-colonel in the infantry, but she requested a legal separation of their assets within six months, her husband already having squandered most of their combined fortune, and she was widowed in 1711. Soon reduced to penury, she returned to Paris in search of gainful employment, where she met the playwright Prosper Jolyot de Crébillon (1674-1762), subsequently known as Crébillon *père* in order to differentiate him from his son, also a writer, and she lived with him until her death. Crébillon *père* served as a crown censor licensing publications, but never gave a privilege to his mistress for any of the four subsequent books that she published during her lifetime, one of which was another collection of tales, *Les Belles solitaires* [The Solitary Beauties] (1745), which remains unobtainable. There is no formal record of who it was that arranged for the posthumous publication of the 1765 *Contes*, and Crébillon *père* was already dead by then; the likeliest candidate seems to be Crébillon *fils* (1707-1777), who might well have inherited the manuscript of "Les Nayades" along with his father's property.

Villeneuve's "La Belle et la bête" became the grandparent of one of the *contes de fées* adapted into modern folklore, but it did so via the more direct parentage of a drastically-abridged plagiarism published by Jeanne-Marie Leprince de Beaumont (1711-1780) in her *Magasin des Enfants*—not a magazine but an educative manual for parents and teachers—in 1743, which had the unusual distinction of obtaining a royal privilege, perhaps because of its stubbornly pious frame narrative, which includes numerous versions of stories from the Old Testament, retold in a manner to which no Catholic clergyman would have objected, as well as several other sternly and crudely moralistic *contes de fées*. Whatever the reason for its granting was, the privilege in question enabled the relentlessly mediocre Leprince de Beaumont to obtain a wider circulation and more frequent reprinting for her handful of *contes de fées* than any other French writer of the century. I have included one of her tales, "Le Prince Fatal et le prince Fortuné" (tr. as "Prince Fatal and Prince Fortunate"), in the exemplary anthology, but more for the sake of completeness than as an expression of approval.

Although Madame de Villeneuve's authentic and infinitely superior version of "La Belle et la bête" was reprinted by Mayer in his *Cabinet*, it virtually disappeared from view thereafter and remained far more difficult to find than the plagiarism for the next two hundred years. The corrupt version featured in the *Magasin des Enfants* is illustrated, and the illustrations depict the Beast as a large dog, but the story lends no encouragement to that depiction, and it does not correspond at all with the four specific details contained in the original story, which are that the Beast is equipped with something resembling an elephant's trunk, has scales that rattle, has paws instead of hands and is extremely heavy. The prolific subsequent imagery associated with recyclings of the neo-folkloristic version of the tale, which routinely equip the Beast with a leonine head but a more-or-less human body, have no warrant in either version, although they are now standardized in cinematic and televisual imagery.

The principal difference between the Villeneuve novella and the Leprince de Beaumont plagiarism is the complete elimination from the latter of a complex back-story detailing a contest of ingenuity between virtuous and malevolent fays, strongly reminiscent of the contests featured in the Comtesse de Murat's novellas but more elaborate and intricate. The *Magasin des Enfants* version also differs from the original in being noticeably harsher in its moralistic sentencing, punishing the Beauty's jealous sisters (reduced to two from the original five) by turning them into statues rather than forgiving them and treating them kindly—a moral policy inherited by Villeneuve from Madame d'Aulnoy and subsequently taken to an unusual extreme in "Les Nayades."

The latter is not, strictly speaking, a *conte de fées*, although it is set in a very similar fictitious world, and the substitution of the titular nymphs for fays might have been a diplomatic move occasioned by the realization—perhaps explicitly confirmed by Crébillon—that *contes de fées* were almost impossible to certify for licit publication and distribution. If so, the substitution evidently did not serve to rescue the story from legal ostracism. Like "La Belle et la Bête," it uses several of the stock motifs of *contes de fées*, featuring a Prince Perfect who falls in love with a shepherdess, unaware that she is really a Princess, as well as employing an exceedingly wicked stepmother and a grotesquely exaggerated ugly sister to supply the beleaguered heroine with an excess of persecution. Like its predecessor, however, the novel is conscientiously concerned to examine those motifs in depth and provide them with much more elaborate explanatory schemas than had been attempted previously. The embedded story of the strange custodian of the Mill of Misfortune and the eventual explanation of Prince Perfect's true identity provided by the gnomide queen are addenda as interesting in their own way as the supplements to the earlier novella detailing the elaborate polity of the land of Faerie.

No other writer of her era carried forward the legacy of Baronne d'Aulnoy and the Comtesse de Murat—both of whom provided abundant raw material for the two long stories—as assiduously and as intensively as Madame de Villeneuve; "Le Belle et la bête" is the evident masterpiece of the contraband Renaissance, and would have remained the longest single work of that renaissance had "Les Nayades" not achieved posthumous publication. We can only speculate as to what she might have achieved had circumstances permitted her to continue with the development of the portmanteaux that she attempted, unsuccessfully, to build for them.

The most prolific of Mademoiselle de Lubert's competitors in the endeavor to carry forward the Comtesse de Murat's quest published two volumes of *Féeries nouvelles* anonymously in 1741, allegedly in The Hague. They were subsequently attributed to an author whose full name is nowadays cited as Anne-Claude-Philippe de Tubières-Grimoard de Pestels de Levis, Comte de Caylus, Marquis d'Esterhazy, Baron de Bransac, but who only used the title Comte de Caylus for purposes of identification and was known to his relatives and friends as Philippe. He published a third anonymous volume, *Cinq contes de fees*, in 1745 without any indication as to its publisher or place of publication.

Some thirty years later, two more stories were published by the widow Duchesne in a small volume, *Tout vient à point à qui peut attendre, ou Cadichon, suivi par Jeannette, ou L'Indiscrétion, contes par feu le comte de Caylus*, ["Everything Works Out for Him who Can Wait; or, Cadichon," followed by "Jeannette; or, Indiscretion," tales by the late Comte de Caylus] (1775), which contains a preface that must have been written with the intention of publishing the volume while the author was alive, apparently in 1760 or thereabouts; although it is unsigned, it confirms that he was the author of the two previous volumes, and also refers to his exploits in Egyptology in a fashion that renders his identity recognizable.

It is possible that the four volumes in question do not contain the full set of the Comte de Caylus's endeavors in the genre of *contes de fées*, but the preface to the final volume implies that they do, and the other stories featuring fays that have sometimes been attributed to him by various speculative bibliographers are probably not his (the Bibliothèque Nationale catalogue notes that *Cinq contes de fées* had been speculatively attributed by Joseph de La Porte—in 1769—to Madame de Villeneuve, so the confusions cut both ways). Although he was a famous and well-connected man, with a considerable reputation as a scholar, Caylus found it politic to publish many of his works anonymously and illicitly, with false title pages. The bulk of the fiction attributed to him, including all of his *contes de fées*, was reprinted under his name in a twelve-volume set of *Oeuvres badines complètes* [Complete Playful Works] compiled in 1787 by Charles Garnier, and that became the definitive compendium of his illicit works, although the accuracy of Garnier's bibliography is inevitably open to slight doubt.

Philippe de Caylus came from an aristocratic military family, his father having been a general and his mother the daughter of a vice-admiral. As previously mentioned, his orphaned mother, Marthe-Marguerite de Mursay, had been brought up by the redoubtable Madame de Maintenon, and her memoirs of Louis XIV's court were edited for initial posthumous publication by Voltaire. None of the members of the salon coterie who invented and popularized *contes de fées* is mentioned in her published memoir—an absence that is probably significant of diplomatic avoidance rather than ignorance, given that she seems to have dabbled in the genre herself.

Caylus had a distinguished military career between 1709 and 1714, but abandoned it after the death of Louis XIV and devoted himself thereafter to antiquarian studies, especially studies in Egyptology, in which academic pursuit he was an important pioneer. He carried out significant research on ancient painting techniques, and was very active as an etcher, leaving behind a rich legacy of engravings as well as his prolific writings. He acquired a posthumous reputation for riotous living, but that was greatly enhanced by a set of licentious fake memoirs published in 1805 and occasional scathing comments by contemporaries who did not like him, the most oft-quoted of whom was Denis Diderot.

Like Lubert and Villeneuve, who preceded him into print, Caylus tried to take up where Murat and d'Aulnoy had been cruelly forced to leave off, in trying to develop the narrative strategies, key themes and imaginative inventiveness of the genre progressively. Like Lubert, with whose work Caylus's has a strong affinity, he had a flair for oddity that continually edges into the surreal, and he never entirely forsook the spirit of amiable parody in which he had apparently commenced. Like Villeneuve, he picked up from Préchac and further elaborated the notion that the community of fays has a kind of parliament or legislative council which regulates their activity, a notion closely connected with the particular use Caylus makes of the term *Féerie* [Faerie].

Although he was already in a position to know that Bourgeant's requiem for Faerie had been a trifle premature, Caylus nevertheless retained a consciousness of the fact that the *fées* seemed to be in a period of decadence, not long for the literary world, which results in a curious combination in his works of sarcasm tinged with nostalgia, a hint of contempt, a blithely casual bizarrerie, and an overripe exuberance. His attitude seems to have been that he was consciously trafficking with absurdities that were already past their sell-by date, but could see no reason why he should not be self-indulgent in that regard.

His work is various in tone and manner, including such exercises in earnest allegory as "Le Palais d'idées" (tr. as "The Palace of Ideas")—which seems to be trying to make a serious point about the psychology of amour, although it is probably not one that many readers would have recognized—and such forthrightly conventional moralistic fantasies as "Bleuette et Coquelico" (tr. as "Bleuette and Coquelicot") and "Jeanette, ou L'Indiscrétion (tr. as "Jeannette; or, Indiscretion"). The curious "Fleurette et Abricot, cadres" (tr. as "Fleurette and Abricot: A Frame Story") poses as the frame story of an imaginary collection of tales, set in a land where the art of faerie has determined the people must change sex every year on their birthday; like several of his other stories, including "Les Dons" (tr. as "The Gifts"), it aspires to the status of a *conte philosophique*. The real strength of Caylus's *contes de fées*, however, is in his longer and more distinctive stories, and in their phantasmagorical elements.

The longest of Caylus's *contes de fées*, the ebullient "Le Prince Courtebotte et la princesse Zibeline" (tr. as "Prince Courtebotte and Princess Zibeline"), covers an enormous amount of colorfully diverse narrative ground at a rapid pace, while the most impressive inclusions in his first two volumes, "L'Enchantement impossible" (tr. as "The Impossible Enchantment"), "La Princesse Azerolle ou L'Excès de la confiance" (tr. as "Princess Azerolle; or, Excessive Confidence") and "Bellinette ou La Jeune vieille" (tr. as "Bellinette; or, The Young Old Woman), achieve a spectacular abundance of hectic imagery. Although "L'Enchantement Impossible" is more heavily dependent on motifs borrowed from Murat than any of the others, it benefits greatly from a brief but spectacular climactic aerial battle to move into unexplored narrative territory in a cavalier fashion. "La Princesse Azerolle" similarly makes use of the vengeance of a nasty fay as a productive plot lever, but complicates it unusually and intriguingly not only by crediting her with an unusual complexity of motivation but also by juxtaposing her with two other fays whose benevolence is awkwardly compromised. "Bellinette" reverts to a more straightforward contest between good and wicked fays, but enhances its plot with some intriguing allegorical episodes.

All of Caylus's *contes de fées* are a trifle slapdash, obviously improvised as the author went along rather than being planned, and sometimes giving the impression that he might have been dictating them to an amanuensis at high speed rather than writing them steadily in his own hand, but their improvisation is so buoyantly inventive as to compensate abundantly for a certain lack of coherency. That imprudently informal methodology has rewards as well as penalties; he admitted in the humorous "advertisement" of his first collection that some of the stories could have done with being tidied up somewhat, but most of them have a reckless brio that that is nevertheless appealing. Caylus does not seem to have been able to maintain that cavalier spirit later in life, and his imaginative reach does not have the same effect or charm in the belated "Cadichon," although that story still retains an admirable eccentricity in parts.

Caylus's bibliography was still somewhat confused when Mayer planned his *Cabinet*, in which he initially reprinted two stories included in the 1745 collection seemingly without being aware of that volume, but he subsequently corrected the error, probably after seeing the collection reprinted by Garnier. While he was alive, therefore, the extent of Caylus's contribution to the genre of *contes de fées* was largely unknown and unappreciated, beyond his immediate circle of friends, but he was certainly an important contributor, and perhaps an influential one. As with Beauchamps, many of the similarities between the stories contained in his first three volumes and subsequent works are probably due to the prevailing *zeitgeist* rather than to direct imitation, but his works were certainly known to several of his contemporaries, who were undoubtedly aware of their authorship via the salons in which they were read and discussed. He did, therefore, make a substantial contribution to setting the tone for the subsequently development of the renaissance, especially for singleton contributions made in the 1740s by male authors, who surely took some license and encouragement from the fact that extravagant examples had been provided by men of the prestige and reputation of Beauchamps and Caylus.

One curious story that apparently took such a license was *Faunillane, ou l'infante jaune* (1741; reprinted 1743; tr. as "Faunillane; or, The Yellow Child"), which bore a humorous title-page alleging publication in Badinopolis by the Frères Ponthommes, at the sign of the King of Egypt. Although written in French and very much in the French tradition, it was the work of a notable Swedish diplomat, Count Carl Gustaf Tessin (1695-1770), who allegedly wrote it in haste specifically in order to be able to commission illustrations for it from the artist François Boucher, who had recently painted his portrait and whose wife he wanted to seduce; the first edition allegedly consisted of only three copies, one of which is in the Bibliothèque Nationale and is reproduced on *gallica*.

Whether that legend is true or not, the story is certainly remarkable for its exaggerated bizarrerie, which might well have taken its lead from Beauchamps and Caylus but outstrips them with deliberately casual effrontery, becoming the most surreal work of its period. Although it is unlikely to have influenced many other writers, even via the 1743 "commercial edition," it is not improbable that it was read aloud, as a joke, in aristocratic salons where the count was reckoned an important guest.

A more substantial quasi-parodic contribution to the genre by a high-profile dabbler was *Acajou et Zirphile* (1744) by Charles Pinot Duclos (1704-1772), allegedly written as a result of a wager, around the illustrations that Boucher had supplied to Tessin's story, thus producing an interesting duplication of imagery in the context of a strikingly different story. Duclos, a close friend of Caylus—who had helped to facilitate his early publications in the genre of libertine fiction—was already a member of the Académie des inscriptione et belles-lettres when he wrote the story, and was subsequently elected to the Académie française; he was a significant contributor to the *Encyclopédie*, but he was regarded by his fellow *philosophes* as something of a lightweight, more adept at *bon mots* than serious endeavors; Voltaire, Diderot and Alembert all disapproved of him. Even so, he replaced Voltaire as France's official historiographer in 1750 when the latter gave up the post. His *Mémoires secrètes des règnes de Louis XIV de Louis XV*, however—derived from and supplementing the memoirs of the Duc de Saint-Simon—could not be published until after the Revolution, although they enjoyed great success then, in English translation as well as French.

Duclos was arguably the most prestigious of the known French dabblers in the genre during the 1740s, and his example might have been significant in prompting Jean-Jacques Rousseau to try his hand at it, Rousseau having appreciated him a little more kindly than the other *philosophes*, probably because of his similar reputation. Although *Acajou et Zirphile* does have inclinations in the direction of a *conte philosophique*, however, it is primarily a colorful joke, most evident in its cavalier employment of chamber pots. Like Caylus, however, the author does seem to have progressed rapidly from a spirit of pure parody to being caught up by the fascination of the genre's toils, and the story's allegorical elaboration exceeds the necessity of its original impulse.

The position of official historiographer of France, inherited by Duclos from Voltaire, was also held for a while by François-Augustin de Paradis de Moncrif (1687-1770), like Duclos a member of the Académie française, whose first publication, in 1717, was *Les Aventures de Zeloïde et d'Amaznaridine, contes indiens*, one of many pastiches of Galland's *Mille et une nuits*, in the genre of *contes merveilleux* that Mayer conflated with that of *contes de fées* in his *Cabinet*. There is a strong element of the *merveilleux* in many of Moncrif's prolific works for the theater, but the handful of his *contes de fées* that Mayer reprinted in the *Cabinet des fées*, the most substantial of which is "Les Dons des fées, ou Le Pouvoir de l'éducation" (tr. as "The Gifts of the Fays; or, The Power of Education"), are more earnestly didactic and moralistic, set very firmly in the tradition of *contes philosophiques*. It was probably one of the first such tales to be written in the context of the contraband renaissance, certainly predating

Duclos's story; although the date of its original publication is difficult to determine, it was prior to 1738.

"Les Dons des fées" deliberately fuses the two genres combined by Mayer—a practice that became increasingly commonplace in the 1750s as *contes de fées* suffered a drastic decline in fashionability, while Oriental fantasies resisted eclipse somewhat more robustly—but in doing so Moncrif was following the same policy of eclecticism previously employed by François Fénelon in the similar service of moral exemplification. As with many earnestly didactic writers, however, Moncrif's *contes* tend to sacrifice literary values entirely to their message, and if they are viewed as stories rather than homilies they are conspicuously weak.

Reprinted in 1751 in Moncrif's *Oeuvres*, and frequently reprinted thereafter, "Les Don des fées" probably provided a more important exemplar than "Faunillane," *Acajou et Zirphile* and Caylus's undoubtedly-related "Les Dons." Although its direct influence was probably limited, it indicated the direction that the path of generic evolution was following. Increasingly, as the 1740s progressed, the element of *conte philosophique* in *contes de fées* became more significant, even in tales written in the same spirit as Mademoiselle de Lubert's. It is probably safe to say that although few of the female writers of such tales would have been recognized as *philosophes* by males jealous of that title, they were certainly acquainted with *philosophes*, respectful of their prestige and capable of competing with them in wit and intelligence.

Among the leading *philosophes*, Voltaire and Montesquieu, in particular, frequently attended Parisian salons in the 1730s and 1740s, and such attendance certainly reflected, if it did not help to cause, the completion of a change in the intellectual direction of those salons. The days when the discussion groups led by the Marquise de Rambouillet and Mademoiselle de Scudéry had separated out literature as the core concern of female salon conversation were long gone, and all salons, following on from examples set in the 1710s and 1720s by the Marquise de Lambert, the Duchesse du Maine and the Marquise de Deffand could be reckoned philosophical as well as literary; in taking her model more directly from Mademoiselle de Scudéry. Madame Le Marchand was attempting a backward step of sorts, but even she borrowed her nickname from Montesquieu.

The *contes de fées* written in the 1740s might not have been evident reflections of an Age of Enlightenment, and some could easily be seen as nostalgic reactions against it, but they were all certainly written with a keen awareness of the advancement of Enlightenment—the manifestations of which, of course, were almost entirely located in the illicit sector of the world of publishing, considered as heresy in a religious as well as a political sense. As that awareness progressed to dominate the production of new tales of Faerie it produced a particular kind of decadence in the genre, not merely reflected in the decline in the production and popularity of such tales after 1750, but also in the style and manner of those that continued an assertive and defiant existence. They were few in number, and considerably removed from their roots in the genre as it had been invented in the 1690s, but perhaps all the more interesting for that.

The Decadence of the Fays

It requires something of a specialist skill to write *contes philosophiques* that not only succeed in embedding their philosophical arguments in engaging stories, but make use of the literary values of their plots to heighten the dilemmas they address. One of the most elaborate satirical comedies cast as a *conte de fées* with a significant element of *conte philosophique* is *Cornichon et Toupette*, which, although attributed by Mayer to Mademoiselle de Lubert, bears a far closer resemblance to the work of Caylus and Duclos, without resembling either closely enough to suggest that one of them might have been its author. Its references to Montesquieu's *L'Esprit des lois* and Alexander Pope's "Essay of Man"—both recent when the novella was published in 1752—are suggestive of an author with his or her finger firmly on the pulse of contemporary thought, and although the Abbé de Saint-Pierre had been dead for some time, the sympathetic citation of his endeavors in the story is also significant. Given that Mademoiselle de Lubert was not only acquainted with Voltaire but probably knew Montesquieu as well, those references do not disqualify her as a possible author of the work, but its cynical attitude to the far-from-*parfait amour* of the eponymous characters is certainly markedly different from the obsession fundamental to work known to be hers.

The most remarkable feature of *Cornichon et Toupette* is the manner in which it creates a series of dilemmas requiring Solomonic judgments on the part of its fays and genii, who, although equipped with the magic power to put them into effect, tend to make a horrible mess of them even with the best of intentions. Although the tone is tongue-in-cheek, and the hypothetical dilemmas highly fanciful, the moral questions underlying them are real, and similar ones have been frequently raised since, in philosophical texts and literary ones alike. Because it is also a hectic and colorful adventure story, *Cornichon et Toupette* is arguably a better story than Jean-Jacques Rousseau's "La Reine Fantasque" (tr. as "Queen Fantasque), which is thought to have been written in 1752 and might conceivably have taken some influence from it, although it was not published until 1769.

Rousseau's story also revolves around a series of moral dilemmas provided with fanciful magically-aided resolutions, and both stories reflect real philosophical debates of which their authors were undoubtedly sharply aware. "La Reine Fantasque" is an uncomfortable narrative, and its discomforts are reflected in its interruptions by fragments of a frame narrative, which sets up a curious antithesis to the thesis of the story.

The story was a kind of experiment that Rousseau did not repeat, and there is a certain significance in the fact that the two *philosophes* who made most prolific use of fantastic *contes philosophiques* in their work, Voltaire and Louis-Sébastien Mercier, wrote no *contes de fées*. Voltaire found Oriental fantasy a more convenient framework for his exemplary needs, and it was only by means of a fleeting reference that he added the name Urgèle to the list of celebrated fays. Mercier was sweeping in his recruitment of fantastic motifs in his many visionary fantasies, but never found a use for fays; it is perhaps not irrelevant to the omission that, unlike Voltaire, Mercier was a devout man, very willing to deploy angels and demons in an earnest fashion, but not attracted to godless milieux.

Few writers in the 1750s followed in the footsteps of Mademoiselle de Lubert, Madame de Villeneuve and the Comte de Caylus in making multiple contributions to the genre, and appearances suggest that, while Lubert and Caylus both gave up on that kind of work, at least for some time, Villeneuve found it impossible to publish such work as she did. A sense that the renaissance had run its course, and that the genre was dying, is evident in several of the works of the period, not least in three stories attributed by modern bibliographies to "Marie-Antoinette Fagnan." The long novella *Kanor, conte traduit du sauvage par Madame ** (tr. as "Kanor: A Tale translated from the Savage") was published in 1750, allegedly in Amsterdam. A short story, "Minet-bleu et Louvette" was then published in the *Mercure de France* in September 1750 with the signature "Madame de Fagnan," accompanied by an editorial note identifying that person as the author of *Kanor*. Another long novella, *Le Miroir des princesses orientales* (tr. as "The Enchanter's Mirror"), followed in two volumes in 1755, without any indication of a publisher or a place of publication, but with the signature "Madame Fagnan."

The Bibliothèque Nationale also credits to Madame Fagnan a pamphlet entitled *Histoire et aventures de Mylord Pet, conte allégorique, par Madame F*** (1755), but the attribution is ridiculous, the story being a scatological skit, evidently by a male author, and the F in the signature is expanded in the humorous dedication to "Fesse" (i.e. buttock). The misattribution, further complicated by a misrendering in the catalogue entry of the actual title of the pamphlet, which has "Milord" rather than "Mylord," does not encourage confidence in the bibliographical expertise of the catalogue's compiler, and adds an extra measure of doubt to the question of whether "Madame Fagnan"—who seemingly could not make up her mind as to whether her signature ought to include a *particule* or not—might have been a pseudonym rather than the name of a real person. *Le Miroir des princesses orientales* had no royal privilege, so the full signature is an oddity, given the risks involved in signing such works with an author's real name. The story also features a fulsome dedication to the Marquise de Pompadour, which gives the impression of being sarcastic.

In 1755 the Marquise de Pompadour (1721-1764) was no longer Louis XV's "official chief mistress," as she had been between 1745 and 1751, but she still had abundant influence at court. She had a reputation as a patroness of the arts and protectress of the *philosophes*, the acquaintance of many of whom she had made in the early days of her marriage to Charles Le Normant d'Étiolles, contracted in 1740, when she attended several of the most celebrated salons in Paris. She had hosted her own salon briefly, attended by Montesquieu and Voltaire, among others, and certainly met some of the writers engaged in the contraband renaissance of *contes de fées*, including the Comte de Caylus and Charles Duclos, but she does not appear to have taken any interest in the genre or assisted any of its practitioners to obtain privileges for the publication of their work. If "Madame Fagnan" knew her, she might have attempted unsuccessfully to use that acquaintance to obtain a privilege, and included the ironic dedication as a perverse revenge when she failed. Perverse and ironic revenge is a central theme of all three of her stories, which depict characters struggling with the effects of sly curses inflicted on them by wrathful fays and male enchanters.

All accounts of "Madame Fagnan" the author appear to be based on the one included by Joseph de La Porte in his 1769 account of French female writers, where he reports that he had been told that her husband worked in "some bureau," but that that was all he had been able to learn about a woman who "appeared to prefer a peaceful obscurity to the literary celebrity that she might have flattered herself with obtaining." There is a reference in the 1787 memoirs of the Venetian playwright Carlo Goldoni, who was the director of the Théâtre Italien in Paris from 1761 onwards, to a Madame Fagnan he had once met briefly, who was the widow of a principal secretary of the royal treasury; Goldoni was certainly acquainted with La Porte, and it might have been from him that La Porte learned verbally that a Madame Fagnan existed whose husband worked in "some bureau." It is presumably that Madame Fagnan who had the forenames Marie-Antoinette and who died in 1770, as Charles-Joseph Mayer and subsequent bibliographers assert, but whether she was the author of the three stories remains open to some doubt.

Whoever used the signature, however, the works are interesting, not least in striking a curious quasi-apologetic attitude similar to that employed by Beauchamps in *Funestine*. The sardonic narrative voice of *Kanor* goes to some lengths to point out the absurdity of many of the conventions of the *conte de fées*, and to emphasize that the age of the fays, if ever there was one, must have reached its twilight long before history became possible. Nevertheless, the story makes constructive use of the vengeful fay Fierotine and the perversity of her enchantments, in contriving a plot that is amusing, unusual and labyrinthine. The satirical opening of the story appears to have been inspired by Jonathan Swift's account of the early travels of Lemuel Gulliver, but casual political satire is soon abandoned in favor of an eccentric celebration of the power of amour far more typical of the genre. The brief "Minette-bleu et Louvette" follows up the latter theme in a literary thought-experiment, in which the conventional perversities of fay magic are again employed as a means to establish a perverse situation that requires authorial ingenuity as well as the power of amour to reach its desired conclusion.

Similarly, the subject-matter of *Le Miroir des princesses orientales* is not so much the magic mirror of the title, which provides its users with magical insight into the minds and hearts of others and supplies the author with a lever to move the plot, but the intense investigation it permits of the operations within the human heart of amour; the story takes to an extreme that element of the original prospectus for *contes de fées* sketched out by Catherine Bernard. Whereas *Kanor* concludes with a moral boldly claiming that Amour can work miracles, and "Minette-bleu et Louvette" focuses more intently on the complication of the kind of miracle-working required, the tripartite plot and eventual conclusion of *Le Miroir des princesses orientales* add the uncomfortable rider that, in order to achieve the desired conclusion of a *conte de fées*, nothing less than a miracle is likely do the job.

Madame Fagnan's three stories are, in effect, an encapsulation of the intellectual thrust of the entire contraband renaissance of *contes de fées*: they constitute a series of probes into the inner working of the human heart, undertaken with a genuine curiosity as to what the thought-experiments contained in the stories might reveal as they unfold, and somewhat distressed to find themselves urged by their own logic to conclude that the problems typical of amorous experience are unamenable to solution, except by means of implausible miracles. That conclusion was inevitably depressing, for Fagnan as for her contemporaries; her work is underpinned and undermined by the awareness—developed and emphasized repeatedly as the genre had progressed—that fays, even if they existed, would not be up to the task of providing such miracles routinely, because the inevitably corrupting effects of their hypothetical power would always be likely to lead them to indifference to human suffering, if not to the malevolence of causing it.

That, rather than any vulgar rational skepticism relating to the workability of magic, was the particular Enlightenment that hammered the nails into the coffin of the genre, and although the final attachments had yet to be added, that coffin was already firmly sealed by 1755. Madame Fagnan, whoever she might have been, was one of the most accurate hammer-wielding undertakers. Part Two of *Le Miroir des princesses orientales* begins with a curious rant against the genre to which it belongs, which summarizes not merely the rational attitude to *contes de fées* obliged by the skepticism of the *philosophes*, but also the tragic aspect of that compulsory clairvoyance.

For Madame Fagnan, clearly, the kind of apology issued by Mademoiselle de Lubert in the introduction to *Tecserion*, that *contes de fées* could be produced and consumed as pure entertainment, disregarding any deeper meanings they might contain, was no longer viable. Whether or not the authors of new *contes de fées* were *philosophes* themselves, they had to operate in an intellectual milieu informed by skeptical philosophy, and even if the stories produced in the

1750s did not actually take leave to examine themselves and their own pretensions—and many of them did—they could not avoid being haunted by that ominous phantom.

Le Miroir des princesses orientales also illustrates further the tendency of *contes merveilleux* produced in the period to edge away from the fictional world adopted by the salon writers of the 1690s, not merely removing the time of the fays to a forgotten prehistory, but also moving it eastwards geographically, in the fashion of Moncrif's didactic works. The tokenistic veneer of Oriental fantasy applied to Fagnan's novella is very light indeed, but its presence as packaging is nevertheless significant of a trend.

A similar example of tokenistic hybridization can be seen in "Durboulour, ou le bonne lionne" (tr. as "Durboulour; or, the Benevolent Lioness") by Marianne-Agnès Pillement de Falques (c.1720-1785?), which was included in a collection entitled *Contes du serrail, traduits du turc* [Tales from the Seraglio, translated from the Turkish] (1753), more for reasons of temptation than accurate description. In spite of one mention of "the prophet," the attribution of a sword that becomes the object of a quest to "the Sufi Solomon," and the brief appearance of a caravan, the story is a pure *conte de fées*, set in the same fictional world as the paradigm examples of the genre, replete with fays, ogres and other standard motifs. Falques did write a much more robust Oriental fantasy, the short novel *Abbassai* (2 vols., 1753), aided by her real knowledge of Oriental languages, as well as a long satirical account of *La dernière guerre des bêtes, pour servir à l'histoire du XVIII siècle* [The Last War of the Beasts, a useful contribution to the History of the Eighteenth Century] (2 vols., 1758), but "Durboulour" is primarily an exercise in affectionate nostalgia.

A defrocked nun who was eventually forced by scandal to flee to England—where she is said to have assisted William Beckford with his translations from the Arabic and might have made a significant contribution to his classic *Vathek*, initially written in French in 1782—Falques can be seen in retrospect as a significant loss to satirical French literature, because rather than in spite of the excessive nature of her contributions to the genre of fake "secret memoirs," but "Durboulour" gives every indication of having written purely for amusement, as a kind of homage to the distant inventions of Murat and d'Aulnoy, and from the 1750s onwards, a nostalgic tone became increasingly inevitable in stories deploying the imagistic apparatus typical of the genre.

Another female writer whose life was touched by scandal, albeit more lightly than in Falques' case, was the actress Marie-Jeanne Riccoboni (1713-1792), who followed her stage career with another, in which she enjoyed even more success, becoming one of the best-selling authors of her day. She followed quite consciously in the footsteps of Mademoiselle de Scudéry in developing her own version of sentimental fiction, which was treated with similar dismissive contempt by critics, without injuring its popularity. She belonged to the great tradition of authors whom no one liked to admit to reading, because rather than in spite of the huge volume of her sales, and many modern authors of "romantic fiction" would recognize and sympathize with that situation. Her contribution to the genre of *contes de fées* is very slight, consisting of a single short story, but it is not at all surprising that she produced one. Nor is it surprising that "L'Aveugle" (1761; tr. as "The Blind Man") has defiant pretentions as a *conte philosophique*, focusing on a dilemma as acute as those featured in *Cornichon et Toupette*." while also manifesting the tone and fluency of what was rapidly becoming standardized as "popular fiction."

The narrative strategy employed by Madame Riccoboni continued to be used in more formal exercises. *Contes philosophiques et moraux* (1765) by Nicolas Bricaire de la Dixmerie (1730-1791) makes extensive use of fantastic fictions in a way that was by then becoming familiar. Almost as a matter of routine, it includes, along with mythological fantasies and Oriental fantasies, a *conte de fées*, "Lindor et Délie" (tr. as "Lindor and Delie"), which makes much of allegorical oppositions in its account of an experimental contest between a fay and an enchanter, in which the eponymous couple become helpless pawns. The author's entire career followed what now looks rather like a standard pattern among prominent *philosophes*, involving a long critical study of the evolution of ideas during the reins of Louis XIV and Louis XV, and a eulogy to Voltaire; like the latter, he was a member the famous Masonic *Loge des Neuf Soeurs* [i.e. the nine Muses], which helped to organize French support for the American Revolution.

The additions to the genre by Riccoboni and Bricaire were tokenistic, and by the 1760s the genre was on the brink of extinction, with only rare exceptions attempting to carry the tradition forward in that decade. The good fay Bonine plays a key role in *Les Ondins* (1768; tr. as "The Water-Sprites") by Marie-Anne de Roumier-Robert (1705-1771), although the term is used rather sparingly, Bonine and her chief adversary being more frequently referred to as "Magiciennes" (their male equivalents are "Génies"). The most important fantasy motif employed in the novella is that of the eponymous elementals, although there is a significant cameo appearance in a subplot by the god Amour. The story is a hectically complex adventure story, which might well owe something to the example of the Comtesse de Murat, but it moves deliberately to the margin of the genre, and can be reckoned an interesting transitional work between *contes de fées* and more generalized fantasy fiction; even so, it is not obvious why Mayer left it to Charles Garnier to reprint in his collection of *Voyages imaginaires* rather than including it in his *Cabinet*.

The renaissance of *contes de fées* begun in the 1730s, probably hatched in Françoise Le Marchand's salon and others parallel to it, spearheaded by the work of Beauchamps, Lubert and Caylus and carried forward into the 1750s by Madame Fagnan and various dabblers, petered out completely, therefore, in the 1760s. The contributions by Riccoboni, Bricaire and Madame de Roumier-

Robert were belated, and the long-delayed publication of Rousseau's "La Reine Fantasque" seemed an eccentric addendum. The belated publication of Caylus's last two stories, in 1775, fifteen years after their composition, was an obvious postscriptum. The genre was not entirely dead even then, however, and one author remained interested in it, who had only just been born when the renaissance began, but whose contributions to it fitted in perfectly with an obsession with originality that caused him to defy every trend he perceived, while relentlessly following up every slight commercial success that he had: Nicolas-Edmé Rétif (1734-1806), who preferred to call himself Restif de La Bretonne.

Restif was the son of a prosperous peasant farmer, the eldest of the eight children of his father's second marriage, following a first that had been almost as prolific. Ostentatiously proud of his peasant ancestry—he took his pseudonym from a field that his family owned briefly—he put it behind him when he set out to make a career as a writer, cannily supporting it by serving an apprenticeship as a typesetter, which supplied him with a day job when he moved to Paris in 1754, initially working in the Imprimerie Royale at the Louvre while moonlighting for printers of illicit texts. He was already working on an autobiography that he intended to be unprecedentedly frank and honest, which he continued to elaborate throughout his life.

Forced to leave Paris for a while in 1760, Restif married and eventually had four daughters, one of whom died in infancy. When the couple returned to Paris his wife worked selling fabrics to help support the family while Restif toiled as a typesetter alongside attempts to make his breakthrough as a writer, eventually succeeding in 1767, and pouring out a long series of prose works thereafter, eventually amassing a total that many of his contemporaries thought excessive, 187 volumes in all. They included a utopian tract entitled *Le Pornographe* [Pornography, a neologism meaning "writing about prostitution"] (1769), offering practical proposals for the legalization and organization of prostitution in the interests of public order and morality, which added a new term to more than one language, soon removed from its intended meaning. The printer Restif worked for most assiduously thereafter, as a writer and typesetter, was the Widow Duchesne, the publisher of the Comte de Caylus's posthumous couplet of *contes de fées* and its apologetic preface, which Restif might well have set in type.

Restif's first considerable success was the quasi-autobiographical *Le Paysan perverti* [The Corrupted Peasant] (1775), which detailed the educative and corrupting effects of life in Paris on an emigrant from a humble principal background, but it was outstripped by *Les Contemporaines, ou Aventures des plus jolies femmes de l'Age présent* [Contemporaries; or, The Adventures of the Prettiest Women of the Present Era] (1780), a collection of short stories detailing the problematic lives of young women of various estates, to which he continued to add further series under various other titles for the rest of his career, alongside the project that eventually appeared as *Monsieur Nicolas ou Le Coeur humain dévoilé* [Monsieur Nicolas; or, The Human Heart Laid Bare] (sixteen volumes, 1794-97).

In the meantime, his marriage broke down and his wife went back to live with her father in 1773, taking the three surviving children with her. Temporarily left alone—two of his daughters eventually came back to live with him—Restif took to prowling the streets of Paris by night, accumulating the observations that were later to provide the raw material for another of his most famous works of quasi-autobiographical fiction, *Les Nuits de Paris ou le spectateur nocturne* [Parisian Nights; or, The Nocturnal Spectator] (four volumes 1788; augmented by others at intervals until 1794).

Restif's contribution to the genre of *contes de fées* consists of a group of six related stories all featuring the character of "la Fée Ouroucoucou," or, as Restif—a propagandist for simplified spelling—later began calling her, "la Fée Wrwcwcw." The name in question is an onomatopoeic rendition of the call of an owl, normally rendered in English as too-wit-too-woo, and it is not irrelevant that during the period in which the stories were written and published, Restif was fond of referring to himself as "le hibou" [the owl], because of his habit of wandering the streets of Paris by night.

The bibliography of the six stories is very peculiar, reflecting the difficulty the author had in packaging them for publication, and at least three of the six published versions obviously underwent considerable modifications between their initial drafting and their publication, in order to fit them to their ultimate context. The first two to be published were the novellas "Le Demi-Coq" (tr. as "The Demicock") and "Les Quatre belles et les quatre bêtes" (tr. as "The Four Beauties and the Four Beasts," which appeared as oft-interrupted interpolations in the text of a long portmanteau work entitled *Le Nouvel Abeilard*, one of Restif's several ripostes to Jean-Jacques Rousseau, in which he borrowed the format of the latter author's *La Nouvelle Héloïse* (1761), in order to dissent fervently from the educational theories elaborated in *Émile* (1762).

Le Nouvel Abeilard appeared in four volumes in 1778-89, illicitly published by the Widow Duchesne. The belated adaptation of pre-existing works as *ad hoc* insertions into works-in-progress was a habit that became increasingly pronounced as Restif's checkered career went on, especially in his more idiosyncratic works. One of the most bizarre of those patchworks is the work into which three of the other four stories featuring the fay Ouroucoucou were introduced as interpolations: *Les Veillées du Marais, ou, Histoire du grand Prince Oribeau, Roi de Mommonie, au pays d'Evinland & de la vertueuse Princesse Oribelle, de Lagénie; tirée des anciennes annales Irlandaises & récemment translatée en français par Nichols Donneraill, du comté de Korke, descendant de l'auteur* [Evenings in the Marais; or, The Story of the Great Prince Oribeau, King of Mommonia, in the country of Evinland, and the Virtuous Princess Oribelle of Lagenia; extracted from the ancient annals of Ireland and recently translated into French by Nicholas Donneraill of the County of Cork, descendant of the author] (tr. as *The Story of the Great Prince Oribeau*), published in four volumes in 1785. The frame story also features the fay. The three interpolated stories, "Mellusine," "Sireneh," and an item untitled within the portmanteau but referred to elsewhere as "La Fée Ouroucoucou," were almost certainly written considerably earlier than 1785, probably in the 1760s or 1770s, and inserted into the narrative of the novel with certain modifications, in order to adapt them to that context.

The sequence of the six stories, and the peculiar manner of their publication, illustrates the awkward problem that Restif had in producing what he called *contes bleus* [fanciful tales] and offering them to an audience once the Age of Enlightenment was in full swing. In the frame narrative of *Le Nouvel Abeilard*, Restif repeated Charles Perrault's apologetic argument that *contes bleus* recycling or modeled on folktales still had an important role to play in a supposedly skeptical society because the marvelous could and ought to function as a "sugar coating" for moralistic apologues that were useful, and perhaps vital, in the "*civilization*" [moral education] of children. As a strident dissenter from Rousseau's argument that children should not be "civilized" at all, but brought up in such a fashion as to allow their supposed innate goodness to develop unhindered, Restif was strongly in favor of methodical moral instruction, and ardent in his assertion that remodeled folktales could be enormously useful—provided that it was explained, eventually, that the elements of the marvelous employed to capture and hold the attention of young listeners must be construed allegorically rather than literally.

The notional narrator in *Le Nouvel Abeilard* and those featured in *Les Veillées du Marais* all insist forcefully that their *contes bleus* are not literally true, and take great pains to explain their supposed moral purpose. The latter portmanteau also goes to considerable trouble, in the complex nesting of its narratives, to explain how it happens that accounts of historical events become distorted by the fancies and exaggerations of contemporary narrators, and further transfigured by the accumulation of imaginary marvels as the tales are repeated and retold over time. Indeed, in its final version, the story of Prince Oribeau goes to great lengths in the attempt to juxtapose and interweave a desupernaturalized version of the imagined "traditional tale" with an "enlightened version" that explains what "actually happened" and how it came to be embellished into a marvel-filled heroic fantasy.

The problem with Restif's appropriation of that argument, however, as with several of its previous employers, is that is it very difficult to believe that any of his *contes bleus*, with the possible exception of "La Fée Ouroucoucou," was actually written as a moralistic apologue. In fact, it seems perfectly obvious that they were initially imagined—or embellished, in the case of the two that recycle familiar legendary tales—as extravagant accounts of marvels, undertaken for the sheer joy of fantasization. Only one—"Les Quatre belles et les quatre bêtes"—really invites a plausible allegorical reading, and then only in the narrow context of Restif's own personal circumstances, as he seems to have gradually identified himself more interestedly with the emotions and predicament of his protagonist. For that reason, at least five of the six stories are manifestly at war with themselves, pretending determinedly, but unavailingly, to be something they are clearly not: a common problem in the literary history of Faerie.

In the autobiographical elements that Restif routinely incorporated into his novels, he often refers to a shepherd who used to narrate local folktales to him in his childhood, while they were watching sheep graze, whom he sometimes names François Courtcrou, linking him phonetically with the Fée Ouroucoucou. His own *contes bleus* seemingly attempt to capture something of the effect that hearing those tales had on his young self. There is no way of knowing whether Restif ever told such tales to his own children, but the fact that he had four daughters undoubtedly has something to do with the fact that "Les Quatre belles et les quatre bêtes" features a hero with four daughters. The eldest of the three survivors would have been in her early teens when Restif eventually began publishing the *contes bleus*, but his wife had taken them away to the provinces when the couple separated in 1773, so they might not have been with him when the stories were written; it was not until 1785 that one of them returned to Paris to live with him, swiftly followed by another. It is surely not irrelevant to its personal significance that the father of the four daughters featured in "Les Quatre belles et les quatre bêtes" is separated from them for many years, and is bitterly at odds with his wife in the meantime.

In fact, "Les Quatre belles et les quatre bêtes" has a footnote as it approaches its denouement, in which the author comments that he has had to change the ending of the "traditional version" of the story because it would be unacceptable to a Parisian audience. Exactly what he meant by that is a matter for conjecture, but the "original" that Restif had in mind was surely his own predicament, and his all-too-sharp awareness that, whereas the father in the story is saved from isolation by a heroic act of self-sacrifice on the part of his wife, which reunites the entire family, his own marriage was irreparably broken, with no fay available to play the role that Ouroucoucou plays in both "Le Demi-Coq" and "Les Quatre belles et les quatre bêtes." Although she is supernaturalized by comparison with the human fays of the 1690s, normally invisible even when active, only appearing on rare occasions in order to wave her wand and sort things out, Ouroucoucou functions as a *deus ex machina* in exactly the same fashion.

In "La Fée Ouroucoucou," the eponymous fay offers conditional supernatural rewards to a virtuous king, which go awry when the King in question is led by moral failures to break the imposed conditions, in a fashion similar to François Fénelon's fays, and leading to a similar moral, but she functions very differently in the frame story and the other interpolated tales. "Mellusine," changes her role very considerably, and elaborates it enormously in integrating it into the imaginary history of Evinland, equipping Wrwcwcw, as her name is now spelled, with an elaborate descendancy via her unlucky daughter Pucellomaneh.

The latter is required by a curse to give birth to ten demi-fay daughters over a period of approximately a thousand years, beginning with Semiramis and Eurydice and extending via Cleopatra, Phryné and other famous *femmes fatales* to Sireneh and Mellusine. Pucellomaneh is said to play a protective role parallel to the one credited to the "original" Mélusine with regard to the House of Lusignan, but she is always backed by the higher authority of Wrwcwcw, here established as the Queen of the Fays and ruler of a Faerie that is carefully positioned by Restif above the earth's atmosphere, while fays themselves are relocated in a more extensive hierarchy of exotic beings. "Sireneh" adapts a conflated version of the legends of Circe and the Sirens to the pseudohistory of Oribeau's world, set on an island in the Shannon; Wrwcwcw is present only in the background, the active role of intervention being delegated to Pucellomaneh.

In the main narrative of *Les Veillées du Marais* too, it is Pucellomaneh who takes the active role, although she is still Wrwcwcw's daughter and Wrwcwcw takes a hand herself more than once in the "marvelous" version of the story, even though she has become a long-dead mortal queen in the desupernaturalized version. The dynasty of fays and demi-fays elaborately outlined in "Mellusine" is transformed by the desupernaturalization of Oribeau's story into a dynasty of human royal families, whose female members become the subtle power behind the thrones of Evinland, deliberately exploiting popular superstition in order to work in mysterious ways, without whose benign influence even good kings are likely to be impotent and bad ones likely to make a terrible mess. As the four volumes of *Les Veillées du Marais* develop, therefore, with many digressions and interruptions breaking up Prince Oribeau's story, the reader is presented with a kaleidoscopic confusion of images from different periods of the imaginary history, and sees the fay Pucellomaneh gradually replaced by Princess Pucellomaneh, whose actions behind the scenes have been responsible for many of the pseudo-supernatural events reported to or witnessed by Oribeau.

That conclusion is not compatible with the early phases of the story, and Restif seems to have changed his mind part way through the writing when he had a flash of inspiration, having seen something in the sky that changed his mind completely with regard to the possibilities of accommodating the marvelous within the literature of an Age of Enlightenment, and adapting the marvelous to the fiction of such an era. We can date that flash of inspiration to the last few months of 1783, when he, along with his wonderstruck neighbors, saw a whole series of balloons take to the Parisian skies, the hot air balloons launched by the Montgolfier brothers being rapidly followed by the hydrogen balloons constructed by the Robert brothers for Jacques Charles.

The impact that the sight of those balloons must have had on Restif is very obvious in *Les Veillées du Marais*, where Princess Pucellomaneh is equipped, in order to carry out all the escapades credited to her fay *alter ego*, with a set of hot air balloons disguised as "rocs," which can either be steered by a mechanism controlled by brass wires or harnessed to a team of eagles and condors. It is not insignificant that two of the notable *contes de fées* included in the exemplary anthology featured flying machines maneuvered by fays—the one in *Cornichon et Toupette* similarly employs balloons to provide lift—nor that such machines can be seen as a modification of one of the standard motifs of the genre: the exotic "*char*" [chariot] with which every fay is equipped. Restif's narrative move in the story of Prince Oribeau, therefore, provides an adept dividing line for a text which is not only an allegory of the fate of Faerie but marks a final chronological boundary in the publication of *contes de fées*.

For the next hundred years, French literary balloons regularly performed miracles that only fays and genii could have achieved before, but they did them in a different spirit, liberated—at least partially—from the thunderclouds of incredulity that Restif and his contemporaries had seen gathering ominously over Faerie. With greater alacrity than any other work of the period, *Les Veillées du Marais* anticipated the direction in which one important flock of *contes bleus* was going to migrate in future, and in substituting Wrwcwcw the pioneering aeronaut for la Fée Ouroucoucou, Restif laid down a template for countless future fictional miracle-workers.

That transformation was not without cost. An objective observer, looking over the five earlier stories in which the fay Ouroucoucou had featured, might well conclude that her role as an agent of morality and *civilization*, helping out the virtuous and punishing the wicked, sometimes left much to be desired, in judgment as well as timing. Like God, she ran into the problem of theodicy: given her capacity to do away with evil with a flick of a wand, why there was so much of it around? Why did the virtuous always have to wait until the end of the story to get things sorted out, and why did they have to jump through lots of hoops in order to get there, when she could have intervened much earlier without laying down so many absurd conditions? In a materialistic sense, that became easier to understand once she and her descendants became cunning women possessed of a dirigible balloon—but their motives also become very muddied and a trifle tawdry, being limited to looking after their own families rather than being superheroic agents of ultimate supernatural good.

In one sense, the career of the fay Wrwcwcw ended rather ignominiously, reducing her far beneath her initial rank of "the noble fay," let alone the sovereignty of Faerie that she had briefly acquired. It has to be admitted, however, that when she was seen, in "Mellusine," apparently in the ninth century or thereabouts, ascending to the realm of Faerie beyond the atmosphere in an aerostat of her own invention, that she was a fay ahead of "the time of the fays," and a fay who knew which way the wind of change was blowing.

Voices in the Wilderness

It may seem puzzling, in retrospect, that the Romantic Movement that flourished in France after the 1789 Revolution, overlapping similar movements in Germany and Britain (one has to say "Britain" rather than "England" because of the vital contribution made to the English-language Movement by Scots such as James Macpherson and Walter Scott), which resulted in a massive resurgence of interest in fantastic literature, not only left *fées* for dead but conducted elaborate obsequies for them. Two of the leading members of the French Movement, Honoré de Balzac and Charles Nodier, produced significant short novels that used the word in their titles: *La Dernière fée* (1823; revised 1825; tr. as *The Last Fay*) and *La Fée aux miettes* (1832; tr. as "The Crumb Fairy") respectively. Both, however, are delusional fantasies, the whole point of which is that fays have no place in the modern world, being an obsolete illusion in which only an innocent raised in isolation from society (in Balzac's tragedy) or a harmless lunatic (in Nodier's whimsical drama) could possibly invest any credulity.

Nodier had previously written several notable works of fantastic fiction, including *Trilby, ou Le Lutin d'Argail* (1822; tr. as "Trilby") which features a "fairy" or sorts—more accurately a brownie—who is emphatically not a *fée*. Indeed, fays of the kind devised in the salons of the 1690 are rigorously excluded, not merely from Nodier's Romantic fiction, except as admittedly-obsolete delusions, but from the entire movement, especially from the abundant fiction its members produced for the consumption of children.

The Movement's most active pioneer as a publisher was Émile Girardin, who founded *Le Journal de Enfants* [The Children's Magazine] and *Musée des Familles* [The Family Magazine] in 1833. The former, edited by Jules Janin, included in its first year of publication a censorious essay by "Michel Raymond" (Raymond Brucker) on "La Morale des contes de fees" [The Morality of Tales of Fays] and the same author's brief "Dernier conte des fées" [Last Tale of Fays], which explained why such material should now be considered unsuitable reading for children, who needed realism in their educational entertainment, and why it would not be featured in the periodical in future.

During the first few months of its publication, the *Musée* followed a format not dissimilar to other magazines of the period, featuring a miscellany of short articles on various subjects, with the occasional short story. When Samuel Henry Berthoud took over the editorship in April 1834, however, he soon adopted very different tactics, running longer stories, mostly novellas; the bulk of the magazine's contents, and the core of its didactic mission, was transferred to these items, which Berthoud labeled "Études." Most were "Études historiques" [Historical Studies] or "Études morales" [Moralistic Studies] but he made an evident effort to gather as many of the topics covered by the magazine as possible under those banners, in obvious pursuit of the theory that educational material was more palatable if it were enclosed in a narrative that had all the conventional reader-appeal of popular fiction—but fantastic fiction was largely banished in favor of naturalism, and of fays there was no sign at all.

That might seem surprising, given that much of Berthoud's own early fiction had been flamboyantly fantastic; he was one of the first people in France to advertise himself as a folklorist and collector of legendary lore, and once set out on a walking tour of his native Flanders in order to collect stories from peasants, although he soon gave up when his blistered feet made it impossible to continue. Over time, however, he collected enough material to fill two volumes with such adapted folktales and pastiches thereof. Significantly, however, there is not a fay in sight, although the Devil and his minions are everywhere, as one would expect in folklore conditioned for more than a thousand years by the Church's moral terrorism. None of the folklorists who followed in Berthoud's footsteps found any trace of fays similar to those devised by the salon writers, although Breton folklorists inevitably found idiosyncratic spiritual entities such as follets and farfadets in abundance. Fays were similarly banished from the *Musée des Familles*, although angels and demons occasionally made figurative appearances therein.

Another of the publishers associated with the French Romantic Movement was Pierre-Jules Hetzel, who followed Janin's and Berthoud's examples in recruiting some of its leading writers—including Nodier, Alexandre Dumas and George Sand—to write for his own periodicals for children. Again, fays were rigorously excluded, and, like his predecessors, Hetzel put a very heavy emphasis on naturalistic fiction, reflecting a conviction that "real marvels" were infinitely preferable as educational instruments to fantasies, and that if the fantastic were to be invoked at all, it was best done in a delusional context. That remained the orthodoxy of French educational theory for the greater part of the nineteenth century.

The orthodoxy in question inevitably had an effect on the tone and manner of the fantastic fiction produced by affiliates to the Romantic Movement who were stubborn in so doing. "Philothée O'Neddy" (Théophile Dondey, 1811-1875), a prominent member of Théophile Gautier's *petit cénacle*, produced a striking novella, "Histoire d'un anneau enchanté, roman de chevalerie" (1841; tr. as *The Enchanted Ring*) which features a heroine very similar to the heroines of many *contes de fées* but is careful only to call her a fay metaphorically. An enchanter plays a minor role but is kept sternly off-stage, and the titular enchanted ring, which enables the heroine to become a powerful enchantress, is a gift from God. The story differs sharply from the original *contes de fées* in giving a central role to the Christian religion and to its most important representative in Carolingian romance, Archbishop Turpin. The author employs an archangel to kick-start his plot and credits its most striking miracle directly to God, but he intrudes a peculiar essay into the narrative in which the author, having tacitly announced in a chapter title that he is going to kill off his heroine, then offers an explanation of why he feels obliged to shun the traditional "happy ending" of *contes de fées*, as a device crucially undermined by modern education.

The absence of fays from French culture in the nineteenth century was not absolute, however, and there was a considerable vogue in Paris for theatrical *féeries* [enchantments] which made much of colorful visual displays, usually contained in tableaux, and special effects. The Théâtre du Chatelet became particularly associated with such productions, thriving on them for much of the latter half of the century. Although many such plays did not feature *fées* at all, and many of those that used the term applied it to "fairies" in the English vein—reflecting the fact that London saw a similar but less enduring boom in "fairy plays" and also in "fairy painting"—the vogue encouraged many adaptations of tales now considered classics, including those by Perrault and a significant number by Madame d'Aulnoy, most notably successful adaptations of "La Chatte blanche" and "Le Biche au bois." Such theatrical adaptations assisted Madame d'Aulnoy's tales considerably to achieve a widespread popularity and respect that her work had struggled to attain and maintain before the Revolution, and helped to elevate her to the classic status she has enjoyed ever since.

The fashionability of *féeries* was responsible the revival of earlier works such as the 1765 opera *La Fée Urgèle*, preserving it for citation by Anatole France, but most of the work was carefully adapted to the staging and available special effects, and designed with that in mind. What it did not do—perhaps surprisingly—was encourage the writing of new prose fiction featuring similar supernatural materials, at least until the end of the century, when the theatrical fashion was well on the wane. A marked cultural divide seemed to be maintained for many years between literary and theatrical writing, and any fays written for the stage would have been at great risk of disappearing without trace because the plays were never printed—a fate that befell enormous numbers of one-act plays, especially those deemed to be "vaudevilles," into which category many *féeries* were considered to fall.

Within the general context of absence there were grudging exceptions. Perrault was already recognized as a classic writer, possessed of the entitlement of antiquity, and Madame d'Aulnoy gradually ascended to that status, but their warrant was not as important in France as the entitlement of being foreign. No French writer active in the first half of the century was as important in France as a recognized writer of fantasies for children as the Brothers Grimm and Hans Christian Andersen—somewhat ironically, as many of the tales popularized by the Brother Grimm were direct or indirect plagiarisms of tales originating in France. It was the works of those writers that became the principal determinants of what would henceforth be called "fairy tales" in English, that being co-opted as the standard translation of both the German *märchen* and the Danish *eventyr*.

Understandably, however, the agents of enchantment deployed by the Grimms and Andersen bear little or no resemblance to the fays of the 1690s French salons. Witches and other minions of the Devil are occasionally featured therein, but in many instances, magic is a kind of common property, not in the specific gift of a particular class of entities.

The Brothers Grimm claimed to be collecting authentic German folktales, and seemingly hoped to find within those supposedly traditional tales something of an authentic German *volksgeist* [spirit of the people], for which an as-yet-hypothetical German nation in search of unification and consolidation was supposedly searching. It is not impossible that they really thought that was what they were doing in asking their middle-class neighbors what stories they knew, and that is a kinder hypothesis than the alternative, so perhaps it ought to be accepted, but what they actually produced is an elaborate tangle of material drawn from various European literary sources, to which any specifically Germanic element was an artificial additive. In any case, what they wrote only bore a remote resemblance to what it is now known that they collected, thanks to the heroic efforts of the literary historian Jack Zipes, based on an examination of their handwritten notes. Andersen was more honest, and made no bones about the fact that he made his stories up, and that any connection they had with Danish folklore was very remote indeed. In both cases, however, legend proved far stronger than truth—as it usually does—and the notion of some such connection proved persistent.

The Brothers Grimm's first collection of *Kinder- und Hausmärchen* was published in 1812, and was augmented by further volumes as it went through ten editions in the next forty years; the stories were widely translated and gradually built up an enormous popularity as some of the tales gave rise to neo-folkloristic versions. The first volumes of Andersen's *Eventyr* were issued between 1835 and 1837, and were similarly augmented in later editions; they too established an international reputation and added considerably to the stock of neo-folkloristic tales, still known in English as "fairy tales," although very few contained "fairies." The fays of the French *contes de fées* are barely echoed in material by Grimm and Andersen, even in those Grimm tales that are actually based on such *contes*. The persistence of fantastic motifs in fiction read to children in nineteenth-century France thus owed little or nothing to native *contes de fées*, having been decisively severed from that root. When characters designated as *fées* were featured in French tales produced during that period they were likely to be more reminiscent of English fairies than the fays designed and developed by Madame d'Aulnoy, the Comtesse de Murat and their followers.

In France, as in England, however, a special license came to be granted from the middle of the century onwards for a fantastic genre of "contes de Noël" [Christmas stories], when writers and readers were given a ticket-of-leave from normal standards and allowed to write fantasies—especially mawkish sentimental fantasies in keeping with the supposed spirit of Christmas. Pierre-Alexis

Ponson du Terrail's "La Fée, conte de Noël" (1854) (tr. as "The Fay: A Christmas Story") is included in the exemplary anthology as a specimen of such work by a writer who became one of the most prolific and popular of his era; its English influences are very obvious.

Although there were few rebels against the prevailing orthodoxy, it would have been very surprising indeed had there been none at all, writers being, in general, an unruly mob. The most widely-read children's writer in France in the latter half of the century was the Russian-born Sophie Rostopchine, Comtesse de Ségur (c.1799-1874), and one of her earliest literary endeavors was a volume of *Nouveaux contes de fées pour les petits enfants* [New Tales of the Fays for Little Children] (1856), containing five novelettes; one that actually features a *fée* "La Petite souris grise" (tr. as The Little Gray Mouse), is reproduced in the exemplary anthology as a sample. When the comtesse became the star of Louis Hachette's *Bibliothèque rose*, however, for which her husband, an important railway pioneer, obtained a monopoly on sales of children's books on railway bookstalls, she never sought to employ that uniquely privileged position to do anything further in the same vein.

None of the several busy collectors of tales active in France during the nineteenth century, understandably collected any authentic folktales featuring fays, and when they wrote pastiches—and almost all published work in that vein consists of pastiches—they very rarely inserted any. One of the most prolific "collectors" of such tales was a famous man of law, Édouard-René de Laboulaye (1811-1883), who published three volumes of *contes bleus* allegedly collected in his travels, as well as a second-hand adaptation of an Oriental fantasy, *Abdallah, ou Le Tréfle à quatre feuilles* (1859; tr. as *Abdallah; or, The Four-Leafed Shamrock*), which proved very popular. *Fées* are almost entirely absent from his work, and the most interesting exception moved them to Italy and made them into nature spirits of a sort. "Le Château de la vie" (1858 in *Souvenirs d'un voyageur*; tr. as "The Castle of Life") is interesting, however, by virtue of its apologetic narrative strategy, which uses a child as a hypothetical narrator, the eccentricity of its dalliance with allegory and moralism, and its grimly downbeat ending.

Against that general background, it is perhaps not surprising that one of the very few nineteenth-century French writers who made any use of *fées* clearly derived from the authentic seventeenth-century tradition, albeit casually, sarcastically and with more than a hint of contempt, was the arch-rebel Charles Baudelaire (1821-1867), in "Les Dons des fées" (written 1862; tr. as "The Gifts of the Fays") one of the ultra-short stories intended for collection in *Spleen de Paris*, which did not see publication until after his death. It represents a kind of dismissal perhaps more fatal than death, but it did make a significant contribution to the preservation of the idea of fays when they were on the brink of literary oblivion. Although a strange and disguised voice in the wilderness, Baudelaire's tale doubtless made a contribution to the preservation of a fugitive foundation on which later writers would rebuild.

It was in celebrating Baudelaire's work that Théophile Gautier—by then the central pillar of declining French Romanticism—popularized the idea of "Decadent style" as an eclectic literary *modus operandi* drawing materials from a wide range of imaginative sources in order to combine them in newly flamboyant ways, reflecting and sarcastically celebrating the alleged decadence of contemporary French culture and civilization. The idea of inevitable cultural decadence had been popularized by Montesquieu, although it did not originate with him, as witness Catherine Durand's account of "L'Origine des fées." Even before the death of Louis XIV, parallels between his reign and the grandiosity of the doomed Roman Empire, had been drawn by jaundiced observers, and the reign of Louis XV added further fuel to the suspicion that the Bourbon Era was heading toward a historical precipice. Baudelaire, Gautier and other writers who were glad to think of themselves as apt commentators on a further slide had the advantage of knowing that the 1789 Revolution had fulfilled Montesquieu's anticipations, and that the hopes of a new grandeur briefly offered by Napoléon Bonaparte had been reduced to tragicomedy by Napoléon III. Those who came after them added to that awareness a knowledge of the catastrophe of the Franco-Prussian War of 1870.

None of the writers concerned was in a situation to link the idea of Decadent fantasy to the work of Madame d'Aulnoy and the Comtesse de Murat, or to *the contes philosophes* of the contraband renaissance of *contes de fées*, because they saw that history through the same distorting lens as Alphonse de Lescure, but in fact, the accounts of the bizarrely perverse consequences of the gifts of the fays offered by the exponents of the genre offer a far more accurate commentary on the phenomenon of aristocratic decadence than Baudelaire's dismissive vignette, the theme of which had already been addressed, squarely and in depth, by the Comte de Caylus in "Les Dons" (tr. as "The Gifts"). Caylus's story was itself a reprocessing of a recurrent theme in the work of Madame d'Aulnoy, also foreshadowed in the Comtesse de Murat's "Anguillette." Given that recurrence of interest and attitude, it is not surprising that there was something of a second renaissance of *contes de fées* toward the end of the century, closely associated with writers heavily influenced by Gautier and Baudelaire, some of whom conceived of themselves as members of a Decadent Movement and all of whom thought of themselves as Symbolists.

The Afterglow

What the French Romantic Movement had deliberately not done, the literary movements that came after it, aspiring to replace it rather than rejuvenate it, did permit, albeit in a faint and eccentric fashion. The faintness was not in the quality of the work—some very fine writers were prepared to toy with the idea of fays after the fall of the Second Empire, and the advent of the Third Republic—but the idea they had of fays was itself very faint by then, so far were they removed from the authentic source in the 1690s.

It was difficult for anyone in the last three decades of the nineteenth century to avoid seeing *contes de fées* in the same fashion as Adolphe de Lescure, who retained Perrault in narrow focus while allowing the Comtesse de Murat, and even Baronne d'Aulnoy, to fade into the background, and practically everyone else involved in the history of *contes de fées* to be obscured entirely. There is a certain ironic propriety in the fact that when the last survivor of the Romantic Movement, George Sand, turned her hand to writing fiction for children late in life, she reprocessed material from several familiar "fairy tales" but nothing from authentic *contes de fées*. The *fées* featured in the titles of two of her stories bear no resemblance to the fays of d'Aulnoy and Murat; the eponymous characters in "La Fée poussière" [The Dust Fay] and "La Fée aux gros yeux" [The Fay with Big Eyes] (both 1876) are metaphorical fays, employed in eccentric attempted popularizations of the scientific world-view.

As previously noted, it required a scrupulous literary historian—more akin to a literary archeologist—of the caliber of Anatole France, to cultivate any kind of awareness of where *contes de fées* had come from, and how they had been reconfigured, and even he put Perrault center stage, albeit not so much to praise him as to bury him. As requiems for the genre go, Anatole France's was certainly eloquent and sharp-witted, and it hit the target at which it was aimed—but it was, in large measure, a false target: a decoy erected by ignorance and misunderstanding. The authentic *contes de fées*, even Madame d'Aulnoy's, remained largely unmourned and uncelebrated, because they were largely unknown and irrecoverable. Nevertheless, a further chapter—or, at least, an epilogue of sorts—was added to the history of literary fées after 1870, and the label enjoyed a further lease of life, even though it came to be applied rather haphazardly.

The first new Movement that attempted to replace Romanticism, considered obsolete by virtue of the manifest historical break of 1870, was the Parnassian Movement, a rather vaguely defined endeavor that was far more manifest in poetry than prose, and perhaps exclusively confined there, depending on the particular conception that each of its participants and commentators had of it.

100

One of the prime movers of the Parnassian Movement was, however, Catulle Mendès, who became a very prolific writer of short fiction, and within a much broader context, a prolific writer of *contes* of various sorts, including *contes de fées* of a sort.

Mendès was aided in that commercial adventure by developments in the literary marketplace. In the last three decades of the century, paper-making and printing technologies made considerable advances, making newspapers and periodicals much easier and much cheaper to produce. There was a remarkable boom in the production of new ones, which created a vacuum of demand for material to fill them in a fashion attractive to potential purchasers, and the pattern of that demand was largely shaped by existing formats. Émile de Girardin's popular newspapers and periodicals had long ago pioneered a tradition of "feuilleton fiction," by which newspapers carried fiction in a section separating from the news section of the paper by a horizontal line—the feuilleton. Traditionally, that space had been employed for interminable serial novels, but after 1870, the pattern of demand shifted as some newspapers began featuring short stories in feuilleton slots, and sometimes publishing weekly "literary supplements" using batches of short stories in slots of similar size—usually between 1400 and 1700 words long. Although it was not difficult to adapt naturalistic "slice-of-life" stories to such narrow slots, they were also hospitable to anecdotal items and *contes* mimicking oral narrations—including *contes bleus*.

Catulle Mendés became an expert in filling those slots, and fantastic *contes* were one of the many instruments he employed; other writers followed suit, especially when the Parnassian Movement faded away, to be replaced by the more robust and ambitious Symbolist Movement, which overlapped to such a considerable extent with the Baudelaire-inspired Decadent Moment that many participants and commentators thought the two identical. The short story slots in the newspapers became an important showcase and source of income for a whole generation of adventurous Parisian writers, and fantastic fiction became a significant feature of their endeavor, in which fays played a fugitive role.

The *fées* routinely featured in Catulle Mendès' *contes merveilleux* have little resemblance to the *fées* of d'Aulnoy and Murat, who were adapted to much more substantial works. They have a much closer resemblance to English fairies, and Shakespeare's Puck became one of his stock characters. There is no evidence in Mendès' work that he ever read any of the original *contes de fées* produced in the 1690s, or the pastiches produced in the mid-eighteenth century. One of his earliest tales in that vein was "La Belle au bois rêvant" (1882; tr. as "The Dreaming Beauty") which is an ironic gloss on the vulgarized abridgement of Perrault's "Le Belle au bois dormant," but synoptic versions of the abridgement had become an element of orally-transmitted folklore long before. One fantastic tale produced toward the end of his career, "L'Azure, l'or et le purple" (1904; tr. as "Azure, Gold and Crimson"), contains echoes of the initiating incident of Madame d'Aulnoy's "La Princesse Belle-Étoile et le prince Chéri" that might not be coincidental, but Mendès story is an allegory that does not feature fays. There is, therefore, a certain irony in the fact that if one simply tabulates titles, Catulle Mendès wrote more tales featuring *"fées"* than any other French writer—more than forty—although a purist might judge that he wrote no "authentic" *contes de fées* at all.

Seventeen stories featuring *fées* of a sort were included in Mendès' first collection to consist almost entirely of fantastic *contes*, *Les Contes du rouet* [Spinning-Wheel Tales] (1885; revised in 1888 as *Les Oiseaux bleus*; tr. as *Bluebirds*). His other collection consisting entirely of fantastic *contes*, *Pour lire au convent* (1887) contains four stories explicitly featuring *fées*, and several associational items, and there are more than twenty further stories in which *fées* play a significant part scattered through his many other story collections. Fays only play a marginal role in Mendès' masterpiece, the novella *Luscignole* (1892); the character featured therein who is called *le roi fée* is a fake, all his "enchantments" being contrived by artificial and mechanical means, and he is clearly a transfiguration of Ludwig II of Bavaria, who was nicknamed the *märchenkönig*, of which *le roi fée* is an approximate translation. *Luscignole* is, in essence, an "anti-fairy tale," in which the fay king's attempt to play the *deus ex machina* role traditionally attributed to good fays goes awry, thus allowing the story to become a graphic horror story, but it retains a strong affinity with the tradition of *contes de fées*, in terms of its tone and the narrative structure that it reproduces in order to undermine its conventions. It has something in common with Balzac's tragic requiem for the genre, *La dernière fée*.

More significantly, *Luscignole* has something in common with the two tales written by Catherine Bernard for the salons of the 1690s, which Mendès had certainly never read. The symbolism of many of Mendès skeptical tales is very similar to the symbolism of "Le Prince rosier," and so is their fundamental philosophy. Even though they feature a different species of fays, therefore, Mendès' belated contributions to the genre have closer affinities with it than he could have suspected, and they represent a significant, if decidedly eccentric, phase in the history of the genre.

In many stories in which Mendès employs fays as a narrative devices, they are simply employed to emphasize his fundamental convictions with flamboyant and absurdly exaggerated irony, as, for instance in "La Fée Menteuse" (tr. as "The Fay Liar") and "Ce que les fées ne peuvent" (tr. as "What Fays Cannot Do"). Other stories, such as "Les Petites fées en l'air" (tr. as "The Little Fays in the Air") and "Le Prince lys et la vague de neige" (tr. as "Prince Lys and the Wave of Snow") employ a much subtler, far more sentimental irony, the latter partaking of a quirky surrealism that became typical of the last phase of his work. Others use fays as allegorical devices in themselves, as in "Le Bon almanach" (tr. as "The Good Almanac") or as instigators of allegorical quests, as in "L'Eau, la glace et le feu" (tr. as "Water, Ice and Fire"). Some, such as "Les Souhaits d'une églantine" (tr. as "The Wishes of an Eglantine") and "Les Solitaries" (tr. as "The Solitaries"), are risqué fantasies, the latter venturing boldly into the territory of the conventionally-unmentionable. Underlying all the work, however, is an insistent consciousness that the chimerical nature of *fées* does not render them irrelevant to the precious functions of literature, any more than the chimerical nature of *amour parfait* renders that Ideal irrelevant to the business of real human life.

None of the writers who followed Mendès' example in writing *contes merveilleux* for *fin-de-siècle* newspapers were as liberal as he was with the term *fée*; the arch-Decadent Jean Lorrain wrote numerous fantastic *contes*, including a striking series of *contes de Noël*, but *fées* are less conspicuous there than witches and sirens. The same is true of other Symbolist writers. It has to be admitted, therefore, that the handful of tales assembled in the final section of the exemplary anthology, although there is nothing amiss with their literary quality, smacks somewhat of scraping the bottom of a murky barrel in terms of their representation and celebration of fays. They are certainly *contes de fées* in the sense that they feature entities identified as *fées,* but they have little or no conscious continuity with the spirit of authentic *contes de fées*, even when the reproduce it partially.

The tales in question are included in the present volume for what they are worth as specimens, illustrating the fact that the spirit of what the English call "fairy tales" was still echoed in France even as the French tradition of *contes de fées* faded into deep obscurity, unredeemed by the belated celebrity won by Madame d'Aulnoy in the theater. Her tales were probably more widely read in the last quarter of the nineteenth century than ever before, but she was regarded more as a literary fossil than a model, and her work had been decisively excised from the collaborative and competitive context that had produced it, relocated in a much broader spectrum, alongside and mingled with the Brothers Grimm and Hans Christian Andersen as well as the parasitic Perrault, rather than linking arms with Mademoiselle de La Force and the Comtesse de Murat.

For the record, Catulle Mendès' "La Dernière fée" (tr. as "The Last Fay") was first published in the newspaper *Gil Blas* on 10 April 1885 before being reprinted in *Les Contes du rouet* and "Le Prince lys et la vague de neige" was reprinted in *Arc-en-ciel et Sourcil Rouge* (1897). Jean Lorrain's "Mélusine Enchantée" (tr. as "Melusine Enchanted") first appeared in the *Écho de Paris* in 1892 (which Catulle Mendès was the newspaper's literary editor) before being reprinted in *Princesses d'ivoire et d'ivresse* (1902). Frédéric Boutet's "La Vallée nommée Solitude" (tr. as "The Valley Named Solitude") was originally published in *Contes dans le nuit* (1898; tr. in *The Antisocial Man and Other Strange Stories*). Anatole France's "Histoire de la Duchesse de Cicogne et de M. de Boulingrin qui dormiront cent ans en compagnie de la Belle-au-bois-dormant" (tr. as "The Story of the Duchesse de Cicogne and Monsieur de Boulingrin") appeared in *Les Sept femmes de Barbe-Bleue et autres contes merveilleux* (1909; tr. as *The Seven Wives of Bluebeard and Other Marvelous Tales*).

The five stories in question barely qualify even as echoes of the extinct genre, and did not constitute a meaningful resurrection; all of them were outshone by the other fantastic tales with which they were mingled by their authors, which were more eclectic in their choice of agents of enchantment and more versatile as arenas of fantastic invention and elegant moralism. Even so, these stories and others contemporary with them did provide a further element to the history of the genre—a footnote if not an epilogue—and no matter how anticlimactic they might seem by comparison with their early predecessors in the anthology, they offer an honest account of what time and tide had made of the genre's aspirations. In the twentieth century a number of writers eventually rediscovered other foundation-stones, especially the work of Madame d'Aulnoy, and began to take some fruitful inspiration from it, but none was able to see those stories in their original context, or gain a substantial understanding of their original purpose and impetus.

Conclusion

If Catherine Bernard's account of a salon game can be assumed to be a disguised account of the manner in which *contes de fées* were invented in the literary salons of Paris in 1690 or thereabouts—and the works support that supposition—then the genre was born of a challenge, not merely in the sense that its practitioners were invited to compete with one another, but in the sense that what they were asked to attempt had a deliberate hint of paradox about it. The players in the game were required to do two things that did not seem, at first glance, to be easily compatible: to make "the charm of the tales…consist of making visible what was happening in the heart," and also to find or contrive "a kind of merit in the marvelous imaginations, which would not be retained by the appearances of verity."

The idea that fiction could and ought to be used as a means of plumbing the depths of the human heart, in order to explore and explain its secret mechanisms, was by no means new in 1690, but the proposition that such exploration and explanation should be a privileged mission and primary purpose of fiction was itself largely a product of the Parisian salons, under the ardent spur of Mademoiselle de Scudéry, which had given rise to a particular species of sentimental fiction. It seemed logical to some writers and commentators, however, that such exploration and explanation was best done, and perhaps could only be done, within a naturalistic narrative framework: that the parameters of the mission required the maximum of realism in the representations of characters and their interactions.

That semblance of logic was, however—arguably, at least—only a semblance, partly because the mission itself was dishonest. Although represented as a descriptive quest, it was actually, in large measure, a prescriptive one; its purpose was not so much to discover the mechanisms of the human heart, but rather to specify how those mechanisms ought to operate, within the context of Virtue. In "making visible" what was happening in the hearts of fictitious characters, writers of fiction were also passing judgment upon it, stigmatizing certain impulses and actions as vice, or evil, while lauding others. That purpose is not necessarily best served by narrative realism; because it deals in hypothetical ideals, it is amenable to extreme representations purified of naturalistic confusions and complications. Extremes are marvelous in themselves, and in order to facilitate their contrivance by narrative artifice, marvelous devices can be an asset. Although it would be an overstatement to call marvelous devices a necessity, they are certainly not an impediment to effective dramatization, and they frequently aid narrative flow that would otherwise be weighed down by the requirements of rational plausibility and the tedium of reportage of everyday circumstance.

The suggestion made by Bernard's princess, however, goes beyond the mere licensing of fantastic devices in honor of their narrative utility; it asks the players of the game to find a merit in the marvelous imaginations themselves: to make an esthetic virtue out of the creativity of the imagination, to seek the fantastic for fantasy's sake. That is unusual, and it rarely features in apologetic arguments for literary marvels, whose makers routinely seek to justify them in terms of their utility, either in terms of moral exemplification, or in terms of providing innocent enjoyment.

It is not obvious that all the participants in the salon game of concocting *contes de fées* fully understood that part of their brief. Most of them, when they felt the need to argue in favor of what they were doing, did so in terms of moral and hedonic utility, perhaps thinking that those were the only arguments that their presumed adversaries would be able to take seriously. One only has to look at the paradigm examples provided by the true pioneers of the genre, however, to realize that they were, indeed, seeking to find a particular esthetic merit in the marvelous imaginations themselves, and the merest glance at the finest productions of the genre as initially prescribed—the later works of Madame d'Aulnoy and the Comtesse de Murat—to understand that that was a significant driving force impelling their work. They did not say so, but it is true, and because the esthetic merit they found in the deployment of the marvelous is real, it has interesting implications regarding fundamental human psychology.

It reveals, in particular, that the delight to be found in the extrapolation of imaginative creativity into the dreamlike realms of the surreal and the absurd carries with it a certain intrinsic embarrassment, responsible for a kind of intellectual allergy that causes some commentators on the genre to suffer a metaphorical anaphylactic shock, and makes even heroic explorers sneeze. On the other hand, no honest analysis of the workings of the human heart would be complete without it, and it is not a coincidence that the writer who tried more heroically than any other before him to write the first honest autobiography also tried, equally heroically, to be the last substantial contributor to the genres of *contes de fées*. There are no secrets that people guard more jealously than the secrets of their daydreams and private fantasies, and any fiction that seems to trespass on that sacred ground is bound to attract a strange combination of fascination and repulsion, especially in a supposed Age of Enlightenment.

The most impressive writers of the second wave of *contes de fées*, who were active in the 1730s and 1740s, did not claim publicly to be serious explorers of the fundamental esthetics of the marvelous either, but it is true of them too; the work of Mademoiselle de Lubert and Madame de Villeneuve would be very puzzling indeed if that aspect of their work were not appreciated. And it is that aspect of their work, more than anything else, that forges a solid link between the finer achievements of the genre of *contes de fées* and the finer achievements of twentieth century fantastic fiction, whether emergent from Symbolism, Surrealism or genre fantasy. Some *contes de fées*, like much genre fantasy, are stereotyped, involving the mere repetition of formulas, but it would be a grave mistake to write off the entire corpus as nothing more than the shuffling of a standardized deck of motifs and narrative moves; at the heart of the enterprise, from its very inception, there was a quest for innovation, for true marvels, and for untried ideas. Some of the new things they discovered soon became familiar, precisely because they struck resonant chords in the minds of their audience, but that does not devalue the effort that went into their origination, and even those motifs that became standardized mostly retain an element of mystery about them that resists insipidity.

Unsurprisingly, it is not the marvelous elements of *contes de fées* that now seem obsolete but the realistic ones. The genre was invented by aristocratic women in the seventeenth century, and in making visible the operations of the human heart it mostly made visible the discomforts, torments, fears and resentments of seventeenth century aristocratic women: the tightly-laced corset of social convention, the catastrophe of arranged marriages; the tyranny and frequent brutality of those in legal control of their lives and fortunes. Such aspects of everyday life are exaggerated by the conventions of the genre: the princesses are the most beautiful in the world, or the ugliest; the prisons in which they are contained are inaccessibly tall towers or lightless subterrains, often guarded by dragons; their captors are ogres, hagwives or giants, often addicted to setting them impossible tasks to complete, under the threat of dire punishment. And the fantasies of their salvation are exaggerated in consequence, beyond all reasonable expectation: the magic wand of the good fay, and, perhaps even more implausibly, the trustworthy amour of a fanciable man.

The plights of seventeenth century princesses—literal princesses like the dowager Princesse de Conti, the Duchesse du Maine and the Duchesse de Bourgogne as well as the multitude of comtesses, marquises and baronnes who were only imitation princesses—no longer apply, even metaphorically, to today's readers, but the plights that have replaced them still contain a few analogues, and, just as it was possible for bourgeois women, and men, to see something of their own existential difficulties mirrored or reflected in the *contes de fées* of the 1690s, so it remains possible today. After all, hearts and malevolence remain constant over time, their operations activated by similar motivational springs, and the imaginative device of an omnipotent magical wand or the possibility that someone we can love might be able reliably to love us back, although still far beyond the bounds of rational plausibility, have not lost their appeal in consequence. Insofar as the marvelous still has merits of its own, that gleam is surprisingly resistant to tarnish, if a reader is capable of taking up an imaginative position from which the light catches it at the right angle. Not everyone is, of course, and opinions have always been divided as to whether the members of the imaginatively-allergic remainder are to be admired or pitied.

At any rate, the achievements of *contes de fées* are not obsolete, for anyone possessed of imagination, and they are not trivial, for anyone hardened to its healthy exercise. The task its inventors set themselves was not straightforward, but it was not impossible; nor was it perverse, although a talent for intellectual contortionism can be useful to its full appreciation.

If, as seems likely, the genre was stamped out when its flame was barely alight because bigots thought it heretical, tacitly hostile to the straightjacket they wanted to impose on human thought, it has to be conceded that the evil bigots in question had an arguable case as well as an allergy. *Contes de fées*, by their very nature, are opposed to dogmatism, opposed to unreasoning tyranny and opposed to the imprisonment of the will. For all the genre's emphasis on the absolutism of virtue and the necessary observation of duty, it is ultimately founded on a commitment to liberty, on the sacred right to say no to coercion and moral terrorism—something that moral terrorists, not unnaturally, cannot tolerate. The genre's persecutors were wrong, obviously, from every rational and moral viewpoint, mistaken as well as evil, but if persecutors could be deterred by cavils of that nature, they would have died out long ago.

Whatever the motive for it was, however, the persecution in question was successful, not merely on a personal level, in putting a stop to the careers of the genre's leading practitioners, but in a general sense. To the limited extent that the genre survived, it was no longer the same, not simply because it was fugitive but because it was penitent. The most powerful weapon of the righteous has always been shame, and from its very inception, the genre's practitioners were persuaded to be ashamed of what they were doing, and of what they were. That was not difficult, in the event, because they were mostly women, and their persecutors were mostly men, with ten thousand years of practice in the art of making women feel ashamed of being women and men doubly ashamed of doing things that were mostly done by women.

Without exception, nobody ever took up her or his pen to write a *conte de fées* without having an apology to hand and guilt peering over their shoulder. That is one of the reasons, but certainly not the only one, why tales of enchantment have always been disguised tales of disenchantment, and why their likeliest path of evolution—the trajectory that the genre of *contes de fées* actually followed—was toward ever deeper disenchantment. Only a tiny minority of the stories in the genre were honest about their disenchantment, but that is understandable; when one goes to a masked ball, one takes a mask—or two, just in case—and the smile on the mask never signifies that the face beneath is smiling; quite the reverse, most of the time.

Why did *contes de fées* usually have happy endings? Because they could—and because their authors know full well that real people don't, because they can't. Such is life, and such is the nature of masks. But masked disenchantment is still disenchantment, and nothing masks disenchantment quite as well as fictitious enchantment. However, it was never difficult to persuade even the most diehard and the most expert writers of *contes de fées* that they ought to feel ashamed of what they were and what they did, and because of that, the genre was probably doomed while it was still in gestation. It could only be born as a game, and no matter how many good fays were sitting around the salon that day, ready and eager to endow the newborn with desirable qualities, there was always a nasty one lurking in the corner, ready to spoil things with a cackle and a curse. But the genre did survive, for a while, and in spite of the cackling and the cursing, it did produce some beautifully grotesque masks, which did make nakedly visible some of the afflictions of the human heart, and did find merits in the marvelous that had been unglimpsed before. Its disenchantment ran long and deep, but its enchantment cannot be written off on that account, and it remains precious—nor was there, or is there, any real need for anyone be ashamed of its preciosity.

It is evident, in retrospect, that the eventual usurpation of the genre by the *philosophes*, whose shadow extended even over its most defiant imaginations, and its consequent transfiguration, in large measure, into a subgenre of *contes philosophiques*, was an unmistakable symptom of its decadence and an augury of its imminent disappearance. Even in that decadence, however, it still had style and occasional verve, and it still contrived to find more merit in its imaginations. The fays could not endure, at least in the manner that they had been devised and designed—such afterlife as they contrived to maintain beyond the Age of the Guillotine was, quite literally, a phantom existence, robbed of flesh and blood—but their brief life was not devoid of achievement, or of merriment.

While they lasted, the new edition fays were not only possessed of beauty and charm themselves, they had the gift of endowing beauty and charm. They were often claimed to be capable of endowing intelligence too, and even though it has to be admitted that the princesses they endowed ostentatiously with that particular quality rarely showed conspicuous evidence of it, it was not a nonsensical claim, and the fact that it was made at all is due a certain credit.

There are limitations, alas, to what a pen can do; in order to make a heroine more beautiful and more charming than anyone else has ever been, it merely has to write that she is, but intelligence has to be seen in action in order to be believed, and even intelligent writers routinely have more difficulty making the intelligent mind visible than they do in performing the same service for the sensible heart. Everybody understands suffering, but only a few of us can suffer understanding, and it is not necessary to be a bigot or a moral terrorist to find that hard. Even freethinkers sometimes cherish chains of intellectual bondage. Seeking and finding merits in imagination requires intelligence, and so does the appreciation of their discovery, and that is one reason why genuinely illustrious fays not only had intelligence but were capable of endowing others with it.

The best *contes de fées* were written by savant women, who did not necessarily want their heroines to have that quality, but wanted nevertheless to have the freedom to gift it to them, and if they did not often give them narrative space in which to exercise it, that has far more to do with the nature of the milieu in which they were writing than their personal limitations, or the limitations of the hypothetical world they invented and mapped. In a fictitious world where evil and good alike are motivated by enchantment, the leverage of intelligence is bound to be somewhat limited, magic being, by definition, immune to its effects, but in a real world where fictitious enchantment often excites reflexive contempt and hatred, the leverage of intelligence is even more narrowly circumscribed.

It is understandable, therefore, that fays, good and evil alike, were more successful in their manipulations of beauty, and in provoking more sweeping metamorphoses, than they were in demonstrating or manipulating cleverness. Because stories are written from without and not from within, however, there is abundant scope for them to be intelligent as well as beautiful, even though success in those projects cannot guarantee success in a mostly-hostile world. It is, inevitably, far harder to write a beautiful story than it is to equip one with a beautiful heroine, and exactly as hard to write an intelligent story as to write a story with intelligent characters. It is a great compliment to say that the best writers of *contes de fées* succeeded in all those regards, but they did—as the exemplary anthology appended to this essay demonstrates clearly enough. The same is true of modern writers of fantastic fiction, for exactly the same reasons, and with exactly the same difficulties—and that is why readers capable of appreciating the merits of imagination contained in modern fantasy fiction will find the stories in the exemplary anthology not merely interesting as historical specimens but enjoyable and rewarding as works of art.

As for the bigoted and the imaginatively allergic, the advice of Madame d'Aulnoy would be to forgive them, for they know not what they are. We might as well, because there is nothing we can do to change them. The poor in spirit, alas, will always be with us.

Further Reading

In addition to the contents of the present volume, English translations of the greater fraction of everything worthwhile produced by the genre of *contes de fées*, as defined for the purposes of this essay, can be found in the following collections and anthologies:

The Robe of Sincerity and Other Stories by Marie-Jeanne de L'Héritier de Villandon. Black Coat Press, 2018.
Contains (among other items):
    The Enchantments of Eloquence; or, The Effects of Mildness
    The Clever Princess; or, The Adventures of Finette
    Ricdin-Ricdon
    The Robe of Sincerity

The Land of Delights: Tales of Enchantment by Charlotte-Rose Caumont de La Force. Black Coat Press, 2018.
Contains:
    More Beautiful than a Fay
    Persinette
    The Enchanter
    Tourbillon
    Green and Blue
    The Land of Delights
    The Power of Amour
    The Good Woman

The Palace of Vengeance and Other Tales of Enchantment by Henriette-Julie de Murat. Black Coat Press, 2018.
Contains:
    Perfect Love
    Anguillette
    Young and Beautiful
    The Palace of Vengeance
    The Prince of Leaves
    The Fortunate Penalty
    The Swine King
    The Island of Magnificence
    The Story of Princess Blanchette and Prince Verdelet
    The Story of Grandimont, King of the Arsacides, and Princess Philomele

The Savage
The Turbot
The Story of the Queen of the Isle of Rocks and the King of Coquerico
The Story of Merline and Prince Fortunate
The Goblins of Kernosy Castle
Bearskin
Starlet
The Fay Princess

Tales of the Fays by Marie-Catherine d'Aulnoy (2 volumes). Black Coat Press, 2019.
Contains:
    Gracieuse and Percinet
    The Golden-Haired Beauty
    The Blue Bird
    The Sprite Prince
    Princess Springtime
    Princess Rosette
    The Golden Branch
    The Orange Tree and the Bee
    The Good Little Mouse
    The Tales of the Fays
    Don Gabriel Ponce de Leon
    The Sheep
    Finette Cendron
    Fortunée
    Babiole
    Don Fernand de Toledo
    The Yellow Dwarf
    Green Worm
    Princess Carpillon
    The Benevolent Frog
    The Woodland Hind
    The New Bourgeois Gentleman; or, Fays à la Mode
    The White Cat
    Belle-Belle; or, The Cavalier Fortuné
    The Pigeon and the Dove
    Princess Belle-Etoile and Prince Cheri
    Prince Marcassin
    The Dolphin

The Queen of the Fays and Other Marvelous Tales. Black Coat Press, 2018.
Contains:

Inès de Cordova by Catherine Bernard
The Rose-Bush Prince
Riquet with the Crest
Stories by Jean de Préchac
Peerless
The Queen of the Fays
Stories by François Fénelon
The Story of Rosimond and Braminte
The Story of Florise
The Story of King Alfaroute and Clariphile
The Story of an Old Queen and a Young Peasant Girl
The Illustrious Fays, attributed to the Chevalier de Mailly
Blanche-Belle
The Magician King
Prince Roger
Fortunio
Prince Guerini
The Queen of the Isle of Flowers
The Favorite of the Fays
Beneficent, or, Quiribirini
The Princess Crowned by the Fays
The Unfortunate Fraud
The Inaccessible Island
Stories from *Nouveaux contes de fees (1718)*
The Little Green Frog
The Flying Ship
Prince Perinet; or, The Origin of Pagodas
Rose-Red, White and Black
Alphinge; or, The Green Monkey
The Satin Physician
The Rainbow Prince

The Tyranny of the Fays Abolished and Other Stories by Comtesse D.L. Black
Coat Press, 2018
Contains:
The Tyranny of the Fays Abolished
The Story of Cleonice
The Story of Melicerte
Agatie, Princess of the Scyths
Princess Leonice
Prince Curious
The Knights Errant
The Story of Princess Zamea and Prince Almanson

The Story of Prince Elmedor of Granada and Princess Alzayde
The Story of Zalmayde, Princess of the Canaries, and the Prince of Numidia
The Story of the Prince of Numidia
The Story of the Prince of Mauretania and the Princess of Castile
The Story of the Fay of Grandeurs and Prince Salmacis
The Story of the Fay of Pleasures and the Cruel Amerdin
The Familiar Spirit: Persian Tales Translated from the Arabic
The Story of Istherie
The Story of the Validated Sultana
Princess Patientine in the Forest of Erimente

Florine and Boca: Tales of Faerie by Françoise Le Marchand. Black Coat Press, 2018.
Contains:
    Florine
    Boca

Funestine and Other Adventures in Romancia. Black Coat Press, 2018
Contains:
    Three *contes de fées* attributed to Catherine de Lintot:
    Timandre and Bleuette
    Prince Sincere
    Tendrebrun and Constance
    The Marvelous Voyage of Prince Fan-Férédin in Romancia by Guillaume-Hyacinthe
    Bougéant
    Funestine by Pierre-François Godard de Beauchamps

The Origin of the Fays and Other Stories. Black Coat Press, 2019
Contains:
    The Fay Lubantine by Catherine Durand
    The Prodigy of Amour by Catherine Durand
    The Origin of the Fays by Catherine Durand
    The Prince of Aquamarines by Louise Cavelier
    Stories attributed to Mademoiselle de Lubert
    Princess Roseate and Prince Celadon
    Prince Typhon and Princess Sensible
    Cornichon and Toupette
    Aglaé or Nabotine by Charles Antoine Coypel
    Acajou and Zirphile by Charles Pinot Duclos
    Faunillane; or. The Yellow Child by Carl Gustaf Tessin
    Queen Fantasque by Jean-Jacques Rousseau

The Gifts of the Fays; or, The Power of Education by François-Augustin de Paradis de Moncrif

Durboulour; or, The Benevolent Lioness by Marianne-Agnès Falques

Princess Camion and Other Tales of Enchantment by Marie-Madeleine de Lubert. Black Coat Press, 2018.
Contains:

Tecserion; or, The Prince of Ostriches

Princess Lionnette and Prince Coquerico

Prince Frozen and Princess Sparkling

Princess Camion

The Impossible Enchantment and Other Tales of Faerie by the Comte de Caylus. Black Coat Press, 2018.
Contains:

Prince Courtebotte and Princess Zibeline

Rosanie

Prince Muguet and Princess Zaza

Tourlou and Rirette

The Yellow Bird

Princess Pimprenelle and Prince Romarin

The Gifts

Nonchalante and Papillon

The Palace of Ideas

Princess Luminous

Bleuette and Coquelicot

The Impossible Enchantment

Princess Minutie and King Floridor

The Prince of Hearts and Princess Grenadine

Princess Azerolle; or. Excessive Constancy

Fleurette and Abricot: A Frame Story

The Mangy Wolf

Bellinette; or, The Young Old Woman

Author's Preface to Cadichon & Jeanette

Cadichon; or, Everything Works Out for Him Who Waits

Jeannette; or, Indiscretion

The Naiads and The Beauty and the Beast by Madame de Villeneuve. Black Coat Press, 2017.
Contains:

The Beauty and the Beast

The Naiads

The Enchanter's Mirror and Other Stories by Marie-Antoinette Fagnan. Black Coat Press, 2019
Contains:
    Kanor: A Tale Translated from the Savage
    Minet-Bleu and Louvette
    The Enchanter's Mirror

The Voyages of Lord Seaton to the Seven Planets by Marie-Anne Roumier-Robert. Black Coat Press, 2015.
Contains (with one other item):
    The Water-Sprites

The Story of the Great Prince Oribeau by Nicolas Restif de La Bretonne. Black Coat Press, 2017.
Contains (in addition to the frame narrative):
    Mellusine
    Sireneh
    The Fay Ouroucoucou

The Four Beauties and the Four Beasts by Nicholas Restif de La Bretonne. Black Coat Press, 2017.
Contains:
    The Demicock
    The Four Beauties and the Four Beasts

The Last Fay by Honoré de Balzac, Black Coat Press, 2016.

Trilby. The Crumb Fairy by Charles Nodier, Black Coat Press, 2015.

The Enchanted Ring by Philothée O'Neddy, Snuggly Books, 2019.

Bluebirds by Catulle Mendès, Snuggly Books, 2017.
Contains (among other items)
    The Dreaming Beauty
    The Maladroit Wish
    Isoline-Isolin
    Golden Kisses
    The Betrothal
    The Bad Guest
    The Moneybox
    The Lost Words
    The Heart's Memory
    The Three Good Fays

The Bonnet Collector
The Three Sowers
The Beauty with the Heart of Snow
The Two Daisies
Puck's Treacheries
The Little Blue Flame
The Last Fay

The Little Fays in the Air and Other Tales of Faerie, Black Coat Press, 2019.
Contains:
The Sufficient Gift
The Enchanted Bed
The Mute Princess
The Bridal Costume
The Roses of the Blue Garden
Puck in the Organ
The Narcissus
The Three Dresses
Courage Recompensed
Vain Betrothals
The Enchanted Ring
The Solitaries
The Flower who was Cold
The Wishes of an Eglantine
What Fays Cannot Do
The Naked Princess
The Most Beautiful Memory
The Good Almanac
The Sweetest Urgency
The Wish Granted
The Little Fays in the Air
The Fay Liar
Luscignole
Water, Ice and Fire
The Clear-Sighted Gold Coin
The Stupidities of Jocelyne
The Poet and the Pearl
Prince Lys and the Wave of Snow
The Flowers' Carnival
Azure, Gold and Crimson

AN ANTHOLOGY OF EXEMPLARY TALES

PART I: 1696-1715

PARADIGMS 1696-1697

Marie-Jeanne L'Héritier: *The Enchantments of Eloquence; Or, The Effects of Mildness*

In the time when there were fays, ogres, follet spirits and other phantoms of the same kind in France—it is difficult to specify that time, but it does not matter—there was a gentleman of great consideration who loved his wife passionately, and that is another reason why I cannot divine what time it was. His wife loved him no less; he was a good man and he merited it. They lived together quite happily for fifteen or sixteen years, but death separated them. The lady died, and only left a unique daughter.

She had been very beautiful, and her daughter was no less so; and, with a thousand charms that appeared in her infancy, she had a complexion so dazzlingly white that it inspired her name, which was Blanche.

Her mother had not had any wealth, but her father had had a good deal. However, he no longer had it when his wife died, because his affairs had turned bad during his marriage, and his daughter found herself reduced to having nothing for her dowry but her white skin and her beauty, which are not usually a great help in finding a considerable match.

Blanche's father, being greatly afflicted by his wife's death, thought that he would not be consoled until he found another, and, as his daughter still seemed young enough to have time to find an establishment at her leisure, he concluded that it was necessary to think of himself first, and he thought seriously about making his choice. The poor state of his affairs made him lean in the direction of wealth, so he attached himself to a widow who was neither beautiful nor young, but very opulent.

Like him, that woman had only one daughter, and she was the widow of a financier, who had not neglected any of the tricks of his métier in order to maximize wealth, and had succeeded in doing so. They had nothing for which to reproach one another with regard to birth, so the point of honor never caused any division between them, but as she had carefully conserved the sentiments and the manner of the family to which she belonged, she had given her daughter an education similar to the one that she had had. Her daughter having a rude character very apt to receive vulgar impressions, it was almost impossible to find two persons more unrefined and rustic than them. In that character they did not fail to include an excessive but ill-extended ambition; they had ideas so ridiculous that they committed a hundred extravagances, in which one saw and discovered the aberrations that their ostentations and vanity inspired in them.

With those dispositions, it is easy to judge that Blanche's father, who bore the title of Marquis, was welcomed with joy by the widow, whose desire to have a great name caused her to make the marriage in a matter of days. Her new husband, who had only envisaged her wealth in marrying her, saw with a great deal of chagrin, as soon as they were married, how numerous and fatiguing the Marquise's faults were, but as he was naturally inclined to be at peace with everyone, and he also had a character of allowing himself to be governed by his wife, such as she was, they lived together quite happily, on condition that he made it a principle never to contradict her and to leave her the absolute mistress in all things. He consoled himself for her inconvenient humor by means of the comforts that the great wealth she had brought him procured. He supported her fits of temper philosophically, and when he saw her begin to scream, as he liked reading, he went to read in his study.

It was only the lovely Blanche who had every reason to complain. Her stepmother had an inconceivable aversion for her; she was in despair in seeing that her beauty caused all her daughter's deformity to appear and rendered her the scorn of society; for Alix—that was the name of the financier's daughter—was a monster of ugliness as well as vulgarity. Such as she was, however, her mother nevertheless loved her to the point of idolatry; she would have sacrificed anything for her satisfaction; and to complete Blanche's misfortune, Alix hated her a hundred times more than her mother. In consequence, she employed all imaginable means to cause her chagrin.

The mother wanted Blanche to be put in a convent, but Alix, who was determined always to see her the victim of her caprices, deflected her mother from that design, fearing that Blanche would then no longer be under their eyes, that some obliging friend might bring all her merit to light and procure her some splendid establishment—which Alix feared more than death.

It was therefore resolved that Blanche would stay in the house and not make or receive any visits. They took measures to hide her carefully from all honest people, and in order to tarnish her beauty they obliged her to occupy herself with the employments of a chambermaid, housekeeper, and even cook.

If I wanted, Madame, to tell you this story entirely in the terms that the storytellers of Provence taught it to our grandmothers, I would tell you a thousand astonishing details about Blanche's cleverness, but there is no need; I shall only tell you that, by virtue of an admirable docility very rare in such a beautiful person, she had the complaisance to employ herself in all the disagreeable tasks that her stepmother prescribe for her; that Blanche added luster to everything she touched; and that no one had ever seen cuffs so well starched and high collars so well-dressed. She acquitted all those things so skillfully that I am sure that if she had lived nowadays she would have been perfectly able to straighten hats, and would have attracted a large court of women who are always in mortal chagrin because their hats go stubbornly askew no matter how much care that they take in giving proof of straightness in their attire. Blanche would have given to that ornament, so useful to women in the land of pygmies, all its symmetry, and she would have outdone Monsieur D***, with whom no coquette dares to quarrel, because she had the fortunate talent of arranging headwear and showing off cornettes better than the finest hairdresser in the world.[2]

That fine prerogative attracted the admiration and complaisance of a large number of women because she did their hair and enabled them to turn heads as she turned them; but let us leave those remarks in order to continue our story.

Not only was Blanche given a thousand fatigues, but she was left in a negligence that would have gone as far as the most disgusting dirtiness but for the natural disposition that she had to be neat in no matter what way she was clad. So, in spite of the care that was taken to give her clothes capable of deforming her, whatever they did, her uncurled hair and her garments of coarse cloth did not prevent her from appearing as beautiful as Amour, while Alix, covered in gold and precious stones and with her hair carefully made up, frightened everyone who looked at her, for the excess of her adornment only rendered her uglier and surlier.

Alix could not stay at home; she was seen incessantly on the promenades and at balls; she never wearied of displaying her pomp everywhere; but if she found pleasure in attracting the gaze of a few bourgeois women, she was also very mortified to hear the pages and musketeers of that era incessantly voicing the most piquant verities behind her. For even in those days, many musketeers, students, young officers and other harebrained individuals had the ridiculous habit of coming to look at all the women they thought poorly adorned in the face, and saying a thousand impertinent things loudly when they did not find them sufficiently beautiful for their liking. Thus, one can imagine how many of

---

[2] The wordplay in this paragraph does not translate, but the references to clothing that I have translated literally could all be construed metaphorically at the time of writing to refer to a woman's character in derogatory terms, in much the same way that many similar terms still can. The term *cornette* refers here to a kind of head-dress, worn by fashionable women as well as nuns.

those young fools exercised the fine talent they had for cold mockery when they saw Alix's repulsive face. But what one cannot easily imagine is how she avenged herself on Blanche for all the insults she had received; calculating that if there were no beauties in the world, ugliness would not be exposed to such scorn, she redoubled her aversion for that lovely individual and engaged her mother to cause her further chagrins.

In spite of Blanche's natural mildness, so much ill-treatment sometimes embittered her to the extent that she made plans to get out of the house no matter what the cost; but the hatred she had for outbursts, the love she had for her father, and the hope of finding an opportunity to escape from of her slavery with decorum took away the resolution to leave noisily. She therefore prepared once again to be patient, and her father, who loved her dearly but did not have the firmness to oppose the barbaric manner in which she was treated, softened her chagrins by sharing them, praised her virtue, and consoled her by promising her, on behalf of Heaven, that she would find herself in a happier state one day.

Those consolations sustained Blanche's constancy in her misfortunes, but as society and all sorts of diversion were forbidden to her, she found the means to obtain it in her room by reading. She amassed a large number of novels,[3] I do not know how; but she did not get as much satisfaction from them as one might think, because she could only read by night, her stepmother occupying her relentlessly while the daylight lasted. Although it required her to cut down on her sleep in order to read, however, that did not stop her; she believed that she was reposing in reading, and when she could slip away for a few moments by day, she returned to her books with haste.

Her stepmother, who kept watch on her incessantly, took umbrage at the ardor that she had to be alone in her room, and, seeking clarification of what it was that attracted her there so powerfully, she surprised her one day as she reached one of the most beautiful passages of a novel as well-written as it was pleasantly invented. The Marquise ought to have been touched to see the innocent amusement to which Blanche was reduced, but although she could scarcely read, she threw herself upon the book and snatched it from her hands, and after having read the title, with a great deal of difficulty, because it was a forbidding Greek name that she pronounced very poorly, she finally understood that the book was a novel, and had commenced to scream strangely at Blanche, when, fortunately for the poor girl, her father came into the room.

---

[3] Translating *romans* as "novels" in this context is undoubtedly anachronistic, but the anachronism is clearly deliberate on the author's part. The works the author has in mind are clearly those of Madeleine de Scudéry, and the following passage is a spirited defense against contemporary prejudice. The reference to a Greek title offers the specific suggestion that the book in question is *Artamène, ou le Grand Cyrus*, [Artamenes; or, Cyrus the Great].

Without giving him time to speak, his wife shouted at him with all her might: "Well, Monsieur Ruinous, with all your chic and sugared arguments, look how well you have brought up your slut of a daughter! I have just caught her reading an amorous book on the sly."

The Marquis found a little more courage than normal that day, and responded to his wife after looking at the book: "Blanche does very well to amuse herself with this reading. You have taken all pleasures away from her; she cannot do better than to take one that will open her mind to politeness. I am delighted when I see young women of quality occupying themselves in reading; if they all applied themselves to it, one would not see them so embarrassed in their pleasure, they would not be running so much from one spectacle to another and from one card game to another."

The Marquise, who knew full well how avid her daughter was for gambling, as well as all other pleasures, thought that her husband had the intention of attacking Alix in what he had just said, so she resumed in an even louder tone: "Truly, I am of the opinion that women of quality, who have wealth in thousands, ought not to be prevented from diverting themselves at their whim; it is as well for paupers,[4] who are of ruined nobility, to entrench themselves in such pleasures, but it is permissible for ladies who have more pistoles than those sluts have pennies to do whatever seems good to them. As for demoiselles who do not have a sou, they only ought to know how to do housework and to be always occupied with it; at least, if they want to be readers, it is necessary that it is in good books, not those in which one learns mischief."

"One does not learn mischief," retorted Blanche's father, brutally, "in these beautiful novels that I see my daughter reading"—for he had loved them even more than her, and he still loved them. "On the contrary," he said, "one only finds great sentiments in them and fine examples; one always sees vice punished therein, and virtue always recompensed. One can even say that for young persons, the reading of novels is in some ways better than reading history itself, because history, being entirely subject to the truth, sometimes presents images very shocking for mores. History paints men as they are, and novels represent them as they ought to be, and they seem by virtue of that to be aspiring to perfection. At least one cannot deny that well-made novels teach social graces and politeness of language. Blanche already has a disposition to speak properly, and I hope that the reading of these agreeable works will finish giving her the habit of it."

The stepmother, who did not understand anything of that philosophy, and was a surly creature who had no intention of relaxing her severity to Blanche in the slightest, could not allow the apology for novels that the Marquis was about to continue to reach completion, because it was all Greek to her.

---

[4] The literal translation of *gueuses* [female paupers] diminishes the insult, the term also being frequently used as a description of common prostitutes.

"What a seeker of midday at four o'clock!" she replied. "Mercy of my life! Let your daughter read as much as she likes, since that game pleases her, and you too, but if the affairs of my house are not done as punctiliously as usual, I shall be able to turn her to that end." She quit them, and the angry conversation finished in that manner.

You, Madame, who only occupy yourself with sublime reading, might perhaps find that Blanche's father was a little too prejudiced in favor of novels. I do not know what you think about it, but I will not tell you what I think either; I will only report what my chronicle contains; I am a historian, and a historian, male or female, ought not to take sides. Do not make fun of these reflections, I beg you, for if you are going to lose your seriousness you will also make me lose mine. I need it, however, in order to have the strength to recount to you tranquilly the rest of this surprising history.

Blanche's father was not mistaken. In very little time, that beautiful girl combined an achieved politeness with her natural mildness; no one can express themselves with greater charm and precision that she did, either by virtue of the commerce that she had with the productions of the intellect or for some other reason. Neither Alix or her mother envied those new advantages; they were too vulgar to sense the delicacy of what they heard her say, so they only continued to be wounded by her personal charms and no longer thought about anything but causing her to lose them forever.

At the height of the summer the Marquis and his family went to the country. It was there that Blanche's stepmother exercised all the talents she had in order to torment her. She employed her in all the most rustic labors, but in spite of the care she took to expose her at every moment to the sun, her complexion, which was naturally incapable of sunburn, still conserved its whiteness.

Her stepmother was dying of chagrin in seeing that nothing was capable of rendering her ugly and could not give up that deign. Finally, after all the means she had attempted, which had not succeeded, she took it into her head also to charge her with going to fetch water for the usage of the entire household from a rather distant spring.

Blanche, who had devoted herself to patience, did not receive that commission with any more repugnance than those that were ordinarily given to her; to go in quest of water was not for her an employment more humiliating than a hundred others to which she had been subjected. In addition, she saw demoiselles who also went there, for the customs of that time were in some ways quite different from the manners of the present time, and the example might have been able to console her if she had been going there of her own free will, like the country demoiselles, or because of the indigence of her father's household.

Although she was well armed with patience, however, she had difficulty holding back her tears when she considered that the crushing toil that was imposed on her was only intended to drive her to despair and destroy her. That was her chagrin. However, not only did she have the example of her neighbors but she had read somewhere that the daughters of kings did the laundry in the times of Homer, and that Achilles did the cooking quite happily; Blanche therefore went, without saying anything about it, to fetch water whenever it was needed.

The spring to which she went to fetch it was surrounded by the most beautiful landscape in the world, but the place was dangerous because it was close to a forest from which wolves often emerged to make brief excursions as far as the water. Muted rumor published that it was for that reason that Blanche's mother liked sending her there so much. The likeable young woman had been warned several times about the danger to which she was exposing herself, but, although the wolves were not what she feared the most, the warnings were quite useless to her, because she could not make her stepmother hear reason.

After having been there several times without finding either beasts or men—to speak like my author—one day, after having drawn the water, she saw a furious wild boar coming toward her, although it was not being pursued by anyone. She was seized by fear, as one inevitably would be, Madame. She was not so frightened, however, that she did not think of self-preservation; she took flight, and had already reached the brushwood when she was struck in the shoulder by a blow that knocked her to the ground. At the same moment, the boar passed by without doing her any harm and hid in the wood.

As she made efforts to get up, in spite of the pain that she felt, she heard someone cry: "What! Beautiful child, it's you that I've wounded instead of the boar! How unfortunate I am!"

At the same time, Blanche saw a richly clad young man, who approached her in order to help her up. Although the blood she had lost rendered her very pale, the hunter had no sooner looked at her than he saw that she was extraordinarily beautiful and felt touched by the gentle and engaging appearance that he found in the young woman, in spite of the rusticity of her clothing.

He did not amuse himself paying her compliments; he was more judicious; he thought about helping her promptly. He tore up his handkerchief and his cravat—or his ruff, if you prefer—in order to try to staunch the blood from the wound. The history says that Blanche's eyes also inflicted a wound on the hunter, but I have difficulty believing that it happened at the first moment; or, if the chronicle is telling the truth, it is necessary that the hunter caught fire as easily as his rifle.

Some critic might say that the hunter could not have had a rifle because, in the days of fays, people did not yet have the use of artillery. I know scrupulous savants who would never let a tale finish without protesting against that anachronism, but if I wanted to get into an argument with such an insensate storyteller, could I not say that Mesdames the fays had performed one of their tricks? One sees many other marvels, so they could well have contrived that one, especially in favor of the hunter in question, who was the godson of Melusine,

Logistille and I don't know how many others among the most celebrated of those obliging ladies.[5]

However, it is true that the weapon that had wounded Blanche was not a firearm, for a historian must always tell the truth, although I am rather sorry that one is lacking here; it was a dart, or a javelin, that the prince had tried to throw at the boar…but I think that I have not yet told you that the hunter was a prince? Well, no matter; I will tell you soon what his genealogy was, for at present it is necessary to return to poor Blanche, whom we have left too long semi-conscious on the grass.

As she found herself in the hands of such a surgeon, she was not afraid, and in a confusion that gave her as much pain as the harm she was suffering. The obliging hunter gave her all the help that he could, and was so penetrated by admiration and dolor that he did not have the strength to say a word.

Finally after having put the best dressing on the beauty's wound that he could contrive and had thrown water in her face ten or twelve times, in such a manner that she no longer appeared to be in danger of fainting, the young stranger said to her: "How extreme my good and ill fortune are today! What good luck to have seen a person as charming as you! What bad luck to have been the cause of the woes she is experiencing!"

"You are an innocent cause of those woes," replied Blanche. "So, Seigneur, such a misfortune does not merit troubling your tranquility."

"Even if you were only an ordinary young woman," replied the stranger, "I would be very sorry to have wounded you; imagine my despair regarding the accident, then, on seeing you as lovely as you are."

"Without responding to your honeyed words," Blanche retorted, "I will tell you, Seigneur, that you are pushing generosity too far. If you had killed me, it would only have been necessary to blame destiny and not yourself. And even then, the loss of the life of a girl like me would not have been anything to merit agitating yours, which appears to me to be one of those fine lives that are ordinarily so useful to the State. I can answer for the fact that people of my character would sacrifice their useless lives with pleasure for gentlemen as necessary to the public as you appear to be. Grant me then, Seigneur, the favor of asking you not to be afflicted by my adventure, for in my turn, I would reproach myself for the chagrin that it would be causing you."

The stranger, who had initially judged Blanche, on the basis of her clothing, to be a peasant, or at most a demoiselle from the village, was extremely surprised by the manner in which she spoke, but he was even more touched by

---

[5] Logistillle is an enchantress who protects the knight Roland in some of the romances detailing his adventures. She appears as a character in the lyric tragedy *Roland* (1685), whose libretto was by Philippe Quinault and music by Raymond Lully, both close associates of Mademoiselle de Scudéry's salon. Quinault is cited by the author a few paragraphs hence.

her mildness than her politeness. The young prince was naturally very violent, and he felt strongly that if anyone, even innocently, had done him as much harm as he had just done to that beauty, nothing that could have stopped him becoming terribly angry against the author of that harm. The less he was capable of such moderation, the more he admired it; by virtue of that, Blanche rendered herself the absolute mistress of his soul, and that example proved admirably in advance the truth of one of the maxims of Quinault, who said with so much justice:

It is beauty which commences to please,
But tenderness that completes the charm.

The Prince was enchanted to such a point that the host of thoughts that presented themselves to his imagination made him remain silent for a few moments, and he only broke the silence in order to say a hundred more gallant things to Blanche. Nevertheless, he did not testify to her any of the impressions that she had made on his heart, because he feared alarming a beautiful person who put as much modesty into her responses as mildness and politeness.

However, the prince was very anxious in seeing that his followers were not catching up with him. He had been separated from them during the hunt, and he was very impatient for someone to find him because he wanted to send immediately for a carriage, to take Blanche wherever she wanted to go.

The beauty, however, to whom he expressed his anxiety and his design, said to him: "Seigneur, I beg you with the utmost urgency not to give orders for that, and if you have as much consideration for me as you have made me see, I assure you that you could not give me a more sensible pleasure than by quitting me without giving me any further thought, and without talking to anyone about encountering me or my wound. I have the strongest reasons in the world for making you those pleas, and I hope that I can return very quietly to my father's dwelling when I have rested here for a little longer."

After a few very obliging protestations on the part of the prince, he said to her: "Well, if that is what you want; I am submissive to your orders; but as for not thinking about you, do not believe, charming person, that one can obey you in that regard."

With those words, the prince quit her, remounted his horse and left Blanche astonished, weak and very anxious about what people might be thinking at home, from which she had been absent for such a long time.

Finally, she set forth, and after much difficulty she arrived at her father's dwelling just as someone was being sent to see what was retaining her at the spring. The stepmother commenced by making a great deal of noise, but when Blanche had said that she had had an accident, that she had been wounded by a wild boar, and that, but for a passer-by who had helped her, she might have died on the spot, the stepmother was constrained to shut up. The Marquis, greatly troubled by that news, ran to his daughter, had her put to bed and resolved not to rely on his wife with regard to the care that Blanche would need.

Since the beautiful young woman is in good hands, let us return to the Prince and his genealogy.

He was related to Urgande, the cousin of Maugis, the great-nephew of Merlin, and also the godson of the wise Lirgandée and the most savant fays, as I have already said.[6] In any case, it is not known exactly of what land he was the future sovereign, for certain narratives say that he was the son of the Duc de Normandie, others affirm that it was the Duc de Bretagne, and other memoirs that it was the Comte de Poitiers that had given him birth. That lack of clarity comes from the fact that no one knows where the spring was to which Blanche went in quest of water. In the final analysis, it does not matter much; it is sufficient that all the narratives agree that the hunter who wounded the beauty was the son and heir of the sovereign of the land.

As the young prince was very occupied by the adventure he had had, as soon as he had rejoined his companions he charged one of his squires, who was very clever, to go and make inquiries in the village regarding Blanche's destiny. The squire acquitted his commission skillfully and came to render an exact account to his master of the birth, the inclinations and the misfortunes of the young beauty. The prince was delighted to learn that she was of illustrious nobility, and thought about taking measures to render fortunate a person who seemed to him to be so worthy of being so.

Blanche was loved in the village of which her father was the Seigneur, as much as Alix was hated, so the peasants had told the squire a hundred amusing tales regarding the fine qualities of the one and the shocking faults of the other. The gentleman, who was quick-witted and jovial, had not forgotten a single word of all the things that had been said to him, and he recounted them to the Prince in the same terms, with a naivety that had the ability to divert a lover who was as occupied with tenderness as the heroes of novels usually are.

The first concern of the Prince was to seek to cure Blanche of the wound he had inflicted, but even though he belonged to a family very knowledgeable in the art of enchantment, he was no more skillful for that in that art, so he had recourse to one of his godmothers, to whom he recounted his adventure. He did not confide to her the amour he had for Blanche; he only requested that the beautiful young woman be cured, but did so with so much ardor, and spoke about her merit with so much exaggeration that any woman with some knowledge of the world, without being a fay and knowing necromancy, would

---

[6] A tragedy entitled *Urgande*, probably by Quinault, was performed in front of Louis XIV's court in January 1679. She also features prominently in his lyric tragedy *Amadis de Gaule* (1684), again with music by Lully, based on the Spanish romance of that title. The name Lirgandée is found in French translations of *Don Quixote*, where she is briefly mentioned as a relative of Urgande.

easily have divined that he was in love. It was, therefore, not difficult for the good fay to make that discovery, and as she loved her godson veritably she was very glad that he had put the affair in her hands, making it a pleasure to see Blanche, and to examine whether she was worthy of the sentiments that she had inspired in a heart insensible until then to tenderness.

Dulcicula,[7] as the fay was named, therefore went to prepare a marvelous balm that cured the most mortal wounds in less than twenty-four hours. Then she adopted the guise of an old peasant woman, and in that apparel she went to present herself at the door of Blanche's father.

The first person she encountered was Alix, to whom she said very civilly, in a village style, that, having an admirable secret, she had come to offer her services to the Marquis for his daughter.

"What has this old madwoman come to tell me?" replied Alix, brutally. "I believe that all the village vermin are frantic to intervene on behalf of that she-ape Blanche. I don't know who they think they all are, to get demented like idiots; this old beast would do better to go make her a box for the cemetery; if it were some good sheepdog, its death would be a greater loss than hers."

Dulcicula was extremely surprised to see a demoiselle covered in gold and gemstones speaking such a strange jargon, but the fay, who was mildness personified, was even more indignant at her evil nature than her vulgarity. She did not make any reply to that brutality, and, having learned that the Marquis was not at home, she addressed herself to the woman whom he had charged with looking after Blanche.

The woman took the fay to the invalid's bedside. Dulcicula said to her, still in terms that were in conformity with her attire, that, her accident having touched her, she had come expressly from her village to offer her a balm that she had, which cured all sorts of injuries very promptly.

Blanche, who had a great deal of intelligence and who was not preoccupied with popular errors, thought that the balm that was being mentioned to her was one of those remedies of which the people are fond, which are known as "innocent little remedies" because they are, in fact, very innocent in their usage. The amiable young woman, however, still retaining her character, replied to the fay: "You are very kind, my good mother, to quit your affairs like this to come and give me pleasure; I don't know how I can recognize what I owe to your zeal, being so far from the state that I would like to be in, but I will mention you to my father, and I hope that he will reward you for your good will. As for the balm, I thank you for it, but I am in the hands of surgeons, and it is necessary not to change remedies every day."

Dulcicula, charmed by Blanche's mildness and honest manners, nevertheless penetrated the poor opinion she had of her balm, but she pressed her to

---

[7] *Dulcicula* is the Latin word from which the French *douceureuse* [sweetness, or mildness] is derived.

make use of it with so much ardor and confidence that the beautiful young woman consented to do so, purely out of complaisance for the peasant woman whom she saw so affectionate for her. The fay therefore put her enchanted balm on Blanche's wound, and, by a marvelous effect, it was not long before the beauty began to feel greatly soothed.

They entered into conversation then. Dulcicula could not cease admiring privately the mildness and other good qualities that she saw combined with so much beauty, and that admiration produced a good effect. The fay was holding a stick on which she seemed to be supporting herself, but it was the enchanted wand of which she made use to accomplish all the prodigies of her art. She touched Blanche with that wand, as if by chance, and gave her a gift of always being more gentle, amiable and decorous than ever, and having the most beautiful voice in the world.

As soon as she left the beautiful invalid's room, accompanied by the woman who was caring for her, she made inquiries regarding Alix. She learned that the scold in question was as coquettish as she was ugly and malevolent, and that because she was always in splendid attire and made a hundred grimaces and contortions in order to make herself seem charming, she was known everywhere, by virtue of irony, as "the beautiful Alix." The woman added that in a thousand places, when a young woman was seen putting on impertinent and affected airs, people said that she was "behaving like the beautiful Alix."

Thus informed, the fay once again encountered the person they had just been discussing in such fine terms in the courtyard, on her own. She approached Alix and said to her, civilly: "Mademoiselle, I beg you to tell me where I can find the back door of this dwelling."

Alix responded angrily: "Can one see anything more ill-informed than this old hag, who comes to ask me such a stupid question?"

Without making any response, the fay began walking behind Alix, and, letting her wand fall on her, as if unintentionally, she made her the gift of always being ill-tempered, disagreeable and ill-behaved. That was only to assure her of qualities that she already had. So, she entered into such a fury at the fall of the wand that she thought about beating the good peasant woman; at least, she vomited against her a torrent of insults. The fay, who had done what she had come to do, withdrew.

Meanwhile, Blanche, who no longer felt such intense pain since the application of the enchanted balm, recalled the adventure in the wood to her memory. The agreeable manners and handsome face of the hunter presented themselves vividly to her idea, and it seemed to her that in all the novels she had read she had never seen anything more marvelous than that incident. She would very much have liked to know who the hunter was, but all her impulses were born of simple benevolence and curiosity. Do not believe, I beg you, that other sentiments played any part in it; you would be doing Blanche wrong.

As for the Prince, he was entirely delivered to amour. What Dulcicula had told him about Blanche's merit further stimulated his fire, and he was so transported that, without the apprehension of his father the Duc, he would have gone in quest of the unfortunate beauty immediately, in order to bring her triumphantly to his palace; but he was able to moderate his transports, not without searching his mind a hundred times for means to content them.

At the end of twenty hours, Blanche found herself completely healed, and a few days there after her pitiless stepmother casually sent her back to the spring. As he was about to draw the water she saw a lady coming toward her who was even more brilliant in her noble attitude and her good grace than in her adornment, although she was dressed in a manner as magnificent as it was gallant. The lady approached Blanche and said to her: "My beautiful child, I beg you to give me something to drink."

"I am in great confusion, Madame," replied Blanche, agreeably, "not to be able to present you with anything but this pitcher, which is scarcely convenient for that." At the same time, the beautiful young woman leaned over the edge of the spring, rinsed out the pitcher carefully, and then presented it, with good grace, to the lady, in order that she might drink.

After drinking, she thanked Blanche very civilly. She found her so amiable in her manners that from thanks she progressed to conversation with her, throwing into it a thousand agreeable and delicate subjects, by which Blanche was not at all embarrassed; she responded to them with so much intelligence, mildness and politeness that she completed charming the person to whom she was talking.

The lady, as I believe that you have already suspected, was also a fay, but you will not have suspected that the fay was named Eloquentia Nativa. That name might appear to some people to be as strange as a Greek name, but, charming Duchesse, you will see clearly that it is very Latin; but, Latin or Greek, it makes no difference, it was by that forbidding name that the fay in question was known, and it is necessary not to be astonished by that; all fays have always had unusual names. Eloquentia Nativa therefore, penetrated by Blanche's eloquence and obliging manners, resolved to recompense her magnificently for the small pleasure that the beauty had given her with such good heart and such good grace.

The savant fay put her hand on Blanche's head and gave her as a gift that pearls, diamonds, rubies and emerald would emerge from her mouth every time she made a finished sentence in her speech. Then the fay bid adieu to the amiable young woman, who returned home carrying her pitcher full of water.

Blanche was no sooner in her stepmother's presence than the woman asked her in a shrill tone what had kept her so long as the spring again. Blanche replied that it was the arrival of the most amiable lady she had ever seen. With those words, a dazzling mass of pearls and precious stones emerged from her mouth.

"What's this!" cried the Marquise.

Blanche recounted to her, eloquently and ingenuously, the encounter she had had with the lady and the conversation that she had had with the admirable stranger, but that story was not told without a rain even more precious than the one that vanquished Danaë falling on to the floor at the end of every sentence, no matter how short it was.

Everyone hastened to pick up what Blanche distributed from her mouth; no one was frightened of the pills that she spilled. She started collecting them herself in her turn, and although she was not mercenary she gradually acquired the habit of speaking in a curt style. The joy of the Marquis was indescribable, which is why I shall say nothing about it.

The Marquise, however, as surprised as she was consternated, resolved to send her daughter to the fountain the next day, flattering herself that she too would find the unknown lady there and that she would do her the same favor as Blanche. People in those days were as they still are today: they did not do themselves justice, and wanted favors without taking the trouble to merit them.

The mother informed Alix of her design, who, being more brutal than ever, replied to her in impertinent terms that she had to be joking in wanting to give her that fine employment, and that she would not do it. The mother told her that she wanted absolutely that it be done and that it was for her own good that she was sending her for water. Finally, Alix, after saying a thousand stupid things, got ready to go.

She adorned herself with as much care as she would have done in order to go to a ball, picked up the most beautiful golden vase there was in the house, and in that pompous display she arrived at the spring. Eloquentia Nativa was, in fact, in the vicinity of the stream; the savant fay had discovered that beautiful solitude a little while before and took great pleasure in it. That day, however, she was strolling in the guise of an agreeable peasant woman, whose naïve attitude and rural costume she had adopted, for Eloquentia was no less beautiful in simple garments than beneath the most brilliant ornaments. On the contrary; when she put on affected attire, it obfuscated her beauty.

Alix sat down on the edge of the spring, and the pretty peasant woman, who was thirsty, because she had been walking for a long time, immediately approached the bank. Alix, whose vulgar mind was only impressed by the glamour of magnificent clothes, to which she rendered the only honor that she was capable of rendering, looked at the pretended peasant with scorn, and did not deign to honor her with a nod of the head, even though Eloquentia rendered her a profound reverence.

The fay was not put off by that; making another curtsey, she said to Alix: "Mademoiselle, I beg you to have the goodness to suffer that I make use of your vase in order to draw water, for I have a violent thirst."

"Look at this small fry," replied Alix, furiously. "One comes here expressly to drink; truly, they need golden vases in order to put their dog's muzzle in.

Go away, stupid scrap, show me your back, and if you're thirsty, go drink from your cattle's trough. "

"You're very brusque, Mademoiselle," replied the fay. "Have I offended you, for you to treat me thus?"

Alix stood up then, and, putting her hands on her hips, shouted with all her might: "I believe that you want to argue, pestiferous slattern, but I advise you not to warm my ears, for I'll have you beaten whenever you go past our door."

The sage fay, full of indignation at the creature's brutalities, wanted to punish her in a manner that conserved a memory full of horror at the insulting torrent of her venomous tongue. She threw Alix to the ground by touching her with the tip of her wand, and in that state she gave her the gift, or rather the punishment, that every time she spoke, toads, snakes, spiders and other vile animals, whose venom would cause everyone to shudder, would emerge from her mouth.

Eloquentia went away immediately, and left Alix full of rage against her.

That malevolent individual waited a long time for the brilliant lady for whose favors she hoped, but, seeing that she was waiting in vain she finally wearied of it and returned home. Her mother was burning with impatience to see her again, and the moment she perceived her from the doorway the Marquise ran toward her.

"Well," she said, "have you had a fortunate encounter?"

"Yes," said Alix. "It was very necessary to send me there to run into a whore."

At these words, a host of snakes, toads and mice emerged in a flood from Alix's mouth.

"Where did you get that, wretch?" cried her mother.

Alix tried to respond, and produced another deluge of vile creatures.

The mother and daughter went back into the house, where it was seen that the fine gift that Alix had was an evil without remedy, and everyone ended up taking that unworthy individual in the utmost aversion. Even her mother could not help doing so.

Meanwhile, the Prince, who was very attentive to everything regarding Blanche, was soon informed of the fortunate gift that she had received from a fay, and as he was aware of the power and generosity of Eloquentia Nativa, who was another one of his godmothers, he had no doubt that the prodigy was due to her. Taking the pretext of wanting to witness it, he manifested a strong desire to have Blanche come to the court and went to ask Eloquentia to go in quest of the beautiful young woman about whom so many marvelous things were said.

"Did you know," the fay said to him, smiling "that it was me who was responsible for it?"

"No," the Prince replied, "but I render you a thousand thanks, for I have an ardent passion for that young beauty."

"You know the zeal I have to oblige you," said the fay, "but you need not thank me on this occasion; I was unaware of the interest you had in Blanche;

you had no part in what I have done for her; the mildness and politeness of that amiable young woman charmed me. Her conversation is entirely admirable; nothing equals the fortunate turn of her expressions, and I wanted pearls and gems to emerge from her mouth in order to mark the sweetness and brilliance that one finds in her speech."

The prince was delighted to hear Blanche's eloquence praised by a fay whose good taste and talents he esteemed a thousand times more than those of rhetoric.

In the end, Eloquentia Nativa quit her godson and went to the house of Blanche's father. It was besieged by an incredible crowd of people. The brilliant things that emerged from her mouth attracted even more people than those which emerged from the mouth of Monsieur de ****, beautiful as they were.

Those people were right; was it not more agreeable to see precious stones emerging from a beautiful small mouth like Blanche's than it was to see flashes of lightning emerging from the wide mouth of that thunderous orator, who was nevertheless so sought-after by the Athenians?[8]

To the great regret of the crowd surrounding Blanche, Eloquentia had her climb into a carriage and took her to the court. There the prince expressed the transports of his tenderness to her. Blanche was not insensible to that, and as the fortunate gift that the beauty had received rendered her richer than the foremost princesses in the world, the Prince married her with the applause of the Duc his father and all the people of his estates.

Blanche's father, who was at the peak of his joy, had great credit in the court, and no longer had to suffer the caprices of his wife; she no longer dared cause him chagrin since the elevation of his daughter.

The envious Alix, whom Blanche's good fortune would have been sufficient on its own to drive her to despair, also had that of seeing that neither her mother nor anyone else could tolerate her presence any longer. She quit her mother's house in a rage and went to wander from one province to another, where she was an object of aversion to everyone and where she experienced all the rigors of necessity. Finally, after having suffered a great deal she died of poverty "under a bush," while Blanche was triumphant.

The happiness of that beautiful person lasted as long as her life, which was long, and her destiny and that of Alix prove what I said to begin with, that often,

Mild and courteous language
Is worth more than a rich heritage.

---

[8] The reference is presumably to Jacques-Bénigne Bossuet, Louis XIV's court preacher, reputed to be the greatest orator of his era, and an habitué of the Hôtel de Rambouillet.

Charles Perrault: *The Beauty in the Dormant Wood*

There was once a king and a queen who were so sorry that they did not have any children, that they were sorrier than one can say. They went to all the spas in the world; prayers, pilgrimages and even devotions were all put to work, but nothing came of it. Finally, however, the queen became pregnant, and gave birth to a daughter.

There was a fine baptism, and the little princess was given for godmothers all the fays that could be found in the land—they found seven—in order that each of them could make her a gift, as was the custom in those days, and by that means the princess had all the imaginable perfections.

After the ceremonies of the baptism, the entire company returned to the king's palace, where there was a great feast for the fays. A magnificent place was set for each of them at table, with a solid gold case in which there was a spoon, a fork and a knife of fine gold, garnished with diamonds and rubies. As everyone took their places, however, an aged fay was seen to enter who had not been invited because she had not emerged from a tower in more than fifty years, and was believed to be dead or enchanted.

The king had a place set for her, but there was no means of giving her a solid gold case like the others, because only seven of them had been made for the seven fays. The old woman thought that she was being scorned and muttered a few threats between her teeth. One of the young fays who was sitting next to her heard her, and judging that she might make some regrettable gift to the little princess, went as soon as they left the table to hide behind the tapestry in order to be the last to speak and to be able, as much as possible, to repair any damage that the old one might do.

Meanwhile, the fays commenced to make their gifts to the princess. The youngest gave her as a gift that she would be the most beautiful young woman in the world, the one who came after her that she would have a mind like an angel, the third that she would have an admirable grace in everything she did, the fourth that she would dance perfectly, the fifth that she would sing like a nightingale, and the sixth that she would play all sorts of instruments with the utmost perfection.

The turn of the old fay having come, shaking her head even more from chagrin than old age, she said that the princess would pierce her hand with a spindle and would die of it. That terrible gift made the entire company tremble, and there was no one who was not weeping.

At that moment, the young fay emerged from behind the tapestry and spoke these words in a loud voice: "Do not worry, King and Queen, your daughter will not die of it. It is true that I do not have enough power to undo entirely what my ancient has done. The Princess will pierce her hand with a spindle, but, instead of dying, she will only fall into a profound slumber, which will last a hundred years, at the end of which the son of a king will come to awaken her."

In order to try to avoid the misfortune announced by the old woman, the king immediately had an edict published throughout the State, by which he forbade anyone to spin with a spindle or to have any spindle in their home, under penalty of death.

After fifteen or sixteen years, the king and the queen having gone to one of their pleasure houses, it happened that the young princess, wandering in the castle one day and going from room to room went all the way to the top of a tower into a small attic where a good old woman was alone, spinning with her distaff. That old woman had never heard mention of the prohibition that the king had made of spinning with a spindle.

"What are you doing there, my good woman?" asked the princess.

"I'm spinning, my beautiful child," replied the old woman, who did not know her.

"Oh, that's nice," said the princess. "How do you do it? Give it to me, so that I can see whether I can do it too."

She had no sooner taken the spindle than, as she was very hasty and a little clumsy, and in any case, the fays' decree ordered it thus, she pierced her hand and fell unconscious.

The good old woman, very embarrassed, called for help; people came from all directions. Water was thrown in the face of the princess, her clothing was loosened, her hands were slapped and her temples were rubbed with the Queen of Hungary's water,[9] but nothing brought her round.

Then the king, who had climbed up in response to the noise, remembered the prediction of the fays, and, judging that it was necessary that it had happened, since the fays had said so, he had the princess placed in the finest apartment in the palace, on a bed embroidered with gold and silver. One might have thought that she was an angel, so beautiful was she, for her unconsciousness had not taken away the vivid colors of her complexion. Her cheeks were rosy and her lips coralline; she only had her eyes closed, but she could be heard breathing softly, which made it evident that she was not dead. The king ordered that she be left to sleep in peace, until the hour for her to wake up had come.

The good fay who had condemned her to sleep for a hundred years was in the kingdom of Mataquin, twelve thousand leagues away, when the accident happened to the princess, but she was informed instantly by a little dwarf who

---

[9] "The Queen of Hungary's water" was a kind of perfume that originated in the fourteenth century and introduced into France by Charles V, made by steeping rosemary and thyme in brandy, although the recipe was elaborated idiosyncratically by numerous subsequent makers. It also became very popular as a medicament, applied externally or internally.

had seven-league boots—they were boots with which one covered seven leagues in a single stride.[10] The fay departed right away and was seen arriving after an hour in a chariot all of fire drawn by dragons.

The king came to offer her his hand to descend from the chariot. She approved everything that he had done, but as she was greatly far-sighted, she thought that when the princess woke up she would be very embarrassed all alone in that old castle; this is what she did:

She touched with her wand everything that there was in the castle, except for the king and the queen: governesses, maids of honor, chambermaids, gentlemen, officers, butlers, cooks, scullions, errand boys, guards, doormen, pages and footmen. She also touched al the horses that were in the stables, with the grooms, the large mastiffs in the farmyard and little Poufle,[11] the princess's little dog, which was next to her on her bed. As soon as she had touched them they all went to sleep, due to wake up at the same time as their mistress, in order to serve her when she needed it. Even the skewers fully laden with grouse and peasants over the fire became dormant, and the fire as well.

All that only took a moment; the fays do not linger over their work. Then the king and the queen, after having kissed their dear child without her waking up, left the castle and went to publish edicts forbidding anyone whatsoever to approach it. Those prohibitions were unnecessary, for in a quarter of an hour such an immense quantity of trees grew all around the park, great and small, with brambles and thorns so intertwined, that no beast or man would have been able to pass through—with the consequence that only the tops of the towers of the castle could be seen, and only from far away. No one doubted that the fay had performed another trick of her trade, in order that the princess would have no fear of curiosity-seekers while she slept.

After a hundred years, the son of the king who was reigning then, who was from a different family than the sleeping princess, having gone hunting in that direction, asked what the towers were that he could see above a dense wood. Everyone replied in accordance with what they had heard said; some said that it as an old castle haunted by ghosts, others that all the witches in the land held their Sabbats there. The most common opinion was that an ogre lived there, and that he took all the children he could catch there, in order to be able to eat them at his ease and without anyone being able to follow him, he alone having the power to pass through the wood.

---

[10] Madame d'Aulnoy employed seven-league boots in "L'Oranger et l'abeille" (tr. as "The Orange-Tree and the Bee") which also features ogres.

[11] The dog's name is usually rendered as Pouffe in modern reprintings of the tale, but the name, rendered in italics in early versions, employs there a compound symbol that is not a double *f* or a double *s* (which are hard to distinguish in the orthography of the time) but something more suggestive of "fl."

The prince did not know what to believe, when an old peasant spoke, and said to him: "My Prince, it is more than fifty years since I heard my father say that there was a princess in the castle, the most beautiful in the world; that she was to sleep for a hundred years, and that she would be woken up by the son of a king, for whom she was reserved."

At this speech, the young prince felt that he was on fire; he believed without hesitation that he could put an end to such a beautiful adventure; and, impelled by amour and glory, he resolved to see immediately what was there.

Scarcely had he advanced toward the wood than all the large trees, the brambles and the thorns, drew apart of their own accord to let him pass; he marched toward the castle, which he could see at the end of a broad avenue into which he entered, and, which surprised him a little, he saw that none of his men had been able to follow him, because the trees had drawn together again as soon as he had passed. He continued on his way nevertheless; a young and amorous prince is always valiant.

He went into a large forecourt, where everything he saw at first was capable of chilling him with fear; there was a frightful silence; the image of death was presented everywhere: there was nothing but the recumbent bodies of men and animals, who appeared to be dead. He recognized, however, by the red noses and crimson faces of the doormen, that they were only asleep, and their cups, in which there were still a few drops of wine, showed clearly enough that they had gone to sleep while drinking.

He went through a large courtyard paved with marble; he went up a stairway and went into the guard-room, where the guards were all lined up, rifles shouldered, snoring loudly. He went through several rooms full of gentlemen and ladies, all asleep, some standing up and others sitting down. He went into a gilded room and saw on a bed, the curtains of which were open on both sides, the most beautiful spectacle that he had ever seen: a princess who appeared to be about fifteen or sixteen years old, whose resplendent glamour had something luminous and divine. He approached, trembling and admiring, and knelt down beside her.

Then, as the end of the enchantment had come, the princess woke up, and, looking at him with eyes more tender than a first sight seemed to permit, she said: "Is that you, my prince? You've certainly been made to wait."

Charmed by those words, and even more so by the manner in with they were spoken, the prince did not know how to testify his joy and his gratitude to her. He assured her that he loved her more than himself. His words were poorly arranged; they were all the more pleasing for that: scant eloquence, much amour. He was more embarrassed than she was and one ought not to be astonished by that; she had had time to think about what she would have to say to him, for it appears—history, however, says nothing about it—that the good fay, during such a long slumber, had procured her the pleasure of agreeable dreams. In the end, they talked for four hours, and still had only said half the things that they had to say to one another.

Meanwhile, the whole palace had woken up with the princess; everyone thought about doing their duty, and, as they were not all in love, they were dying of hunger. The maid of honor, pressed like the others, became impatient, and said loudly to the princess that the meat was served. The prince helped the princess to get up; she was fully dressed, and quite magnificently, but he refrained from telling her that she was dressed like my grandmother, but that she was no less beautiful for having a high collar. They went into a hall of mirrors, and had supper there, served by the officers of the princess; violins and oboes played old pieces, excellent although no one had played them for a hundred years.

After supper, without wasting any time, the grand almoner married them in the castle chapel and the maid of honor drew the curtain for them. They did not sleep much—the princess had no need of it—the prince quit her in the morning in order return to the city, where his father was doubtless worried about him.

The prince told him that while hunting he had got lost in the forest and had slept in the hut of a charcoal-burner, who had given him black bread and cheese to eat. The king, his father, who was a good man, believed him, but his mother was not convinced. Seeing that he was going hunting almost every day, and that he always had a reason in hand to excuse himself when he had slept away from home for two or three nights, she had no doubt that it was some love affair. He lived with the princess for two entire years, and she had two children, the first of which, who was a daughter, was named Dawn, and the second a son, who was named Day because he seemed even more beautiful than his sister.

The queen said to her son several times, in order to make him explain, that he must be content with his life, but he dared not confide his secret to her; he feared her, although she loved him, because she was of the ogress race. The king had only married her because of her great wealth, and it was whispered in the court that she had the inclinations of ogres and that when she saw little children pass by she had all the difficulty in the world restraining herself from throwing herself upon them; so the prince never wanted to tell her anything. When the king died, however, which happened at the end of the two years, and he saw that he was the master, he declared his marriage publicly and went in great ceremony to find the queen, his wife, in her castle.

She was given a magnificent reception in the capital city, which she entered between her two children.

Some time afterwards the king went to make war on his neighbor, the Emperor Cantalabutte. He left the regency of the realm to the queen, his mother, and recommended his wife and two children to her strongly. He had to be at war all summer, and as soon as he had gone the queen mother sent her daughter-in-law and her children to a country house in the woods, in order to be able to sate her horrible desire more easily.

She went there a few days later and said to her butler: "I want to eat little Dawn for my midday meal tomorrow."

"Oh, Madame!" said the butler.

"I want it," said the queen—and she said it in the tone of an ogress who wants to eat fresh flesh—"and I want to eat her with sauce Robert."[12]

The poor man, seeing clearly that it was necessary not to trifle with an ogress, took his large knife and went up to little Dawn's bedroom. She was then four years old, and she came jumping and laughing to throw her arms around his neck and ask him for a bonbon. He started to weep; the knife fell from his hands, and he went into the farmyard to cut the throat of a little lamb. He made such a good sauce for it that his mistress assured him that she had never eaten one so good. At the same time he had taken little Dawn away and given her to his wife in order to hide her in the lodgings she had at the back of the farmyard.

A week later the wicked queen said to her butler: "I want to eat little Day for my evening meal."

He made no reply, but resolved to deceive her as he had before. He went to look for little Day, and found him with a little foil in his hand, with which he was fencing with a large monkey, although he was only three years old. He took him to his wife, who hid him with little Dawn, and substituted for him a tender little goat-kid, which the ogress found admirably good.

All had gone well so far, but one evening the wicked queen said to the butler: "I want to eat the queen with the same sauce as her children."

It was then that the poor butler despaired of being able to deceive her. The young queen was over twenty years old, not counting the hundred years that she had slept; although beautiful and white, her skin was a trifle firm, and what means were there of finding an animal with such a firm skin in the menagerie?

He made the resolution, in order to save his life, to cut the queen's throat, and he went up to her room with the intention of not having to do it twice. He excited his fury, and went into the young queen's room dagger in hand. He did not want to surprise her, however, and he told her very respectfully what order he had received from the queen mother.

"Do your duty," she said, holding out her neck. "Carry out the order you have been given; I shall go to see my children again, my poor children that I loved so much." For she believed that they were dead, because they had been taken away without saying anything to her.

"No, no, Madame," replied the poor butler, moved to compassion. "You shan't die, but you'll see your dear children nevertheless, in my house, where I've hidden them, and I'll deceive the queen again by giving her a young hind to eat in your stead."

---

[12] Sauce Robert is a mustard sauce featured in *Le Cuisinier François* (1651), compiled by Henri IV's cook and thus granted classic status.

He took her to his room immediately, where he allowed her to embrace her children and weep with them. Then he went to butcher a young hind, which the queen ate for her supper with the same appetite as if it really had been the young queen. She was quite content with her cruelty, and planned to tell the king, when he returned, that rabid wolves had eaten his wife and his two children.

One evening, when she was prowling, as was her wont, in the courtyards and farmyards of the castle in order to sniff out some fresh meat, he heard little Day weeping in a ground-floor room because the queen, his mother, wanted to have him whipped because he had been naughty. She also heard little Dawn, who was asking for mercy for her brother.

The ogress recognized the voices of the queen and her children, and, furious at having been deceived, she commanded the next morning, in a terrible voice that made everyone tremble, that a large tub should be brought into the middle of the courtyard, which she had filled with toads, vipers and other snakes, in order to have the queen and her children, the butler, his wife and his maidservant, thrown into it. She had ordered them to be brought out with their hands tied behind their backs.

They were there, and the executioner was preparing to throw them into the tub, when the king, who was not expected so soon, came into the courtyard on horseback. He had come post-haste, and he demanded, utterly astonished, what the horrible spectacle meant. No one had dared to inform him when the ogress, enraged to see what she saw, hurled herself head first into the tub and was instantly devoured by the nasty beasts that she had had put into it.

The king was sorry about that; she was his mother, after all; but he soon consoled himself with his wife and children.

MORAL

To wait a while in order to have a husband,
Who is rich, handsome, elegant and mild,
Is something that is natural enough.
But to wait a hundred years, while always asleep?
Women are no longer found
Who sleep so tranquilly.

The fable seems to want to make us think
That the agreeable knots of Hymen are often
No less happy for being deferred,
And that one loses nothing by waiting.

But the female sex with such ardor
Aspires to the conjugal oath,
That I have neither the strength nor the heart
To preach that moral to it.

Henriette-Julie de Murat: *Perfect Love*

The redoubtable Danamo reigned in one of the pleasant lands dependent on the Empire of the Fays. She was knowledgeable in her art, cruel in her actions and glorious in the honor of being descended from the celebrated Calypso, whose charms had glory and power in stopping the famous Ulysses and triumphing over the prudence of the vanquisher of Troy. She was tall, and grim of face, and her pride had only submitted with great difficulty to the harsh laws of marriage, amour never having been able to reach as far as her heart, but the design of uniting a flourishing kingdom with the one of which she was the Queen and another that she had usurped had caused her to espouse an old King, one of her neighbors.

The King died a few years after the marriage and he left to the fay a daughter named Azire, who was extraordinarily ugly, but did not appear so in the eyes of Danamo; she found her charming, perhaps because she resembled her perfectly. She was to be Queen of three realms, a circumstance that compensates for many faults, and she was requested by all the most powerful princes of neighboring lands. That urgency, combined with the blind amity of Danamo, ended up rendering her vanity insupportable; she was desired with ardor, therefore she must be worthy of it. Thus the fay and the princess reasoned between themselves, and enjoyed the pleasure of the deception.

Danamo only thought about rendering happiness to the princess so perfect that she thought her deserving of it, and she brought up in her palace a young prince, the son of her brother. His name was Parcin Parcinet. Everything he wanted to do he did well; he danced perfectly, he sang likewise and he won all the prizes in any tourney that he took the trouble of disputing. The young prince was the delight of the court, and Danamo, who had her designs, did not oppose the respect and admiration that everyone had for him.

The king who was Parcin Parcinet's father being the fay's brother, she had declared war on him without even seeking a reason. The king fought valiantly at the head of his army, but what could an army do against the power of a fay as knowledgeable as Danamo? She only allowed the victory to remain in the balance for as long as was necessary for her unfortunate brother to perish on that occasion. As soon as he was dead, killed by a thrust of a wand, she dispersed her enemies and rendered herself mistress of the kingdom. Parcin Parcinet was still in the cradle; he was brought to Danamo; it would have been vain to try to hide him from a fay. He already had the seductive graces that win hearts; Danamo caressed him, and a few days later she took him with her to her own realm.

The prince was eighteen years old when the fay, wanting to carry out the designs formed so many years before, resolved to unite Parcin Parcinet with the princess, her daughter. She did not doubt for a moment the infinite joy that the young prince would experience, having been born ambitious but destined by his misfortunes to live as a subject, in one day becoming the sovereign of three empires. She sent for the princess, and finally revealed to her the choice that she had made for her.

The princess listened to that speech with an emotion that caused the fay to judge that the resolution in favor of Prince Parcinet did not please her daughter.

"I can see," she said, on remarking her disturbance increasing further, "that you want to take your ambition higher and combine with your empire that of one of the many kings who have asked for you. But what king can Parcin Parcinet not defeat? His courage is above all; the subjects of a prince so perfect might well become rebels one day in his favor; by giving you to him I am assuring you of the possession of his kingdom. For his person there is no need to speak; you know that the proudest beauties cannot resist his charms."

The princess, suddenly throwing herself at the fay's feet, interrupted her speech and admitted to her that her heart had not been able to resist the young victor, famous for so many conquests, but she added, blushing: "I have given a thousand marks of my tenderness to the insensible Parcin Parcinet, but he has received them with a coldness that makes me despair."

"That is because he dared not raise his thoughts as far as you," replied the proud fay. "He doubtless fears displeasing, and I am grateful for his respect."

That flattering opinion was too convenient for the inclination and vanity of the princess for her not to allow herself to be convinced by it.

Finally, the fay sent for Parcin Parcinet. He came to find her in a magnificent cabinet, where she was waiting with the princess, her daughter.

"Summon all your courage to your aid," she said to him as soon as he appeared, "not to sustain your woes, but in order that you should not succumb under your good fortune. You are to reign, Parcin Parcinet, and to complete your happiness, you are to reign by marrying my daughter."

"Me, Madame!" cried the young prince, with an astonishment in which it was easy to remark that joy had no part. "I am going to marry the Princess?" he continued, recoiling several steps. "What god has come to meddle with my destiny, to whose care alone I can ask for aid?"

These words were pronounced by the prince with a haste in which his heart played too great a part for them to be arrested soon enough by reason.

The fay thought that Prince Parcinet's unexpected happiness had overwhelmed him, but the princess loved him, and love sometimes renders lovers more perspicacious than intelligence. "Whatever god it is whose aid you are imploring so tenderly, Parcin Parcinet," she said to him, emotionally, "I know only too well that I have no part in the prayers you have made to him."

The young Prince, who had had time to recover from his initial astonishment, and had understood the imprudence of what he had just done, summoned his intelligence to the aid of his heart. He replied more gallantly to the princess than she had hoped and thanked the fay with an air of grandeur, which showed clearly enough that he was not only worthy of the empires that she was offering him, but that of the whole world.

Danamo and her proud daughter were satisfied by his speech; they arranged everything before emerging from the cabinet, and the fay only deferred the day of the wedding for some time in order to give the entire court the leisure to prepare for that great celebration.

On their emergence from the queen's cabinet, the news of the marriage of Parcin Parcinet and Azire spread throughout the palace instantly; a crowd gathered to rejoice with the prince. Although the princess was scarcely likeable, it was a great fortune to which she was about to enable him to climb.

Parcin Parcinet received all those honors with a cold expression that surprised his new subjects all the more because it seemed to be mingled with a chagrin and an extreme anxiety. It was necessary throughout the day for him to receive the congratulations of the entire court and sustain the testimonies of amour that Azire incessantly gave him. What a situation for a young prince occupied with a vivid dolor!

Night appeared to him to have delayed its return a thousand times longer than usual. The impatient Parcin Parcinet pressed it with his wishes; it finally came. He emerged precipitately from the place where he had suffered so much and went back to his apartment. After having sent everyone away, he opened a door to the palace gardens and traversed then, only accompanied by a young slave.

A beautiful but not very extensive river flowed at the end of the gardens and separated from the fay's magnificent palace a small castle flanked by four towers and surrounded by a deep moat filled by the same stream. It was to that place that the prayers and desires of Parcin Parcinet incessantly went. What a marvel was contained therein! Danamo had that treasure guarded carefully; it was a young princess, the daughter of her sister, who had confided her on her deathbed to the fay's care. Her beauty, worthy of the admiration of the whole world, appeared too dangerous to Danamo to allow Azire to be seen beside her. Sometimes, the charming Irolite—that was her name—was permitted to come to the palace to see the fay and the princess, her daughter, but she was never allowed to appear in public. Her charms were unknown—but not unknown to everyone.

They had appeared in Princess Azire's apartment to the eyes of Parcin Parcinet and he had adored them as soon as he had seen them. The proximity of the blood relationship gave no privileges to the young Prince with regard to Irolite; since the young princess was no longer a child, the pitiless Danamo did not permit anyone to see her.

However, Parcin Parcinet burned with a flame as ardent as the charms of Irolite were bound to ignite; she was fourteen years old, her beauty was perfect; her hair was a charming color, without being entirely black or blonde; her com-

144

plexion had all the freshness of spring; her mouth was beautiful, her teeth admirable and her smile gracious; she had large brown eyes, bright and touching, and her gaze appeared to say a thousand things of which her young heart was unaware.

She had been brought up in great solitude; although the castle where she lived was close to the fay's palace, she saw no more people there than she would have done in the middle of a desert. Danamo had that order followed exactly; the beautiful Irolite spent her life with the women destined to accompany her. Their number was small, but however little fortune could be expected in a Court so solitary and limited, renown, which did not fear Danamo, published so many marvels regarding the young Princess that the noblest young women of the Court offered to be imprisoned with the young Irolite. Her presence did not belie the expectations raised by renown, and they always found much to admire in her.

A governess of extreme intelligence and sagacity, formerly attached to Irolite's mother, had remained with her, and often bemoaned the rigors of Danamo for the charming Irolite. Her name was Mana; the desire to render the Princess the liberty she ought to enjoy and the rank she ought to have had caused her to tolerate the love of Parcin Parcinet. It was three years since, having been introduced into the castle one evening, dressed as a slave, he had found Irolite in the garden, and he had spoken to her tenderly. She was then only a child, but an admirable child; she loved Parcin Parcinet as if he were her brother, and could not yet understand that one could love differently.

Mana, who was rarely far away from Irolite, had surprised the young prince in the gardens; he had told her about his love for the princess and the design he had formed either to render her liberty one day or to die trying, and to go thereafter to show the people of his realm a glorious means of avenging themselves on Danamo and placing Irolite on the throne. The nascent merit of Parcin Parcinet was able to render the most difficult projects credible, and it was the only aid that was offered to the liberation of Irolite, so Mana permitted him to come to the castle sometimes when night had fallen. He only saw Irolite in her presence, but he spoke to her about his love and incessantly tried, by means of tender speeches and constant cares, to inspire an ardor in her as keen as his own.

For three years, Parcin Parcinet had only been occupied by his tenderness; almost every night he went to the princess's castle, and every day he did nothing but think about her.

We left him traversing Danamo's gardens accompanied by a slave, penetrated by the dolor to which the fay's resolutions had reduced him. He arrived at the edge of the stream; a small gilded boat moored to the bank, in which Azire sometimes went out on the water, served to take the amorous prince across. The slave rowed, and as soon as Parcin Parcinet had climbed a silken ladder that was thrown down to him from a small terrace that overlooked the façade of the castle, the faithful slave rowed the boat back to where it ought to be. He only approached the castle again in response to a signal that Parcin Parcinet made, by showing a lighted torch on the terrace momentarily.

This evening, the prince followed his ordinary route; the silken ladder was thrown down to him and he entered without obstacle all the way to young Irolite's bedroom; he found her there, lying on a bed of repose, in tears. She was so beautiful in that dolorous state that her charms had never seemed so touching to the young Prince.

"What's wrong, my Princess," he said to her, throwing himself to his knees beside the bed on which she was lying. "Who can have made those precious tears flow? Alas," he continued, sighing, "I have even more bad news to tell you."

The tears and sighs of the young lovers were confounded, and it was necessary that they let them run their course before he could tell her the cause of that sharp dolor. Finally, the young prince begged Irolite to tell him what new rigor the fay had imposed upon her.

"She wants to make you marry Azire," the beautiful Irolite replied, blushing. "Could these cruelties ever be so dolorous?"

"Oh, my dear princess," cried the Prince, "you dread that I am marrying Azire! My fate is a thousand times sweeter than if I had not thought so."

"Can you praise destiny," said young Irolite, languidly, "when it is in haste to separate us? I cannot express the pain that fear is making me feel. Oh, you are right, Parcin Parcinet, one loves a lover differently from a brother."

The amorous Prince thought that he should thank fortune for his woes. Never had Irolite's young heart appeared to him to know amour, but finally, he could no longer doubt the happiness of having inspired the princess to tender sentiments. That felicity, which he had not expected, raised all his hopes.

"No," he cried, transported. "I no longer despair of vanquishing our misfortunes, since I am assured of your tenderness. Let us flee, my Princess; let us flee the fury of Danamo and her odious daughter; let us go confide to a less dreary abode the ardent amour that alone can render us happy.

"If I depart with you," the young princess said, with astonishment, "what will the entire kingdom say about my flight?"

"Forget such vain considerations, beautiful Irolite," Parcin Parcinet interjected, impatiently. "Everything presses us to quit this place; let's go..."

"But where will you go?" asked the prudent Mana, who had been present all along, and who, being less preoccupied than the young lovers, foresaw all the difficulties of their flight.

"I have designs that I shall explain to you," said Parcin Parcinet, "but how have you learned the news of the fay's Court so soon here?"

"One of my relatives," said Mana, "wrote to me as soon as the rumor spread through the palace, and I thought I ought to inform the Princess."

"How I have suffered since that moment," said the lovable Irolite. "No, Parcin Parcinet, I could not live without you."

The young Prince, transported by amour and charmed by those words, gave Irolite's beautiful hand an ardent and tender kiss, which had all the grace of a precious favor, and of a first favor.

The daylight, which was beginning to appear, warned Parcin Parcinet too soon that it was time to withdrew. He assured the princess that he would come back the following night in order to make her party to his plans.

He went back to the boat and the faithful slave, and retired to his apartment. He was transported by the pleasure of being loved by the beautiful Irolite, and agitated by the difficulties that he foresaw clearly that he would encounter in his flight; sleep could not calm that anxiety, nor make him forget his happiness for a moment.

Scarcely had the morning entered his apartment than a dwarf presented him with a beautiful sash on the part of Princess Azire, who, in a note more tender than Parcin Parcinet would have liked, begged him insistently to wear the sash from that day forward. He sent a reply that embarrassed him greatly, but it was necessary to liberate Irolite, and to what constraint would he not have exposed himself in order to free her?

He had just sent the dwarf back to Azire when a giant came on the part of Danamo to present him with a saber of extraordinary beauty, the hilt of which was a single stone brighter than a diamond, which cast a light so dazzling that it illuminated the night. Engraved on the saber were the words: *For the hand of a Victor*.

That present pleased Parcin Parcinet; he went to thank the fay for it, and appeared before her wearing the marvelous saber that she had just sent him and Azire's beautiful sash. The tenderness that Irolite had for him suspended all his anxieties; it had spread in his heart the joy, so sweet and so perfect, that fortunate love makes felt. That air of contentment appeared in all his actions; Azire attributed it to her charms and the fay to Parcin Parcinet's satisfied ambition. The day was spent in pleasures that did not diminish in the slightest the insupportable impatience in which Parcin Parcinet found himself.

In the evening they went for a walk in the gardens and an excursion on the river that the Prince knew so well; his heart felt a keen emotion on entering the little boat; no matter how different from the pleasure to which it ordinarily led him was the mortal boredom he felt then, Parcin Parcinet could not help gazing several times at the dwelling of the charming Irolite. She did not appear on the terrace of the castle, for there was an express order that she should not emerge from her bedroom when the fay or Azire was out on the water.

The princess, who was attentive to all the prince's actions, noticed that his gaze often turned toward the castle.

"Why, Prince," she said, "in the midst of the honors that surround you, are you looking at Irolite's prison? Is it worthy of your attention?"

"Yes, Madame," said Parcin Parcinet, imprudently. "I am sensible to the suffering of those who have not attracted their misfortunes."

"You have too much pity," said Azire, disdainfully. "But to extract you from your trouble," she said, lowering her voice, "I will tell you that Irolite will not be a prisoner for long."

"And what will become of her?" asked the young Prince, brusquely.

"The Queen will marry her in a fortnight to Prince Ormond," Azire replied. "He is, as you know, of the same blood as us, and in accordance with the Queen's intentions, the day after his marriage, he will take Irolite to one of his fortresses, from which she will never return to the Court."

"What!" said the Prince, with an extraordinary emotion. "The Queen will give that beautiful Princess to such a frightful Prince, whose bad qualities even surpass his ugliness? What cruelty!"

The last word escaped him involuntarily, but he could not betray his courage and his heart any longer.

"It seems to me that it is not for you, Parcin Parcinet," replied Azire, proudly, "to complain of Danamo's cruelties."

That conversation would doubtless have been extended too far for a young Prince who had to pretend, but, fortunately for Parcin Parcinet, the young women of Azire's retinue approached her, and, the fay having appeared on the water's edge a moment later, Azire wanted to go and join her. On emerging from the boat, Parcin Parcinet feigned illness, in order at least to have the liberty to go and lament the unfortunate news without witnesses.

The fay, and Azire especially, testified a great anxiety regarding his illness. He retired to his apartment; there he criticized destiny a thousand times for the woes that threatened the charming Irolite, and he abandoned himself to all his dolor and all his tenderness. Finally beginning to remedy his woes, so dolorous for a faithful lover, he wrote, with the most touching expressions that his amour was able to dictate to him, to one of his aunts, who was a fay like Danamo, but who had as much joy in relieving the unfortunate as Danamo took in making them. Her name was Favorable. He explained to her, therefore, the cruel situation to which amour and fortune had reduced him, and, not daring to leave Danamo's Court himself for fear of betraying the designs that he had formed, he sent his faithful slave to Favorable.

When everyone had retired, he left his apartments, as usual, traversed the gardens and got into the little boat, taking an oar himself, without really knowing whether he would be able to make use of it properly. But what cannot amour teach? It achieves much more difficult things. It made Parcin Parcinet row with as much skill and diligence as the most expert in that métier, and he went into Irolite's castle. He was surprised only to find the sage Mana in the princess's bedroom, in tears.

"What's wrong, Mana?" the prince said to her, urgently. "And where is my dear Irolite?"

"Alas, Seigneur, she is no longer here," Mana said to him. "A troop of the Queen's guards, and a few women, to whom she is apparently confiding her, took her away from the castle three or four hours ago."

Parcin Parcinet did not hear the end of those sad words; he had fainted as soon as he learned of the Princess's departure. Mana brought him round with infinite trouble, and he only emerged from that torpid state to enter suddenly into fury. He drew a little dagger that he wore at his waist and would have pierced his heart with it if the sage Mana had not retained his arm as much as was possible for her.

Throwing herself to his knees, she said: "What, Seigneur! You want to abandon Irolite and life, to deliver her to Danamo's fury? Alas, without you, where will she find aid against the fay's cruelties?"

Those words immediately suspended the unfortunate Prince's despair. "Alas," he said, shedding tears that all his courage could not hold back, "where is my Princess? Yes, Mana, I shall live at least to have the sad satisfaction of dying for her and expiring while avenging her on her enemies."

After those words Mana implored him to leave that fatal abode, in order to avoid further misfortunes. "Go, Prince," she said to him. "We do not know whether the fay has someone here ready to give her an account of what is happening here; preserve a life so dear to the Princess you adore; I will let you know whatever I can learn about her."

The Prince left after that promise and returned to his apartment with all the dolor that a very tender and very unfortunate amour can inspire. He spent the night in a chair, on to which he had thrown himself on entering; daylight surprised him there, and it was already some hours after its commencement that he heard a noise at his bedroom door. He ran to it with the impatience one experiences when one is expecting news in which one's heart is keenly interested. He found his servants there, bringing him a man who wanted to speak to him without delay. He recognized him as one of Mana's relatives, who put a letter in Parcin Parcinet's hands. He went into his cabinet to hide the emotion that the letter caused him; he opened it precipitately, having recognized Mana's handwriting, and found these words therein:

Mana,
to the greatest Prince in the world.

    Be reassured, Seigneur, our Princess is safe, if that word is permissible so long as she is in her enemy's power. She has asked Danamo for me, who has permitted me to rejoin her. She is being kept in the palace. Yesterday evening, the Queen had her come to her cabinet, and ordered her to look proudly at Prince Ormond, who would become her husband in a few days; and she introduced her to that Prince, so unworthy of being your rival. The Princess was so afflicted that she only replied to the Queen with tears. They have not dried up. It is up to you, Seigneur, to discover whether aid is possible against such pressing woes.

At the bottom of the letter, written in a tremulous hand, were these words, which seemed to be effaced in several places:

How sorry I am, my dear Prince; your woes are even more dolorous to me than mine; I will spare your tenderness the recitation of what I have suffered since yesterday; why should I trouble the repose of your life without, alas, my being able to make you happy?

What movement of joy and dolor did the heart of the young prince not feel? What kisses did he not bestow on that precious evidence to the divine Irolite's love? He was so beside himself that he had all the difficulty in the world forming a reply that would have some consequence. He thanked the sage Mana, he informed the Princess of the aid that he anticipated from the fay Favorable, what did he not say about his dolor and his amour? Finally, he brought the letter to Mana's relative and gave him a clasp of precious stones of inestimable price and beauty, in order to begin to recompense him for the pleasure that he had just given him.

Mana's relative had only just left when the queen and Princess Azire sent someone to enquire as to how the Prince has spent the night; it was easy for them to judge by his face that he was not in good health, and he was urged to go to bed. He understood that there would be less constraint than if he went to see the fay, and he consented to do that.

In the afternoon the queen came to see him, and she talked to him about the marriage of Irolite and Prince Ormond as a matter that she had decided. Parcin Parcinet, who had made the resolution to constrain himself in order not to render his design futile, appeared to approve of the fay's intentions, and only begged her to wait until his health was fully restored, because he wanted to attend the celebration of that great marriage. The fay and Azire, who were in despair at his illness, promised him whatever he wanted, and at least Parcin Parcinet had delayed Irolite's sad wedding for a few days.

The conversation he had had with Azire on the water had bought forward the misfortune of the beautiful Princess he loved so tenderly. Azire had told the queen what Parcin Parcinet had said, and about his pity for Irolite. The queen, who never delayed in the execution of her will, had sent for Irolite that same evening, and resolved with Azire to complete the princess's marriage and hasten her departure before Parcin Parcinet had a more established authority.

After ten days, however, the Prince's faithful slave arrived. What a joy it was for him to find, in the letter that Favorable had written to him, marks of her compassion and amity for him and for Irolite. She sent him a little ring forged from four different metals: gold, silver, bronze and iron; the ring could protect him four times from the persecutions of the cruel Danamo, and Favorable assured the prince that the evil fay would only be able to command that he be pursued as many times as the ring had the power to save him. That good news rendered health to the young prince, and he sent someone to search for Mana's relative urgently. He gave him a letter that informed Irolite of the fortunate success that they had achieved.

There was no time to lose; the queen wanted to complete Irolite's marriage in three days; the same evening there was to be a ball in Azire's apartment; Irolite was to be there. Parcin Parcinet could not resolve to appear neglected; he put on magnificent attire and appeared a thousand times more brilliant than during the day. At first, he dared not speak to the divine Irolite, but what did they not say when their eyes sometimes dared to meet?

Irolite had the most beautiful costume in the world; the fay had given her marvelous jewels, and, only having to have her in the palace for four more days, had resolved to treated her as she ought to be treated. Her beauty, which was not accustomed to being accompanied by so much ornamentation, seemed marvelous to everyone, and even more so to the amorous Parcin Parcinet; he even judged by some movement of joy that he saw shining in her beautiful eyes that she had received the letter.

Prince Ormond often spoke to Irolite, but he appeared so ugly of face beneath the gold and precious stones with which he was decked that he was not a rival worthy of the jealousy of the young prince. The ball was nearly at an end when Parcin Parcinet, carried away by his amour, wished with an extreme ardor to be able to speak to his princess.

Cruel Queen, and you, odious Azire, he said to himself, *will you take away from me any longer the charming pleasure of saying a thousand times to the beautiful Irolite that I adore her? Will you not quit this place, jealous witnesses of my amour? Amour can only triumph in your absence.*

Scarcely had Parcin Parcinet formulated that wish than the fay felt a slight indisposition, and summoned Azire, who went with her into the next room, where Ormond followed them. Parcin Parcinet had on his finger the ring that the fay Favorable had sent him, which could deliver him four times from Danamo's persecutions. He should have kept that assured help for more urgent occasions, but can a violent amour accord with prudence?

The young prince had no doubt, given the departure of the fay and Azire, that the ring was beginning to serve his amour. He flew to the beautiful Irolite and spoke to her about his tenderness, with expressions more insistent than eloquent. He knew that he had perhaps employed Favorable's charm lightly, but he could not repent of an imprudence that had secured him the sweet pleasure of speaking to his dear Irolite.

Together they decided the place and time when they would finally free themselves from their painful slavery.

The fay and Azire returned after some time. Parcin Parcinet drew away from Irolite with regret. He looked at the fatal ring and perceived that the iron was confounded with the other metals and was no longer visible at all, so he could see all too clearly that he only had three wishes still to make, and resolved to employ them more usefully than the first for the benefit of his princess. He only made the confidence of his departure to his faithful slave, and spent the rest of the night disposing all the things necessary for his flight.

The next day he seemed tranquil in the queen's apartment, and even in a livelier humor than usual. He exchanged pleasantries with Prince Ormond regarding his marriage, and acted, in sum, in a manner capable of calming any suspicions that anyone might have regarding his amour.

At two hours after midnight he went into the fay's park; he found his faithful slave there, who, on his master's orders, had brought four of his horses. The prince did not have long to wait for the beautiful Irolite to appear, walking unsteadily and leaning on Mana. The young princess was taking the step with difficulty; it had required all of Danamo's cruelties and all Ormond's bad qualities to determine her to do it; amour alone might not have been sufficient.

It was summer, the night was fine and the Moon, which was illuminating the sky with the brilliant stars, provided a light more pleasant than daylight. The prince advanced hastily; they had no time for long speeches. Parcin Parcinet kissed Irolite's hand tenderly and helped her to mount a horse; fortunately she had a marvelous seat, riding being one of the pleasures that had amused her during her imprisonment. She sometimes rode with her companions in a little wood a short distance from the castle, where the fay had permitted her to go.

After speaking for a few more moments to the princess, Parcin Parcinet mounted his own horse; the other two were for Mana and the faithful slave. Then the young prince drew the shiny saber that the fay had given him, swore to the beautiful Irolite to adore her as long as he lived and to die, if necessary, to defend her from her enemies. After those words, they set forth, and it seemed that the Zephyrs were on their side, or that they mistook Irolite for Flora, for they always accompanied them.

Daylight, however, revealed the unexpected news to Danamo.

The ladies who were with Irolite were astonished that she was sleeping later than usual. But, following the order that the sage Mana had given them the previous evening, they dared not go into the princess's room without being summoned. Mana slept in Irolite's bedroom, and they had left by a little door that opened to a courtyard of the palace where few people went; that door was in Irolite's cabinet; it had been locked, but with a little difficulty, in two or three evenings, they had found a means of opening it.

Finally, the queen sent someone to Irolite's apartment to summon her to her presence; everyone obeyed the fay's orders; they knocked on the door of the princess's bedroom; there was no reply. Prince Ormond arrived, having come to take Irolite to the queen; he was very astonished to see them knocking in vain.

He had the door broken down; they went in and, seeing that the little door in the cabinet had been forced, no longer doubted that the Princess had fled the palace.

That news was taken to the queen; she quivered with anger on hearing it. She ordered that people should search everywhere for Irolite, but it was in vain that they sought information out her flight; no one had been informed of it. Prince Ormond set forth by himself to search for Irolite, and the fay's guards were sent in all diligence along the roads that it was judged that they might have taken.

Meanwhile, Azire perceived that in the general turmoil, Parcin Parcinet had not appeared; she sent people to his apartment immediately, and jealousy finally opened Azire's eyes, causing her to think that the prince had abducted Irolite.

As she had not yet suspected him of being in love with her, the fay could not believe it, but she went to consult her books, and found that Azire's suspicion was a verity. Meanwhile, the queen having learned that Parcin Parcinet was not in his apartment, nor anywhere in the palace, she sent men to the castle where Irolite had lived for such a long time, to see whether anything could be found there that might justify or condemn the prince.

The sage Mana had taken care not to leave anything there that might betray the intelligence of Irolite with Parcin Parcinet, but near the chair on which the young Prince had fainted for such a long time, they found the sash that Azire had given him, which she had detached during his faint, and which neither the Prince nor Mana, occupied with their dolor, had perceived.

What did the vainglorious Azire not feel at the sight of that sash? Her amour and her vanity made her suffer equally; she was excessively afflicted, and had everyone who had been in Irolite's service and that of the prince put in the fay's prisons. The ingratitude that the queen believed that Parcin Parcinet had shown to her pushed natural fury to the extreme, and she would willingly have given one of her realms to be able to avenge herself on the two lovers.

Meanwhile, they were pursued in all directions. Ormond and his troop found fresh horses everywhere, by order of the fay; Parcin Parcinet's were weary and no longer responded with their ardor to their master's impatience. Ormond caught up with them as they emerged from a forest.

The first impulse of the young prince was to go to combat that unworthy rival. He was already running toward him, carrying his saber in his hand, when Irolite shouted to him: "Don't seek unnecessary danger, Prince; obey Favorable's orders."

Those words arrested Parcin Parcinet's anger and, in order to obey the princess and the fay, he wished that the beautiful Irolite would be in security from the persecutions of the cruel queen.

Scarcely was that wish formed than the earth opened up between him and Ormond; before his eyes a somewhat deformed little man appeared, magnificently dressed, who made him a sign to follow him. The slope was gentle and very smooth; he descended on horseback with the beautiful Irolite, Mana and the faithful slave, and the earth closed up again.

Ormond, surprised by such an extraordinary event, ran diligently to tell the story to Danamo.

Meanwhile, our young lovers followed the little man along a very obscure route, at the end of which they found a vast palace, which was only illuminated by a large quantity of torches and lamps. They were invited to dismount, and they went into a hall of prodigious grandeur. It was sustained by columns of shiny earth covered with golden ornaments; the walls were of the same material.

A little man covered with jewels was sitting on a golden throne at the back of the hall, surrounded by a large number of people of similar build to the one who had guided the Prince to the place. As soon as he appeared with the charming Irolite, the little man stood up from his throne and said to him: "Come, Prince; the great fay Favorable, who has been my friend for a long time, has asked me to save you from the cruelties of Danamo. I am the King of the Gnomes; be welcome in my palace, with the beautiful Princess who accompanies you."

Parcin Parcinet thanked him for the aid he had just given him. The king and all his subjects were delighted by Irolite's beauty; they took her for a star that had come to illuminate their abode. A magnificent meal was served to Parcin Parcinet and the princess. The King of the Gnomes honored them; a very harmonious but slightly barbaric music was the evening's entertainment; the charms of Irolite were sung to it, and these lines were repeated several times:

What Star descends beneath the earth
To embellish this tenebrous domain?
Let us not look too long at that bright light,
Which seduces and charms the eyes;
The bright star that illuminates us
Is very dangerous to the heart.

After the music, the prince and the princess were each conducted to a magnificent chamber. Mana and the faithful slave served them. The next day they were shown the king's palace; he disposed of all the treasures contained in the earth; it was impossible to add anything to those riches; there was a confused mass of beautiful things, but art was lacking there in everything.

The prince and the princess remained in that subterranean place for eight days, Favorable having given that order to the King of the Gnomes. In the meantime, the prince and princess were given feasts every day, which were not very elegant, but magnificent. On the eve of their departure, in order to immortalize the memory of their sojourn in his empire, the king had their statues erected to either side of his throne. They were made of gold, and the pedestals were white marble. These words were written with letters formed of diamonds on the pedestal of the statue of the prince:

We no long desire the sight of the sun;
We have seen this Prince;
He is more handsome and brilliant.

And on the pedestal of the statue of the princess were these words, written in the same manner:

To the immortal glory
Of the goddess of beauty;
She has descended down here
Under the features and the name of Irolite.

On the ninth day the prince was given the most beautiful horses in the world; their harness was gold, covered in diamonds. They emerged from the somber abode of the gnomes with the little troop, after having expressed their gratitude to the king. They found themselves in the same terrain where Ormond had attacked them. The prince looked at the ring, and only found the silver and the bronze in evidence.

He continued his route with the charming Irolite, and they were hastening to arrive at Favorable's dwelling, where they would finally be safe, when all of a sudden, on emerging from a valley, they encountered a troop of Danamo's guards, who were still searching for them. The guards were preparing to fall upon them when the prince promptly made his wish, and immediately, a large area appeared between Parcin Parcinet's party and the Fay's, covered with water.

A beautiful semi-naked nymph appeared in the middle of the water in a little boat of woven reeds. She drew nearer to the bank, and begged the prince and his beautiful mistress to enter the little boat. Mana and the faithful slave followed them; their horses remained on land, and the little boat suddenly sank beneath the water, which made the fay's guards believe that they had perished in wanting to save themselves with their sailors.

Meanwhile, they found themselves in a palace, the walls of which were nothing but large sheets of water, which fell incessantly, forming, halls, rooms and cabinets, and surrounded by gardens, in which a thousand water jets of bizarre shape formed the design of flower beds. There were only naiads in the empire where they were, who were able to live in that palace, as beautiful as it was singular. In order, therefore, to give a more solid dwelling to the Prince and the beautiful Irolite, the naiad who was conducting them took them into grottoes of shells in which coral and pearls shone, and all the other riches of the sea. The beds were made of foam; a hundred dolphins guarded Irolite's grotto and twenty whales Parcin Parcinet's.

The naiads admired Irolite's beauty in their turn, and more than one triton was jealous of the gazes and cares that the young prince attracted. As soon as they were in the princess's grotto they were served a superb collation of all sorts of glazed fruits; twelve sirens came to charm the anxieties of the young prince and the beautiful Irolite with their sweet and gracious songs. They finished their concert with these words:

> In whatever places Amour leads us.
> That God is able to render us happy.
> Perfect lovers, charmed by your chain,
> In the water's depths make your fire shine.
> In whatever place Amour leads us,
> That God is able to render us happy.

In the evening there was a feast in which only fish were served, but of an extraordinary size and an exquisite taste; after the meal the naiads danced a ballet with garments of fish-scales of different colors, which had the most beautiful effect in the world; the horns of tritons, and other instruments unknown to mortals, composed the symphony; it was bizarre but new and very pleasant.

Parcin Parcinet and the beautiful Irolite were in that empire for four days, Favorable having thus ordered; on the fifth day, the naiads came in a host to escort the prince and princess. The two lovers were in a boat made of a single shell, and the naiads, half out of the water, accompanied them as far as the bank of a little river, where Parcin Parcinet found his horses again. He set forth with all the more diligence because he perceived, on looking at his ring, that the silver had disappeared, and nothing remained but the bronze; but they were not far from Favorable's dwelling, so much desired.

They traveled for another three days, but on the fourth, the sun, which had just risen, glinted on distant weapons, and when the men carrying them came a little closer, they recognized them as Prince Ormond and his troop. Danamo had sent them back to pursue them, with orders not to quit them if they found them, not to leave any place where something extraordinary might happen and above all, to try to engage Parcin Parcinet in combat.

Danamo had realized, after Ormond had told his story, that a fay was protecting the prince and the princess, but she was so knowledgeable that she did not despair of vanquishing her by means of charms more powerful than hers.

Ormond was delighted to see the prince and Irolite again, for whom he had been searching with so much difficulty and care. He ran at Parcin Parcinet, sword in hand, in order to try to fight him, following the orders he had received from Danamo. The young prince also drew his saber, in such a proud manner that Ormod repented of his enterprise more than once; but Parcin Parcinet, who perceived Irolite all in tears and softened by that sight, made his fourth wish.

Immediately, a great fire that rose up almost to the clouds separated Parcin Parcinet and his enemy. That fire made Ormond and his troop retreat. The young prince and Irolite, still followed by the faithful slave and the sage Mana, found themselves in a palace the sight of which initially caused young Irolite a great deal of fear. It was entirely composed of fire, but she was entirely reassured when she perceived that that she did not feel any heat more ardent than that of the sun, and that the fire only had the brilliance and the flame of the one she feared without having all the other qualities that rendered it insupportable.

A large number of young and beautiful persons clad in garments that appeared to be undulating flames came to receive the princess and her lover. One of them, whom they judged to be the queen of the realm by virtue of the respect that was rendered to her, said to them:

"Come, charming Princess, and you, handsome Parcin Parcinet; you are in the realm of the Salamanders; I am its Queen, and it is with pleasure that I am charged with hiding you in my palace for seven days in accordance with the orders of Favorable; I only wish that your sojourn here could be of longer duration."

After these words they were taken into a huge apartment, made of fire like the rest of the palace, and which shone with a brighter light than that of the sun. That evening, in the queen's abode, there was a very delicate and well-prepared supper; after the meal they went on to a terrace, in order to watch a firework display of marvelous beauty and very singular design, which was held in a large courtyard of the salamanders' palace. Twelve amours were on as many columns of differently colored marble; six of them appeared to be ready to fire arrows, and the other six were sustaining a large cartouche, on which these words were written in letters of fire:

> *The beautiful Irolite in this place*
> *Has victory for her share,*
> *However ardent our fires might be,*
> *The one that shines in her eyes*
> *Burns better, and pleases more.*

Young Irolite blushed at her own glory, and Parcin Parcinet was delighted that they found her to be as beautiful as she appeared in his own eyes. Meanwhile, the amours fired arrows of fire, which crossed paths in the air, forming in a thousand places the monogram and the beautiful name of Irolite, and raising it as high as the sky.

The seven days that they remained in the palace were spent in pleasures. Parcin Parcinet remarked that all the salamanders had intelligence and a charming vivacity, and that they were all gallant and amorous; even the queen did not seem exempt from that passion, for a young salamander of marvelous beauty.

On the eighth day they emerged with regret from an abode in such conformity with their tenderness. They found themselves in a beautiful country. Parcin Parcinet looked at his ring and found that on the four metals, mixed together, these words were engraved:

You have wished too soon.

Those words afflicted the prince and the young princess, but they were so close to Favorable's dwelling that they hoped to be able to arrive there that very day. That thought suspended their dolor; they went on, invoking Fortune and Amour, but those are often infidel guides.

Parcin Parcinet was finally close to entering Favorable's lands, but Ormond, following the fay's orders, was not far from the place where the fire had separated them; he had camped behind a wood and sentinels that he had placed on perpetual guard came to warn him that the prince and the princess had just reappeared in the plain. Had his men mount up, and caught up with the unfortunate prince and the divine Irolite that evening.

Parcin Parcinet was not frightened by the large number of those who were attacking him all at the same time. He ran at them with a valor that frightened them.

"I am keeping my promise, beautiful Irolite," he said, drawing his saber. "I shall die for you, or deliver you from your enemies."

After those words he struck the first who presented himself before him and laid him at his feet; but—an unexpected dolor—the marvelous saber that he had obtained from the fay shattered into a thousand pieces. That was what Danamo had anticipated of the young prince's combat when she gave him weapons; she had charmed them in a particular manner, so that they could not be used against her; the first blow they struck caused them to break into smithereens.

Disarmed, Parcin Parcinet could not resist for long; numbers overwhelmed him; he was captured and laden with chains, and young Irolite had the same destiny.

"Oh, Fay Favorable," cried the Prince, sadly, "abandon me to all Danamo's rigors, but save the beautiful Irolite."

"You have disobeyed the fay," replied a young man of surprising beauty who appeared in the air. "It is necessary for you to bear the penalty; if you had not been prodigal with the aid of Favorable today, we would have saved you forever from the cruelties of Danamo. The entire empire of the sylphs is afflicted by not having the glory of rendering such a charming prince and such a beautiful princess happy."

After those words, he disappeared, and Parcin Parcinet groaned then at his imprudence; he seemed insensible to his own misfortunes, but he resented those of Irolite keenly; the regret of having contributed to them would have made him die of dolor if Destiny had not resolved to make him suffer the most cruel punishments.

Young Irolite gave evidence of a courage worthy of the illustrious blood from which she was descended, and the pitiless Ormond, far from being softened by a spectacle so touching, tried to redouble the misfortune that he was causing her. He caused them to be conducted separately, and took away from them by that means the sad sweet sadness of lamenting together a misfortune without remedy.

After a journey so cruel, they arrived at the Court of the evil fay; she felt a malign joy on seeing the prince and the young princess in a state so worthy of giving birth to pity in any other soul than hers. Azire felt some for Parcin Parcinet but she dared not express it in front of the fay.

"I shall, therefore," said the cruel queen, addressing the young prince, "have the pleasure of avenging myself for your ingratitude. Instead of mounting the throne that my generosity had destined for you, go into the Prison of the Sea, where I shall end your unhappy life in frightful tortures."

"I prefer the most frightful prison," said the prince, looking at her proudly, "to the favors of a queen as unjust as you."

Those words irritated the fay further. She had expected to see him humiliated at her feet. She had him taken to the prison she had destined for him.

Irolite wept on seeing him leave; Azire could not retain her sighs; and the entire court groaned in secret at an order so pitiless.

As for the beautiful Irolite, the queen had her taken back to the castle where she had lived for such a long time, had her guarded with care, and treated her with all the inhumanity of which she was capable.

The prison to which the prince was taken was a frightful tower in the middle of the sea, built on a little desert island, and he was locked up there, charged with irons, and treated with all the harshness imaginable. What an abode for a prince worthy of ruling the entire world! The memory of Irolite was his sole occupation; he only appealed to Favorable to help his dear Princess, and he wished a thousand times a day to die, in order to expiate alone the fault that he had committed.

His faithful slave was locked in the same prison, but he did not have the satisfaction of serving his illustrious master; Parcin Parcinet only had with him grim soldiers devoted to the fay, who, while obeying her, nevertheless could not help respecting the unfortunate Parcin Parcinet. His youth, his beauty and, above all, his courage, touched them with admiration, which made them regard the prince as a strong man, above others.

The sage Mana was treated in Irolite's castle like the prince's slave in the Prison of the Sea. Only Danamo's women approached the princess, and on the fay's orders they heaped her continuously with further dolor by relating the sufferings of Parcin Parcinet. The prince's woes made Irolite forget the memory of her own, and everything renewed her tears in a place where she had so often seen the charming prince swearing an eternal fidelity to her.

Alas, she said to herself, *had you only been less constant, my dear Prince, your infidelity would have cost me my life; but what would it matter? You would be living happily, after three months of suffering.*

One morning, Danamo, who had spent the time making a charm of extraordinary power, sent Irolite two lamps, one of gold and the other of crystal; the one of gold was lighted, and Danamo had her given an order always to keep one of the two lamps lit, but she was told that she could light them in accordance with her choice. Irolite replied with her natural meekness that she would obey, without even seeking to comprehend what the fay's command signified. She carried the two lamps carefully into a cabinet; the one of gold was lit and did not go out all that day, and the next day she lit the other; she continued thus to obey the fay.

She had kept the lamps for fifteen days when her health began to deteriorate; she did not doubt for a moment that her dolor was the cause, and she was told, in order to redouble her distress, that Parcin Parcinet was very ill. What news for Irolite! Her intense dolor and dejection softened all the women who were with her. One evening, when they were all asleep, one of them approached the princess quietly and, seeing her light the crystal lamp, she said: "What are you doing, great Princess? Extinguish that fatal light; your days are attached to it; save such a beautiful life from the cruelties of Danamo."

"Alas," said the sad Irolite, in a languid fashion, "she has rendered my life so unhappy that it is a kind of favor on the part of the fay to give me the means of ending it." A moment later, however, she continued, with an emotion that brought beautiful colors to her face: "But what life is the golden lamp menacing, the light of which I take the same care to maintain?"

"The days of Parcin Parcinet," replied Danamo's confidante, for she was speaking to the princess by her order; the evil fay wished to torment her by informing her of what her cruel destiny was.

At that news, the dolor of having to take care of herself by terminating the days of Parcin Parcinet caused her to fall unconscious for a long time. She came to, and, in recovering her senses, she also recovered all her despair.

"Odious fay," she said, when she had the strength to speak, "barbaric fay, my death is not sufficient for your fury, you also want to make a prince who is so dear to me, and is so worthy of the most perfect and the most mutual love, perish by my hand. But death, a thousand times gentler than you, will soon deliver me from all the woes that your rage can invent against a passion so violent and so faithful."

The young princess wept incessantly over the fatal lamp that was attached to the days of Parcin Parcinet, and only lit her own henceforth; she watched it burn joyfully, as a sacrifice that she was making to her amour and to her lover.

160

Meanwhile, the prince was tormented by tortures that all his courage could not resist. The fay had had one of the soldiers guarding him in his prison, and who pretended be sensible to the dolors of the illustrious prince, tell him that Irolite had consented to marry Prince Ormond a few days after he had been taken to the frightful prison in which he was still groaning, that the princess seemed content after her marriage, that she had been present at all the fêtes that had been held to celebrate it, and finally, and that she had departed with her husband.

That was the only dolor that the prince had not expected, and it was also the only one that could possibly be stronger than his constancy.

"What, my dear Irolite," said the sad prince, "you are Ormond's? You have not even lamented my misfortunes? You have only thought of ending those that my tenderness caused you? Live happily, ingrate Irolite. I still adore you, inconstant as you are, and I want to die for my amour, since you have not wanted me to have the glory of dying for my princess."

While the unfortunate Parcin Parcinet was afflicting himself thus, and the tender Irolite was giving her life to prolong her lover's, Danamo was touched by Azire's despair. She was dying of dolor for the woes of Parcin Parcinet. Finally, the cruel fay, who saw clearly that, in order to save her daughter's life, it was necessary to pardon the prince, allowed her to see him, and to promise him all the wealth for which he had once hoped, provided that he would marry her; and the fay resolved to kill Irolite as soon as the prince had accepted those propositions.

The hope of seeing Parcin Parcinet again rendered life to the sad Azire, and the queen permitted her to send to Irolite's castle for the golden lamp, which she wanted to keep herself in order to be more assured that it would not be lit. That order appeared more cruel than all the others that afflicted Irolite.

"What anxiety for the life of Parcin Parcinet!" said the women who were with her. "Don't worry so much; he's going to marry Princess Azire, and it's because she is careful of his life that she has just sent for the lamp to which his life is attached."

The torment of jealousy had been lacking the woes of the unfortunate Irolite. After those words she sensed it born within her heart.

Meanwhile, Azire went to see the prince, in order to offer him marriage and her kingdoms. Then, pretending to be unaware that he had learned that Irolite had married Ormond, she tried to convince him by means of that example that he had pushed confidence too far.

Parcin Parcinet, to whom nothing was precious without the charming Irolite, preferred prison and his woes to liberty and empires. Azire was in despair at that refusal and her dolor rendered her as unhappy as him.

In the meantime, the fay Favorable, who until then had made a glory of the insensibility of her heart, had been unable to resist the charms of a young prince who was then shining in her Court and was in love with her. At first Favorable could not resolve to let him hear that the pride of her soul had allowed itself to be vanquished by his care. Finally, she yielded to the desire no longer to leave him unaware of his triumph. The pleasure of speaking to the person one loves then appeared to her to be so charming and so worthy of being desired that, approving of the fault that she had criticized so much, she came diligently to the aid of Parcin Parcinet and the beautiful Irolite.

A little later and she would no longer have had the time to aid them; Irolite's fatal lamp was due to run out in ten days, and Parcin Parcinet's dolor was near to ending his life.

Favorable arrived in Danamo's palace; her power was well above her rival's, and she had herself obeyed in spite of the anger of the wicked fay. The prince was taken out of his prison, but he only came out after being assured by Favorable that the beautiful Irolite could still be his. In spite of his pallor he appeared more handsome than the daylight that he had just seen again. He went with the fay Favorable to the princess's castle. The lamp was now only giving off a feeble light, but the dying Irolite did not want to consent to its being extinguished until she had been assured of the fidelity of her fortunate lover.

There is no expression vivid enough and tender enough to express the perfect joy they felt on seeing one another again. Favorable enabled them to recover all their charms in a moment, and endowed them with a long life and a constant happiness, but could find nothing to add to their tenderness.

Danamo, furious in seeing her authority overturned, killed herself. The fate of Azire and that of Ormond were placed by the prince in Irolite's hands; she only wanted to avenge herself by marrying them to one another forever. Parcin Parcinet, as generous as he was faithful, only wanted to recover his father's kingdom, and allowed Azire to reign in Danamo's.

The marriage of the Prince and the divine Irolite was made with an infinite magnificence, and after having expressed their gratitude to Favorable and heaping the slave and the sage Mana with benefits, they departed for their kingdom, where the Prince and the lovable Irolite enjoyed the rare happiness of always burning with a amour that was as tender and as constant in tranquil good fortune as it had been ardent and faithful during their misfortunes.

Charlotte-Rose Caumont de La Force: *More Beautiful than a Fay*

There was once a king in Europe who, having already had several children by a princess that he had married, had a desire to travel and go from one end of his kingdom to the other. He stopped agreeably in various provinces, and when he was in a beautiful castle at the extremity of his states, the queen, his wife, went into labor and gave life to a daughter, who seemed so prodigiously beautiful at the moment of her birth that the courtiers, either because of her beauty or the desire to pay court to her, named her More Beautiful than a Fay. The future made it very evident that she merited such an illustrious name.

The queen was scarcely on her feet again when it was necessary for her to follow the king, her husband, who departed urgently to go and defend a distant province that his enemies were attacking. Little More Beautiful than a Fay was left with her governess and the ladies that were necessary to her. She was raised with a great deal of care, and as her father had to sustain a long and cruel war, she had the leisure to grow and be embellished. Her beauty rendered her famous throughout the surrounding lands; people talked about nothing else. At twelve years old she might have been mistaken for a divinity rather than a mortal person. One of her brothers came to see her during a truce and linked himself with her in a perfect amity.

However, the renown of her beauty and the name that she bore irritated the fays against her to such an extent that they thought about nothing but avenging themselves on her for the pride of her name and destroying a beauty that caused them so much jealousy.

The queen of the fays was not one of those good fays who are the protectors of virtue and who only take pleasure in doing good. After the passage of several centuries, when she had succeeded to her royalty by means of her great knowledge and her artifice, the number of her years had rendered her very small, and no one any longer called her anything but Nabote.[13]

Nabote therefore assembled her council and made it known to its members that she had resolved to avenge the many beautiful persons that she had in her court, and all those who were in the entire world, that she wanted to absent herself and go personally to see and steal the beauty that was causing so much talk disadvantageous to their charms.

Having said it, that was what she did. She departed, and, putting on simple clothes, she transported herself to the castle where the marvel was contained.

---

[13] i.e., Dwarf.

She soon made herself familiar there, and by means of her intelligence she persuaded the princess's ladies to receive her among them.

Nabote was struck by a great astonishment, however, when she realized, by the force of her art, after having studied the castle, that it had been constructed by a great magician, and that he had attached such virtue to it that people could only emerge voluntarily from its enclosure and its promenades, and it was not possible to make use of charms of any kind against its inhabitants.

That secret was not unknown to More Beautiful than a Fay's governess, who, knowing full well what a priceless treasure had been confided to her care, nevertheless loved her without dread, knowing that no one in the world could take the child away as long as she did not leave the castle or its gardens. She had forbidden her expressly to do that, and More Beautiful than a Fay, who already had a good deal of prudence, was careful not to fail in that precaution. A thousand lovers that she had made futile efforts to abduct her, but, living in security, she had no fear of any violence.

It did not take long for Nabote to insinuate herself into her good graces; she taught her to do beautiful needlework; during tasks that she rendered amusing, she told her little stories, and neglected nothing to entertain her. She pleased her so much that soon, neither of them was seen without the other.

In all these cares, Nabote was no less occupied with her vengeance; she was seeking a means to seduce More Beautiful than a Fay and to oblige her, by means of cunning, simply to set foot outside the threshold of the castle; she was always ready to make her move and kidnap her.

One day, when she had taken her into the garden, where young women, after having picked flowers, were ornamenting More Beautiful than a Fay's lovely head, Nabote opened a little door that opened to the countryside, and, having gone through it, she performed a hundred capers that made the princess and the young people with her laugh. Then, suddenly, the wicked Nabote pretended to feel ill, and a moment later she let herself fall, as if she had fainted. A few of the young women ran to help her; More Beautiful than a Fay hastened too.

Scarcely had the unfortunate princess passed through the fatal doorway than Nabote got up again, seized her with a powerful arm and, making a circle with her wand, formed a thick black fog. Although it dissipated immediately, the earth opened up and two moles with wings of rose-leaves emerged, drawing an ebony chariot. Nabote got into it with More Beautiful than a Fay, and it rose into the air, traveling with an incredible speed. It was swiftly lost to the sight of the young women, who, by their tears and their screams, soon announced to the entire castle the loss that it had just suffered.

More Beautiful than a Fay only recovered from her initial astonishment to fall into one more frightful; the rapidity with which the chariot flew through the air left her so dazed that she almost lost consciousness. Eventually, recovering her senses, she looked down; how terrified she was to find nothing beneath her but the prodigious extent of a vast sea!

She uttered a piercing scream and turned round. Seeing her dear Nabote close by she embraced her tenderly and clasped her tightly in her arms, as once does customarily to reassure oneself; but the fay pushed her away rudely.

"Get away, brazen child," she said to her. "Recognize in me your most mortal enemy. I am the Queen of the Fays; you are going to pay for the insolence of the name you bear."

More Beautiful than a Fay, more tremulous on hearing those words than if a thunderbolt had landed at her feet, was even more frightened by them than by the horrible route she was taking.

The chariot finally landed in the middle of the magnificent courtyard of the most superb palace that was ever seen.

The sight of such a beautiful place reassured the timid princess slightly, especially when, on emerging from the chariot, she saw a hundred young beauties, who came very courteously to make reverence to the fay. Such a cheerful abode did not seem to announce misfortune. She even had a consolation, which could not fail to be welcome in a misfortune as great as hers; she noticed that all those beautiful persons were struck with admiration as they looked at her, and she heard a confused murmur of praise and envy, which gave her a marvelous satisfaction.

But that moment of vanity did not last long! Nabote ordered imperiously that More Beautiful than a Fay's beautiful clothes should be taken away, believing that that would rob her of a part of her charms. She was therefore stripped, but Nabote's fury only increased in consequence. What beauties came to light! What confusion for Fay society!

She was dressed in wretched rags, but one might have thought that simple and naïve beauty was determined to triumph in that state over the most ostentatious display; she had never been more charming.

Nabote ordered that she be taken to the place that she had organized for her, and given her task.

Two fays took hold of her and escorted her to the most sumptuous and beautiful apartments that could ever be seen. More Beautiful than a Fay considered them; in spite of the sight of her misery she said to herself: *Whatever torments are being prepared for me, my heart tells me that I shall not always be unhappy in this beautiful place.*

She was made to go down a large black marble staircase, which had more than a thousand steps; she thought she was going into the bowels of the earth, or that she was being taken to Hell. Finally, she went into a small cabinet paneled in ebony, where she was told that she would sleep on a little straw, and where there was an ounce of bread and a cup of water for her supper. From there she was taken into a large gallery, the walls of which were made of black marble from top to bottom, and which only received illumination from five lamps made of jet, which emitted a somber glow, more capable of inducing alarm than reassurance. Those sad walls were hung with cobwebs from top to bottom, the fatality of which was such that the more one removed them, the more they multiplied.

The two fays told the princess that the gallery had to be cleaned by daybreak, or else she would be made to suffer frightful tortures. Placing a ladder in her hands and giving her a rush broom, they told her to get to work, and left her to it.

More Beautiful than a Fay sighed, and, not knowing the fate of the cobwebs, even though the gallery was huge, she decided courageously to obey the order. She took her broom and climbed the ladder nimbly. But—Oh God!—imagine her surprise when, thinking that she was clearing the marble and getting rid of the cobwebs, she found that they only increased. She soon wearied, and, seeing sadly that her efforts were futile, she threw away the broom, came down, sat on the bottom step of the ladder and started to weep softly, aware of the extent of her misfortune.

Her sobs had become so precipitate, one after another, that she no longer had the strength to sustain her beautiful body, when, raising her head slightly, her eyes were struck by a bright light. The entire gallery was illuminated in an instant, and she saw a young boy on his knees before her, so handsome, so agreeable and so well-dressed that she mistook him for Amour. But she remembered that Amour was depicted nude, and the handsome boy had a coat covered with gems. She also suspected that all the light might be coming from his eyes, which she saw so beautiful and so brilliant.

The youth considered her, still on his knees, and she wanted to kneel down too.

"Who are you?" she asked him, astonished. "Are you a god? Are you Amour?

"I'm not a god," he replied, "but I have more amour in myself alone than there is in Heaven or on earth. I'm Phraates,[14] the son of the queen of the fays, who loves you and wants to help you."

Then, taking the broom that she had thrown away, he touched all the cobwebs, which immediately became a golden fabric of marvelous workmanship; the glow of the lamps became bright and luminous, and Phraates gave the princess a golden key.

"You'll find a lock," he told her, "in the paneling of your cell; open it very quietly. I'll go, for fear of rendering myself suspect; go and rest, you'll find everything you need. Adieu."

And, putting one knee on the floor, he kissed her hand respectfully.

---

[14] Phraates was the name of several kings of ancient Parthia; the name would have been familiar in the salons of Louis XIV's court because of the publicity given to it there by Bossuet's history of the world.

More Beautiful than a Fay, more astonished by that encounter than by anything that had happened to her during the day, went back into the little room and tried to find the lock that had been mentioned to her.

On approaching the paneling, she heard a voice, the most likeable in the world, which seemed to be lamenting dolorously; she thought that it was an unfortunate like herself who was being tormented. She listened curiously.

"Alas, what can I do?" said the voice. "They want me to change the acorns in this basket into Oriental pearls."

More Beautiful than a Fay, less surprised by that than she would have been two hours before, knocked on the wood two or three times and said, quite loudly: "If punishments are inflicted here, miracles are also worked; don't give up hope. But tell me, I beg you, who you are, and I'll tell you who I am."

"It's more pleasant for me to satisfy you, "replied the other, "than to continue my employment. I'm the daughter of a king; it's said that I was born charming; the fays were not present at my birth, and you know that they are cruel to those they don't take under their protection at birth."

"I know that only too well," said More Beautiful than a Fay. "I'm beautiful like you, the daughter of a king, and unfortunate, because I'm lovable without the aid of their gifts."

"We're companions, then?" said the other. "But are you in love?"

"There has scarcely been time," said More Beautiful than a Fay to herself, in a low voice, but she went on, loudly: "Go on, and don't ask me any more questions."

"I was deemed," the other went on, "to be the most charming thing that there had ever been; everyone loved me and wanted to possess me. I was named Desire; all wills were submissive to me and I had a place in all hearts. A young prince, more smitten with me than any other, attached himself uniquely to me; I filled him with hope and satisfaction. We were going to unite ourselves forever when the fays, jealous of seeing me the object of universal passion and unable to tolerate the charms that they had not bestowed, abducted me one day in the midst of my glory and put me here in a vile place. They have told me that they will strangle me tomorrow morning if I haven't carried out a ridiculous order that they've imposed on me. Now tell me who you are."

"I'll have told you everything," replied More Beautiful than a Fay, "when I've told you my name, which is More Beautiful than a Fay."

"You must be very beautiful, then, said Princess Desire. "I have a great desire to see you.

"I have as much desire for my part," replied More Beautiful than a Fay. "Is there a door that opens in this wall, for I have a little key that might be useful to you?"

While searching, she found one, which she was, indeed, able to open. She pushed it, and, suddenly appearing to one another, they were both greatly surprised by the marvelous beauty that they each possessed.

After they had embraced one another fervently, and saying many obliging things, More Beautiful than a Fay started laughing on seeing that Princess Desire was constantly rubbing her acorns with a little white stone, as she had been ordered to do. She told her about the task that she had been given to do, and how a kind unknown force had assisted her miraculously.

"But what can it be?" Princes Desire asked her.

"I believe it's a man," replied More Beautiful than a Fay.

"A man!" cried Desire. "You're blushing; you love him!"

"Not yet," she replied, "but he told me that he loves me, and if he loves me, as he says, he'll help you."

Scarcely had she spoken those words than the basket shivered, agitating the acorns, as the oak from which they had been collected might have done. They suddenly changed into the most beautiful pear-shaped pearls, of the highest clarity; it was one of them of which Cleopatra made such a rich banquet for Mark Antony.

The two princesses were very content with that change, and More Beautiful than a Fay, who was beginning to get accustomed to prodigies, took Desire by the hand, and drew her into her room. There she found the panel that contained the lock that had been mentioned to her; she opened it with the golden key and went into a room whose magnificence surprised and impressed her, because she saw evidence of the cares of her lover everywhere therein. It was strewn with the most beautiful flowers and exhaled a divine perfume.

At one of the ends of the charming room there was a table covered with everything that could content delicacy of taste, and two fountains of liquid that flowered into porphyry basins. The young princesses sat down in two ivory chairs enriched with emeralds. They ate with appetite, and when they had supped, the table disappeared. In the place where it had been, a delightful bath appeared, into which they both climbed. A few steps away they saw a superb dressing-room containing large hampers with gold clasps, full of linen so clean that it communicated a desire to make use of it.

A bed of singular form and extraordinary richness terminated the marvelous room, which was bordered by orange-trees in golden pots garnished with rubies and cornelian columns that sustained the sumptuous vault all around its perimeter; they were only separated by huge crystal mirrors that extended from the floor to the ceiling. A few small tables in rare materials supported vases of precious stone full of flowers of all kinds.

Princess Desire admired her companion's good fortune. Turning toward her, she said: "Your lover is gallant; he can do a great deal, and he wants to do everything for you. Your luck is uncommon."

A pendulum clock chiming midnight caused them to hear the name of Phraates at every stroke. More Beautiful than a Fay blushed, and threw herself on to her bed; she thought she would seek repose, which was troubled by the image of Phraates.

The next day there was a great astonishment in the fay court, on seeing the gallery so richly decorated and the beautiful pearls filling the basket. They had thought that they would be able to punish the young princesses; their cruelty was disconcerted, and they found each of them withdrawn to her little room.

Agitating their council again to give them further tasks in which they would see them defeated, they told Desire to go to the sea shore and write in the sand, with the express order that what she wrote would never be effaced, and they commanded More Beautiful than a Fay to go to the foot of Mount Adventurous, fly up to the summit and bring them back a vase full of the water of immortality. To that effect, they gave her feathers and wax in order for her to make wings and doom herself like another Icarus.

Desire and More Beautiful than a Fay looked at one another after that frightful command, embraced one another tenderly, and separated, as if saying their final adieu. One was escorted to the shore and the other to the foot of Mount Adventurous.

When More Beautiful than a Fay was alone, she took the feathers and the wax and assembled them as best she could. After she had toiled fruitlessly, her thoughts turned to Phraates. "If you love me," she said, "you'll come to my aid again."

Scarcely had she finished the last word than she saw him before her eyes, a thousand times more handsome than the previous night. Broad daylight was very advantageous to him.

"Do you doubt my love?" he said. "Is anything difficult for someone who loves you."

Then he asked her to take off some of her clothes and, having taken his usual recompense, which was a kiss on her hand, he suddenly transformed himself into an eagle. She experienced some chagrin in seeing that lovable figure change in that fashion, but he placed himself at her feet, spreading his wings, and easily made her understand his design. She lowered herself on to him, and put her beautiful arms around his superb neck. He rose gently into the air. One would not have been able to say which of them was the most content: her, in evading death by carrying out the order given to her; or him, in being charged with such a precious burden.

He carried her gently to the top of the mountain, where she heard an agreeable harmony of a thousand birds, which came to render homage to the divine bird that had carried her. The top of the mountain was a florid plain surrounded by beautiful cedars, in the middle of which was a little stream, the silvery waters of which flowed over golden sand strewn with brilliant diamonds. More Beautiful than a Fay knelt down and, before anything else, she put her hand in the precious water and drank some of it. After that she filled her vase and turned to her eagle.

"Oh," she said, "how I wish that Desire had some of this water!"

Scarcely had she said that than the eagle flew down, picked up one of More Beautiful than a Fay's slippers, came back to fill it with water, and went to take it to Princess Desire on the sea shore, where she was employed in writing on that arena, futilely.

The eagle came back to find More Beautiful than a Fay and resumed his beautiful burden.

"Alas," she said, "what is Desire doing? Bring us together."

He obeyed. They found her still writing, but as she wrote, a wave came to efface what she had written.

"What cruelty," said the princess to More Beautiful than a Fay, "to order me to do what cannot be done. I judge by the strange mount that I see you astride that you've succeeded."

More Beautiful than a Fay got down and, touched by her companion's misfortune, she turned to her lover and said: "Show me your omnipotence."

"Or rather my love," retorted the prince, reverting to his ordinary form.

Desire, seeing the beauty and the grace of his person, made surprise and joy shine in her eyes.

More Beautiful than a Fay blushed, and with an involuntary movement, she placed herself in front of him in order to hide him from her companion. "Do as you're told," she continued, with a charming anxiety.

Phraates, aware of his good fortune, and wanting to terminate her embarrassment, said: "Read," and disappeared more rapidly than a flash of lighting.

At the same moment a wave came to break at More Beautiful than a Fay's feet, and, on retreating, allowed her to see a bronze tablet mounted in the arena, as if it had been there for all eternity and as if it would still be there until the end of the world. As she looked at it she saw letters that were formed, profoundly engraved, which composed these lines:

> *The faith of vulgar lovers,*
> *Their ardor and all their oaths,*
> *Are only written in sand,*
> *But what one senses for your lovely eyes*
> *In characters of starlight, is written in the skies;*
> *Whoever tried to erase it would strive in vain.*

"I understand," exclaimed Desire. "Whoever loves you must love forever. How well your obliging lover expresses his tenderness!" Then she embraced More Beautiful than a Fay, who, dissipating in her arms the slight jealousy she had just felt, confessed to her friend the conflict that had taken place, and, both satisfied in their amity, they abandoned themselves to an agreeable conversation full of sincerity.

Queen Nabote sent someone to the foot of the mountain to discover what had become of More Beautiful than a Fay. Nothing was found but scattered feathers and some of her clothes; it was judged that she had been crushed, as desired.

Thinking that, the fays hastened to the sea shore. They cried out on seeing the bronze tablet, and were frightened on seeing the two princesses enjoying themselves tranquilly on a spur of rock. They called out to them; More Beautiful than a Fay gave them her water of immortality and laughed softly, along with Desire, at the fays' fury.

The queen did not see the joke; she knew that an art as great as her own had assisted them, and her rage increased to such a point that, without hesitation, she decided on their complete ruination by the last and most cruel of proofs.

Desire was condemned to go the following day to the Fair of Time, in order to obtain the make-up of youth, and More Beautiful than a Fay to go to the Forest of Marvels, in order to capture the hind with the silver hooves.

Princess Desire was taken to a great plain, on the edge of which was a prodigious building divided into halls and galleries full of boutiques so superb that in order to find a comparison one had to remember the magnificent banks of Marly.[15] In each of those boutiques there were young and agreeable fays, and next to them, to assist them, the persons they loved the most.

As soon as Desire appeared, her beauty charmed everyone; she took possession of all hearts. In the first boutiques she went into, she excited great pity when she asked for the make-up of youth; no one wanted to tell her where it could be found, because, when it was not a fay who came in search of it, a torture was designated for the person charged with that dangerous commission.

The good fays told Desire to turn back and not to ask any longer for what she was seeking. She was so beautiful that everyone ran toward her wherever she went. Her bad luck brought her to the boutique of a malevolent fay. Scarcely had she asked for the make-up of youth on the part of the queen of the fays than, launching a terrible glance at her, she told her that she had it and would give it to her the next day, and ordered her to go into a room to wait while it was being prepared. But she was put into a dark and stinking place where she could not see anything. She was gripped by terror.

"Ah!" she said. "Obliging lover of More Beautiful than a Fay, hasten to help me, or I'm doomed."

He was either deaf to her voice or incapable of acting in that place as he had done in others. Desire was in torment for part of the night, and slept for the rest. She was woken up by an agreeable young woman, who told her, while bringing her a little nourishment, that she had come on behalf of the favorite of the fay who was her mistress, who had resolved to help her; that she would be fortunate if that happened, because the fay had sent for an evil spirit, in order

---

[15] There was a so-called *banque* [bank, in the financial sense], associated with retail establishments, in Marly, where Louis XIV's court frequently employed the Château de Marly as a base before the completion of the Palais de Versailles.

that he might come to blow ugliness into her nose, and in that deformed and ignominious state she would send her back to the queen of the fays in order to serve for the triumph of her resentments.

Princess Desire thought she would die of fright at the threat of suddenly losing all her charms, and she wished that she might die. Her torment was horrible, she was groping her way around her dark abode when someone took her by the arm and she felt a very tender emotion in her heart. She was taken toward a little light, and when her sight was restored it was struck by the most charming object of all. She recognized the dear prince that loved her so much, from whom she had been separated on the eve of her wedding.

Her transports and joys were extreme. "Is it really you?" she said, a hundred times.

Finally, when she was fully convinced, forgetting all her present misfortunes, she continued: "But is it you who are the favorite of that wretched fay? Is it with that fine title that I see you?"

"Have no doubt about it," he replied, "And we shall owe to her the end of all our troubles and our good fortune."

Then he told her that, in despair at her abduction, he had gone to find a sage, who had told him where she was, and that he would only ever recover her from the realm of the fays; that he had given him the means to find her, but that he had been stopped initially by the cruel fay, who had fallen in love with him; that, following the advice of his sage, he had amused her and, by his tenderness, had rendered himself so much the master of her mind that he retained all her treasures and was the minister of all her desires; that she had just departed on a voyage of six thousand leagues and would not be back for twelve days, so it was necessary to run away; that he had gone to her cabinet to take a fragment of the stone of the ring of Gyges, which she put on in order that she could go anywhere she liked invisibly; that, as for himself, he could show himself freely.

"Don't forget the make-up of youth," she said to him. "I want to put it on and give it to a companion I have."

The prince laughed.

"Where are we going" she asked.

"To the home of the queen of the fays," he said.

"Not that!" she cried. "We'll perish there."

"The sage who advises me," he went on, "told me to take you back to the last place from which you had departed if I wanted to ensure my happiness; he has never lied to me about anything whatsoever."

"All right," said Desire. "Let's go, then."

The prince gave her a precious box that contained the make-up of youth, and in the desire to appear more beautiful in her lover's eyes she rubbed it on her face precipitately, forgetting that she was invisible because of the stone he had given her. She took him by the arm. They traversed the entire fair in that fashion, and went all the way to the queen's palace.

There the prince took back the stone of Gyges. The amiable Desire showed herself and he became invisible, to the great regret of the princess, whose arm he took in his turn, and they went into Nabote's court.

All the fays gazed with a marvelous astonishment on seeing Desire return with the make-up of youth, and the queen frowned.

"Let her be strictly guarded," she said. "Our cleverness is vain; it's necessary to cause her death without going about it in such a roundabout way."

That was the sentence pronounced. Desire trembled with fear on hearing it; her lover reassured her as best he could.

But let us return to More Beautiful than a Fay. She had been taken to the Forest of the Marvelous; and this is why she had been required to hunt the hind with the silver hooves.

There had once been a queen of the fays who had succeeded to that great title naturally; she was beautiful, good and wise; she had had several lovers, whose love and cares were wasted in her regard; uniquely occupied in protecting her virtue, she did not amuse herself listening to the sighs of lovers. There was one of them whom her rigors rendered most unhappy, because he loved her more than any of the others. One day, seeing that he could not bend her, he protested to her in his despair that he would kill himself; she was unmoved by that threat and considered it as one of those follies by which the minds of men are often attained but which do not go any further. However, some time afterwards he threw himself into the sea.

A sage who had brought up the young man complained to the supreme intelligences, and the chaste fay was condemned to be a hind for a hundred years, as a penance for her rigor, unless an accomplished beauty who wanted to risk hunting for ten days in the Forest of Marvels could capture her and return her to her original form. Nearly forty years had already passed since she had been transformed.

In the beginning, several beauties had taken the risk of attempting such a bold adventure, which promised so much glory, each of them believing that they would be the most fortunate; but as none of them had come back, after ten years no more mention was heard of it, the ardor having cooled, and no beauty had been seen to offer herself for a long time, so that those who had been taken there since had only gone by order of the fays, in order to abandon them to certain death.

It was also to get rid of More Beautiful than a Fay that she was taken to the Forest of Marvels. She was given a small provision of food, purely for form's sake, and a silken rope with a noose, with which to catch the hind. That was the whole of her hunting equipment.

She set down what she had been given at the foot of a tree, and when she saw that she was alone she directed her sight into the vast forest, in whose profound silence and solitude she could only see an object of despair.

She wanted to remain on the edge of the forest and not go any deeper into it, and in order to get her bearings she marked the place from which she departed. She was abused, however, one always went astray in that forest, without being able to get out of it.

She perceived the hind with the silver hooves walking gravely along a trail, and went after her with her rope in hand, thinking she could capture her, but the hind ran, sensing that she was pursued, stopping from time to time and turning her head toward More Beautiful than a Fay. They were together all day without getting any closer to one another, and night separated them.

The poor huntress found herself very weary and very hungry, but she did not know where the meager provisions she had been given were, and she could not obtain any repose because of the hard ground. She lay down under a tree, very sadly; she could not sleep for long; she was too scared; the slightest sound frightened her, an agitated leaf making her tremble. She turned over and over in that wretched state, her thoughts directed toward her lover. She appealed to him several times, and, seeing that he was lacking when she was in such great need, she shed a few tears and said to herself: "Oh, Phraates, Phraates, have you abandoned me?"

She was falling asleep when she felt an agitation beneath her, and it seemed to her that she was in the best bed in the world. Her slumber lasted a long time without being interrupted. She was woken up in the morning by the song of a thousand nightingales, and, turning her beautiful eyes, she saw that she was two feet above the ground; the grass had grown under her beautiful body and had acquired the virtue of making a delightful couch. A huge orange tree extended its branches over her to serve as an awning; she was covered with flowers. Alongside her, two turtle-doves announced to her, by means of their love, that she ought to put her hope in Phraates' amour. The ground around her was covered with strawberries and all kinds of the most excellent fruits; she ate some, and found herself as sated and as strong as the finest meat would have achieved. A stream that was running nearby served to slake her thirst.

"Oh, cares of my lover," she exclaimed, when she was fully satisfied, "how necessary you were to me. I won't murmur any more, but don't give me so much, and show yourself."

She would have continued if she had not seen the hind with the silver feet, sitting on her hindquarters and gazing at her tranquilly. She thought she had her this time; she presented her with a handful of grass in one hand, and held her rope in the other, but the hind drew away with short bounds, and when she had covered a short distance she stopped and looked at her.

They played that game all day.

Night fell, and she spent it as she had the one before.

The awakening was like the first, and four days and four nights passed in the same fashion.

Finally, on the fifth morning, More Beautiful than a Fay, on opening her eyes, thought that she was seeing a light brighter than daylight when she perceived in her lover's eyes the amour that she had inspired in him. He was sitting beside her and kissing the tip of her foot. His presence and his respectful action pleased her a great deal.

"It's you then?" she said. "If I haven't seen you in recent days, at least I've received marks of your generosity."

"Say my amour, More Beautiful than a Fay," he said. "My mother suspects that it's me who is helping you, and she has me guarded. I escaped briefly, thanks to a friendly fay. Adieu; I only came to reassure you; you'll see me his evening, and if Fortune wishes it, we'll be happy tomorrow."

He went away, and again she hunted all day. When night fell, she perceived a little light nearby, which sufficed for her to look around for her lover.

"Here is my lighted wand," he said. "Hold it in front of you and go, without being frightened, wherever it takes you. When it stops, you'll find a large heap of dry leaves. Set fire to them, go into the place that you see, and if you find the remains of an animal there, burn it. Our friends the heavenly bodies will do the rest."

More Beautiful than a Fay would certainly have liked to receive more ample instructions, but, seeing that there was no remedy, she held the wand in front of her, which showed her the way. She walked for nearly two hours, rather bored with doing nothing but that. She finally stopped, and did, indeed, see a large heap of dry leaves, to which she did not fail to set fire.

The light was soon so bright that she was able to perceive a fairly high mountain, in which she perceived an opening partly hidden by brushwood. She parted it with her wand and went into a dark place. Soon afterwards, she found herself in a large hall ornamented with an admirable architecture and illuminated by several lights. What struck her with some astonishment, however, was seeing the skins of several wild and terrible beasts hanging from golden hooks, which she mistook at first for the beasts themselves. She turned her eyes away with some horror and they paused in the middle of the room, where there was a beautiful palm tree; and on one of the branches was the skin of the hind with the silver hooves.

More Beautiful than a Fay was delighted to see it, and, picking it up with her wand, she immediately took it to the fire that she had lit at the entrance to the lair. It was consumed in an instant. Returning to the hall, she penetrated into several more magnificent rooms. She stopped in one, where she saw several small beds standing on the Persian carpet, one of which was more beautiful than the others, under an awning of gold cloth. But she did not have the leisure to contemplate for long something that seemed so singular to her; she heard loud bursts of laughter and several people talking loudly.

More Beautiful than a Fay turned her steps in that direction. She went into a marvelous place where there were fifteen young women of divine beauty.

She did not surprise them any less than they surprised her; the excellence of her person charmed them all, and caused a suspension of all their senses. An attentive silence was followed by cries of admiration. But one of the beautiful women, more beautiful than all the rest, advanced with a jovial expression, laughing, toward the charming princess.

"You are my liberator," she said to her. "I cannot doubt it; no one enters here who has not put on the skin of one of the animals that you have seen at the entrance to this cavern; that has been the fate of all these beautiful persons you see beside me. After ten days of fruitless attempts to capture me, they were changed into animals during the day, and by night we recover our human faces. And if you had not liberated me, charming princess, you would have been changed into a white rabbit."

"A white rabbit!" cried More Beautiful than a Fay. "Oh, Madame, it's much better that I have conserved my ordinary form, and that such a marvelous person as you is no longer a hind."

"You have set all of us free," said the fay. "Let's spend the rest of the night joyfully, and tomorrow we shall go to the palace and fill the entire court with astonishment."

It is impossible to describe the delight that resounded in that charming dwelling and the excitement of all those beautiful young women who were about to enjoy the sweetness of living again, so to speak. They were all the same age at which they had commenced their hunt in the Forest of Marvels, and the oldest of them was not twenty years old.

The fay wanted to go to bed for three or four hours; she had More Beautiful than a Fay go to bed with her, and desired to know her adventure. She related it to her in such a touching fashion, her speech was so simple and truthful that the fay promised without reserve to serve her amour and render her happy. More Beautiful than a Fay did not forget to speak to her about Desire, and the fay was immediately favorable to her.

They went to sleep after a rather long conversation, which they interrupted agreeably with the charming caresses that they gave one another.[16]

The following day they all took the road to the palace, wanting to surprise the fays agreeably. They quit the Forest of Marvels without regret, and arrived at the palace quietly. When they were near the final courtyard they heard a thousand harmonious voices, which composed an excellent music.

"It's some kind of celebration," said the fay. "We've arrived at a good time."

And, on advancing, they found the courtyard filled with an incredible crowd.

---

[16] This is a remarkable passage to find in a story published in 1697, with a royal privilege.

They fay had the door opened and passed through it with her troop. The first to recognize her uttered cries to the heavens, and they were soon the subject of a great joy; but as they advanced further she was struck by a strange spectacle. She saw a young woman, more charming than the Graces and as fair as Venus, who was attached to a stake next to a pyre, where she was apparently about to be burned.

More Beautiful than a Fay uttered a loud scream, recognizing Desire, but she was very surprised when, at the same moment, she could no longer see her, and a young man appeared in her stead, so beautiful and so well-built that one could not weary of looking at him.

At that sight, More Beautiful than a Fay uttered a much louder scream, and, running without any further restraint, she threw her arms around him, crying a thousand times: "It's my brother!"

It was her brother, who was also the fortunate lover of Princess Desire, and who, fearing that she might die, had just given her the ring of Gyges in order to shield her from the cruelty of Queen Nabote. By that means, he had revealed himself.

While the brother and sister were giving one another that evidence of tenderness, the invisible Desire mingled hers with them, and her voice made itself heard although her body did not appear. All the fays, in an unparalleled astonishment, gave striking evidence in a thousand different fashions of their joy at seeing their virtuous queen again. The good fays came to throw themselves at her feet, kissing her hands and her garments. They wept, they lost the power of speech; each one expressed herself in accordance with her character. The bad fays, the partisans of Nabote, also hastened around her, and politics gave an air of sincerity to their false demonstrations.

Nabote herself, in despair at that return, constrained herself with an art of which she alone was capable. She was obliged to yield her power immediately to the veritable queen, who, in a grave and majestic manner, asked why the young woman she had seen merited such a torture, and since when had such a cruel death been solemnized by feasting and games. Nabote excused herself very poorly, and the queen was listening impatiently when Desire's lover spoke out.

"That princess was being punished," he said, "because she was too lovable. The princess my sister was tormented for the same reason. They were both born as you see them." Then he asked his mistress to take off the stone of Gyges, and she became visible. Having reappeared, Desire charmed everyone who saw her.

"They're beautiful," the prince went on, "they have a thousand virtues that they did not obtain from the fays; that is what has roused them and obliged them to persecute them. What injustice, to want to extend tyrannical power over everything that does not depend on you!"

The prince fell silent. The queen turned to the assembly with an agreeable expression. "I demand," she said, "that these three persons are given to me; they shall have the happiest of fates that mortals can have. I owe a great deal to More

Beautiful than a Fay and I shall recompense her for what she has done for me with the most constant happiness."

Turning toward Nabote, she continued: "You shall reign, Madame; this empire is large enough for you and me. Go to the beautiful isles, which will belong to you. Leave me your son; I shall associate him with my power and I want him to marry More Beautiful than a Fay; that union will reconcile us all."

Nabote was enraged by everything the queen ordered, but what could she do? She was not the stronger; she had no alternative but to obey. She was about to do so with an ill grace when the handsome Phraates was seen arriving, followed by a gallant company of youths which composed his court; he came to render his homages to the queen and to rejoice in her return. In passing however he glanced at More Beautiful than a Fay and enabled her to see, by his passionate gaze, that it was only his first duty,

The queen embraced him and introduced More Beautiful than a Fay to him, asking him to receive her hand. It was unnecessary to ask him whether he obeyed with joy, as he cried with delight:

> God of lovers you repay the confidence
>   Of a thousand amorous labors;
> You will become, to fulfill all my wishes,
>   My pleasure and my recompense.

The two marriages were celebrated on the same day; they were so happy that it was said that they were the only spouses who earned the golden vine, and that those of whom there has been mention since have only had the idea of it.

Thus, virtue triumphs over the misfortunes it provokes. Envy and jealousy only serve to make it shine, and the justice of heaven often permits it to be happy.

There is a destiny that watches over the conduct of humans, and enables them to overcome everything that tries to oppose her happiness.

> Born under a prosperous star,
> Without being fashioned by art;
> Everything will succeed for you, the cruelest affair
> Will be rendered good one day by a stroke of luck.
> Fortune overwhelms us for a while,
> But only to assist us better;
> Happiness makes itself taste better
> To those who remember a wretched state.
> A wicked fay displays her power,
> Always raising obstacles to virtue,
> In these times fays are no longer seen
> But one no longer sees miracles.

EXPLORERS 1697-1698

Marie-Catherine d'Aulnoy: *Green Worm*[17]

There was once a great queen who, having given birth to twin girls, invited a dozen fays of the neighborhood to come and see them and to endow them, as was the custom in those days—a very convenient custom, for the power of fays almost always repaired what nature had spoiled; but sometimes, it spoiled what nature had done well.

When the fays were all in the banqueting hall a magnificent meal was served to them. Everyone was about to sit down at table when Magotine came in; she was the sister of Carabosse, who was no less malevolent than her. At that sight, the queen shivered, fearing some disaster, for she had not invited her to come to the feast. Hiding her anxiety carefully, however, she went in quest herself of a green velvet armchair embroidered with sapphires. As she was the oldest of the fays, all the others moved aside to make room for her, and each one whispered: "Let's hasten to endow the little princesses, my sister, in order to forestall Magotine."

When she was offered an armchair she said rudely that she did not want one, and that she was big enough to eat standing up; but she was mistaken, for the table being a little high, she could not even see it, she was so small. She had a chagrin in consequence that augmented her ill humor further.

"Madame," the queen said to her "I beg you to take a place at the table."

"If you wanted to have me there," the fay replied, "You should have invited me, like the others; you only want pretty, benevolent and magnificent people like my sisters at your court; as for me, I'm too ugly and too old; but with that, I have no less power than them, and without boasting, perhaps I have more."

All the fays pressed her so much to go the table that she consented to it. First, a golden basket was placed on it with a dozen bouquets of gems inside; the first comers each took theirs, with the result that none remained for Magotine. She started to mutter between her teeth. The queen ran to her cabinet and brought her a casket of perfumed Spanish leather covered with rubies and filled

---

[17] The original title, *Serpentin vert*, could refer to anything green and serpentine; the noun often refers to a paper streamer or the coiled tube of a still, but it rarely refers to a snake (and the author deliberately avoided titling the tale *Le Serpent vert*). The creature in the story, although initially introduced as a snake, is possessed of wings and claws, and is thus clearly a kind of dragon, so I have preferred the translation "worm."

with diamonds; she begged her to receive it, but Magotine shook her head and said: "Keep your jewels, Madame, I have plenty of them; I only came to see whether you had thought about me, but you have neglected me greatly. With that she tapped the table with her wand, and all the meat with which it was laden was changed into fricasseed snakes; the fays were so horrified that they threw away their napkins and quit the feast.

While they were talking about the bad turn that Magotine had just done them, that barbaric little fay approached the cradle where the princesses were enveloped by sheets of golden cloth, and were the prettiest in the world. "I endow you, she promptly said to one, with being perfect in ugliness." She was about to give some malediction to the other when the fays, who were very emotional, came running and stopped her from doing so, with the consequence that the evil Magotine broke a glass panel and, passing through it like a flash of lightning, disappeared from sight.

The queen hardly felt the bounty of a few gifts that the benevolent fays were able to endow the princess; she only felt the dolor of finding herself the mother of the ugliest creature in the world. She took her in her arms and had the chagrin of seeing her become uglier from one moment to the next. She tried in vain to do herself violence in order not to weep in front of the fays, but she could not help it, and the pity they felt for her was immeasurable.

"What can we do, my sister?" they said to one another. "What can we do to console the queen?"

They held a great council, and then told her to listen less to her dolor, because there was a time marked where her daughter would be happy."

"But will she be beautiful?" the queen interrupted. "Will she be beautiful?"

"We can't explain ourselves further," they replied. "Let it suffice for you, Madame that your daughter will be content."

She thanked them very much, and did not fail to charge them with presents, for even though the fays are very rich, they always like to be given something, and that custom has passed since to all the people of the earth, without time having destroyed it.

The queen called her elder daughter Laidronnette the younger one Bellotte; their names suited them perfectly, for Laidronnette became so frightful that whatever intelligence she had, it was impossible to look at her; her sister was embellished, and appeared utterly charming, with the result that Laidronnette, having already reached twelve years of age, came to throw herself at the feet of the king and the queen to beg them to permit her to go and shut herself away in the Castle of Solitude in order to hide her ugliness and not desolate them any longer. They loved her in spite of her deformity, with the consequence that they had some difficulty consenting to it, but they still had Bellotte, and that was enough to console them.

Laidronnette asked the queen only to send her nurse with her and a few officers to serve her. You need have no fear, Madame," she said, "that anyone will abduct me; and I confess that, being made as I am, I would even like to avoid the light of day."

The king and queen accorded her what she wanted; she was taken to the castle she had chosen. It had been built several centuries before; the sea came all the way to beneath its windows, and served it as a moat. A vast nearby forest furnished promenades, and several meadows terminated the view. The princess played instruments and sang divinely well.

She remained in that agreeable solitude or two years, where she even wrote a few book of reflections, but the desire to see the king and queen again obliged her to mount a carriage and go to the court. She arrived as Princess Bellotte was about to be married; everyone was joyful. When they saw Laidronnette they had chagrined expressions; she was not embraced or caressed by any of her relatives, and for her only welcome she was told that she had grown even uglier.

She was advised not to appear at the ball, but that if she wanted to see it they would contrive some hole through which she could look. She replied that she had not come to dance or listen to violins; that she had been in the solitary castle for such a long time that she had been unable to help quitting it in order to render her respects to the king and queen; that she knew with a sharp dolor that they could not suffer her; and that she would therefore return to her desert, where the trees, the flowers and the springs did not reproach her for her ugliness when she approached them.

When the king and queen saw that she was so annoyed they told her that by doing some violence to themselves they could allow her to stay with them for a few days. As she had courage, however, she replied that she would have too much difficulty quitting them if she spent that time in such good company. They wanted her to go away too much to retain her, so they told her coldly that she was right.

Princess Bellotte gave her for a wedding present an old ribbon that she had worn all winter on her sleeve, and the king she was marrying gave her some purple taffeta with which to make a skirt. If she had followed her impulse she would have thrown the ribbon and the taffeta in the faces of the generous people who regaled her so poorly, but she had so much intelligence, sagacity and reason that she did not want to testify any bitterness; she departed, therefore, with her nurse to return to her castle, her heart so full of sadness that she made the entire journey without saying a word.

One day, when she was in one of the darkest paths of the forest, she saw a large green serpent under a tree, which raised its head and said to Laidronnette: "You're not the only unfortunate one; look at my horrible form, and know that I was born more beautiful than you."

The frightened princess only heard half those words; she fled, and did not dare to go out for several days, so fearful was she of a similar encounter. Finally, bored with being always alone in her room, she went downstairs in the evening and went to the sea shore.

She was walking slowly, thinking about her sad destiny, when she saw a small boat coming toward her, gilded and painted with a thousand different devices. The sail was gold brocade, the mast cedar-wood and the oars carambola. It seemed that hazard alone was navigating it, and when it stopped near the shore, the princess, curious to see all those beauties, climbed into it. She found it garnished with crimson velvet with a gold backcloth, and what served as nails were made of diamond.

Suddenly, the boat drew away from the shore. The princess, alarmed by the peril she was running, took the oars in order to try to go back, but her efforts were futile; the wind that was blowing elevated the waves and she lost sight of the land. No longer perceiving anything but the sky and the sea, she abandoned herself to fortune, convinced that it would scarcely be favorable to her, and that Magotine was doing her another bad turn.

It's necessary to die, she said to herself. *What secret movements make me fear death? Until now, alas, have I known any of the pleasures that can make it hated? My ugliness frightens even my nearest relatives; my sister is a great queen and I am relegated to the depths of a desert, where the only company I have found is a talking snake. Isn't it better for me to perish than to drag myself through a life as tedious as mine?*

These reflections dried up the princess's tears. She looked with intrepidity to see from which direction death would come. She seemed to be inviting it not to be late, when she saw something serpentine in the water that was approaching her boat, and which said to her: "If you were in a humor to receive some help from a poor Green Worm like me, I'm in a position to save your life."

"Death scares me less that you," cried the princess. "If you want to give me some pleasure, never show yourself to my eyes."

Poor Green Worm uttered a long hiss—that is the fashion in which snakes sigh—and without making any reply, it sank beneath the waves.

What a horrible monster, the princess said to herself. *It has green wings, its body is a thousand colors, its claws are ivory, its eyes fiery and its head is bristling with long hairs. Oh, I'd rather perish than owe my life to it. But*, she went on, *what attachment does it have to following me, and by what adventure can it speak, as if it were reasonable?*

She was still thinking about it when a voice, responding to her thought, said to her: "Know, Laidronnette, that it is necessary not to scorn Green Worm, and if it were not saying something harsh to you, I would assure you that he is less ugly in his species than you are in yours. Far from wanting to annoy you, though, one would like to soothe your pains, if you would consent to it."

That voice surprised the princess greatly, and what it had said appeared so unbearable that she would not have had enough strength to retain her tears, but she suddenly made a reflection and cried: "What! I don't want to mourn my death because I'm reproached for my ugliness. What good would it do me, alas, to be the most beautiful person in the world? I would perish nonetheless; it ought to be a motive of consolation, to prevent me from regretting life."

While she was moralizing thus, the boat, still floating at the whim of the wind, broke up against a rock; no two pieces of wood remained together. The poor princess felt that all her philosophy could not hold out against such an evident peril. She found a few fragments of wood, which she took in her arms, and feeling herself buoyed up, she arrived fortunately at the foot of the huge rock.

Alas, what became of her when she saw that she was tightly embracing Green Worm! As it perceived the terrible fear that she had, it drew away slightly, and shouted at her: "You'd fear me less if you knew me better; but it's the rigor of my destiny to frighten everyone."

Immediately, it threw itself into the water, and Laidronnette remained alone on a rock of prodigious size.

In no matter what direction she cast her eyes, she saw nothing to soften her despair. Night was approaching; she had no provisions to eat, and did not know where to retire.

I thought, she said, sadly, *that I'd end my days in the sea; doubtless their final period will be here. Some marine monster will come to devour me, or lack of nourishment will take my life.*

She went to sit down on top of the rock. As long as there was daylight, she gazed at the sea, and when night had fallen completely she took off her purple taffeta skirt, covered her head and face with it; and then remained thus, very anxious about what was going to happen.

Finally, she went to sleep, and it seemed to her that she heard various instruments. She persuaded herself that she was dreaming, but a moment later, she heard these lines being sung, which seemed to be made for her:

Suffer that here Amour wounds you,
That his tender fires are felt here.
That god banishes our sadness;
We please ourselves in this happy abode;
Suffer that here Amour wounds you,
That his tender fires are felt here.

The attention that she paid to those words woke her up completely. *With what good and ill fortune am I menaced?* she wondered. *In the state I am in, do fine days still remain to me?* She opened her eyes with a sort of dread, apprehensive that she might find herself surrounded by monsters; but what was her surprise when, instead of that savage rock she found herself in a chamber paneled with gold; the bed on which she was lying responded perfectly to the magnificence of the most beautiful palace in the world.

She asked herself a hundred questions about that, unable to believe that she was really awake. Finally, she got up, and ran to open a glazed door that opened on to a spacious balcony, from which all that the beauties of nature, seconded by art, can contrive on earth was revealed: gardens full of flowers, fountains, statues and rare trees; forests in the distance; palaces, the walls of which were ornamented with precious stones, and the roofs with pearls, so marvelously made that they were as many masterpieces; a calm and placid sea, covered with a thousand different sorts of boats, whose sails, banners and streamers, agitated by the wind, had the most agreeable effect on the sight.

"Gods!" she cried. "Just gods! What do I see? Where am I? What a surprising metamorphosis! What, then, has become of that frightful rock, which seemed to threaten the stars with its sullen points? Was it me that nearly perished yesterday in a boat and was saved by a Worm?"

She spoke thus; she walked back and forth; she stopped; finally, she heard a noise in her apartment; she went in and saw a hundred pagodas coming, clad in a hundred different fashions; the largest were a cubit high, the smallest no more than four fingers; some were beautiful, gracious and agreeable others hideous, of a frightful ugliness; there were some made of diamonds, emeralds, rubies, pearls, crystal, silver, brass, bronze, iron, wood and clay; some had no arms, others had no feet, mouths extending to the ears, eyes askew and noses crushed; in a word, there was no more difference between the creatures that inhabit the world than there was between those pagodas.[18]

The ones that presented themselves before the princess were the delegates of the realm; after having made a speech mingled with a few very judicious reflections, they said to her, in order to divert her, that for some time they had been traveling the world, but that in order to obtain permission from their sovereign, they had sworn an oath to her on departure not to speak; that they had been so scrupulous that they did not want to move their heads, nor their feet, nor their hands, but that the majority had not been able to help it, having traveled the world thus, when they returned, entertaining their king with the story of everything most secret that happened in the various courts where they had been received.

"It is, Madame," the delegates added, "a pleasure that we will give you sometimes, for we have orders not to neglect anything to distract you; instead of bringing you presents, we have come to divert you by means of our songs and dances. Immediately, they started to sing these words, while dancing a round dance with Basque tambourines and castanets.

Pleasures are charming

---

[18] The model for these "pagodas" is not the building itself but the humanoid figures often found at the entrance or in association with them; pagodas and their decorations became fashionable in seventeenth-century France; there was a notorious example at Versailles, and the Pagoda of Chanteloup commissioned by the Duc de Choiseul can still be seen, along with its Oriental garden.

When they follow pains
Pleasures are charming
After long torments.
Don't break your chains.
Young lovers.
Pleasures are charming
When they follow pains
Pleasures are charming
After long torments.

By dint of suffering inhumane rigors,
You'll find happy moments;
Pleasures are charming
When they follow pains
Pleasures are charming
After long torments.

When they had finished, the delegate that had served as spokesman said to the princess: "Here, Madame, are a hundred pagodines who are destined for the honor of serving you; everything you could want in the world will be accomplished, provided that you stay among us."

The pagodines appeared in their turn; they were holding baskets proportionate to their stature, filled with a hundred different things, so pretty, so useful, so well made and so rich that Laidronnette could not weary of admiring them, of praising them and exclaiming about the marvels she saw.

The most apparent of the pagodines, which was a little figure of diamond, proposed that she go into the bath grotto because the heat was increasing. The princess walked beside the one that showed her the way, between two rows of bodyguards of a stature and bearing to make one die of laughter. She found two crystal tubs garnished with gold, full of water of an odor so fine and rare that she was surprised by it. An awning, gold mingled with green, rose above it.

She asked why there were two tubs; she was told that one was for her and the other for the sovereign of the pagodas,

"But where is he?" she exclaimed.

"Madame," one said, "he is presently at war; you will see him when he returns."

The princess asked whether he was married, she was told that he was not, and that he was so lovable that he had not thus far found anyone worthy of him.

She did not take her curiosity any further; she undressed and got into the bath. Immediately, the pagodas and pagodines began to sing and play instruments; some had theorbos made of walnut shells, others had viols made from almond shells, for it was necessary that the instruments be proportionate to their stature, but all of it was so accurate and harmonized so well that nothing was more enjoyable than concerts of that sort.

When the princess got out of the bath, she was presented with a magnificent dressing gown; several pagodines playing flutes and oboes marched ahead of her singing verses praising her. She entered thus into a chamber where her clothes were laid out. Immediately, pagodine wardrobe mistresses and chambermaids came and went, coiffing her, dressing her, praising her and applauding her; there was no longer any question of ugliness, purple skirts or dirty ribbons.

The princess was veritably astonished. *Who*, she wondered, *can have procured me such an extraordinary good fortune? I was on the point of perishing, I was awaiting death, I could not hope for anything else, and yet I suddenly find myself in the most agreeable and magnificent place in the world, where everyone testifies more than joy on seeing me.*

As she had infinite intelligence and good will, she conducted herself so well that all the little creatures that approached her were charmed by her manners.

Every day, when she got up, she had new garments, new lace, new gemstones; it was still a pity that she was so ugly, but because she could not suffer from it she began to find it less disagreeable, by virtue of the great care that was taken to adorn her. There was no time when a few pagodas did not arrive and render an account of the most secret and most curious things that were happening in the world: peace treaties, leagues to make war, treasons and ruptures of lovers, infidelities of mistresses, despairs, reconciliations, disappointed heirs, broken marriages, old widows remarrying inappropriately, treasures discovered, bankruptcies, fortunes made overnight, fallen favorites, sieges of forts, jealous husbands, coquettish women, bad children, and destroyed towns—in sum, what did they not tell the princess in order to amuse or occupy her?

Sometimes there were pagodas who had bellies so inflated and cheeks so swollen that it was surprising. When she asked them why they were like that they told her: "As it's not permitted for us to laugh, not to talk, in society and we incessantly see such risible things there, and almost intolerable stupidities, the desire to mock is so powerful that we swell up, it's really a hydropsy of laughter, of which we're cured as soon as we're here."

The princess admired the good minds of the pagodine population, for one could indeed have swelled up with laughter if it were necessary not to laugh at all the impertinences they saw.

There was no evening when one of the best plays of Corneille or Molière was not performed. Balls were very frequent; the smallest figures, in order to take advantage of everything, danced on tightropes in order to be more visible. Furthermore, the meals that were served to the princess could have passed for feasts at solemn festivals. She was brought serious, gallant and historic books.

In sum, the days flowed by like moments, although, in truth, all those witty pagodas appeared to be insupportably tiny, for it often happened that when she went for a walk she put thirty or so in her pockets in order to entertain her; it was the funniest thing in the world to hear them chatting with their little voices, as clear as those of marionettes.

Once, it happened that the princess, not sleeping, said: "What will become of me? Will I always be here? My life is passing more agreeably than I would have dared to expect, but my heart lacks something. I don't know what it is, but I'm beginning to feel that this succession of the same pleasures, which isn't varied by any events, seems insipid."

"Oh, Princess," said a voice, "isn't that your fault? If you wanted to love, you'd discover very quickly that one can remain for a long time with the person one loves in a palace, or even in a frightful solitude, without wanting to go out."

"What pagoda is speaking to me?" she asked. "What pernicious advice is it giving me, contrary to all the repose of my life?"

"It's not a pagoda," was the reply, "that is warning you about something you will do sooner or later; it's the unfortunate sovereign of this realm, who adores you, and who only dares tell you so while trembling."

"A king adores me!" replied the princess. "Has that king eyes, or is he blind? Has he seen that I'm the ugliest person in the world?"

"I've seen you, Madame," replied the invisible individual. "I haven't found you such as you represent yourself, and whatever your person, your merit or your disgraces might be, I repeat to you that I adore you, but my respectful and fearful amour obliges me to hide."

"I am obliged to you for that," said the princess. "What would I do, alas, if I loved something?"

"You would be the felicity of the person who cannot live without you," he said, "but if you do not permit him to appear, he will not dare to do so."

"No," said the princess, "No, I don't want to see anything that engages me too strongly."

The other ceased to respond to her, and she spent the rest of the night very occupied with that adventure.

Whatever resolution she had not to say anything that had the slightest relationship to that adventure, she could not help asking the pagodas whether their king had returned. They said no. That response, which accorded poorly with what she had heard, worried her; she nevertheless asked whether the king was young and well made. She was told that he was young, that he was well made and very lovable. She asked whether they often had news of him; she was told that they received it every day.

"But does he know that I'm in his palace?" she added.

"Yes, Madame," was the reply. "He knows everything that happens in your regard. It interests him, and couriers depart every hour who go to tell him your news."

She fell silent, and commenced to dream much more frequently than she had been accustomed to do.

When she was alone, the voice spoke to her. She was sometimes afraid of it, but it sometimes gave her some pleasure, for there was nothing so gallant as everything that it said to her.

"Whatever resolution I've made never to love," the princess replied, "and whatever reason I have to defend my heart from an engagement that can only be fatal, I confess to you that I would be very glad to know a king whose taste is as bizarre as yours; for if it is true that you love me, you are perhaps the only person in the world who can have such a weakness for a person as ugly as me."

"Think whatever you please about my character, my adorable princess," the voice replied, "I find enough to justify you in your merit; it isn't that alone that obliges me to hide. I have reasons so sad that if you knew them you wouldn't be able to refuse me your pity."

The princess then pressed the voice to explain, but the voice no longer spoke; she only heard it uttering long sighs. All those things worried her. Although he was an unknown and hidden lover, he rendered her a thousand cares. To add to that, the place where she found herself made her wish for a company more appropriate than that of pagodas. That was why she began to suffer ennui everywhere. Only the voice of the invisible individual had the ability to occupy her agreeably.

On one of the darkest nights of her tears, when she was asleep, she perceived, on waking up, that someone was near her bed. She thought that it was the pagodine of pearls, which, having more intelligence than the others, sometimes came to converse with her. The princess reached out to pick her up, but someone took her hand, held it tightly, kissed it, and a few tears fell upon it; the individual was so emotional that he could not speak. She had no doubt that it was the invisible king.

"What do you want with me, then?" she said to him, sighing. "Can I love you without knowing you and without seeing you?"

"Oh, Madame," was the reply, "what conditions do you attach to the sweetness of pleasing you? It's impossible for me to allow myself to be seen. The malevolent Magotine, who did you a bad turn, is the same one who condemned me to a penitence of seven years; five have already gone by; two still remain, all the bitterness of which you would soothe if you would accept me as a husband. You will think that I am very bold, and that what I ask of you is absolutely impossible, but Madame, if you knew how far my passion goes, and how far the excess of my misfortunes goes, you would not refuse the favor that I ask of you."

Laidronnette became annoyed. As I have already said, she found that the invisible king had everything that could please intellectually, and amour took root in her heart under the specious name of a generous pity. She replied that she required a few more days in order to make up her mind. It was a great deal to have got her to the point of only deferring for a few days something with which one ought to flatter oneself.

The fêtes and concerts redoubled; nothing was sung to her any longer but wedding songs; she was brought presents incessantly, the magnificence of which surpassed anything that had ever been seen; the assiduous amorous voice paid court to her as soon as night fell, and the princess went to bed early in order to have more time to converse with it.

Finally, she consented to take the invisible king for her husband, and she promised him not to see him until after his penitence was finished. "It would be all over for you and for me," he said, "if you had that imprudent curiosity; it would be necessary for me to recommence my penitence and for you to share the punishment with me; but if you can prevent yourself from following the bad advice that will be given to you, you will have the satisfaction of finding me in accordance with your heart, and rediscovering at the same time the marvelous beauty that the malevolent Magotine took from you.

Delighted by that new hope, the princess swore a thousand oaths to her husband to have no curiosity contrary to his desires. Thus, the wedding was completed without noise and without splendor, but the heart and the mind settled their account nonetheless.

As all the pagodas sought urgently to divert their new queen, one of them brought her the story of Psyche, which a very fashionable author had just put into beautiful language.[19] She found many things in it that related to her own adventure, and such a violent desire took hold of her to see her father and her mother in her home, with her sister and her brother-in-law, that nothing the king could say was capable to getting rid of that fantasy.

"The book that you are reading," he added, "can tell you into what misfortunes Psyche fell. Please profit from it in order to avoid them."

She promised more than he asked. Finally, a vessel laden with pagodas and presents was dispatched with letters from Queen Laidronnette to the queen, her mother. She implored her to come and see her in her realm, and the pagodas were given permission for that one time only to speak elsewhere than in their own land.

The loss of the princess had not failed to touch the sensibility of her near relatives; she was thought to be dead, with the result that her letters were infinitely agreeable to the court; and the queen, who was dying to see her again, did not resist for a moment departing with her daughter and son-in-law. The pagodas, who alone knew the way to their realm, conducted the entire royal family there, and when Laidronnette saw her parents she nearly died of joy. She read

---

[19] The reference is to the story of Cupid and Psyche, the earliest surviving written version of which is found in Lucius Apuleius' *Metamorphoses*, better known as *The Golden Ass*. The specific citation is an expanded version, composed in the early 1690s, of Jean de La Fontaine's poem "Les Amours de Psyche et de Cupidon" (1669); the longer version, combining verse with prose, proved very popular.

and reread the story of Psyche, in order to be on her guard against all they might say, and above all what she ought to reply, but however hard she tried she went astray in a hundred places. Sometimes the king was with the army, sometimes he was ill and in such a bad humor that he did not want to see anyone, sometimes he was making a pilgrimage, and then he was hunting or fishing. In sum, it seemed that she was engaged to say nothing that would hold up, and that the barbaric Magotine had disturbed her mind.

Her mother and father conferred together, and concluded that she was deceiving herself, with the consequence that, by virtue of an ill-judged zeal, they resolved to talk to her. They acquitted that task with so much skill that they cast a thousand dreads and a thousand doubts into her mind. After having defended herself for a long time against agreeing with what they said, she confessed that, until then, she had not seen her husband, but that he had so much charm in his conversation that it was sufficient to hear him to be content, that he was in penitence for two more years, and that after that time, not only would she be able to see him, but she would become as beautiful as the day star.

"Oh, you poor woman!" cried the queen. "How crude the snares that are extended for you are! Is it possible that you believe such tales with such a great simplicity? Your husband is a monster, and it cannot be otherwise, for all the pagodas of which he is the king are true apes."

"I would rather believe," said Laidronnette, "that he is the god Amour himself."

"What an error!" cried Queen Bellotte. "Psyche was told that she had a monster for a husband, and she found that it was Amour; you're obstinate that Amour is yours, and surely he's a monster. At least put your mind at rest; enlighten yourself in such an easy matter." The queen, her mother, said the same, and her son-in-law too.

The poor princess was so confused and troubled that, after having sent all her family away with presents that paid for the purple taffeta and the sleeve-ribbon, she resolved, whatever might happen, to see her husband.

Oh, fatal curiosity, which a thousand fatal examples cannot correct, how dear you are going to cost that unfortunate princess!

She would have regretted not imitating her predecessor Psyche, with the result that she hid a lamp in her room and made use of it to see the invisible king so dear to her heart. But what frightful screams she uttered when, instead of tender Amour, blond, pale, young and utterly lovable, she saw the frightful Green Worm, with long bristling hair.

He woke up, transported with rage and despair. "Barbarian!" he cried. "Is this the recompense for so much love?"

The princess did not hear him; fear had made her faint, and Worm was already far away.

At the noise of all that tragedy, several pagodas had come running. They put the princess to bed, they helped her, and when she had come round they

190

found her in a state that imagination cannot attain. How many times did she reproach herself for the woe she was going to procure her husband? She loved him tenderly but she abhorred his form, and she would have given half her life not to have seen him.

However, her sad reveries were interrupted by a few pagodas that entered her bedroom fearfully. They had come to tell her that several ships full of marionettes, with Magotine at their head, had entered the port without obstacle. The marionettes and the pagodas had been enemies at all times; they were in competition in a thousand things, and the marionettes even had the privilege of talking everywhere, which the pagodas had not. Magotine was their queen; the aversion that she had for the poor Green Worm and the unfortunate Laidronnette had obliged her to assemble troops with the resolution of coming to torment them at the moment when their dolors were most intense.

The fay had no difficulty succeeding in her projects, for the queen was so desolate that although she was pressed to give the necessary orders, she refused to do so, saying that she did not understand war. The greatest captains among the pagodas that were in the besieged cities and in the capital were assembled on her orders; she ordered them to take care of everything, and then shut herself away in her cabinet, regarding all the events of life with an almost equal eye.

Magotine had for a general the famous Polchinelle, who knew his métier well, and had a large reserve corps composed of wasps, cockchafers and butterflies, which wrought marvels against a few lightly-armed frogs and lizards. They had been in the hire of the pagodas for a long time, and were, in truth, more redoubtable in name than by their valor.

Magotine amused herself for some time watching the battle; the pagodas and pagodines surpassed themselves therein; but with a thrust of her wand the fay dissipated all those superb edifices. Those charming gardens, those woods, those meadows and springs were buried in their own ruins, and Queen Laidronnette could not avoid the harsh condition of being a slave of the most malign fay there ever was.

Four or five hundred marionettes obliged her to come to where Magotine was.

"Madame," said Polchinelle, "this is the queen of the pagodas, whom I dare to present to you."

"I've known her for a long time," said Magotine. "She is the cause of my receiving an affront on the day of her birth, which I shall never forget."

"Alas, Madame," said the queen, "I believe that you are sufficiently avenged. The gift of ugliness that you bestowed on me to the utmost degree could have satisfied a person less vindictive than you."

"How she talks," said the fay. "Here's a doctor of a new edition. Your first employment will be to teach my ants philosophy; prepare to give them a lesson every day."

"How can I do that, Madame?" replied the afflicted queen. "I don't know philosophy, and if I did, would your ants be capable of learning it?"

"See, see the argumentative chit!" cried Magotine. "Well, Queen, you might not teach them philosophy, but you'll give the whole world, in spite of yourself, a lesson in patience that it will be difficult to imitate."

With that she had iron shoes bought for her so narrow that half her foot would not go in, but it was necessary nevertheless or her to be shod; the poor queen had to weep and suffer all the time.

"By the way," said Magotine, "here's a distaff charged with cobweb; I intend you to spin it as fine as your hair, and I only give you two hours."

"I've never spun. Madame," the queen said to her, "but even though what you want appears impossible to me, I'll try to obey you."

She was immediately taken into the depths of a very obscure grotto. It was sealed with a large stone after she had been given a loaf of brown bread and a jug of water.

When she tried to spin the dirty cobweb, her excessively heavy spindle fell to the ground a hundred times over; she had the patience to pick it up as many times and to recommence the work several times, but it was always futile.

"I know all too well now," she said, "the excess of my misfortune. I am delivered to the implacable Magotine; she is not content to have stolen all my beauty, she wants to find pretexts for making me die."

She began to weep, passing through her mind the fortunate state she had enjoyed in the realm of Pagodia, and dropping her distaff on the ground. "Let Magotine come when she pleases," she said. "I can't do the impossible."

She heard a voice that said: "Oh, Queen, your indiscreet curiosity has cost you the tears that you are shedding. However, there is no means of seeing the person one loves suffering. I have a friend that I have not mentioned to you; she is known as the Protective Fay. I hope that she will be a great help to you."

Immediately, there were three raps, and without her seeing anyone, her distaff was spun and unwound.

After two hours, Magotine, who was seeking a quarrel, had the stone sealing the grotto removed and she came in, followed by a numerous cortege of marionettes.

"Let's see, let's see," she said, "the work of an idler who can neither sew nor spin."

"Madame," said the queen, "I didn't know, in fact, but it has been necessary to learn."

When Magotine saw such a strange thing, she took the ball of spider-silk and said: "Truly, you're so skillful that it would be a great pity not to occupy you. Here, Queen, make nets with this thread that are strong enough to catch salmon.

"Oh, please," she replied, "consider the difficulty with which flies are caught therein."

"You argue a great deal, my beautiful friend," said Magotine, "but that won't do you any good." She left the grotto, had the large stone replaced in front of it, and assured her that if the nets were not finished in two hours she would be doomed.

"Oh, Protective Fay," said the queen, then, "if it's true that my woes can touch you, don't refuse me your help."

Immediately, the nets were finished. Laidronnette was surprised to the utmost degree; with all her heart she thanked the helpful fay who did so much good, and thought with pleasure that it was doubtless her husband who had procured that friend for her.

"Alas, Green Worm," she said, "you're very generous still to love me after all the harm I've done you."

There was no reply, for Magotine came in, and was very surprised to find nets so industriously wrought that an ordinary hand would not have been capable of doing such work.

"What!" she said. "Will you really be bold enough to sustain that it's you who wove these nets?"

"I have no friend at your court, Madame," the queen said to her, "and even if I had one, I've been so securely imprisoned that it would be difficult for anyone to speak to me without your permission."

"Since you're so skillful and so adroit," said Magotine, "you'll be very useful to me in my realm."

She immediately ordered that ships be equipped and that all the marionettes should be ready to depart. She had the queen attached with heavy iron chains, for fear that by some movement of despair she might throw herself into the sea.

The unfortunate princess was deploring her sad destiny one night when she perceived Green Worm by the light of the stars, who was approaching the ship quietly.

"I still dread frightening you," he said, "and in spite of the reasons I have for not protecting you, you are infinitely dear to me."

"Can you forgive my indiscreet curiosity?" she replied, and can I say to you without displeasing you:

Is that you, Worm, dear lover, is that you?
Can I see again the object for which my heart sighs?
What! I can see you again, my dear and tender spouse!
O Heaven, what a rigorous martyrdom I have suffered!
How I have suffered, alas,
In not seeing you.

Worm replied with these lines:

How the dolors of absence
Trouble amorous hearts!
In the frightful realm
Where the gods exact their vengeance.
One cannot suffer more rigorous woes
Than the dolors of absence.

Magotine was not one of those fays who sometimes sleep; the desire to do evil always kept her awake. She did not fail to overhear the conversation of King Worm and his wife; she came to interrupt it like a Fury.

"Aha! You're dabbling in poetry and lamenting in the tone of Phoebus. Truly, I'm very glad. Proserpine, who is my best friend, has begged me to give her some poet for her wages; she has no lack of them, but she wants even more. Let's go, Green Worm, I order you, to complete your penitence, to go to the somber manor and give my compliments to the noble Proserpine."

The unfortunate Worm departed immediately, with long hisses, leaving the queen in the most intense dolor. She thought she had nothing more to lose, in her transport she cried: "By what crime have I displeased you, barbaric Magotine? I was scarcely in the world when your infernal malediction took away my beauty and rendered me frightful. Can you say that I was guilty of anything, since I did not have the usage of reason yet and did not know myself? I am certain that the unfortunate king that you have just sent to the Underworld is as innocent as I was; but finish it—kill me promptly; it's the only favor I ask of you."

"You would be too content," Magotine said to her, "if I granted you that prayer. It's necessary before then that you draw water from the bottomless well."

As soon as the ships had arrived in the realm of the marionettes, the cruel Magotine took a millstone, attached it to the queen's neck and commanded her to climb to the summit of a mountain that was far above the clouds; when she was there she was to pick four-leaved clover and fill her basket with it, and then descend into the bottom of the valley in order to draw, in a pitcher pierced with holes, the water of discretion, of which she was to bring her enough to fill her large glass.

The queen told her that it was impossible for her to be able to obey, that the millstone weighed ten times as much as she did, that the pierced pitcher could never retain the water that she wanted to drink, and that she could not even attempt such an impossible thing.

"If you fail in it," Magotine said to her, "be assured that your Green Worm will suffer in consequence."

That threat caused the queen so much fear that, without examining her weakness, she tried to walk; but alas, it would have been futile if the Protective Fay, to whom she appealed, had not come to her aid.

"This," she said to her, as she approached her, "is the just payment for your fatal curiosity; you only have yourself to blame for the state to which Magotine has reduced you."

Immediately, she transported her to the mountain and put the four-leafed clover in her basket, in spite of the frightful monsters that guarded it. They made supernatural efforts to defend it, but with a stroke of her wand, the Protective Fay rendered them meeker than lambs

She did not wait until the grateful queen had thanked her to finish giving her all the pleasure that depended on her. She gave her a little chariot drawn by white canaries, which talked and whistled marvelously. She told her to go down the mountain, to throw her iron shoes at two giants armed with clubs that were guarding the spring, and that they would fall unconscious. She advised her then not to stay at the spring, nor to go back up the mountain, but to stop in an agreeable little wood that she would find in her path; that she could spend three years there; that Magotine would always think that she was still occupied in drawing water in her pitcher or that the other perils of the journey had caused her death.

The queen embraced the knees of the Protective Fay and thanked her a thousand times for the particular favors she had received from her. "But Madame," she added, "neither the fortunate success that I ought to have, nor the beauty that you promise me, will be able to touch me with joy until Worm has been devermified."

"That is what will happen after you have been in the wood on the mountain for three years," the fay said to her, "and, on your return, you have given the water in the pitcher and the clover to Magotine."

The queen promised the Protective Fay not to fail in anything that had been prescribed to her. "However, Madame," she added, "will I be three years without hearing mention of King Worm?"

"You deserve to be deprived of his news as long as you live," replied the fay, "for can there be anything more terrible than to condemn that poor king, as you have done, to recommence his penitence?"

The queen made no reply; the tears that flowed from her eyes and her silence were evidence enough of the dolor she felt. She climbed into the little chariot; the canaries did their duty and conducted her into the depths of the valley, where the giants were guarding the spring of discretion.

Promptly, she took off the iron shoes, which she threw at their heads; as soon as they were touched they fell like lifeless colossi. The canaries took the pierced pitcher and repaired it with such a surprising skill that it did not appear that it had ever been broken.

The name the water bore gave her a desire to drink it. *It will render me*, she thought, *more prudent and discreet than I have been in the past; if I had had those qualities, I would still be in the realm of Pagodia.* After she had drunk a long draught she washed her face, and became so beautiful, so beautiful, that she might sooner have been taken for a goddess rather than a mortal person.

Immediately, the Protective Fay appeared and said to her: "You have just done something that pleases me infinitely. You knew that that water could embellish your soul and your person; I wanted to know which of the two would have preference. In the end it was your soul that had it; I praise you for that, and that action will abridge your penitence by four years."

"Don't diminish my punishments," relied the queen, "I merit them all; but relieve Green Worm, who does not merit any."

"I will do what I can," said the fay, embracing her, "but wait; since you're so beautiful, I want you to quit the name of Laidronnette, which no longer suits you. It's necessary that you call yourself Queen Discreet."

With that she disappeared, leaving her a small pair of shoes, so pretty and so well embroidered that she almost regretted putting them on.

When she had remounted her chariot, holding her pitcher full of water, the canaries took her straight to the wood on the mountain. There has never been a more agreeable place; the myrtles and the orange trees linked their branches to form long covered pathways and arbors that the sun could not penetrate; a thousand streams that flowed gently contributed to refreshing that beautiful abode; but what was rarest of all was that all the animals there talked, and they gave the best welcome in the world to the little canaries.

"We thought," they said to them, "that you had abandoned us."

"The time of our penitence is not yet finished," replied the canaries, "but here is a queen that the Protective Fay has charged us with bringing; take care of diverting her as much as you can."

At the same time she found herself surrounded by animals of every species, which paid her great compliments.

"You shall be our queen," they said to her. "There are no cares and respects that you ought not to expect from us."

"Where am I?" she exclaimed. "By means of what supernatural power can you talk to me?"

One of the little canaries, which had not quit her, twittered to her: "It is necessary that you know, Madame, that several fays, having set out to travel, were chagrined to find people falling into essential faults; they thought at first that it would be sufficient to warn them in order to correct them, but their cares were futile, and, suddenly becoming irritated, they put them in penitence; they made parrots, magpies and chickens of those who talked too much, pigeons, canaries and little dogs of lovers and mistresses, monkeys of those who mimicked their friends, pigs of certain people who were excessively fond of good cheer and lions of angry people. In the end, the number of those they put in penitence became so large that this wood is populated by them, with the consequence that one finds individuals of all qualities and humors here."

"By what you have just told me, my dear little canary," the queen said to him, "I have reason to believe that you are only here for having loved too much."

"That's true, Madame," relied the canary. "I was the son of a Spanish grandee: Amour has rights so absolute over all hearts in our country that one cannot escape him without falling into the crime of rebellion. An English ambassador arrived at the court; he had a daughter of extreme beauty, but whose arrogant and piquant humor was insupportable; in spite of that I attached myself to her, I loved her to the point of adoration; she sometimes seemed sensible to my cares, but at other times she rejected me so forcefully that she drove my patience to the limit.

"One day, when she had driven me to despair, a venerable old woman accosted me, reproaching me for my weakness, but all that she could say to me only served to make me more obstinate. She perceived that, and became irritated. 'I condemn you,' she said, 'to become a canary for three years, and your mistress a wasp.' Immediately, I sensed the most extraordinary metamorphosis take place in me.

"In spite of my affliction, I couldn't help flying into the ambassador's garden to discover the fate of his daughter, but I was scarcely there when I saw her become a huge wasp, buzzing four times as loudly as any other. I fluttered around her with the urgency of a lover whom nothing can detach; she tried several times to sting me. 'If you want my death, beautiful wasp,' I said to her, 'it isn't necessary for that to employ your sting; it's sufficient for you to order me to die.' The wasp made no reply; she alighted on flowers that were to suffer her ill humor.

"Dejected by her scorn and my condition, I flew away without taking any particular route. I eventually arrived in one of the most beautiful cities in the world, which is called Paris. I was tired; I threw myself into a clump of large trees enclosed by walls, and without knowing who had caught me I found myself at the door of a cage painted green and garnished with gold. The furniture and the apartment had a magnificence that surprised me; immediately, a young woman came to caress me, and spoke to me with so much affection that I was charmed.

"I had not been in her room long before I was informed of the secret of her heart. I saw a kind of braggart come to see her, always furious, who could not be satisfied, not only charging her with unjust reproaches but beating her and leaving her for dead in the hands of her women. I was not a little afflicted to see her suffer such unworthy treatment, and what displeased me even more was that it seemed that the blows with which he hurt her had the virtue of reawakening all that pretty lady's tenderness.

"I wished day and night for the fays that had rendered me a canary to come to put some order into such ill-matched amours. My desires were accomplished; the fays appeared abruptly in the room, just as the furious lover was commencing his ordinary Sabbat; they charged him with reproaches and condemned him to become a wolf. As for the patient young woman who allowed herself to be beaten, they made her a ewe and sent her to the wood on the mountain. As for myself, I easily found the means of flying away.

"I wanted to see the different courts of Europe. I went into Italy, and hazard caused me to fall into the hands of a man who, often having affairs in his city, and not wanting his wife, of whom he was very jealous, to see anyone, took care to lock her up from morning until evening, with the result that he destined me with the honor of diverting that beautiful captive, She was, however, occupied with other cares than that of listening to me. A certain neighbor whom she had loved for a long time, came to the top of the chimney in the evening and let himself slide down, blacker than a demon. The keys that the jealous man had taken away only served to put his mind at rest.

"I always feared some unfortunate catastrophe, and the fays came in through the keyhole, causing the tender couple a surprise that was not mediocre. 'Go in penitence,' they said to them, touching them with their wands, so that the chimney-sweep became a squirrel and the lady a she-monkey, because she was adroit; and the husband who took so much care to keep the keys of his house became a mastiff for ten years.

"I would have too many things to recount to you, Madame," added the canary, "if I told you all the different adventures that have happened to me. I am obliged to return, from time to time, to the wood on the mountain, and I hardly ever come without finding new animals, because the fays are still traveling, and people continue to irritate them with infinite faults; but during the sojourn you spend here, you will be able to divert yourself with the stories of all the adventures of the persons who are here."

Several immediately offered to tell her theirs whenever she wished; she thanked them very politely, but as she had more desire to think than to talk, she searched for a solitary spot where she could be alone. As soon as she had marked one, a little palace appeared there, where the finest meal in the world was served to her; it only consisted of fruits, but very rare fruits; the birds brought them, and for as long as she was in the wood, she did not lack anything.

Sometimes there were fêtes more agreeable by their singularity than anything else; lions were to be seen dancing with lambs there, bears sweet-talking doves and snakes showing affection for linnets. A butterfly could be seen intriguing with a panther. In sum, nothing was matched in accordance with its species, for it was not a matter of being a tiger or a sheep, but only people that the fays wanted to punish for their faults.

They loved Queen Discreet to the point of adoration; they all rendered her the arbiter of their disputes. She had an absolute power over that petty republic, and if she had not reproached herself incessantly for the misfortunes of Green Worm she would have been able to support her own with a kind of patience; but when she thought about the state to which he was reduced, she could not forgive herself or her indiscreet curiosity.

When the time came for her to leave the wood on the mountain, she informed her little conductors, the faithful canaries, who assured her of a fortunate return. She slipped away one night in order to avoid adieux and regrets that would have cost her a few tears, for she was touched by the amity and deference that all those reasonable animals had testified to her.

She did not forget the pitcher full of the water of discretion, or the basket of clover, or the iron shoes, and while Magotine believed her to be dead she suddenly presented herself before her, with the millstone round her neck, the iron shoes on her feet and the pitcher in her hand. On seeing her, the fay uttered a loud cry, and then asked her where she had been.

"Madame," she said to her, "I've spent three years drawing water with the pierced pitcher, and the end of which I found the means of making it hold some."

Magotine burst out laughing, thinking about the fatigue the poor queen had had, but, looking at her more attentively, she cried: "What's this? Laidronnette has become quite charming! Where, then, have you obtained that beauty?"

The queen told her that she had washed herself with the water of discretion and that the prodigy in question had occurred.

At that news, Magotine threw the pitcher to the ground.

"O power that is defying me," she cried, "I shall be able to avenge myself. Prepare your iron shoes," she said to the queen, "it's necessary that you go on my part to the Underworld, to ask Proserpine for the essence of long life. I always fear falling ill, and even dying; when I have that antidote, I shall no longer have any reason for apprehension. Refrain, therefore, from taking the stopper from the bottle or tasting the liquor she will give you, for you'd diminish my share."

The poor queen had never been more surprised than she was by that order. "By what route does one go to the Underworld?" she asked. "Can those who go there come back? Alas, Madame, will you not weary one day of persecuting me? Under what star was I born? My sister is far more fortunate than me; it's necessary no longer to believe that the constellations are equal for everyone."

She started to weep, and Magotine, triumphant at seeing her shed tears, burst out laughing. "Let's go, let's go," she said. "Don't defer for a moment a journey that will bring me so much satisfaction." She filled a satchel with old nuts and brown bread for her.

With that good provision, she departed, resolved to break her head against the first rock for her pains. She walked for some time without taking any route, going one way and turning the other, thinking that it was a very extraordinary command to send her thus to the Underworld. When she was tired she lay down at the foot of a tree and started to dream about the poor Worm, no longer thinking about her journey; but she suddenly saw the Protective Fay, who said to her: "Don't you know, beautiful queen, "that in order to extract your husband from the somber abode where Magotine's orders retain him, that it's necessary for you to go to Proserpine's dwelling?"

"I'd go much further if it were possible for me," she replied, "but Madame, I don't know where to descend into that tenebrous domain."

"Here," said the Protective Fay, "this is a green branch; strike the earth with it and pronounce verses distinctly."

The queen embraced the knees of that generous friend, and then she said:

You who are able to disarm the master of thunder,
Amour, give me aid,
Come to stop the course
Of rigorous ennuis that are tearing my soul.
Open for me, as you can, the path to the Underworld;
In that subterranean realm you can make your flame felt,
Pluto for Proserpine has moaned in your irons;
Open for me, tender Amour, the path to the Underworld.
A faithful husband has been snatched from me;
I feel the rigors of the most terrible fate.
My dolor is more than mortal,
And I cannot find death.

She had scarcely finished her prayer when a young child, more beautiful than anything we see, emerged from the depths of a cloud mingled with gold and azure; he flew and came to alight at her feet; a crown of flowers circled his head. The queen knew by his bow and his arrows that it was Amour. He said to her as he approached:

Your sighs have been heard,
I have abandoned the heavens,
And come to dry the tears flowing from your eyes.
For you I can attempt anything;
You shall see again the object you love the most;
Recall Worm to the pleasures of life,
And punish thus his cruel enemy.

The queen, astonished by the splendor that surrounded Amour, and delighted by his promises, cried:

Into the Underworld I am ready to follow you;
That horrible abode will seem charming to me,
If I see again the lover
Without whom I can no longer live.

Amour, who rarely speaks in prose, struck three blows, singing these words marvelously well:

Earth, obey my voice,
Recognize Amour, open a passage
All the way to the dismal shore
Where Pluto imposes his laws.

The earth obeyed; it opened its large bosom, and by means of an obscure descent, in which the queen had need of a guide as brilliant as the one who had taken her under his protection, she arrived in the Underworld. She feared encountering her husband there in the form of a serpent, but Amour, who sometimes mingles rendering a few good offices, having foreseen everything that could be anticipated in that regard, had already ordered Green Worm to become what he had been before his penitence. However powerful Magotine was, alas, what could she do against Amour?

The first thing that the queen found, therefore, was her amiable husband. She had never seen him in such a charming form, nor had he seen her as beautiful as she had become; however, a presentiment—and perhaps Amour, who made a third party with them—enabled them to divine who they were. The queen immediately said, with an extreme tenderness:

I have come to his place in order to bend destiny's law,
If you are arrested here by a barbaric order
Let us unite our hearts, let nothing separate us;
The Underworld that is deemed full of fear
Will have nothing sad for me.

The king, transported by the most intense passion, responded to his wife everything that could mark his ardor and his joy; but Amour, who does not like to waste time, invited them to approach Proserpine.

The queen paid her a compliment on behalf of the fay, and begged her to charge her with the essence of life. That was a password agreed between those good persons; she immediately gave her a phial rather poorly sealed, in order to facilitate the desire to open it. Amour, who was not a novice, warned the queen to refrain from a curiosity that might again be fatal, and, emerging promptly from that sad abode, the king and the queen saw the light again.

Amour did not want to abandon them; he conducted them to Magotine, and, in order that she would not see him, he hid in their hearts. However, his presence inspired sentiments so humane that the fay, although she did not know the reason for it, received the illustrious unfortunates very well; making an effort of supernatural generosity, she returned the kingdom of Pagodia to them; they went back there immediately, and lived with as much good fortune as they had previously experienced disgrace and annoyance.

> *Often, a curious desire*
> *Is the source of the most frightful woes;*
> *Upon a secret that might make us miserable,*
> *Why desire to open our eyes?*
> *The fair sex especially has that cruel audacity.*
> *Let us take as a witness the first mortal;*
> *On her were modeled Pandora and Psyche,*
> *Who, wanting to penetrate a mystery,*
> *Which the gods wanted to keep hidden from mortals,*
> *Became the authors of their own misery.*
> *Laidronnette, who wanted to know Worm,*
> *Experienced a similar destiny;*
> *The example of Psyche could not render her sage;*
> *Alas, that of their past misfortunes*
> *The majority of mortals, curious and insensate*
> *Have not made a better usage.*

Henriette-Julie de Murat: *The Prince of Leaves*

In one of the parts of the world to which poets alone have the right to give names, commonly known as the land of the fays, a king once reigned who was so renowned by his fine qualities that he attracted the esteem and admiration of all the princes of his times. He had lost his wife, the queen, some years before, of whom he had not had a son; but he had no longer desired one since he had had a daughter of such marvelous beauty that he had given her, as soon as she was born, all his tenderness and all his attachment.

She was named Ravissante by a fay who was a close relative of the Queen, who predicted that the intelligence and the charms of the young Princess would surpass everything seen thus far, and similarly the hope that they ought to have of the beauty she would be; but she added to that agreeable prediction that the happiness of the princess would be perfect, provided that her heart was always faithful to the first impressions that it received of amour.

With only that circumstance able to assure a happy destiny, the King, only wanting Ravissante to be happy, desired passionately that her happiness had been attached to any other fatality, but one does not make one's destiny at will. He begged the fay a thousand times to make young Ravissante the gift of constancy, as he had seen her make others the gifts of intelligence and beauty, but the fay, who was knowledgeable enough not to be mistaken regarding the various effects of her knowledge, told the king sincerely that the power of fays cannot extend over the qualities of the heart. She promised him, however, that she would apply all her cares to imprinting the young Princess with the sentiments to which her happiness was attached.

On the strength of that promise, the king confided Ravissante to her as soon as she reached the age of five years, preferring to deprive himself of the pleasure of seeing her rather than risking by that pleasure becoming contrary to her fortune. The fay took the little Princess away, whom the joy and novelty of traveling through the air in a brilliant little chariot consoled in a few moments for having quit her father's court.

On the fourth day after her departure, the flying chariot stopped in the middle of the sea, on a rock of prodigious grandeur. It was made of a smooth and shiny stone, the color of which imitated that of the sky perfectly. The fay remarked with pleasure that young Ravissante found that color very beautiful, and drew from that a fortunate presage for the future, because it is the one that signifies fidelity.

Shortly after arriving, the fay touched the rock with the golden wand she was holding in her hand. The rock immediately opened, and Ravissante found herself, along with the fay, in the most beautiful palace in the world. The walls were of the same substance as the rock, and the same color was found in all the paintwork and all the furniture, but it was so ingeniously mingled there with gold and precious stones that, far from being tedious, it was equally pleasing everywhere.

Young Ravissante stayed in that beautiful palace, with beautiful young women that the fay had transported from various lands to serve and amuse the princess; she spent her childhood there in all the pleasures appropriate to her age. When she had reached the age of fourteen years, the fay consulted the stars again in order to discover very precisely the time at which Ravissante's heart was due to be touched by a passion that pleases even more than it is redoubtable, redoubtable though it is, and she saw distinctly in the stars that the fatal term was approaching when the destiny of the young princess was to be accomplished.

The fay had a nephew who was infinitely dear to her; he was the same age as Ravissante, born on the same day and at the same hour. She had also found, in consulting the stars on his behalf, that they promised him the same fate as the princess—which is to say, a perfect happiness, provided that he had a fidelity that nothing could vanquish. It was, however, easier to ensure his constancy than his happiness.

In order to render him amorous and faithful, she only had to enable him to see Ravissante; no one could escape her eyes, and the fay hoped that the attentions of the young prince might one day touch her heart. He was the son of a King who was the fay's brother; he was lovable, and not only had the young princess not yet had a lover, she had not even seen a man since she had been on the rock. The fay flattered herself that the novelty of the pleasure of being loved tenderly might perhaps engage her to love in her turn.

She therefore transported the prince, whose name was Ariston, into the rock that served the beautiful Ravissante simultaneously as a palace and a prison. He found that she was amusing herself making garlands of flowers with the young women of her Court in a forest of blue hyacinths, where she went for walks, for the fay, in giving the rock the ability to produce plants and trees, had enclosed that power in the very color of the rock.

Some time before, the fay had told the princess that Prince Ariston would be coming to the island, and she had added, in favor of the prince, everything that she thought capable of making him desired, but she was disappointed this time, and when Ariston arrived, she did not recognize in the beautiful eyes of the princess the disturbance and surprise that ordinarily presages a tender passion.

As for the prince, his sentiments were in accord with the fay's hopes; he fell passionately in love as soon as he had seen Ravissante. It was not possible to see her without adoring her; never had grace and beauty been so perfectly united as they appeared to be throughout the person of that lovable Princess. She had a complexion of marvelous beauty, and her brown hair further enhanced its paleness; her mouth had infinite charms, her teeth were more admirably white than pearls; her eyes, the most beautiful in the worlds, were blue-brown, and they seemed so simultaneously bright and touching that it was not possible to sustain their gleam and their vivacity without yielding one's heart forever to the fatal power that amour had attached to their gaze; her stature was not very tall, but she was perfectly beautiful and all her actions had a particular grace; everything that she did, and everything that she said, was equally pleasing, and a smile or a single word was often sufficient to prove that she had as many charms in her intelligence as in her person.

Such as I have just described her, and a thousand times more lovable, it would have been very difficult for Ariston not to fall madly in love, but the princess received his cares without attention, and did not appear to be touched by them at all. The fay remarked that, and had a dolor in consequence that was only surpassed by the one that the prince felt. She had seen in the stars that the individual who was destined to possess Ravissante would extend his power over the entire earth, and even as far as the seas, so it was as much by virtue of ambition that she wished that her nephew might be able touch the heart of the princess as because Ariston desired it by virtue of amour.

She believed, however, that if the prince were as knowledgeable as she was in her art, he might find some secret to render himself more lovable in Ravissante's eyes. The fay, who had never loved, did not know that the secret of pleasing is not always to be found, whatever the urgency and ardor with which one seeks it. She therefore taught Prince Ariston, in a short time, all the sciences that are only known to fays.

He had no pleasure in learning them, and only thought of employing them with regard to his tenderness. He began by making use of them to provide the princess with new amusements every day; she admired the prodigies, and even deigned to praise what she found most elegant in what the prince did for her, but she received his attentions and devotions as homages justly due to her beauty, and of which she believed herself to be worthy by virtue of the generosity she had in receiving them without anger.

Ariston despaired of the scant success of his passion, but he was constrained thereafter by further information to admit that the time of which he complained so justly, and during which he felt the misfortune of his amour so keenly, had nevertheless been the happiest of his life.

A year after his arrival on the island, the day, so remarkable for him, on which he had seen Ravissante for the first time, was celebrated by games; in the evening he gave her a fête in the forest of hyacinths; there was marvelous music, which was heard equally in all the parts of the forest, without it being possible to see where such agreeable sounds were coming from. Everything that was sung by the invisible musicians expressed Ariston's amour for the Princess tenderly; they finished their admirable concert with these words, which were repeated several times:

Neither reason nor my rigorous fate
Would be able to end my cruel suffering
Without the aid of sweet hope;
I sense my heart burning with the same fires.
Amour would not know the excess of his power
If I had not felt the power of your eyes.

After the music, a superb collation suddenly appeared under a tent of silver gauze, held up by strings of pearls. It was open on the side that faced the sea, which bordered the forest in that place, and it was illuminated by a large number of chandeliers of brilliant diamonds, which cast a light little different from that of the Sun. It was by that light that the nymphs of Ravissante's court drew her attention to an inscription on the entrance to the tent, written in golden letters on a ruby of prodigious grandeur, sustained by twelve little Amours, who flew away as soon as the princess had read the inscription, which contained these lines:

No matter to how many places in the world
Your beautiful eyes will carry irons
You will not find a heart as faithful
As the one that burns for you in this desert;
But to ensure you of an immortal glory
And to see the world entire at your feet,
Princess, we shall publish to mortals
How beautiful you are.

The fête continued, and Prince Ariston at least had the pleasure of occupying the princess's leisure, if he could not occupy her heart. But he was deprived of that satisfaction by a surprising spectacle that appeared in the distance over the sea, and which attracted the curiosity and the attention of Ravissante and the entire court. What they saw drew closer, and they discerned that it was an arbor formed of myrtles and laurels mingled together, closed on all sides, which an infinite number of winged fish were pushing with great rapidity.

The spectacle was all the more novel for Ravissante because she had never seen the color of that arbor. The fay, having foreseen that the color in question was to cause some misfortune to her nephew, had banished it absolutely from her island.

With an impatience that appeared to Ariston to be an evil presage for his amour, the princess desired that what she could see might come closer; she did not have long to wait, for the winged fish pushed the arbor in a matter of moments all the way to the foot of the rock, where they stopped, and the attention of the Princess and her entire court was redoubled.

The arbor opened, and a young man of marvelous beauty emerged, who appeared to be sixteen or seventeen years old. He was only clad in a few myrtle branches interlaced with a sash of roses of different colors.

The handsome stranger experienced an astonishment similar to the one that he caused; Ravissante's beauty did not leave him the liberty to amuse himself by gazing at the rest of the spectacle, the glare of which had attracted him to the rock from far away. He approached the princess with a grace that she had never seen, even in herself.

"I am so surprised," he said, "by what I find on these shores, that I have even lost the liberty of being able to express my astonishment. Is it possible," he continued, "that a goddess like you does not have temples all over the world? By virtue of what charms or what prodigies are you still unknown to mortals?"

"I'm not a goddess," said Ravissante, blushing. "I'm an unfortunate princess, sent away from the Estates of my father, the king, in order to avoid I know not what misfortune, which I am assured was predicted for me at the moment of my birth."

"You appear to me," said the handsome stranger, "to be far more redoubtable than the stars that might have attached some fatal influence to your beautiful days. Over what ill fortune can a beauty so perfect not triumph? I sense that it can vanquish anything," he added, sighing, "since it has vanquished in a moment a heart that I flattered myself that I could conserve insensible forever."

Without giving her time to respond, he continued: "But Madame, it is necessary that I go away, reluctantly, from this charming place where I see you, and where I have just lost my repose. I shall return soon, if Amour is favorable to me."

After those words he went back into the arbor, and in a short time he was lost to sight.

Meanwhile, Prince Ariston remained so bewildered and so afflicted by that adventure that he did not have the strength to speak to begin with; a rival had arrived by virtue of an event as surprising as it was unexpected; that rival had appeared to be only too charming, and it seemed to him that he had remarked in the beautiful eyes of the princess, while the stranger was speaking, a languor that he had always desired to see there, but had never seen thus far. Transported by a despair that he dared not allow to burst forth, he took Ravissante back to the palace, where she spent a part of the night occupied with her agreeable adventure, of which she had the circumstances repeated several times by the nymphs of her court, as if she had not been there herself.

As for Prince Ariston, he went to consult the knowledge of the fay, in order to seek to oppose some secret to the violent dolor by which he was tormented, but she had none against jealousy, and it is even said that none has been found since.

The prince and the fay then redoubled their enchantments in order to forbid entry to the rock to the redoubtable stranger, whom they assumed to be an enchanter. They surrounded the island with frightful monsters, which occupied a large area of the sea, and which, animated by their own fury and the force of charms, seemed to assure Ariston and the fay that it would be impossible to take away from them the beautiful princess whom they were guarding with so much care.

Ravissante felt more keenly the power of the handsome stranger's charms by virtue of the dolor caused to her by the obstacles that had been placed around the island against his return. She resolved at least to avenge herself on Prince Ariston; she began to hate him, and that was quite enough to ensure her vengeance. Ariston could not console himself for having attracted Ravissante's hatred by virtue of a passion that, it seemed to him, ought to have produced exactly the opposite effect.

The princess lamented in secret the neglect of the stranger; it seemed to her that amour ought already to have made him keep the promise that he had made to return, but sometimes, also, she ceased to desire that return in remembering the perils by means of which the fay and Ariston had forbidden the approach of the island.

One day, when she was occupied with these various reflections, she was walking on her own along the sea shore, for Ariston no longer dared follow her, as he had done before, and the princess even refused to see the fêtes with which he was accustomed to divert her. She had just arrived at the same place that the adventure of the unknown had rendered so recognizable, when she saw a tree of extraordinary beauty on the sea, which was floating toward the rock. Its color, which was that of the stranger's myrtle arbor, immediately gave her joy.

The tree drew nearer to the rock, and the monsters tried to prevent its passage, but a little wind agitated the leaves of the tree, and having dispersed a few of them against the monsters, they yielded to arms so slight and lacking in danger, and even arranged themselves in a circle, with a kind of respect, around the tree, which approached the rock without encountering any other obstacles. It opened, and the stranger appeared within, sitting on a little throne of verdure.

He stood up precipitately at the sight of Ravissante, and spoke to her with so much intelligence and amour that after she had told him in a few words what her fortune was, she could not hide from him that she was touched by his return and even by his tenderness.

"But," she said to him, "is it just that I should know the sentiments that you have inspired in me before I even know the name of the person who has given birth to them?"

"I had no intention of hiding my birth from you," the charming stranger replied, "but in your presence one can only talk about you. However, as you want it I shall obey you by telling you that my name is the Prince of Leaves. I am the son of Spring and a sea-nymph related to Amphitrite, and that is what enables me to extend my power even over the waters; my empire is in all the places of the world that recognize Spring, but I prefer to live, almost always, on a fortunate island where no season ever reigns except the pleasant season that my father is accustomed to provide. The air there is always pure, the fields there are always florid, the sun does not make its ardors felt, only approaching it in order to illuminate it; night is banished therefrom, and that is why it is called the Isle of Day. It is inhabited by a people as gallant as the climate is agreeable; it is there that I offer you a mild and tranquil empire, where you would reign with even more sovereignty over my heart than everything else.

"It would be necessary, however, beautiful Princess," he continued, "for you to consent to be taken away from this rock, where you are retained in a veritable slavery, with a few honors, which are rendered to you in order to disguise it."

Ravissante could not resolve to go with the Prince of Leaves to his empire. In spite of the fear she had of the power of the fay and the counsels of her amour, she flattered herself that her constancy in refusing Ariston's pleas would perhaps resolve him to cease loving her and that the fay would return her to her father, from whom the Prince of Leaves could obtain her.

"But I want at least," she said to him, "to be able to tell you what is happening on this island, and I don't know how that can be possible, for everyone is suspect to me here."

"I shall, therefore, leave you subjects of a Prince who is among my friends," said the Prince of Leaves, "who will always remain with you, and by means of whom you can often give me your news. Only remember, beautiful Princess, the impatience with which I shall await that news."

After those words, he approached the tree that had brought him, and touched several of its leaves; two butterflies emerged therefrom, the prettiest in the world, one the color of fire and white, the other yellow and flax gray. Ravissante was looking at them when the Prince of Leaves, smiling, said to her: "I see that you're surprised by the form of the confidants that I am giving you, but these butterflies are not only what they appear to you to be; that is a mystery that those I am leaving you will explain to you, when you permit them to converse with you."

After that, Ravissante noticed in the distance some of the nymphs, coming to search for her in her solitude; she begged the Prince of Leaves to embark again. He obeyed her, in spite of the infinite pain that he felt in quitting her; but he could not depart quickly enough not to be seen.

The fay and Ariston were informed of his return to the island, and from that moment on, in order to remove from the beautiful Ravissante the means, and even the hope, of seeing him again, they built on the summit of the rock a tower of the same stone, and in order to be absolutely sure, as the adventure of the monsters had surprised them, they rendered the tower and the rock invisible for all those who came in search of it, no longer wanting to trust ordinary enchantments.

Ravissante despaired of an imprisonment so cruel and so difficult to break; Prince Ariston had not hidden from her that he had rendered it invisible; he had even tried to represent that care as a certain sign of his tenderness; but Ravissante's hatred and scorn for him were increasing every day, and he hardly dared appear before her any longer.

Meanwhile, the butterflies had not quit her, and she often gazed at them with pleasure, because they had come from the Prince of Leaves. One day, when she was even sadder than usual, dreaming on a terrace that was at the top of the tower, the butterfly the color of fire flew over one of the vases filled with flowers that ornamented the balustrade.

"Why not send me to inform the Prince of Leaves?" it said, suddenly, to the princess. "He will come to your aid infallibly."

Ravissante was astonished at first to hear the butterfly speak, although her lover had prepared her for that novelty. For a few moments, she did not say anything, but the name of the Prince of Leaves enabled her to dissipate her astonishment.

"I was so surprised," she said to the butterfly, "to hear you talking like us that I took some time to reply to you. I see clearly that you can go to inform the Prince of Leaves of my misfortune, but what can he do except suffer a futile affliction? He will not be able to find me in a place that the cruelty of my enemies has taken care to render invisible."

"It is less so than you think," replied the yellow butterfly, flying close to the princess in order to join the conversation. "I have soon observed your prison: I have flown, and even swum, around it; it disappears when one is in the water, but it ceases to be invisible when one is high in the air. Doubtless the fay did not believe that route easy enough for her to think of defending it like that of the sea. That is advice that I was going to give you," the butterfly continued, "when my brother broke the silence that we have maintained until now."

Such agreeable news had rendered some hope to the princess. "Is it possible," she said, "that Ariston has neglected some precaution to satisfy his cruelty and his amour? Undoubtedly, his power and that of the fay, which can do anything over the sea and the land, does not extend as far as the air; that is the reason that has prevented the prince and the fay from rendering the isle invisible from the direction of the sky."

After a few moments of reflection, Ravissante added: "But can the Prince of Leaves do anything in the air?"

"No, Madame," said the butterfly the color of fire, "he can do nothing there, and your prison will be as invisible to him, even though he is a demigod, as it would be for a human, but..."

"The prince will, therefore, be as unfortunate as me," interjected the sad Ravissante, shedding tears that augmented her beauty, and which moved the two butterflies extremely, "and I sense that I will be even more unfortunate by virtue

210

of the woes of the Prince of Leaves than my own." With a sigh, she continued: "What should I do, then?"

"Send me forth immediately," replied the butterfly the color of fire, brusquely. "I will go and inform the Prince of Leaves of your misfortunes, and he will come to your aid; although his power does not extend over the air, one of his friends is a prince who can do anything there, and of whom he can dispose, as of himself; that is what my brother, who will remain with you, can explain to you during my voyage.

"Adieu, beautiful Princess," the butterfly continued, fluttering above the balustrade. "Cease being anxious and count on my diligence; I will fly with as much rapidity as you wish."

After those words the butterfly was lost in the air, and the princess then felt the joy, so keen and so charming, that is given by the hope of soon seeing someone whom one loves. She returned to her room, and the yellow butterfly followed her there; she felt an extreme impatience to know from what prince her lover could expect an aid so necessary to their happiness. In order not to be ignorant any longer, she begged the yellow butterfly to tell her everything that might contribute to augmenting and flattering her hope. She put it in a little basket of flowers, which she brought to a table next to her, and the butterfly, which made it an honor to please her, commenced its story.

Near the Isle of Day, where the Prince of Leaves reigns, there is another isle, smaller but just as agreeable. The ground there is always covered with flowers, and we are sure that that is a grace which Flora has granted to our land in order to immortalize the memory of the happy days when she came to find Zephyr there; for it is said that it was to our isle that they came when their love was still secret and new. It is called the Isle of Butterflies. Its inhabitants do not have the form in which you see me; they are little winged humans, very pretty, very gallant, very amorous and so fickle that they scarcely love the same thing for longer than a day.

When the Golden Age was still reigning on earth, Amour, who flattered himself then that all hearts would always be tender and faithful, feared that, by virtue of the facility that we had of flying all over the world, we might go to teach mortals the agreeable science of changing in loving, which that god called an error capable of destroying the happiness of his empire forever. In order to forbid us any commerce with the rest of the world, he came to our island, touched the ground there with one of his arrows, and then rose up again on the brilliant cloud that had brought him.

"If you wish," he said to the inhabitants of the island, "to continue to go through the air like the gods, I have just ensured my vengeance; you can no longer trouble the felicity of my empire without dangerous commerce." After those words he disappeared.

Amour's threats did not take away from the butterflies the desire for change, nor that of flying through the air, in order at least to have the pleasure of sometimes quitting the earth. Some of them rose into the air and found that they had the same facility there as before the time when Amour had come to forbid it, but as soon as they emerged from the limits of our island, they were changed into little animals such as you see me, all of different colors. Vengeful Amour had wanted to mark by that diversity how inclined to inconstancy they were.

Surprised by their metamorphosis, they returned to our island, and as soon as they had touched the ground they resumed their original form. Since that fatal time, Amour's vengeance has always continued among us; when we quit our homeland, nothing human remains to us except intelligence and the liberty of speech; but we never make use of the latter faculty outside our island, in order not to render that vengeance celebrated by publishing it ourselves throughout the world, and in order not to frighten those who, like us, have a penchant for inconstancy; but we have the pleasure of seeing and traveling the world.

Destiny has avenged us on Amour, without our having to interfere; inconstancy reigns with as much power as him throughout the extent of his empire. Some centuries after that change had occurred in the Empire of the Butterflies, the Sun, who seems to take pleasure in enabling the birth of flowers, applauded himself so well for his own work that he fell in love with a rose of extraordinary beauty. He was loved tenderly in return, and she sacrificed for him all the cares that the Zephyrs took of her; after a time, the rose became somewhat different in form from others; the Sun immediately enabled the birth of others similar to her, in order that she would be more easily confounded in that quantity of flowers, which then appeared to be specimens of a new plant. It is the one that has subsequently been called the rose with a hundred leaves.[20]

Eventually, a demigod was born of the Sun and that flower, whom the Sun destined to rule over our island. Until then we had not had a sovereign, but the son of a god who favored our land so constantly was received as its King with an extreme joy; he was named the Prince of Butterflies. It is that prince, beautiful Princess, who will be able to help you by way of the route of the air, and whom the adventure I shall relate to you has rendered the friend of the Prince of Leaves forever, and so perfectly.

In a land far away from that of the butterflies, a fay reigns who makes her dwelling in a very obscure cavern; she is known as the Fay of the Grotto; she is extraordinarily tall, and her face is a mixture of green, aurora and blue; her form renders her almost as redoubtable as her power, and she is so feared by mortals, that none of them has been bold enough to dare to approach the land she inhabits.

---

[20] i.e. *Rosa centifola*, sometimes known in English as the Provence rose or the cabbage rose.

One day, the Prince of Butterflies, who was traveling for his diversion in the vicinity of her empire, perceived the fay, and, surprised by that encounter, he followed her for a long time in order to see what would become of such a frightful monster. She did not notice that she was observed, for the prince, although a son of the Sun, has not been able to obtain from destiny the liberty to travel in any other form than the one we all take on when we leave our realm, because he was born on our island after the time when Amour made us feel his vengeance. However, he was not inconstant, as all his subjects are, and Amour, in order to grant him at least a small mercy, had permitted that when he changed form he would only be a single color, and that that color would be the one that signifies fidelity.

In that form, he followed the Fay for as long as he wished; he saw her enter her somber dwelling; urged by an impulse of curiosity, he flew after her, but what a spectacle awaited him in the depths of that cavern! He saw there a young woman more beautiful and more brilliant than the daylight, who was lying on a bed of grass, and who seemed to be extremely sad. From time to time, she shed tears, which fell from her beautiful eyes; her dejection and languor only served to make her seem more lovable.

The Prince of Butterflies remained so touched by that sight that he almost forgot a thousand times over the form that he had, only to remember that he was madly in love and burning to say so. He was extracted from such a sweet reverie by the terrible voice of the fay, who spoke to the young woman with a frightful harshness. He sensed dolor and anger in consequence, and was in despair at being unable to express either one.

The fay, who, by virtue of a natural restlessness, could not remain long in the same place, soon went out of the cavern; then the prince approached the young woman by whom he was so charmed; he fluttered round her, and, wanting to enjoy the only liberty that his form permitted him, he alighted on her hair, which was the most beautiful blonde in the world, and then on her face.

He was dying of the desire to tell her how touched he was by her beauty and her dolor, but what means did he have of making her believe that he was a son of the Sun, without being able to appear before her in his own form? And how could he tell her about the vengeance of Amour and the inconstancy so natural to the inhabitants of his isle, while wanting to persuade her that he would never cease to love her?

He remained for several days in the cavern or in the forest that surrounded it; he could not resolve to quit that beauty, whom he adored, and although he dared not speak to her, he wanted to, and that was enough to make him prefer that frightful abode to the agreeable place where he had the pleasure of reigning, and that of being the most handsome prince in the world.

During the time in which he did not quit that young person, he always saw the fay treat her with an incredible inhumanity, and he learned from their speech that the unfortunate beauty was the Princess of Linnets; that the fay, who was one of her relatives, had kidnapped her in her most tender youth in order more easily to usurp her realm, which was a little island situated not far from that of the butterflies. The prince had been there many times; he had even heard mention that its princess had been kidnapped and that no one had ever been able to discover what had become of her. That land was called the Isle of Linnets because of the large quantity of little birds of the species bearing that name to be found there.

The Prince of Butterflies pitied the misfortune of that lovable princess, and in order finally to discover whether it was possible to liberate her, he resolved to go away. He flew to the Isle of Day without a moment's repose; he found the Prince of Leaves there, with whom he had been linked for some time in tender amity, and who had just spent a year in the Isle of Butterflies. He related his adventure to that prince, and, after having examined all the means they might employ to set the young princess free, the Prince of Leaves resolved to go himself to the fay's forest in order to inform the Princess of Linnets of the violent amour that that the Prince of Butterflies had for her, and of the reasons that still prevented the unfortunate prince from appearing before her in his veritable form, if she would not consent to allow herself to be taken to the Isle of Butterflies.

However, the Prince of Leaves appeared to his friend to be too redoubtable a confidant; he feared, with reason, that the princess might be more touched by the charms of such a perfect prince than by the story of the amour of another prince of whom she had never heard mention. He bemoaned the cruelty of his destiny, and searched for some other means of declaring his amour to the princess, but in vain; no one other than a demigod could approach the fay's dwelling without immediately feeling the deadly effects of her vengeance.

He therefore embarked with the Prince of Leaves, agitated by a jealous dread; it seemed to him that the prince would not be able to conserve for a single minute, at the sight of the beautiful princess, the insensibility in which he had always gloried. Amour, touched by the awful state to which he had reduced him, wanted at least to reassure him against that just dread, and at the same time to triumph himself over the insensible heart of the Prince of Leaves.

It is by means of you, beautiful princess (the butterfly continued) that the god expected the victory, and you alone were worthy of obtaining it. It was on the same day as the embarkation of the two princes that they saw from afar, on a rock, an illumination so brilliant that the Prince of Leaves, pushed by his destiny, ordered the winged fish that were conducting the arbor of myrtles in which he was traveling to approach the place from which the bright light was coming.

You know the rest of that adventure. The Prince of Leaves found you in the forest of hyacinths and left at your feet a liberty that was so dear to him, and which, until that moment, he had always conserved. Pressed by the impatience of the Prince of Butterflies, who had only suffered with regret the pause on that shore, he tore himself away with an infinite difficulty from a place where his heart and his desires would have liked to arrest him forever. They continued their voyage, and the Prince of Butterflies was so satisfied to see the Prince of Leaves veritably amorous and so far from becoming his rival, that he did not doubt that it was a sufficiently favorable presage to promise him perfect good fortune in the remainder of his enterprise.

They arrived in the forest of the Fay of the Grotto; they went into the sad dwelling, and Amour, who had resolved to favor them, enabled them to find the Princess of Linnets alone and asleep.

There was no time to lose; the Prince of Leaves bore her away to the arbor of verdure, to which the Prince of Butterflies followed him. The fay returned at that moment. She uttered horrible cries at the sight of that abduction. She believed that she could prevent it by the power of her art and avenge herself on the person who had just taken the Princess of Linnets away, but her enchantments were useless against the Prince of Leaves, who drew away from that dismal shore in very little time.

Meanwhile, the young princess woke up, and was equally surprised by the place where she found herself and the presence of the Prince of Leaves. It was, however, an agreeable astonishment, which was augmented by the discourse of the prince, who informed her of the effects of her beauty, that she was liberated from the tyranny of the fay, that she could reign henceforth in her empire, and in a realm even more beautiful than her own.

The Prince of the Butterflies spoke to her about his amour with so much vivacity and tenderness that the Princess felt an infinite curiosity to see him in his veritable form, of which she had formed from that moment on the finest idea in the world. They continued their journey, and in a few days they arrived at the Isle of Butterflies, the ground of which the prince hastened to touch, in order finally to appear to the eyes of the princess as he was. The sight of him did not belie the idea that she had formed of him; he was fortunate enough to please her, and he loved her all the more tenderly for that.

The Princes of Linnets sent word to her own island to inform her subjects about her adventure; they came to find her in a crowd, and it was in their presence that she accepted the heart and the Empire of the fortunate Prince of Butterflies. Meanwhile, the Prince of Leaves had quit him as soon as he had conducted him to his island in order to return to you, Princess, where his impatience and ardent amour pressed him incessantly to render.

Ravissante was listening to the butterfly with an extreme attention when she saw Prince Ariston enter her room with a fury in his expression whose effects she feared.

"Destiny is threatening me," he cried as he came in, "and it promises me a great misfortune; it is doubtless that of losing you, there is no other that my heart can find sensible enough to merit being predicted to me! Look, Madame," he continued, addressing Ravissante, "look what color the walls of the tower are becoming: it is a certain sign for me of imminent misfortune."

As Ariston's woes were a source of pleasure for Ravissante, she looked at what the prince was pointing out to her, and perceived that the blue stone had lost its original color and was beginning to turn green; she felt joy, because she had no doubt that it was a sure presage of the arrival of the Prince of Leaves. That joy, which the unhappy Ariston remarked, increased his despair. What did he not say to Ravissante? Rendered sincere by the excess of his dolor, he told her that he loved her enough not to cease adoring her, although he was assured of being unhappy all his life.

"I cannot doubt my misfortune," he said to the Princess. "Destiny has promised me, as it has you, that I will always be miserable if I were not faithful to the first impression amour made in my heart, and what means is there of accomplishing that cruel order? When one sees you, after having already become sensible, one forgets everything, even the care of one's happiness, only to think of loving you and only to seek to please you. A young princess of my father's Court had appeared worthy of my vows; I believed that I would only think about returning to her when I had spent some time here, but a moment of seeing you overturned all my projects; my reason and my heart were equally in accord in my change, and I believed that nothing was impossible for the tender amour that you had inspired in me. I even flattered myself that it could change destiny, but your ever-constant rigors taught me that I was mistaken, and that no hope any longer remains to me but that of soon dying for you."

Prince Ariston had just finished that speech, which made him seem to Ravissante at least worthy of some pity, when they saw a throne of foliage in the air sustained by an infinite number of butterflies. One of them was entirely blue, and that color enabled Ravissante to recognize the son of the Sun; he flew toward her and said: "Come, beautiful Princess; it is today that you will recover your liberty and render the most amiable Prince in the world happy."

The butterflies set the throne down next to Ravissante. She sat on it, and they lifted it up.

Ariston, in despair at having lost the princess, only consulted the excess of his dolor, and hurled himself into the sea. The fay immediately abandoned the rock, which that death had just rendered too disastrous for her, and in order to mark her fury she shattered it, along with the tower, by means of a thunderbolt, into an infinite number of pieces, which were transported by the waves and winds into various parts of the sea.

That is the species of stone from which rings have since been made that are named turquoises; those which are still named turquoise de la vieille roche[21] are all made from residues of that dispersed rock, and the others are only stones that resemble them. The memory of the misfortune predicted to Prince Ariston by the change in the color of the walls of the tower has been passed down to us; it is

---

[21] A variety that normally retains that designation in English, although it is also known as odontolite.

still said that if those rings turn green, some misfortune will occur to those who wear them, and it is even asserted that it is ordinarily amorous misfortunes that are thus predicted.

While the fay expressed her dolor by the destruction of her island, the Prince of Butterflies, satisfied to have rendered the Prince of Leaves a service similar to the one that he had received from him, conducted Ravissante through the air as far as a ship of rushes ornamented with garlands of flowers, where the Prince of Leaves was waiting with all the impatience that a violent amour can cause. Words cannot express the pleasure he felt on seeing the princess arrive; joy and amour had never appeared more vividly than in the heart and in the speech of that prince. He set sail diligently for the Isle of Day.

The Prince of Butterflies flew away to rejoin the lovable Princess of Linnets instead. Ravissante sent two butterflies to her father, the king, in order to inform him as to what her fortune had been; the good king praised Destiny and went as soon as possible to the Isle of Day, where the Prince of Leaves and the beautiful Ravissante reigned with all imaginable felicity and were always happy, because they never ceased to be amorous and faithful.

> *One ought to envy the fate of Ravissante;*
> *Because of a keen and constant ardor,*
> *Amour lavished his precious treasures upon her.*
> *To be able to enjoy them like her,*
> *Alas, how happy one would be,*
> *If it were sufficient to be faithful.*

Marie-Catherine d'Aulnoy: *Princess Belle-Etoile and Prince Cheri*

There was once a princess to whom nothing any longer remained of her past grandeurs than her bed-canopy and her hair-grip; one was velvet embroidered with pearls, the other gold enriched with diamonds. She kept them as long as she could but the extreme necessity to which she found herself reduced obliged her from time to time to detach a pearl, a diamond, an emerald and sell it secretly in order to nourish her equipage. She was a widow charged with three very young and very amiable daughters. She understood that if she brought them up with an air of grandeur and suitable magnificence they would feel their disgrace more afterwards. She therefore made the resolution to sell the little that remained to her and go away with her three daughters, in order to establish herself in a house in the country where their expenditure would be appropriate to their petty fortune.

While passing through a dangerous forest she was robbed, with the result that almost nothing remained to her. The poor princess, more chagrined by that last misfortune than all the ones that had preceded it, knew full well that it was necessary to earn her living or die of hunger. She had once loved good cheer, and knew how to make excellent sauces. She never went anywhere without her little gold cooking-pot, which people came from far away to see. What she had once done to amuse herself, she now did in order to subsist.

She settled near a big city, in a very pretty house; she made marvelous stews there; people were very greedy in that region, with the result that everyone flocked to her house. There was no talk of anything but the good fry-cook; she was scarcely given time to breathe. Meanwhile, her three daughters grew up and their beauty would have made no less noise than the princess's sauces if she had not hidden them in a room from which they rarely went out.

On one of the most beautiful days of the year a little old woman came into her house who seemed very tired. She was leaning on a stick; her body was bent over and her face full of wrinkles. "I've come," she said, "in order for you to give me a good meal, for I want, before going to the other world, to treat myself in this one." She took a wicker chair, placed it next to the fire, and told the princess to hurry up.

As she could not do everything, she summoned her three daughters. The eldest was named Roussette, the second Brunette and the youngest Blondine. She had given them those names with reference to the color of their hair. They were dressed as peasant girls, with bodices and skirts of different colors. The youngest was the most beautiful and the mildest. Their mother ordered one to go in quest of little pigeons in the aviary, another to kill pullets and a third to make the pastry. Finally, they set before the old woman a very proper place-setting, with a very white table-cloth and well-varnished earthenware crockery, and served her several courses. The wine was good, there was no lack of ice, the glasses were rinsed continually by the most beautiful hands in the world; all of that gave the little old woman an appetite. If she ate well, she drank even better. She complimented the wine and said a thousand things in which the princess, who seemed not to pay any heed to it, found a good deal of wit.

The meal finished as cheerfully as it had begun. The old woman got up, and said to the princess: "My good friend, if I had any money I'd pay you, but I was ruined a long time ago; I needed to find you to have such good cheer; all that I can promise you is to send you better custom than mine."

The princess smiled, and said, graciously "Go on, my good mother, don't worry about it; I'm always paid well enough when I give some pleasure."

"We've been delighted to serve you," said Blondine, "And if you'd like to sup here, we'd do even better."

"Oh, how fortunate one is," cried the old woman, "When one is born with a heart so benevolent! But do you believe that you won't receive the recompense? Be certain," she continued, "that the first wish you make without thinking of me will be granted."

At the same time, she disappeared, and they had no reason to doubt that she was a fay.

That adventure astonished them; they had never seen one before; they were fearful, with the result that for five or six months they talked about it, and as soon as they desired something they thought about her. Nothing succeeded, with the result that they were very angry against the fay.

One day, however, when the king had gone hunting, he went to the house of the good fry-cook, to see whether she was as skillful as people said, and as he approached the garden with a lot of noise, the three sisters, who were picking strawberries, heard him.

"Ah!" said Roussette, "if I were fortunate enough to marry Milord the Admiral, I could boast that I'd make so much thread with my spindle and my distaff, and so much cloth with that thread, that he wouldn't have any more need to buy any for the sails of his ships."

"And I," said Brunette, "if fortune were favorable enough to enable me to marry the king's brother, could boast that I'd make so much lace with my needle that he'd see his palace filled with it."

"And I," added Blondine, "could boast that if the king married me, at the end of nine months I'd have two beautiful boys and a beautiful girl, that their hair would fall in ringlets, spread out with precious stones, with a brilliant star on the forehead and a neck circled by a rich gold chain."

One of the king's favorites, who had come in ahead in order to inform the hostess of his coming, having heard people talking in the garden, stopped without making any noise, and was very surprised by the conversation of the three beautiful young women. He immediately went to repeat it to the king in order to amuse him; he did, in fact, laugh, and commanded that they be brought before him.

They appeared immediately, with a marvelous manner and grace. They curtseyed to the king with a great deal of respect and modesty, and when he asked them whether it was true that they had just been talking about the husbands they desired, they blushed and lowered their eyes. He pressed them to admit it; they agreed, and he immediately cried: "Certainly, I don't know what power is acting upon me, but I won't leave here until I've married the beautiful Blondine."

"Sire," said the king's brother, "I ask your permission to marry that pretty Brunette."

"Grant me the same favor," added the admiral, "for the redhead pleases me infinitely."

The king, very glad to be imitated by the noblest men in his realm, told them that he approved of their choices, and asked the mother if she was agreeable to it. She replied that it was the greatest joy she could ever have. The king embraced her, and the prince and the admiral did no less.

When the king was ready to dine, a table with seven gold place-settings was seen to come down the chimney, and everything that can be imagined of the most delicate to make a good meal. The king hesitated to eat, however; he feared that he meat might be the product of the Sabbat, and that manner of serving via the chimney seemed slightly suspect to him.

The sideboard was arranged; nothing could be seen but gold vases and bowls, the workmanship of which surpassed the material. At the same time a swarm of honey-bees appeared in crystal hives and commenced the most charming music that can be imagined. The whole room was filled with hornets, flies, wasps and midges, and other small creatures of that sort, which served the king with a supernatural skill. Three or four thousand gnats brought the drinks, without a single one daring to drown in the wine, and with astonishing discipline.

The princess and her daughters realized soon enough that everything that was happening could only be attributed to the little old woman; they blessed the hour when they had met her.

After the meal, which was so long that nightfall surprised the company at table, of which His Majesty felt slightly ashamed, because it seemed that in that marriage Bacchus had taken the place of Cupid, the king stood up and said: "Let's finish the feast as it ought to have begun." He took his ring from his finger and put it on Blondine's; the prince and the admiral imitated him. The bees redoubled their songs. They danced, they rejoiced, and the people who had followed the king came to salute the queen and the princess. For the admiral's wife they did not make as much ceremony, of which she was in despair, for she was older than Brunette and Blondine and found herself less well married.

The king sent his chief squire to inform the queen, his mother of what had happened and to summon his most magnificent carriages in order to bring back Queen Blondine and her two sisters. The queen mother was the cruelest of all women and the most ill-tempered. When she knew that her son had married without her participation, and, above all, a young woman of such obscure birth, and that the prince had done the same, she became so angry that she frightened the entire court. She asked the chief squire what reason had been able to engage the king in such an unworthy marriage. He told her that it was the hope of having two sons and a daughter in nine months, who would be born with long curly hair, stars in the forehead and golden chains around the neck, and that such rare things had charmed him. The queen mother was disdainful of her son's credulity; she said many offensive things about that, which gave sufficient evidence of her fury.

The carriages had already arrived at the little house. The king invited his mother-in-law to go with him, and promised her that she would be treated with every sort of distinction, but she immediately thought that a court is a perpetually-agitated sea.

"Sire," she said to him, "I have too much experience of society to quit the repose that I have only acquired with great difficulty."

"What!" said the king. "You want to continue to keep a hostelry?"

"No," she said, "You can give me something on which to live."

"At least," he said, "suffer that I give you an equipage and servants."

"I thank you for that," she said, "but if I'm alone, I shall have no enemies to torment me; if I had domestics, I'd fear finding some among them."

He king admired the intelligence and moderation of a woman who thought and spoke like a philosopher.

While he was urging his mother-in-law to come with him, Admiral Rousse's wife hid in the back of her carriage all the beautiful golden bowls and vases from the sideboard, wanting to profit from them without leaving anything behind, but the fay, who saw everything, even though no one saw her, changed them into earthenware pitchers. When she had arrived and wanted to take them to her cabinet she found nothing worth the trouble of so doing.

The king and the queen embraced the sage princess tenderly, and assured her that she could dispose at will of everything they had. They quit the rural abode and came to the city, preceded by trumpets, oboes, timpani and drums, which could be heard a long way away. The queen mother's confidants had advised her to conceal her ill-humor, because the king would be offended by it, and that might have unfortunate consequences. She restrained herself, therefore, and only manifested amity to her two daughters-in-law, giving them gems and praising indifferently everything they did, well or badly.

The blonde queen and the brunette princes were closely united, but with regard to Admiral Rousse's wife, she hated them mortally. *Look at the good fortune of my two sisters*, she said to herself. *One is a queen, the other a prin-*

cess of the blood; their husbands adore them, but I, the eldest, a hundred times more beautiful than them, only have an admiral for a husband, by whom I am not cherished as I ought to be. The jealousy she had against her sisters caused her to ally herself with the queen mother, because she knew full well that the tenderness she manifested to her daughters-in-law was only feigned, and that she would be glad to have an opportunity to harm them.

The queen and the princess became pregnant. Unfortunately, a great war had broken out and it was necessary for the king to put himself at the head of his army. The young queen and the princess, being obliged to remain under the power of the queen mother, begged to be allowed to return to their mother, in order to console themselves with her for such a cruel absence. The king was unable to consent to that. He implored her to remain in the palace; he assured her that his mother would treat her well. In fact, he begged her with the utmost insistence to love her daughter-in-law and to take care of her. He added that she could not oblige him more sensibly, that he hoped that she would have two beautiful children, and that he would await news of them with great anxiety.

The malevolent queen, delighted that her son was confiding his wife to her, assured him that he could leave with an entire peace of mind. Thus, he left, with such a strong desire to return soon that he risked his troops in all encounters, and his good fortune not only ensured that his temerity always succeeded but that he advanced his affairs strongly.

The queen gave birth before his return. Her sister, the princess, gave birth to a beautiful boy on the same day, but died immediately thereafter.

The admiral's wife was very occupied with means of harming the young queen. When she saw her with such pretty children, while she had none, her fury augmented. She made the resolution to speak to the queen mother promptly, for there was no time to lose.

"Madame," she said to her, "I am so touched by the honor that Your Majesty does me in giving me a part in her good graces, that I would gladly deprive myself of my own interests in order to further yours. I understand all the displeasure by which you have been overwhelmed since the unworthy marriages of the king and the prince. Now here are four children who will eternalize the fault that they have committed. Our poor mother is a poverty-stricken villager who had no bread when she took it into her head to become a fry-cook; believe me, Madame, make a fricassee of all those little brats and remove them from the world before they make you bluish."

"Oh, my dear Admirale," said the queen, embracing her, "how I love you for being so equitable and for sharing, as you do, my just displeasures. I had already resolved to execute what you are proposing to me; it is only the manner that embarrasses me."

"Don't let that trouble you," said Madame Rousse. "My mastiff bitch has just had three pups, two dogs and a bitch; they each have a star on the forehead and a mark around the neck that makes a chain of sorts. It's necessary to make the queen believe that she had given birth to those little beasts and to take her two sons, her daughter and the princess's son, and kill them."

"Your design pleases me infinitely," she cried, "And I've already given orders to that effect to Feintise, her maid of honor, so it's necessary to have the little pups."

"Here they are," said the Admirale. "I've brought them." Immediately, she opened a large purse that she always had at her side, and took out three mastiff puppies, which she and the queen wrapped up as the queen's children would have been, all ornamented with lace and golden embroidery. They arranged them in a covered basket, and then the wicked queen mother, followed by the red-head, went to see the queen.

"I've come to thank you," she said to her, "for the beautiful heirs you've given my son; here are heads well made to wear a crown. I'm not astonished that you promised your husband two sons and a daughter with stars on their foreheads, long hair and gold chains around the neck. Here, nurse them yourself, for there's no woman able to suckle dogs."

The poor queen, overwhelmed by the misfortune she had suffered, nearly died of dolor when she perceived the three canines and saw that litter making a desperate howling on her bed; she started to weep bitterly. Then, putting her hands together, she said: "Alas, Madame, don't add reproaches to my affliction; it can surely be no greater. If the gods had permitted me to die before I had received the affront of seeing myself the mother of these little monsters, I would estimate myself too fortunate. Alas, what am I going to do? The king will hate me as much as he loved me."

Sighs and sobs stifled her voice; she no longer had the strength to speak, and the queen mother, continuing to heap her with insults, had the pleasure of spending three hours thus at her bedside. She went away thereafter and her sister, who pretended to share her displeasure, told her that she was not the first to whom a similar misfortune had occurred, that it was obvious that it was a trick of the old fay who had promised them so many marvels, but that, as it might be dangerous for her to see the king, she advised her to go to their poor mother's house with her three canine children.

The queen only responded with tears. It was necessary to have a very hard heart not to be touched by the state to which she was reduced; she suckled the wretched dogs, believing that she was their mother.

The queen mother ordered Feintise to take away the queen's children, with the son of the princess, to strangle them and bury them so well that no one would ever know anything.

As Feintise was on the point of carrying out that order, and already had the cord in her hand, she cast her eyes on them and found them so marvelously beautiful, and that they were marked in such an extraordinary manner by the stars that were shining on their foreheads, that she dared not put her criminal hands on such an august blood. She had a small boat brought to the edge of the sea, and she put the four children in the same cradle, along with a few strings of precious stones, in order that if fortune carried them into the hands of a women charitable enough to nourish them, she would be sufficiently recompensed.

The boat, pushed by a strong wind, drew away so rapidly along the shore that Feintise lost sight of it; but at the same time, the waves swelled, the sun was hidden, the clouds dissolved in the water and a thousand thunderclaps resounded all around. She had no doubt that the little boat had been submerged, and felt joy that the poor innocents had perished, for she would always have dreaded some extraordinary event in their favor.

The king, incessantly occupied with his dear wife and the state in which he had left her, having a brief truce, returned post-haste; he arrived twelve hours after she had given birth. When the queen mother saw him she went to meet him with a composed expression of dolor. She held him in her arms for a long time, moistening his face with tears; it seemed that dolor was preventing her from speaking. The king, trembling, dared not ask her that had happened, for he did not doubt that there were great misfortunes.

Finally, she made an effort to tell him that his wife had given birth to three dogs. Immediately, Feintise presented them. The Admirale, in tears, threw herself at the king's feet, and begged him not to put the queen to death, and to content himself with sending her back to her mother, which she had already resolved to do, and that she would receive that treatment as a great mercy.

The king was so bewildered that he could hardly breathe; he looked at the puppies, and remarked with surprise the star that each had in the middle of the forehead, and the different color circling the neck. He let himself fall into an armchair, rolling a thousand thoughts round his head, unable to make any firm resolution; but the queen mother pressed him so forcefully that he pronounced the exile of the innocent queen.

Immediately, she was put in a litter with the three dogs, and without having any regard for her, she was taken to her mother's house, where she arrived almost dead.

The gods had looked with compassionate eyes upon the boat containing the three princes and the princess. The fay who protected them caused milk to fall instead of rain into their little mouths; they did not suffer from the frightful storm that had blown up so suddenly.

In the end, they floated for seven days and seven nights; they were as tranquil in the open sea as on a canal when they were encountered by a corsair ship. The captain having been struck, although from a distance, by the brilliant gleam of the stars they had on their foreheads, lowered a launch, convinced that the boat was full of gems. He found some, in fact, but what touched him more was the beauty of the four marvelous children. The desire to conserve them engaged him to return home, in order to give them to his wife, who had none and had wanted some for a long time.

She was very anxious on seeing him return so promptly, for he had gone to make a long voyage, but she was transported with joy when he put such a considerable treasure in her hands; they admired the marvel of the stars together, the golden chains that could not be removed from their necks, and their long hair. That was something else entirely when the woman combed it, for pearls, rubies, diamonds and emeralds of various sizes fell from it continually, all of them perfect. She talked about it to her husband, who was no less astonished than she was.

"I'm very weary," he told her, "of the profession of corsair. If the hair of these little children continues to give us treasures, I don't want to run the seas any longer, and my wealth will be as considerable as that of our greatest captains."

The corsair's wife whose name was Corsine, was delighted with her husband's resolution; she loved the children all the more for it. She named the princess Belle-Etoile, her elder bother Petit-Soleil, the younger one Heureux, and the son of the princess, Cheri. He was far above the other two for beauty, and although he had no star or chain, Corsine loved him more than the others.

As she could not raise them without the help of a nurse she asked her husband, who was very fond of hunting, to trap some little fawns; he found the means, for the forest where they lived was very spacious. When she had them, Corsine exposed them to the wind. The hinds, which scented them ran to suckle them. Corsine hid them, and put the children in their place, who adapted very well to hinds' milk. Twice every day four of them came in company to Corsine's house in search of the princes and the princess, whom they took for fawns.

It was thus that the tender infancy of the princes passed. The corsair and his wife loved them so passionately that they gave them all their care. The man had been well brought-up, it was less by inclination than the eccentricity of fortune that he had become a corsair. He had married Corsine in the house of a princess, where her mind had been fortunately cultivated; she knew how to live, and although she found herself in a kind of wilderness, where they had only subsisted on the larcenies he committed in his expeditions, she had not yet forgotten the usages of society. They had the utmost joy in no longer having the obligation to risk all the perils attached to the profession of corsair, and they became rich without that. Every three days, as I have said, considerable gems fell from the hair of the princess and her brothers, which Corsine went to sell in the nearest city, from which she brought back a thousand nice things for the four children.

When they had emerged from early childhood the corsair applied himself seriously to cultivating the fine nature with which Heaven had endowed them. As he did not doubt that there were great mysteries hidden in their birth and the encounter that he had had with them, he wanted to recognize by their education that present of the gods, with the consequence that, after having rendered his house more capacious, he attracted persons of merit there who taught them various sciences with a facility that surprised all those great masters.

The corsair and his wife had never told anyone about the adventure of the four children. They passed them off as their own, although they marked by all their actions that they emerged from a more illustrious blood. They were closely united with one another; they found that natural and polite; but Prince Cheri had sentiments more urgent and more vivid for Princess Belle-Etoile than the other two. As soon as she wanted something, he would even attempt the impossible to satisfy her; he hardly ever quit her; when she went hunting, he accompanied her; when she did not go, he always found excuses to forbid him to go. Petit-Soleil and Heureux, who were her brothers, spoke to her with less tenderness and respect. She noticed that difference, held it to Cheri's credit, and loved him more than the others.

As they advanced in age, their mutual tenderness increased; at first they had nothing but pleasure therein. "My tender brother," Belle-Etoile said to him, "if my desires were sufficient to render you fortunate, you would be one of the greatest kings on earth."

"Alas, my sister," he replied, "don't envy me the good fortune that I enjoy with you; I prefer spending an hour where you are to all the elevation you wish for me."

When she said the same thing to her brothers, they replied naturally that they would be delighted by it, and to test them further, she added: "Yes, I'd like you to occupy the finest throne in the world, even if I were never to see you."

Immediately, they said: "You're right, my sister, the one is far better than the other."

"You would consent, then," she replied, "to no longer seeing me?"

"Of course," they said. "It would be sufficient for us sometimes to hear your news."

When she was alone, she examined those different fashions of loving, and felt her heart disposed exactly like theirs, for even thought Petit-Soleil and Heureux were dear to her, she did not want to remain with them all her life, but with regard to Cheri, she dissolved in tears when she thought that their father might perhaps send him to roam the sea, or put him in the army. It is thus that amour, masked by the specious name of good nature, was established in their young hearts.

At fourteen years of age, however, Belle-Etoile began to reproach herself for the injustice she believed that she was doing her brothers by not loving them equally. She imagined that Cheri's cares and caresses were the cause of it. She forbade him to seek further means of making himself loved. "You've found too many of them," she told him, agreeably, "and you've succeeded in making me put a great difference between you and them."

What joy did he not feel when he heard her say that! Far from diminishing his eagerness, she augmented it; he made her a new gallantry every day.

They did not know as yet how far their tenderness went, and they did not know its species, until Belle-Etoile was brought several new books. She took the first one that came to hand; it was the story of two young lovers, whose passion had begun while believing themselves to be brother and sister; then they had been recognized by their relatives, and after infinite troubles they had married. As Cheri could read perfectly well, had a fine understanding and made himself understood in the same manner, she asked him to read the book to her while she finished some silk-floss needlework that she wanted to complete.

He read that adventure, and it was not without a great anxiety that he saw in it a naïve description of all his sentiments. Belle-Etoile was no less surprised, and it seemed that the author had read what was happening in her soul. The more Cheri read, the more touched he was; the more the princess listened, the more emotional she was; whatever effort she could make, her eyes filled with tears and her face was covered with them. Cheri made futile efforts on his part; he went pale, changed color and the tone of his voice; they both suffered all that one can suffer,

"Oh, my sister," he cried, looking at her sadly and dropping his book. "Oh, my sister, how fortunate Hippolyte was not to be Julie's brother!"[22]

"We would have a similar satisfaction," she replied. "Alas, is it any less due to us?" As she finished speaking, she knew that she had said too much; she remained nonplussed, and if anything could console the prince, it was the state in which he saw her.

From that moment on they fell into a profound sadness, without explaining themselves further; they penetrated a part of what was happening in their souls; they were careful to hide from everyone a secret that they would have liked not to know themselves, and which they did not discuss with one another. However, it is so natural to flatter oneself, the princess nevertheless took account of the fact that Cheri was the only one who did not have a star on his forehead or a chain around his neck, although, like his cousins, he had long hair with the gift of shedding precious stones when it was combed.

When the three princes went hunting one day, Belle-Etoile shut herself in a little cabinet, which she liked because it was dark and she could dream there with more liberty than elsewhere. She did not make any noise. That cabinet was only separated from Corsine's bedroom by a partition, and the woman thought she had gone out for a walk. She heard her say to the corsair: "Belle-Etoile is of an age to be married now; if we knew who she is, we could try to establish her in a manner appropriate to her rank; or if we could believe that those we represent as her brothers aren't, we could give her to one of them, for who could she ever find as perfect as them?"

---

[22] The coupling of these two names reveals that the book in question is Madame d'Aulnoy's historical romance *Hypolite, comte de Duglas* (1690).

"When I encountered them," the corsair said, "I didn't see anything that could instruct me as to their birth; the stones that were attached to their cradle made it known that the children belonged to rich people. What was singular about it is that they were all twins, for they seem to be the same age, and it's not ordinary that there are four of them."

"I suspect too," said Corsine, "that Cheri isn't their brother; he doesn't have a star or a chain around his neck."

"It's true," replied her husband, "but diamonds fall from his hair, like that of the others, and after all the riches we've amassed by means of those dear children, nothing more remains for me to wish than to discover their origin."

"It's necessary to leave that to the gods," said Corsine. "They have given them to us, and doubtless when the time comes, they'll develop what is hidden from us."

Belle-Etoile listened attentively to that conversation. The joy she had in being able to hope that they came from illustrious blood was inexpressible, for although she had never lacked respect for those to whom she believed she owed the light of day, she had nevertheless felt the pain of being the daughter of a corsair. But what flattered her imagination most was the thought that Cheri might not be her brother; she was burning with impatience to talk to him, and to tell them all about such an extraordinary adventure.

She mounted a light bay horse whose dark mane was attached with diamond buckles, for she had only had to comb her hair once to garnish an entire hunting equipage; its green velvet saddle-cloth was studded with diamonds and embroidered with rubies. Once mounted up, she set off into the forest to search for her brothers. The sound of horns and the barking of the dogs allowed her to hear where they were, and she joined them after a moment.

At the sight of her, Cheri detached himself and came toward her more rapidly than the others. "What a pleasant surprise!" he shouted. "You've finally come hunting—you, whom we couldn't distract for a moment from the pleasures that music gives you, and the sciences you're learning!"

"I have so many things to tell you," she replied, "and wanting to do it in private, I came to look for you."

"Alas, my sister," he said, sighing, "What do you want with me today? It seems that for a long time you've no longer wanted anything from me."

She blushed; then, lowering her eyes, she sat on her horse, sad and pensive, without replying to him. Finally, her two brothers arrived; she woke up at the sight of them as if from a profound sleep, and leapt to the ground, walking ahead. They all followed her, and when they were in the middle of a small patch of grass shaded by trees, she said: "Let's sit down here and I'll tell you what I've just heard."

She related to them, exactly, the corsair's conversation with his wife, and how they were not their children. Nothing could be added to the surprise of the three princes; they debated between them what they ought to do. One wanted to depart without saying anything, another did not want to depart at all, and the third wanted to depart and tell them everything. The first sustained that it was the surest means, because the profit they obtained from combing their hair would oblige them to retain them; the second replied that it would be good to quit them if they knew of a definite place to go, and what condition they had, but that the title of vagabonds was not agreeable; the third added that it would be ingratitude to abandon them without their agreement, and stupidity to want to stay any longer with them in the middle of a forest where they could not learn who they were, and that the best course was to talk to them and make them consent to their going away. They all came round to that opinion. Immediately, they mounted up in order to go and find the corsair and Corsine.

Cheri's heart was flattered by all that hope could offer of the most agreeable to console an afflicted lover; his amour enabled him to divine a part of future things; he no longer believed that he was Belle-Etoile's brother; his constrained passion, obtaining a new impetus, permitted him a thousand tender ideas, which charmed him.

They joined the corsair and Corsine with expressions mingling joy and anxiety.

"We haven't come," said Petit-Soleil—for he was the spokesman—"to deny you the amity, the gratitude and the respect that we owe you. Although we're informed of the manner in which you found us at sea, and that you're neither our father nor our mother, the pity that you had in saving us, the noble education you've given us, and all the cares and benevolence you've had for us are engagements so indispensable that nothing in the world can free us from your dependency. We've come to renew our sincere thanks to you, to beg you to recount such a rare event to us, and to advise us, in order that, guiding us by your sage advice, we'll have nothing for which to reproach ourselves."

The corsair and Corsine were very surprised that something they had hidden so carefully had been discovered. "You're too well informed," they said, "And we can't hide it from you that you're not our children and that fortune alone enabled you to fall into our hands. We have no illumination as to your birth, but the gems that were in your cradle could be evidence that your parents are either great lords or very rich. Apart from that, what can we advise you?

"If you consult the amity we've had for you, you'd doubtless remain with us and console our old age with your amiable company; if the château we've built in this place doesn't please you, or the abode of this solitude caused you chagrin, we'll go wherever you wish, provided that it's not to court; a long experience has disgusted us with that, and you'd probably be disgusted if you were informed of the continual agitations, feints, envy, inequalities, veritable evils and false goods that are found there. We could tell you more, but you'd believe that our counsels were interested; they are, too, my children; we desire to arrest you in this peaceful retreat, although you're free to quit us whenever you wish.

"Consider, however, that you're in port and you'll be setting forth on a stormy sea; that pains almost always surpass pleasures; that the course of life is limited; that one often quits it in mid-career; that the grandeurs of society are false diamonds by which one allows oneself to be dazzled by virtue of a strange fatality, and that the most solid of all goods is to know how to limit oneself, to enjoy tranquility and to become sage."

The corsair would not have finished those remonstrations so soon if he had not been interrupted by Prince Heureux. "My dear father," he said, "we have too much desire to discover something about our birth to bury ourselves in the depths of a desert. The morality that you establish is excellent, and I would like us to be capable of following it, but a kind of fatality is summoning us elsewhere. Permit that we fulfill the course of our destiny. We will come back to see you and render you an account of all our adventures."

At those words the corsair and his wife began to weep. The princes were moved to compassion, especially Belle-Etoile, who had an admirable nature and who would never have thought of leaving the wilderness if she were sure that Cheri would always remain with her.

That resolution having been made, they no longer thought about anything but preparing their equipage in order to embark; for having been found at sea, they had some hope that they might receive the enlightenment there regarding what they wanted to know.

They took aboard their small ship a horse for each of them, and, after having combed their hair to the point of skinning the scalp in order to leave gems for Corsine, they asked her to give them in exchange the diamond chains that had been in their cradle. She went to look for them in her cabinet, where she had kept them carefully, and she attached them to Belle-Etoile's garments. She embraced her incessantly, moistening her face with her tears.

No separation has ever been so sad; the corsair and his wife nearly died of it; their dolor did not come from an interested source, for they had amassed so much treasure that they did not want any more. Petit-Soleil, Heureux, Cheri and Belle-Etoile boarded the ship. The corsair had made it very good and quite magnificent. The mast was ebony and cedar, the rigging green silk mingled with gold, the sails cloth of gold and green, and the paintings excellent. When it set sail, Cleopatra with her Antony, and even all the oarsmen of Venus would have lowered the flag before it. The princess was sitting under a rich awning at the poop; her two brothers and her cousin were standing beside her, more brilliant than the stars, and their own stars projected long beams of dazzling light.

They resolved to go to the same place where the corsair had found them, and they did, in fact, go there. They had planned to make a grand sacrifice to the gods and the fays there in order to obtain their protection, and that they might be guided to their birthplace. They took a turtle-dove in order to immolate it, but the compassionate princess found it so beautiful that she saved its life, and to protect it from a similar accident, she released it. "Go, little bird of Venus" she said to it, "And if I have need of you some day, don't forget the favor I've done for you."

The turtle-dove flew away; the sacrifice being finished, they commenced a concert so charming that it seemed that all of nature was keeping a profound silence in order to listen to them. The waves of the sea did not rise; the wind did not blow. Zephyr alone agitated the princess's hair and put her veil in slight disorder.

At that moment a siren emerged from the water, who sang so well that the princess and her brothers admired her. She turned toward them and cried to them: "Cease to worry; let your vessel go; descend where it stops, and let those who love one another continue to love one another."

Belle-Etoile and Cheri felt an extraordinary joy at what the siren had just said. They did not doubt that it was for them, and, making one another a sign of intelligence, their hearts spoke without Petit-Soleil and Heureux perceiving it. The ship sailed at the whim of the winds and the waves; their navigation had nothing extraordinary; the weather was always fine, and the sea always calm. Nevertheless, their voyage lasted three entire months, during which the amorous Prince Cheri often conversed with the princess.

"How many flattering hopes I have, charming Star!" he said to her one day. "I am not your brother; this heart, which recognizes your power, and which will never recognize another, was not born for crimes, although it would be one to love you as I do, if you were my sister; but the charitable siren who came to counsel us has confirmed what I had in mind in that regard."

"Oh, my brother," she said, "don't trust too much in something that is still so obscure that we cannot penetrate it. What would our destiny be if we irritate the gods by sentiments that could displease them? The siren explained herself so obliquely that it is necessary to have a great desire to divine in order to apply what she said to us."

"You are forbidding yourself to do so, cruel woman," said the afflicted prince "much less because of the respect you have for the gods than by virtue of aversion for me."

Belle-Etoile made no reply, and, raising her eyes to the heavens, she uttered a profound sigh, which he could not help interpreting in his favor.

They were in the season when the days are long and hot; toward evening the princess and her brothers went up on deck in order to watch the sun set in the bosom of the waves; she sat down, the princes placed themselves beside her; they took up instruments and commenced their agreeable concert.

Meanwhile, the vessel, impelled by a fresh wind, seemed to sail more lightly and hastened to double a little promontory that hid a part of the most beautiful city in the world; but suddenly, it was revealed; its aspect astonished our amiable young folk. All the palaces were marble, the roofs gilded, and the rest of the houses of very fine porcelain. Several evergreen trees mingled the enamel of their leaves with the various colors of the marble, gold and porcelain, with the consequence that they wished that their ship would enter the port; but they doubted that it could find a place there, there were so many others, the masts of which composed a floating forest.

Their desires were accomplished; they dropped anchor, and the shore was immediately covered with people, who had perceived the magnificence of the ship. The one that the Argonauts had constructed for the conquest of the fleece did not shine as much; the stars and the beauty of the marvelous children delighted those who saw them. Some ran to give the king the news; as he could not believe it, and the great terrace of the palace extended as far as the sea shore, he went there promptly.

He saw that the Princes Petit-Soleil and Cheri, holding the princess in their arms, were carrying her ashore; afterwards, their horses were brought out, the rich harness of which responded well to everything else. Petit-Soleil was mounted on one blacker than jet; Heureux had one that was gray, Cheri one as white as snow, and the princess her light bay. The king admired all four of their horses, which were marching so proudly that all those who approached them moved aside.

The princes, having heard people say: "There's the king," looked up, and having seen him, his attitude full of majesty, they immediately made him a profound reverence, and passed by slowly, keeping their eyes fixed on him.

For his part, he watched them and was no less charmed by the incomparable beauty of the princess than the good looks of the young princes. He commanded his squire to go and offer them his protection and everything they might need in a country where they were apparently strangers.

They received the honor that the king did them with much respect and gratitude, and told him that they only needed a house where they could be in private, that they would be very glad if it were a league or two from the city, because they were very fond of walking. Immediately, the chief squire had them given one of the most magnificent, where he lodged them comfortably with all their retinue.

The king's mind was so full of the four children he had just seen that he went immediately to the room of the queen, his mother, to tell her about the marvel of the stars shining on their foreheads, and everything that he had admired about them.

She was utterly nonplussed; she asked without any affectation what age they appeared to be; he replied fifteen or sixteen years; she did not manifest her anxiety but she had a terrible fear that Feintise had betrayed her.

Meanwhile, the king was striding back and forth, and said: "How fortunate a father is to have sons so perfect and a daughter so beautiful! As for me, unfortunate sovereign, I am the father of three dogs; they are illustrious successors, and my crown is very secure!"

The queen mother listened to these words with a mortal anxiety. The brilliant stars and the approximate age of the foreigners had so much in common with that of the princes and their sister that she had strong suspicions of having been deceived by Feintise, and that instead of killing the children she had saved them. As she had great self-possession, she did not give any evidence of what was happening in her soul; she did not even send anyone that day to seek information about many things that she desired to know, but the next day she commanded her secretary to go there and, under the pretext of giving orders in the house for their comfort, to examine everything, and see whether they had stars on their foreheads.

The secretary left early in the morning; he arrived as the princess was dressing; at that time one's complexion could not be bought from merchants; what was white remained white and what was black did not become white, with the result that he saw her uncoiffed; her blonde hair, finer than gold thread, which was being combed, descended in curls all the way to the floor; there were several baskets around her in order that the stones that fell from her hair would not be lost; the star on her forehead projected fires that could hardly be sustained, and the gold chain around her neck was no less extraordinary than the precious diamonds that were tumbling from the top of her head.

The secretary had a great deal of difficulty believing what he saw, but the princess, having chosen the largest pearl, begged him to keep it as a souvenir of her; it is the same one that the kings of Spain esteemed so much under the name of Peregrina, which means Pilgrim, because it came from a traveler.[23]

The secretary, confused by such great liberality, took his leave of her and saluted the three princes, with whom he stayed for a long time, in order to be informed of a part of what he wanted to know. He returned to give an account of it to the queen mother, who was confirmed in the suspicions that she already had. He told her that Cheri had no star, but that stones fell from his hair as from that of his brothers, that in his opinion he was the best made, that they came from far away, and that their father and mother had only give them a certain time in order to see foreign lands.

That article deflected the queen slightly, and she sometimes imagined that they were not the king's children. She was thus suspended between dread and hope when the king, who was very fond of hunting, went in the direction of their house. The chief squire, who accompanied him, told him in passing that it was there that he had lodged Belle-Etoile and her brothers, by his order.

"The queen has advised me not to see them," said the king. "She fears that they might have come from some country infected with the plague, and that they might bring bad air therefrom."

---

[23] The pearl known as La Peregrina became part of the Spanish crown jewels in 1558, having previously been worn by Queen Mary of England. In a more recent era, it was famously owned by the actress Elizabeth Taylor.

"That young foreign woman," said the chief squire, "is indeed very dangerous, but sire, I fear her eyes more than bad air."

"In truth," said the king, "I think as you do," and, immediately spurring his horse, he heard instruments and voices. He stopped close to a large drawing room, the windows of which were open, and after having admired the sweetness of the symphony, he advanced.

The noise of horses obliged the princes to look out; as soon as they saw the king they saluted him respectfully and hastened to come out, approaching him with cheerful faces and so many marks of submission that they embraced his knees and the princes kissed his hands, as if they had recognized him as their father.

He caressed them abundantly and sensed his heart so emotional that he could not divine the cause of it. He told them that they should not fail to come to the palace, and that he wanted to converse with them and introduce them to his mother. They thanked him for the honor that he was doing them, and told him that as soon as their garments and equipages were complete, they would not fail to pay their court to him.

The king quit them in order to finish the hunt that had commenced; he sent them half of the kill, obligingly, and took the other half to his mother.

"What!" she said. "Is it possible that you have had such a meager hunt? You usually kill three times as much game."

"That's true," replied the king, "but I've regaled the handsome strangers; I feel an inclination for them so perfect that I'm surprised by it myself, and if you had less fear of contagious air, I would already have had them come to lodge in the palace."

The queen mother was very annoyed; she accused him of lacking regard for her and made him reproaches for risking himself so lightly.

As soon as he had left her she sent word to Feintise to come and speak to her. She shut herself in her cabinet with her. She took her by the hair with one hand and held a dagger to her throat. "Wretch," she said. "I don't know what reserve of generosity prevents me from sacrificing you to my just resentment; you've betrayed me; you didn't kill the four children that I put into your hands to be rid of them. At least confess your crime, and perhaps I'll pardon you."

Feintise, half-dead with fear, threw herself at her feet and told her what had happened; that she believed it to be impossible that the children were still alive, because a tempest had blown up, so terrible that she had thought they would be crushed by the hail. In the end, though, she asked for time and said that she would find a means to get rid of them, one after another, without anyone in the world being able to suspect her.

The queen, who only wanted their death, was slightly appeased. And, in fact, old Feintise, who saw that she was in great peril, neglected nothing that depended on her. She waited for a time when the three princes were hunting, and, carrying a guitar under her arm, she went to sit under the princess's window, where she sang these words:

> *Beauty can overcome anything,*
> *Fortunate who can profit from it!*
> *Beauty is effaced,*
> *The age of ice*
> *Comes to tarnish all flowers;*
> *How painful it is*
> *When one remembers*
> *The attractions one has lost!*
> *One is in despair.*
> *And one takes, to please*
> *Superfluous cares.*
> *Young hearts, let yourselves charm,*
> *In the fine age one ought to love.*
> *Beauty is effaced,*
> *The age of ice*
> *Comes to tarnish all flowers;*
> *How painful it is*
> *When one remembers*
> *The attractions one has lost!*
> *One is in despair.*
> *And one takes, to please*
> *Superfluous cares.*

Belle-Etoile found those words rather pleasant; she advanced on to a balcony in order to see the person singing them. As soon as she appeared, Feintise, who had dressed very properly, made her a great reverence. The princess saluted her in her turn, and as she was cheerful, she asked her whether the words she had just heard had been made for her.

"Yes, charming person," Feintise replied, "they are for me; but in order that they will never be for you, I've come to give you some advice from which you ought not to fail to take advantage."

"And what is it?" said Bell-Etoile.

"As soon as you've permitted me to come up to your room," she added, "You'll know it."

"You can come up," the princess replied.

Immediately, the old woman presented herself, with a certain air of the court that one does not lose once one has it.

"My beautiful girl," said Feintise, without losing a moment—for she feared that they might be interrupted—"Heaven has made you very lovable; you are endowed with a brilliant star on your forehead, and many other marvels are recounted about you, but you still lack one thing that is essentially necessary to you; if you do not have it, I feel sorry for you."

"And what do I lack?" she replied.

"The dancing water," replied the malign old woman. "If I have had some of it, you wouldn't see a white hair on my head, not a wrinkle on my brow; I'd have the most beautiful teeth in the world, which a childish air that would charm. Alas, I knew the secret too late; my attractions were already effaced. Profit from my misfortunes, my dear child; it would be a consolation for me, for I sense movements of extraordinary tenderness for you."

"But where can I get this dancing water?" asked Belle-Etoile.

"It's in the luminous forest," said Feintise. "You have three brothers; does one of them not love you enough to go in search of it? Truly, they would scarcely be affectionate. In sum, there is no other means to be beautiful a hundred years after your death."

"My brothers cherish me," said the princess. "There is one of them who would not refuse me my anything. Certainly, if that water does everything you say, I will give you a recompense proportionate to its merit."

The perfidious old woman retired diligently, delighted to have succeeded so well. She told Belle-Etoile that she would be careful to come to see her."

*

The princes returned from hunting; one brought a young boar, another a hare and the third a red deer; all were laid at the feet of their sister. She gazed at that homage with a kind of disdain; she was occupied with Feintise's advice; she even seemed anxious about it, and Cheri, who had no other occupation than studying her, was not with her for a quarter of an hour without remarking it.

"What's the matter, my dear Star," he said to her. "Is the country where we are not to your liking? It that's the case, let's depart immediately. Perhaps, too, our equipage isn't large enough, the furniture beautiful enough, the table delicate enough. Speak, please in order that I have the pleasure of obeying you first and making the others obey you."

"The confidence that you give me to tell you what is passing in my mind," she replied, "engages me to declare to you that I can no longer live if I don't have the dancing water; it is in the luminous forest. With it, I shall have nothing to fear from the years."

"Don't be upset, my lovely Star," he added. "I'll depart and bring it to you, or you'll know by my death that it's impossible to obtain."

"No," she said, "I'd rather renounce all the advantages of beauty; I'd rather be frightful than risk a life so dear. I implore you not to think any longer about the dancing water, and, if I have any power over you, I even forbid you to do so."

The prince pretended to obey, but, as soon as he saw that she was occupied, he mounted his white horse, which only went by leaps and curvets, he took money and a rich coat; of diamonds he had no need, for his hair would furnish

236

enough, and three strokes of a comb sometimes caused a million's worth to fall. In truth, that was not always similar; they even knew that the disposition of their mind and that of their health regulated the abundance of the stones. He did not take anyone with him, in order to be more at liberty, and in order that, if the adventure were perilous, he could risk it without enduring the remonstrations of a zealous and fearful domestic.

When time for supper had come and the princess did not see her brother Cheri appear, anxiety gripped her to such a point that she could neither eat nor drink. She gave orders to search for him everywhere. The two princes, knowing nothing about the dancing water, told her that she was tormenting herself excessively; that he could not be far away; that she knew that he abandoned himself voluntarily to profound reveries; and the he had doubtless stopped in the forest. She acquired a little tranquility, therefore, until midnight, but then she lost all patience, and told her brothers, weeping, that she was the cause of Cheri having gone away, that she had testified an extreme desire to have the dancing water of the luminous forest, and that he had doubtless taken the road there.

At that news they decided to send several people after him, and she charged them to tell him that she implored him to return.

Meanwhile, the malevolent Feintise was very intrigued to know the effect of her advice. When she learned that Cheri was already on campaign, she had a sensible joy, not doubting that he would have more diligence than those who were following him, and that he would be overtaken by misfortune. She ran to the palace, proud of that hope; she gave the queen mother an account of what had happened.

"I admit, Madame," she told her, "that I cannot doubt that they are the three princes and their sister; they have stars on the forehead, gold chains around the neck, their hair has a ravishing beauty, and precious stones fall from it continually. I've seen on the princess the jewels that I put in her cradle, with which she adorns herself, although they aren't worth as much as the ones that fall from her hair, with the result that it isn't possible for me to doubt their return, in spite of the care I believed I had taken to prevent it. But Madame, I'll rid you of them, and as that's the sole means that remains for me to repair my fault, I only beg you to grant me the time. One of the princes has already departed to go in search of the dancing water; he'll doubtless perish in that enterprise, as I've prepared several occasions to doom him."

"We shall see," said the queen, "whether the success responds to your expectations, but remember that that alone can save you from my just fury."

Feintise withdrew, more alarmed than ever, searching in her mind for everything that could make them perish.

The means that she had found with regard to Prince Cheri was one of the most certain, for the dancing water could not be drawn easily; it had cause so much rumor by virtue of the misfortunes of those who searched for it that no one know the route.

His white horse went at a surprising speed; he spurred it without quarter, because he wanted to return to Belle-Etoile promptly and give her the satisfaction that she expected from his journey. Nevertheless, he traveled for a week without reposing anywhere but in the woods, under the first tree, without eating anything other than the fruits he found on the way, and scarcely leaving his horse time to browse the grass.

Finally, at the end of that time, he found himself in a region where the air was so hot that he began to suffer considerably. It was not that the sun had more ardor; he did not know to what to attribute the cause until, from the top of a mountain, he perceived the luminous forest All the trees were burning, without being consumed, and throwing flames into places so distant that the country was arid and deserted. The hissing of serpents and the roaring of lions could be heard in the forest, which astonished the prince greatly, because it seemed that no animal except the salamander could live in that kind of furnace.

After having considered such a frightful thing he descended, thinking about what he was going to do, and he said to himself more than once that he was doomed. As he drew nearer to the great conflagration he was dying of thirst. He found a spring that emerged from the mountain and fell into a large marble basin. He dismounted, approached it, and bent down in order to draw water in a small golden vase that he had brought in order to put the water that the princess desired into it.

He perceived a turtle-dove that was drowning in the spring; its feathers were soaked; it no longer had any strength, and sank to the bottom of the basin. Cheri took pity on it; he rescued it. First he suspended it by its feet; it had drunk so much that it was bloated by it. Afterwards, he warmed it up; he wiped its wings with a fine handkerchief. He helped it so much that after a while, the turtle-dove was more cheerful than it had ever been sad.

"Sire Cheri," it said to him, in a soft and tender voice, "you have never obliged a little animal more grateful than me. It's not only today that I have received essential favors from your family; I am delighted to be able to be useful to you in my turn. Don't believe that I'm unaware of the subject of your voyage. You've attempted it a trifle recklessly, for no one knows the number of people who have perished here. The dancing water is the eighth wonder of the world for the ladies; it embellishes, it rejuvenates and it enriches; but if I don't serve as your guide, you'll never be able to reach it, for the spring emerges seething in the middle of the forest and precipitates into a gulf there. The path is covered by tree branches that all hang down ablaze, and I can see no other means of going there than to go underground. Repose here without anxiety, therefore, and I will organize what is necessary."

At the same time the turtle-dove rose into the air, came and went, swooped and soared, again and again, so much that at the end of the day it said to the prince that everything was ready. He took the obliging bird, kissed it, caressed it, thanked it and followed it on his beautiful white horse.

He had scarcely gone a hundred paces when he saw two long files of foxes, badgers, moles, snails, ants and all sorts of creatures that hide underground. There was such a prodigious quantity of them that he could not understand by what power they were assembled thus.

"It's by my order," the turtle-dove told him, "that you see this little subterranean population in this place; they've just worked for your service and have done so with an extreme diligence. You'll give me the pleasure of thanking them."

The prince saluted them and told them that he would like to meet them in a less sterile place, that he would regale them with pleasure. Each small creature seemed content.

When he reached the entrance of the vault, Cheri left his horse there. Then, bent over, he went on with the benevolent turtle-dove, which led him safely all the way to the spring. It was making such a loud noise that would have deafened him if the bird had not given him two of its white feathers, with which he blocked his ears.

He was strangely surprised to see that the water was dancing with the same precision as if Favier and Pecout had taught it. It is true that they were only old dances, like the Bocane, the Mariée and the Saraband. Several birds that were fluttering in the air were singing the tunes to which the water wanted to dance.

The prince drew enough to fill his golden vase; he drank it in two draughts, which rendered him a hundred times more beautiful than before, and refreshed him so well that he scarcely perceived that of all the places in the world, the luminous forest is the hottest.

He departed by the same route by which he had come; his horse had drawn away but, faithful to his voice, as soon as he called it, it came at a fast gallop. The prince jumped on to it lightly, very proud to have the dancing water.

"Tender turtle-dove," he said to the bird he was still holding, "I still don't know by what prodigy you have so much power in this place; the effects that I have felt engage me to an enormous gratitude, and as liberty is the greatest of goods I return yours to you, to equal the favor that you have done me."

As he finished speaking, he let it go. It flew away as swiftly as if it had stayed with him against his will.

What inequality! he said to himself, then. *There is more of the human about you than the turtle-dove; one is inconstant, the other is not.*

The turtle-dove replied to him from up above: "Ah! Do you know who I am?"

Cheri, astonished that the turtle-dove had replied thus to his thought, judged that it was very clever; he was sorry to have let it go. *It might have been useful to me,* he said to himself, *and I could have learned many things from it that might have contributed to the repose of my life.* However, he agreed with himself that it is necessary never to regret a benefit accorded; he found himself greatly in debt when he thought about the difficulties that it had smoothed out for him in order to obtain the dancing water.

His golden vase was sealed in such a manner that the water could not escape or evaporate. He was thinking agreeably about the pleasure that Belle-Etoile would have in receiving it, and the joy he would have in seeing her again when he saw several horsemen riding at full tilt, who had no sooner seen him than they pointed him out to one another.

He was not afraid; his soul had an intrepid character that was not alarmed by perils; but he felt a great deal of chagrin that something was stopping him. He pushed his horse abruptly toward them, and was agreeably surprised to recognize a party of his domestics, who presented him with little notes, or, more accurately, orders, that the princess had given them for him so that he would not expose himself to the dangers of the luminous forest. He kissed Belle-Etoile's handwriting, sighed more than once, and, hastening to return to her, he extracted himself from the most sensible pain that one can experience.

When he arrived he found her under a few trees, where she had abandoned herself to all her anxiety. When she saw him at her feet she did not know what welcome to give him; she wanted to scold him for having departed against her orders and she wanted to thank him for the charming present he had brought her. In the end, tenderness prevailed, and the reproaches she made him had nothing unpleasant about them.

Old Feintise, who was not asleep, heard from her spies that Cheri had returned more handsome than he had been before his departure, and that the princess, having put the dancing water on her face, had become so exceedingly beautiful that there was no means of sustaining the slightest of her gazes without dying more than half a dozen deaths.

Feintise was quite astonished, and very afflicted, for she had expected that the prince would perish in such a great enterprise; but it was no time to be put off. She waited for a moment when the princess went to a small temple of Diana with little accompaniment. She approached her and said to her, in a manner full of amity: "How joyful I am, Madame, at the fortunate effect of my advice! It is only necessary to look at you to know that you now have the dancing water; but if I dare to offer you an advice, you ought to think of rendering yourself mistress of the singing apple. That is something else entirely, because it embellishes the mind to such a degree that there is nothing of which it is incapable. Does one want to be persuasive? It is only necessary to sniff the singing apple. Does one want to speak in public, make verses, write in prose, be diverting, makes people laugh or cry? The apple has all those virtues, and it sings so well and so loudly that one can hear it eight leagues away without being deafened by it."

"I don't want it!" cried the princess. "You nearly caused my brother to perish with your dancing water, your counsels are too dangerous."

"What, Madame!" replied Feintise. "You'd be sorry to be the most knowledgeable and intelligent person in the world? In truth, you're not thinking about it."

"Ah, what would I have done," Belle-Etoile continued, "if my brother's body had been brought back to me, dead or dying?"

"That one," said the old woman, "need not go again; the others can be obliged to serve you in their turn, and the enterprise is less perilous."

"It doesn't matter," said the princess. "I'm not in a humor to risk them."

"In truth, I feel sorry for you," said Feintise, "for losing such an advantageous opportunity; but you'll think about it. Adieu, Madame." She withdrew immediately, very anxious about the success of her speech, and Belle-Etoile remained at the feet of the statue of Diana, irresolute as to what she ought to do. She loved her brothers, and she loved herself too; she understood that nothing could give her a more sensible pleasure than to have the singing apple. She sighed for a long time, and then she started weeping.

Petit-Soleil was coming back from hunting; he heard the noise in the temple and went in. He saw the princess, who covered her face with her veil because she was ashamed of having moist eyes. He had already remarked the tears and, approaching her, he implored her insistently to tell him why she was weeping. She would not do it, replying that she was ashamed of herself, but the more she refused her secret, the more desire he had to discover it.

Finally, she told him that the same old woman who had advised her to send someone to conquer the dancing water had come to tell her that the singing apple was even more marvelous, because it gave so much intelligence that one became a species of prodigy; that the truth was that she would have given half her life for such an apple, but that there was too much danger in going to search for it."

"You won't be afraid for me, I can assure you," said her brother, smiling, "For I don't have any desire to render you that good office. What! Don't you have enough intelligence? Come on, my sister," he continued, "and cease afflicting yourself."

Belle-Etoile followed him, as saddened by the manner in which he had received her confidence as the impossibility she found of possessing the singing apple.

Supper was served, and all four of them went to table. She could not eat. Cheri, the lovable Cheri, who only had attention for her, served her the best of what was there, and pressed her to taste it; at the first morsel her heart swelled, tears came to her eyes and she left the table, weeping.

Belle-Etoile weeping! O gods, what a subject of anxiety for Cheri! He demanded to know, therefore, what was wrong with her. Petit-Soleil told him, joking in a fashion that was rather disobliging to his sister. She was so piqued in consequence that she withdrew to her room, and did not want to speak to anyone all evening.

As soon as Petit-Soleil and Heureux had gone to bed, Cheri mounted his excellent white horse, without telling anyone where he was going. He only left a letter for Belle-Etoile, with an order to give it to her when she woke up, and all night long he rode at hazard, not knowing where he could obtain the singing apple.

When the princess got up, the prince's letter was presented to her. It is easy to imagine everything she felt of anxiety and tenderness on an occasion like that. She ran to her brothers' room in order to read it to them. They shared her alarm, and immediately sent almost all their men after him, to oblige him to return without attempting the adventure, which would doubtless be terrible.

Meanwhile, the king had not forgotten the beautiful children of the forest; his footsteps continually took him in that direction, and when he passed close to their house and saw them he reproached them because they had not come to his palace. They made excuses, first because they were working in their equipage, then because of their brother's absence, and assured him that when he returned they would be sure to take advantage of the permission he had given them to render their very humble respects to him.

Prince Cheri was too driven by passion to fail to make great diligence. At daybreak he found a young man reposing under trees, reading a book. He approached him in a civil manner and said to him: "Permit me to interrupt you, in order to ask you whether you know where the singing apple can be found."

The young man looked up, smiling graciously. "Do you want to make the conquest of it?" he asked.

"Yes, if it possible for me," the prince replied.

"Oh, Sire, you don't know all the perils then. This is a book that speaks about it, and it is frightening to read."

"It doesn't matter," said Cheri. "Danger is incapable of putting me off. Only tell me where to find it."

"The book indicates," the young man continued, "that it is in a vast desert in Libya; that one can hear it singing eight leagues away; and that the dragon guarding it has already devoured five hundred thousand people who have dared to go there."

"I'll be the five hundred thousand and first," the prince replied, smiling in his turn and saluting him.

He took the road that went in the direction of the deserts of Libya. His beautiful horse, which was of the zephyrian race—for Zephyr was his ancestor—went as rapidly as the wind, with the result that he made incredible diligence.

He listened hard, but he did not hear any singing from that direction; he was afflicted by the length of the road and the fruitlessness of the journey, when he perceived a poor turtle-dove that had fallen at his feet; it was not yet dead, but very nearly. As he could not see anyone who might have wounded it, he thought perhaps that it belonged to Venus and that, having escaped from her dovecot, the little mutineer Amour, in order to try his arrows, had launched one at it. He felt sorry for it; he dismounted from his horse, picked it up, and wiped its white feathers, already tinted with vermilion blood. He took a small golden flask from his pocket, in which he carried a balm admirable for wounds; he had scarcely applied some to the injured turtle-dove than it opened its eyes, raised its head, spread its wings and preened its feathers.

Then, looking at the prince, it said: "Handsome Cheri, you are destined to save my life, and perhaps I can render you great services. You have come to conquer the singing apple. The enterprise is difficult, and worthy of you, for it is guarded by a frightful dragon, which has twelve feet, three heads, six wings and a body of bronze."

"Oh, my dear turtle-dove," said the prince, "what a joy it is for me to see you again, and at a time when your help is so necessary to me. Don't refuse it to me, my little beauty, for I would die of dolor if I had the shame of returning without the singing apple, and since I obtained the dancing water by your means, I hope that you can find someone again to enable me to succeed in my enterprise."

"You have touched me," replied the turtle-dove, tenderly. "Follow me. I'll fly ahead of you, and I hope all will go well."

The prince let it go; after having traveled all day, they arrived near a mountain of sand.

"It's necessary to dig here," said the turtle-dove.

Immediately, without being deterred by anything, the prince started digging, sometimes with his hands and sometimes with his sword. After a few hours he found a helmet, a breastplate and the rest of a suit of armor, with the equipment for his horse, entirely made of mirrors.

"Arm yourself," said the turtle-dove, "and have no fear; the dragon, when it sees itself in all these mirrors, will be so frightened that it will flee, thinking that they are monsters like itself."

Cheri approved strongly of that expedient. He armored himself with the mirrors, and, picking up the turtle-dove, they went on together into the night. At daybreak, they heard a delightful melody. The prince begged the turtle-dove to tell him what it was.

"I'm convinced," it said, "that only the apple can utter such agreeable sounds, for it makes all the orchestral parts by itself, and, without making use of any instruments. It seems to be playing them in a delightful fashion."

They were still getting closer; the prince thought privately that he would like the apple to sing something appropriate to the situation he was in, and at the same time he heard these words:

Amour can overcome the most rebellious heart;
Do not cease to be amorous.

You who are following the laws of a cruel beauty,
Love, persevere, and you will be happy.

"Oh!" he cried, responding to those lines. "What a charming prediction! I can hope to be more content one day than I am; it has just been announced to me."

The turtle-dove said nothing about that; it had not been born loquacious, and only spoke about indispensably necessary things.

As they advanced further, the beauty of the music was augmented, and no matter what urgency he had, there was something so rapturous about it that he stopped without being able to think about anything but listening to it. The sight of the terrible dragon, however, which suddenly appeared with its twelve feet and more than a hundred claws, its three heads and its body of bronze, extracted him from that species of lethargy; it had scented the prince from far away, and was waiting for him in order to devour him like all the others, of whom it had made excellent meals. Their bones were distributed around the apple tree where the beautiful fruit was; they rose up so high that it could not be seen.

The frightful animal advanced, bounding. It covered the earth with an exceedingly dangerous poisonous foam. Fire emerged from its infernal maw, along with little dragonets, which it launched like darts into the eyes and ears of the knights errant who wanted to take away the apple. When it saw its terrifying figure, however, multiplied hundreds of times in all the prince's mirrors, it was frightened in its turn; it stopped, and, looking proudly at the prince charged with dragons, it no longer thought of anything but fleeing.

Cheri, perceiving the fortunate effect of his armor, pursued it all the way to the entrance to a profound cavern, into which it precipitated itself in order to evade him; he quickly sealed the entrance, and hastened to return toward the singing apple.

After having climbed over all the bones that surrounded it, he saw the beautiful tree with admiration; it was amber, with topaz apples, and the most excellent one of all, for which he had searched with so many cares and perils, appeared at the top, made of a single ruby, with a crown of diamonds above it. The prince, transported by joy to be able to give such a rare and perfect treasure to Belle-Etoile, hastened to break the amber branch, and, proud of his good fortune, he mounted his white horse; but he no longer found the turtle-dove. As soon as its cares were unnecessary, it had flown away.

Without wasting time in superfluous regrets, as he feared that the dragon, the hissing of which he could hear, might find some route to reach the apples, he returned with his own to the princess.

She had lost the usage of sleep during his absence; she reproached herself incessantly for her desire to have more intelligence than others; she dreaded Cheri's death more than her own.

"Oh, wretched woman!" she cried, uttering profound sighs. "Was it necessary that I had that vain glory? Was it not sufficient for me to think and speak well enough not to do and say anything impertinent? I shall be well punished for my pride if I lose the one I love! Alas," she continued, "perhaps the gods, irritated by the sentiments that I might be forbidden to have for Cheri, want to take him away from me by means of a tragic end."

There was nothing that her afflicted heart had not imagined when, in the middle of the night, she heard a music so marvelous that she could not help getting up and going to the window in order to listen better; she did not know what to think. Sometimes she believed that it was Apollo and the Muses, sometimes Venus, the Graces and the Amours. The symphony was still coming closer, and Belle-Etoile listened.

Finally, the prince arrived. The moonlight was bright. He stopped under the balcony of the princess, who had withdrawn when she perceived a rider in the distance. The apple immediately sang: "Wake up, beautiful sleeper."

Curiously, the princess looked out promptly to see who could be singing so well, and, recognizing her dear brother, she nearly leapt down from the window in order to be near him sooner. She shouted so loudly that the whole household woke up, and someone went to open the door to Cheri. He came in with an urgency that can easily be imagined. He was holding the amber branch in his hand, at the end of which was the marvelous fruit, and as he had often respired its scent, his intelligence was augmented to such a degree that nothing in the world was comparable.

Belle-Etoile ran to him with great precipitation.

"Do you think that I will thank you, my dear brother," she said to him, weeping with joy. "No, there is no possession that I am not buying too dearly when you risk your life in order to acquire it for me."

"There is no peril," he said, "that I do not always want to risk in order to give you the smallest satisfaction." He continued: "Receive, Belle-Etoile, this unique fruit; no one in the world merits it as much as you; but what can it give you that you do not have already?"

Petit-Soleil and his brother came to interrupt that conversation; they had a sensible pleasure in seeing the prince again. He recounted the story of his journey to them, and that relation took them all the way to daybreak.

The evil Feintise had returned to her little house after having talked to the queen about her projects; she was too anxious to sleep tranquilly; she heard the sweet song of the apple, which nothing in nature could equal. She had no doubt that the conquest had been made. She wept, she moaned, she scratched her face and she tore her hair; her dolor was extreme, for, instead of harming the beautiful children, as she had projected, she had done them good, even though nothing but perfidy had entered into her advice.

As soon as it was daylight, she learned that the return of the prince was only too true. She returned to the queen mother.

"Well, Feintise," that princess said, "are you bringing me good news? Have the children perished?"

"No, Madame," she said, throwing herself at her feet, "but Your Majesty should not be impatient; I still have an infinite number of means to deliver you from them."

"Oh, wretched woman," said the queen, "You're only in the world to betray me; you're sparing them."

The old woman protested that it was entirely the contrary, and when she had appeased her somewhat, she returned home in order to think about what it was necessary to do.

She let a few days go by without appearing, at the end of which she spied so well that she found the princess on a forest path where she was walking alone, awaiting the return of her brothers.

"Heaven is heaping you with benefits, charming Star," the rascally woman said, approaching her. "I've learned that you possess the singing apple; certainly, when news of that good fortune reached me, I could not have had more joy, for its necessary to confess that I have an inclination for you that interests me in all your advantages. However," she continued, "I can't help giving you a further advice."

"Oh, keep your advice!" cried the princess, drawing away from her. "Whatever benefits it brings me, they can't repay me for the anxiety it has caused me."

"Anxiety isn't such a great evil," she replied, smiling. "There are sweet and tender ones."

"Shut up," said Belle-Etoile. "I tremble when I think of it."

"It's true," said the old woman," that you have a great deal to lament, being the most beautiful and most intelligent woman in the world; I apologize for that."

"One more blow," replied the princess. "I have had enough of the state to which my brother's absence has reduced me."

"It's necessary, in spite of that," Feintise continued, "that I tell you that you still lack the little green bird that says everything; you would be informed of your birth, the good and bad successes of life; there is nothing so private that it could not reveal it to you. When everyone in the world says: 'Belle-Etoile has the dancing water and the singing apple,' they will say at the same time: 'but she does not have the little green bird that says everything,' and it would be almost as if she had nothing."

After having spoken thus what she had in mind, she withdrew.

The princes, sad and thoughtful, commenced to sigh bitterly. *That woman is right*, she said to herself. *What use to me are the advantages I receive from the water and the apple, since I do not know who I am, who my parents are, and by what fatality my brothers and I were exposed to the fury of the waves? It is necessary that there was something very extraordinary in our birth for us to be abandoned thus, and a very evident protection of Heaven to have saved us from so many perils. What pleasure I would have in knowing my father and my mother, in cherishing them if they are still alive, and honoring their memory if they are dead!*

With that, tears came in abundance to cover her cheeks, similar to the droplets of dew that appear in the morning on the lilies and the roses.

Cheri, who always had more impatience to see her than the others, had hastened to return from the hunt; he was on foot, his bow hanging negligently by his side, his hand holding a few arrows, his hair bound up. In that state he had a martial appearance that was infinitely pleasing. As soon as the princess perceived him, she went into a dark pathway, in order that he would not see the impressions of dolor that were on her face, but a mistress cannot draw away so rapidly that an urgent lover cannot overtake her.

He had scarcely cast his eyes upon her that he knew that she had some distress. He was anxious about that; he begged her and pressed her to tell him the reason for it, but she refused obstinately. Finally, he turned the point of one of his arrows against his heart. "You do not love me, Belle-Etoile," he said to her. "I have nothing more to do than to die."

The manner in which he spoke threw her into the utmost alarm; she no longer had the strength to refuse him her secret; but she only told him on condition that he would not seek as long as he lived the means of satisfying the desire that she had. He promised her everything she demanded, and gave no indication that he wanted to undertake that last journey.

As soon as she had retired to her bedroom and the princes to theirs, he went downstairs, took his horse out of the stable, mounted up and set forth, without speaking to anyone.

That news threw the beautiful family into a strange consternation. The king, who could not forget them, had sent an invitation to come and dine with him; they replied that their brother had just absented himself, and that they could not have any joy or repose without him, but that when he returned, they would not fail to go to the palace.

The princess was inconsolable; the dancing water and the singing apple had no more charms for her; without Cheri, nothing was agreeable to her.

The prince went forth, wandering through the world. He asked everyone he encountered where he might find the little green bird that says everything. Most of them did not know, but he encountered a venerable old man who, having invited him into his house, agreed to take the trouble to look into a globe that played a part in his study and his amusement. He said afterwards that it was in a glacial climate, on the summit of a frightful rock, and informed him of the route that he ought to take. The prince, full of gratitude, gave him a small bag of large pearls that had fallen from his hair, took his leave of him and continued his journey.

Finally, at dawn one day, he perceived the rock, very high and very steep, and on the summit, the bird that spoke like an oracle, saying admirable things. He understood that with a little skill it would be easy to catch, for it did not appear to be wild. It went back and forth, leaping lightly from one pinnacle to another. The prince dismounted, and, climbing silently in spite of the harshness of the mountain, he promised himself the pleasure of giving a sensible one to Belle-Etoile.

He was so close so the green bird that he thought he could catch it, when the rock suddenly opened up and he fell into a spacious hall; as motionless as a statue, he could no longer stir or complain of his deplorable adventure. Three hundred knights who had attempted the quest before him were in the same state. They looked at one another; it was the only thing that was permitted to them.

The time seemed so long to Belle-Etoile that, not seeing her Cheri return, she fell dangerously ill. The physicians knew full well that she was being devoured by a profound melancholy. Her brothers loved her tenderly; they talked to her about the cause of her malady; she confessed to them that she reproached herself day and night for Cheri going away; and that she sensed clearly that she would die if she did not receive news of him. They were touched by her tears, and in order to cure her, Petit-Soleil resolved to go in search of his brother.

The prince departed; he discovered where the famous bird was; he went there; he saw it; he approached it with the same hopes; and at that moment the rock engulfed him, he fell into the great hall, and the first thing that arrested his gaze was Cheri; but he could not speak to him.

Belle-Etoile was slightly convalescent; she hoped continually to see her two brothers return; but her hopes were disappointed; her affliction took on new force; she did not cease to lament day and night; she accused herself of her brothers' disaster, and Prince Heureux, having no less compassion for her than anxiety for the princes made the resolution in his turn to go in search of them. He said so to Belle-Etoile; immediately, she tried to oppose it, but he replied that it was only just that he risk himself in order to find the persons who were the dearest in the world to him. With that, he departed, having bid the princess tender adieus. She was left alone, prey to the sharpest dolor.

When Feintise heard that the third prince had set forth she rejoiced infinitely; she informed the queen mother, and promised her more than ever to doom the whole of that unfortunate family.

Indeed, Heureux had an adventure similar to Cheri and Petit-Soleil; he found the rock; he saw the beautiful bird; and he fell like a statue into the hall, where he recognized the princes for whom he was searching, without being able to speak to them. They were all arranged in crystal niches; they never slept, did not eat, and remained enchanted in a manner so sad that they only had the liberty to dream, and to deplore their adventure.

Inconsolable, Belle-Etoile, not seeing her brothers return, reproached herself for having waited such a long time to follow them. Without further hesitation, she gave orders to all her servants to wait for her for six months, but that if she or her brothers had not returned in that time they were to return to inform the corsair and his wife of their death. Then she put on male clothing, thinking that there was less risk for her, thus disguised, in her journey than if she had gone to travel the world as an adventuress.

Feintise saw her depart on her beautiful horse, and, at the culmination of her joy, she ran to the palace to regale the queen mother with that good news.

The princess was only armored by a helmet, the visor of which she hardly ever raised, for her beauty was so delicate and so perfect that no one would have believed, as she wanted them to, that she was a cavalier.

The rigor of the winter made itself felt, and the land where the little bird that says everything lived did not receive the fortunate influences of the sun in any season.

Belle-Etoile felt a strange cold, but nothing could deter her, when she saw a turtle-dove that was scarcely less white and scarcely less cold that the snow on which it was lying. In spite of her impatience to arrive at the rock, she did not want to let it die, and, descending from her horse, she took it in her hands, warmed it with her breath and then put it in her bosom. The poor little thing was no longer moving. Belle-Etoile thought it was dead; she regretted that. She took it out, looked at it, and said to it, as if it could understand her: "What can I do, lovely turtle-dove, to save your life?"

"Belle-Etoile," the small creature replied, "A soft kiss from your mouth can finish what you have so charitably begun."

"Not one," said the princess, "but a hundred, if necessary."

She kissed it, and the turtle-dove, recovering courage, said to her gaily: "I know you, in spite of your disguise; know that you are attempting something that would be impossible without my help; do as I advise you, then. As soon as you arrive at the rock, instead of seeking a means to climb it, stop at the foot, and commence singing the most beautiful and melodious song that you know. The green bird that says everything will listen to you and will remark where the voice is coming from. Afterwards, pretend to go to sleep. I will stay with you; when it sees me it will descent from the summit of the rock in order to peck me; it is at that moment that you will be able to catch it."

The princess, delighted by that hope, arrived at the rock almost immediately; she recognized her brothers' horses browsing the grass; that sight renewed all her dolors; she sat down and wept bitterly for a long time. But the little green bird said such beautiful things, so consoling for the unfortunate, that there was no heart that did not rejoice, with the consequence that she wiped away her tears and began to sing so loudly and so beautifully that the princes in the depths of their enchanted hall had the pleasure of hearing her. That was the first moment in which they sensed some hope.

The little green bird that says everything listened, and looked to see where that voice was coming from. It perceived the princess, who had taken off her helmet in order to sleep more comfortably, and the turtle-dove, which was fluttering around her. At that sight, it descended stealthily and came to peck it, but it had not plucked out three feathers when it was already captured.

"Ah! What do you want with me?" it said "What have I done to you to come so far to render me so unfortunate? Accord me my liberty, I implore you; say what you want in exchange, there is nothing I cannot do."

"I desire," said Belle-Etoile, "that you return my three brothers to me; I don't know where they are, but their horses, which are grazing near this rock, tell me whether you are retaining them in some place."

"I have a rose-red feather under my left wing," it said. "Pull it out and make use of it to touch the rock."

The princess was diligent in what she had been ordered to do; at the same time, she saw flashes of lightning and heard the sounds of wind and thunder mingled together, which caused her an extreme dread. In spite of her terror she kept hold of the green bird, fearful that it might escape. She touched the rock with the red feather again, and the third time, it split from the summit to the foot. She entered victoriously into the hall where the three princes were, with many others.

She ran to Cheri; he did not recognize her with his coat and her helmet, and the enchantment had not yet ended, with the consequence that he could nether speak nor act. The princess, who perceived that, asked further question of the green bird, to which it replied that it was necessary to rub the eyes and mouth of all those she wanted to disenchant with the red feather.

She rendered that good office to several kings and several other sovereigns, and especially to the three princes. Touched by such a great benefit, they threw themselves at her feet, naming her the liberator of kings. She perceived then that her brothers, deceived by her costume, did not recognize her, She took off her helmet promptly, held out her arms to them, embraced them a hundred times, and asked the other princes, with a great deal of civility, who they were.

Each one told her their particular adventure, and offered to accompany her wherever she wanted to go. She replied that, although the laws of chivalry might give her some right over the liberty that she had just rendered to them, she did not want to prevail upon it. With that, she retired with the princes, in order for them all to take account of what had happened to them since their separation.

The little green bird that says everything interrupted them in order to beg Belle-Etoile to set it at liberty; she immediately looked for the turtle-dove in order to ask its advice, but she no longer found it. She replied to the bird that it had cost her too many difficulties and anxieties for her to get such scant enjoyment from its conquest. All four of them mounted up, and left the kings and emperors to go away on foot, for in the two or three hundred years that they had been there, their equipages had perished.

The queen mother, rid of all the anxiety that the return of the beautiful children had caused her, renewed her entreaties to the king to marry again, and importuned him so much that she chose a princess for him from among her relatives.

As it was necessary to break his marriage with poor Queen Blondine, who had always remained with her mother in their little house in the country, with the three dogs that they named Chagrin, Mouron and Douleur because of all the troubles they had caused them, the queen mother sent for her; she climbed into a carriage, dressed in black, with a long veil that fell to her feet, taking the dogs with her.

In that state, she appeared more beautiful than the day star, although she had become pale and thin, for she no longer slept and only ate out of complaisance. Except for the queen mother, everyone felt very sorry for her; the king was so moved by compassion that he dared not look at her, but when he thought that he was at risk of having no heirs but dogs, he consented to everything.

The day of the wedding having arrived, the queen mother, begged by Admirale Rousse—who had always hated her unfortunate sister—said that she wanted Queen Blondine to be present at the celebration. Everything was prepared to make it grandiose and sumptuous, and as the king would not be sorry for the foreigners to see that magnificence, he sent his chief squire to the house of the beautiful children to invite them to come, and ordered that if they could not come yet, he was to leave orders that they could be informed when they returned.

The chief squire went to search for them and did not find them, but, knowing the pleasure that the king would have in seeing them, he left one of his gentlemen to wait for them, in order to bring them without any delay.

The happy day arrived, which was that of a great banquet. Belle-Etoile and the three princes arrived; the gentleman told them the king's story: that he had once married a poor girl, perfectly beautiful and good, who had had the misfortune to give birth to three dogs, and that he had expelled her in order no longer to see her; that he had loved her so much that he had spent fifteen years without wanting to listen to any proposal of marriage; that the queen mother and his subjects had pressed him so forcefully that he had resolved to marry a princess of the court, and that it was necessary to come promptly to witness the whole ceremony.

At the same time Belle-Etoile put on a rose-colored velvet robe garnished with brilliant diamonds; she let her hair fall in long curls over her shoulders, and tied it again with ribbons. The star that she had on her forehead emitted so much light, and the golden chain that ran around her neck without her being able to remove it seemed to be of a metal far more precious even than gold. In sum, nothing so beautiful had ever appeared to mortal eyes. Her brothers were no less so, especially Prince Cheri, who has something about him that distinguished him very advantageously.

All four of them climbed into an ebony and ivory carriage, the interior of which was cloth of gold, with similar cushions, embroidered with gems; twelve white horses drew it; the rest of their equipage was incomparable.

When Belle-Etoile and her brothers appeared, the delighted king came to receive them with his entire court at the top of the staircase. The singing apple made itself heard in a marvelous manner; the dancing water danced; and the little green bird that says everything spoke better than oracles. All four knelt down before the king, took his hand and kissed it with as much respect as affection.

He embraced them and said: "I am obliged to you, amiable foreigners, for having come here today; your presence gives me a sensible pleasure. As he finished speaking he went with them into a large drawing room, where musicians were playing all sorts of instruments and several splendidly-served tables left nothing to be desired of good cheer.

The queen mother arrived, accompanied by her future daughter-in-law, Admirale Rousse and all the ladies, among whom the poor queen was brought, with a long leather thong around her neck and the three dogs tethered in the same fashion. She was taken into the middle of the room, where there was a cauldron of bones and rotten meat, which the queen mother had ordered for their meal.

When Belle-Etoile and the princes saw her so unfortunate, although they did not know her, tears came to their eyes, either because the revolution of the grandeurs of the world touched them, or they were moved by the force of the blood, which made itself felt.

But what did the evil queen think of a return so unexpected and so contrary to her designs? She darted a furious glance at Feintise, who desired ardently then that the earth might open up in order to precipitate herself into it.

The king introduced the beautiful children to his mother, saying a thousand good things to her about them, and in spite of the anxiety by which she was gripped, she spoke to them nevertheless with a cheerful expression, and looked at them as favorably as if she had loved them, for dissimulation was customary in those days.

The feast passed very gaily, although the king was extremely pained to see his wife eating with her dogs, like the least of creatures. Having resolved to have complaisance for his mother, however, who was obliging him to remarry, he allowed her to organize everything.

At the end of the meal, the king addressed Belle-Etoile, saying: "I know that you are in possession of three treasures that are incomparable; I congratulate you, and I beg you to tell us what it was necessary to do to conquer them."

"Sire," she said, "I will obey you with pleasure. I had been told that the dancing water would render me beautiful and that the singing apple would give me intelligence; I wanted to have them for those two reasons. With regard to the little green bird that says everything, I had another; it is that we do not know our fatal birth; we are infants abandoned by our relatives, of whom we do not know any. I hoped that this marvelous bird might enlighten us on a matter that occupies us day any night."

"To judge your birth by you," replied the king, "it must be of the most illustrious; but speak sincerely, who are you?"

"Sire," she told him, "my brothers and I have deferred interrogating it until our return; on arrival we received you orders to come to your wedding; all that I have been able to do has been to bring you the three rarities in order to divert you."

"I am very glad," cried the king, "not to defer such an agreeable matter."

"You're amusing yourself with all these bagatelles that are proposed to you." said the queen mother, angrily. "They're clowns, with their rarities; the names alone ought to tell you that nothing is more ridiculous. Fie! I don't want petty foreigners, apparently from the dregs of the people, to have the advantage of abusing your credulity. All this consists of some tricks of sleight-of-hand and without you, they wouldn't have the honor of sitting at my table."

On hearing a discourse so disobliging, Belle-Etoile and her brothers did not know what would become of them; their faces were covered with confusion and despair at enduring such an insult before that great court. But the king, having replied to his mother that her procedure was exaggerated, begged the beautiful children not to be chagrined, and extended his hand to them as a sign of amity.

Belle-Etoile took a crystal bowl, into which she poured all the dancing water; the water was immediately seen to leap in cadence, going back and forth, rising up like a little irritated sea, changing a thousand colors, and moving the crystal bowl along the king's table; then it suddenly threw a few drops in the face of the chief squire, to whom the children had some obligation. He was a man of rare merit, but his ugliness was no less so, and he had lost an eye. As soon as the water had touched him, he became so handsome that he was no longer recognizable, and his eye was cured.

The king, who loved him dearly, had as much joy in that adventure as the queen mother felt displeasure, for she could not hear anything but the applause that was given to the princes.

After the great noise had died down, Belle-Etoile put on the dancing water the singing apple, made of a single ruby crowned with diamonds, with its amber branch; it commenced a concert so melodious that a hundred musicians could not have done as much. That delighted the king and the entire court, and they only emerged from their admiration when Belle-Etoile took from her sleeve a little golden cage of marvelous workmanship, in which was the green bird that says everything. It was nourished on powdered diamonds and only drank the liquid of distilled pearls.

She took it, very delicately, and placed it on the singing apple; she fell silent out of respect, in order to give it time to speak. It had plumage of such great delicacy that it agitated when one closed one's eyes, and when they were reopened near to it, it was all the shades of green imaginable.

It addressed the king, and asked him what he wanted to know.

"We all want to know," said the king," who this beautiful young woman and these three young men are."

"O King," replied the green bird, in a strong and intelligible voice, "she is your daughter, and two of the princes are your sons; the third, named Cheri, is your nephew." With that, it recounted the entire story, with an incomparable eloquence, without neglecting the slightest detail.

The king dissolved in tears, and the afflicted queen, who had quit her cauldron and had approached slowly, wept with joy and amour for her husband and her children—for could the verity of the story be doubted, when all the marks that allowed them to be recognized were visible?

The three princes and Belle-Etoile got up at the end of their story; they came to throw themselves at the king's feet; they embraced his knees and kissed his hands; He held out his arms to them, he hugged them to his heart; nothing could be heard but sighs and cries of joy.

The king got up and, seeing the queen, his wife, who was still fearful, lurking near the wall in a humiliated fashion, he went to her, made her a thousand caresses, presented her with an armchair next to his own and obliged her to sit in it. Her children kissed her feet and hands a thousand times; no spectacle was ever more tender or more touching.

Everyone wept on their own account, and raised their hands and eyes toward Heaven, to render thanks to it for having permitted such important and obscure things to be known.

The king thanked the princess who had had the design of marrying him, and gave her a large quantity of gems. But with regard to the queen mother, the admiral's wife and Feintise, what would he not have done to them if he had listened to his resentment? The thunder of his anger was beginning to rumble when the generous queen, her children and Cheri implored him to calm down and to render against them a judgment more exemplary than rigorous.

He had the queen mother imprisoned in a tower, but the admiral's wife and Feintise were thrown into a black damp dungeon, where they only ate with the three dogs named Chagrin, Mouron and Douleur, which, no longer seeing their good mistress, bit them continually. They ended their lives there, which were long enough to give them time to repent of all their crimes.

As soon as the queen mother, Admirale Rousse and Feintise had been taken away, each to the place that the king had ordered, the musicians recommenced playing their instruments and singing. The joy was unparalleled. Belle-Etoile and Cheri felt it more than everyone else put together; they saw themselves on the eve of being happy. In fact, the king, finding his nephew to be the most handsome and most intelligent man in his court, said to him that he did not want such a great day to pass without celebrating his wedding, and that he would grant him his daughter.

The prince, transported by joy, threw himself at his feet, and Belle-Etoile testified no less satisfaction.

But it was only just that the aged princess, who had lived in solitude for so many years should quit it in order to participate in the public joy. The same little fay who had come to dinner in her house and whom she had received so well, suddenly came in there again, in order to tell her what was happening at the court.

"Let's go," she continued. "I'll tell you on the way the cares I have taken for your family."

The grateful princess climbed into her carriage; it was brilliant with gold and azure, preceded by martial instruments and by a corps of six hundred guards, who appeared to be great lords. She told the princess the whole story of her grandchildren, and said that she had not abandoned them, that in the form of a siren, and that of a turtle-dove—in sum, in a thousand fashions—she had protected them.

"You see," the fay added, "that a benefit is never wasted."

The good princess wanted to kiss her hands continually to mark her gratitude; she could not find terms that were not below her joy.

Finally, they arrived. The king received them with a thousand testimonies of amity. As one can believe, Queen Blondine and the beautiful children hastened to testify amity to the illustrious lady, and when they knew what the fay had done in their favor, and that she was the gracious turtle-dove who had guided them, nothing could be added to what they said to her.

To complete heaping the king with satisfaction, she told him that his mother-in-law, whom he had always taken for a poor peasant, had been born Princess Souveraine. That was perhaps the only thing that the monarch's happiness lacked.

The celebrations finished with the wedding of Belle-Etoile and Prince Cheri. They sent in quest of the corsair and his wife, in order to recompense them for the noble education they had given the beautiful children. Finally, after long troubles, everyone was satisfied.

Amour, not to displease the censors
Is the origin of glory,
He can animate great hearts
To brave peril and seek victory.
He it is who, throughout the world,
Has conserved the memory of Prince Cheri,
And who made him attempt the various exploits
That are marked in his story.
As soon one wants to pay his court to the fair sex,

One must be prepared to serve its caprices;
But a heart does not fear the greatest precipices
If it has, to animate it, glory and amour.

Henriette-Julie de Murat: *The Isle of Magnificence*

In the century when the fays were in vogue, one of the most famous had her Court on an island surrounded for a league around by a deep and profound lake, over which one could never pass without the consent of Queen Pleasure—as the fay was named—even by supernatural means such as riding on the back of a monstrous fish, a flying chariot, or something similar.

The island was called the Isle of Magnificence. The Queen's palace was in the middle of it; the architecture was of a new order, and very agreeable, for the material was the most brightly polished white ivory. The interior, even more superb, displayed wall-panels, ceilings and floors of Oriental agate, turquoise, onyx, cornelian and aventurine of all colors. Those rich materials served as frames for the most beautiful paintings in the world; the furniture was made of the same substances. Here one saw an aventurine sofa the color of fire, there an agate banquette, lapis armchairs, cornelian stools and amber settees, expertly carved. The wood of the beds was no less precious than the other furniture, and the fabrics sustained gold, silver, pearls and precious stones. The cabinets, desks, tables and sideboards were unequaled, they were inlaid with precious stones representing landscapes, flowers, fruits, birds and animals.

Only golden vessels were employed there, but not for cooking, none being done on the entire island; cooks and scullions were unknown there. A quarter of an hour before serving, all the dishes to be served were arranged on large cedar tables in the servants' parlor, and on the bottom of each one the name of the foodstuff that ought to fill it. The door was closed, and a quarter of an hour later, the meats and the fruits were done to perfection.

The gardens were no less marvelous than the palace was surprising. The water features, flowers and fruits were distributed with an order and artistry so out of the ordinary that it was not difficult to judge, on seeing them, that nature played no part in it.

The fay Pleasure combined a rare beauty with a flourishing youth that was not subject to time. Her mild and cheerful humor won the hearts of her subjects, who loved her passionately; she only liked to do good.

The entire island was filled with small, comfortable and magnificent buildings occupied by the inhabitants, who were all noble Lords and beautiful Ladies, the majority of whom had quit crowns in order to be subjects of Queen Pleasure. Some of those buildings were in marble of several different colors, others of jasper, porphyry and nacre. There were some of burnished silver and Corinthian copper; their design was various, but the symmetry and the arrangement of colors had an effect so regular that what was on one side was found on the other.

The beautiful fay's Court was one of the most charming and most numerous. There was nothing but amusing diversions, sumptuous meals, balls, operas, comedies and apartments. Although the Queen had no affair of the heart, she was not sorry that her subjects became happy by means of unions in which only amour played a part. She did not confine her cares to her realm alone; she had a secret commerce with elemental peoples who rendered her an account of everything that was happening in the world, and when some extraordinary accident happened to persons distinguished by their merit or quality, she did not refuse her help, and sometimes quit her charming empire in order to be useful to them.

One day, that beautiful Queen was informed by her usual couriers that one of the most powerful realms of the earth, governed by a valiant and sage King, had been attacked by several neighboring Kings who, jealous of his prosperity, had joined forces in order to crush him. He had already been opposing that torrent of enemies successfully for several years, but the fay, who knew that arms are transient, was concerned for the glory of that great King, and, without being requested, she departed from the Isle of Magnificence in a coral chariot pulled by two swans, and went to the Courts of the Kings and Princes in league, where she appeared in forms appropriate to her designs.

She insinuated in one a desire for repose, rendered another amorous and caused a few to run out of money, and even went as far as making use of maladies and tempests in order to stop others. Finally, she arrived at making them accept the advantageous offers of peace made by their generous enemy, and when she saw that they were all in accord, she resolved to spend some time in the Court of the great King.

She appeared there in her ordinary form and with her veritable name. For as long as she was in that Court she received homages of every kind, and when she departed, she left everyone amorous for Pleasure.

Although fays do not always make use of seven-league boots, they nevertheless make their journeys with diligence; the beautiful Queen only employed hers for a single day and night, during which she heard a woman crying very loudly as she passed through a hamlet. Her inclination, which always rendered her ready to help the unfortunate, obliged her to go down to the ground, and, approaching a small window in which she saw a light, she recognized that the cries were coming from there.

She lent an ear and heard the voice of one woman saying to another: "Courage, my child, you have just put into the world two beautiful boys; you still have the strength to deliver this one. You will be no less fortunate than your neighbor, who has just done as much. She has only had three girls, and to all appearances, you will have three boys; if they live, it might well be that they will make three marriages.

The fay understood by this discourse that there was a woman in labor. The novelty of the circumstance made her curious; she knocked on a small door that she perceived. A peasant came to open it, without a light, but a carbuncle that she had, of which she made such use occasionally, soon illuminated the little hamlet, whose inhabitants were no less frightened than delighted to see a Lady so beautiful and adorned.

"Don't be astonished, my children, I am only here for your relief."

At that moment, the woman gave birth to a third boy. Pleasure had them brought, and after having looked at them attentively she said to their mother: "What will you do with these children? You're poor, and I believe that it would give you pleasure if someone were to relieve you of the responsibility of their nourishment. If you want to give them to me, I will take care of them; they will be more fortunate than you; but as their happiness depends on your neighbor's three daughters, it's necessary to know whether she wants to do the same."

Those good folk were very surprised to see a Lady so savant and so charitable. The peasant woman, poor as she was, nevertheless had difficulty in resolving to lose her children, but her husband, to whom such a great fecundity gave no pleasure, said to the fay: "Take them, Madame, you won't do me so much good as long as I live; treat them like the cabbages in your garden. I believe that my friend will be no less glad to be rid of his three daughters than I am of my three sons, and I'll take him the good news right away."

So saying, he ran toward the door, but Pleasure said to him: "Wait, my friend, I'll go with you in order to let your friend know who it is that wants to have his daughters."

She followed the peasant, by the light of her carbuncle. As soon as he had gone in he told the husband and the wife what it was about, and after they had recovered somewhat from their astonishment they showed the fay the three most beautiful little creatures that had ever been seen. She made her intentions known to them, and they consented to it; then she made them presents capable of enriching them, and when she had returned to the first hut she did as much for the father and mother of the three boys, without forgetting the midwife, whom she told to take from a little trunk that she would find behind the door everything necessary to wrap the three children richly. Their astonishment increased continually. Finally, she put the babies with her in her chariot and having rubbed their lips with an essence that put them to sleep, she continued her route.

The Queen arrived before dawn at her palace, where she gave the children nurses and put them in separate apartments, the girls on one side and the boys on the other. The six children were raised in the same fashion until the age of fifteen, without ever seeing one another.

The three boys were handsome and well made; they had good minds, but of different species; that is why the fay gave each of them a name appropriate to his capacity. She named one Intelligence, because he had a penetrating mind capable of all sciences and all arts; the second she called Memory because he remembered everything with a surprising facility; and the third, who had a great deal of solidity and who seemed capable of great things, she called Understanding. Nothing was lacking in their education.

The girls were raised with similar care and as persons of quality. Their beauty was different, as was their humor. One of them was blonde, white and silvery, with lively and cheerful eyes, took pleasure in everything, took no chagrin and gave none to anyone. Pleasure named her Felicity. One of the others was neither brunette nor blonde, but her beauty attracted everyone's respect; she spoke fluently and in good terms, reciting everything she knew with verity and charm, observing the smallest circumstances. Her name was History. The other spoke little, justly, and never without necessity, knowing perfectly how to discern what it was necessary to say or not to say, in accordance with the occasion. Her beauty was regular, her complexion pale and bright, and her hair black. She was named Prudence.

One day, the charming Queen of the Isle of Magnificence had those six agreeable young people dressed in very rich and well designed garments that suited them perfectly. She had them come into her cabinet, where she was alone. They had never seen one another, and after having given them some time to consider one another she told the young men to give their hands to the beautiful young woman and to choose freely and without constraint the one that they liked the best. They did that, after having bowed to them politely. It happened, by a fortunate effect of sympathy, that Intelligence gave his hand to Felicity, that Memory took that of History and that Understanding offered his to Prudence. The six young people were quite content with their choice, and it was not long before they perceived a reciprocal passion for one another.

Queen Pleasure gave the three brothers the three principal responsibilities in her household. Intelligence had the conduct of her enchanted gardens and he was the Grand Bostangi.[24] Memory had the care of the stones of the crown and the fay's magnificent wardrobe and was the Guardian of the Royal Treasury. As for Understanding, he had the direction of the furniture, the vessels and golden vases, and organized all the feasts and amusements, with the quality of Treasurer of Small Pleasures. The three beautiful young women, their mistresses, were Ladies of the Palace.

Two years went by in that fashion; the six young people were the delight of the superb Court. Only one year remained until the time that Pleasure had destined to render them happy, when one of the great Lords of the Court married one of the Queen's maids of honor, who was a very beautiful young woman. Magnificent celebrations were held, and Pleasure did not forget anything to solemnize the wedding.

On the night that followed the last of the diversions, as he traversed the gardens to return to the palace, Intelligence found all the fruits on the ground, and the fountains that were accustomed to play uninterruptedly had dried up. He was frightened by such a surprising thing, and, having thought about how such

---

[24] Bostangi is a Frenchification of the Turkish word for gardener, also used as a title for a member of the Imperial Guard of the Ottoman Empire.

an accident could have happened, he remembered that when Felicity had joined him in order to tell him about something pleasant that she had just seen, he had amused himself chatting with her for so long that he had forgotten to release the fatal crow to whose nocturnal liberty the beauty of the gardens was attached. A fault so terrible in the most essential point of his responsibility, the rest being nothing but ceremony, almost caused him to die of dolor.

He ran to the crow's cavern, but the bird refused to come out, telling him that Pleasure merited the chagrin that the disorder of her gardens would cause her, since she had entrusted their conduct so lightly to an amorous young man. That crow was something more than he appeared to be; he was a famous magician that the fay had transformed thus, as a punishment for some disorders he had caused on the island.

The unfortunate Intelligence, fearing the anger of the Queen, decided to run away. His amour wanted to retain him. Lose his mistress and lose her forever! That was something he could not envisage without horror. But when he thought that the fay's anger might cause him to lose it forever by virtue of some change of form, as had happened to the magician, he preferred to follow his initial plan.

How could he get away from the island, though, since no one could traverse the lake without Pleasure's permission? That difficulty, which appeared insurmountable, did not stop Intelligence. He ran toward the lake without knowing what he was going to do; on the way he tripped over something; it was a coil of thick rope. When he got closer to the lake he heard a noise in the water, and perceived in the moonlight that it was a diving bird. All the animals of that land had reason, so he spoke to it in this fashion:

"Diver, dear friend, come to my aid, I implore you."

The diver immediately came to him, saying: "What do you want of me, Sire Intelligence? You have only to command me, and I will follow your orders to the extent that is possible for me."

"What I want of you," said Intelligence, "is for you to take the end of this rope in your beak, traverse the lake, and when you reach the other shore, attach the rope to the nearest tall tree, and then come back to find me here."

The adroit diver set about carrying out the order that he had been given. As he advanced, Intelligence let out the rope proportionately. The diver was diligent; he came back in a short time to find Intelligence, and assured him that the rope was firmly attached. Intelligence did the same for his part, thanked the obliging bird, and told him to add to the pleasure he had just had the one of telling the charming Felicity, as soon as he found the opportunity, what he knew about the adventure, and assuring her on his behalf that, no matter where he might be, he would love her eternally.

Having said that, he climbed up the tree to which the rope was attached, on which he walked, making use of his arms adroitly as a counterweight, and traversed the lake in that manner. He had previously practiced that kind of amusement, and it served him usefully on this occasion.

While these extraordinary things were happening to Intelligence, his two brothers were not experiencing any better luck. Memory had gone to shut the Queen's jewel-cases and close her wardrobe, which had five different locks. He had already closed four of them when he heard History laughing; she was defending herself from the pursuit of a young Lord who was in love with her. That laughter offended Memory; he thought he ought to forbid such liberties with the utmost seriousness. Jealousy seized him, and, no longer thinking about closing the last lock, which had to be done in uninterrupted sequence, he ran to his mistress, whom he had no sooner joined than the gallant who was following her fled, laughing.

"I believe, Madame," Memory said to her, with a chagrined expression, "that if it were not for my presence, you would not have been sorry if some favor had been stolen from you."

"That is very insulting," she replied, proudly, "and I would like to think, Sire, that you know me well enough not to accuse me so lightly. You have not seen History emerge from the gravity that is natural to her, either for you or any other; I have never allowed any indiscreet complaisance to escape me." As she quit him she continued: "Go away; you do not merit my tenderness."

Those words struck Memory like a thunderbolt; he saw the fault that his jealousy had caused him to commit, and he stopped the beautiful young woman by throwing himself at her feet and begging her pardon a thousand times. He obtained it without difficulty; the anger of lovers is never difficult to calm. He tried to repair his fault by means of a thousand protestations of love and respect, and as they saw the Queen, who was returning to her apartment, Memory escorted his mistress as far as the door of her room.

When he was alone he remembered that he had not closed all the locks. He knew the consequence of that and fear seized him; he ran to the wardrobe, which he opened. But gods, what became of him on finding it empty, and the jewel cabinet as well? He made almost the same reflections that Intelligence had made, and although it seemed to him that he could never separate from his dear mistress, he resolved, by virtue of the fear of punishment, to flee that charming place.

He ran to the edge of the lake and saw the impossibility of traversing it. Then, in the moonlight, he spotted a herb, about the virtue of which he had been informed by an old inhabitant of the island. It was such that by running the herb in question on the soles of the feet, one could walk on water as solidly as on firm ground. He made the experiment immediately, and, having found it veritable, he made use of it and traversed the lake.

For his part, Understanding had put away the vessels that had been employed in the feast, as well as a quantity of magnificent carpets and rich rugs; he had closed the door of the cupboard in which the moneyed gold was kept that served for gambling, and only had to rub the lock with the water of security that he obtained from a little spring at the most remote part of the island, of which he always kept a small bottle about his person, when he heard Prudence cry out.

He ran to her; she had tripped and fallen. He lifted her up; she had hurt her foot slightly, and as she had difficulty sustaining herself, he helped her to walk as far as her room. While her maids were taking off her shoe and stocking and applying a few remedies, Understanding expressed to her the chagrin he felt in not having been close enough to her to prevent the accident; and, as lovers make use of all sorts of opportunities to say pretty things to their mistress, Understanding did not fail to say very tender and obliging things to his. But the solidity of her mind, which put her above bagatelles, made her say to her lover:

"Sire, I wonder whether the urgency you felt in coming to my aid might have made you forget some circumstance of your duty. You know how important it is for you not to fail in it, and I'd be very sorry if the help that you have just rendered me were to cost you any of the repose of your life."

That reflection on the part of Prudence caused Understanding to tremble. He quit her without expressing any of his dread, and ran to the cupboard. But imagine his surprise when he opened it and no longer found any of the riches he had put away therein. He realized, too late, the fault he had just committed of forgetting the water of security.

All the cruel thoughts that had agitated the minds of his unfortunate brothers tormented him even more cruelly. His penetration enabled him to envisage his misfortune with terrible circumstances.

"Oh, Prudence, my dear Prudence," he cried. "How wise you are and how unwise I am!"

Afflicted and amorous as Understanding was, he concluded that it was necessary to think of his safety, which he did by seeking a means of traversing the lake. He had been unable to think of anything useful to him when, while leaning sadly against a tree that he recognized as one of those from which cinnamon is obtained, he took a small dagger from his belt, which was the only weapon of which people made use on the island, more for convenience than defense, and he employed it to slit the bark of the tree, which proved to be very thick. He removed it in its entirety, and then cut four small branches from the tree. He put two of them across the two ends to hold the bark open, and the other two served him as oars. He put the bark into the water and, making use of it as a boat, he traversed the lake without any danger.

The three charming sisters, who knew nothing of what had happened, felt an extreme dolor on learning the sad news of the departure of the three Princes. Nothing was capable of consoling them, and they accused themselves of being the cause of their lovers' misfortunes.

Meanwhile, the fay, who had been woken up in order to inform her of all the disorder and the flight of the Princes, was extremely angry, and if the three brothers had not been out of her lands, they would have felt its effects. It was not the impossibility of remedying the losses that afflicted her—her art was capable of anything—but the shame of having been mistaken in her choice. The Art of Enchantment has rules, like the others, and the prodigious power that it gives to those who possess it almost always depends on certain secret conditions that are its soul, and which must only be confided to people who are capable of observing them and who know their consequences. That is what Pleasure had thought she was doing in choosing those three young pupils, but what had deceived her is that, not knowing amour herself, she did not know how dangerous it is to give employments of that consequence to people attained by the passion in question, which has too much power over the heart and the mind.

She had seen in her prophetic mirror how it had all happened. She sent for the three sisters, who had not dared to appear before her. The loss of Understanding was afflicting Prudence with despair; History was half-dead at the loss of Memory; as for Felicity, she had never experienced dolor until the moment when she had been deprived of Intelligence. When they came into the Queen's chamber, Prudence took the lead in order to hide the disorder of her sisters; she threw herself at Pleasure's feet along with them and said to her, respectfully, in a touching manner:

"Madame, we alone are culpable; only punish us, and pardon those who have failed in what they owe you because of having too much urgency for us. Their passion is innocent, Madame, since you have given birth to it, but the effects are not."

Those words spoken by Prudence touched Pleasure. She shed a few tears over them, which were surely the first of her life. "Get up," she said to Prudence. "I alone am criminal; I have put the youth of your lovers to too delicate a proof; I'm not sorry that they have escaped my anger; perhaps I would not have been the mistress of it. Console yourselves, and continue to live as usual; the absence of the lovable fugitives will not be long, and I shall take care of their fortune."

The disorder of the palace was soon reestablished, and the three sisters no longer felt any chagrin except that of the absence of their lovers. Let us see now what had become of them.

*

When Intelligence had passed over the lake, he walked for several days through a deserted country without encountering any towns or villages, only finding water with difficulty, and only small quantities of a few wretched wild fruits for nourishment.

"Alas, dear Felicity," he said, "what has become of you? I don't regret the loss of so much magnificence, I only feel yours, and I would be even more unhappy if I lost your heart."

After many difficulties and fatigues, he arrived in a beautiful forest, the cover of which was proof against the most penetrating rays of sunlight. There were beautiful springs there, the waters of which were marvelous, and one could not take twenty steps without finding trees laden with all sorts of fruits. Millions of birds of every species made continuous concerts there, and little branches that one encountered from time to time formed cabinets appropriate for repose. Intelligence went into them by night, and if he had not been in love, he would have found them very tranquil.

The forest was so vast that although he marched almost all day, he did not find an issue. "I can see," he said, sometimes, "that I shall spend my life here, that the anger of the Queen of the Isle of Magnificence has limited itself to depriving me forever of the sight of the one I love, and that in order to avenge herself more fully, she is augmenting my passion." People of intelligence are always unhappier than others.

He applied himself so well in that solitude to studying the song of birds that he discovered mysteries therein hidden thus far from everyone but him. He found that some were mocking the stupidities of humans; that others were giving them advice they did not heed; and that a few of them were informed of a few surprising events of which they had been the only witnesses.

Above all, however, he studied the nightingales with so much care that he knew that they had invented music, and that they expressed all the sentiments of amour by means of their song. Intelligence understood when they were lamenting absence or infidelity, whether they were happy or unhappy, and, in sum, he knew that they entered perfectly into all the delicacies of that passion. He became so fond of that little masterpiece of a voice that he followed it everywhere.

One day, when he was listening to one of them that seemed to him to be more knowledgeable than all those he had heard, filled with admiration, he cried: "Oh, most charming of all the animals, if only you could be understood by the Queen of the Isle of Magnificence. I'm sure that she would make you the gift of speech in order to be understood all over the world."

He had no sooner uttered that exclamation than the bird replied to him: "I'm much obliged to you, charming mortal, for the wish that you have just made in my favor, and which has been granted so promptly; I shall only make use of it to give you pleasure."

Intelligence was agreeably surprised by that adventure, all the more so as it made him know that the Queen was no longer irritated against him.

"All that I ask of you," replied Intelligence, "is that you enable me to get out of this forest."

"I'll do that," the bird replied, "and even more, if it's possible for me." As she spoke she came to perch on Intelligence's shoulder, and, having been told to march, he soon emerged from the forest, on the edge of which he found a little cabin, the door of which was open.

He went in. It was rather neatly furnished. What surprised him was not seeing anyone in it, and finding a table there on which a well-prepared supper was set. As night was about to fall, he decided to spend it there; to that effect, he waited for the mistress of the house to appear, in order to ask her for permission to do so. However, seeing that it was already late, and not having seen anyone appear, he thought that it must be a favor of Queen Pleasure.

The joy that he experienced put him in a good mood; he supped better than he had done for four months, and his little friend kept him company by entertaining him agreeably with the following story.

The Story of Princess Blanchette and Prince Verdelet

There is a land not far from here that is named the Realm of the Cabbage Lettuces. All its inhabitants are gardeners, and the great lords are florists. There are no great riches, but the land is very agreeable. The Queen of the Cabbage Lettuces was a good Princess, whom I often diverted in her garden, and it appeared that she took great pleasure in hearing me sing. She died some time ago, and she left a son who was the heir to her estates, who is one of the most gallant Princes one could ever see. His name is Verdelet, and he fell in love with a beautiful Princess named Blanchette, the daughter of the King of the Frivolities, his neighbor.

Those people are stupid; they only amuse themselves by making bad verses and songs to sing on street corners. Their speech is filled with nothing but proverbs, sayings, quips and insipid jokes that are not very funny. Some of them travel the world and become tightrope walkers, operators of marionettes, Tabarins, Marquis d'Embreville and d'Angely.[25] The wittiest are Italian comedians under the names of Arlequin, Mesetin, Scaramouche and Doctor Balouade.[26] There are also women, some are Leances, others Columbines, Diamantines, etc., and by that means they enrich themselves, for they are all vagabonds in their homeland.

There are also people of another species, whose are not the most maladroit, but are the least esteemed; they are jesters and fools who, in the homes of Kings and Princes, often counterfeit madmen, telling them truths that sages dare not think.

---

[25] Tabarin was the pseudonym of a famous street performer, Antoine Girard (1584-1633), who engaged in comic dialogues with his brother, known as Mondor, while selling quack medicines. Any claims to fame or notoriety possessed by the other two names remain enigmatic although both marquisats do seem to have existed in the seventeenth century, the latter as St. Jean d'Angely.

[26] All stock characters in the French adaptation of the Italian commedia dell'arte. The original of the second, Mezzetino, is a schemer and drunkard; the original of the last-named, Dottor Balanzone is a decadent scholar. The female characters, except for Columbine, are far less well-known, and the other two named were probably *ad hoc* improvisations.

The King of those peoples is a Prince who has nothing of their manners; he is as sage as can be, and is named Peudacquets.[27] It is very annoying for a Prince who has such merit to command fools, but, in order to make use of a proverb of the country, where the goat is tethered it is necessary to browse.

Princess Blanchette, the daughter of the King of the Frivolities, with whom, as I have already said, Verdelet the King of the Cabbage Lettuces had fallen in love, is a small person with a good figure; her breasts, her arms, her hands and her face are in marvelous proportion, and nothing was ever whiter than her skin; an imperceptible incarnadine is mingled with it on her cheeks, and has the same effect as pomegranate juice mingled with milk curds. Her eyes are large, blue, nicely spaced, mild and intelligent; they are crowned by two eyebrows as black as ebony, and seem to be made with a brush. Her hair is the same color, and it is necessary to agree, on seeing her, that she is utterly charming.

Verdelet had no difficulty in making himself loved, since he is entirely lovable. Because they were neighbors they saw one another often; he made her presents of salad vegetables garnished with flowers and admirable fruits in baskets so well wrought that their gallantry more than made up for the magnificence they lacked. The King of the Frivolities approved of his suit, and to all appearances, their happiness was imminent when a malevolent fay named Berlinguette, who dwelt in the hollow of a nearby mountain, took it into her head to fall in love with Verdelet.

She was ugly and old, as malevolent fays ordinarily are, the good ones always being young and beautiful. Berlinguette did what she could to hide her faults under ceruse, carmine and beauty spots; jewels, ribbons and decorations were not spared therein. She came to the Court of the King of the Cabbage Lettuces under rather poorly-inventive pretexts; she made him presents adroitly in the manner of Sapates;[28] sometimes he found a sword garnished with diamonds on his dressing-table; once, rummaging in his pocket, he pulled out a snuff-box of great value filled with projection powder instead of tobacco; another time, they found at his feet a locket garnished with gems, in which there was a portrait of Berlinguette painted by Largillière,[29] who has the gift of rendering an ugly woman beautiful without changing her features; on waking up he found magnificent rings, purses full of gold, or barbs and Turkish horses in his stables. He found superb collations in out of the way places, to which he was conducted without thinking about it, and where Berlinguette did not fail to explain her sen-

---

[27] i.e. "few acquisitions."

[28] Sapate is a Frenchification of the Spanish *zapato*, a a kind of shoe put out at Christmas, as stockings were and sometimes still are put out in England to receive presents.

[29] Nicolas de Largillière (1656-1746) spent his early years in England, but returned to Paris in the 1680s, where he was taken under the wing of Louis XIV's court painter Charles Le Brun.

timents to him, making him know that if he wanted to marry her, he would be the happiest and the richest Prince on earth.

He was embarrassed, as an honest man would be, when he did not find himself in a humor to take advantage of the advances that were made to him, and, at the same time, did not want flatly to contradict a Lady. One day, after one of those collations during which it started to rain heavily, she sent him home in her sedan chair, because he had no carriage. It was very elegant; the porters were two huge monkeys dressed in scarlet with silver Brandenburgs. Instead of taking him to his own palace they took him to Berlinguette's, which one entered through an opening at the foot of the mountain. She tried to reconcile him to that deception by telling him that it was in order to let him see the treasures of which she wanted to make him the owner.

Nothing was finer or richer than that dwelling. It would take too long for me to describe it, as I could do, because I followed the King without being perceived. All the riches had no effect on him, and he got himself out of it as best he could.

Until then he had not said anything to Princess Blanchette about the fay's amour, but her portrait, which he dropped inadvertently, and which put a hammer in the Princess's head, obliged him to reveal the whole mystery, and in order to make her see that he did not intend any trickery he went to see her father the King, with whom he fixed a day for the marriage, which he wanted to be made in secret.

On the morning of the happy day Verdelet set forth at dawn; he did not have far to go and he arrived in good time at the palace of the King. It was not yet daylight there, so he went to stroll in the garden, where he spent his time, as speculative lovers do, gazing at the window of his mistress's apartment. I had followed him, because I wanted to be at the wedding, and I was amusing myself singing in a cherry tree, occasionally nibbling a few cherries for my breakfast, when I saw the malevolent Berlinguette descending from the sky. She was not adorned, because she was angry, and her little eyes were sparkling like two hot embers. Her carriage was a rusty iron chariot as poorly greased as a fiacre; two dirty griffins with mud all the way up to their backs were pulling the rig. It was very close to Verdelet before he saw it.

"I've got you, traitor," she said to him, catching him by the arm and striking him with her wand. "You're not yet where you think."

Immediately, he found himself in the chariot, which rose up, and was surrounded in an instant by a black cloud that hid it from sight.

I was in despair over his misfortune, but all that I could do for my own satisfaction was to follow him. He arrived in a short time in an old half-ruined castle a day away from here. Berlinguette set her carriage down in the courtyard and took the poor King into a low apartment, unfurnished and very dirty. After having made him traverse three rooms, she went into a chamber hung with black, entirely closed and only illuminated by four green candles.

Showing the Prince a kind of coffin, she said: "This is where you'll be until you decide to marry me."

"I'll be here a long time, then," he told her, his eyes full of wrath, "since I'd rather die than do that."

Scarcely had the Prince uttered those words than he found himself in the coffin, which Berlinguette enveloped in a black cloth. She closed all the doors with so much promptitude that I had difficulty getting out, and then she climbed back into her chariot and left; the drawbridge of the castle was immediately raised.

I am the only one who knows about that adventure; since that time, the King and the Princess of the Frivolities have believed the Prince to be lost. I have no doubt that the savant Queen who has made me the gift of speech has done so with the design of extracting the unfortunate Prince from the sad abode where he has been detained for a year, and that that adventure is reserved for you.

Intelligence was surprised by the story that the nightingale had just told him, and had no more doubt that there was something supernatural about the bird. He lay down with that thought in his mind.

As soon as day dawned he got up, and was astonished to see beside him a sword and magnificent clothes, in which he found a very rich locket containing a portrait of Felicity. He kissed it a thousand times, with delight, and no longer doubted his reconciliation with Queen Pleasure. He took off his clothes and put on those presented to him. The nightingale, who was present, rejoiced with him at his good fortune.

He ate what remained of the supper, and when he opened the door to leave he found a beautiful, well-harnessed horse there; he mounted it without further ado, with his little friend, and set forth into a large and beautiful pastureland, where he rode almost all day. Toward evening he saw an ancient castle, which, the nightingale told him, was the one in which Verdelet was imprisoned.

He drew closer, all the way to the edge of the ditch, which was filled with brambles and thorns. The drawbridge was raised and he was thinking about how he might overcome those obstacles when the confidence that he had in the fay Pleasure caused him to address these words to her: "Since I am sure, charming Queen, that you are no longer angry with me, enable me to know what you want me to do to help the unfortunate King of the Cabbage Lettuces."

He had no sooner finished speaking than the drawbridge was lowered. Promptly, he traversed the courtyard, where he left his horse. The nightingale showed him the first door of the apartment where she had seen Verdelet imprisoned. Intelligence had drawn his sword, and he knocked on the door. It opened, as well as the windows, through which, the light having entered, he saw that the place was occupied by thick spider-webs, filled with a prodigious quantity of those vile insects, of supernatural dimensions.

The nightingale was afraid, and went to hide beneath the Prince's hair. He brought down the spider-webs by cutting through them with his sword, and all the monstrous spiders were enveloped by them; after which, finding the path free, he knocked on the second door, which opened, like the first.

He found that room full of large wasps, which were making a frightful noise, by which he was not astonished. Whirling his powerful sword, he obliged all those insects to get out of the way and thus leave him free passage.

Promptly, he touched the third door, through the opening of which he perceived four huge snakes, which rose up on their tails, surrounding him. Without being astonished, however, he touched them with his enchanted blade, and immediately, they fled through the windows, uttering horrible cries.

Only one door remained, which was open, like its predecessors, and through which Intelligence went into the black room, which he found exactly as the nightingale had described it. He approached the coffin, and, touching it with his sword, he said: "Prince, a power greater than the one that retains you in this place has send me to aid you; emerge from that long sleep and return to the charming Blanchette."

Immediately, a long sigh was heard, and the black drape fell away of its own accord. The King of the Cabbage Lettuces appeared. The Prince gave him his hand in order to help him climb out, which he did promptly. He was richly dressed, but his beautiful blond hair was rather unkempt.

"Oh! Who are you?" he said, embracing his liberator. "How obliged I am to you, and for the fact that you have just pronounced a name that gives me joy."

"Sire," said Intelligence, "It is not a time to amuse one another with compliments; it is necessary to get out of a place where your enemy is omnipotent." As he said that, he took him by the arm and drew him out of that sinister dwelling.

When Intelligence reached the courtyard, he found a second horse with his own; he presented it to the King, and they drew away promptly from such a deadly place.

Without perceiving it, they took the road to the forest, and in a short time they find themselves in the cabin where Intelligence had spent the night. It was well-illuminated, and a very adequate supper was set out there, as well as a second bed. The King of the Cabbage Lettuces was very hungry, and he ate with a hearty appetite. The nightingale, whose acquaintance he had made, told him everything she knew about his adventures. What pleased him the most was that she gave him news of Princess Blanchette, whom she had seen not long ago, and who had appeared very touched by his loss.

Verdelet and Intelligence made the resolution to go as promptly as possible to the home of the King of the Frivolities. The nightingale offered to guide them there, and they set forth early the following morning.

While they are traveling cheerfully, let us see what had become of Memory.

When he had crossed over the lake with dry feet, thanks to the aid of his miraculous herb, Memory found himself on a road that led to a very populous city. While traversing it he saw a number of people assembled in a large square, in the middle of whom were several magistrates in ceremonial garb, who were examining people occupied in weighing herbs, powders and various sacks. There were others who were lighting furnaces and adjusting alembics of various shapes.

After Memory had examined those things without being perceived he moved closer. His fair face and the richness of his attire soon caused people to make way for him, and he asked what the purpose of the apparatus was. One of the magistrates told him that they were men who claimed to know the composition of theriac.[30]

"They're mistaken," said Memory. "I've seen reliable manuscripts of that composition, and they don't have what they need in order to succeed."

All the magistrates, informed by the one he had just told, asked Memory to take charge of the enterprise himself. He did so, and in a very short time he brought the operation to perfection, to the great contentment of all the people, whom he promised to teach the secret of the veritable tincture of the purple of the ancients, which was accepted with pleasure.

Memory was given magnificent lodgings, people to serve him, a good table and more money than he wanted. He carried out his experiments with so much success that the people found themselves in a position to furnish the whole world with purple dye and theriac.

If Memory had had no other design than enriching himself, he had found the means of doing so, but that was not his intention. He was still thinking about his dear mistress, as well as the anger of Queen Pleasure.

One night, when those cruel thoughts had prevented him from sleeping, he got up with the sun and, on opening a window, he saw a sword on his table, sparkling with gems, to the hilt of which a locket was attached by a golden chain. He opened it, and found that it contained a portrait of History. I leave you to imagine his joy and surprise.

He knew that the present came from the Queen, of whose anger he was so justly fearful, but who, to all appearances, was appeased. He also thought that the sword was destined for some use that he would discover in due course. He resolved, therefore to quit that place, and he got dressed. He did not forget to

---

[30] Theriac was a medicine invented by the Greeks in the first century A.D., the use of which spread throughout the world and which acquired a reputation as an omnipotent curative agent, for which reason the term was often used by alchemists as a synonym for the mythical panacea. The famous French apothecary, Moyse Charas (1619-1698), published an ostensible (very elaborate) formula in 1676, with which Murat would probably have been familiar.

arm himself with the miraculous sword, and mounted a horse. Without wanting anyone to go with him, he left the city, and in order to conceal his tracks, he went into a large forest that was a few leagues away.

After having ridden for part of the day, a storm blew up, mingling rain, hail and thunder, which obliged him to seek shelter in a cavern he perceived. The obscurity of the place, and that of the forest, augmented by the storm and the decline of the day, prevented him from examining the cavern, which might have been a den of thieves, or that of some wild beast; that obliged him to remain on his guard.

After having been in the place for some time, he heard movement close by; large yawns followed. Then, looking attentively, he saw a gleam, which he recognized as the eyes of a large lion that was waking up. His first thought was to flee, but an unknown impulse prevented him from doing so.

Meanwhile, the lion woke up, stretching its limbs and, striking the ground with its tail, it approached Memory quietly. Having gazed at him, it caressed him in the same fashion as a dog he had known. Those manners, not usual to those sorts of animals, reassured him to the extent of giving him the boldness to return the caresses by stroking the animal's back and head.

The animal quit Memory and walked toward the back of the cavern. Turning toward him from time to time, it seemed to be inviting him to follow it. That uncommon procedure obliged our adventurer to take the risk. And, ready for any eventuality, he followed it. His eyes adapted to the obscurity; at the back of the lair he saw an opening, from which a faint light emerged, by the favor of which he and the lion entered another cavern.

It was illuminated by a lamp wedged into the rock, and he saw by the light of the lamp that the place was very tidy. A little bed of moss occupied one side, on the other was a kind of table of the same substance, on which there were beautiful fruits in a rush basket, with soft white bread.

In order to do the honors of his home, the lion tugged Memory's coat gently, to oblige him to sit down on the bed. When he had obeyed, the lion set itself at his feet, and, looking at him with as much mildness as its face would permit, it sighed several times, while placing its head on his knees.

Memory, who suspected the mystery of the extraordinary things he was seeing, said to the lion, while striking it: "What do you want with me, poor animal? With what design are you asking me for so many caresses? Can I render you some service? If I were still in the home of the Queen of the Isle of Magnificence, I would beg her to give you the means of explaining your troubles. I am sure that, being as powerful as she is, she would give you that relief."

He had no sooner finished speaking than the lion stretched itself, put its paws around his neck, and said to him, in a human voice: "Oh, dear stranger, whom the gods have doubtless sent me in order to put a end to my woes, or at least to ameliorate them by giving me the ability to express them, the unfortunate King of the Arsacides is greatly obliged to you."

Memory's surprise was extreme, and if the lion's embrace had frightened him, he was at least as alarmed to find a King under that terrible form. Seeing his astonishment, the Lion King continued, saying: "You're right to be surprised by an adventure so uncommon, but you will be even more so when I've told you the details of it."

"I only want to learn them, Sire," said Memory civilly, "in order to be useful to you, being persuaded that the prodigy that has just occurred is an effect of the power of Queen Pleasure, who wants to make use of me to liberate you from such a frightful condition, which can only be an effect of an unjust power."

"Alas," said the lion, "what you say is all too true, and you are going to be instructed by the story that I shall tell you. But before commencing, let us eat a few of these fruits, which are doubtless presents from your benevolent Queen, since, during the year in which they have been made to me daily, I have not known where they came from."

They ate together, and after the meal, they sat down on the little bed in the attitudes that were appropriate to them, and the lion spoke in these terms.

The Story of Grandimont, King of the Arsacides, and Princess Philomele

My name is Grandimont, King of the Arsacides. If the happiness of a King depends on commanding savant and bellicose peoples, I ought to be the happiest Prince on earth, and I would have been, in fact, if I had never fallen in love. For several centuries the crown of the Arsacides has been in my house; in the same family there was a princess named Philomele, who was, without exaggeration, the most beautiful, the most sage and the most charming person there ever was. I loved her with all the passion of which a heart can be capable, and I was fortunate enough to inspire a parallel one in her.

A few wars I had had to sustain against my neighbors delayed our union, but after they had been fortunately concluded, I saw myself in a state to be happy, when a famous magician named Cameleor arrived in my country. He chose for his abode a high mountain near my capital, and in a single night, a castle of burnished gold appeared there, which, when struck by the Sun's rays, was the most splendid object that has ever been seen.

That magician took on different forms every day; he was sometimes young and sometimes old. He sometimes appeared with a very ugly face, and in an instant he became the most handsome of all men. He often transformed himself into a ferocious or domesticated animal, a bird or a fish.

He saw Princess Philomele and he fell madly in love. He did not fail to adopt his most agreeable face in order to please her, but he could not achieve his goal. He employed promises and presents in vain. She told me, with chagrin, about Cameleor's amour, to which I could find no other remedy than begging her to conclude our marriage secretly; but the scrupulous virtue of the Princess prevented her from consenting to that, and she wanted to accomplish it formally, with the ordinary solemnities. I prepared myself for that as promptly and as secretly as possible, but I could not do so well enough for Cameleor not to be alerted. He no longer held back, he resolved to do by the power of his art what he had not been able to achieve by that of his amour.

One evening, when it was hot and the Princess's maids were undressing her in her chamber, the windows of which were open, Cameleor entered in the form of a great eagle and carried poor Philomele away. The cries of her maids put the entire palace into upheaval, and I learned the terrible news as I was about to go to bed. I spent the night in the most cruel dolor of which a lover who loses the person he loves can be capable. I only interrupted my cries and plaints to give the necessary orders and to go at the head of my officers to ruin the fantastic palace of the thief of my wealth and snatch her from his power: a design as futile as it was reckless, since, when I advanced at daybreak toward the palace, I did not see the slightest vestige of it.

It was then that despair took entire possession of my soul, the cruel dolor of which overwhelmed my body with so much violence that it would have required very little to succumb to it. I was put to bed because I no longer had the strength to sustain myself. When night fell, I wanted to be alone, in order to afflict myself with more liberty. As I was engaged in that cruel occupation, I saw a man of evil appearance enter my chamber through the window, with a yew branch in his hand. He approached me, and said to me, with a grim expression. "You have only to make appeal to your Philomele and you will never see her again as long as you live,"

"Oh, traitor!" I cried "So it's you who have stolen the charming Philomele from me; what have you done with her, execrable enchanter?"

"I have not done with her what I wanted to do," he replied, "but no matter; I am content, since you will never have her; she is a bird and you shall be a lion, and you shall not change that form unless you have aided in the slaying of a horrible dragon, which must be the work of the scorned passion of an amorous and cruel fay."

As he finished speaking, he touched me with the yew branch. I became a lion at the same instant. My change did not astonish me, and I wanted to make use of it to devour him, but he escaped me and disappeared.

I remained in that state until my servants, coming into my chamber, gave me the means of getting out of it; their fear was extreme on seeing a lion in a place where they expected to find their King, and I promptly ran to the nearest forest, which is this one. My amour and my dolor had no part in my change, and the speech that was taken away from me rendered me even more unhappy. I counted for nothing the loss of my kingdom, only that of my dear Princess was sensible to me. I found this first cavern, which serves as my retreat by night, and I spend the day listening to the birds, always believing that I might find the object of my tenderness among them.

I only have the form of a lion, and I have never been able to nourish myself by carnage; men and beasts had nothing to fear from me but fear, my aliments being nothing other than herbs and a few wretched spoiled wild fruits, only being able to eat those that fell from trees. I sometimes made the resolution, in the most violent fits of my despair, to allow myself to die of starvation, but a certain natural penchant, mingled with a faint and confused hope, gradually diminished the resolutions that I made against my life.

One day, when I had found almost no nourishment and my weakness had made me return to my cavern earlier than usual, I was very surprised to see a new opening. I approached it and it led me into this cavern where we are. It was illuminated as it is at present; I found bread and fruits here. Since that time, the lamp has always burned, and for a year, as I have already told you, I have not lacked that nourishment. That, amiable stranger, is the story of the deplorable fortune of the unhappy Grandimont.

Memory thanked him, and assured him that his misfortunes would soon be over, since, to all appearances, they were known to the fay Pleasure. They had some further conversation, and then they reposed until daylight, at the commencement of which they emerged from the cavern, which immediately closed again.

Memory found his horse, over which it appeared that the fay had extended her cares, for it was still eating. He mounted it, and obliged Grandimont to take the rump. They emerged from the forest, and when they reached the high road, their frightening equipage caused everyone to flee. They took the most out-of-the way roads, where they found nourishment from time to time, and as for the night, they spent it under a few trees, where they had no fear of being attacked.

They had traveled thus for several days without knowing where they were going, or where they wanted to go, when one evening, they were surprised by such a heavy downpour that they were obliged to seek a shelter other than the wood in which they had resolved to spend the night.

Memory perceived a light, which did not appear to be far away; he followed it, and it led him to a little hermitage, where he knocked. The hermit came to open the door, but when he saw the lion he tried to close it again; Memory, who was on the alert, prevented him from doing so, assuring him that the lion was a domesticated animal, as gentle as a lamb. The hermit had difficulty believing it, but he was not the stronger, and they entered in spite of him. Memory asked him whether he had anything to eat; he gave them what he had, with which they made a very frugal meal.

The lion was still leaning on the knees of his friend, who was stroking him gently. Memory asked the hermit what country they were in, and he said that it was that of the Frivolities, and that he was not far from the capital, where everyone was in great desolation since a cruel fay named Berlinguette, who had a grudge against King Peudacquets and his daughter, Princess Blanchette, had sent a horrible dragon into the country, which had caused a frightful disorder, eating all the people it could catch and spoiling the crops. By virtue of a surprising prodigy, it had said that if people wanted it to leave the country in repose, they had only to give it a daughter of the city every day, and the magistrates had resolved to make that decision, for the public good, while awaiting some means by which the cruel fay could be appeased.

To that effect, they had taken the names of all the daughters, not even excepting the Princess, which they had put into an urn in order to draw them by lot, and the first name that had been drawn was that of the Princess, who was to be taken to the dragon the following day, in spite of the anger of the King. He had not been able to do anything other than have it cried throughout the city that if someone should be fortunate enough to kill the dragon, he would give them his daughter the Princess in marriage.

It was said that she was not alarmed by a death so cruel; the dolor that she had felt for a year since the loss of her lover, the King of the Cabbage Lettuces, who had been abducted by the malevolent Berlinguette, who was in love with him, had rendered her insensible to the point of scorning life."

Memory asked the hermit whether the dragon was far away. He said no, that it had withdrawn to a cavern at the extremity of the wood.

The good hermit ceded his cell to his guests, and, as the company of the lion did not give him pleasure, he retired into another place, where he shut himself in as best he could.

When Memory was alone with Grandimont he told him that he could see clearly that the magician Cameleor's prediction was about to be accomplished, and that he would surely kill the dragon, whose death would liberate the Princess and return him to his original form.

"Alas," said the King of the Arsacides, "what good will it do me to emerge from this state if I cannot recover my lovable Philomele?"

"Worry not, Sire," Memory said to him. "Abandon yourself to the guidance of the powerful Queen."

As soon as daylight appeared they found a good breakfast. They summoned their host in order for him to share it: the good man was a little surprised by that fare, but he ate it nevertheless, after which Memory asked him to be kind enough to show them the route that led to the dragon's cave, because he had resolved to liberate the princess.

The hermit did what he could to dissuade him from that design, but his rhetoric was wasted. He therefore led him through the wood, the greater number of whose trees had perished by the dragon's breath. He left them, recommending them to the gods.

At the same time, Memory and the lion saw several people coming from the direction of the city; it was the Princess, escorted by her maids, who were in tears.

When they were closer, they were surprised to see Blanchette's beauty. It was not sustained by any adornment; her clothes were very simple and negligent, her attitude was modest and her stride firm. Her gaze was sad, but no fear was visible therein.

Memory approached her and after having bowed to her, he said: "Madame, it is not just that so many charms should be prey to a monster; your subjects must be very cowardly for all of them not to be armed for your defense. I hope, beautiful Princess, that I shall extract you from this peril."

"Sire," Blanchette replied, "I do not love life enough to suffer that you should risk yours for my conservation. Furthermore, Sire, I would like to tell you that if the promise of the King, my father is engaging you in this enterprise, I warn you that, whatever merit you appear to me to have, I will not be the prize of your victory. I owe myself entirely to the unfortunate Prince to whom I have pledged my faith, and who might have lost his life in order to conserve mine."

"Although that recompense," Memory replied, "would be capable of arming all the Princes in the world for your defense, amiable Princess, it is not the motive that animates me. My heart would be too unworthy a present to offer you, since it has no longer been mine for a long time; so you will be satisfied. It is solely the glory of rendering you a service that will engage me in this perilous enterprise." He showed her the lion, who was a few paces away, and of which the Princess's maids were very frightened, and continued: "I hope to share the glory with this generous animal."

As he finished speaking, the frightful howls of the monster were heard in the distance. It emerged from its lair and came at a rapid pace toward its beautiful prey. It was enormous; its body was covered in black scales sown with red patches; it had six horrible claws; three tongues—or, rather, three darts—emerged from its frightful mouth, which was armed with four rows of teeth; it had four horns like those of a bull, and two huge wings soiled with blood.

At that sight, the Princess's resolution abandoned her and she fell almost dead in the arms of her women, who were scarcely in a better state. A few of the King's guards and a few young lords, who had followed her, fled, but Memory and the lion, losing no time, advanced toward the dragon.

The lion leapt on to its back and, seizing one of its wings, rendered it unusable. While it was making efforts to disengage itself, Memory delivered a sword thrust to its throat. That fatal blow, greater in effect than in force, caused the monster to fall backwards, covering the ground with a black liquid that emerged from the wound in abundance, and a moment later it lay lifeless.

Immediately, the lion disappeared, and in its place was seen the handsome and valiant King of the Arsacides, in his natural form. He ran to embrace his liberator, to whom he said everything that gratitude can produce in a great heart. Memory defended himself with modesty, making him know that he had not had the best part.

They ran to the Princess, who had recovered somewhat from her fear, her women having told her that the dragon was dead.

"Madame, the deal of the cruel monster that threatened your days has not only delivered you; it has also broken the charm that has retained the illustrious King of the Arsacides in the form of a lion for two years. Here he is, Madame," Memory showed her Grandimont, who approached her, and said to her the most intelligent things in the world, to which the Princess replied as much as her surprise would permit.

As Grandimont offered his hand to Prince Blanchette in order to return to the city, and Memory asked her to accept his horse, they saw two riders coming through the wood at a gallop. When they were thirty paces away, they descended from their horses, and one of them, who ran toward the Princess with open arms, was recognized by her as Verdelet.

Joy had almost the same effect on her as fear had just done a moment before; she leaned on one of her women while the Prince threw himself at her feet. Embracing her knees, he said: "Oh, my dear Princess, how happy I am to see you delivered from the peril that I learned you were in; but at the same time, I am covered in confusion because it is not to my arm that you owe your deliverance."

The Princess gave him the response that tenderness and joy inspired in her; she introduced her liberators to him, although she did not know them herself, and Verdelet did not fail to express his gratitude.

While that scene had unfolded between the two lovers, another had unfolded full of amity between Intelligence and Memory; the two brothers, who had recognized one another, could not find terms to express their sentiments.

Meanwhile, renown had informed the King of the Frivolities of the news of the dragon's death. He promptly put his horses to his caleches and came to meet his daughter, whom he found in better company that he expected. After several compliments on one part and the other, they resumed the route to the city and entered it in triumph. The Frivolities had at least as much joy at the death of the dragon as the deliverance of the Princess. The King regaled his guests marvelously.

When Intelligence had recovered somewhat from the surprise that the unexpected encounter with his brother had given him, he thought about his dear nightingale, whom he had not seen since the death of the dragon. He did not know what to think about her absence, and it gave him a veritable anxiety. He retired early with his brother to the apartment that had been prepared for them. It was there that they rendered one another an exact account of their adventures

Intelligence had reached the chapter of the nightingale, whose loss he regretted, when he saw the bird enter through the window. His joy was extreme; he asked the reason for their separation, and she replied to him as follows:

"Since the happy day when you made that wish, so advantageous to me, since it enabled me to recover the use of speech..."

"What!" Intelligence interrupted. "You were recovering speech? Had you had it before?"

"Yes, of course I had had it before," said the nightingale, "since I am more than I appear to you, and my misfortunes have constrained me to hide for two years in this paltry form the unfortunate Princess of the Arsacides."

"What!" cried Memory. "You are the incomparable Philomele, mistress of the charming and unfortunate King Grandimont, who has just resumed his original form, by virtue of the death of a frightful dragon, and has quit that of a lion, in which he has been groaning for two years, by virtue of the malice of the same enchanter who reduced you to the form in which you still are?"

"What!" responded the illustrious bird. "Grandimont has been a lion?"

"Yes, certainly," said Memory. "If you wish, I will tell you what I know of the story."

"You would give me pleasure," said the sad Princess, bathing her little eyes with tears. She perched on a table while Memory told her what he knew about the Prince.

When he had finished, he said to the Princess: "But Madame, I am astonished that you hid from the eyes of a man whom you love with so much passion, and who is suffering cruel pains in his uncertainty regarding your fate."

"Alas," said Philomele, "I am more to be pitied than criticized, since the cruelty of my destiny has reduced me to refusing him that consolation, which would be, in my regard, the most sensible that I could have. In order to inform you both of that cruel circumstance of my misfortune, I will tell you what Grandimont was unable to tell you, because he does not know it.

"Know, then, amiable brothers, that when the cruel Cameleor, in the form of an eagle, abducted me from within the arms of my women, he took me to his brilliant castle, where he tried to shake my constancy by means of the sight of his treasures and the promise of all imaginable grandeurs and pleasures, but he gained nothing by it and I always remained firm in the resolution never to belong to anyone but the King of the Arsacides.

"My firmness irritated the magician so much that his amour was converted into fury. He lost the respect that he had so far had for me, and he resolved to make use of force in order to satisfy himself. That resolution, which he made known to me in a manner that gave me no room to doubt it, frightened me. 'Alas,' I cried, on seeing the terrible state to which I found myself reduced, 'is there no propitious power that can help me? A Princess that had my name was once changed into a nightingale in similar circumstances; oh, I would be glad if I could have such a favorable fate.'

"I had no sooner formed that wish than it was accomplished; my body was covered in feathers and my natural size was reduced to that if this small animal, of which I no sooner had the form than I had the lightness, in flying away through a window.

"As I cleaved through the air, drawing away from the deadly castle of the enchanter, I heard something flying after me. Alas, imagine my fear when I saw that I was being pursued by a falcon, that could not be anyone but Cameleor, who, to all appearances, had had recourse to that transformation in order to oppose my flight. My dread diminished, however, when I saw that cruel bird stopped by a sparrow-hawk, which, having battled it for some time, obliged it to flee.

"I recovered my courage and, seeing that I was being visibly protected against the power of the enchanter, I began to fear him less, and I no longer found myself afflicted by anything but the absence of my lover, whom I imagined to be in despair at my loss. I retired to the hollow of a tree in order to spend the night, during which I made terrible reflections on my condition. I made the resolution to return to the palace and do enough by my behavior in Grandimont's presence for him to be able to suspect who I was.

Daylight appeared, and I was about to cry out my plan when I heard a voice, which said to me: 'Refrain, unfortunate Princess, from carrying out your resolution. If Grandimont sees you in this form, you will remain in it all your life. The magician, in despair at your transformation, was unable to do anything worse than attach that fatal circumstance to it. It is therefore necessary to avoid the sight of your lover, and allow the time prescribed by destiny to pass, after which you can recover your original form, but that can only happen on the Isle of Magnificence. Follow me, and I will take you to a place where you can await tranquilly the opportunity to be conducted to that fortunate abode.'

"Immediately, I saw the sparrow-hawk that had fought against the falcon. I followed it, and learned on the way that I had been correct when I thought that the falcon was Cameleor; but my guide told me that I need not fear his power any longer.

"We arrived in the forest in which you lived for such a long time," she said to Intelligence, "and where I found you. The obliging sparrow-hawk told me that it was the place of my exile, and permitted me to go as far as the Kingdom of the Frivolities, about which it told me what I said to you. It also told me to go to the home of the Queen of the Cabbage Lettuces, and that I would be able subsequently to be useful to the Prince, her son. After those instructions, it left me.

"I had been in that place for two years when I found you. As soon as I had heard you mention the Isle of Magnificence, I had no doubt that you were the person who would take me there, and I followed you constantly. When we arrived in this country and I found Grandimont here, I hid, for fear of being perceived, and I shall continue to do so until we are on that island, so much desired."

The two brothers promised Philomele to help her, and they remained in accord with her that she would remain hidden in that room, where she would not be at risk of being exposed to the sight of the King of the Arsacides, and that when they left that place she would hide in Intelligence's hair, as she had done before.

The King of the Frivolities made preparations for the marriage of his daughter with King Verdelet, and it was due to be celebrated in a few days when the people were suddenly struck by a malady so sudden that in less than three days the kingdom was deserted, with the exception of a few people who fled by sea and took refuge where they could—and it is those who are the Frivolities of today.

The King suddenly found himself devoid of servants, and the most annoying thing was that his treasures and his most precious furniture were stolen in a single night. He had no doubt that all that disorder was an effect of the rage of his detestable enemy. That was true, and if they had not all been under the protection of the fay Pleasure, she would have caused them to perish.

Intelligence and Memory advised them to embark with them for the Isle of Magnificence, to which they had no doubt that they would soon find the route.

As they were getting ready to leave, Princess Feverolle and her lover, Prince Petitpois arrived at the palace. They each had a small estate belonging to the Kingdom of the Cabbage Lettuces, They were coming to inform their King, Verdelet, of the destruction of his palace and theirs. The fay Berlinguette had sent a wind that had entirely dried up the gardens, killed the gardeners and toppled all the houses, not excepting the King's palace.

While everyone is regretting their losses, let us see how Understanding's affairs had progressed.

When he had passed over the lake with his cinnamon bark, he took the road to the sea, which was not very far away. He found a ship ready to set sail, and without knowing how or why, he embarked on it. The dolor that the loss of his dear Prudence caused him, and the indignation that Queen Pleasure must have against him, occupied him so forcefully that he did not even take the trouble to ask where the ship was going.

He had already been sailing for several days with the same indifference when, on emerging from his cabin one morning, he was very surprised to see that there was no longer anyone on the ship; the pilots, sailors and passengers had all disappeared. He searched the vessel all the way to the utmost depths of the hold, but he found the same solitude everywhere.

Although he was perfectly instructed in everything that it is necessary to know in order to sail a ship, being alone, he would not have been able to carry out the maneuvers. Understanding was not unaware of all those difficulties, and that is why he decided to perish whenever it pleased the fay Pleasure, whom he believed to be the cause of such an unnatural event.

He shut himself in his cabin to await his last moment. A storm blew up, which made him see a more certain death. Sometimes the vessel was borne up into the clouds, sometimes it was precipitated into abysses. The wind, the hail, the thunder and the lightning were making a terrible din, when a great calm suddenly succeeded them, and a silence so profound that even the sound of the waves was inaudible.

Understanding thought at first that the vessel had perished, but he changed his mind a moment later, seeing that it was impossible that it had done so, not being in the water and not even feeling the wetness of the rain. He went up on deck in order to clarify what was happening, but all that he was able to determine was that the ship was motionless; not the slightest breath of wind could be felt, and a thick darkness did not allow the sight of either the sky or the water.

"Where am I?" he said. "And what is this prodigy? What ought I to expect of my destiny? Which of the elements will contribute to my doom? Has any mortal ever been in such cruel uncertainty? How frightful this profound silence is! Am I suspended in the air? Have I sunk to the center of the earth? Alas, I know nothing, and what appears to me to be most probable is that I am going to perish, in whatever manner it might be.

"Well," he continued, "let's perish, since we must."

Having made that resolution, he remained tranquilly on the deck, where he spent several hours, at the end of which he heard a rather pleasant, but very distant, sound. The sound was augmented, in such a fashion that he discerned that it consisted of voices accompanied by instruments, such as theorbos, viols and flutes.

"I'm doubtless dead," said Understanding, "and the vessel has passed in an instant from the waves of the agitated sea to the dormant waters of the Styx. What I can hear can only be coming from the Elysian Fields."

After that reflection he continued to listen for some time, after which a bright light struck his eyes, with all the more force because he had been in darkness for such a long time. At first it occupied very little space, and appeared to be coming from some profundity, but its clarity and extent were gradually extended. After an hour or so, it appeared close enough for him to determine that it was on land, but a land obscured by a dark night; nothing could be glimpsed by the means of that profound light but a great void in which the sight was not arrested by any object.

Finally, the light, which appeared to be occupying a hollow path, rose as far as the surface of the ground, on which he saw two men appear, each of whom was holding a large candle of white wax. He recognized by the light of those candles that the men were almost naked, except for a small sheath, which descended from the belt to the knees. It was made of a fabric decorated with several colors on a silver background. They each had a double bandolier of the same fabric, as broad as a hand, which crossed over the stomach. The skin of their bodies and faces was olive in color; their features were not disagreeable, but they had slightly crooked noses, fingers and toes. Their eyes resembled two grains of black jet, without any apparent whites. The little hair they had was black and curly, and only covered the top of the head, leaving their ears visible, which were very large.

Those two figures, marching abreast, slightly apart, had no sooner appeared than they were followed by two others, and then by two more, until they numbered twelve, after which a man appeared on his own. His stature was a little shorter than average, but noble and well formed. He was perfectly handsome, and seemed to be between twenty-six and thirty years old. His complexion was slightly brown, but nevertheless fine, smooth and polished. He had large black eyes, soft and intelligent; his hair, of the same color, fell in thick curls over his shoulders; his costume, almost Roman, was velvet, patterned with leaf-green on a bright gold background. Silk stockings the color of fire covered his legs and thighs; light shoes of a cloth similar to his coat, attached with diamond buckles, formed his footwear. His coiffure was a little toque of similar adornment, around which was a string of precious stones, from beneath which six or seven feathers the color of fire protruded negligently, the shafts of which were covered with pearls and diamonds mixed together.

After that charming object, twelve more attendants similar to the first were marching, in the same order. No spectacle had every appeared more beautiful than that brilliant march in that tenebrous place, and Understanding, who was accustomed to magnificence, was charmed by it. After having marched for a few strides, one of the attendants was detached on his master's order, and approached the vessel where Understanding was. When he was close, he struck the ground with his foot, and immediately appeared on deck near Understanding, to whom he said, in an unknown language, which was nevertheless understandable: "My master, the King, having learned of your arrival in this country, asks you to come to find him."

"And who is your master, the King?" asked Understanding.

"He is the person you see" replied the envoy. "His name is Antijour, and this land is the Realm of Lost Riches." He continued: "Give me your hand and stamp your foot like me."

He did so, and found himself on land outside the ship. He approached King Antijour with a great deal of respect and was received very civilly.

"Amiable stranger," the King said to him, "you must be something marvelous, and the prodigious manner in which you have arrived in my domain leaves me in no doubt of that."

Understanding, although slightly surprised, was about to reply to him, when the other said, offering him his hand: "This is not the place where I want to learn about your adventures; follow me."

Immediately, the King and his entire retinue returned whence they had come, resuming the hollow path, which descended gradually.

When they had marched for about an hour, always descending, they found themselves in a flat country where the same silence and the same obscurity reigned in which Understanding had seen something very bright shining from afar. When he was closer he discerned that there were seven great porticos built in varnished clay, so beautiful and so lustrous that they resembled mirrors: ornaments of architecture were marked there by an infinite number of small lamps, which had the same effect in that obscurity as the stars in a beautiful night.

Understanding noticed that those lamps and the candles that Antijour's attendants were carrying did not produce any smoke, and that although he had seen them burning for more than an hour, they had not diminished.

When the King had passed under the middle portico with Understanding and all of his magnificent retinue, they came into a large courtyard paved in squares of black and white marble, like a checkerboard, at the back of which seven more porticos corresponded to the first. They supported a large building of the same material, illuminated in the same way. The two sides of the courtyard were each limited by seven porticos similar to the others and filled with the same illuminations, but the greatest marvel was that the porticos at the back of the courtyard and those at the sides were as many theater decorations, composed and illuminated like those in the Opéra. Some represented gardens as far as the eye could see, ornamented by fountains, flowers and figures; others enabled the sight, in the distance, of seas, ships and marine monsters. Others were visible that represented magnificent palaces, forests, meadows, fields and, in sum, everything that the art of perspective has of the finest and most natural.

Antijour allowed his new guest to admire these marvels for a while; then, having entered a kind of vestibule, he went up a great staircase illuminated at intervals by crystal chandeliers filled with candles. From there he went into an apartment, the first room of which was a hall hung with beautiful haute-lisse tapestries, and furniture in proportion, as well wrought as in France. The second and third rooms were equally neat but with different adornments; admirable paintings and portraits were visible everywhere, and they only walked on the most exquisite Persian and Turkish carpets.

Finally, the King entered his bedroom, which could have passed for a masterpiece of magnificence, especially the bed, which was at least as beautiful and rich as the one that Aubelle once showed in Paris in the Hôtel de la Ferté. A quantity of lords followed His Majesty there. They were sufficiently well made and quite magnificent, but it would have needed a great deal for them to be as handsome as the King.

That Prince took Understanding into his cabinet, which was full of the rarest curiosities; he invited him to sit down beside him, and asked him to tell him who he was and how he had been brought to his realm.

Understanding gave him the satisfaction he desired, and gave him a description of the beauties and riches of the Isle of Magnificence, as well as the charms and the profound intelligence of Queen Pleasure, above all her power and her science. He did not say anything about himself except the circumstances that had been advantageous to him, carefully refraining from making him the confidence of his flight. Intelligent people always know how to be sparing when the occasion demands.

When he had finished his story, Antijour made known the pleasure that he had obtained from listening to him, and seemed charmed by the great things that he had just learned about the beautiful fay. He said to Understanding:

"I suspected strongly that you were an extraordinary man, since no one else has come to this land in the manner in which you were brought here, and we will see in due course what might have produced such an uncommon event. It is necessary that your art penetrates the entire depth of the sea, that it has traversed the realm of the undines and the earth that separates us, the routes of which are only known to those people. My kingdom has as much extent as the seas that are above us; all the riches that are swallowed up in their bosom are ours. The undines, whom I have just mentioned, and who live on the sea bed, receive them and send them to us, being my subjects and belonging to my empire. All the rich furnishings you have seen, and will see, come to us by that route.

"Ordinarily, we live entirely on fish and a few marvelously good vegetables that come from the sea bed; the undines furnish us with both. When vessels perish, those people, who know physiognomy perfectly, rescue and revive, in order to send them to us, the people who are useful to us, such as painters, set-designers, musicians, sculptors, architects, butlers, cooks, tailors, upholsterers and several sorts of artisans. They do not live long here, the air not being appropriate to them, but they teach our subjects what they know, and succeed in that quite well.

"The music that you might have heard when you arrived here is made by persons of that sort. Two years ago, the undines of the Rhône, who have commerce with ours, sent us an entire Opera company, which had perished in the river. We also have knowledge of the sciences, by way of scholars who are also sent to us, and the books that fall into our hands. Our soil produces hardly anything because of the lack of air. We have worms that make wax, like your bees, and that wax has the property of not making any smoke and lasting ten times as long as yours. As for the oil of our lamps, it is the undines who furnish us with it, which they prepare in a manner so particular that it is almost inextinguishable, and our lamps which burn permanently, only have to be filled at intervals of several years.

"We have no women, we live for two hundred years, and we worship darkness; our generation is accomplished by taking an ounce of powder taken from a substance desiccated by fire, the composition of which was taught to us by the gnomes, who also have commerce with us; that desiccated substance is also what makes us stronger and more robust. We soak that powder in a precious liquid that flows from a unique tree that we have in this land; then we put it in a particular soil, and after nine revolutions, which are measured like your days, we find an egg there, which is placed in a box made of a whale's egg, filled with halcyon down. After nine more revolutions, a little embryo emerges from that egg, which is enclosed in a glass bottle a cubit high and sealed hermetically. When the embryo is as large as the bottle, which always happens after forty-nine revolutions, it breaks of its own accord and the child that emerges is clothed and nourished like us, and reaches adulthood within a year.

"There is never more than one Prince; his generation is made like those of others, from the body of a dead and desiccated Prince, except that his formation requires double the number of revolutions."

When Antijour reached that point in his story, a little carillon was heard, composed of tiny bells of a marvelous softness and harmony. "Let's go to supper," said the King. "Those bells inform us of it; as we have no light to regulate our days, they mark our hours; there are some of them at the doors of all the rooms, which are rung by mechanisms like clocks. In the morning they tell us to get up; they do the same at the mid-day meal and supper, and when it is time to go to bed."

As he was speaking, they arrived in a hall, where the supper was served with an admirable abundance and neatness. The salvers, plates and all the garniture of the sideboards were silver. After having washed his hands the King sat down at table. He had Understanding placed facing him, and ten or twelve lords sat down in the adjacent places. All the dishes were very well prepared. Fine Mayence and Bayonne hams were served as entremets, as well as sausages of good quality; fat capons and other poultry were not forgotten.

"Hazard is giving us extraordinary fare today," the King told his guest. "A French vessel, which sank near here this morning, has furnished us with these meats. We are also drinking champagne, of which there was an abundant provision. Our undines are faithful; they send us even the slightest things."

The dessert was very tasty; there were solid and liquid marmalades, royal marzipans and all kinds of pastries and conserves, as well as an abundance of all sorts of fruits. They drank liqueurs, and wines from Spain, the Canaries, Muscat and Assiotat; distilled liquors and Ratafia were not lacking.

When the meal was over the King asked Understanding what opera he would like to see. He replied very respectfully that his desire would be regulated by his. "In that case, said the King, we'll see *Issé*,[31] which is the latest."

Immediately, the flame-colored curtains of Gennes damask, garnished with golden fringes, that closed the windows of the palace were opened. There were no other closures. The windows opened over one of the decorations I mentioned.

---

[31] *Issé*, a pastoral opera by André Destouches, with a libretto by Antoine Houdar de La Motte, had its official première at Versailles on 17 December 1697, as part of the celebrations of the Marriage of Princess Marie-Adélaïde of Savoy to the Duke of Burgundy. The title role was played by Marthe Le Rochois and the role of Apollo, disguised as a shepherd, by Louis Gaulard Dumesny. The librettist was a member of Madame de Lambert's salon, and his name suggests that he was a distant relative of Baron d'Aulnoy.

The opera of *Issé* was performed there; the younger actors took the roles of women, who never entered that land. Everything was very well staged, and the music almost as good as in Paris, when Le Rochois and Dumesny were not singing.

After that diversion, coffee, tea and chocolate were brought, served in the rarest Chinese and Japanese cabinets, garnished with the finest porcelain. The little golden bells—for they were made of that metal—rang not long thereafter, and they were informed that it was time to retire. Understanding took his leave of the King, who had him conducted to a very beautiful apartment, where he lay down on a beautiful and good bed.

His mind was so full of the marvelous things that he had seen and heard that he had a great deal of difficulty going to sleep, although it was much easier to repose tranquilly in that world than in ours.

The next day he was woken up by the clockwork carillon, and a short time afterwards, one of the King's courtiers came into his room, followed by servants carrying magnificent clothes, in the fashion of the country; they presented them to Understanding on behalf of the King, who wanted him to wear them. He accepted the present politely, and had himself dressed in a blue and gold brocade coat with rose-colored silk stockings. His toque was surrounded by a string of rubies and pearls, and feathers of the same color as the silk stockings. That outfit suited him perfectly, with his fine complexion and black hair.

As he finished dressing, he wanted to take a fine watch from the pockets of the coat he had been wearing the day before in order to carry it with him, but he was strangely surprised, when he took it out, that it was not the one that he had brought from the Isle of Magnificence, but another, far richer, on the lid of which was a portrait of Queen Pleasure, surrounded by large diamonds of an infinite value. The courtier who was present, dazzled by the richness of the jewel, asked Understanding whose painting it was. Without making known his astonishment, he told him that it was the portrait of a beautiful Queen, of whom he had the honor of being the subject.

He understood that there was a mystery hidden beneath that adventure, and what gave him more pleasure was that he believed that, since the Queen had made him that present in such an impenetrable place, she had the design of making use of him, and that, in consequence, her anger must have relented in his regard.

While he was making those reflections, he was conducted to the King's apartment, where he found a large Court gathered for his rising. That Prince received him perfectly, and after he was dressed he went into his cabinet with him. He was no sooner there that the King asked him to tell him a few particularities about his homeland, principally concerning its beautiful Queen.

Understanding satisfied the King's desire, and after having left him with a very advantageous idea of his homeland and its princess, he continued: "Sire, I was so occupied with the extraordinary things that happened to me yesterday that I did not think of showing you the portrait of the Queen of the Isle of Magnificence."

So saying, he took it out of his pocket and presented it to Antijour, who was struck by an extreme surprise. He remained motionless for some time gazing attentively at the portrait, and then collected himself.

"Amiable stranger," he said, "Would you like to confide such a precious jewel to me?"

"It's yours, Sire," Understanding replied, bowing profoundly.

"Thank Heaven," replied the King, sighing. He left the cabinet without saying anything more, and when he had returned to his room he ordered one of his courtiers to show Understanding the rarest things that he had.

He was taken to the library, where he saw an infinite number of books and manuscripts containing marvelous secrets, secret negotiations and original histories that it has never been possible to recover. He saw all the riches and all the beauties of the palace, after which his conductor invited him to sit down in a chair carried by two men similar to the King's attendants. The courtier took one like it, and the men carried them so rapidly that no postillion would have been able to keep up with them.

In that vehicle Understanding was carried to the factories of foreigners and those of the country; then his conductor took him to see the productive land, which was of small extent. It was enclosed by a golden wall, as was the place where the powder of desiccated bodies was kept, of Kings as well as their subjects. In another closed space he also saw the unique tree that the King had mentioned to him.

Afterwards he was taken to the Temple of Night, which was built in black marble. The goddess was represented there in the form of a golden bat, covered in black crepe; poppies were sacrificed to her, those being the only flowers that grew in that land, the leaves and stems being dead-leaf in color and their flowers brown violet. They were burned on an altar of black stone, washed with all the poppy-syrup that was found in sunken ships. No one ever spoke in loud voices in the Temple, nor for a league around; it was only illuminated by one lamp. The King only came to make his devotions there once a year, and that devotion consisted of sleeping in the Temple for one night, on an ebony bed set up for him, with a black velvet awning.

Understanding went for a walk on the bank of a river whose water seemed as black as ink, but when it was drawn therefrom, it was very clear and very good. The only animals seen in the land were the worms that made wax, their work being done in soft earth where they made holes similar to our hives.

After having shown him all the beauties of the land, the lord who had accompanied Understanding, took him to his house, where he regaled him. It was very clean and well-illuminated inside and out. What seemed most surprising to Understanding was the infinite number of lamps and candles that illuminated those somber dwellings continuously.

The entire revolution, to use the local term, passed in that manner, and they covered more territory in that space of time that one would have done in a fortnight in our world.

Understanding returned to have supper with the King, where everything happened as it had the day before, except that the King seemed pensive and ate very little, and there was no opera. When the meal was over, Antijour took Understanding to his cabinet, sat down in an armchair, made him a sign to do likewise, and then, leaning on a marble table and supporting his head in his hand, he remained silent for some time. Then he took the portrait of Pleasure out of his pocket.

He gazed at it tenderly, and, turning to Understanding, he sighed, and said: "You're right to say that the power of your Queen is great; it must be so, since her painting has put my heart into a state that it had not yet known. There are portraits in my palace of the most beautiful women in the world, but I have never felt anything in seeing them except the pleasure that a beautiful work of art gives. Alas, it is not the same with this one; the hours marked by this fatal watch, which it accompanies, have caused me to find the last of my repose, and although amour is a passion that is only known here by way of books, I sense that it has taken possession of my heart, and that I can no longer live happily without the possession of that incomparable person. I have sensed in the time of a single revolution the most delicate sentiments of amour; jealousy, absence and impatience have made themselves felt in my heart with all their force.

Understanding was very surprised to hear the King of Lost Riches speaking thus, but, making an instant's reflection on his adventure and the manner in which the portrait of Queen Pleasure had been sent to him, he had no doubt that she had played a large part in it. That is why he said to the King: "Sire, I am not astonished by the sentiments that you have for the Queen of the Isle of Magnificence. Her power is great enough to extend into these subterranean places, and it adds to her grandeur to receive the homage of a Prince whose merit and origin are so extraordinary. Abandon yourself, Sire to the sweetness of the passion that you are beginning to feel, and be sure that, provided that you can find a means to get out of this region, it will not be impossible for you to become happy."

Antijour was charmed by the beautiful hopes that his dear confidant gave him; he embraced him a thousand times and told him that he would send for a magician who had given talismans to several of his subjects that enabled them to accomplish impossible things. Understanding quit the King and retired to his apartment.

The next day, the magician came to find Antijour, to whom he promised everything that he wished. He told Understanding that, and expressed the joy that he felt. He also told him of his fear that his people might oppose his departure. He was going to think about the production of another Antijour, that name being annexed to all the Kings of the land. He did not lose any time, and after eighty-six revolutions, the new Prince was in a fit state to emerge from his bottle, that being the time at which he had the use of his reason.

In the meantime, Antijour became ever more amorous of the fay Pleasure. He talked about her continually with Understanding, for whom he provided all the diversions that were in his power. For himself, he no longer cared about them, finding no other pleasure than thinking about his passion. After he had put the young Antijour in the hands of those of his subjects he thought most capable of his education, he no longer thought about anything but leaving.

He had given orders to the undines to send him the crew of the first ship that fell into their hands; they had already done that, and he had put Understanding on the vessel, which was equipped with everything necessary, and on which immense riches were embarked, although Understanding had told him that it was quite unnecessary to carry treasures to a place that was the source of them.

Finally, when everything was ready, Antijour had the new King recognized, and then he departed, greatly regretted by his subjects, to whom that departure seemed all the more surprising because there was no precedent for it.

The King, who had not wanted anyone to accompany him, boarded the vessel alone with Understanding. As soon as he was there, the magician caused a wind so violent and impetuous to emerge from the earth that it lifted the vessel up, with so much promptitude that it pierced the solid ground and was in the realm of the undines in an instant. Antijour stopped there for some time in order to give those people a few orders regarding their new monarch, and the utility of the kingdom that he was quitting.

Meanwhile, Understanding remarked the surprising situation of that place and the form of its people, who live on the sands of the sea, the suspended waters of which serve as the sky, from which a faint light emerges similar to that of dusk. The men there are tall and well-made, the women rather beautiful, but pale, as are the men. The women have long hair, almost white; the men have blue hair. Both are semi-clad in a fabric made of green mesh, so beautiful and so delicately worked that it resembled velvet.

Their retreats are hollowed-out rocks, which compose very neat and very comfortable habitations. The points of those rocks, rising above the waves of the sea, are the reefs that cause so many vessels to perish. One also sees large well-cultivated market gardens, where there are quantities of vegetables. Understanding remarked amphibious animals there, strolling in large numbers over the sand, strewn with shells of all kinds.

As soon as Antijour had finished his conversation, the magician, who had followed him, raised another wind, with lifted the ship again, caused it to pierce the waves and immediately set it afloat. Understanding saw the light again with great pleasure. The King was greatly inconvenienced by it for several days, during which he was obliged to keep to his cabin. He gradually accustomed himself to it, his amour and the sight of the portrait of the charming fay completing his cure.

After three or four days of navigation, the pilot notified them that he could see land, and that the wind was impelling them toward a very comfortable port. Understanding advised the King to drop anchor there, which they did in very little time, Antijour and Understanding went ashore in order to discover what land they were in, for the pilot, who did not seem to be very experienced, or had lost his memory during his resurrection, did not know.

After they had gone a short distance, Understanding, who had better eyesight than Antijour, who was not yet accustomed to seeing so far, perceived several people coming toward them. They went forward, and when they were closer, it appeared from the richness of their clothing that they were not common people. There were men and women, but how surprised Understanding was to recognize his two brothers, who were among them. It was, in fact, them, who had come in search of a vessel in order to escape with King Peudacquets of the deplorable kingdom of the Frivolities. He was accompanied by Princesse Blanchette, Grandimont, Feverolle and Petitpois.

If Understanding had recognized his brothers, they had done likewise in his regard; they all came together and embraced with a great deal of joy and astonishment. Intelligence introduced his brother to the illustrious persons he was accompanying, and Understanding did as much for Antijour, whose beauty and fine manners won the admiration of the beautiful troop. The merit of the latter had the property that it was only necessary to see him to hold him in esteem. All those distinguished individuals exchanged reciprocal civilities, and when Antijour had learned the design that they had of embarking for the Isle of Magnificence his joy was extreme. He offered them his vessel, which was accepted with pleasure.

They embarked immediately, and, the wind being favorable, they set sail promptly. The conversation was agreeable, and everyone recounted his adventures. For the three brothers, they could not quit one another, and could not find enough time to tell one another everything that had happened to them. Understanding was chagrined when he learned from his brothers that they had portraits of their mistresses, while he did not have one of his.

"You have no grounds for complaint," Intelligence said to him, "since you have that of the Queen in exchange."

"That's true," he said, "but that portrait is not a favor for me, since, to all appearances, it was only sent to me in order to surrender it to the King of Lost Riches." As he finished speaking, without thinking about it, he put his hand in his pocket, and was agreeably surprised to take out a painting of the beautiful and sage Prudence.

There was only poor Philomele who had no part in the conversation; she was still hiding in Intelligence's hair; but when he was with his two brothers he told Understanding that, to whom he related his adventure in a very low voice, for fear of being overheard by the King of the Arsacides.

Their navigation was short and fortunate, and they landed to the great contentment of everyone. Antijour wondered where he could find a means of conveying his riches, but he was soon relieved of the embarrassment, because scarcely had they all disembarked than the ship disappeared.

"I told you, Sire," Understanding said to Antijour, "that that apparatus would not be to the liking of Queen Pleasure; she is doubtless sending your treasures back whence they came."

That Prince had too great a soul to be touched by that loss; it could only have been sensible to him in relation to his amour, but what Understanding said to him made him know that it had no part to play therein, and he did not think about it any longer.

The agreeable troop had not taken a hundred paces over the strand than they found themselves at the entrance of a long avenue of myrtles as large as oaks. One walked there over short grass dotted with flowers, and thousands of birds were singing marvelously there.

"These trees," said Memory, "have been the symbol of amour in all times, and as there is no one here who does not feel that passion, I believe that we would do well to make crowns of it to ornament our heads triumphantly."

Everyone applauded that speech, and as they prepared to break the lowest branches in order to employ them for that purpose, fourteen doves as white as snow, each of which was carrying a crown of myrtle enriched with gems, came to flutter over the heads of the lovers, whom they crowned. Antijour, Grandimont and the three brothers each received two. They deciphered that mystery clearly, and understood that the double crowns were for their mistresses.

There was only the King of the Arsacides who sighed dolorously, saying: "Alas, unfortunate Prince and even more unfortunate lover, what will you do with that crown, and where will you find the one who would like to receive it from your hand?"

"Don't be afflicted, great King," Intelligence said to him. "You are not far from the end of your troubles, and the charming Queen that we are going to see will not fail to bring a conclusion to them."

With those agreeable adventures, they found themselves at the end of the avenue of myrtles, which terminated at the shore of the lake that served as the limit of the isle so much desired. Three launches, shining with gold and gems, appeared on the lake, advancing propelled by oars. One was furnished in green, another the color of rose and the third in blue, all fringed and braided with silver. The oarsmen were dressed in the same livery.

When the launches were within range, the three brothers recognized their mistresses in the middle one. They were as beautiful as stars and ornamented like goddesses. The other two launches were empty. As soon as they had touched the shore, Understanding, Intelligence and Memory ran to give their hands to the charming sisters; they were so transported that they could only speak with their gazes; the responses were in the same language.

Prudence advanced first and made her compliments on the Queen's behalf to the illustrious individuals, whom she then obliged to enter the launches. When they were all aboard, the oarsmen did their duty, and reached the other shore in very little time. While those magnificent vessels were making the waters of the lake seethe, which seemed to be proud of such a beautiful charge, the lovers were at the feet of their mistresses, full of joy and hope.

Finally, they touched that beneficent soul. Intelligence had no sooner set foot on it that Philomele appeared as she had been before Cameleor had abducted her. Although everyone was touched with admiration for such perfect beauty, Grandimont thought he would die of pleasure; he threw himself at her feet, saying: "Is it you, charming Princess? Is it you, my lovable Philomele? Alas, where have you spent so much time, and how have you escaped the hands of the cruel Cameleor?"

"Sire," she said, raising him up and looking at him tenderly, "I cannot tell you those things now; I'll inform you of them at a more convenient time. It's sufficient that we can see one another, that our misfortunes have not diminished our tenderness, and that we no longer have anything to fear from our enemies." She indicated Intelligence. "This is the man to whom I have the obligation for my transformation."

Without knowing any more, Grandimont testified his gratitude to him.

As they advanced into the island, the beauties that they discovered at every moment augmented their pleasure and admiration, but it was another matter entirely when they approached the palace. All the lords composing the magnificent Court advanced to meet the Princes and Princesses and conducted them to the Audience Hall, which was the most beautiful, the most grandiose and the richest room imaginable. But nothing could compare to the beautiful Queen who presided in that place. She was seated on a throne elevated by several steps, which was filled with carbuncles whose glare was unsustainable, considerably augmented by a sun of diamonds by which the architecture was terminated.

The Queen was wearing a costume so covered in gems that its color could not be distinguished. She was holding a golden wand garnished with emeralds, at the end of which there was one that represented a cock. Her necklace was composed of thirteen pearls, each of such great value that the great Queen Cleopatra's were only fit for making a stew for her lover. She had no crown, because she was awaiting one from the hands of Amour. All the ladies of the Court, dressed in various colors and brilliant with gold and gems, were sitting on the steps of the throne, which were covered in blue velvet sown with golden stars. All the officers were lined up on the two sides of the hall

The first who entered was King Antijour; he stopped at the first step; the sight of the beautiful Queen surprised him so much that he was immobilized. For her part, Queen Pleasure was not exempt from agitation; her hour had come, and her heart, which had never been sensible, became so at the sight of the man who was to vanquish it.

The initial surprise of the King of Lost Riches having diminished slightly, he advanced and threw himself at the feet of the beautiful fay, where he placed his two myrtle crowns. He said to her: "Incomparable Queen, I have no other crowns to offer you but these; the one I possess at the center of the Earth is not worthy of you, so I have quit it forever, and I have reserved nothing but my heart, of which I make you a sincere homage, and although it was formed in an extraordinary manner, it was nevertheless sensible solely to the features of your painting. If you care to accept it, charming Queen, I will doubtless be the happiest of all men, but if I am unfortunate enough to displease you, I shall die at your feet of amour and dolor."

He said the last words in such a touching fashion that Pleasure was moved by them. "Get up, Prince," she said to him, holding out her hand, which he kissed. "I am not unjust, and although my heart has never been sensible, I cannot respond for the future. Love, hope and repose on your merit."

She blushed as she spoke those words, which appeared to have escaped her against her will. Antijour perceived that, and he thought he would die at the feet of Pleasure, who made him a sign to get up in order to make way for the King of the Frivolities, who was followed by his daughter, Princess Blanchette and the King of the Cabbage Lettuces.

The King explained all his misfortunes to the Queen. She knew them at least as well as he did; she commiserated with him and promised him her protection. She was charmed by the beauty of Blanchette, on whom she lavished a thousand praises. It can be said that no one ever merited them more than that admirable Princess. The Queen congratulated Verdelet on his good fortune.

The King of the Arsacides came in his turn with the beautiful and intelligent Princess Philomele. The Queen made them know that all the help they had received in their transformations had come from her, and that it was her who had changed Philomele into a nightingale, in order to extract her from the hands of Cameleor.

Petitpois and Feverolle had their turn, and although that young Princess only had a mediocre beauty, she nevertheless had a certain air of freshness, as had her lover, who also had his merit.

Finally, the audience was terminated by the three brothers, whose pardon was duly signed.

The Queen descended from her throne and was conducted by Antijour to her apartment, where she was followed by the most beautiful and most numerous Court imaginable. It was already late, and a supper was soon served, the description of which would require an entire volume.

After that meal, there was a ball of great magnificence; the newly arrived Princes and Princesses shone therein, the liberalities of the Queen having augmented their adornments with jewels of consequence, of which she made them a present. Antijour danced there perfectly well; no one was astonished by that, for he had learned from a master of the Opéra. Above all, however, Petitpois and Feverolle carried off the prize. When they danced together nothing was more agreeable; no one had ever seen such a disposition until then, and it seemed that they were not touching the floor.

After the ball, all the Kings, Princes and Princesses were conducted to apartments proportionate to their quality and the Queen's wealth, but principally Antijour, who advanced his affairs so far in such a short time that everyone perceived by the manner in which he was served and respected that he would soon become the King of that Magnificent Isle, in possession of its charming Queen.

In a quarter of an hour, she gave orders for the next day's fête, in which so many lovers were to become spouses. Everything there was grandiose, superb and beyond all description. Antijour married Queen Pleasure. Grandimont became happy by virtue of the possession of a person for whom he had suffered so many woes, and who had suffered no fewer for her part. As for Blanchette and Verdelet, they completed the wedding so often interrupted by the malicious and cruel Berlinguette. Feverolle and Petitpois were united forever, and that agreeable union is still seen today, perpetuated over the centuries. The three brothers and the three sisters were to enjoy a perfect happiness together; Intelligence would never be separated from Felicity; History would always shine with Memory; and Understanding was so charmed with Prudence that he never did anything without her advice.

The pleasures and the diversions that followed the sumptuous weddings lasted for a long time. Afterwards, Queen Pleasure summoned the King of the Frivolities, his son-in-law Verdelet, the King of the Arsacides and Petitpois to her cabinet one day, and asked them what they wanted to do. She said that if Peudacquets wanted to return to his homeland she would send him more intelligent and more laborious people; and that she would reestablish the Kingdom of the Cabbage Lettuces, with the Principality of Petitpois and Feverolle, and assured them that they no longer had anything to fear from Berlinguette, since she had imprisoned her in the Fearful Castle with the griffins, the spiders the wasps and the snakes, who were nothing but four magicians, one of whom was Cameleor.

The Princes thanked the fay very much for her advantageous offers, but told her that they would rather remain on the Isle of Magnificence and become subjects of such a powerful Queen than command peoples, whoever they might be. Petitpois made the same decision, and there was only Grandimont who wanted to return to his kingdom. He loved glory, and he could not see any to acquire among the pleasures of the Court. He departed some time after, with the charming Queen of the Arsacides. The fay heaped them with presents and gave them an equipage worthy of their rank.

Pleasure went a long time without having any children, and it was believed that she might never have any, because of the difference of origin between King

Antijour and herself, but she finally became pregnant, to the great contentment of her husband, for it is usually husbands who love their wives who want them to have their children. She gave birth to a Prince who was a marvel of intelligence and beauty. He was named Antinuit, and after two or three centuries he inherited his mother's realm, and had a long posterity, who still bear his name.

FELLOW TRAVELERS 1697-1715

Catherine Bernard: *The Rose-Bush Prince*

The queen of a realm that is not found on the map, being the widow of a king she had loved tenderly, lived in a dolor proportionate to the amour she had had. A daughter, the unique fruit of their marriage, gave her an occupation of sorts capable of dissipating her chagrin, but Florinde—that was the daughter's name—was to cause her some in her turn.

One day, when all the queen's women were in her room with the princess, a little ivory chariot appeared drawn by six butterflies with wings painted in a thousand colors. A person whose stature corresponded to the carriage, and whom they suspected to be a fay, after having circled them in the chariot several times, threw this note:

> *Florinde was born with many charms,*
> *But her misfortune will be extreme*
> *If she has to love one day*
> *A lover whom she cannot see.*

The fay disappeared, and left a great surprise in all minds. The queen was more disturbed by it than she ought reasonably to have been; the eccentricity, and even the apparent impossibility, of that misfortune, did not reassure her against the caprices of amour and those of destiny combined. She thought of forestalling them, and did not wait until Florinde had reached the age of amour to make her known to all those who might be potential suitors.

Among the neighboring princes there was one hidden from the eyes of the world, but Florinde's portrait did not fail to reach him by way of the fays, for whom nothing is impossible. The king, his father, being the widower of a wife who had made him suffer all the horrors of jealousy, had married a second one unlikely to inspire it but born to feel it. She took the caprices of her passion so far that the prince in question knew that he had only exchanged troubles, and did not know which of his woes was the greater. In that uncertainty he had concluded that marriage was a frightful bond, and he resolved to keep the only son he had far from commerce with all women. He had him brought up in a magnificent castle, and delivered him to all the diversions of his age.

The young prince was taught all the sciences that could not instruct him of what it was desired to keep hidden from him. In sum, all his amusements were lavish, except the one for which he was born; but Amour allows no one to escape.

The prince, who found Florinde's portrait under his feet, initially looked at it in surprise. Admiration followed close behind, accompanied by a disturbance unknown to a young man accustomed to exercises and reflections that had nothing in common with those sentiments.

His first desire was to see the original of the portrait; it was a face more delicate than those he had seen until then, and, either because of the instinct of a mystery natural to amour or because he realized that something was being hidden from him, he did not communicate to anyone the design he had to quit a place that had always appeared agreeable to him, but which he began to regard as a prison as soon as he wanted to leave it.

He was able to escape his surveillance, and he set forth without knowing where he was going. He had only taken a few steps when he encountered the fay that we have already mentioned.

"Where are you going, unfortunate prince?" she said to him. "You're running toward all the misfortunes that your father wanted to enable you to avoid, but you can't escape your destiny."

Meanwhile, Florinde's mother ordered a magnificent tourney, which attracted to her court all the princes of the neighboring realms. They wanted to show off their handsome faces and their skill splendidly; but, although Florinde could not help holding them in esteem, amour did not enable a choice, and a pity that was cruel to all of them prevented her from determining in favor of any of them. They had acquired for her the sentiments that her beauty was bound to inspire, and she would have made too many of them miserable if she had made one of them happy.

The queen sent away those princes dolorously; her daughter did not like any that she had seen, so half of the prophecy had been fulfilled, and the rest remained to be dreaded.

Sometime after that, Florinde, weary of the court and having nothing to keep her there, obtained permission from her mother to retire to a country house. It was an agreeable place, appropriate to amuse a young person free of the cares of amour.

One day, while she was walking in a flower-garden, she perceived a rose-bush that was greener and more florid than the others, which curbed its little branches as she approached, seemingly giving her approval in its fashion.

An action so novel in a rose-bush surprised the princess; the prodigy made in her favor pleased her; it was a kind of homage by which she was touched. She went around the flower-bed several times; the rose-bush bowed every time she went past. She wanted to pick a rose that seemed to her to be very red, but she pricked her finger painfully.

The sting of the wound prevented her from sleeping at night, and the next morning she got up earlier than usual, and went to walk in the flower-garden.

The rose-bush redoubled its reverences with an urgency that delighted the princess and made her forget the pain, only to think about the marvel. Finally, while musing, she approached the rose-bush too closely, and found herself caught on it without being able to free herself. As she tried to pull away she felt an extraordinary resistance.

She struggled nevertheless, but she heard a sound emanating from the leaves that resembled sighs.

"What!" she exclaimed. "A rose-bush can sigh?"

"It can do more, Madame," it said to her, "and you have the power to make it talk. Permit it to tell you its sad story.

"I am a prince," it went on. "The most precious thing in the world had been hidden from me. I lived without seeing you, and this is what it has cost me to come in search of you. A fay has given me this form, and told me that I would keep it until the day when I would be loved by the most beautiful person in the world; but what I see here must be reserved for the gods, and I am running the risk of always being a rose-bush."

The princess made to reply. Something serious took the place of the joy that the reverences of the rose-bush had given her; she even thought it too bold in having dared to embrace her with its branches. She quit it, but not without looking toward the flower-bed more than once.

Her night was agitated by sentiments that were quite similar, although she thought that they were different. The animated rose-bush caused her astonishment; the prince it concealed caused her pity; she felt a sort of anger because it had had the audacity to speak to her about amour, but in the end, she pardoned the lover in favor of the bush. How can one be angry with a rose-bush?

The princess returned to the flower-garden the next day. In truth, she took care to keep her distance from the rose-bush, but she could be perceived by it, and could even hear its plaints. After circling it several times she drew nearer to it, and tried to console it for its metamorphosis, without answering for anything else.

A few days later, seeing that it was too exposed to the insults of the atmosphere, she had a little marble cabinet built for it, sustained by pilasters, where she went to visit it frequently.

Gradually, she became accustomed to giving it a human face in her mind, and even a pleasant face. Little by little, she permitted it to speak to her about amour. It seemed to her that the discourse of a tree could not be dangerous.

The rose-bush was able to take advantage of that favorable disposition; it said a great deal, but it made it understood that it was suppressing even more; and by means of a disorder above eloquence, it convinced her that she was loved very tenderly.

The princess thought so often about the prodigy of the rose-bush that she no longer thought about anything else. The marble cabinet was the place to which her steps naturally conducted her; it even escaped her to say excessively tender things to the prince, for whom she felt a great compassion, but the fay's menacing oracle could not be effaced from her mind, Perhaps she already loved what she had not seen, but she doubted it as long as she only saw a tree; she was afraid of returning its original form, but sometimes wished it involuntarily.

For its part, the rose-bush found room for laments amid the most flattering words that the princess said to it. "If I can believe your words and your cares," it said to her, "I excite your pity, but you do not have enough if you give me nothing more; and that mild sentiment of the most beautiful person in the world cannot give me back my form."

Meanwhile, the queen could no longer support the absence of her daughter, and gave her an order to return immediately. That was a thunderbolt for the princess; it was necessary to separate from the rose-bush, for which she found, at that moment, that she had a veritable passion. She shed a quantity of tears over its leaves, which could not be washed by them without sensing their virtue.

Immediately, the rose-bush disappeared, and Florinde no longer saw anything at her feet but a charming prince. He embraced her knees with all the certainty of being loved: a pleasure that is almost never sure for other lovers, all the ordinary evidence being suspect by comparison with that marvelous event. Thus, the idea of his happiness transported him to such a point that he lost, so to speak, the usage of his senses; when he recovered them, he seemed by virtue of his immobility still to retain something of the tree that had hidden him.

At the sight of such a lovable prince, Florinde's amour was augmented, but her modesty increased proportionately; she regretted the veils that had hidden her own sentiments from herself.

She returned to court, and the prince went with her. The queen, who did not know anything about the adventure of the rose-bush, and who only knew the birth of the prince, permitted him to be a suitor for her daughter.

He saw his mistress every day, but it was no longer without witnesses, and he often regretted his tree-bark; it had constrained him less than all the decorum that was required of him.

The prince pressed for his marriage, but Florinde, frightened by the prodigy of her amour, which gave her reason to fear the fay's oracle, engaged the queen to agree that she send that lover away in order to make sure of his constancy before giving herself to him.

She summoned the prince and said to him: "Prince, you know that I love you, and in accordance with that word I have the right to dispose of you. The prediction of my misfortunes frightens me; everything that ought to make me fear them has happened. If you were not sure of being loved infinitely, my alarms can convince you of it; if you were less so, I would anticipate my disgrace by breaking with you, but in spite of my terrors, I cannot, and it is better that, in giving me certain marks of your fidelity, you belie the oracle. You had only seen me when you loved me. Perhaps I was only able to please you by virtue of the novelty. It is necessary to test you; go and live on the Isle of Youth until I recall you. Go; I want to flatter myself that the more charming the abode is, the more the voyage will afflict you."

What a proposition for a beloved lover! Since he had known amour he had always seen the person he loved, and he had never had the idea of absence. To live far from Florinde seemed so terrible to him that he thought his last moment had come. He did not have the strength to complain; his tears flowed without him sensing them, and his action marked such a great amour that the princess, judging that she could not resist such a great passion, fled to the queen's apartment. From there she sent an order to her lover that he obey her without seeing her again, that he simply leave, and that she would take care of soothing her woes.

The prince set forth with a submission of which few examples have been seen since. He was ill when he arrived on the Isle of Youth, and thought he would find physicians there, but there had never been any need for them on an island of that name. Laughters, Games and Amours welcomed him by throwing roses at him; immediately he breathed an air that restored his health, and at the same time, all the charms that dolor had caused him to lose.

He was taken to the palace of the queen of the realm by way of a path covered with the flowers that are born with the commencement of spring. He saw a person who had all the graces of beauty with all the naivety and joy of childhood; she was only fourteen years old. She was sitting on a jasmine throne; a thousand Amours were playing around her, some of them enchaining her with orange-blossom and others spreading it over her head; others were undoing her hair and allowing the tresses to fall over a nascent cleavage. She was exchanging badinage with her women and throwing them flowers with a marvelous grace.

That spectacle had the wherewithal to distract him from his sentiments for Florinde. The Queen of Youth was not married, because she wanted a husband of her own age, and gallant, whom she had not been able to encounter. The prince was twenty-four and bearded. A few of the followers of youth asked him for news of past centuries, but the queen began to look at him favorably. The century of ten years that distinguished their ages disappeared because of all the charms with which the prince was replete.

The queen did not neglect anything to engage him: gazes, flattering words and little teasing actions, the meaning of which is very serious, everything was put to use, and everything was understood, although the prince, who was cleverer than her, pretended not to pay any attention to it. She explained herself more overtly, and made him proposals of marriage, with the advantages most capable of touching an amiable man, such as always being his, and possessing forever and without interruption all the benefits without which the others are nothing, all the graces and all the pleasures.

It was difficult for the prince to refuse the dowry that the she was offering to bring him. Gradually, he forgot Florinde, and it was just in time that she forced him to remember that she was still in the world.

Scarcely had she spent a day without seeing the prince than she had sensed the horror of living without the person one loves; however, she strove to vanquish her sentiments; she had already loved without seeing; she did not want to marry without knowing that she was loved constantly. A fortnight passed in those agitations, but she was about to succumb to them, dread and jealousy coming to join the dolors of absence. It was necessary to sacrifice reflections to amour, and she sent for the prince, who was given this letter on her behalf:

If you are suffering as much as me, you have much of which to complain. I cannot support my dolors and yours; I cannot risk losing you for having wanted too much to make sure of you; it is enough, you are already worthy of being recompensed for having obeyed the cruelest of all orders. Alas, I did not know their rigor very well, but I have felt it, and I judge that you cannot sustain it. Depart and come back; why are you not here?

That note arrived very appropriately; the prince, to whom his solitude had given a severe education, had not yet had the leisure to be spoiled by society; he believed that it was not permitted to him to be inconstant, and in spite of the liking that he had for the Queen of Youth, he left the island. As he drew away slowly from a place that had charms for him, however, he read the news of his proscription on a few placards that he encountered on his road. The queen promised anyone who delivered her fugitive, dead or alive, the same favors that she had offered him.

It did not require any more to cure the prince. He hastened his flight, and he arrived at Florinde's feet; seeing him return, she did not have the strength to examine whether he had been faithful.

They were married, and, the prince having become king by virtue of the death of his father, he took his wife to his own estates, where the marriage, in accordance with custom, ended all the charms of their life. Fortunate are those who live therein in honest indifference, but people accustomed to love are not as reasonable as others, and hardly ever provide an example of good households.

The prince, by virtue of idleness, told Florinde that he had had a slight weakness for the Queen of Youth. Florinde made him as many reproaches as if she had not been his wife; he was shocked and importuned by them; he wanted to lament them and console himself with the ladies of the court; she spied on him, surprised him, and heaped him with insults.

Finally, persecuted by her furies, he asked the fays to become a rose-bush again, and obtained that as a favor.

For her part, the jealous Florinde had a head so weak that she could not bear the odor of a flower that reminded her of her amour; it is since that time that roses have always caused the vapors.

François Fénelon: *The Story of King Alfaroute and Clariphile*

There was a king named Alfaroute who was feared by all his neighbors and loved by all his subjects. He was wise, good, just, valiant and clever; nothing was lacking in him. A fay came to find him and told him that great misfortunes would soon befall him if he did not make use of the ring that she put on his finger. When he turned the diamond of the ring inside his hand, he immediately became invisible, and as soon as he turned it outwards again, he was visible, as before.

That ring was very convenient for him and gave him great pleasure. When he was suspicious of one of his subjects, he went into the man's cabinet with his diamond turned inwards; he heard and saw all domestic secrets without being perceived. If he feared the designs of some neighboring king, he went to all his most secret councils, where he learned everything without ever being discovered. Thus, he anticipated without difficulty everything that anyone wanted to do against him; he thwarted several conspiracies formed against his person, and disconcerted the enemies who wanted to crush him.

He was, however, not content with his ring, and he asked the fay for a means of transporting himself in an instant from one country to another, in order to be able to make prompter and more convenient use of the ring that rendered him invisible.

"You're asking too much," the fay replied, with a sigh. "Fear that the last gift might be harmful to you."

He did not listen, and still pressed her to grant it to him.

"Well," she said, "it's necessary, then, for me to give you, reluctantly, what you'll repent of having."

Then she rubbed his shoulder with an odorous liquid. Immediately, he felt two small wings born on his back. Those little wings would not show under his clothing, but when he had resolved to fly, he had only to touch them with his hand; they would immediately become so long that he would be able to surpass infinitely the rapid flight of an eagle. As soon as he no longer wanted to fly, he had only to touch his wings again; they would shrink immediately, in such a way that they could no longer be perceived under his garments.

By that means, the king could go anywhere in a matter of moments; he knew everything, and no one could imagine how he divined so many things, for he shut himself away and appeared to remain in his cabinet almost all day long, without anyone daring to enter it. As soon as he was there he rendered himself invisible by means of his ring, extended his wings by touching them and traveled immense distances.

By that means he engaged in great wars, in which he won all the victories he wanted, but as he saw the secrets of men incessantly he knew that they were so wicked and deceptive that he no longer dared to trust anyone.

The more powerful and redoubtable he became, the less he was loved, and he saw that he was not loved even by those to whom he had given the greatest wealth. In order to console himself, he resolved to go into all the countries in the world to search for a perfect woman whom he could marry, by whom he could be loved, and by means of whom he could render himself happy.

He searched for a long time, and as he saw everything without being seen, he knew the most impenetrable secrets. He went into all courts; he found deceptive women everywhere, who wanted to be loved but who loved themselves too much to love a husband in good faith. He went into all private houses. One woman had a light and inconstant mind, another was hypocritical, another arrogant, another eccentric; almost all were false, vain and idolaters of their own person.

He descended as far as the lowest conditions, and finally found the daughter of a poor laborer, as beautiful as the day, but simple and ingenuous in her beauty, which she counted for nothing, and which was, in fact, the least of her qualities, for she had an intelligence and a virtue that surpassed all her personal graces. All the youth of her neighborhood hastened to see her, and every young man believed that he would assure the happiness of his life by marrying her.

King Alfaroute could not see her without being impassioned by her. He asked her father for her, who was transported with joy to see that his daughter would be a great queen.

Clariphile—that was her name—passed from her cabin into a rich palace, where a numerous court received her. She was not dazzled by it; she conserved her simplicity, her modesty and her virtue, and she did not forget where she had come from when she was heaped with honors.

The king's tenderness for her was redoubled, and he finally believed that he would succeed in being happy. It would not have taken much for him to be happy already, so proud was he commencing to be of his queen's good heart. He rendered himself invisible continually in order to observe her and to surprise her secrets, but he did not discover anything in her that was not worthy of admiration. He no longer had any but a residuum of jealousy and suspicion that still troubled him slightly in his amity.

The fay who had predicted the fatal consequences of her last gift warned him frequently, and he was importuned by her. He gave orders that she was no longer to be allowed to enter the palace, and told the queen that he forbade her to receive her. The queen promised to obey, with a great deal of difficulty, because she liked the good fay very much.

One day, the fay, wanting to instruct the queen with regard to her future, entered her apartment in the guise of an officer, and told the queen who she was. Immediately, the queen embraced her tenderly. The king, who was then invisible, perceived it, and was transported by jealousy to the point of fury. He drew his sword and ran the queen through, who fell into his arms, dying.

At that moment, the fay resumed her veritable form. The king recognized her, and understood the queen's innocence. Then he tried to kill himself. The fay stopped the thrust and tried to console him.

As she died, the queen said to him: "Although I am dying by your hand, I am dying entirely yours."

Alfaroute deplored his misfortune in having wanted, in spite of the fay, a gift that was so deadly. He returned her ring and begged her to take away his wings. He spent the rest of his days in bitterness and dolor. He had no other consolation than going to weep over Clariphile's tomb.

Jean de Préchac: *The Queen of the Fays*

There was once a king who was known as King Guillemot. He was the best prince on earth, who asked for nothing but love and simplicity; it is even affirmed that he wiped his nose on the sleeve of his doublet. He was in no hurry to get married. However, as the Guillemot race was very ancient, his people wanted him to give them successors. There had been talk of several different marriages, but he had always found invincible difficulties in them.

A neighboring princess, whose name as Urraca, had estates that were much to the liking of King Guillemot, but Urraca had always shown a marked repugnance for marriage and a great deal of insensibility to the efforts that several sovereigns, particularly Comte d'Urgel, had made to please her. Her dominant passion was astrology, and she was determined not to marry until she had read in the stars that she would be the mother of a perfect princess, who would be a prodigy of beauty and virtue, who would do infinite good, and would have no other concern than relieving the afflicted.

That knowledge obliged her to listen to the proposals that came to her from all directions. Her nurse often spoke to her in favor of Comte d'Urgel, who had put her in his interests by means of great liberalities, but Urraca, who had the same humor as most other women in being sensible to distinguished ranks, would rather have been a queen than Comtesse d'Urgel.

King Guillemot, informed of the dispositions of the princess, sent an ambassador with an authority to marry her on his behalf, and sent her at the same time a gilded belt, a packet of pins, a small knife and a pair of scissors—ordinary presents in those days. The marriage was soon concluded, and the wedding ceremony too.

The new queen requested that the king should come to find her himself and stay for a time in her estates before taking her back to his kingdom, but King Guillemot rejected that proposal and insisted that the queen come to find him.

The proud Urraca could not reconcile herself to such an absolute order, and the malevolent nurse, who had not received any present from the Guillemots, animated the mind of her mistress in such a way that they spent more than a year in that situation.

Comte d'Urgel, who had found means of seeing the queen without her perceiving him, had fallen passionately in love with her, and still continued to heap the nurse with presents, in order to be informed of the sentiments and the slightest occupations of the queen.

The pride of the princess left him nothing for which to hope, but his amour did not permit him to be disabused, and he believed that he might be able to achieve anything by means of the advice of the deceitful nurse. Although those

307

early times were far from the corruption of the present century, Amour, who has always been subtle and full of inventions, inspired the comte to engage the nurse to introduce him to the queen's presence, persuading her that he was King Guillemot, who was coming to see her incognito. That appeared to him to be all the easier because the queen had never seen her husband. He proposed it to the nurse, and presented her at the same time with a purse full of gold guillemots, which were then very rare.

The nurse, dazzled by such a rich present, promised him everything and they agreed together that the comte would dress as a page in King Guillemot's livery; that the page would bring a garland of flowers to the queen, and would tell her that, his council not having wanted to permit him to go to see her in the apparel of a king, he desired to enter her presence secretly, and had sent her to ask for her permission.

That project was carried out in its full extent, and the nurse did not fail to make much of the gallantry of King Guillemot, with the result that the poor queen found herself pregnant and gave birth after nine months to a beautiful princess without her having heard any further mention of King Guillemot. She nevertheless sent a courier to him to inform him of the birth of his daughter.

King Guillemot became very angry on learning that news, and wanted to put the courier to death, but his council prevented him from doing so, and sent him back with a very piquant letter against the honor of the queen.

As the race of Guillemots was very ancient had had for a motto *Rather death than dishonor*, the entire house was mortified by that insult, especially the king, who was inconsolable and threatened his subjects with allowing himself to die of hunger. It was a primitive century, in which husbands, less polished than those of today, had the simplicity of punishing themselves for their wives' faults.

King Guillemot, having nearly gone mad, was walking along a pathway one day when he heard a voice that followed him, crying *cuckoo, cuckoo*, which was in those days the greatest insult that one could address to a married man. The king flew into a fury, called his guards, and commanded that the reckless individual be hacked to pieces. In spite of all his threats, the voice did not stop. The king was informed, in order to calm him down, that it was a bird, but that only served to irritate him further, convincing him that the entire world was laughing at his adventure, even the birds, which were saying aloud what people were only thinking.

In his wrath, he ordered that all the birds in his kingdom should be exterminated. His vengeance not being satisfied by that cruel massacre, he also wanted them to be eaten. All the courtiers ate some, in order to be obliging, and found them so good that people have continued to do so ever since, although they had previously been horrified by any human who ate a bird, and the pleasure that King Guillemot had in avenging himself caused him to change the resolution he had made to allow himself to die of hunger.

While King Guillemot was exterminating innocent poultry, the queen, who was waiting the return of her courier, nursed the little princess herself, fearing that if she drank the milk of an ordinary nurse, she might also absorb any bad inclinations she might have. As the fays meddled with everything in those days, she sent word to a fay named Belsunsine, one of her friends, who lived in the Pyrenees, asking her to be godmother to the princess.

The fay, sensible to such a great honor, endowed her with an infinite number of good qualities and named her Meridiana. The queen gave a magnificent fête in order to do more honor to the fay, which would have continued for several days but for the arrival of the courier bringing King Guillemot's outraged letter. The poor queen, who had acted in good faith, nearly died when she learned that King Guillemot disavowed the child and was treating her with the utmost indignity.

In her despair, she found no better remedy than to assemble her council; she explained the entire affair to them as it had happened, assuring them that the nurse was a reliable witness to all her conduct. Then she demanded justice against the bad conduct of King Guillemot. It was resolved with a common voice that war should be declared, and although King Guillemot's estates were of far greater extent than Queen Urraca's, her subjects were so convinced of the perfidy of King Guillemot and the innocence of the queen that they all swore to risk their wealth and their lives for the reparation of the insult.

War was declared on King Guillemot, and troops were levied everywhere; serious preparations for battle were made and everyone debated such an extraordinary adventure. Those who knew of the simplicity of King Guillemot and his scant urgency for women judged that the child was not his, knowing full well that he was incapable of making such a voyage or of performing a similar gallantry. The queen had the reputation of being the most virtuous princess on earth; the more her actions were examined, the less occasion was found, or even any pretext, for suspecting her conduct.

Several neighboring potentates wanted to involve themselves in mediation, but the Guillemots, jealous of the point of honor, rejected all the propositions that were made to him to recognize the child, and the queen, who believed that she had been abused under the faith of marriage, preferred to perish with all her subjects if King Guillemot would not admit the fact and beg her pardon for his perfidy.

Comte d'Urgel was one of those who pressed hardest for that element, and as he still loved the queen and did not think much of the Guillemots, he proposed, in order to spare the blood of so many people, to settle the matter in single combat, offering to defend the honor of the queen in the capacity of her champion.

King Guillemot would not accept that challenge, but Prince Guilledin, his brother, who had a courage worthy of the ancient Guillemots, begged the assembled estates of the realm to permit him to fight Comte d'Urgel. As it was a matter of nothing less than the loss of the kingdom, the estates permitted the combat, with great acclamations, and having rendered on the appointed day to the capital city of the queen's estates they found Comte d'Urgel there, who testified much scorn for a champion that he believed to be far beneath his courage.

The combat took place in the presence of the queen and her council, and either because Prince Guilledin was more adroit than Comte d'Urgel or because victory is always declared for the truth, the Prince felled the Comte with a thrust of his lance, which wounded him mortally.

The judges having run to him, he declared before dying that he had deceived the queen with the help of the nurse. The wicked woman was arrested and did not have the strength to contradict what the Comte had just said.

The unfortunate queen, enlightened as to a mystery that, in spite of her good faith, made her appear culpable, would have died of dolor if, on the advice of Belsunsine, she had not suspended her despair for love of Meridiana. She nevertheless ordered that the nurse should be handed over to Prince Guilledin, and that the gilded belt, the pins, the little knife and the scissors that King Guillemot had sent her should be returned to him.

Prince Guilledin returned victorious, and was received in his brother's estates with extraordinary applause. The nurse, imprisoned in an iron cage, was dragged through the streets for a long time, and then thrown into the sea. King Guillemot, who had refused Comte d'Urgel's challenge, was deposed and imprisoned, and Prince Guilledin mounted the throne.

Urraca, ashamed of her misfortunes, did not have the courage to suffer the sight of any of her subjects and retired, with her dear daughter and the fay Belsunsine, to a mountain in the Pyrenees, the highest of all, which is named the Pic du Midi. She put all her application into educating Meridiana well, inspiring her with scorn for all men, and teaching her everything she knew about astrology.

The young person in question was becoming more lovable every day, and already had more intelligence and reason than is usual for children of her age. Belsunsine loved her as tenderly as her own mother, and while Urraca made her party to her science, the fay revealed her supernatural secrets to her. She remembered everything she was told once, and had a nature so mild that she always obeyed without question everything that was demanded of her.

Meridiana's great beauty, her docility and the continuous progress that she made in the sciences and all the secrets of the fays consoled her sad mother greatly, but as all the happiness in life is of short duration, another fay, whose name was Balbasta, jealous of the beauty and the extraordinary talents of the young princess, abducted her secretly. For fear that Belsunsine might discover her retreat she burned juniper and other berries in all the places through which she passed, and imprisoned the princess in a high tower in the Château de Pau, which is at the foot of the Pyrenees. She gave her the task of drawing water from a very deep well, putting it in a sieve, and then climbing five hundred steps, in order to take it to the top of a tower where the fay had a little garden that she made her water.

Queen Urraca, already overwhelmed by misfortunes, was unable to survive the loss of her dear daughter, and died not long after Meridiana's abduction, without the amity that Belsunsine testified for her, or all the assurances that she gave her of taking no repose until she had discovered her retreat, being able to console her.

Meanwhile, Meridiana, far from complaining about her difficult task, acquitted it with a great deal of success, aided by the secrets that Belsunsine had already taught her, without Balbasta ever perceiving it, with the consequence that every time the evil fay appeared, the princess received her very graciously, always begging her to order her to do something more difficult, assuring her that she would never be able to take enough trouble to please such a benevolent fay.

Balbasta, surprised by the rude labor and patience of the princess, nevertheless gave her new occupations every day, the latest of which were always more difficult than the previous ones, all the way to making her pick up a bushel of millet, one seed at a time, threatening to make her suffer horrible tortures if she missed a single one and if she could not tell her how many seeds here were in the bushel.

Meridiana always acquitted herself in the same manner, and never failed to thank Balbasta for her generosity. The fay, vanquished by the docility of the princess, finally wearied of persecuting her, and, having visited Belsunsine one day, whom she found very afflicted, she asked her the subject of her chagrin.

The good fay naturally told her the source of her affliction, exaggerating the beauty, the good nature and the admirable talents of Meridiana; she dissolved in tears in telling her the story. Balbasta, who was convinced of the princess's merits, allowed herself to be softened by her companion's tears, and promised her to discover her retreat and bring her back to the Pic du Midi, on condition that she engaged the charming princess to love her.

Belsunsine, delighted by the mere thought of seeing her dear Meridiana again, promised everything.. The next day, Balbasta returned to the Pic du Midi and presented the princess to Belsunsine, who almost died of joy on seeing her again. She tried to console her for the death of her mother, and the two fays, having embraced her tenderly, both promised her to serve as her mother and not to hide any of their secrets from her. They gave her, in advance, a ring that shielded her from any insults that other jealous fays might make her.

It was a long time before she was able console herself for the death of her mother. She built her a magnificent mausoleum on top of the mountain, and that death did not fail to engage her in further meditations on the unfortunate condition of mortals, who are exposed to so many different miseries, without great princes being dispensed from that fatal vicissitude. She was confirmed then in the resolution she had already made, which her mother the queen had so often inspired in her, to practice virtue, to renounce commerce with humans, to apply herself anew to the knowledge of the stars, and to profit from the goodwill that the fays had for her. Filled with those sentiments, she attached herself strongly to Belsunsine, who finished teaching her everything she knew.

Balbasta, who loved her no less than her companion, made her party to all her secrets; Meridiana attended several assemblies of fays, where she was much admired and applauded. As they remarked that she was informed of all their secrets, and that she was entirely detached from life, they resolved to receive her among the number of fays. She seemed touched by the honor that was being offered to her, but when, in the ceremony, it was proposed that she take the form of a dragon, in order to have the gift of illusions, and to be able to make a magnificent palace appear where there was nothing but smoke, she refused to do it, and affirmed that she did not want to deceive anyone. Many of the fays murmured against that delicacy, but it was passed by a majority vote, because of her beauty and her high birth.

As soon as she was a fay she thought of nothing but using her power of enchantment to relieve a host of oppressed individuals. She chose for her dwelling a grotto in the Pyrenees, which she ornamented with a large number of beautiful statues, and which is known today as Meridiana's Espalungue. She traveled to all the countries in the world under the pretext of visiting her companions the fays, to whom she gave rich presents, although she only undertook the voyages in order to acquaint herself with the mores of all nations. She recognized, however, that there was malice, infidelity and weakness everywhere, and that the majority of humans had almost the same faults in whatever country they lived. She did not find any who were perfectly happy and did not desire anything more; that knowledge gave her a great deal of compassion for their miseries, and fortified her in the resolution she had made always to relieve the unfortunate.

Throughout her voyage, she never missed an opportunity to do good. Having arrived in India, at the home of the fay Mamelec, she remarked in her palace a young woman of surprising beauty, who was occupied in cutting stubble to make litter for fifty camels.

Judging that there might be something extraordinary in that, Meridiana asked her who she was. The beauty admitted that she was the daughter of the king of Monomotapa, and told her that her stepmother, seeking to avenge herself for the fact that she had not wanted to marry one of her brothers, had asked the fay Mamelec to abduct her, and that the fay had enchanted her for three hundred years, of which only two hundred had passed as yet. She started to weep as she finished speaking, and begged Meridiana not to distract her from her labor, because if she did not finish by the marked time, four old women who were her overseers would take turns to beat her; the first would give her fifty strokes of a rod on the soles of her feet, the second as many on her shoulders and the other two twenty-five each, half on her belly and half on her buttocks.

Meridiana, moved by the story of so many cruelties, tapped a stone with her wand, and the camel stables were furnished with litter in an instant. The beautiful Indian woman, astonished by that marvel, judged that Meridiana was a great divinity and implored her, her eyes bathed with tears, to have pity on her misery. The fay consoled her and promised to employ herself in her service; she spoke about her to Mamelec, and asked her with such great entreaties for mercy for the beautiful princess that it was granted to her with a good heart.

Meridiana ran to the princess and assured her, while presenting her with a white rose, that in an hour she would find herself in the room from which she had been abducted, in the same garments, with the same youth and beauty that she had had on the day of her abduction.

It is true that she arrived in the palace of her father, the king, but as the kingdom had passed to another house in such a long interval of time, no one recognized her. The king, who had several children, was very surprised to see the princess; her great beauty was admired, but as it was a matter of ceding the kingdom to her, no one dared declare themselves in her favor. The archives were examined, and it was found that it was true that a princess of the royal blood had been abducted by the fays, but what appearance was there that she had returned after two hundred years? In brief, the king did not find it appropriate to get to the bottom of a question that might have cost him his throne.

As all peoples like novelty, and those of Monomotapa were very curious to see such an extraordinary person, the king was led to fear that there might be an uprising in favor of the princess, and he was told that, in order to set his mind at rest and assure his children of the crown, it was necessary, as a matter of good politics, to put her to death. Others, less cruel, suggested that he marry the princess to his eldest son, but the king, who was miserly and hoped to make enough money from the prince's marriage to marry his two daughters, rejected the latter advice and resolved to put the princess to death, accusing her of seducing his people.

She was arrested, but during her trial, the king's eldest son, touched by the charms of the beautiful person, went to declare to his father that if he put the princess to death he would throw himself on the same pyre that had been built to burn her. The king was so offended by his son's declaration that he hastened the execution of the unfortunate princess, but the fay Meridiana, who had foreseen what would happen, went to visit her in her prison and found her much more afflicted by the resolution that the prince had made to die with her than her own misfortune.

The fay approved of the gratitude she had for the young prince, and after having promised her never to abandon her, she told her that her father had hidden a rich treasure in a place that she indicated to her, assuring her that the reigning king would let her marry his son gladly if she revealed that treasure to him. Then she went to the king's cabinet, spoke to him in a menacing tone and called him cruel and a usurper, adding that he was very fortunate to be able to assure the kingdom to his children by means of the marriage of the beautiful princess, who had more treasure than all the other princes of India put together.

She disappeared after saying that, and the king, frightened by that vision, was agitated by a host of confused and various thoughts. His avarice prevailing over all those impulses, however, he resolved to obtain clarification from the princess herself as to whether she had treasure, and, judging that the queen would be better able than him to extract that secret, he charged her with that commission.

The queen, as cunning as all Indians, flattered her and caressed her, already addressing her as her dear daughter-in-law and exaggerating the strong passion that her son had for her, since he wanted to die for her service. The princess, who had already seen the prince several times and knew the obligations she had to him, assured the queen that she would be delighted to conserve that dear son, and told her that if the rights she already had over the crown were not sufficient, she would give her a treasure of inestimable price. The queen embraced her a thousand times, and, that treasure having been found in the place that the fay had indicated, the marriage was made with extraordinary magnificence and the reciprocal satisfaction of the two lovers.

Delighted to have finished such a great favor, Meridiana returned to her grotto in the Pyrenees. Her vigilance and her good heart did not permit her to remain tranquil for long; she was at the childbirth of all the queens, and, not content with preventing the tricks of other fays, she endowed the princesses with an extreme beauty and the princes with great valor, and even sometimes rendered them invulnerable. The consequence of that was that in past centuries, the children of kings had no need of their sword to conquer several kingdoms. Meridiana's reputation extended throughout the world, and whatever envy the other fays had against her, she treated them with so much civility and was able to make them such agreeable little presents and speeches that she hardly had any enemies, and was greatly esteemed in all the corps of fays.

The help that she gave crowned heads did not prevent her from rendering services to people of mediocre condition, and if she found a poor shepherdess who did not have the strength to defend her sheep against a hungry wolf, she flew to her aid and took her to a good pasture, which the wolves would not have dared to approach. If a sleeping woodcutter had lost his ax, she did not disdain to bring it back to him, and if a poor traveler fell into the hands of thieves she came to his defense and protected him from their cruelties. In sum, everyone who appealed to the fay Meridiana was sure of being helped promptly. It was by such actions that she won the hearts of persons of all conditions, finding all her pleasure in procuring good and preventing evil.

As there is no one who does not approve of good deeds, although not everyone had the strength to do them, the fays were delighted by all the good they heard said of their companion, and perceived with pleasure that the terror they had once inspired was turning to affection, that they were welcome everywhere and summoned to all the councils of kings, even of particular families.

Belsunsine and Balbasta published everywhere the obligation they had to the beautiful Meridiana, and the other fays did not contradict them.

The ambition that slips into all sorts of estates caused the fays to judge that if they chose a queen their corps would become much more considerable, since that queen would be ranked among the other crowned heads. That project having been applauded by all the fays, they met one day in order to hold the election. Having rendered to the marked place, the affair was discussed. It was proposed that the power of the person elected should be limited, but, the choice having fallen on Meridiana, all the fays had so much esteem for her and so much confidence in her probity that they gave her a boundless authority, to the point of being able to interdict those who displeased her.

Meridiana was then crowned, in spite of her resistance, and notwithstanding the reasons that she gave the assembly for preferring Princess Merlusine to her. However, she did not abuse her authority, and had even more regard for the fays than she had had before. That good conduct charmed them to such an extent that they had no difficulty in obeying her.

The new queen having firmly established her monarchy, sent the fays away with the order to inform her regularly of everything that was happening in the different countries in which they lived, and she retired herself to her grotto in the Pyrenees, where she received several ambassadors on the part of a large number of sovereigns who had obligations to her, and who congratulated her on her new dignity.

Her elevation gave her new cares, and did not spare her any. Always eager to find, in all the places that she went, that she could be useful to someone, she suffered with impatience anyone thanking her for a benefit, assuring them that she had far more pleasure in giving it than they had in receiving it. She criticized the great for the scant attention they paid to the fortune of their inferiors, since it cost them so little; she excused the faults of everyone, and did not understand how one could resolve to return a bad deed or do any harm to anyone. In sum, there never was anyone who honored virtue more, or who had so much indulgence for human weakness.

She sometimes allowed herself to be seen in her grotto, sometimes on the Pic du Midi, and often in different places, where she listened to all those who wanted to speak to her, even making use of treasures that she discovered for the indigent, giving a princess to be married a bushel of gold as liberally as she gave a modest sum to a shepherdess to repair the loss of a ewe that had died.

A marquise who has been married for a long time without having children was finally fortunate enough to become pregnant; she chose a woman of confidence who had already served as nurse to her son. That nurse having very subtly exchanged her own child with the son of the marquise, the young man had inclinations so base, and gave a thousand chagrins to his supposed parents, to the point that the marquis accused his wife of infidelity, it not being possible that he was the father of such a bad lot. The marquise, who had nothing for which to reproach herself, groaned and wept continually because, as the false marquis grew older, his bad inclinations were further revealed. She had heard mention of the Queen of the Fays and her marvels; that obliged her to undertake a journey to the Pyrenees to implore her aid.

The marquise threw herself at the feet of the fay, imploring her to enable her to die or to change the inclinations of her son. The fay lifted her up very graciously, and told her that she had no reason to lament either for her son or herself, since that son resembled her in body and mind. Mortified and shamed by a response that seemed so disobliging, the marquise was already disposed to leave when Meridiana embraced her and told her how her son had been exchanged by the nurse, how it was easy to prove that by means of a little yellow mark that he had on his left arm. The marquise remembered that immediately, and was impatient to quit the fay in order to go in search of her son. Meridiana, who perceived that, judged that the journey to return to her husband and tell him that good news would be very long, made her a present of two horses that could cover a hundred leagues in an hour, and sent her away very content.

The marquis, who could not console himself for having an heir so unworthy, nearly died of joy on hearing his wife's story. His first impulse was to kill the wicked nurse, but the marquise calmed him down and they went to see the nurse together, who lived on one of their lands. First they asked her for news of her son; she replied, weeping, that he was the worst son in the entire regions, that he had lost their flock, and that he spent entire days hunting, adding that he would make a better marquis than a shepherd.

"Would you like to exchange him with ours?" the marquise asked her.

"You think you're joking," retorted the malign shepherdess. "Perhaps you'll do him as much honor as yours, but do better and take charge of both of them."

During that dialogue the young hunter arrived, laden with game, which he presented to the marquis with a politeness worthy of his birth. The marquise, who thought she was looking into a mirror on looking at the young man, who resembled her very closely, could not retain the impulses of nature for long and embraced him several times, her eyes bathed with tears.

"We're talking," the marquis said to him, "of making an exchange of you for my son. Would you be sorry?"

"If that could be," replied the young man, "without doing any wrong to your son, I feel that I have enough courage to sustain such an illustrious rank."

"Yes," the father continued, "but it's necessary, in order to be a marquis, to have a yellow mark on the left arm."

The young man immediately rolled up his sleeve and showed his yellow mark. The marquis and his wife, unable to doubt the truth, embraced him again, and the nurse, seeing the mystery discovered, did not have the strength to maintain her imposture and admitted everything.

316

It was by similar actions that the Queen of the Fays acquired the esteem and veneration of a infinite number of people, Her generosity was admired by all the fays, but very few were found who wanted to imitate her; on the contrary, the majority made use of their power to cause a thousand woes to humans, either out of envy or malice; they ordinarily devoted themselves to persecuting beautiful women, especially great princesses, which caused Queen Meridiana a great deal of pain. She would have liked to be everywhere, in order to remedy that. She tried several times to give them a horror of evil and inspire noble sentiments in them, but it was futile. There were old hunchbacks who only nourished themselves on the tears and sobs of persecuted princesses, and who would rather have died than cease their malice.

Seeing that bad habits had got the upper hand, and that the matter could not be remedied, Meridiana finally resolved to make use of her authority and the power she had to forbid them the use of their functions as fays for as long as she wished. She assembled them all and expressed to them the sensible displeasure she had in seeing that the fays, who might be honored as divinities if they applied themselves to good, were only thinking, for the most part, of tormenting illustrious persons; that humans were unfortunate enough, by virtue of their short lives, maladies, the lack of possessions and an infinity of unexpected accidents that happened to them on a daily basis, without the fays putting all their industry into persecuting them; that seemed to her so unjust that she had resolved to prohibit it for three centuries, and only to allow them the liberty to do good, in order that they might have time to apply themselves to exercises of virtue and correct their inveterate malice.

She ordered them thereafter to come, in the final years of the third century, to the hall of the Château de Montargis, which was large and spacious, in order to render her an account of the progress they had made, promising to reestablish in their functions all those whose conduct had been benevolent and who had some good deed in their favor.

That fulminating sentence made the entire troop murmur, but it was necessary to obey. The majority of the fays abandoned the mountains and almost all of them retired to old châteaux, where they amused themselves spinning and waiting for the end of their interdiction, and since that time no more mention has been heard, of abductions or other similar vexations that the fays used to make, and the memory of them would have been lost if their tales did not remain to us.

Queen Meridiana, always applied to good, made a voyage to Fortunate Arabia, from which she brought back cinchona, sage, betony and several other herbs that have the virtue of prolonging life. She planted them in the Pyrenees, where they are still found today, and established a marvelous flower garden, garnished with all sorts of flowers, on the heights of the Pic du Midi, without time having been able to destroy that agreeable flower garden, which still subsists and which curiosity-seekers can see with pleasure. Then she devoted herself, for several years, to studying the crystalline waters that emerged from the

Pyrenees, and, having perceived that those waters have several different virtues, she judged that if she could make them pass throughout the mines of gold, lead and sulfur that there are in those mountains, the waters would take on the virtues of those minerals, and would be a great help for the relief of humans. She examined their sources, caused them to flow through new conduits, and mingled them so well that those waters cure all sorts of maladies. It is to the cares of that illustrious fay that we owe the waters of Bagnères, for fevers and various other maladies; those of Bares, for all sorts of wounds; those of Cautères, for indigestions; Aigue-bonne, for ulcers; and Aigue-caure, for rheumatisms.

Although Meridiana was a benefactress for the whole world, she had a particular predilection for her homeland, and, thinking that the majority of kings in those times were cowards or imbeciles, she was touched with compassion by seeing people governed by such princes. The opinion she had that the people of her homeland were all borne to goodness, and the knowledge she had of their intelligence, often made her hope that a prince of Béarn might reign one day in the beautiful realm of France, but as she was an enemy of injustices and that could not be one without dethroning the legitimate kings, she deferred the execution of that project for a long time. Finally, she found an opportunity by virtue of the marriage of Antoine de Bourbon with Jeanne d'Albret, heir to Navarre and Béarn;[32] the fay disposed minds so well that the affair succeeded.

The queen gave birth to four different children, whom the fay, who had long views, abandoned to destinies, not finding that they had the qualities necessary to fulfill her project. But in the end, the queen having become pregnant for a fifth time, the fay endowed the child with a good mind and great valor, and then enabled him to be brought up without any delicacy, just like the children of commoners; and it was him who succeeded to the crown of France by virtue of his merit, and perhaps also the help of the fay.

That prince had a son whom the fay endowed with a great deal of intelligence, valor and justice, but having forgotten to endow those first two with a long life, and perceiving that humans had need of examples who would be present for a long time in order to excite them to virtue, she resolved to repair that fault at the first opportunity; in fact, she gave the sin of the latter prince the justice of his father and the valor of his grandfather, and also added a great piety and a long life.

Satisfied with so many good deeds, and above all in thinking that the Béarnais, for whom she had a great deal of esteem, would have the opportunity in future to make use of their talents and their intelligence, by the favor of the kings that would be their compatriots, she wanted to efface from human minds the memory of the fays and retire to her grotto, where she would remain for several years without seeing anyone.

---

[32] Antoine de Bourbon married Jeanne d'Albret in 1548; their son succeeded to the French throne as Henri IV.

It was only about two years before the three centuries of the fays' interdiction would elapse when their queen, who had assigned them to the Château de Montargis, perceived that it was in too much disorder to receive such good company. Nevertheless, as the situation of the castle was very advantageous, there was a very spacious hall there, a charming view, a great forest and a beautiful river, Meridiana wanted the assembly to be held there.

Not wanting to make use of her art to reestablish it, however, she remembered that the great prince who was its master took his origin from the region of the Pyrenees, and she was informed that he was able to embellish houses with the same facility as he won battles. She made use appropriately of that knowledge and insinuated to that prince the desire to reestablish the Château de Montargis, which was executed with as much diligence as if the fays had done the work, with the result that the house, abandoned for several years, was soon in a state to lodge several great princesses comfortably.[33] Meridiana having arrived there, all the other fays, impatient to have their interdiction lifted, also went there.

The queen, having received them very favorably, testified the joy that she had in seeing them again, and was the first to render an account of her occupations during the three centuries of their absence. Her modesty caused her to pass succinctly over all the good things she had procured, and she only spoke about the impatience she had had to see them gain, convinced that each of her sisters had done well and had conducted herself much better than she had.

Merlusine, having made a profound reverence, assured the queen that she had never missed an opportunity to do good to those of her house and to many others, and although she had been living for a long time in the mountains of Dauphiné, she had cede her retreat to the Chartreux and retired to the Château de Sassenage, where she did all the good of which she was capable secretly, without any other motive than the satisfaction that well-born souls find in practicing virtue. The queen treated her very civilly, and after having done her much honor and given her great praise, she lifted her interdiction.

An old fay, bleary-eyed and poorly-built, presented herself before the queen and told her that she had retired to the Château de Pierre-Encise, where she had prevented the prisoners receiving letters from anyone, and, none of them having escaped from that rude prison, demanded for recompense that the queen permit her to perform enchantments as she had before. The queen replied that since the employment of jailer was so much to her taste she ordered her to continue in it, without meddling in anything else. That judgment was applauded, and the poor old fay was jeered loudly.

Then a tall good-looking fay advanced before the queen and told her that she had chosen for her retreat the Château de Moncalieri on the Po; that she had

---

[33] The restoration of the Château de Montargis in the 1560s was actually carried out by Princesse Renée de France, the younger daughter of Louis XII.

found a duchesse in childbed, who was about to be on a par with queens, that she had endowed the little princess to whom she had given birth with a great deal of intelligence, solid virtue, the most beautiful eyes in the world, a beautiful complexion and even good conduct, very premature, because as soon as she was born she had destined her to occupy the most august throne on earth. She added that her confidence in the good qualities of that amiable princess had gone so far that she had persuaded the duchesse, her mother, to put her to proof for a year, assured that the better one knew her, the more one would love her, which had succeeded, as she had said.

The fay then wanted to talk about many other advantages that she had procured for her homeland, but the queen, seeing that she was entering into details that were too delicate, interrupted her and assured her that what she had done for the charming princess was more than sufficient to merit that she continued to employ enchantment with the same liberty that she had had before her interdiction, and in order to mark how much her conduct was agreeable to her she also lifted in her favor the interdiction of another fay, one of her friends, who had done nothing to merit that favor.

Another fay appeared who had a very composed manner; she told the fay that she had retired a long time ago to the Castello Ferrara; that she had prevented neighboring princes rendering themselves masters of it on several occasions and that her zeal for the religion had engaged her to make that beautiful duchy fall into the hands of the Pope. The queen, without entering into any detail, criticized her for allowing the house of the ancient Dukes of Ferrara to become extinct, and dismissed her.

Then another fay presented herself who wore a black velvet toque on her head, and told the queen that she lived in the Château de Boussu in Flanders, and that in order to imitate the good deeds of the Queen of the Fays she had thought that she could not do better than to purge the world of a large quantity of libertines; that in order to succeed in that she had attracted to the château several thousand men of all sorts of nations, and had caused a large proportion of them to perish. The good queen was horrified by that great cruelty, and, having reproached her for the death of several heroes, she forbade her ever to appear in her presence again.

Another fay in hunting costume presented herself before the queen and told her that she had lived in the Château de Fontainebleau a long time before François I had augmented the building; that she had been exposed to an infinity of slanders; thus far, she had been made to pass for a phantom under the pretext that she sometimes hunted in the forest; that she assured Her Majesty that she had never done any harm to anyone, even avoiding frightening shepherds; and that she had had the satisfaction of being present at the first childbirth of a sage queen and had given her child all the virtues of a hero and, above all, a generosity similar to that of the queen, his mother, and that she saw with pleasure that the prince had never told any lie, whether his father had put him at the head of his armies, had summoned him to his council or charged him with other cares. The queen, who was very interested in the prince that the fay had just mentioned, lifted her interdiction and even praised her.[34]

Another fay, who appeared after the one from Fontainebleau, threw herself at the queen's feet and told her that she lived in the Château de Chambord, where she had had almost no opportunity to do good or evil;[35] that she had nevertheless had good will; and that, unable to do any better, she had often prevented the foxes from eating the pheasants; she even admitted that the only malice she had ever done was to present herself to a hunter in the form of a fox, made him fire several rifle shots and come back in the same form to ask the hunter whether he had seen two of her little comrades go by. The entire company laughed, including the queen. The fay begged the queen, however, to reestablish her prerogatives as a fay; the queen consented to that, but limited her to doing harm to foxes, wolves, cats and other animals that eat game.

Another fay, who had a very intelligent appearance, presented herself before the queen and said that she had retired to the Château de Chantilly, where she had contributed a great deal to the education of several great heroes; that in recent times she had taken particular care to embellish the house and gardens, and that she had had the skill to attract a princess there who was so charming that she alone, without the help of the waters and the gardens sufficed to render the château the most agreeable abode on earth.[36] The queen, who liked actions in which virtue and industry appeared, permitted her to enchant as before.

A new fay presented herself, with rather extraordinary garments, and told the queen that she had once lived in Heidelberg Castle; that other fays, enemies of the house Palatine, had been at the childbed of the Electress and had given several nasty predictions to the princes and princesses born there; that she had only been there once, by chance, at the time when the Electress gave birth to a princess whom she had endowed with great virtue, a good mind, much probity and elevation and a very noble souls; that she had not even neglected to give her beautiful teeth and beautiful hair; but that princess having passed into other states and the electorate into distant branches, in which she did not know anyone, she was resolved no longer to return to Heidelberg, begging the queen to assign her another mansion for her dwelling.[37] The queen, satisfied with the

---

[34] The price in question succeeded to the throne as Louis XIII in 1610 and reigned until 1643. His mother was Marie de' Medici.

[35] After the death in 1547 of François I, who had it built as a hunting lodge but hardly used it, the Château de Chambord was abandoned until Louis XIV ordered its restoration in the mid-17th century, but he abandoned it in 1685.

[36] Charlotte de Montmorency, Princess de Condé (1594-1650).

[37] The Electress Charlotte of Hesse-Kassel (1627-1686) was the mother of Princes Elisabeth Charlotte, who married Philippe I, Duc d'Orléans, the younger brother of Louis XIV.

good faith of the German fay, reestablished her former privileges and assigned for the Château de Montargis and its forest for her ordinary dwelling.

Another fay, very replete, prostrated herself before the queen and told her that she lived in the Château d'Amboise and its forest, that once when she was bathing in the Loire she had prevented a boat from capsizing, and that that action alone merited the restoration of her privileges; but the queen remembered that the fay had been part of the conspiracy that had once been woven around the Château d'Amboise, and dismissed her without listening to her any further.[38]

The fay of the Château de Blois presented herself before the queen and told her that she had taken care to conserve in Bois fine language and fine cream, asking to the reestablished in her rights, but the queen, who remembered that she had given occasion to everything that had happened in the last estates of Blois and had a more recent memory of pernicious advice that she had inspired not long ago in a great prince who lived in the château, ordered her to work perfecting Blois cream, and forbade her to meddle in anything else.

Another fay was presented, simply clad, who said to the queen that she was one of the oldest fays in the world, that she lived in the Château de Pons in Saintonge, that she had seen it change master several times, dolorously, and, dreading that it might finally fall into the hands of a bad master, she had procured its possession by a prince who was no less commendable by his intelligence and a host of good qualities than for his high birth.[39] The queen, in favor of that good action, permitted the fay to continue to work enchantments as of old.

Another fay came forward, who told the queen that she lived in the Château d'Epagny in Bourgogne, of which she had procured the possession by a great princess, who, by virtue of her extreme beauty, her majestic air and her good conduct merited being compared to the Queen of the Fays, since her reputation was known throughout the world, to the point that peoples of the extremities of the earth had made her their divinity; the fay asked that her privileges be reestablished, and even added that she had never done other malice than once breaking the drawbridge of the château in order to retain for longer the most august company in the world, which she had attracted there. The queen found that she had good taste and lifted her interdiction.

One appeared who had a very serious expression, and said that she lived in the Château de Nancy, that she had seen with a great deal of regret the absence of her prince, that if anything had contributed to console her for that, it was the alliance he had made with a queen of august blood who had a great deal of virtue and piety; that she had abandoned the Château de Nancy for some time to attend the first childbirth of that queen and had endowed the child with a hand-

---

[38] The Amboise conspiracy of 1560 was an alleged Huguenot plot to abduct François II and seize political control of the realm.

[39] The Château de Pons was besieged and destroyed by Louis XIII in 1621.

some face, great valor and a strong inclination to return to his estates; that, the prince having reached an age to be married, she had conducted his affairs so well that she had procured him a young princess who only counted kings and emperors among her ancestors, but much less considerable by her high birth than her docility, her intelligence and her noble manners.[40] "I flatter myself, great Queen," the fay continued, "that in favor of that illustrious couple, you will reestablish me in my former rights, in the assurance that I give out that the first child born to that marriage will not fail to be endowed very advantageously." The queen started laughing, and lifted the interdiction.

Another fay presented herself, who spoke a corrupt French and told the queen that she lived in the Château de Ryswick, to which she had attracted by means of her skill the ambassadors of the greatest princes on earth, and after several conferences, had finally obliged them to conclude a good peace.[41] Then she wanted to talk about the merit of the princes of the house of Nassau, to whom the house belonged, but the queen, who was fully convinced, told her that she did not need any other reasons to engage her to lift her interdiction. She praised her zeal highly and not only reestablished all her ancient functions, but accorded her the same favor for another fay, whom she could choose.

A very decrepit fay appeared before the queen, and told her that she had lived in the Château de Loches for a long time, where nothing had ever happened against the service of the princess; that even the English, having besieged the castle, which they thought they would take by famine, and having reduced the besieged to the last extremity for want of food, she had imitated the squeal of a pig and started crying night and day on the ramparts, with the result that the English, convinced that here were still abundant provisions within the castle, lifted the siege. In addition, she had exercised such delicacy in the choice of governors of the place that she had only ever suffered persons of great merit and known probity, and that in recent times, when the castle no longer had a garrison or fortifications, she had never relented on the probity of the governor. The queen, who admired actions of honor, reestablished her privileges as a fay.

Another fay presented herself, who told the queen that she lived in the castle of Barcelona, that she had always loved fine actions; that in spite of whatever predilection she might have had for her homeland, she had been so touched by the extreme valor of the two princes who had attacked its ramparts that she had not been able to refuse them entry to her castle. The queen replied that all women were virtuous if they were touched by someone's merit, that since she had paid more attention to the valor of the two heroes than to her duty, she ordered her to leave the castle of Barcelona and go to that of Aner, where she could

---

[40] Probably a reference to the Duc de Bourgogne and his marriage in 1697 to Marie-Adelaïde de Savoie.

[41] The Treaty of Ryswick, signed in September-October 1697, can only have been concluded very shortly before the story, published in 1698, was written.

watch over the establishment of that house; she left her the liberty of all her former privileges for that.

The queen was trying to end the session when another fay appeared, dressed in the Turkish style, who said that she had lived for a long time in the castle of Andrinople, where she had often changed the condition of a slave into that of a sultana and that, in order to conform with the character of the Queen of the Fays, she had watched over the conservation of the Ottoman princes, and had even prompted the abolition of the barbaric custom of strangling they younger ones for the security of the eldest. By virtue of that, three brothers had ruled successively, and then the son of the first had succeeded his father and his uncles.

The queen lifted her interdiction, gave great praise to the vigilance of the fay, and said that it was to be wished that all fays had the same attention and watched continuously over the conservation of great princes, lamenting that none had been found to go into Spain to watch over the royal house; but the fays responded that they only chose old castles for their retreat and Her Majesty knew very well that there were no castles in Spain.

Several foreign fays then presented themselves, but the queen, who was convinced of great vexations that they had caused in the countries where they lived, did not want to listen to them, and after having made a very eloquent speech, to exhort those who remained under interdiction to apply themselves to virtue, she closed the session after having signed them to return in three centuries to the hall in the Château de Pau to render her an account of the progress they had made in the exercise of virtue.

Chevalier de Mailly: *The Magician King*

There was once a king who was powerful as much by virtue of the extent of his domination as the secrets of magic that he possessed. After having spent the years of his youth in all the pleasures that a rich magician prince could not lack, he encountered a princess of great beauty who fixed his fickle humor, for he had always flown from beauty to beauty before. He asked for her in marriage, and having obtained her, he thought himself the most fortunate of men in possessing such a lovable person, by whom he was loved perfectly.

Before the end of the year that beauty gave birth to a son worthy of his heritage, for he appeared as soon as he entered the world so marvelously beautiful that he won the admiration of the whole court. As soon as the queen, his mother, thought she was strong enough to undertake a short journey, she used the pretext of taking him for some fresh air to carry him secretly to the home of a fay who was her godmother. I say secretly because the fay had warned the queen that the king was a magician, and as there has always been a fierce war between sorcerers and fays, the king would not have approved of anyone having commerce with the latter.

The queen's godmother had a palace in a forest that was not far from the court. The queen, as I said, took her son there in order that he might receive the gifts of faerie, so useful in the adventures for which princes are destined.

The fay, who was particularly interested in everything concerning the queen, and who found the young prince very pretty, gave him the art of pleasing everyone, so to speak, from the cradle, and in the fullness of time, a marvelous facility to learn everything that might render him an accomplished prince one day. He made such rapid progress therein that all those charged with his education were charmed to see that he surpassed their expectations every day.

The prince, for whom so much was hoped, was not very old when he lost the queen, his mother, who gave him, as a final item of advice, as she died, to resolve nothing of consequence without having asked the opinion of the fay who had taken him under her protection.

The prince received the queen's advice with all possible respect, and her last sighs with an affliction that cannot be expressed without having seen it, and which nothing could equal but that of the king, his father, who was inconsolable in losing a charming princess with whom he had hoped to spend the happiest life that he could have desired.

Neither time nor reason could console the king, and, the sight of all the places in his palace where he had conversed with that charming person renewing his grief every day, he resolved to go traveling with a few companions. As he was a magician, however, he often abandoned those companions for several days, and sometimes for several weeks; but after having traveled, under different forms, in all the countries that awakened his curiosity, he returned to the place where he had left his retinue.

After having roamed for a long time from one realm to another without finding anything that touched him, he decided to transform himself into an eagle, and in that guise he cleaved the air, traversing a host of countries into which he had not yet been, and finally reached a region that he found very agreeable by virtue of the sweetness of the air one breathed there, caused by the odor of the jasmine and the orange-blossom with which the ground was covered.

Charmed by that odor, he descended to fly a little lower in order to see at closer range what was giving him so much pleasure. Finally, he perceived gardens below him that appeared to him to be of enchanted beauty, flower-beds planted in different fashions, charged with all the most beautiful flowers imaginable; fountains full of clear fresh water threw a hundred different figures into the air in as many jets of water, which rose up to a prodigious height. In another direction, waterfalls whose sound was appropriate to entertain melancholy were presented to his eyes.

There were also several canals lined with marble and porphyry, charged with small galleys and gondolas, on which gold and azure could be seen shining all the way to the oars. But objects even more brilliant caught the eyes. Several women of great beauty, clad in a manner to dazzle, by virtue of the quantity of pearls and diamonds with which their woven garments were decorated, filled the galleys and gondolas. It was the queen of the country, with her daughter the princess beside her, more beautiful than the day star, and all the ladies of her court, who had emerged from the palace in order to take the air as soon as the sun had set.

No mortal had ever appeared as brilliant as that adorable princess appeared then, and the king needed his eagle's eyes in order to sustain her splendor. He was so charmed by such a beautiful spectacle that he lost the use of his wings, and was stopped by a power that it was impossible to resist. He perched at the top of a tall orange-tree on the edge of the canal that bore that superb fleet, and from there he contemplated the attractions of the divine princess for a long time.

As an eagle that has the heart of a king is audacious, he formed instantly the design of carrying off the princess. He was so touched by her beauty that he anticipated that he could no longer live without possessing her. That design was great, and far beyond the strength of an ordinary eagle, but the king found forces in his art proportionate to his project, and being provided with them, he did not think any longer of anything but making it succeed.

He waited until the princess had emerged from the galley, and, seeing her slightly separated from her companions, he judged his time so well that he lifted her up into the air before her squire, who was preparing to give her his hand, had perceived him. The princess uttered cries and plaints so touching between the claws of her abductor that it would not have taken much for him to repent of his enterprise. However, as it would have been weakness to fail to complete the execution of such a fine design, the eagle continued to traverse the air with a rapidity that took away the means of making the princess understand the tender and respectful sentiments that he had for her.

When he thought that he was safe, however, he gradually lowered his flight and set the princess down gently in a meadow dotted with flowers. It was there that, after having asked her for a thousand pardons for the violence her had done to her, he explained that he was taking her to a flowery kingdom where he was the master, of which he wanted to put her in possession, with more authority than he had himself.

He neglected nothing to express his tenderness, and spared none of the oaths that lovers make in order to persuade her that it would be eternal. The princess, still frightened by the peril in which she had found herself, did not speak for some time, but when she had recovered her wits somewhat and saw that she was no longer in the arms of her dear mother the queen, penetrated by a profound dolor, she shed a torrent of tears.

The king, who loved her veritably, was touched by that. "Cease to be afflicted, adorable princess," he said to her. "I am only seeking to make you the happiest woman in the world."

"If you are telling me the truth, Sire," the princess retorted, "I demand the liberty that you have stolen from me, or suffer that the violence you have done me today will make me regard you as my cruelest enemy."

She tried to appease him then, by telling him that if he asked the king her father for her, there was every appearance that he would obtain her, since, if he was a powerful king, as he said, her father would have no reason to refuse the alliance.

The king replied to the princess that he was in despair at seeing her so opposed to his design, but he flattered himself that he would render her more agreeable by taking her to a place where she would be respected by everyone, and where, he could assure her, pleasures would be born beneath her footfalls. At the same moment, he picked the princess up again, and in spite of the cries that she redoubled with all her might, he transported her with the same rapidity all the way to the capital of his estates.

He set her down gently on a lawn, and scarcely was she there when she saw emerging instantly from beneath her feet a palace of extraordinary magnificence. Its architecture was very beautiful and very regular; gold glittered equally outside and in all the apartments, which were ornamented with precious furniture. Everything that could flatter the senses and ambition was encountered there in abundance, and it was impossible to wish for anything that was not found there. The princess, who thought she was alone there, was agreeably surprised to see herself surrounded by a number of beautiful and very amiable young women, who hastened to compete with one another in serving her. A parrot with admirable plumage said the pettiest things in the world to her.

The king had resumed his natural form on arrival at that palace, and although he was no longer very young, he had what was necessary to please anyone but the princess. She was prejudiced against the prince by such a great hatred because of the violence that he had done to her, however, that although she saw that she was in his power and far from any hope of rescue, it was not possible for her to regard him as anything but her enemy, and she could only respond to all that he said to touch her with words full of her resentment.

The king hoped, however, that time might soften the mind of the princess, and that, not seeing any other man than him, she would become accustomed to him. He took the precaution of surrounding the princess's palace with an impenetrable cloud, and went thereafter to show himself his court, where everyone was in great anxiety, not having had any news of him for a long time. The prince, his son, and all the courtiers were overjoyed to welcome their king, for he was loved perfectly by all his subjects.

They were to have the displeasure thereafter of seeing him more rarely than in times past; he employed the pretext of affairs that he had found on his return to shut himself in his cabinet, but it was actually to be able to spend that time with the princess, whom he had the dolor of finding still inflexible.

Not knowing what remedy to apply to such a great misfortune, nor what the cause could be of the princess's obstinacy, he was afraid that, in spite of his precautions, she might have heard mention of the merit of his son, the prince, who was young and handsome and adored by the court for his benevolence. He was in a horrible anxiety, and could only find relief therefrom by sending his son away. He proposed to him that he travel, and gave him a magnificent equipage.

The prince visited several courts, where he stayed for various lengths of time, in accordance with how agreeable he found them, and finally arrived in the one where mourning was being worn for the abducted princess. The king and queen gave him a very gracious welcome. Time and the presence of an amiable young prince having lessened the dolor that the loss of the princess had caused, the pleasures of the court were gradually revived, and the young prince took a full part therein.

One day, when the court was in the queen's cabinet, the prince, having perceived the portrait of a great beauty, was suddenly struck by it and demanded eagerly who it was. The queen, who overheard him, spoke for the young woman that the prince had asked, and said that it was all that remained of her dear daughter, who had been abducted, no one knew how or by whom. The queen could not talk about that sad adventure without shedding tears.

The prince was sensibly touched by that, and instantly promised the queen to search for the princess throughout the world, and not to take any repose until he had returned her to her hands. The queen assured him that she would receive such a singular favor with an eternal gratitude, and even said that if the princess were agreeable to it, she would give her to him in marriage, with the estates of which she was the sovereign. The queen was the heiress of a neighboring realm, of which the king approved of her disposing as she pleased.

The prince, more touched by the hope of possessing the princess than the kingdom he was offered, took his leave of the king and queen and set forth on his enterprise. The queen had given him a portrait of the princess that she wore on her arm, "in order," she told him, "that you do not lose the idea of her and do not have any difficulty in recognizing her when you encounter her."

The prince, already very passionate for the charming princess, of whom he had only thus far seen the resemblance, departed with his heart full of hope, and went in long stages to find the fay whom his mother the queen had recommended to him. He begged her to aid him with her art in such an important matter.

Having learned all the circumstances of the adventure, the fay asked for time to consult her books, and told the prince, after having thought about it, that the princess he sought was close by, but that it was too difficult to penetrate into the enchanted palace where his father, the king, was holding her, because he had covered it with a thick cloud. The only expedient she could imagine was to capture a parrot that the princess had, which she did not think impossible, because it sometimes went out and flew some distance from the palace.

The fay, who had a great passion to give pleasure to the son of a princess she had loved uniquely, went out immediately and tried to find the parrot. She came back shortly thereafter holding it in her hand, and immediately locked it in a cage. Having touched the prince with a mysterious wand, she transformed him into a parrot, and told him what he had to do in order to reach the princess.

The prince, well instructed as to how to be a parrot, went to the charming princess, whom he found to have a beauty hundred times greater than he had believed. He was so nonplussed that the princess was surprised; she was afraid that her parrot might be ill, and as he was her only consolation, she picked him up and caressed him, which reassured the prince and gave him the boldness to play his character well. He said a thousand pretty things, and the princess was charmed by them.

The king arrived, and the parrot had the pleasure of seeing him hated. When the king had gone, the princess went into her cabinet alone; the parrot flew in there and witnessed the laments she made regarding the persecutions of the king, who had begged her insistently to determine herself to marry him.

In order to console her, the parrot said a thousand things to her, in which she found so much intelligence that she sometimes doubted whether it was, in fact, her parrot that was talking to her so agreeably. He said even more forceful things, by which she was very astonished. When he saw that she was in the disposition he desired, he said to her:

"Madame, I have a very important secret to confide to you. I beg you not to be alarmed by the things that I am going to tell you. I am here to liberate you, Madame, and it is on the part of the queen, your mother, that I have come. To prove to you what I am saying, look at this portrait, which your mother gave me."

He took the portrait from beneath one of his wings. The princess's surprise was very great, but she she could not help conceiving hopes on the basis of what she saw and heard, because she had recognized the portrait as the one that the queen wore on her arm.

Seeing that the princess was not greatly alarmed, the parrot told her who he was, what the queen had promised him, and about the help he had already received from the fay, who had assured him that she would give him all the means of transporting the princess all the way to the cabinet of the queen, her mother.

When he saw that the princess was listening to him attentively, he begged her to permit him to appear before her in his natural form. The princess having made no response, he plucked a feather from his wing, and the princess immediately saw a prince of surprising beauty; she allowed herself to be flattered pleasantly by the hope of owing her liberty to a man who appeared to be so lovable.

The fay who had taken responsibility for the conduct of the adventure had made a chariot capable of containing the prince and princess and had hitched it to two eagles so powerful that they were capable of taking them to the ends of the earth. Having put the parrot she was keeping in a cage into the chariot, she charged the eagles with taking it as far as the window of the princess's cabinet, which was done in a moment; the princess, having climbed into the chariot with the prince, was very glad to find her parrot there too.

As soon as the princess was in the chariot, she saw someone riding an eagle that was flying ahead of the chariot; she was astonished by that, but the prince reassured her, telling her that it was the good fay, to whom she was obliged for all the help that had reached her, who wanted to escort them all the way to her mother's cabinet.

The king, who had not slept tranquilly since the day when he first saw the princess, woke up with a start. He had just seen in a dream that someone was taking his mistress away. He resumed the form of an eagle and flew to her palace, where, not having found her there, he entered into a terrible fury. He returned home as quickly as possible in order to consult his books.

Having understood that it was his son who had stolen his precious treasure, he transformed himself instantly into a harpy, and, possessed by rage, he resolved to devour his son, and even the princess, if he encountered them.

He pierced the air with an extraordinary rapidity, but he had set out too late, and the fay, anticipating that he would follow them, had raised impetuous winds in the air behind them, which retarded his flight and gave the prince and the princess the time to arrive safely in the queen's cabinet. She was there, in an impatience of which she did not know the cause, as if she had had a presentiment of some extraordinary event. With what joy, as you can imagine, she received the princess she had regretted so much, and the amiable prince who had enabled her to see her again!

The fay also came to the cabinet, and warned the queen that the magician king, from whom something had just been stolen that was dearer to him than his crown, would soon arrive, and that nothing could protect the prince and princess from his fury, aided by his enchantments, if they were not married. As soon as they were united by the bond of marriage, however, he would be unable to do anything against them.

The queen sent a warning to the king immediately, and the marriage was made. The magician king arrived at the end of the ceremony; the despair that he was in at having arrived too late having troubled his mind, he appeared in his natural form, and tried to throw a black liquid over the married prince and princess capable of killing them, but the fay advanced a wand that she was holding in her hand, and turned the liquid back on the king who had just thrown it, whereupon he fell down, having lost the usage of all his senses.

The king in whose home he had just tried to carry out such a cruel vengeance, feeling deeply offended, had him picked up and put in prison. Magicians no longer having any power when they are in prison, the imprisoned king, when he came round, was very embarrassed to find himself in the power of a prince he had offended so gravely, but he was not subjected to any cruelty on a day of such great rejoicing.

The prince, having asked for mercy for his father, obtained it, and had his prison opened. It was no sooner open than the king was seen in the air in the form of an unknown bird; he only said as he departed that he would never forgive his son, or his neighbor the fay, for the cruel insult they had dealt him.

The fay was asked to establish herself in the realm where she was; she agreed to that, and transported her books and her secrets of enchantment there. She built a new palace there, which she made her residence; no one in the court thought any longer of anything but rendering thanks to the generous fay to whom they owed so many obligations, and enjoying the perfect felicity into which she had put the entire royal family.

The prince and the princess spent a long and very happy life together, and left in possession of the kingdom thereafter a posterity that was always covered in glory.

Catherine Durand: *The Fay Lubantine*

There was once a fay in Asia whose power had no limits; the likes of Circe and Armide did not come up to her waist. She loved her husband infinitely; destiny, which has always gone its own way, took him away from her in her early youth; nothing remained of him but a daughter so beautiful and so charming that her graces were infinite even in the cradle.

The young princess was seen from a very tender age to have an inclination for pleasure that astonished all those who approached her; no tears ever emerged from her eyes; her little mouth did not open to cries, its only usage being a gracious smile that inspired joy; games were invented for her; her little arms opened to embrace and thank the women who contributed to her amusement; violins, oboes, dances and spectacles made her delights; she showed a marked distaste for symphonies whose tones were melancholy, and anyone in the court who was sad did not appear before her with impunity; a delicate but piquant mockery made them sense the antipathy she had for them. Her mother, the fay, who had never seen anything like it, although she had seen everything, gave her a name that suited her character; she called her Lubantine, and that is how the ancients made their goddess Lubantine, known in their theology as the goddess of joy and liberty.

In fact, young Lubantine could not abide anything that constrained her; when her mother tried to moderate that violent love of liberty slightly, she sulked as prettily as anything in the world, but soon resumed a serene face, employing supplicant badinage to beg the fay not to exclude her from the only wealth one has in this life.

When she was fourteen years old and her person was formed, her mother consulted her books regarding the destiny of such an extraordinary young woman. She found that she would always live happily and amid pleasures, if she could avoid seeing a foreigner. That fatality appeared easy enough to deflect; we shall soon see what order her powerful mother brought to it.

Lubantine's stature was mediocre and slender; her arms were placed by the Graces, her feet were small and well-turned; her hair was a bright brown, her eyes had a dazzlingly brilliant finesse; her nose was small and made for the rest of her features her face was round, her full, delicate and vivid cheeks each had a little dimple formed by the very hand of Amour; there was also one in her chin; her mouth was one of those that it has never been possible to depict, small, fashioned, red, laughing, ornamented by two rows of perfect teeth; her breasts were full, white and youthful.

She had intelligence; her imagination was sparkling, if one can speak thus, and one sensed a secret charm in her conversation, but she was libertine; she gave in to all her desires. Lubantine's mother, however, no sooner saw that she was at an age to be established than she proposed a very advantageous marriage to her. As you can imagine, that was not calculated to please her; she manifested such a strong opposition to it that her mother, who thought her the prettiest person in the world—as, in fact, she was—and who only thought of making her happy, established her with cheerful young people made to please her in a palace that has never had an equal. It was built of precious stones; the doors were never closed; there were magnificent baths, aviaries filled with birds, halls for spectacles; a regulated Opera whose inimitable actors never caught a cold; actors who never grew old; players of all sorts of instruments; gaming tables where the women became more beautiful and the men more gracious.

The general order of that court was to surprise Lubantine every day, and not to have any sad thought; malady and mortality were banished from that beautiful abode, amour made its pleasure felt, absolutely separated from its pain—for no one there believed that its pains were pleasures.

Four different gardens were seen from the four facades of the palace. In one of them there were swings of a particular form; Lubantine often availed herself of that amusement, and for the rest of the day her retinue performed plays. There were stakes planted with rings attached, and those who used the swings were obliged to carry away the rings; when they did not succeed, a penalty was ordered, which went no further than making up a garland of flowers for Lubantine or composing a madrigal in her honor. When hazard caused it to fall, one could laugh in safety, for then the previously beaten and solid terrain softened and became a padded mattress.

In the second garden there were acrobats, rope-dancers and jumpers, all so sure of their skill that no one was afflicted by the anxious attention caused by the fear of seeing them fall, even though they performed surprising feats.

The third garden was occupied by female bathers who worked in shifts incessantly. One pool of Cordovan water had, as well as the odor, the faculty of rendering skin whiter. Lubantine had a separate one in the palace, but she often went to amuse herself by pestering the bathers; teasingly, she tugged their bathing costumes, which were woven from nettle-cloth garnished with Malines lace; those women played countless different instruments on the edges of the pools; neat and elegant beds extended under magnificent tents served them for repose after that pleasant exercise. Men were excluded from the enclosure of that garden, but the walls were so low and people knew so little restraint in the place that they often violated the refuge with their gaze.

The fourth area was a park rather than a garden; it was filled with beautiful, clean and gentle wild beasts, which allowed themselves to be hunted by Lubantine and her court, and which enjoyed themselves afterwards with the same dogs that ran after them without doing them any harm; the hunting equipages were superb, and Lubantine's livery crimson and gold.

At the center of the palace there was a large courtyard surrounded by four facades. It was there that the ladies watched tourneys, jousts, ring-races and carousels, which the young princes admitted to Lubantine's court often put on in order to amuse her. Their skill was astonishing, and they received prizes from the hand of their sovereign when they merited them. She always had some new petty intrigue, but her heart was only engaged to the exact extent required to amuse her.

The three gardens I mentioned were, in any case, so beautiful, and everything that could render them delightful was so unsparing, that they were a spectacle themselves; as for the park designed for hunting, there were woods, streams, plains and a hill that was often preferred by arrangement to other places. Lubantine did not have to take the trouble to express a wish; her desires were always anticipated; but as she had exquisite taste in everything, she treasured delicate cheer; never has there been anything to compare with what she was served at every meal; the wines were chosen carefully, and I have even heard it said that champagne was often served, even though no mention of it in that century is known.

When the fay put her daughter in that place she made her this speech, or very nearly: "My age and my cares, my dear Lubantine, no longer permit me to savor the pleasures that suit you. I don't envy you them; on the contrary, I'm lavishing them upon you. Live happily, since I don't anticipate that your destiny can change, I'm going to retire to my manor in the woods; come to visit me there occasionally. Remember me and be a fay like your mother, since I've been able to allow you to participate in my art."

The savant fay refrained from prescribing to Lubantine never to receive any foreigner and not to leave the enclosure of her palace—that would have given birth to the desire to do so—but she extended that enclosure prodigiously. It did not have any appearance of a prison; one would have searched in vain elsewhere for what was found in that delightful abode, but there were stakes planted on all the roads that ended there on which the following inscription could be read:

> *Refrain from having the desire*
> *To see the lovely Lubantine;*
> *Death would follow closely the dangerous pleasure*
> *Of contemplating her divine person.*

Travelers, frightened by that warning, turned away from such a terrible path immediately, and Lubantine remained in the midst of delights for six years without ever experiencing any dolor or chagrin.

She sometimes went to see her mother. One day she found her bathed in tears; the young fay's first impulse was to flee an apparition so contrary to her humor; she had already taken a few backward steps when the afflicted mother said to her: "Come closer, Lubantine; your fate causes me compassion; you will soon be delivered to great misfortunes. I don't know yet what form they will take; it only depends on you to avoid them; it's necessary to deprive you of some pleasure; I can see that the fatal point is there, but as I can't disentangle which one will be deadly to you, deprive yourself of all those you take for a while; you'll discover more taste for them afterwards."

"Me, Madame," said Lubantine, "deprive myself of joy and liberty? I might as well be deprived of daylight. You're naturally sad," she added, "the situation of your humor might have made you dread imaginary perils, and I should deprive myself of real and imaginary possessions for that? No, no, rather..."

"Well, my daughter," said the sage fay, "The future is developing a little to my eyes; I can see that a hunt is going to cause you horrible misfortunes; don't go hunting for three months."

"Oh, Madame," said Lubantine, "you know that it's to liberty in particular that I attach my happiness. I might well have no desire to go hunting for ten years in succession, but the necessity of depriving myself of it would inconvenience me. I'll quit you, Madame," she added, "for fear of participating momentarily in the melancholy that I see in your eyes."

In fact, the free Lubantine went to leap into a carriage harnessed to six lions, which were meeker than lambs, and raced to the Palace of Pleasures.

She was embarrassed by a dream all that night. Until then the god of sleep, respectful of her repose, had only presented agreeable images to her, but this time she thought she saw an unknown individual whose appearance pleased her greatly; he had a little dart in his hand with which he teased her; she acquired a taste for that teasing; the dart had already inflicted a wound in the middle of her heart; she sensed her pleasures redoubling, but soon afterwards a beautiful woman whose features she did not know plunged it in so cruelly that she thought that she was falling, bathed in her own blood, and all that she could do was to kill the people who had just taken away her life.

She uttered a cry that woke her up and attracted her women; the agitation of the dream did not permit her to pull herself together until she had been awake for some time; then she started to laugh at her fear, and got up as quickly as possible, in order to dissipate that baleful imagination.

The pleasure she chose for that day was hunting; she even released the deer herself, which hurtled out of the park where the hunt usually concluded. It was the first time that had happened, for her journeys to see her mother were made by air; but destiny was conducting her, with the aid of her love of liberty.

Lubantine found herself somewhat fatigued; she suspended the hunt and dismounted from her horse. She sat down in a forest at the foot of a large tree that she chose.

"Go away," she said to the hunters. "I need repose; let me sleep."

Immediately, a bed of moss and flowers rose up beneath her; cushions of magnificent fabric were placed under her head, and an elegant awning was attached to the branches of the tree.

She had not yet savored the charms of slumber when she heard a man who was saying in a very agreeable tone of voice: "Is it possible that you can repent of having made me happy? Yes, divine Melisene, I am happy, since you have been good enough to confide yourself to my faith and have quit your father's kingdom to follow me. What my happiness lacks is essential enough, but I await your kindness with a respect with which you ought to be content. Don't be afflicted, then, and don't tarnish what you have done for me by an appearance of repentance."

"No," said a woman to whom the speech was addressed, "that isn't the subject of my tears. The fatal time is approaching when you are to endure proofs that frighten me. I only know you; will my feeble charms hold out against those of a..."

"Oh," interrupted the man who had spoken first, "don't alarm yourself ahead of time; the obscurity that encloses predictions might be hiding an agreeable verity from you, and whatever might happen, I shall belong as long as I live to my dear Melisene."

Lubantine thought that the man's promises were reckless, and that the woman to whom they were addressed was very imprudent to have followed a lover into such a solitary place: a severity that an unfamiliar impulse caused her.

Have these lovers come to spread the poison of amour in this locale? she wondered. *We only know its pleasures,* she added, *let them leave the places of my dependence.*

With those words she got up and soon found what she was seeking. A young blonde woman, pale and possessed of a perfect beauty, clad in an elegant but neglected costume, was sitting on the grass; a man was at her feet in a tender and respectful attitude. He was tall and handsome, with large dark eyes.

"Who are you," said Lubantine, "who come on to my land to talk about amour?"

The voice of the fay, her charms and her magnificence, attracted the gaze and the veneration of the lovers. The stood up diligently, and the man spoke. "We are, Madame, an unfortunate brother and sister seeking a refuge against the fury of a cruel and implacable family."

"A brother and a sister!" said the fay. "Who, then, said the passionate things that I have just heard you saying to one another?"

The young woman blushed; her lover threw himself at Lubantine's feet.

"It's necessary to admit to you, Madame," he said, "that I love the beautiful Melisene, whom you see here, passionately. Cruel relatives have forbidden us to see one another; a mutual love had made us seek means of never being apart, and we beg you, Madame," he added, "to suffer us in this place, where you apparently command."

336

The good looks and noble appearance of the man did not permit the fay to refuse his plea. I know not what impulse even gave her response a tender softness different from the joy that normally shone in her eyes. The beautiful young woman had no part in that mild welcome; on the contrary, she looked at her disdainfully. Then, turning back to the agreeable stranger, she said to him: "After having granted you what you request," she said to him, "don't refuse me your name. As for your birth, it would be difficult to hide it; the appearance you have is not encountered in ordinary people, and the title of king struck my ears when you were talking to this person." She pointed at Melisene.

"My name is Ciridor, Madame," he replied, "and my father is King Absolute, a name that has been imposed on him because he never yields to anyone, and everyone has always done his will. The princess you see is the daughter of the King of the Gentle Isle, and her mildness does not belie her origin."

"That's sufficient," Lubantine interrupted. "You can tell me the rest of your adventures at your leisure; not only will I receive you in my lands, but I'll take you to my palace; we'll seek there the means of rendering you happy, and prescribe for Princess Melisene a life a little less vagabond than she is leading at present."

With those words she sounded a small enameled gold hunting horn garnished with diamonds that she wore at her side, and the whole of her brilliant court soon gathered around her. Prince Ciridor's squire and Princess Melisene's governess came to mingle with that elegant troop. Ciridor aided Lubantine and his princess to mount their horses, and mounted his own with such grace that he attracted the attention of all the spectators. The deer that had rested in company with the pack gave a further hour of pleasure to the hunt, after which everyone returned to the palace.

The magnificence and the pleasures that were savored there gave Ciridor a sort of agreeable distraction, which cost the tender Melisene sighs. Lubantine allotted her an apartment whose views only overlooked the hunting park. She conducted her there personally and told her as she quit her that she would send ambassadors to her father's court to inform him that she had her in her power and was taking her under her protection; and that while awaiting his response she was obliged to keep her in a kind of solitude more appropriate to the estate of her destiny. With those words she embraced her and left her with her governess, in a kind of dolor that had something so piquant that tears soon covered her beautiful cheeks.

"Has anything ever been seen comparable to my misfortune, my dear Celinte?" she cried, as soon as she was alone with her. "What a bizarrerie of my star! You know everything that I have done for Ciridor; the virtue of which I make a profession ought to give him an eternal gratitude for the excess of my tenderness, and yet I see in him the deadly penchant of which a cruel prediction had warned me."

Celinte interrupted the dolorous reflections of the princess, and asked her what one could dread of a lover like Ciridor.

"What can I dread?" said Melisene. "Lubantine is charming; Lubantine is a fay; her power, her beauty, the pleasures that follow her everywhere and the fickleness of men all give me a mortal apprehension. And have I not seen Ciridor looking at her, admiring her and forgetting me momentarily?" she added, redoubling her sighs.

Celinte employed all her eloquence in consoling the princess, and promised to report to her faithfully what she knew, but the means were forbidden to her; she was not permitted to leave the apartment, where they were given in abundance, however, everything that might satisfy the senses.

Meanwhile, the prince, who was young, gallant and who loved pleasures, had an admiration for Lubantine that could already be called a liking; he spent the first days in a transport that made him forget Melisene. The fay had an inexplicable charm in all her actions; her fêtes were very extensive; the sighs that a commencement of amour was causing her to utter had a grace from which it was not possible for him to defend himself, and, as her sighs only marked the passion that gave birth to them, without having the sadness appropriate to them, her lovely smile followed close behind them.

Ciridor, heaped with joy by the effect of his merit, was more handsome and wittier than usual; Lubantine and he gave themselves gradually to amour and joy. The spectacles multiplied, the Palace of Pleasures finished new ones continually.

Lubantine went out on her own one day in order to stroll in the hunting park; her heart was already sensing the more impetuous movements of amour, but until then everything had passed in gazes. She plunged into the wood in order to dream at her ease. Ciridor, driven by the same desire, encountered her in that remote location.

"How I have wanted this moment," he said to the fay, "and how I have dreaded that it might not be favorable to me! You only like pleasures," he added, "I am not their enemy, but I am so jealous of them and I am audacious enough to wish that you only loved me."

That declaration was rather bold, but Lubantine was naturally too distant from the furious impulses of anger to invoke them on this occasion, and the tenderness that she felt added its effect to her temperament.

"Thus far, Prince," she replied, "you have no reason to complain of my rigors. I have not hidden the penchant I feel for you; I find pleasure in seeing you, I have an infinite one in hearing you. Let us love one another with ardor," she added, "since we are summoned to it. Is it not necessary to seize the opportunities that are presented to savor new felicities?"

That morality pleased Ciridor infinitely. He added further impetus to it in his fashion. They had a very long and very agreeable conversation. Lubantine agreed on emerging from the wood that only Ciridor could bring her pleasures to a culmination, and they plunged into sensual pleasures.

The fay's example gave birth the countless new amours in her court; everyone was in love; everyone abandoned themselves to its delights, while the unhappy Melisene was dying of dolor and jealousy. She had seen her lover and her rival from her window emerging from the hunting park; their appearance was so contented and so amorous that she had no reason to doubt her misfortune. She abandoned herself to everything that a delicate soul is capable of suffering.

One day, losing the little patience that remained to her, she tried to force her way past her guards in order to go and reckon with the fay for her detention and her lover for his infidelity. Her emergence was opposed, but that action caused rumor; Ciridor was informed of it; a slight return to the past caused him to lament the situation of the princess. He tried to say something in her favor, but Lubantine, who did not want to be troubled by anything, replied that she would release her from her prison and that she even wanted to render her witness to their amusements.

"I have no fear," she added, "that she would dare to dispute anything with me, nor that you might return to her."

In fact, the fay went to fetch Melisene, in a gracious and mild manner. "Come, Princess," she said to her. "It is time that you had your part in our fêtes."

The sad Melisene left with her. But what a change! She no longer had the perfect beauty that might have been able to generate amour in the most insensible; her figure and the sound of her voice remained to her, but her face became so frightful, her features so irregular and her sort of ugliness so bizarre, that when Lubantine presented her to Ciridor he took several steps back, and even let an exclamation of disgust escape. The princess turned toward a large mirror, in which she saw herself as beautiful as usual, and became more indignant against her infidel lover; for the fay. in taking away her beauty and making her ugly for everyone else, had left her the slight satisfaction of appearing beautiful in her own eyes, and that was the origin of a self-esteem unknown before.

Celinte saw with astonishment the prodigious ugliness of the princess and forgave the prince his inconstancy. "Let us flee, Princess," she said to her. "let us flee a court whose voluptuous mores cannot fail to corrupt; no one will try to stop us."

"Why flee?" replied Melisene, sadly. "Could I resolve myself to do it? Ciridor is fickle, but his fickleness will bring him back to me."

Then Celinte could not hide from her the degree to which she had become horrible; she was not sparing in the portrait she made of her. The princess, who still found herself beautiful, nearly became angry with her confidante, and flattered herself that her displeasures had only brought a slight change to her charms.

On the other hand, Ciridor, whose ingratitude was confirmed by Melisene's appearance, told Lubantine, laughing, that she had taken a strange path to make sure of his heart, and that even if she had changed nothing in the person of the princess, he would not have broken his new chains.

"I assure you," she said, "that that vengeance is not excessive; it is always necessary to take precautions against reversions. And then," she added, "what harm have I done her? She still believes herself to be beautiful; her imagination will always be satisfied."

"Good, Madame," said Ciridor. "Not content with having rendered her ugly, you also want to render her ridiculous, and the security she has regarding her attractions will make her play the part of a pretty woman."

They had the inhumanity to mock her for a long time because of a misfortune that she only had because of them, and when they wanted to enjoy their malevolence they made her appear, pompously adorned, to see the spectacles that were prepared for them.

The prince, intoxicated by amour, decided that he wanted to render an effective worship to the fay. You are too charming," he told her, "only to merit adoration by virtue of your face. It's necessary to set up an altar to you, to burn incense to you, to immolate victims to you."

"Oh, as for bloody victims," Lubantine interjected, "I don't want any. People can offer them to me, but I shall give them liberty with my own hands."

That same day, an altar was constructed in a great hall of crystal; two thousand candles burned there incessantly before the figure of the fay, which was a single pearl with draperies of brilliant rose-colored diamonds. Behind the transparent walls of the hall, large hollow figures had been disposed, painted in perfection, which represented the peoples of all the continents of the world, adoring the beautiful Lubantine. Inextinguishable candles always made those bodies appear luminous. Each of them held an offering, which related to the character of the fay. There were pocket mirrors, diamonds, snuff-boxes, boxes of beauty-spots, ribbons and all the rest of the elegant equipment of ladies.

The interior of the hall, which had become a temple, was full of players of instruments and singers; sarabands and chaconnes were danced there in favor of tenderness or libertinage, and a perpetual commerce of love letters, gazes and pretty amorous larcenies was seen; a continual distribution was made of the most exquisite dishes and the most delectable liqueurs; the ice creams and chocolate there surpassed ambrosia, and if no one acquired immortality, at least the women there were always young and beautiful, and the men always well made and elegant.

A sofa with a golden back enriched with rubies was beside the altar, destined for the pretended goddess, when she wanted to receive her incense in person; a cushion of the same kind was below the sofa for the amorous Ciridor. The superb awning that covered the area descended in a curtain when it pleased Lubantine to disappear from the eyes of her subjects. Perfumes were lavished there. In sum, everything that luxury and adulation could invent was put to use in favor of the fay.

She had the cruelty of wanting the unfortunate Melisene to witness the consecration of the temple; she nearly died of dolor there. Her rival was as beautiful as Venus. Ciridor picked up a censer himself in order to be the first to adore her, and as he had the most beautiful voice in the world, he began this hymn, to which the chorus responded:

Alone you know the fine sensual pleasure,
Before you there were only feeble images,
Sweet joy with liberty
Are your gifts, receive our homages.
Queen of hearts, games and pleasures,
Who can drive away the ridiculous censors
And, braving remorse and scruples
Accord everything to your desires;
Goddess Lubantine, may our incense always
Rise above your altars;
Can we envy the fate of the immortals
When we contemplate your divine grace?

Alone you know the fine sensual pleasure,
Before you there were only feeble images,
Sweet joy with liberty
Are your gifts, receive our homages...

The hymn went on for a long time, but it is so pleasant to be praised, Ciridor's voice was so harmonious and the choir so marvelous, that Lubantine sensed what expression cannot represent; there was even something tragic in the ceremony, which did not spoil its savor at all.

The princess could not bear the bitterness of her affliction; she fainted in Celinte's arms. Ciridor turned his head in her direction, allowed himself to be carried away without admitting pain into his life and ran to throw himself at Lubantine's feet.

"Let everything perish, my goddess," he said, kissing one of her hands, which she held out to him, "provided that I adore you all my life."

That transport caused others in the fay.

When the ceremony had finished everyone went to occupy themselves with the customary pleasures. No one enquired about Melisene. She was suffering woes that would have given rise to pity in cruelty itself, but the fay only felt precisely what was necessary to make her suffer more—which is to say, that her life should be preserved and that she should be prevented from harming herself.

Several days passed in the worship of the new goddess. Amid that vaunted sensual pleasure the princess recovered in spite of herself, and, impelled by an unknown emotion, she ran once again to the fatal temple where all the objects renewed her dolor.

The high priest Ciridor was brilliant with gems and even more brilliant by virtue of his beauty; the fay was contemplating him with eyes in which amour was painted. Even the princess had more passion for him than when he was faithful; those sentiments furnished her with courage. Her voice was heard in the middle of the ceremony, which rose up to pronounce these words:

> Charming Queen of Cythera,
> Whose wrath Psyche once ignited,
> Beautiful Venus, will you suffer
> The offense that a prince dares to make you in this place?
> It is little that he violates his oath,
> That crime only injures me,
> But that ingrate, that reckless fool
> Profanes his incense for another than you;
> Render him forever the usage of his senses,
> Charming Queen of Cythera.

When Melisene commenced that prayer to Venus everyone attempted to interrupt her, but no one was able to succeed in that; tongues were tied. Ciridor, the infidel Ciridor, opened his mouth in vain in order to impose silence; he could not articulate anything. Lubantine felt the same prodigy in herself, and that silence, which had a mysterious cause, was only broken after the princess had been seen to resume her original beauty.

Then the fay uttered a dolorous scream, and the assembly murmured a few words in praise of Melisene. As if recovering from an enchantment, Ciridor quit the worship of the false goddess and returned submissively to the feet of his first mistress.

Venus was recognized in those changes.

The temple was not destroyed; the statue of Lubantine remained standing; but the veritable Lubantine appeared ugly, with the same ugliness that she had previously given her rival, without the same consolation remaining to her. She found herself so frightful that, her love of pleasure changing into fury, and the goddess not having taken away her power of faerie, she no longer thought about anything but avenging herself on the innocent causes of her misfortune.

She had the princess imprisoned again, with terrible menaces. Ciridor, who wanted to repair his faults, opposed that with all his courage, but what could he do, alone against an absolute and sovereign fay?

Venus, the jealous Venus, had avenged her outrage; that alone was interesting for her; what did the success of the amours of Ciridor and Melisene matter to her? Lubantine went every day into a horrible prison where she had locked her up; there, with an unparalleled inhumanity, she disfigured her beautiful face with a diamond that she wore expressly; then she labored on her incomparable breasts, and did not quit that mortal exercise until the force of dolors had caused her death.

Celinte implored her at least to send her body back to the sovereign of the Gentle Isle; the fay granted her that.

The poor king had no sooner seen that sad spectacle than he died of affliction; before his death he ordered that a magnificent sepulcher be built for his daughter, for himself and for Ciridor.

The fay attempted in vain to make Ciridor return to her; her ugliness and the repentance he felt excluded her from his heart. She applied herself to making him take a dose of poison every day, which weakened him gradually and often caused him furious pains; they only finished with his life, and the prediction of which Melisene had made mention was verified. No one has ever known the wording of it, but in essence, the prince was menaced with being unable to resist terrible ordeals, and then being exposed to a tragic end.

After that, Lubantine was tormented by remorse; she discovered too late that excessive sensual pleasure leads into profound abysms, and that, if one cannot have perfect happiness without amour, amour that is not regulated by virtue causes all the woes of life.

However, as the commencement of Lubantine's life presented a cheerful image, and the pagans sacrificed to much stranger divinities than Liberty and Joy, they erected temples to them under the name of the goddess Lubantine. But as no one was ever able to prescribe just limits to those two things, people only had imperfect ideas of them and always went beyond or fell short of joy and liberty.

Author Unknown: Princess Patientine in the Forest of Erimente

There was an ogre named Insacio who made his dwelling in a lair into which the sun's rays had never penetrated. He was cruel and devoid of justice, and the Furies of Hell, which had presided over his birth, having spread the foam of Cerberus over his tongue, it was so penetrated by it permanently that as soon as he touched a woman with his tongue she was doomed to die, without any remedy being able to save her. To possesses all the wealth of the earth was the sole passion that occupied his heart; neither amour nor amity had ever found any place there. The devouring avidity by which he was tormented to amass riches gave him an anxiety that never allowed him any repose.

He had two sisters who were similar to him in humor. They lived with him. The elder was named Aigredouce; she had beauty and some mildness in her temperament; that sometimes made her take the part of the unfortunates whom the ogre tormented cruelly; in particular, she often stopped him from touching with his piercing tongue those who were unfortunate enough to enter his lair. But with that benevolence she nevertheless had a bitterness in her facial expression and all her words which was very displeasing. The younger, whose name was Bizarrine, had a humor so capricious, so imperious and so chagrined that no one could invent torments more insupportable than to oblige someone to live with her. Her amity was no less to be dreaded than her hatred, giving no more repose to those she loved than to her enemies.

The ogre often went to take lessons from the goddess Avarice, whose dwelling was not far from his lair. When he consulted her one day regarding his destiny, she told him that if he could make himself loved by a princess named Patientine, the daughter of Lycaon, and have her in his power, he would be the richest of all the ogres of his era. He thanked Avarice for her good advice, and, having returned home, he disposed his equipage with diligence. He quit his natural form for fear of frightening Patientine. He took that of a well made young man with good manners, and changed his bristling hair into the most beautiful blond hair in the world.

Under that new metamorphosis he appeared at the court of the Queen of Lydia, Patientine's mother, who had been a widow for some years. He was received there under the name of the Prince of Thrace, and was able to disguise himself so well that he won the hearts of the queen and the princess in a very short time.

Patientine had a very strong amity for a young woman of her court named Espritée. She held the first place in her heart, as she held it by her rank with regard to the queen, and she did not hide anything from her. She confided to her the nascent tenderness she had for Insacio.

Espritée, who, by virtue of a presentiment of whose cause she was unaware, feared that the princess might be unfortunate if she married the false Prince of Thrace, tried to turn her away from that alliance, but eventually, seeing that the queen wanted it as much as Patientine, she no longer opposed it. The marriage was therefore concluded in a matter of days, and that amiable princess, whose beauty, sweetness and virtue had made all the neighboring princes sigh, was delivered to the barbaric Insacio.

The ogre, impatient to return to his lair with his prey and get out of a court whose magnificence wounded his humor so much, departed with his wife and Espritée, who did not want to quite Patientine, no matter what opposition Insacio raised.

After a few days' travel, the princess arrived in the Forest of Erimente, and a short time later at the terrible lair. She found Aigredouce and Bizarrine there, who attempted to please her by means of urgent attentions. How can the astonishment of the princess, on finding herself in such a frightful place, be described? She nearly died of dolor, and all the influence that Espritée had over her mind could not console her.

The ogre, who had resumed his ordinary form and his natural cruelty, was not touched by Patientine's tears, Aigredouce tried to make her understand that she was wrong to be afflicted by being united with Insacio, that all princesses would envy her good fortune if they knew about it; and that if, by her complaisance, she could win his heart, nothing would be lacking to her happiness. Bizarrine, who happened to be in a compassionate mood, believing that her presence might soothe Patientine's chagrins, did not quit her, and made her so impatient with the advice she gave her regarding her conduct, that she augmented the princess's dolor greatly.

Espritée employed all the intelligence that the gods had given her to win the amity of the ogre and that of his sisters, in order to diminish Patientine's chagrin. She thought she had succeeded in that, but she realized subsequently that nothing touched that heart insensible to pity.

Meanwhile, Insacio, wanting to take advantage of the good fortune of having Patientine in his power, in order to become rich, began to put Avarice's lessons into practice. He made the unfortunate princess get up before dawn and forced her to go into the forest in search of herbs, which he made her put into huge cauldrons over the fire in order to extract the juice from them. Then he made her carry them into the animal sheds to give them to the monsters that he kept there. Fattened on the juice of those herbs, the beasts were infinitely valuable, and worth a great deal of money. The merchants of Thrace and Bosnia often came to buy them from him.

When Patientine came back from such a difficult employment, in order to relax, she was given a distaff and made to spin wool in order to make the crimson fabric in which all the kings of the Orient dressed themselves. She was only allowed to rest when she had filled several spindles. At other times, she employed her sad days searching in the nearby mountains for the marvelous seed from which the crimson dye was made, and she was made to spend every evening making the dye. The poor princess did not have a moment's rest. If she had been able to win the ogre's cruel heart with so much hard labor, she would have been consoled, but Insacio, always tormented by the desire for sordid gain, never thought that she worked hard enough, and scolded her incessantly for not doing more.

The princess suffered all those reproaches and obeyed him with a meekness that would have touched anyone but Insacio. Aigredouce told him sometimes that he ought to be content with Patientine, but Bizarrine said that her brother did very well not to be sensible to the unhappiness of his wife, that it was necessary to profit from the opportunity to enrich himself, and that if any relief were given to Patientine, she would find her more insupportable work.

"At least," said Aigredouce, "I could give her nourishment that might sustain her in such hard employments, for she can't live on acorn-bread and the little piece of goat's cheese that you give her for the whole day. You ought to remember that she hasn't been brought up with so much harshness, and you ought to fear that she might soon succumb to those fatigues."

"My sister," said the ogre, angrily, "you've already corrupted that girl, nourished in a superb court, but I shall certainly refrain from following such pernicious advice. I don't intend to eat in one day, in overly delicate fare, everything that I've accumulated with so much difficulty."

Insacio's natural anxiety did not permit him a longer conversation; he quit his sister and went into the mountains to see whether he could find Patientine there collecting seeds. He found her lying at the foot of a tree conversing with her dear Espritée, The furious Ogre vomited all the most horrible insults at the unfortunate princess and swore to take away the only consolation she had by sending Espritée away. He would have done so right away had it not been for the fear that the young woman might tell the queen about all her daughter's woes.

Without responding to the barbarian with a single word, Patientine wiped away her tears and, having finished stripping the earth in that area of its precious seeds, returned to the lair. She found Bizarrine there, who made a crime of her sadness, and Aigredouce, wanting to console her, told her that with an affected air that she thought she was driving her patience to an extreme.

All the ogre's subjects experienced his cruelty, and in order to content the insatiable thirst he had for riches he made them work night and day digging in the soil in a valley near his lair, where Avarice had told him that he might finds a treasure. That was a further misfortune for Patientine. He wanted her to be with those unfortunate diggers incessantly, in order to prevent them taking a moment's rest. That new employment did not dispense the poor princess from her spinning; she took her distaff with her, and, sometimes burned by an ardent sun and sometime pierced by rain and fog, she remained exposed to the insults

of the weather all day long. What heart would not have been sensible to impulses of pity on seeing the evils that the young princess suffered?

One day, when she was with the workers, Courageous, the Prince of Bosnia, who had seen her at the court of the Queen of Lydia and who had always
had an inclination for her, which all his reason had had difficulty vanquishing,
passed close to her. Surprised by such an unexpected encounter, he dismounted
from his horse and approached her urgently. He found her beautiful, in spite of
the change that so many misfortunes had brought about in her charms, and testified to her in respectful terms the pleasure he had in seeing her again.

The princess, ashamed of being found in a state so different from the one
in which the prince had seen her before, did not say anything for some time, but
the fear of being found with him by Insacio caused her to speak in order to beg
him to go away.

As she finished speaking a furious lion emerged from the forest and came
to hurl itself upon Patientine. The prince drew his sword and set himself to defend her; by means of a menacing cry and a blow he struck the lion at the same
time, he obliged the furious beast to turn its rage against him. Courageous defended himself for a long time, but not without receiving a large wound in the
belly from the lion's claws, and if the diggers had not run to his aid he might
have perished in the combat, but they overwhelmed the lion with so many blows
that it fell dead at Patientine's feet.

Insacio, attracted by the screams of the princess, arrived as the prince, losing consciousness because of his wound, let himself fall on to the grass.
Touched by pity for the first time in his life, he had him carried to his somber
abode, and ordered that his wounds should be dressed. Penetrated by gratitude,
Patientine bandaged him with her beautiful hands and took the trouble to go
with Espritée to look for simples to put on the wounds.

How sensible Prince Courageous was to the benevolence of the princess!
His amour acquired new force; he could not express sufficiently how apprecia-
tive he was of the evidence of her gratitude, and praised a hundred times a day
the two wounds he had received in saving her life.

In the meantime, the ogre was obliged to go away with his sisters for a few
days. Courageous took advantage of those fortunate moments to tell the princess
everything he felt for her, but Patientine, whatever reasons she had to be discon-
tented with her cruel husband, responded to him with so much discretion that
she fully merited the prince's tenderness.

Insacio came back sooner than expected, and finding his wife with the invalid, he entered in a fury and heaped her with outrageous reproaches. He repented of having Courageous brought to his home, and, his avarice combining
with his jealousy, he forbade Patientine to furnish the prince any longer with the
necessities of life, and told her that she was not to enter the cave that he was in
again. Patientine received that order dolorously, but did not murmur in protest,
and recommenced her hard labors.

The amorous prince suffered the misfortunes of the princess with impatience. His cave was so close to the ogre's that he heard all the ill-treatment that the latter meted out to the beautiful Patientine, and, not wanting to augment it, as soon as he could ride a horse, he took care to depart from a place that was so dear to him. That was not without having consulted with Espritée as to what he could do to extract the princess from such a hard slavery. First of all they made the resolution to inform the Queen of Lydia, but Espritée told him that she did not have the power to break her daughter's chains, and that it was necessary for her to go and find a fay who was a close relative of Patientine, who, by means of her science, could give them the means to remove the princess from the ogre's cruel hands. She said that she would leave with him the next day at dawn in order to find the fay, without telling the princess, who would not want to consent to her happiness.

After having made all their preparation, Courageous took his leave of Insacio and the charming Patientine, and departed the next day with Espritée. The princess did not learn about her friend's departure without chagrin, and could not understand what had obliged her to leave her, knowing the tender amity that she had for her.

While Courageous and Espritée were making their journey, a very powerful prince arrived with his wife in a castle near the Forest of Erimente. His name was Entreprenant and his wife was named Froidine. The ogre was told by the goddess Avarice that he would need Entreprenant's help to preserve him from a great misfortune that was menacing him, and as he knew of no misfortune except those regarding the loss of wealth, he followed the advice of the goddess; he went to see the newcomer and took Patientine with him. Emerging from her natural humor, Froidine received the beautiful princess very well, and Entreprenant was unable to see without paying for the pleasure of gazing at her with the loss of his heart. He made the ogre a thousand amities, in order to have the liberty of seeing his lovely wife, in spite of the natal aversion that he conceived for him at first sight.

Entreprenant often went to Insacio's home and, not being able to hide his passion for long, talked about it to Patientine. That beautiful person, abandoned to the ogre's furies, listened without anger to a declaration that she would not have wanted in better times, in order to assure herself of an aid against Insacio's cruelties, and the prince, charmed not to be rejected, obliged Froidine to visit Patientine often, and to testify amity to her; but the ogre, seeing that it took Patientine away from her ordinary labors, ordered her not to go see Froidine so frequently, and made a crime of what he had ordered her to do.

He searched for new work for her, and the princess, with her usual meekness, obeyed him. Entreprenant often surprised her breaking reeds, from which she extracted a cotton that was very rare in the region, which served to make cloth with which she dressed herself. She would have liked to hide from everyone the ill-treatment she received from the ogre, but, that not being possible, she tried to excuse it. Entreprenant wasted no time in trying to make Patientine comprehend that her husband did not merit that tenderness. His concern was futile; the virtuous person replied that, the gods having given her Insacio for a husband, it was her duty to obey him and to love him with the same fidelity as if he were the best of all men.

Bizarrine often came to interrupt these conversations, and warned the ogre about them. She put him in such a bad humor that, in spite of the advice of Avarice, he quarreled with Entreprenant and Froidine and shut the princess in his lair, not allowing her to go out into the forest any longer. His fury did not stop there; he no longer gave Patientine any rest, and every day was employed in furnishing her with new torments, which the amiable person suffered with an admirable patience.

Insacio, fearful of losing Patientine, not because of any sentiment of amity, but because of the great wealth that she amassed by her labor, surrounded his lair with clouds so dense that he rendered it invisible to everyone, and, changing his two sisters into monsters, he put them at the entrance to the cavern in order to forbid entry to anyone who might penetrate the enveloping cloud. Having taken his precautions so well to take away the anxiety of losing Patientine he savored some tranquility.

Meanwhile, Prince Courageous and Espritée arrived at the palace of the fay Clementine, and were received by her with the air of benevolence that made everyone love her. She took them into her cabinet, and, having invited them to sit down beside her, she said: "I know the purpose of your journey, charming Espritée; Patientine needs my help; she is at the extremity of misfortune, and the gods, who wanted to give a model to humans by the example of her virtue, will extract her by means of my art from the tyranny of the cruel ogre. It will need a few days for me to prepare for the journey; spend them here in all the pleasures that can be obtained in this palace."

After those few words, the fay dismissed the prince and Espritée; he found in the hall a troop of nymphs, who came toward them and conducted them to a superbly furnished apartment. After they had rested there for a few hours, the nymphs had Espritée pass into a cabinet, where they dressed her in a silver and pink garment and decocted her head with a feather capeline of the same color. In that new apparel they brought her to Prince Courageous's room, and served them a light meal of fruits and preserves. After the collation they took them into a garden, which responded to the beauty of the palace, and, leaving them in an arbor of jasmine and pomegranate, they gave them the liberty of listening to a charming orchestra, which was in a myrtle arbor next to theirs.

Courageous and Espritée gave a few moments to the pleasure of such a pleasant symphony, but as nothing could prevent them from thinking about the woes of Patientine, they talked about that beautiful person for such a long time that it was night when they returned to the palace. The time having come to repose, Courageous left Espritée in her apartment.

The next day, at dawn, the nymphs came to wake the amiable Espritée in order to take her to the fay's park. They gave her a very elegant hunting costume and took her into the courtyard of the palace. There she found a small ebony chariot with golden suns, drawn by four tigers, into which she climbed. The nymphs followed her in other chariots of a similar beauty, and Prince Courageous, mounted on a superbly harnessed black horse, came to join them at the rendezvous.

The whole day passed as agreeably as possible; the deer only ran for as long as was required to provide pleasure without fatiguing the ladies, and when night constrained them to return to the palace they arrived there with all the joy that such a charming amusement had inspired in them. Afterwards, the fay sent word to Espritée and Courageous to come to see her, which they did urgently.

"Espritée," she said, "my charms are ready; it requires no less power than mine to extract Patientine from Insacio's irons. He has employed all the art of Hell to form an enchantment that renders her invisible to our eyes; Avarice has given him advice, but I shall render his power useless and render the princess to you. Let us depart right away, in order to arrive at his tenebrous abode at sunrise. And you, Prince Courageous, forget your valor, and without using your arms to vanquish the monsters—they would be impotent against them—leave me the care of breaking Patientine's chains."

Without waiting for a response, the fay presented her hand to the prince, and, telling Espritée to pick up a small bottle that was on her table and follow her, she went on to a large terrace that was at the end of her apartment, where they found a chariot drawn by eagles. The fay, having placed herself therein, had the prince and Espritée enter it, and, the eagles having flown into the air, they arrived with the first ray of sunlight at the cloud that hid the ogre's lair.

Clementine told Espritée to spread a few drops of the essence in the bottle over the cloud, and it dissipated immediately, allowing Espritée and the prince to see the entrance to the lair, guarded by the two monsters.

"Remember," the fay said to Courageous, seeing him already putting his hand on his sword, "that to combat the princess's guardians, your sword is useless, and only my power will suffice to destroy the enchantment."

The prince, ashamed of having disobeyed the fay's command, stopped, and presented his hand to Clementine to help her descend from her winged chariot. Espritée followed her, impatient to see the princess again. Approaching the monsters, the fay touched them with her enchanted wand, which constrained them to resume their natural form, and, fearful of the presence of Clementine, to flee into the forest. The fay, scornful of objects unworthy of her anger, went into the cavern, and, expelling the obscurity by her presence, she saw the beautiful Patientine, who was removing a cauldron full of herbs from above the fire.

Ashamed to be surprised in an exercise so unbefitting to her birth, and dazzled by the fay's splendor, she dropped the cauldron. No sooner had the water and herbs it contained touched the ground than the cavern was seen to be full of brilliant gold instead of what had been in the cauldron. More astonished than ever, Patientine uttered a loud cry.

The ogre, who was in his animal shed, heard Patientine scream and ran to see what had happened to her. Charmed to see his cavern full of a metal that was so dear to him, without perceiving the fay, the prince or Espritée, who was holding the princess in her arms, he bent down precipitately to pick up that precious gold, but as he touched it, it became once again what it had been before. The water, running through his avid hands, formed a stream in the cavern. The ogre's astonishment at such an extraordinary sight is inexpressible, and, raising his haggard eyes, he saw the fay, who said to him, with a severe expression:

"Tremble, unfortunate Insacio, and recognize the justice of the gods by the torments to which they condemn you. You will lose this unfortunate princess, whom you have rendered yourself unworthy of possessing by the evils that your avarice has made her suffer. I want to take her back to her realm, where she will find the recompense for her virtues, while you will employ your misfortunate days in amassing riches that will disappear from your hands as soon as you have touched them, without you being able to correct your desire to amass them by the experience that you will accumulate, at every moment of your life, of being unable to possess them.

"You will serve as an example to all those who see your torture, and to take away the only pleasure that might remain to you, of making use of your poisoned tongue to avenge yourself on those who approach you, you shall no longer have that dangerous power; it will only be possible to spread that venom over those who resemble you. The evil that your tongue pronounces against mortals will not do them any harm, and will only serve to add a new splendor to the innocence that you have oppressed."

The cruel ogre trembled with rage at the fay's discourse, but, the gold taking the place of the stream again, without remembering his torture, he bent down to pick it up.

Clementine made use of that moment to take Patientine away, and, making her enter her chariot with Courageous, and Espritée, she sat down next to her. The eagles having resumed their flight, they were soon far away from the fatal lair.

While they made their voyage through the air, the ogre, without remembering Patientine, was occupied in picking up the liquid gold; but, the fay's enchantment taking effect, it changed its nature as soon as he had touched it, and flowed away as it had the first time, becoming gold again as soon as it was on the floor of the cavern.

Since that terrible moment the ogre has experienced a torture in conformity with the frightful vices that had led him to commit so many crimes. Without giving himself a moment's repose, he spends his misfortunate days in a continuous rage, like the unlucky Tantalus in Hell, persecuted by a continuous thirst that he cannot slake, unable to approach the water that recoils when he tries to drink it. All his neighbors and subjects, charmed by such a just torment, come to see it every day, and make him know, by the lack of power that the venom of his tongue over those of which he wishes to avenge himself, that the fay's words were veritable.

Meanwhile, Clementine and the beautiful Patientine arrived in Lydia and descended into the courtyard of the Palace of Sardis, surprising the queen agreeably by her presence. She embraced her dear daughter a thousand times, and threw herself at the feet of the fay to thank her for having liberate Patientine from the cruel yoke of Insacio. She heaped Espritée with caresses, and assured Courageous of an eternal esteem.

After having heaped the charming Patientine with benefits, the fay returned to her palace. Courageous remained at the court of the Queen of Lydia, and, adapting his passion to the virtue of the princess, adored her in secret. Espritée shared the fay's gifts with Patientine, and, charmed to have her with her, knew no greater happiness than being loved by Clementine and her dear princess.

PART II: 1716-1788

THE CONTRABAND RENAISSANCE 1716-1750

Author Unknown: The Flying Ship

Several centuries ago, all the princes of the earth, as well as their subjects, fatigued by the tyranny that fays exercised incessantly, resolved with a common accord to declare war on them. They were convinced that their power ordinarily caused great evils, and was only beneficial for very few people. And how was that done? Most often, it was on conditions so rigorous that it was necessary to be delivered to the most terrible ordeals before succeeding in accomplishing one's desires, and sometimes before obtaining the slightest favor.

The fays were immortal then, as they are today, but they were nevertheless submissive to that fatal day every week when, appearing in the form of some animal, they were exposed to the insults of their enemies. At the moment of their metamorphosis all their power vanished, and, subject to the same poverties as the beasts whose form they had been obliged to take, it was only by fleeing or hiding that they could escape the outrages in preparation for them. In spite of all the precautions they took, however, they were often surprised, and all the aforementioned kings took advantage so successfully of the advantage that the day fatal for the fays gave them that in a short time they perished in large numbers and were reduced to making the decision to retreat.

They were rather irresolute about the choice of a country where they could live together without mingling with any mortals when one of their number, who surpassed the others in prudence and industry, offered an opinion that was universally applauded. She proposed the construction of an enormous vessel of extremely light wood, the external surface of which would be covered by ostrich plumes. Those plumes ought only to be attached to the hull of the ship by the end of the quill, in order that the air, by agitating them, would sustain the machine and cause it to progress in a rapid and certain fashion. The interior of the great vessel ought, according to the plan, to be lined with the skins of swans; and two phoenix plumes, so dazzling that they had the virtue of rendering invisible everything that surrounded them, ought to be attached to the poop and the prow of the beautiful machine, in such a fashion that nothing in the world could separate them from it.

As soon as the design of that vessel was approved, the work was complete; the simple wish of the fays sufficed for its execution. They embarked in haste, firmly resolved not to determine their residence until they had examined the whole world with the greatest attention. They were lifted up instantly, without the ship making the slightest movement, and no mortal has been able to boast of having seen their embarkation.

When they had reached the highest region of the air, the vessel traveled with perfect smoothness, as it would have done on the calmest and most placid sea. The stars appeared in that place with a splendor that was never obscured, which one cannot imagine in our hemisphere; their glare did not cause any dazzle and their proximity was not inconvenienced by their heat. When one looked at the earth through that immensity of air, it resembled a sad and tenebrous chaos, which would naturally inspire no regret in persons who had abandoned that abode.

But what cannot habitude achieve? The fays had been too long accustomed to the habitation of the earth; they valued their art too much, which could only be exercised on humans, to resolve to separate themselves from it entirely. Nor did they want to be distant from the vicinity of the heavens. Torn between those two desires, which appeared to them to be incompatible, they were assisted by encountering a mountain, against which their vessel was in danger of breaking.

That mountain was the only one in the world that rose up to such an excessive height. The precipices that surrounded it rendered it inaccessible; the summit far exceeded the denser air; in consequence it was exempt from all bad weather; but the closer the slope of the mountain approached the earth, the more it was covered by snow and ice. The fays amassed them in one place and used them to construct a vast and very high hall. The cold and the tempests were forbidden to approach that entire section in future; flowers and fruits took the place of frosts and the zephyr had orders never to cease to embellish them. The situation of the summit of the mountain was admirable and delightful, but unfortunately, its area was small in extent.

The fays organized the terrain, therefore. In the middle they placed a basin of a precious substance; they gave birth there to a spring that would never dry up, the water of which would spread out incessantly, by means of agreeably distributed cascades, over the flowers and fruits with which the mountain was henceforth clad. That water, which participated in the celestial matter with which it was mingled, was much purer than that we use down here; furthermore, it had the property of procuring the immortality and maintaining the beauty of the persons who bathed in it, at the same time as it procured a perfect health for those who made use of it as their beverage. In a moment, the fays erected a magnificent palace on one side of that spring, where they established their dwelling, and that palace was placed symmetrically with the aforementioned hall.

The fays had made that hall a place of enchantment; they had converted its walls, which had previously only been masses of ice, into diamond, and the sun, by virtue of its proximity, had finished giving them solidity without altering their transparency. That was, however, one of the least of the prodigies that rendered the hall marvelous and worthy of being inhabited by the gods. When one entered it and looked upwards, the movement of the heavens was developed with the same clarity as if one had been in the sky; similarly, when one looked downwards, one could distinguish the immensity of the sea and the entre earth; one could penetrate all the way to its entrails. As for the walls of the beautiful hall, they represented by turns, In accordance with the will of those considering them, all the individuals inhabiting the world. Not only were their faces depicted naturally, but all the actions presented there were retraced with the most exact verity.

To the miracle of sight was added that of hearing. Without the latter article its curiosity would have been lacking something. In the same place, therefore, several sorts of instruments were found ranged on ruby tables, which produced the same effect for conversations as the walls did for visible objects, so that, in knowing the faces, it was also possible to know the character of their hearts and minds. In order to operate the instruments, it was sufficient to order the one whose sound one preferred to bring the words that the persons about whom one was curious were speaking; the instrument obeyed immediately, with a great deal of fidelity and melody. It had, in addition, the advantage of only rendering it intelligible to the person interrogating it, in order not only to be discreet but also not to be an obstacle to those who might have a similar desire at the same time.

The fays found themselves in the obligation of employing the utmost industry in order to live easily in such a small area. Furthermore, it was necessary for them, in order to come safely to earth, when they desired to do so, to render themselves unrecognizable by changing their form; otherwise, what hope could they have had of exercising their talents freely? That last expedient was to reduce their stature to the height of the smallest children, while nevertheless conserving the proportions of the best made adults. They also gave their skin a hardness approaching that of stone and covered that skin with a varnish that allowed the pallor of their complexion to be seen and the rouge with which they liked to adorn themselves. By that means, their beauty became splendid and very solid.

When they had a desire to come into the world they presented themselves before the walls of the hall; they passed in review all the persons, especially the prettiest children, that were then on earth and determined, on the basis of the physiognomy, to attach themselves to them, sometimes in order to harm them, and sometimes to give them pleasure. In sum, they acted in that regard as almost everyone does, following the prejudices of hatred or inclination.

On arrival on earth they ordinarily forbade themselves the usage of speech. It was, therefore, only children who would have consideration for them, but it was unimportant to them by what title they entered palaces and the simplest houses, provided that they were, in fact, received there. Their complexion had, as I have said, a whiteness, a redness and a polish above the natural and their adornment was always very carefully chosen. Children amused themselves dressing and undressing them; they became common in society; they were found everywhere. It was therefore necessary to choose a name for them, and people gave them that of Doll, in memory of an empress on the same name,[42] who became famous by virtue of the continuous application she had had all her life to making up her face and ornamenting herself. Dolls, received in the world without anyone having the slightest suspicion of them, did all the good and evil they wished without either being attributed to them, and it appears that they still conduct themselves in the same fashion, in spite of the prejudice people have that their power is finished and that their bodies have been converted into inanimate plaster.

At any rate, seven or eight thousand years ago, one of the fays, whose treasures are inexhaustible—the same one who, as everyone knows, had raised to royalty by a bizarre route a young woman of mediocre condition whom she had taken in amity—resolved to seek again some occupation worthy of her. She entered the hall and, having sat down negligently on a sofa facing one of the walls, she was struck during the review she made of the human race by a little princess four years old, whose beauty and charms surpassed anything that had ever been seen. She consulted regarding her intelligence a sort of violin, which reported speech so brilliant and jovial that she judged that she was nothing less than perfect. The princess, her mother, who was very young, very beautiful and very witty, charmed her no less.

She felt ready to fly toward that amiable family, and nothing put any obstacle in her design except the discovery she made, to her chagrin, that there was no further perfection to give them. She could not, however, resolve herself to being unnecessary to them; when one is keenly interested in people, only easily distinguishes how one might be useful to them. She perceived that their fortune

---

[42] The *Cabinet des fées* text has a note at this point, presumably inserted by the author, to explain (in jest) the origin of the French *poupée* [doll]: "Sabine Poppée, the second wife of the Emperor Nero, famous for coquetry and the care she took for the conservation of her beauty. Some people attribute the invention of make-up to her." The reference is to Poppaea Sabina the Younger (30-65 A.D.), who was, like every other wife of an emperor, snidely slandered by Roman "historians" in much the same way that the mistresses of French kings were slandered.

was not proportionate to their birth and their merit; that the little princess had a brother to whom all the wealth of the house belonged, and that, in consequence, she might have great need of her assistance in future—for in those remote times, the fay of treasures was necessary and desired in the world.

That discovery determined the fay to depart, but in order to be received more favorably by that amiable child, she found the means of being sent by an aunt whom she loved very much. That aunt spent her life retired in a desert, and only saw her niece very rarely. She was delighted to have such a present to give her, and no one had been able to tell me which of them had the greater pleasure, in giving or receiving. The aunt dressed the Doll in clothes similar to her own, and those of the persons with whom she lived in her desert.

The little princess received the present; she called the Doll her aunt and gave her amities and caresses, as if she were indeed her aunt. The rest of the house gave her a welcome no less warm, and was so content with it that she engaged one of her sisters to come and keep her company. The later consented gladly, and was given by the same hand in the same costume.

The two fays, unable to add anything to the graces of the princess, applied themselves to inspiring her with a courage capable of resisting all the misfortunes of life. They did the same favor for the mother, and as the child was at the age when the education of children begins, the fays rendered her very knowledgeable in a short time without putting her to the trouble of studying; her vivacity would never have become accustomed to that difficulty.

When she had attained the age of twelve, they took her away one night in the launch of the ship whose description has been given. Ostrich plumes gave it the same lightness. They took her into the beautiful hall that might be called the mirror of the world. Then they passed in review before them all the kings of the world, with the design of knowing which one she found most to her taste. The princess dared not make a choice to begin with; it appeared that that would wound her modesty in some way. Finally, after an absolute command, she noticed a young king, and it was the same one that the fays destined for her.

They had heaped that prince since his birth with their most precious gifts; they had rendered him extremely lovable, and he still had a free heart. It was only a matter of inspiring desire in him equal to the one to which he had given birth. The fays caused a portrait of the princess to fall into his hands; that was not very difficult for them, and the prince fell madly in love even more easily. Although he was in earliest youth, his sagacity and his extraordinary merit rendered him the absolute master of himself and his estates; thus, he did not want an ambassador to negotiate the affair that was to him the most important in the world; he came in person, with a court and a pompous equipage, to ask for the hand of the princess. He had no difficulty obtaining it; even in those remote times it was no longer merit alone that determined fortune.

That happy event appeared incomprehensible to everyone; no one knew to whom the little princess and her mother could have such an obligation. They alone, who were in the confidence of the fays and took advantage of their benefits every day, had knowledge of it.

The flying ship, which the fays had conserved preciously in a grotto in the mountain, was given to the newlyweds, who rightly preferred that equipage to any other to go to their kingdom. They were received there with acclamations and a joy that is indescribable, and which did not relent with time. The ship always remained with those two amiable spouses, along with the power to take aboard anyone they wished, and that of being visible or invisible. It will be remembered that, in order to do that, it was only necessary to cover and uncover the phoenix feathers at will.

The newlyweds went in their beautiful vehicle to pay a visit to the aunt who had given the Dolls. They no longer wanted to permit her to live in her desert; they took her away with them. They did more, and associated her with all the privileges accorded by the fays. The one that touched her the most was the pleasure of bathing with her sister and her niece in the celestial water that communicates immortality. That circumstance allows the well-founded judgment that the company still enjoys all the felicity that has just been depicted, and they are perhaps diverting themselves at this very moment traveling through the air on the flying ship—and some day, the phoenix plumes, differently placed, might permit us to see them pass by.

Louise Cavelier: *The Invisible Prince*

A fay whose power extended over the four elements had four sons. Her tenderness for them engaged her to divide her empire between them. She gave the eldest that of fire, as the noblest of the elements. He was an active, lively prince with a brilliant imagination. She made her second son sovereign of earth. A depth of sagacity and prudence made up for the scant vivacity that was seen in him. The third was monstrously large, barbaric and savage, so his mother, in order to hide so many effects from mortal eyes, gave him the empire of the sea.

The last of all had that of air. He had an uneven, slightly mercurial humor, and was easily drawn away by his passions. His mother, who loved him tenderly, brought him up with a horror of women, and was pleased to see it augmenting with age. She maintained it in his early years with stories of princes whose misfortunes had been caused by Amour alone; she depicted that god with colors so dark that the prince had no difficulty allowing himself to be convinced that his flame was the poison of hearts.

"Fear the flattering sweetness of Amour, my son," she said to him. "He only seduces our hearts in order to render them unhappy; his slightest pleasures poison the rest of life; and if his sharp arrows do not bring death to a soul, at least they bring idleness and laxity, more to be feared than death."

Such was the advice of that sage mother, who also inspired the young prince with such a strong inclination for hunting that he spent the best days of his life in it. She even had a forest of prodigious extent planted for him, which she populated with all the animals found in the four continents of the world. She brought him up in the middle of that forest in a palace so magnificent that nothing could equal it, and the desires of the young prince would have been satisfied if they had been limited to the charms of a delightful abode.

The young prince occupied himself primarily with making war on the inhabitants of the forest. Sometimes, mounted on a chariot harnessed to four chargers that he guided himself, he raced deer that fled tremulously before him. Sometimes, pike in hand, he took pleasure in fighting against a furious boar, whose bristling fur, glittering eyes and foaming mouth would have frightened the boldest mortals. Not a day passed when he did not give proof of his skill or strength, and the praise that his mother gave him always ended with some plaint against Amour.

But she could speak ill of the god as much as she liked; one cannot force nature. The heart of the young prince disapproved secretly of all the speeches that the fay made him, and although that tender mother, in quitting him for some affair that took her elsewhere, expressly instructed him not to leave his palace, because she foresaw the misfortunes that might befall him, he could not help disobeying her.

Abandoned to his own devices, the prince soon forgot the sage advice of his mother, and, ennui gradually overtaking him, he had himself transported one day by the aerial spirits to the court of a neighboring king. That was on the Isle of Roses, a fortunate clime in which winter does not extend its power. There, the grass is always green; the rose-bushes, perpetually in flower, perfume the air with a charming odor and incessantly present to the eyes the cheerful image of spring.

The first glance arrested the prince of genii for some time; the spacious sea, the waves of which came to die on the shore and broke noisily against the rocks, astonished him; the gilded wheat that covered the countryside and the grapes with which the hills were charged, were as many objects that surprised him with their novelty.

The king of that island had a daughter, a princess of unequaled beauty. Her name was Rosalie. The prince of genii had no sooner seen her than he no longer remembered the misfortunes that had been predicted for him. He lost in an instant the horror of Amour that had been inspired in him almost since birth. Alas, it only takes that god an instant to overturn projects of twenty years.

A prince like him did not sigh for long without thinking about means to render himself happy. He could not imagine a shorter one than having Rosalie abducted from her palace by his genii.

Imagine the dolor of the king, whom the beauty and goodness of his daughter consoled, having no one but her! He groaned night and day; his loss was always present to him; he no longer had any other pleasure than that chatting to a young prince who was previously unknown in his court. Alas, he did not know the secret interest that prince had therein; he had seen Rosalie, and had been unable to resist her charms.

One day, the king appeared more downcast than usual, and he went for a walk along the sea shore along a coast of steep cliffs, a place where, avoiding the tumult and importunate homages of his court, he came to bemoan the abduction of his daughter. The unknown prince, by whom alone the king wanted to be accompanied, finally broke the silence.

"There are still remedies for your woes," he said to the king, "and if you would care to promise me your daughter, my cares and my courage will bring her back to your estates."

"You're trying to flatter my dolor," the king replied. "I've seen my daughter abducted through the air; her cries would have moved to compassion anyone but the barbarian who has stolen her from me. That unfortunate princess is languishing in an unknown land, perhaps forbidden to the rest of men; I shall not see her again. However, go, generous stranger; bring back Rosalie, and may you be happy forever in this realm, of which I shall make you the emperor right away."

That stranger was the son of the King of the Golden Isle, of which a single city occupied the whole extent. An ever-tranquil sea beat its walls; they were decorated with golden bas-reliefs representing fables. The birth of Jupiter could be seen there; along with the dances of Corybants; the fall of the Titans, monstrous children of the earth; Daphne fleeing Apollo; the amours of Mars and Venus; those of her son and Psyche; the abduction of Proserpine; and a thousand other stories that the sculptor had represented carefully. The top of the walls was ornamented by orange trees, lemon trees and green trees, forming agreeable groves.

All the houses were built with the same symmetry, and all were made of sculpted gold. The windows were sealed with large squares of rock crystal mounted in the gold. A balustrade of the same metal terminated the roof of every house. All the streets were paved with sheets of gold, and they all ended in a large square, in the middle of which stood a temple, which could be entered by four different doors. The frontispiece was ornamented with columns and statues of gold and silver, placed on pedestals decorated with bas-reliefs representing the amours of the youth of Plutus. He was also the god to whom the temple was consecrated, and it was there that he rendered oracles.

At the moment of his son's birth, the king had not failed to consult the god regarding the destiny of the young prince; the minister, the faithful interpreter of his edicts, having considered the victims for a long time, after a shudder and a fearful murmur, had dictated this oracle:

What baleful stars dominate today!
On this newborn prince everything declares war.
I see the winds, the waves and the earth
Rising up against him.
By the furies of a giant, to save a woman,
I see him plunged into the seas;
But finally I see him in a palace of flame,
In spite of all the various efforts
Of the angry earth, the waves and the air.

A fay, the protectress of the Golden Isle, was at the king's court at the time when Plutus rendered this oracle, and, wanting to give the young prince a mark of her amity and protection, she made him a present of a stone that rendered one invisible by putting it in one's mouth; but one could not talk when one held it; that was the only condition attached to the virtues of the stone. The fay thought that it was a means of delivering the prince from all the misfortunes with which the edicts of destiny seemed to menace him.

As soon as his early youth was past, he had a desire to know whether the rest of the world responded to the magnificence of his father's estates. He embarked under the pretext of visiting several islands dependent on the Golden

Isle, but, a horrible tempest having thrown his vessel on to unknown coasts, where barbarians massacred the greater part of his crew and made the rest slaves, he had no other resource to escape their barbarity than to make use of his stone and render himself invisible. With that artifice he passed through the middle of them and reached a forest in which he marched for a long time; finally, however, he arrived at the edge of the sea, where he embarked.

He landed on the Isle of Roses, and went right away to the court of Rosalie's father. He had no sooner seen the princess than he fell in love with her. He had already spent several months sighing for her in secret when the prince of the genii came to abduct her.

Rosalie was an accomplished princess. Her graces even surpassed her beauty, and the most insensible man could not see her without loving her.

> *Her bright and lively eyes bore amour into the soul;*
> *Her complexion was fresher than a morning rose;*
> *With a gracious and delicate smile*
> *She set hearts ablaze with the most ardent flame.*
> *Nothing so lovely ever appeared beneath the skies;*
> *No, Jupiter himself never*
> *Made anything so gracious,*
> *After the amiable object that I love,*

The Prince of the Golden Isle could not resist so many graces. He loved her from the first moment that he saw her, and swore never to love anyone but her. He was inconsolable at her abduction; he spent days and nights in tears and sighs. "Alas," he cried, "perhaps I shall never see my lovable princess again as long as I live. Captive in an unknown palace, what can a mortal who has nothing in his favor but his amour do against the power of a demigod? But no matter; what would I not attempt? What can an extreme amour not achieve?"

It was in that hope that he quit the court of the unhappy king whose daughter had just been abducted.

He traveled for a long time without hearing any news of the princess; and he had already been walking for several days through a forest so dense and dark that one could hardly see to guide oneself therein when he found himself in a broad avenue of fir-trees, the crowns of which touched the skies. A green carpet dotted with the most beautiful flowers occupied the middle of the avenue; the spaces between the trees were ornamented by marble and porphyry statues, and the sun's rays, which could not pierce the rest of the forest, as if taking their revenge, appeared to illuminate that place with a purer and bright light.

The invisible prince perceived a palace at the end of that avenue. On seeing it, he sensed a secret transport in his heart, which was for him a presage that it was Rosalie's abode. That was the sole joy he had felt since her abduction. He arrived at the door of the palace, which was made from a single agate. He went through three courtyards, which were surrounded by moats of fresh pure water. The border was fitted with a balustrade at elbow height, made of brilliant diamonds with ruby tablets. The rarest birds were walking along the edges of the channels; others were perched on the balustrade and others on the roof of the palace, which was rock crystal, of magnificent architecture. A hall ornamented with fluted emerald pilasters led to terraced gardens that overlooked meadows as far as the eye could see. Water jets of a prodigious height further embellished that enchanted place, and beds of the most sought-after flowers perfumed the air with the most delectable odors.

The magnificence of the place, in which nature and art seemed to be exhausted, did not stop the invisible prince for a moment. He was only thinking about his princess; he was only looking for her; he did not find her in that palace, so what charm could it have for him? In vain he had traversed the halls and cabinets; in vain he had already explored almost all the gardens; only one wooded area remained to see.

Trembling, he went into a pathway bordered with bronze statues, alternating with pools of water. The path led him to a grove of orange trees taller and stouter than our largest chestnut trees. In the corners of the grove there were four arbors.

In the first he only found a jasper basin with a golden figure in the middle representing the serpent Python, which seemed to want to obscure the sun again with its open mouth, eyes and ears.

In the second, in the middle of an emerald basin, there was a bronze Aeolus surrounded by winds that he had just unleashed in order to inundate the earth with torrential rain.

In the center of the topaz basin of the third rose a rock of white marble, from which a spray of water of prodigious size emerged; at the foot of the rock was a weeping Ariadne, from whose eyes tears emerged, drop by drop, that one might have thought natural.

Only the fourth cabinet remained, the basin of which was ruby and the statues black marble. It was a Memnon, whose soldiers were mourning his death; he was lying at the foot of a trophy of arms, from which a thousand water jets emerged. Imagine the surprise and the joy of the invisible prince when he found Rosalie there! But by what frightful despair they were followed when he saw the prince of the genii at her knees!

"Will you always reproach me for a crime," he said to her, "of which amour was the cause? Alas, you would pardon me easily if you knew what it is to love."

"No," replied Rosalie, "You have taken me away from my father. All the magnificence that you have displayed to my eyes, all your power and all your amour, will never be able to console me. Go away, cruel man, hope for nothing henceforth from me but hatred and scorn."

She stood up immediately and, marching with a long stride, she retired to her apartment. The invisible prince followed her. Fearing that the surprise of seeing him might reveal his presence, he thought it better to wait all night. The princess spent it lamenting her captivity. That gave the invisible prince time to write these verses, which she found when she awoke on the edge of her bed:

> *You sigh, beautiful princess,*
> *And captive in this abode,*
> *You are seen to pass every day*
> *In languor and in sadness;*
> *But in the somber ennui that oppresses you*
> *Do you say nothing about amour?*

The princess did not doubt for a moment that it was the prince of genii who had written those lines in order to make his sentiments known; she kept them nevertheless and felt a discreet pleasure in reading them.

The invisible prince did not stay there; and when the prince of the genii had departed in order to meet his brothers in the abode of his mother, who assembled them every year, he no longer thought about anything but means of liberating Rosalie. He did not want to reveal himself immediately. He wanted to sound out the heart of the princess and make certain of the aversion that she seemed to have for the prince of genii.

One day, when she was alone in her cabinet, thinking about her woes, Rosalie was surprised to see a quill emerge from the writing equipment that was on her table and write of its own accord on a sheet of white paper. She could not see the hand that was guiding it, for it was that of the invisible prince. The prodigy astonished her. When the pen had finished writing, however, carried away by curiosity, she got up in order to read what had been written.

She found the following lines:

> *Slave of a jealous prince*
> *Whose amour is greatly to be feared,*
> *Of a frightful fate you suffer the blows;*
> *But you are not alone in lamenting,*
> *There is someone unhappier than you.*

"Whoever you are, favorable genius," said Rosalie, "for I do not doubt that you are one, whom my chagrin renders sensible to the woes I am suffering, whoever you are, what misfortune gives you more to lament than me?"

The same pen immediately traced this response on the same piece of paper:

> *You are suffering rigorous woes;*
> *But for me, my pain is extreme;*

Your fate is cruel, mine is frightful;
You do not love and I love you.

"You love me!" cried the princess. "Oh, may your amour render you a hundred times unhappier, for doubtless you are a subject of the prince who is keeping me captive here; perhaps you are the prince himself. Yes, may Amour avenge me forever for the woes I am suffering here."

The invisible prince was charmed to see the aversion that Rosalie had for the prince of genii. It is always a pleasure for an unfortunate lover to see his rival maltreated. However, the princess could not help shedding a few tears.

"Alas," she said, sighing, "if you only knew the deplorable state that I am in your valor would make you confront all risks in order to liberate me from it; but you do not know my woes, and the greatest of all for me is to be unable to see you."

The invisible prince shivered at those words. He knew from the beautiful Rosalie's tears that he had a beloved rival. What was his dolor! So it was only tremulously that he wrote the following:

Confide in me, Princess,
I swear by that same amour
Of which the tender confession wounds you
To extract you from this abode.
But if liberty has such charms for you,
For the price of my generous cares,
Name me the fortunate mortal
Who costs your eyes so many tears.

What can the desire for liberty not make us do? Whatever risk there was for the princess is confessing that she loved, after having hesitated for some time, she broke the silence and said: "What are you asking of me, and ought I not to fear a confidence like the one I am about to make to you? I foresee all the misfortunes that might happen to me, but your promises reassure me, and something in the depths of my heart draws a confession from me that I would rather keep silent.

"One day, I was in my father's gardens surrounded by a numerous court and occupied with the pleasure of receiving its homage, when a young stranger, whose grace and beauty surprised us all, emerged from a wood that bordered a long canal along which I was traveling. He seemed astonished by the sight of our gilded boats ornamented by banderoles of flowers. He stopped and followed us for a long time with his eyes, but I finally lost sight of him, and on losing it, I felt a disturbance that I had not known previously. I was pensive for the rest of the day, and it was only when I went into my father's apartment that I emerged from my reverie.

"I found the same stranger there. I blushed on seeing him and could not listen without trouble to the story he was telling my father about his adventures. He never wanted to reveal his identity. I saw him every day, and every day I felt a new pleasure in seeing him. I did not oppose that nascent amour; I found the stranger worthy of my tenderness. I believed that I remarked in his gaze that I was not indifferent to him. Far from offending me, my passion was augmented by the pleasure of thinking that I was loved. How happily I lived! I saw incessantly that I was loved. Why did a barbaric prince have to separate me from him?"

Rosalie could not hold back her tears, and the invisible prince could not remain hidden any longer. He immediately removed the stone and threw himself at Rosalie's feet.

Judge their secret transports,
You, young hearts of which Amour is the master,
It is for you alone that these pleasures are made;
It is necessary to love to know them.

After having talked for a long time about their tenderness, they discussed measures for getting out of the palace of the prince of the genii. But the stone that rendered one invisible could only be used by one person, and it would be necessary for the Prince of the Golden Isle, in order to save Rosalie, to expose himself to all the fury of the prince of genii. He did not hesitate, however.

"Let me," he said to her, "Let me, my princess, expose myself alone to the wrath of the prince of genii, and flee this place forever."

Rosalie could not resolve herself to do that. "No, Prince," she replied, "this abode no longer seems frightful to me, since I can see you here. You have a fay who protects you and returns in all the seasons of the year to your father's court. This is the time when she ought to go there. Depart, Prince, depart, and try to obtain from her a stone similar to yours. It will be easy for us thereafter to escape together."

The prince of genii having returned, the invisible prince left a few days later. He could not liberate Rosalie too soon. He hastened to go to the court of the King of the Golden Isle, but the detours of the forest hindered him in getting out of it; he was unable to arrive quickly enough, and the fay had already gone. His dolor was extreme. It was for another three entire months that Rosalie had to suffer.

He was inconsolable, and had already resolved to return to the palace of the prince of the genii in order to spend the three months with Rosalie when, while traversing an avenue that led to the sea shore where he was due to embark, he saw a monstrous oak tree open up, and two princes emerged from the hollow of the tree who were conversing. As they could not see the invisible prince, they thought they were alone and had no fear of talking aloud.

"Are you going to torment yourself forever," said one of them, "with a passion that you know can never be fortunate, and have you nothing in your empire that can console you for it?"

"What use is it to me," replied the other, "to be prince of gnomes, and for my mother to be sovereign of the four elements, since I can never be loved by Princess Argentine? Remember the day when we were walking in her gardens and, hidden behind the thick palisade that surrounded a spring ornamented by shells and stones, the waters of which formed baths as pure and clear as crystal, we saw Argentine, whom the heat of the day obliged to come and seek the cool of woods the sun was never able to penetrate in spite of its ardor, the breath of the zephyrs conserving a delightful freshness there at all times. She sat down on a grassy bank dotted with a thousand flowers that bordered the spring, and, the brilliance and murmur of the water inviting her to bathe in it; you saw her dive into it, as I did.

"Her trouble appeared extreme. Ashamed of being visible, although alone in that place; stark naked exposed to the light of the sky, she scarcely dared, alas, to look at herself. My soul was moved by her hidden treasures; what was the freshness of her breasts, and of her arms! No, Venus herself, stark naked, would have a thousand times fewer charms. And I judged by those she offered to my sight, all those I could not see.

"Since that moment, I have not ceased to think about her. Her image follows me night and day. I love her, and I am certain, alas, that she will never love me. You know that I have the cabinets of time in my palace, and that in the first, large mirrors represent the past to us, that in the second, the present is depicted for our eyes, and that one discovers the future in the third. It was to the last that I ran as soon as I had quit Argentine, but alas, in spite of all my tenderness, I saw nothing but scorn and rigors. Judge my amour and my woes, since, in spite of that certainty, I feel that I love her still."

The Prince of the Golden Isle was delighted to know that the gnome prince loved Argentine. She was his sister, and he hoped to be able to obtain by means of him, from his brother the prince of genii, the liberty of the Princess of the Isle of Roses. He would have liked to be able to go into the cabinets of time, but, Argentine having appeared at the end of the avenue, the gnome prince and his confidant went back into their tree and returned to their realm.

The invisible prince took note of the tree and did everything he could to open it, but found it impossible; it was closed by a secret he did not know. However, the desire to know whether Rosalie still loved him, and whether he would love her forever, obliged him to defer his departure for a few days. He remained in the avenue, hoping that the gnome prince would return to it.

He was not mistaken; he saw him one day, and while he was conversing with his confidant the invisible prince went into the tree, which they had not closed, and went down an ebony and ivory stairway that led him to a sculpted red copper door, which he opened. He found himself in a gallery of surprising length and breadth. It was pierced on both sides; one side overlooked delightful gardens, the other a lake that extended as far as the eye could see, lined with marble and surrounded by a forest.

He advanced into the gallery. All the furniture was solid gold and silver; the most beautiful vases and statues could be seen there, and the cornice was ornamented by the rarest porcelains. At the end of the gallery there was a sculpted silver door, above which the invisible prince read this inscription:

> Here of all times is the faithful image,
> Here all is revealed to the curious gaze;
> The present is depicted here, the past recalled,
> And the obscure future is unveiled to our eyes.

The invisible prince tried in vain to open the door; his efforts were futile. It was closed by secrets that he could not discover. The gnome prince knew them, and it was not until he had seen him open it that the invisible prince entered the cabinet of the past.

It was there that he saw again the canal where he had encountered Rosalie for the first time; he saw her abducted by the prince of genii; he saw that prince on his knees in the arbor with the statue of Memnon; but all of that only renewed sad memories. He could not even retain his tears when he saw everything that the prince of genii had made Rosalie suffer since his departure; he pressed her incessantly; his threats and his anger appeared painted in his eyes; he kept her increasingly confined; she no longer had the liberty to leave her apartment. The unfortunate princess spent days and nights in tears.

Such a cruel state was too sensible to the invisible prince. He covered his eyes in order to abandon himself entirely to his dolor; he even emerged from the fatal cabinet momentarily, but amour drew him back involuntarily. What was his surprise on seeing, when he went back in, Rosalie at a window overlooking a magnificent expanse of water, writing a letter by moonlight. He trembled, approached the mirror and read:

> Arrest your course, dear night,
> Of which the star that shines for us,
> Has just pieced the somber veils.
> Have pity on my dolors;
> It is by favor if its darkness
> That I dare to shed tears here.
>
> From the moment it emerges from the waves,
> Sowing the gold of its blonde tresses,
> The sun will spread the daylight.
> Reentering my sad slavery,

It will be necessary to hide my amour
From the jealous eyes of my tormentor.

What torment does he make me suffer?
He even takes away the pleasure
Of shedding tears in secret;
While there is not a moment
In which, full of dread and alarms,
I do not tremble for my lover.

Under the law of a barbaric prince,
Whose cruelty separates me
From what I love forever;
O gods, how extreme is my pain;
I always see the one I hate,
And I never see the one I love.

Oh, who beneath your law, Amour,
Ever had more to lament than me?
And who was ever more faithful?
How rigorous your empire is!
Alas, a chain so beautiful
Merits a happier fate.

And you, worthy object of my flame.
You, dear prince, from whom my soul
Wants never to be disunited,
You who cause me such alarms,
As a mark of my memory
Receive my sighs and my tears.

But a rival too odious
Will soon appear in this room;
Of the night day will take the place.
How excessive is my misfortune?
I must efface in the morning
Even the trace of my tears.

Reading those verses softened the heart of the invisible prince. He lamented Rosalie's fate; but his dolor was extreme when he saw the prince of genii enter the princess's apartment furiously. He appeared to be threatening her with rendering her captivity even harsher if she did not respond to his desires. His

369

eyes inflamed by anger, his precipitate stride, his somber expression and his menacing gestures marked his barbarity and his fury.

The invisible prince could not stand such a cruel spectacle, He emerged from the cabinet of the past and went into that of the present. It was there that he saw Rosalie sitting on the bank of a canal. She was holding in her hand what she had written while she had been in the palace of the prince of genii. She appeared to be reading it with pleasure, and the tender and passionate gaze marked her trouble and her amour.

The invisible prince would dearly have liked to go into the cabinet of the future, but the gnome prince never went into it. He knew that he would only see Argentine's indifference and scorn there, and he was too sensitive to want to convince himself of it. It was in the cabinet of the present that the invisible prince spent the little time that he had before the return of the fay who protected him. The absence of Rosalie was less rude; he saw her incessantly; he followed her from moment to moment; but in the end, the time arrived when he had to tear himself away from that place in order to be present when the fay arrived.

The invisible price emerged from the cabinets of time, and returned to the court of the King of the Golden Isle, his father. He asked the fay for a stone similar to the ne he had received from her previously. The fay, who loved him, gave it to him instantly. He departed immediately to go and liberate the princess.

He arrived at the edge of the forest that surrounded the palace of the prince of genii; he traversed it by means of the paths he had frayed the last time, and finally arrived at the door of the palace. He went through all the apartments without finding Rosalie. There were no arbors in the gardens that he did not visit, but he searched in vain, and did not find her. Seized by a sincere dolor, he was ready to kill himself a thousand times over.

He waited there for some time, but, nothing being offered to his sight, he left that fatal place, not knowing where to go. He remembered the cabinets of time, where he was sure of seeing what had happened to Rosalie and where she might be. He went back through the forest, embarked, and reached the Golden Isle. Having arrived at the foot of the oak from which one descended to the palace of the gnome prince, he went down the stairway and opened the gallery and the door of the cabinet of the past.

What was his surprise when he saw that Rosalie had dropped one of the pieces of paper on which he had written to her while he was in the palace of the prince of genii, and that the prince, having picked it up, had entered into such a furious anger that he had removed her immediately to a palace at the top of a mountain that surpassed the clouds.

He wanted to see what Rosalie was doing at the moment, and went into the cabinet of the present. There he saw her in a long room, where the prince of genii had a crystal retrenchment made. All the princess's actions were visible through it, and the prince had her guarded day and night by genii, which surrounded her, and which never quit her. She was tearful, she sighed incessantly, and her dolor was apparent in the dejection of her expression and the tears that trickled from her eyes.

The despair of the invisible prince is indescribable. He saw his princess removed at the moment when he was about to liberate her, and reproached himself for having been the cause of it. He did not know where to find the palace in which she was living; it was covered in clouds, and he did not know the mountain, or even the country, where it was located. However, he emerged from the palace of the gnome prince resolved to travel the world in order to find Rosalie. He went to the sea shore, where he embarked.

The waves were tranquil. Favorable wind inflated the sails of his ship, and he had already lost sight of the shore when the atmosphere suddenly darkened, the wind changed and the sea, becoming more agitated by the minute, announced by the foam of its waves an imminent tempest. Its fury suddenly increased, and the Prince of the Golden Isle's ship, after having wandered over the waves for a long time, was finally pushed by the violence of the waves against the breakers of a coast. It was wrecked, but amid the debris of his ship he seized a plank. He was the plaything of the winds and waves for a long time, but he was finally cast up on an unknown island.

His surprise was extreme to hear frightful screams resounding, and a moment later a symphony and songs that charmed him. Such a great singularity obliged him to advance. He found himself at the entrance of a wood guarded by two dragons. Their entire bodies were covered in yellow scales; their curved tails covered the ground with their long coils; they projected fire from their mouths and nostrils; and their glittering eyes would have made the boldest mortal tremble.

As the prince was invisible, those monsters did not oppose his passage. He went into the wood. It was a labyrinth in which the multitude and diversity of the pathways prevented him from finding the entrance again. He walked for a long time without encountering anyone; he only found an infinite number of human hands, each of which emerged from the ground as far as the wrist, which had a band of gold around it, on which a name was inscribed. He read several of them, but they told him nothing.

His curiosity increased as he went further into the labyrinth. Eventually, in the middle of a grove of cypresses, he found two dead bodies. He recognized by a residue of warmth that it was not long since they had been killed. What astonished him more was that each of them had a silken cord the color of flame around the neck, one end of which they were holding, and they appeared to have strangled themselves. Both had gold bands on the arm, on which their names were written, and those of two princesses.

The invisible prince recognized them as the sovereigns of two islands that were connected to the Golden Isle, but the names of the two princesses were unknown to him. He lamented the destiny of the unfortunate princes, and, knowing the respect that is owed to the dead, he immediately dug a grave at the edge

371

of the path and buried them in it. Scarcely were they covered with soil than the hand of each of the unfortunate princes emerged from the ground and remained elevated, as far as the gold band that encircled the wrist.

The invisible prince continued on his way, thinking about the singularity of that adventure. He had not yet encountered anyone except those two princes when, on turning a corner, he perceived a tall man whose dolor was painted in his face. Long sighs were emerging from his breast, and a torrent of tears was flowing from his eyes. He was holding in his hand a silken cord the color of flame like those the invisible prince had found around the necks of the two dead princes.

He followed that stranger for some time without him saying a single word. Hazard appeared to be guiding his footsteps; always overwhelmed by dolor, nothing extracted him from his reverie. Finally, he turned into an avenue of sycamores, where the invisible prince perceived another man, as sad and no less meditative than the first.

The two unknown men came together, and embraced one another without speaking; each passed his red silken cord around his neck, and immediately the cord tightened of its own accord. They fell, side by side. The invisible prince could not get to them quickly enough to alter their destiny. He tried in vain to loosen the silken cords, but it was impossible. He buried them, like the other two, and their hands immediately emerged from the soil as far as the gold band that each had around the arm.

The invisible prince dared not reveal himself; he feared some enchantment. He was already beginning to despair of being able to get out of the labyrinth when he perceived the dragons that defended the entrance. He emerged, and, advancing further into the island, he found himself at the portal of a delightful park, where he perceived a large number of people, some of whom were lying on beds of grass, others walking along the bank of a stream and others sitting under bushy trees, spending all day dancing and feasting. A charming music resounded in that place; birdsong mingled with that harmony, and, in sum, everything in that enchanted abode appeared to respire nothing but joy and pleasure.

The invisible prince approached, drawn by curiosity, and found himself within range of hearing the conversation of a young prince and a young princess.

"You love me," said the prince, "and you have sworn to love me until death, but perhaps, in spite of your oaths, you will not love me forever, and perhaps, by your lightness, you will soon force me to have recourse to the Fay of Despair, the sovereign of half this island. It is there to which lovers are removed who, in despair at the infidelity of their mistresses, want to renounce life.

"The fay who seizes them puts them in a labyrinth made in such a fashion that they can walk for an infinite time without encountering one another. When each one goes in she attaches a circlet of gold to his wrist, on which his name is inscribed, with that of his faithless mistress. Then she gives him a silk cord the color of flame, which can only tighten at the moment when one desperate lover finds another. Then, approaching one another, they pass the cords round their necks, which immediately tighten and strangle them. The first person who finds them buries them, and their hands immediately emerge from the ground as far as the gold band, remaining thus as eternal evidence of the infidelity of their mistresses.

"However frightful that death might be," the prince continued, it would be sweet for me, if I had lost your heart."

It was by the conversation of those two lovers that the invisible prince learned that he was on the Isle of Lovers, and that he had emerged from the Labyrinth of Despair, where unhappy lovers went to end their days. It was adjacent to the Park of Fortunate Lovers, from which it was only separated by a simple palisade.

> *On the faith of Amour you can scarcely rely;*
> *Lovers, whatever pleasures you might enjoy,*
> *From his favors to despair*
> *There is only a single step to take.*

The invisible prince explored the gardens; everywhere he only found lovers charmed by one another; but their happiness only served to render him more miserable. He left, and sought places more remote, the solitude and silence of which were more appropriate to his passion.

Sitting on a rock, the spurs of which advanced into the sea, he spent days thinking about Rosalie.

Will destiny never cease to persecute me? he said to himself. *My misfortunes and my shipwreck would be sufficient to overwhelm me with dolor, even if Amour had not added his cruelest penalties to them. Far from my father's estates, without the hope of ever seeing him again, I am dragging out a languid life here, where the gods have only left me in order to augment my torments further. If I were suffering alone, my woes would seem light to me, but Rosalie is a captive; I was sailing in order to save her. Cruel sea, fatal shipwreck, how much you have cost my heart in bitter dolor!*

The prince's eyes filled with tears then; he was almost drowned by them. He thought of nothing night and day but means of getting off the island, and was despairing of ever finding one when he heard a horrible noise. The waves of the sea rose up all the way to the clouds; the shore resounded with the noise of long roars, and he finally saw a woman emerge from the depths who was fleeing as fast as she could from a furious giant. The pitiful screams that she uttered moved the invisible prince; he ran to combat the giant, in order to give the unfortunate woman time to get away, but scarcely was he within range when the giant touched him with a wand that he was holding in his hand and rendered him motionless.

The giant had soon overtaken his prey, and, lifting her in his arms, he plunged back into the sea with her. Tritons then emerged, who put the Prince of the Golden Isle in chains and who, in returning the usage of his senses to him, put the unfortunate prince into the most horrible state in which he had ever found himself. His pity cost him dear; he could no longer make use of his stone; he was dragged down to the sea bed, without any hope of ever liberating his princess.

The giant, who was the third son of the Fay of the Four Elements and the sovereign of the sea, had touched the Prince of the Golden Isle with a wand that had the virtue of rendering a mortal capable of living under water. Thus, the prince, led by the tritons that had put him in chains, passed through places where only horrible monsters live, traversed forests of immense extent and descended into frightful abysms.

He finally arrived in a large space surrounded by frightful rocks. In the middle of those rocks rose one on which the Prince of the Golden Isle perceived the giant who had struck him with his wand. He was sitting there as if on a throne; a long beard hung down to his waist; his bald and wrinkled forehead, his sunken eyes, his terrible gaze and his menacing voice would have made anyone but the Prince of the Golden Isle tremble.

"Temeritous individual," the giant said to him, "death ought to be the price of your insolence, but live and suffer a torture even crueler; augment here the number of unfortunates whom I take pleasure in tormenting."

The Prince of the Golden Isle was attached to a rock. He was not alone in lamenting; all the rocks were garnished with princes and princesses that the giant was holding captive. That monster, whose fury raised tempests expressly to be able to augment the number of his victims, seized with joy all those who perished therein.

The Prince of the Golden Isle could not make use of his stone because he was enchained. He sighed night and day; of all the woes he suffered, the memory of Rosalie was the most sensible for him.

Finally, one day, the giant wanted to give himself the pleasure of seeing some of the unfortunates that he kept in chains fight one another. The lot fell upon the Prince of the Isle of Gold. He was untied; and as soon as he was free, he put the stone in his mouth and rendered himself invisible.

What was the giant's surprise when he saw the Prince of the Golden Isle disappear! He ordered that all the passages by sealed, but the invisible prince had already slipped between two rocks.

He marched for a long time through forests in which he encountered nothing but monsters of frightful form. He climbed rock after rock, slid from tree to tree, and after infinite troubles he finally found himself on a shore, at the foot of a mountain that he recognized as the same one that he had seen in the cabinet of the present, and the one where Rosalie was kept captive.

It is thus that fortune plays with the projects of men, and the disasters that seem to us without remedy are often the source of an imminent good fortune.

He climbed all the way to the summit of the mountain, which pierced the clouds. He found a palace there, which he entered. He penetrated as far as a broad pathway, in the middle of which he saw the crystal chamber where Rosalie was guarded night and day by genii. It did not have the smallest opening.

The embarrassment of the invisible prince was extreme; he did not know how to inform Rosalie that he had finally returned. He saw her incessantly dissolving in tears. The dolor of the unfortunate princess pierced the heart of the invisible prince. It was necessary to avoid awakening the jealousy of the Prince of Genii, for at the slightest suspicion he would transport her to the other extremity of the earth. It was, however, necessary to alert Rosalie—and what can love not imagine?

One day, when Rosalie was pacing back and forth in her chamber, having approached the crystal that served as a wall, she was astonished to see it tarnished, as if someone had breathed on it. She tried to wipe it away, but her surprise was even greater when she saw that it was not on her side. The vapor was dissipated. Rosalie changed places, but as soon as she stopped, the same vapor tarnished the crystal.

It did not require any more to make the princess suspect that her lover had returned. She immediately began to treat the prince of genii more kindly, flattering him with the hope that she might listen to him if he made the captivity in which he was holding her a little milder. She only asked him for the favor of being able to walk around the long room for an hour a day. The prince of genii permitted that. She emerged right away, and the invisible prince immediately gave her the stone, which she put in her mouth.

The fury of the prince of genii is indescribable. He ordered his aerial spirits to fly throughout the world and to bring Rosalie back as soon as they could discover the place to which she had gone. The genii left in order to carry out that order and spread out all over the earth.

Meanwhile, Rosalie and the invisible prince, holding one another by the hand, had first reached a door, which gave access to a terrace that descended into the gardens. They traversed them in silence, thinking that they were already saved, and their hearts were already applauding in secret the pleasure of soon seeing one another again when a furious monster chance to launch itself between Rosalie and the invisible prince, and scared the princess so badly that she let go of her lover's hand.

They searched for one another for a long time. They could not speak, because they were unable to do so while invisible. They had heard the order of the prince of genii to seize them as soon as they appeared, so the slightest sound might have given them away.

How short the duration of their joy was, alas! And it was followed by a sensible dolor. After having wandered in the forest for a long time, the princess finally stopped on the edge of a spring. She spent every moment of the day writing on trees: *If ever the prince my lover is guided to this place, let him know that it is here that I live, and that I shall return to the bank of this spring every day, the waters of which are augmented by my tears.*

A genius read those words and repeated them to the prince of genii, who, rendering himself invisible, had himself taken to the bank of the spring. He waited there for Rosalie, and extended a hand to her, which the princess mistook for that of her lover, and by virtue of that mistake he passed a silken cord around her arms. Immediately rendering himself visible, he cried to his genii to take her into the most frightful abyss imaginable.

The invisible prince arrived at that moment. He saw the prince of genii rise into the air holding a silk cord in his hand. He did not doubt that it was Rosalie that he was taking away. He abandoned himself entirely to his despair, and his first impulse was to take away his life

Can I survive my misfortunes? he said to himself. *Are there any comparable to those to which fortune has condemned me? It seems that it only allows me to envisage an end to my woes in order to render them even more sensible. What will become of me, alas? Will I ever be able to discover the place to which that barbarian has taken Rosalie?*

The unfortunate prince had resolved to let himself die, and his extreme dolor was sufficient to terminate his days, but the hope of discovering once again by means of the cabinets of time where the princess might be sustained him against his woes. He continued his route through the forest, and after having walked for some time he found himself at the entrance of a temple defended by two lions of extreme dimensions. Being invisible, he went in.

In the middle of the temple was an altar, on which there was a large book. A curtain hid the back of the temple. Curiosity caused the invisible prince to open it. He saw a bed on which a child was asleep. He knew by his weapons that it was Amour. He stood there for some time looking at the god whose irons he wore. He sensed a secret pleasure in seeing his conqueror asleep.

Alas, he said to himself, *that cruel child is savoring the repose that he takes away from the rest of the world; is it necessary that I still love him in spite of all the evils he has made me suffer? Oh, how dearly I am paying for the pleasure of bearing his chains!*

The invisible prince, fearful of waking Amour, closed the curtain again and approached the altar on which he had seen the book. He opened it. It was the register of lovers. The invisible prince found Rosalie's name there. He read that she had been abducted by the prince of genii to the bottom of an abyss to which only the Gilded Spring gave access.

The land irrigated by that spring was unknown to him.

Where shall I go? he wondered. *How can I find a place of which I only know the name? Perhaps every step I take in order to find it will only take me*

further away, alas. But no matter; it's very fortunate that there is still a means of saving Rosalie.

When he emerged from the temple the invisible prince found himself at the intersection of six paths that pierced the forest. He was hesitating as to which to take when he perceived two people at the end of the one to his right who were coming toward him. He soon recognized them; it was the prince of gnomes and his confidant. The pleasure of hearing news of Argentine obliged the invisible prince to follow them and listen to their conversation.

"I believe your advice," said the gnome prince, "and I would break the irons whose rigor is crushing me if reason were able to vanquish amour. I know that Argentine will never love me, and yet I adore her. Every day she becomes dearer to me, and I would believe myself to be happy if I were sure that she would love me some day, but of all the pains of amour the only one that remained for me to know was jealousy, and to complete my woes, my dear Lisistrate, with the thought of never being loved by Argentine I have the horror of thinking that she loves someone else. It was at the last fête I gave her that I perceived it. Her anxious gaze marked the trouble in her heart. Inattentive to the cares I showed her, she scarcely deigned to look at me.

"She's in love, my dear Lisistrate, she's in love; I cannot doubt it. However indifferent Argentine was, at least my amour amused her before, if it did not please her. I tremble, however, to be enlightened, now that I am ready to attempt the fatal adventure of the Gilded Spring; it is in the depths of these woods that the spring's waters flow. A golden sand as fine as dust surrounds its edges. A single drop of water dropped thereon instantly traces in the sand the name of a rival as soon as he is loved. How fearful I am, my dear Lisistrate—and that dread is already a near-certainty of my misfortune."

The invisible prince was careful not to quit the gnome prince, since hazard had allowed him to find the spring, the place where the prince of the genii was keeping Rosalie.

After several turnings, the gnome prince finally arrived on the edge of the Gilded Spring. He bent down, sighing, and, letting a drop of water fall on to the sand, he immediately saw the name of his brother, Prince Flame, traced in the same sand. Dolor seized him, and he fainted in Lisistrate's arms.

The invisible prince, who had no suspicion regarding Rosalie, only thought of rescuing her. As he had the facility of going into water without suffering any harm, he did not hesitate to dive into the spring. In a corner he perceived a door, which he opened. It opened on to a mountain. He descended it precipitately, sure that he was going to liberate Rosalie.

At the foot of the mountain he only saw a single rock, to which a ring was attached, and to that ring a silk cord, which the invisible prince immediately cut. Immediately, he seized the hand of the princess, who sensed in her heart that the hand gripping hers was that of her lover. She had not wanted to remove the stone, and whatever entreaties, pleas and enticements the prince of genii had been able to employ, she had remained invisible. The stone that rendered one invisible could only be removed by the person who was making use of it, and Rosalie was afraid that the prince of genii would steal it from her if she once removed it.

The invisible prince and the princess climbed the mountain together, but Rosalie, not having the virtue of passing through water like the invisible prince, could not traverse the gilded spring.

They were on the edge of a stream, holding one another in an incessant embrace, bathing in their tears. They were unable either to see one another or to speak to one another; tears and sighs were the only language the unfortunate couple had. The fury of the prince of genii made them tremble. He had excited a horrible storm in the atmosphere when, on returning from hunting, he had found Rosalie gone. The unleashed winds marked by their whistling the fury and wrath of their sovereign.

The storm had already lasted for several days when a frightful heat suddenly spread through the air. In the midst of lightning flashes and the frightful sound of thunder, long whirlwinds of flame fell from the sky, setting the forests and verdure ablaze as they fell. Even the stream on the edge of which the princess and her lover were sitting dried out instantly.

The invisible prince, ever attentive, did not doubt that the Gilded Spring had experienced the same fate. He opened the door and found the water dried up. He immediately took hold of Rosalie and took her through.

They traveled for a long time before arriving at the Golden Isle but they finally reached it. They found the inhabitants of the island desolate at the abduction of Princess Argentine.

On his return from the Gilded Spring, the gnome prince, overwhelmed by jealousy, had had her brought to his palace in order to get her away from his brother, Prince Flame. That prince had entered into such a furious chagrin that he had resolved to avenge himself by setting the world ablaze, and it was his wrath that had saved Rosalie and the Prince of the Golden Isle.

The invisible prince moved to compassion by his sister's misfortunes, revealed himself to Prince Flame, who no longer emerged from the gardens of the King of the Golden Isle, the place where he had so often seen Argentine. He showed him the tree by means of which one descended to the palace of the gnome prince.

Prince Flame went into it and brought Argentine out. In order to recompense the amity of the invisible prince he took him with Rosalie and Argentine to an empire where they no longer had to fear the power of either the prince of the genii or the gnome prince.

Charmed by the beautiful knot that binds them,
And more amorous at every moment,
Those lovers spend their life

In pleasure and games;
But their fate has nothing I envy.
And I find myself happier
When I see Silvie for a moment.

Prince Flame married Argentine, who was named Princess Flame. She it is who presides over that noble and brilliant element.

A few days after their marriage, the prince took his new wife to the end of a gallery that terminated his palace, and there, after having opened a subterrain that was only illuminated by a single lamp, the somber glimmer of which scarcely allowed objects to be distinguished, Princess Flame would have trembled if she had not been with her lover, but does one fear anything when one is with the person one loves?

Then the prince, clasping her tightly in his arms, kicked with his foot, and a trapdoor immediately opened. The princess felt herself dragged down as if into the depths of an abyss.

Finally, the shaft ended in the middle of a cabinet brilliant with light. At each end was a crystal urn filled with flames.

The prince then broke the silence that he had maintained his far. "You see in these two urns, lovely princess," he said, "the most precious things I have in all my empire. Destiny reposes on me the care of guarding them, but it is you that I want to share these benefits and my power. Choose one of these two keys. One opens the urn in which the fire of life is enclosed. A single spark is capable of reanimating the blood of the iciest old man, and if its flame escaped, all humans would be immortal. In the other are the fires of amour."

"Oh, can I hesitate over the choice?" cried Princess Flame. "What affair would I have with life if I had lost your heart? The present that you make me today assures me of an eternal fidelity. I no longer need fear your indifference, since I shall be mistress of the flames of amour."

That blind god ceased from that moment on to dispose of them at his whim, and it is Princess Flame who, in accordance with her will, dispenses her fires to mortals, only opening the urn when it pleases her.

But given the secret fire of which my soul
Feels the vivid ardor night and day,
It is necessary that all the flame
Of the urn has passed into my heart.

Attributed to Catherine de Lintot: *Tendrebrun and Constance*

There was once a fay named Vicious. She made her abode on one of the highest mountains in the realm of Pentasila. The number of years had augmented both her ugliness and her malevolence. She was rarely seen to emerge from her castle; what was the point of tiring herself out unnecessarily? Her children, the Vices, served her at the whim of her desire, traveling the world and causing infinite disorder there. Kings and noblemen had been warned always to be on their guard against such monsters, but they had the secret of slipping into the most carefully sealed palaces. All doors opened at the mere sight of Flattery, their beloved sister. The great, especially, and the rich, allowed themselves to be drawn by her sweet insinuations, and Vicious's children obeyed her everywhere.

King Judicious was the only one who closed entry to his estates to them. It would be difficult to express how much he hated that numerous family. In spite of all his precautions, however, one of the little Lies was clever enough to penetrate all the way to his bedroom without being recognized, and lived there for a long time.

One day, the king, who was in front of his mirror having his hair combed, took it into his head to ask his courtiers how old he appeared to be. They all replied with sincerity that he looked to be about forty-five—which was, in fact, the number of his years—but the Lie assured His Majesty that he had the appearance and freshness of a man of forty.

At that speech the king looked at him attentively, recognized him as one of the Vices, and ordered that he be whipped and immediately expelled from the kingdom. Several noblemen spoke in his favor, but were unable to obtain clemency for him.

"The child you can see," the prince said to them, "is a monster to be feared a thousand times more than the cruelest beasts in my forests. He pleases and amuses you because he is small, but he will grow, and if I tolerate him he will soon introduce all his brothers here in spite of me. Let him leave promptly and let him be chastised as he merits."

Judicious was obeyed and the Lie, after having been punished, retired weeping to the home of the fay, to whom he related what had just happened to him. Vicious frowned, took him in her arms, kissed him twice on the forehead and, in order to console him, assured him that in future, he would be protected from such disgraces.

She kept her word, but she swore by the green and blue bonnet that she wore that she would avenge herself on the king and all his race before the end of the day. As she spoke those words she uttered five frightful shrieks, leapt three times over an ardent ember that she kept in a brazier full of fire, and spat on a spider-web that she found in a corner of her room; after which she touched the cobweb with her wand, which became a winged toad of monstrous size, wearing a green saddle embroidered with glow-worms

The fay caressed the toad, gave it a cake made with milk, sugar, almonds and caterpillars, and, having told it to wait, went to sit down at her dressing-table; for she was extremely coquettish, although she was more than two thousand years old, and never went out without a great deal of rouge and numerous beauty-spots. She put on a large quantity that day, and coiffed herself and dressed herself like a young woman. All that adornment certainly rendered her even more frightful than she was. Content nevertheless with her appearance, she imagined, like several old women of my acquaintance, that the attire in question prevented anyone from perceiving her wrinkles and her emaciation.

Finally, Vicious mounted her toad, traversed the air with an incredible velocity, and in very little time rendered to the abode of King Judicious.

That prince was in an arbor in his garden, sitting on a little throne of leaves that young Constance, his unique daughter, had taken care to ornament with different flowers. She was at his feet, leaning over the edge of a stream, which formed a sheet of water. She told the king several stories that she had made up in order to amuse him. Her narration was interrupted by a frightful clap of thunder, which almost made her faint, and which tipped Judicious off his throne. Overwhelmed by dolor at the sight of that fall, she tried, in spite of her lack of strength, to run to pick him up, but a frightful darkness spread instantly and prevented her from helping him.

Rendered desperate by that new prodigy, Constance went in all directions, searching in the obscurity and calling out in a voice as sad as it was faint to the person to whom she owed the light of day. Several bursts of laughter that she heard stopped her tremulous steps; then the darkness dissipated and she perceived nearby an old woman, whom she took for one of the three Furies, so horrible did she appear.

It was the malevolent Vicious, who, charmed by all the woes that she was commencing to make felt, was laughing with all her might. She ceased laughing, however, seeing that the young princess wanted to go away, in order no longer to see her, and to try again to find the king. She seized her by the arm and, touching her with her wand, said: "Don't look for your father; he's in my power. Only prepare yourself to suffer the torments that my hatred is getting ready."

With those words she took a pinch of red powder, which she threw into the air, pronouncing a few words, and immediately, a rain of fire fell that consumed the entire realm of the unfortunate Judicious.

Turning then to Constance, she said: "You've just seen the fashion in which I've avenged myself on everything that belongs to you. Now I'm going to make you experience how I treat people who dare to displease me. Then she made her toad hop over the princess's head. The animal let three drops of a black liquid fall, which immediately metamorphosed her into a crayfish. In that form she conserved the memory of what she had been, but she lost the use of speech. Then the fay tapped the ground with her wand and caused a frightful abyss to appear, into which she precipitated the unfortunate Constance.

The princess fell for a week, with great rapidity, into that frightful gulf, of which she could not find the bottom. At the end of that time, she realized that she was in a pool, which appeared to her to be immense. She sensed that she was swimming there and living as if she had spent her entire life in that element. However, she did not eat anything, for fear of being caught by a fisherman's hook. The smallest fish that she saw or heard made her tremble, because she imagined that it was some animal come to devour her.

One evening, when the aquatic troop was sleeping tranquilly, Constance became bolder, and resolved, by courtesy of a beautiful moonlight, to go for a swim on the surface of the water. The first thing that was offered to her sight was a young man of about twenty-two lying under foliage that the brilliant night star illuminated perfectly. He appeared to be overwhelmed by sadness and ennui, and seemed quite indifferent to the officious cares that Zephyr was rendering him by blowing softly in the air and displacing slightly from his cheeks long thick curls of hair that were falling negligently over his shoulders. His reverie no longer permitted him to take any pleasure in the soft concerts of nightingales that were striving close by to make the echoes repeat their melodious sounds. In sum, nothing seemed capable of distracting his thoughts.

The princess stopped in order to consider him, and found a thousand charms in him that obliged her to sigh several times, and made her sense more than she had done before the misfortune of being a crayfish. She swam nearby for a long time without him noticing her, but in the end, she made so many jumps in the water that he looked in her direction. She perceived that, but for the moment, the dread she had of being caught and put on the fire did not present her approaching him, in such a fashion that he could easily have caught her with his hand.

The young man was the son of a great Tartar Emperor. Vicious had abducted him from his father's court. For two years the fay had kept him imprisoned in that frightful abode. How hard she had tried to make him love her! All her artifices were futile; the hatred that the prince had conceived for her was invincible; he could not look at her without horror. Vicious soon discerned his sentiments; that might have put an end to his life; she would have sacrificed him to her rage and her chagrin if the violence of her passion had not calmed a fraction of the fury by which she was agitated.

The prince was named Tendrebrun. He was tall and well built, and all his features were agreeable; he had an air of majesty and the politeness of the noblest society attracted all hearts to him. In sum, he had been born with a great penchant for amour, and when he wanted to please, he pleased.

The indolent life that he led in the fay's abode bored him infinitely; he was retained there by an enchantment that all his courage was unable to overcome;

he had the liberty to stroll in the gardens of the palace, but he usually only made use of it when night had deployed its wings, because he dreaded encountering Vicious or someone from her retinue. The edge of the pool where Constance was confined was the place he almost always chose to repose and to think about means he might employ to get out of his prison.

He had already been savoring the agreeable coolness of the night for some time when he saw the crayfish, which, as I have said, was looking at him very attentively. He thought at first that it was dead, but, after picking up a little twig, he touched it, and knew that it was not. Astonished by the fact that it did not appear to want to escape, and that its eyes were attached to him in a particular fashion, he considered it attentively. Then, picking it up, he heard it sigh; after that, he had no doubt that it was some unfortunate person whose metamorphosis was the work of Vicious. He voiced that idea, and noticed that it made all the signs that a crayfish can employ to make him understand that he was not mistaken. He therefore carried it rapidly to his apartment, put it in a golden bowl full of water, which he found in his cabinet, and threw himself on his bed.

Curiosity soon came to trouble the mildness of the repose that he had begun to enjoy, however. The memory of his prisoner snatched him from the arms of sleep; he ran to the cabinet, visited his crayfish, and gave it a piece of biscuit. Having perceived that it ate it with pleasure, he felt sorry for it again and promised to keep it company as often as he could.

Sometimes, he looked at it and thought he remarked something in its eyes so tender and so touching that he could not help uttering imprecations against the person who had reduced it to that state.

One day, when he assured her that no one was interested in her misfortunes as much as he was, she emerged from the water, took a pen and a sheet of paper that he had left on the table, and, making use of her paw, wrote her name and the causes of her metamorphosis. She thanked Tendrebrun for the care he had taken of her and implored him not to abandon her, and to be careful that the fay did not discover her.

The prince, charmed by what she had just done, swore that he would rather lose his life than suffer that the slightest harm be done to her; in order to reassure her, he told her that Vicious ought to be away from her palace for a month.

From that day on he was more assiduous toward her; he read her several amusing stories in order to relieve her boredom, and he anticipated her in everything that might give her pleasure. Constance listened to him with an infinite satisfaction, and although amour made further progress in her heart every day, she refrained nevertheless from letting him know the extent to which she was smitten with his charms. Such a confession appeared to her to be shameful, and she did not hope that Tendrebrun would ever fall in love with a crayfish. Those thoughts caused her so much pain that she made the resolution one evening to allow herself to die of starvation.

She therefore stopped eating. The prince perceived that, and asked her the reason, but she refused to tell him, which gave him a great deal of chagrin. He imagined that perhaps she did not like what he gave her, and that she would rather eat fish. With a view to making sure, he took a line and went straight to the pool.

A small fish was caught on his hook; he took it with al diligence to his dear crayfish and threw it into the bowl, imploring her to eat it; but the fish was no sooner there than it agitated the water and troubled it in such a fashion that the prince could no longer see anything.

A moment later the water calmed down and became clear. Tendrebrun saw his crayfish again, but instead of the small fish he saw a little old man, whose cheerful and agreeable expression reassured those his sudden appearance might have frightened.

"Have no fear, Prince," he said to the son of the Tartar Emperor. "My name is Beneficent; the fay who is retaining you was irritated against me because I had removed a young princess that she had taken to the court of a king, one of my neighbors, in order to give her in marriage to a monster, one of his friends. She changed me into a small fish, because her power is far greater than mine, and told me as she threw me into the pool where you caught me that I would remain there until someone fished me out. I've been there for three hundred years. I owe you my liberty and I want to render you happy."

As he was speaking he took a little golden box from his pocket, and a flame-colored bird emerged from the box.

"This bird," he said to the prince, "will take you in a short time to wherever you wish, provided that you hold on to the tip of its wing without ever letting go. That's not all I can do for you. This crayfish is a charming princess in whom you have inspired a great deal of tenderness. I want to return her original form; you can take her with you by letting her hold on to the other wing of the bird."

Having said that, the old man took the crayfish and cut off its head, to the great astonishment of the prince, who was preparing to make him the sharpest reproaches, but he was prevented from doing so by a loud noise that he heard.

It was Vicious, who was arriving home sooner than she was expected. The fay remarked the disturbance of the prince and the bird that he was already holding in his hands. She quivered with rage on seeing that the animal would have stolen her lover a moment later. She snatched it from his hands furiously, therefore, and crushed it, searching in all directions to see whether the person who had made him a present of it might be; but he had disappeared, and her search was futile.

Tendrebrun, in despair, said to the fay everything he could imagine of the most insulting, but she only heard a part of his reproaches, because she went out, in order to go and augment the prince's enchantment.

The latter was no sooner alone than he ran to the unfortunate crayfish, whose head the old man had cut off. Scarcely had he touched it, however, than the chamber appeared to be ablaze and he found himself in the midst of flames. Immediately thinking of saving himself, he left the crayfish in order to look for the window or the door. The fire dissipated as he was about to go out, and he perceived that it had not done him any harm. Seeing then that he had been alarmed unnecessarily, he searched for the crayfish, in the hope that some new prodigy might have brought it back to life.

After a futile search, he had no doubt that it had been consumed by the flames, a misfortune for which he blamed the fay. He felt a dolor so sharp in consequence that, scarcely able to sustain himself, he collapsed on a sofa, which fortunately happened to be behind him, and lay there for a long time, his eyes looking at the floor, without making the slightest movement.

Finally, he perceived something moving at his feet, which appeared to him to be extremely bright. Having leaned over to see what it might be, he was greatly surprised to see a tiny young woman about the size of a large pin, all of whose features were charming. She was wearing a dress of white gauze, sown with tiny carbuncles, and he discovered on her head a spray of feathers garnished with precious stones.

Astonished by that new prodigy, Tendrebrun picked her up very delicately, placed her on the table in order to consider her more easily, and found her so beautiful that he gave no further thought to the crayfish he had just lost. Instantly, he felt for that admirable little person a passion so violent that he thought he was going mad, on making the reflection that he would never be able to do anything but gaze at her, since she was so small, and it was impossible for him to unite himself with her by means of bonds stronger than those of amity.

Those thoughts would have rendered him even unhappier than he had been before if he had had time to deliver himself to them, but the beauty with whom he was occupied, gazing at him with eyes capable of inflaming the least tender hearts, said to him in a voice as soft as it was charming:

"Prince the old man you saw had just returned me to my original form. A moment ago I was a happy crayfish, since, in that for, you had the generosity to take care of me and I lacked nothing. Presently, I'm an unfortunate princess, devoid of parents, devoid of support and devoid of a realm, only too content, however, to be able to assure you of the gratitude that I shall have all my life for the services that you have rendered me.

"What! It's you, beautiful Constance, that I had the good fortune of conserving here for a few days?" Tendrebrun said to her. "It's you whom I was regretting so deeply a moment ago, and who, if I can believe Beneficent, will suffer without difficulty that I adore you for as long as I live? How can it be that the old man's knife has not caused you to perish, and that you have escaped the flames that surrounded you on all sides?"

"Everything the magician did was necessary to disenchant me," she told him. "He was the one who made the fire appear that alarmed you so much. He took me at the instant you abandoned me, and, touching me with a coral wand, he returned my natural form, at a reduced stature. He also gave me this crystal egg, telling me that as soon as you have touched it with a branch of jasmine that you will find on the ground at the entrance to the garden, you and I will no longer be in the power of the fay."

Constance then gave the mysterious egg to the prince, and implored him to go in search immediately of the jasmine that would set them free. Before obeying her, however, he wanted to tell her how much he loved her, and to let her know how desperate he was in seeing her so tiny.

"I'll become taller," the young princess said, smiling. "The worthy old man assured me that within an hour, I'll be as tall as I was before the fay turned me into a crayfish. So don't worry, but don't delay, and run to search for the jasmine that alone can get us out of here."

The prince, full of pleasure and hope, was about to follow that advice when Vicious suddenly came back into the room and forbade him to go out. The princess, seeing her cruel enemy, ran to hide, but fell off the table-top, albeit without injuring herself.

Tendrebrun, wanting to pick her up without the fay perceiving it, forgot that he was holding the crystal egg and dropped it, with the consequence that it shattered into a thousand pieces. To complete the misfortune, Vicious advanced so promptly that he did not have time to put Constance in his pocket, and the poor princess found herself directly underneath the dress of her mortal enemy.

The prince trembled, seeing that the fay might crush her by making the slightest movement, but fortunately, she remained in the same place. In one of her hands she held a gilded vellum book, and in the other an ebony wand, with which she tapped him on the shoulder.

"Don't think of escaping me, ingrate," she said. "I've just rendered the charms that retain you close to me so powerful that all the powers of Hell couldn't break them. Resolve, therefore, to see me incessantly by your side to torment you if you don't accept immediately the heart and the hand that I still want to offer you; on the contrary, imagine all that might make the happiness of a mortal, and be assured of enjoying it is you respond to my desires. Speak quickly, and remember that your response will decide the good or ill fortune of your days. I'll give you a quarter of an hour to make up your mind."

The prince, to whom the discourse and threats of the fay caused scant anxiety, was only occupied with what he could see. His eyes were attached to her dress, because he perceived that it was stirring, and had no doubt that it was the unfortunate Constance who was visibly growing. The excess of his dolor was unimaginable when he thought that his lovely princess was soon about to appear before the fay, and would then be exposed to new punishments. How he repented amusing himself talking about the amour that she caused him; he ought instead to have run after the jasmine branch that was so necessary to them—but regrets were futile; the moment when he was about to lose the princess had arrived.

She was growing so prodigiously and so rapidly that Vicious finally sensed her, and her head suddenly emerged from the split in her skirt.

"Aha!" she said, extremely surprised. "What does this mean? How, little creature, have you dared to come so close to me? Does the fellow who gave you back your original form think that I'm not sufficiently powerful to take it away from you again, and that you can show yourself to my eyes with impunity? I'll prove the contrary to him."

"Stop, cruel woman!" said the prince, hastily. "Don't maltreat a princess who has experienced your fury excessively."

"And what interest do you have in her?" she replied, in a tone that made Constance feel faint and the prince go pale. "How do you know her and what renders you so sensible to her?"

"Only the pity that I have for the unfortunate," said Tendrebrun, who dared not confess the truth.

But the fay turned her head, and, showing her long black teeth as she muttered a few words, opened her book, and discovered everything that had happened between the two lovers.

That knowledge put her into such great wrath that it made the earth tremble. Her first impulse was to kill them, but, changing her resolution, she uttered a screech similar to that of an owl, and spun for a quarter of an hour without stopping, holding the prince by the hair without him being able to make use of his strength to extract himself from her frightful hands. Then a frightful griffin appeared and an enormous bat, which asked her what her orders were. She showed them the prince and the princess.

"Take them," she said. "Go away, and do your duty."

She was obeyed, and both of them took directly opposite routes with their prey.

The griffin, charged with the prince, traversed a number of countries, and after having traveled through the air for three hours descended at nightfall in the middle of a wood, where Tendrebrun imagined that he was about to be devoured. The animal having placed him on the ground gently, however, flew away without touching him.

The obscurity was so great that the prince did not know whether he ought to go forwards, backwards, or stay where he was. After having remained irresolute for a few moments, however, he made the decision to walk, groping, awaiting all the catastrophic events that might happen to him.

He had only taken a few paces when he perceived a light, which seemed very distant as yet. He walked for more than a quarter of an hour in order to reach it. Finally, he found himself next to a castle whose windows were illuminated.

He examined the building, but he was extremely surprised when he realized that it was that of the emperor, his father. Suspecting that it was a dream, he advanced as far as the door of the guard-room with an agitation that did not leave him the liberty of speech. The first people who saw him uttered cries of joy and ran to his father's apartment to tell him the good news.

That prince, curbed by the weight of years, was lying on several piles of cushions, of golden cloth embroidered with pearls, and lending a very mediocre attention to a concert of voices and instruments that some of his women were performing. When he saw the men enter who had come to tell him that Tendrebrun was in the palace, and perceived that dear son in person, whose loss had been so sensible to him, the joy that the two individuals felt is imaginable, if one knows the tender emotions of nature. I shall not describe them, therefore; I shall simply say that no prince had ever found his father and his subjects again with more pleasure than Tendrebrun felt.

The emperor was very old; he obliged his son to take the reins of the empire, finding him more capable of governing than he was himself.

The prince took charge, reluctantly, of the care of a state that had been rather neglected for some years. The splendor of his crown and the pleasure of reigning over a numerous people did not prevent him from thinking about Constance. He sighed continually and regretted the moments that he had spent with her.

How lovable she is, he sometimes said to himself. *What tenderness, grace, delicacy and intelligence are assembled in that divine person! What would I not sacrifice to find her again? Alas, perhaps the Fate has already cut the thread of her beautiful days; or, if she is still alive, it is doubtless only to experience the further furies of the malevolent Vicious. Are you thinking about me in your misfortunes, charming princess? Do you remember that Tendrebrun will never cease to love you, and that he will put everything to work to deliver you from your troubles? Yes, you must be convinced of that, you must believe that my dolor will soon put me in the grave if I do not see you again promptly.*

It was thus that he conversed with himself in thinking about young Constance; he imagined the methods of Vicious very often; he could not understand how he had escaped from her hands, or why she had sent him back to his estates without doing him any harm, because he had experienced until then such violent marks of her amour and her anger. He was far away from her, but he was still fearful of her fury and malevolence.

That dread, combined with his passion, troubled the tranquility of his days infinitely. Unable to live overwhelmed by so many anxieties, he resolved to go to the island of Tintarinos in order to ask Beneficent for news of Constance and obtain from him some talisman that might preserve him from the fay's enchantments.

Having confided his design to the emperor he had a ship equipped, charged it with rich presents, and left the court accompanied by a dozen of the youngest and bravest lords of the empire.

The god of winds, impelling his vessel rapidly, soon allowed him to perceive the tip of the island he was seeking, but when he was only a short distance away, the sky darkened and was covered with thick cloud. The sea changed color and the waves swelled, colliding with one another with such a great impetuosity that the prince's ship could not continue its route and ran aground on a sandbank, on which they would all have perished if the sea had not calmed down some time thereafter.

The air then became as tranquil as the waves. The clouds dissipated, and permitted the prince to run his eyes over the vast empire of Neptune, by which he was surrounded, to see if he could discover any ship.

He had not been looking for long when he saw something shiny appear, albeit a long distance away, which came towards him at a prodigious speed. When the object was within visual range, he saw that it was a mother-of-pearl boat, in the middle of which was a rose-bush that served it as a mast; the leaves were large enough to serve as sails. Eight tritons and eight sirens, who were conducting it, brought it very close to Tendrebrun.

Then one of the sirens spoke to him, saying; "Prince, we have been sent here by young Bounty, our mistress, to tell you that she is waiting for you on her island. She is the daughter of Beneficent, and is only occupied, following his example, with the care of rendering mortals happy. The art of faerie, which she possesses, has informed her of your misfortunes. Touched by the troubles you are suffering, she wants to deliver you from them by giving you the talisman of which you were going in search on the island of Tintarinos. Here is a bracelet that we have brought on her behalf; never take it off; it will return to you the lovely princess from whom you are separated. It is to our mistress that you owe your liberty and your return to Tartary, in spite of the efforts of the wicked Vicious. Hasten, then, to go and thank her for all that she has done for you.

The prince, delighted to have found such a fortunate adventure at the time he least expected it, climbed into the boat without delay, with all his retinue. After having sailed for six minutes, at the most, he landed on the island where he was awaited.

It was only planted with rose-bushes and jasmines, which formed long covered pathways; the flowers of those trees, mingled with the green leaves, produced a charming effect. Verdant grass, dotted with little pink and white flowers, covered the ground. In fact, any other color than the ones I have just mentioned, was banished from the island. That is why the prince had no sooner disembarked from the boat than he saw the blue and gold coat that he was wearing change into another, of pink gauze embroidered with emeralds and diamonds.

A sheep with a fleece of silver thread and horns of diamond presented itself to serve as his guide. It conducted him, making several bounds over the grass, to an arbor where Tendrebrun saw a hundred young women of an admirable beauty. They were surrounding a young woman of about sixteen years, who surpassed them in grace and beauty. She was lying negligently on a bed of jasmine on the edge of a crystal basin where several swans were swimming. Palisades and a vault of flowers prevented the god of the day from spreading too much light in that agreeable enclosure.

The sheep went to lie down next to its beautiful mistress, and the prince, realizing that she was the daughter of the old man of Tintarinos of whom mention had been made, expressed his gratitude to her with as much respect as intelligence. The young fay received it with a mildness and grace that he had only found previously in Constance.

She asked him whether he had the bracelet, and recommended that he never remove it from his arm, because as long as it was there, the fay Vicious and others would not be able to do him any harm. Then, presenting her hand to him, she got up and led him into a labyrinth ornamented with very well-wrought ivory statues. After having traversed the labyrinth, she led him over a terrace that overlooked the sea shore to a crystal castle, which the prince admired for a long time. She told him that he could rest there for a few days, and promised to transport him thereafter to his dear Constance.

The fay warned the prince not to go out of the apartment that he chose in the palace, during the time he spent on the island, once midnight had chimed. "If you go out," she said, "and if you even open the windows between then and four o'clock in the morning, misfortunes will overtake you from which I will not be able to protect you. In the meantime, I am obliged to quit my palace and go to visit my father."

Tendrebrun assured her that he would follow her advice exactly, and consented without difficulty to remain in that beautiful abode for as long as the sun took to travel the celestial vault three times.

The first day was spent savoring all the pleasures that a powerful fay can procure, and talking about the daughter of Judicious. He was astonished by the attention that Bounty had in talking to him about the person he loved, although it is true that it was always him who commenced the conversation. However, making the reflection that it was lacking in prudence, and even politeness to repeat the same thing so often and continually to exaggerate the amour one has for someone else before a person as charming as the fay, he gradually corrected himself, and his discourse was soon no longer filled with the impatience he had to see his princess again. On the contrary, he often said that he wished that he might be away from her for longer than he had said, in order to discover the effect that absence would produce in his heart. Then, remaining silent for a few moments, he kept his eyes attached to Bounty, sighed, no longer able to sustain the tenderness of her gaze without experiencing a disturbance that was not usual for him.

He eventually perceived that Constance no longer reigned over his soul, and that the beautiful fay occupied it uniquely. He no longer thought about anything, therefore, except making his passion known to her. At first he allowed his eyes and his sighs to speak, and he became sad and pensive. The fay perceived that, and proposed to him that he leave, in order to rediscover the person who was causing his languor; but Tendrebrun threw himself at her feet, took one of her hands, which he kissed with transport, and implored her not to send him away from her, to suffer that he adore her and that he might wear her chains all his life.

Bounty seemed astonished by that declaration, and blushed extremely, but assured him nevertheless that she would not refuse his request, because his inclination responded to the desire she had to content him. But she said at the same time that he could only remain with her on condition of marrying her the same day, because she had sworn an inviolable oath not to permit any man to love her who was not her husband, or to allow him to stay on her island for longer than a brief interval.

That condition pleased the prince extremely; he assured her that he accepted it with all the joy imaginable, and pressed her not to defer his happiness. As she quit him she promised to go and augment her charms, if possible, by donning a costume even more elegant.

She came back after an absence of an hour, and, everything having been prepared for the ceremony, their marriage was concluded. Nymphs came to rejoice with them, by means of their dances and songs, for such a beautiful union. They all had garlands of flowers, with which they enchained the two spouses. Several of them also married young lords in the prince's retinue. Fauns and satyrs made the woods resound with their instruments and celebrated the happy day with games and fêtes that they invented. In sum, everything on the island that breathed was animated by pleasures, except for the unfortunate Constance, whom hazard had caused to encounter it.

She was still in the power of the bat; that monster, after having taken her away from Vicious's palace, had traveled over the four continents of the world with her, pretending to be unable to find the realm to which the malevolent fay had ordered it to take her. They had been traveling for a month when they passed over the Isle of Roses. The bat stopped then, and asked Constance whether she wanted to rest for a few moments. The princess, fatigued by the journey, consented to that gladly, and the night-bird descended slowly to deposit her behind an arbor where Tendrebrun and Bounty were swearing an eternal amour.

What a spectacle for a lover! What despair did she not feel on seeing the infidel prince make a thousand caresses and say a hundred things each more passionate than the last to a young person that she found only too lovable. She thought twenty times of standing up in order to go and heap Tendrebrun with the reproaches that he merited, but, making the reflection that she would only cause, at the most, a little shame and that she would only receive from him a few excuses full of indifference, which would be a further triumph for her rival, she preferred to constrain herself and enclose within herself the mortal dolor that the change caused her.

She contented herself, therefore, with letting a torrent of tears flow from her beautiful eyes, and begged the bat to continue its voyage and to remove her promptly from a place so fatal to her repose. The latter, charged with the will of Vicious, was as malevolent as its mistress. Seeing the extreme affliction of the princess, therefore, it wanted to augment it, by telling her about the facility with which the Tartar prince had forgotten her and the pleasures that he had savored since he had been with his new bride.

Constance made no reply, silently charging his perjury with ingratitude and treason. *How perfidious he is*, she said to herself, *but in spite of that, how lovable he is! How much amour I have just seen in his eyes! Gods, can it be that he has ceased so promptly to love me and that I am deprived forever of his tenderness? Amour, it is you who is presently causing my greatest misfortune: you are taking away all that I love, to give it to another. At least render me my indifference. But alas, I sense that it is no longer in my power to recover it, or to extinguish the fire that I feel in my soul, and that fate is condemning me to eternal dolor.*

That was what the princess was thinking. When the bat had consented to depart, it stopped after a few hours of flight and told her that she had arrived in the realm of Indolent, to whom Vicious had sent her in order to marry him that same day, and it was taking her down to the palace that the king had prepared for her—which it did, immediately. It put her in the hands of several women destined to serve her and flew away, after having gone to Indolent's apartment in order to give him the fay's compliments and inform him of the arrival of Constance.

That prince received the news with joy, for he had a great desire to get married. He was tall, young and well made, but he had no head, and, in consequence, he could do nothing for himself. The Vices, to whom he had given free entry to his kingdom, reigned there with more authority than him.

All those monsters had taken such firm possession of all his subjects that the unfortunate king dared not do anything without their advice. Debauchery and ignorance extended their empire over the men of war and the persons of the highest status; injustice and interest made the magistrates act; hypocrisy and avarice were followed secretly by the dervishes and other ministers of altars, and gallantry by the female sex.

In sum, all of Vicious's children had their courtiers, and commanded, independently of all that, the men and women of the realm, without fear that Indolent would have anything to say about it. So, the complaisance the king had for the Vices procured him the amity of their mother. That fay had made him a present, a few days before the arrival of the daughter of Judicious of a beautiful polished head, which replaced—in appearance, at least—the one that nature had refused him. That head was attached to the shoulders, and, by means of a few springs, made all the necessary movements. At first he had a little difficulty in wearing it, but he became accustomed to it.

It might be difficult to imagine how he could see, hear and talk; I shall explain. He had a mouth in a dimple in his neck, an ear in the left hand and an eye in the right. I agree that the arrangement had its inconveniences, but in sum, a fay who had wanted to avenge herself on his mother, the queen, had placed them in that fashion when she became pregnant with the unfortunate prince. As for a nose, she had not given him one because it appeared to her that it was unnecessary, so he could not smell anything.

The prince, formed in that fashion, had no doubt that Constance would consent joyfully to marry him. He therefore went to visit her, and proclaimed to her that the day would not pass without her being his wife.

She was in a beautiful apartment; gold and silver gleamed there in abundance, but her eyes, although full of tears, spread an even greater splendor there than all the riches put together.

Indolent approached her, and, in order to see her more clearly, put his right hand near her face. He was delighted to find her so beautiful, and paid her a compliment on her beauty that he had spent two days learning by heart, and which had been found for him in a new book. Then he gave her his hand in order to conduct her to the temple, where she would, he said, receive her crown and be united with him. But the princess pushed him away gently, assuring him that she would never accept the honor that he wanted to do her and begging him to permit her, on the contrary, to retire to one of the temples in the city where a number of young women were enclosed, consecrated to the service of the gods.

That response astonished the king so much that he did not say anything for several moments. Recovering slightly from his surprise, he tried by means of his pleas to make her resolve to what he desired, but, everything he said being futile, he got carried away in such a fashion that his head, which was not attached very well, fell to the floor and revealed to the princess a species of monster that appeared to her to be frightful.

The accident augmented the prince's anger; he said a thousand offensive things, and warned her that he would only give her a week to decide to marry him, after which he promised to put her to death if she were obstinate in refusing him. Going out then, he left the unhappy Constance unintimidated by his threats, still occupied with the infidelity of the ingrate she loved.

The week passed without her reflecting even once on the fate that was in preparation for her. No sooner had the time expired than Indolent came to visit her, in order to discover whether her sentiments were in conformity with those he had; but, having found them opposed to his own, he ordered immediately that she be taken to the Black Forest.

That forest was thus named because it was never illuminated by the sun's bright rays. Thick fogs reigned there from the commencement of the year to the end. A continuous cold wind made itself felt there violently, and blew with such force that it shook the largest trees in the forest, which were only charged with yellow and faded leaves. The cries of barn owls and long-eared owls and the howls of ferocious beasts with which it was filled were heard in all directions. A wall a hundred feet high surrounded it on all sides and prevented anyone from getting out of it. In sum, one could not find a more frightful abode.

However, the exceedingly unfortunate Constance was imprisoned there, and found herself less unhappy there than in the palace she had just quit, because the most somber and deserted places seemed more appropriate to hide her dolor.

As soon as she found herself in the sad place, she expected to become the prey imminently of some of the wolves or wild boars that she saw running all around her; and although she had no appetite for life, she felt gripped by horror and dread in thinking that she was about to be devoured. Directing her tremulous footsteps toward the places that seemed to her to be the least accessible, therefore, she went to hide there, in order to avoid encountering cruel animals, and to wait there for a milder death that dolor and weakness could not fail to procure for her.

Incessantly agitated by those various thoughts, she saw a lion of enormous size coming toward her, the fierce and proud appearance of which left her no hope. At that sight, she started running at top speed; but the furious animal, more skillful in running than the young princess, caught up with her promptly and, seizing her by the dress, caused her to fall unconscious on a pile of dry leaves that the wind had assembled.

The lion in question, less cruel than Constance had imagined, did not do her any harm. On the contrary, touched by the state she was in, it promptly went to fetch water in its mouth and spat it out over the face of the dying princess.

That aid brought her round. She opened her beautiful eyes, and seemed astonished to see the light again and to perceive nearby the lion she had feared so much, which was licking her hands and washing them with its tears.

"What a prodigy!" she exclaimed. "I've found humanity among ferocious animals, and I only encountered cruelty among humans. Why has this lion not taken away my life? My misfortunes would be over and I would not have the chagrin of thinking at this moment that the ingrate I adore has forgotten the oath that he swore to love me eternally, and is enchanted by the pleasures that he is savoring with my rival."

As she finished speaking she allowed a great quantity of tears to flow, and would doubtless have made a few resolutions fatal to her days if the lion had not moderated her dolor somewhat by means of its caresses and attentions.

Sensible to what it was doing in order to calm her, she stroked it, in spite of her chagrin, and even thanked it, as if she were certain that it had understood her. Two frightful bears that she saw passing by terminated her discourse and caused her to forget the desire that she had had to die. She therefore got up in order to run away again, without thinking that she had a defender beside her stronger than those animals. Seeing her design, however, the lion, which was still lying beside her, tugged her gently by the dress and made her sit on its back.

Then, immediately rising to its feet with a surprising lightness, it ran through the forest.

The princess, feeling herself carried away, was uncertain of her fate, and did not know whether she ought to feel dread or hope. She was finally informed. The lion took her to the foot of a rock, which the sea beat with its waves. It was the only place that was not surrounded by walls, because it was inaccessible. The lion placed her on the sand gently, and then went to look for oysters and other shellfish, which it presented to her very politely. She ate some, and drank, with pleasure, water from a spring that was not far away, which the lion had collected in a large shell.

After that light meal, which would not have displeased the princess in a less unfortunate situation, the lion pushed her into a cavity in the rock, and, having followed her in, it closed the entrance with a large stone.

In spite of the marks of amity that Constance had received from the animal, she trembled when she found herself alone with it in that obscure lair. It was vast and only received daylight through a few cracks that time had made. Several piles of dry leaves seemed to have been piled up to serve as a seat and a bed; in fact, they had been gathered there with that design. The cavern was her defender's, who had only taken her there to defend her during the night from the animals of which the forest was full.

Seeing that the daylight had almost faded away, and observing that the lion was not seeking to do her any harm, the princess understood its intention and sat down on the leaves—not in order to go to sleep; her mind was too agitated, but in order to recover somewhat from the fatigues she had endured. The sad master of the place lay down beside her and spent a part of the night sighing, kissing her hands from time to time

The princess, who could not sleep, reflected on all everything that had just happened to her, unable to divine the reason for the animal's sadness, or why it was treating her with so much kindness. She spent two thirds of the night in those reflections.

Finally, she fell asleep, and only woke up at daybreak. She was surprised not to see the lion beside her and got up to see whether it was in some other place in the rock, but her efforts were futile; she could not find it. Anxious that it might have quit her, she found the stone disturbed and went outside to see whether it was on the sea shore. She went there, but without discovering anything.

Alarmed to have lost her companion, she was about to go back into the cavern to hide from the animals she feared when she perceived a man among the trees, who was defending himself with a sturdy staff against a monstrous boar. That spectacle frightened her, but did not cause her to run away. She had no doubt that it was some unfortunate condemned, like her, to end his days in the forest. She hoped that he would be victorious over the boar and that he might be able to get her out of this horrible place. She therefore waited, some distance away, for the battle to end. It did not take long; the boar received several blows on the head, delivered so vigorously, that it soon fell dead. That was not, however, without having wounded its valiant enemy, who immediately leaned against a tree, only able to sustain himself with difficulty because of the quantity of blood he had lost.

Seeing him in that state, Constance thought she could not refuse him help without lacking humanity. She therefore ran to him with the design of helping him to staunch the blood.

Gods! What became of her, as she approached, when she recognized Tendrebrun? He was pale, sad and dying, and no less charming for that. What did she not experience on seeing the danger he was in? She forgot all her anger and asked him, in a tremulous voice, with tears in her eyes, whether he still recognized her, and whether he wanted to accept the feeble service that she could offer him.

The prince stared at her, and, without replying a single word, drew away so promptly, in spite of his lack of strength, that he was soon lost to sight. Her despair, after that astonishing behavior, is imaginable.

"How he flees me!" she cried. "The sight of me horrifies him more than the most cruel beasts, than death itself. Unfortunate as I am, can I still resolve to live after so much scorn? No, let us run to death, since it alone can terminate my pains."

As she finished speaking she turned her steps back toward the sea, and threw herself into it without hesitation. She would have found death there if the lion, returning to its cavern, had not perceived her and immediately thrown itself in after her, in order to rescue her.

That prompt rescue was necessary; an instant later and the beautiful days would have ended. The lion prolonged them by means of its cares, so well that she recovered her senses. Carrying her into its cavern then, it laid her down on the bed of leaves, started a fire with stones that it struck together, lit a few tree branches with it that it went to fetch, and which it lay on the dry leaves, and warmed up the unfortunate princess.

She was about to reproach it for the pity that had engaged it to help her when she heard a voice, which said to her: "Find the door that is here if you want to find the end of your troubles."

That oracle rendered her strength and appeared to give great pleasure to the lion.

They both searched the extent of the rock for that door, therefore, even advancing into places so dark that they feared getting absolutely lost.

Hazard finally enabled Constance to encounter the door so much desired. She stumbled and tried to lean against the rock, and placed her hands precisely on the door, which opened instantly under the thrust she had provided.

She alerted the lion to the discovery, and climbed a stairway within it that was presented to her. It was less dark than the interior of the rock. After having climbed about ten thousand steps they arrived on a green lawn, which occupied the entire summit of the crag.

It was so prodigiously high that the tallest trees in the forest seemed no more than a foot in height.

It was only possible to reach that lawn by way of the stairway that Constance had discovered. She did not have time to examine the summit because she perceived a young woman attached to a stake by thick iron chains, who was making every effort to prevent a steel box poised on a feeble pivot at the very edge of the rock from falling into the precipice.

The lovely young woman had a tranquil, mild and modest physiognomy. Virtuous people could not have seen her without experiencing an infinite esteem and respect for her, so she inspired a good deal in the princess, who, touched by her situation, ran toward her in order to make efforts to set her free. She advanced, therefore, with that design, in company with her faithful companion, but they had scarcely reached the unfortunate woman when her chains fell and she stood up—without, however, quitting her box.

Looking at the princess then, with an air of recognition and majesty, she said: "For a long time, beautiful Constance, I have been lamenting your fate, and have desired to see you in this place. Don't be surprised; several centuries ago I read in the book of destinies that you would one day render me the power that I lost an infinite time ago. Although I appear young to you, I have seen an infinite number of centuries go by, and I am the one who enabled my voice to pass through the rock in order to advise you to seek the door through which you have just passed in coming here.

"My name is Virtue; I once reigned in the world and I was loved and adored by sovereigns and their subjects. No one envied my empire except Vicious, who, jealous of the happiness that I procured for mortals, spread all the weaknesses in the human heart and gave birth to all the Vices. She took advantage of my absence and employed the time of a voyage I was making to a country unknown to anyone but me. In the end, the Vices expelled me when I returned, and took away the splendid radiance by which I was surrounded. Since then I have been misunderstood, and generally abandoned. There was no king who wanted to lend me his support; that completed my doom, because I cannot reign over any people if I am not cherished by their princes.

"Not content with having made me lose my authority, Vicious brought me to this rock, where she chained me, in order to prevent me from troubling her new domination. Her superior strength does not, however, prevent me from quitting my chains for two days every year, during which I travel all over the world, visiting those who have not forgotten me. I have often traveled without finding a single person who still remembers my name.

"Once, however, in passing through your father's estates, I saw him and found that he had the sentiments for me that I desired. I perceived with pleasure the aversion that he had for Vicious and her children: since that time I limited my excursions to his realm and I visited him every year. In the year when you came into the world I witnessed your birth, in the form of an old woman, and I gave you all the gifts that might render you perfect.

"I consulted the destinies in order to know what would happen to you; I discovered that a great many misfortunes were reserved for you, but I read then that you would overcome them and that destiny had chosen you to restore my initial splendor—in sum, that you were to extract me from the undignified slavery that I was in. Content with that knowledge, I returned to my mountain; since that time I have continued to see you without making myself known and without showing myself.

"One day, when I was coming here to resume my chains, I saw Vicious arrive in a chariot of fire; she stopped it close to me and, showing me the box you see, she told me that it contained one of my most faithful friends, who was about to be precipitated at that moment into the depths of the sea. The malevolent fay then placed the box that she had in her chariot on the tip of the rock, and went away, convinced that it would not take long to fall. Fortunately, I've had enough strength to retain it until now. I've tried several times to open that prison, but in vain. Now that I'm free, I'm going to deliver the unfortunate friend. Only interest yourself in me, beautiful princess, and you shall soon see the effect of my power."

The lovely Virtue then pronounced a few words; the box opened, and allowed her and Constance to see King Judicious, chained by the midriff. What a surprise it was for the king to see the light again, and to rediscover a daughter whose loss he had mourned! What a joy it was for that charming daughter to see again a father who had cost her so many tears! Finally, what a pleasure it was for Virtue to make the happiness of those virtuous individuals! It is easy to imagine the contentment of all three, and one ought not to think that a long time passed before Judicious was completely liberated.

He gave Constance a hundred caresses, as well as his friend, and told them that he had been imprisoned in the box ever since he had been abducted from the gardens of his palace; that he would have died of despair and hunger if the malevolent Vicious, who wanted to prolong his suffering, had not made him drink a liquid that had preserved his life in spite of him.

Constance was so penetrated by joy that she could not speak; she contented herself with taking his hands, kissing them and bathing them with her tears.

The lion, who had been a tranquil witness thus far to what was happening, approached the king and kissed his robe respectfully. Turning then toward Virtue, it looked at her in a fashion that seemed to be asking whether he was to be the only unfortunate one.

That person, who could do anything, read his thoughts and said to him: "It is just, amiable prince, that I also compensate you for having conserved the sentiments that I inspired in you." Immediately placing her hand on his forehead, she pronounced these words in a soft and gracious voice: "Resume your natural form, never to quit it again."

Then the lion disappeared, and allowed to be seen in its stead the son of the Tartar Emperor.

After having thanked his benefactress in a few words, which marked his keen gratitude, he ran to throw himself at the feet of the princess, in order to obtain a pardon that, he said, she could not refuse him without injustice and cruelty.

Constance, seeing him so close to her and seeing him tender and charming again, felt an extraordinary emotion. Her first impulse was to tell him that she had forgotten everything, since he still loved her, but what she had seen him do with Bounty and the last mark of indifference that he had given her in the forest returned to her mind so forcefully, that she resolved not to forgive him

Turning her eyes away from him, she told him that he ought not to think about her any longer, that she never wanted to see him again, and that he had offended her too deeply for him to be able to hope to occupy in future the place that he had had for a long time in her heart.

Seeing the despair that that response caused the prince, Virtue addressed the daughter of Judicious and said to her: "Cease, beautiful Constance, to drive a lover who adores you to despair. Believe that he only loves, and has only ever loved, you. Only deign to listen to him, and you will be convinced of it."

After having denied herself that briefly, the princess consented to it, and the prince, charmed that she was permitting him to justify himself, told her how he had found himself in the palace of his father, the Emperor, after having been taken away from her, and made her a sincere confession of all the woes that he had suffered since the cruel moment when he had been distanced from her.

The time that he employed in expressing his pains and his love for the princess interrupted the thread of his narrative somewhat, and gave Virtue the time necessary to inform the king briefly about the adventures of his daughter. After that account, Tendrebrun continued, in the following fashion:

"The sojourn I spent on the Isle of Roses will no longer appear to you to be a crime, my dear Constance, when I have told you that I was forced to land there and remain there by the enchantments of Vicious, who, in the form of a young and beautiful person named Bounty, offered me her help in order to take me to you, with the sole design of attracting me to her by means of deceptive charms. She could not retain me otherwise; she therefore had me given a bracelet, which, she said, would protect me from all sorts of misfortunes as long as I had it on my arm; but it was, in fact, a powerful talisman that inspired in a short time a violent passion for the person who had composed it, and which prevented me from discovering her faults. I soon felt its effects, since I became the most passionate of men in the fay's presence. I forgot you in spite of myself, and put all my felicity into pleasing my greatest enemy. I did not imagine that anything could be found more perfect than her. I would have remained in that error for a long time but for what happened to me one night when I could not sleep.

"I heard a sound of voices in the gardens, which did not seem to me to be ordinary, and I saw such a large quantity of torches passing the windows of my apartment that, curious to know what it could be, I got up and went to my window without thinking about the prohibitions that had been imposed on me.

"I had no sooner opened it than I perceived in the air and in the pathways of the wood an infinite number of frightful monsters, some of which were carrying lanterns and the others torches, and they were all heading for the arbor where I had seen Bounty for the first time.

"That surprising spectacle caused me to make the resolution to slip close to that enclosure in order to see what would become of those frightful figures. I left my room quietly and traversed the wood by way of the darkest places. I soon repented of having followed those dense routes because, as I tried to move aside a few tree branches that covered my route, they hooked on to that fatal bracelet. It fell off, and I could not find it again in the darkness.

"That loss, which I thought considerable, afflicted me greatly, but it could not prevent me from continuing on my way. I finally arrived at the enclosure, where I was gripped by fear on seeing Vicious surrounded by that troop of monsters.

"They were her children, the Vices. My first impulse was to flee, but, far from following it, I made the decision to listen to what the members of that horrible company were saying. I heard Vicious recounting to her sons that it had been a long time since she had made use of all the artifices of which she was making use in order to deceive me, and telling them how she had composed the mysterious bracelet that had made her appear so beautiful to my eyes.

"I learned then that the reason she had forbidden me to open my windows during four hours of the night was because she feared that I might see all the Vices arriving for the audience she was obliged to give them during that interval. In sum, I heard enough to know how I had been deceived and the unfortunate state to which I had been reduced.

"I thought about you, then, beautiful princess; the idea of your charms presented itself to my imagination, and rendered me the most miserable of all mortals. Overwhelmed by a thousand different thoughts, I perceived that the assembly was about to finish, and I returned to my apartment, determined to pretend that I had not discovered anything, in order to find an opportunity to escape and to travel the earth in order to search for you.

"As daylight had not yet appeared I went to bed in order to dream there at my ease, but as I undressed I found the bracelet that I had lost; it had hooked on to one of the buckles of my gaiters. I was very glad to have it in my hands in order to convince myself of the effect that it produced.

"Night had no sooner given way to day than I saw the false Bounty arrive, accompanied by a numerous retinue. The sight of her would have inflamed me as usual, if I had not removed instantly the powerful charm that deceived me. Scarcely was it unfastened from my arm than all those beauties disappeared and allowed me to see in their stead the hideous face of the cruel Vicious and all her daughters.

"In spite of the efforts that I made to constrain myself to caress the fay, she perceived the change in me; it made her suspicious. She stared at me, and, seeing me nonplussed, she wanted to see whether I was still wearing the bracelet.

"Not having found it, she trembled and rose into the air to a height of six feet, after which she touched me with her wand, changed me into a lion and swore that she was going to invoke all the infernal powers in order to hate me as much as she had loved me. She added that I ought to expect to feel the cruelest effects of her hatred. Then she sent me to her friend King Indolent, in order that he could make me combat several animals of my species on his birthday, which he ordinarily celebrated with similar fêtes.

"She ordered him to enclose me in the Black Forest after I had served as a spectacle for his subjects, and I learned before my departure that when I was in that forest I would resume my natural form for one hour every day, in order not to be in a state to defend myself against the animals that inhabit it. However many wounds I might receive I would not lose my life, because she wanted me to live for a long time in order to have the pleasures of prolong my suffering. While I was a man I would not have the liberty of talking and I would be forced to flee the sight of any person of either sex.

"The sentence was carried out. I fought twelve lions in the presence of Indolent's entire court; you were a witness, reluctantly, to that frightful spectacle. I had the joy of seeing you there, and the mortal displeasure of not being able to tell you about my misfortunes. Then I was taken to the Black Forest. There I discovered the cavern that served you as a retreat and made it my habitation.

"A few days later I encountered you. On seeing you, I experienced an incredible joy, but it was not of long duration because I could not make myself known to you, and, in spite of all the cares I took to enable to you avoid death, you were exposed to a thousand dangers.

"Those thoughts caused me a great deal of sadness and made me shed tears, which you noticed. Several times I heard you say things that proved to me that you still loved me. I saw with extreme satisfaction the dolor you experienced when you had seen me wounded by the boar. I have never sensed the malevolence of Vicious more sharply than when I was forced to draw away from you at a time when you were offering me your help with so much generosity.

"In sum, until now I have been the most unfortunate of men. It is you, divine Constance, who can render me the most fortunate. Do not delay, then, and let me read in your eyes that I still possess your heart entirely; I flatter myself that the king, your father, touched by my troubles, will not disapprove of you."

Judicious immediately spoke, assuring him that he would not raise any objection if his daughter wanted to give him her heart and her hand.

Constance, seeing that her lover was faithful, promised to love him as long as she lived. That assurance compensated him for all that he had suffered. Virtue told the king that it was necessary to unite those lovable individuals immediately, but that, as the place where they were was inappropriate to such a beautiful celebration, she was going to take them to the Tranquil Isle, which was a thousand times more charming than the Isle of Roses; nothing would trouble their felicity there.

As she finished speaking they saw a magnificent chariot appear, carried on a shining cloud, which came to settle at their feet. She made the princes and the princess climb into it, and took her place with them. They were all carried into the air and taken to the island that was to be their abode.

That island was a land of delights; nothing was lacking there. The beauty of the gardens, arbors and waters surpassed anything that they had seen thus far. Palaces of flowers, diamonds and crystal were built in different places The Fountain of Youth flowed in that beautiful place. Virtue made Judicious drink from it, and the prince became again what he had been in his early youth.

Tendrebrun, who still conserved a veritable amity for his father, begged the amiable sovereign to permit him to drink that marvelous water too. She wanted to take charge of that personally; she departed immediately, and returned with him two hours later.

The good emperor blessed the day a hundred times that had enabled him to find his dear son again; he gave Constance a thousand caresses, as well as her father, and urged them both to render his son happy. He drank the water of youth and recovered the strength and the features that the great number of years had taken away from him.

Those illustrious individuals reposed for two or three days, in order to recover from the fatigues they had endured, after which the two lovers were taken to the temple of Hymen, where they swore an eternal love to one another joyfully.

Virtue rendered them immortal, as well as their fathers, and promised always to dwell with them. There were charming fêtes for an infinite time. The inhabitants of the island were delighted with the princes and the princess that Virtue had given them. They were all subjects of that divine daughter, and had always loved her; that is what had brought them to assemble in that beautiful abode.

After the first days of the happy marriage, Virtue proposed to the two spouses to accompany them in the voyage they wanted to make in the world. They consented to that with pleasure and departed, each mounted on a white eagle.

First they went to the Isle of Roses where Vicious had made her abode, but they no longer found her there. She had returned to her mountain. They therefore took the road there, and found her boiling in a huge cauldron a quantity of spiders and vipers with quicksilver, in order to make a spell that she wanted to use that same evening. She uttered a frightful screech when she perceived Constance and Tendrebrun and trembled on seeing the person who was accompanying hem.

Her design then was to flee and hide, but Virtue said to her: "Remain attached to this mountain until the end of centuries, and stay here without it being permitted for you to do the slightest harm. That is what I order you to do to punish you for all the crimes you have committed; but I want you to give me the little box that you keep in your pocket."

The malevolent fay, finding herself powerless against her enemy, was obliged to obey; she therefore gave her the box and remained chained next to her cauldron, without being able to move.

Virtue knocked her down, tore up all her magic books and left her in that horrible place uttering howls that could be heard for at least a league around. Then she opened the box, and showed the prince and princess the little magician of the island of Tintarinos, whom the malevolent Vicious had imprisoned there some time ago.

Beneficent, charmed to find himself among friends again, made them a thousand amities and begged Virtue to permit him to follow her everywhere. She consented to that with pleasure, and traveled with that amiable company through several realms, which she found governed by Vices. She could have expelled them if she had wanted to do so, but the people of whom they had rendered themselves the masters were so wicked and corrupt that she resolved to punish them for not having followed her by leaving them under the domination of those monsters.

She renounced thereafter the empire that she had once had over the earth, and only formed the design to make a voyage from time to time to remove the small number of men and women who had an extreme aversion to the Vices, in order to transport them to her island—which she has executed until the present day, and that is why there are so few virtuous people to be found in the world.

After having traveled all over the world, she returned to the Tranquil Isle with the prince, the princess and Beneficent. Their return caused extreme joy to the Emperor, the king and all the inhabitants of the beautiful country. Constance augmented that joy a short time afterwards by bringing into the world a charming princess, who was subsequently as perfect as those who gave her life.

The happiness of all those individuals has not deteriorated since; they live content in that unknown land, because they refuse entry to the children of Vicious. Only Virtue makes their felicity; they love her and respect her, and never ceases to say that those she protects and who do not abandon her are fortunate.

Marie-Madeleine de Lubert: *Princess Camion*

There was once a king and a queen who had only one son; he was their unique hope. In the fourteen years since he had been born, the queen had never had the slightest suspicion of pregnancy. The prince was marvelously handsome; he learned everything that was wanted of him. The king and the queen loved him madly, and their subjects had put all their tenderness into him; for he was affable to everyone, and yet knew how to make the distinction of the people who approached him. His name was Zirphil.

As he was an only son, the king and queen resolved to marry him as soon as possible, in order to see princes born who could sustain their crown if Zirphil, unfortunately, were to be taken away from them. A search was therefore made on foot and on horseback for a princess worthy of the dauphin, but none was found who was suitable.

Finally, after a great investigation, someone came to tell the queen that a veiled woman wanted to speak to Her Majesty in private, about an important matter. The queen went swiftly to her throne in order to give her an audience.

The lady approached without removing her white crepes, which fell all the way to the ground. When she was at the foot of the throne she said: "I am astonished, Queen, that you thought about marrying your son without consulting me; I am the fay Marmotte, and my name has made enough noise to have reached you."

"Oh, Madame," said the queen, descending promptly from the throne in order to go and embrace the fay, "you will easily forgive me for my fault when you know that I have only listened as if to a tale to all the marvels that I have been told about you; but now that you have done me the favor of coming to my palace, I no longer doubt your power, and I beg you to be kind enough to honor me with your advice."

"It does not go thus with the fays," said Marmotte. "Such an excuse might satisfy a common one, but I am mortally offended, and to commence your punishment, I order you to have your Zirphil marry the person that I am bringing you."

With those words she rummaged in her pouch and took out a little toothpick case; she opened it and took out a little enamel doll, so pretty and so well made that the queen, in spite of her dolor, could not help admiring it.

"This is my goddaughter," the fay continued, "and I have always destined her for Zirphil."

The queen was in tears; she implored Marmotte in the most touching terms not to expose her to the ridicule of her people, who would mock her if she announced that marriage to them.

"What is there to mock, Madame?" said the fay. "Oh, we shall see whether anyone will mock my goddaughter, and whether your son will not adore her. I want to tell you that she has merit; she is small, it's true, but she has more intelligence that your entire realm put together; when you hear her, you'll be surprised, for she speaks, I can assure you. Go on, little Princess Camion,"[43] she said to the doll, "Speak to your mother-in-law a little, and show her what you can do."

Then the pretty Camion jumped on to the queen's tippet and paid her a little compliment so tender and so reasonable that the queen suspended her tears in order to kiss Princess Camion with all her heart.

"Here, Queen," the fay said to her. "Take my case and put your daughter-in-law back into it; I want your son to become accustomed to her before marrying her; I believe that won't be long delayed, your obedience might soothe my anger; but if you go against my orders, you, your husband, your son and your kingdom will feel the effect of my wrath. And above all, put her back in her case this evening, for it's important that she doesn't stay up late."

With those words she lifted her veil, and the queen fainted in fear when she perceived a veritable living marmot, black, hairy and as large as a human. Her women came to her aid, and when she had recovered from her faint she could no longer see anything except the case that Marmotte had left her.

She was put to bed and the king was informed of the accident; he arrived, very frightened. The queen sent everyone away, and, with a torrent of tears, related her adventure to the king, who did not believe it until he saw the doll, which the queen took out of its case.

"Just Heaven!" he cried, after having meditated a little, "can it be that kings are exposed to such great misfortunes? Oh, we are only above other men in order to feel more dolorously the pains and misfortunes attached to life."

"And to give greater examples of firmness, Sire," said the doll, in a tiny, soft and clear voice.

"My dear Camion," said the queen, "you speak like an oracle."

Finally, after an hour of conversation between the three individuals, it was concluded that they would not divulge the marriage as yet, and would wait for Zirphil, who was away for three days, hunting, to decide whether to follow the fay's orders, of which the queen took charge of informing him.

In the meantime, the queen, and even the king, shut themselves away in order to converse with little Camion. She had a very well-ornamented mind, she spoke well, and with a singular turn that was very pleasing; however, although she was very animated, her eyes had a fixity that was unpleasant, and the queen

---

[43] *Camion* is nowadays the French term for a truck or wagon carrying goods; at the time when the story was written, however, its far more common referent was a small pin used by dressmakers, and that is the resemblance that the name is supposed to evoke.

was only shocked by that because she had begun to love Camion, and feared that the prince might acquire an aversion to her.

More than a month had already passed after Marmotte had appeared, and the queen had not yet shown him his intended bride. One day, however, he came into her apartment when she was still in bed.

"Madame," he said to her, "the most surprising thing in the world happened to me some time ago while I was hunting; I wanted to continue to hide it from you, but it has become so extraordinary that it's absolutely necessary that I tell you.

"I was following a wild boar very ardently into the depths of the forest, without noticing that I was alone, when I saw it hurtle into a hole in the ground. My horse having gone after it, I fell for half an hour, but found myself at the bottom without having been wounded. There, instead of the wild boar, which, I confess, I dreaded seeing again, I found an exceedingly ugly woman, who invited me to dismount from the horse and follow her. I did not hesitate, and gave her my hand. She opened a little door that had previously been hidden from my sight, and I went with her into a green marble hall, where there was a golden vat covered with a curtain of very rich fabric. She lifted it up, and I saw in that vat a beauty so marvelous that I nearly fell backwards.

"'Prince Zirphil,' said the lady who was bathing there, 'the fay Marmotte has enchanted me here, and it is by means of your help alone that I can be liberated.'

"'Speak, Madame,' I said. 'What is it necessary to do to recue you?'

"'It is necessary,' she said, "to marry me directly, or to flay me alive."

"I was as surprised by the first proposal as I was frightened by the second. She read my embarrassment in my eyes, and continued speaking: 'Don't imagine,' she said, 'that I'm making fun of you or that I'm proposing to you something that you might repent. No, Zirphil, be reassured; I am an unfortunate princess, to whom the fay has taken an aversion; she has made me half woman and half whale, for not having wanted to marry her nephew, King Merlan,[44] who is frightful, and even more wicked, and she has condemned me to the estate that I am in until a prince named Zirphil has fulfilled one of the conditions that I have just proposed to you. In order to achieve that end, I had my maid of honor take the form of a wild boar, and she is the one who lured you here. I even have to tell you that you will not get out until you have fulfilled my desire in one way or the other. I am not the mistress of that, and Citronette, whom you see here with me, will tell you that it cannot be otherwise.'

---

[44] *Merlan* is the French term for a whiting. The word is used in the story both as a proper name, when I have left it untranslated, and as a trivial noun, when I have translated it, as with Marmotte/marmot and other words employed in the same dual fashion. I have, however, always translated *baleine* as whale, because it is not really used as a proper name with reference to the princess in the vat.

"Can you imagine, Madame," said the prince to the queen, who was listening attentively, "the state in which that last speech put me? Although the face of the whale princess pleased me infinitely, and her graces and misfortunes rendered her extremely touching, the whale part gave me a frightful horror; however, when I thought that it was necessary to flay her alive, I was in despair. 'But Madame,' I said, finally—for my silence had become as stupid as it was insulting, 'is there not a third means?'

"I had not finished speaking when the whale princess and her maidservant made cries and lamentations to pierce the vault of the hall. 'Ingrate! Cruel man! Tiger! Everything there is of the most savage and inhuman!' she said to me. 'You want me, then, to be condemned to the torture of seeing you expire? For if you do not resolve to grant me what I request, you will perish, the fay has assured me, and I will be a whale all my life.'

"Her reproaches pierced my heart; she raised her beautiful arms out of the water, and joined her charming hands in order to beg me to choose promptly. Citronette was at my knees, which she was embracing, screaming as if to render me deaf.

"'But how can I marry you?' I said. 'What sort of ceremony is necessary for that?'

"'Flay me,' she said to me, tenderly, 'and don't marry me; I love you as much as that.'

"'Flay her,' said the other, still screeching, 'and don't be embarrassed by anything.'

"I was in a perplexity that I cannot describe, and while I thought about what I ought to do, their cries and tears redoubled, and I no longer knew what would happen. Finally, after a thousand combats, I raised my eyes to the beautiful whale princess again, and I confess that I found her inexpressibly charming. I threw myself to my knees next to the vat and took her beautiful hand. 'No, Princess,' I said to her, 'I will not flay you; I would rather marry you.'

"At those words, joy spread over the face of the princess, but a modest joy, for she blushed, and, lowered her beautiful eyes. 'I shall never forget the service that you are rendering me,' she said. 'I am so penetrated with gratitude that you can expect anything from me after that generous resolution.'

"'Don't waste time!' cried the insupportable Citronette, 'Tell him quickly what he has to do.'

"'It is sufficient,' said the whale princess, 'for you to give me your ring and that you receive mine. Here is my hand, receive it as a pledge of my faith.'

"I had no sooner made that exchange and kissed the beautiful hand that she presented to me than I found myself back on my horse in the middle of the forest. Having called my men, they came to me and I returned here, without being able to say a word, so astonished was I. Since then, every night, I have been transported, without knowing how, into the beautiful green hall, where I spend the night next to an invisible person; she speaks to me, and tells me that it is not yet time for me to know her."

"Oh, my son!" cried the queen. "It is really possible, then, that you are married."

"But Madame," said the prince, "although I love my wife infinitely, I would have sacrificed that tenderness if I had been able to get out of it without doing that."

At those words, a little voice emerged from the queen's pouch, which said: "Prince Zirphil, it was necessary to flay her; but your pity might perhaps be fatal to you."

The prince, surprised by that voice, remained quite nonplussed. The queen tried in vain to hide the cause of that adventure from him; he promptly rummaged in that pouch, which was on the armchair next to the bed and took out the case, which the queen took from his hand and which she opened. Immediately, Princess Camion emerged, and the astonished prince knelt down next to the queen's bed in order to consider her at closer range.

"I swear to you, Madame," he cried, "that this is the miniature of my dear whale. Is it, then, a gallantry that you are making me, and did you want to frighten me by letting me believe any longer that you did not approve of my marriage?"

"No, my son," said the queen, "my chagrin is veritable, and you have exposed us to the cruelest misfortunes by marring that whale, because, in sum, you were promised to Princess Camion, whom you see in my hands."

Then she told him everything that had happened with the fay Marmotte, and the prince let her say everything she wanted without interrupting her, so surprised was he that she and his father had lent themselves to an affair that seemed so ridiculous.

"God forbid, Madame," he said, finally, when the queen had finished, "that I would ever oppose Your Majesty's designs and go against my father the king, even if he had ordered me to do things as impossible as these seem; but even if I had wanted to, even if I had fallen in love with this pretty princess, how would your subjects ever have…?"

"Time is a grandmaster, Prince Zirphil," said Campion, "but it's over; you can no longer marry me, and my godmother appears to me to be a person who will not suffer it easily when someone breaks their word to her. Tiny as I am, I feel as much as another the annoyance of this adventure, but as it was not entirely your fault, except that you were a little too stupid, perhaps I can persuade the fay to reduce her vengeance."

After those words, Camion fell silent, for she was exhausted by having said so much.

"My darling," said the queen, "I beg you to rest, for fear of doing yourself harm, in order that you will be in a fit state to speak to the fay when she comes to desolate us. You are our consolation, and if we are punished, mine will be mild if Marmotte does not take you away from us."

Little Camion felt her tiny heart moved by the queen's words, but being completely out of breath, she could only kiss the queen's hand, over which she shed a few tiny tears.

Zirphil was touched by that situation, and asked Camion for her own hand, in order to kiss it in his turn. She gave it to him with a great deal of grace and dignity, and then she went back into her case.

After that tender scene, the queen got up in order to go and tell the king what had happened and to take reasonable measures against the anger of the fay.

The following night, in spite of the guard having been doubled in his apartment, the prince was removed as midnight chimed, and found himself, as usual, next to his invisible companion; but instead of hearing the pleasant and touching things that she was accustomed to say, he heard her weeping, and the person drew away from him.

"What have I done?" he said, finally, after tiring himself out running after her. "What have I done for you to treat me so badly? You're weeping, my dear whale, when you ought to be consoling me for what I have to dread for my tenderness!"

"I know everything," said the whale princess, in a voice punctuated by sobs. "I know everything cruel that can happen to me, but, ingrate, it is of you that I have the most to complain."

"O Heaven!" cried Zirphil. "For what have you to reproach me?"

"The amour that Camion has for you," said the voice, "and the tenderness with which you kissed her hand."

"Tenderness!" said the prince, hotly. "My dear whale, do you know mine so little that you accuse it so lightly? Furthermore, if Camion could have amour for me, which is impossible, since she only saw me for a moment, how could you fear it, after the love I have for you, after the proofs that I have given you? It is you that I ought to accuse of injustice, for if I looked at her with some attention, it was only because her face represents yours, and, deprived of the pleasure of seeing you, everything that resembles you pleases me extremely. Don't hide any longer, my dear princess, and I will never look at another woman."

The invisible woman seemed consoled by those words and drew nearer to the prince. "Forgive me," she said, "that little fit of jealousy; I have enough reasons to fear that I might be separated from you to have been afflicted by something that seemed to commence announcing that misfortune to me."

"But may I not know why it is not permitted for you to show yourself?" said the prince. "For, if I have delivered you from the tyranny of Marmotte, how it is possible that you are still submissive to it?"

"Alas," said the invisible princess, "if you had chosen to flay me, we would have been much more fortunate; but you had so much horror for that proposal that I did not dare to proffer it again"

"By what hazard," the prince interjected, "is Camion informed of that adventure, for she said something very similar to me?"

Scarcely had he finished pronouncing those words that the whale princess uttered a frightful scream and leapt out of the bed. The surprised prince got out precipitately. What was his fear, though, when he perceived the hideous Marmotte in the middle of the room, holding the beautiful whale princess—who was no longer either a whale or invisible—by the hair. He wanted to draw his sword, but the whale princess, in tears, begged him to moderate his anger, because it would serve no purpose against the power of the fay. The horrible Marmotte ground her teeth, and a violet flame emerged therefrom, which singed the hairs of his beard.

"Prince Zirphil," she said to him, "a fay who is protecting you against me prevents me from exterminating you, your father, your mother and everything that belongs to you, but you will suffer no less in that which is dear to you for having married without consulting me, and your torment will not end, nor those of your princess, until you have submitted to my orders."

As she finished speaking, she disappeared, along with the princess, the room and the palace, and he found himself in his apartment, naked except for a chemise, sword in hand. He was so astonished and so beside himself with anger, that he did not think that it was freezing cold, for it was the middle of winter. At the noise he made, his guards entered his room and begged him to go to bed or allow himself to be dressed. He made the latter decision and went to the queen's room.

For her part, she had passed the night in the cruelest of all anxieties. She had not been able to sleep on going to bed, and in order to try to succeed in that she had wanted to talk about her chagrins with little Camion; but she had shaken her case in vain; Camion was no longer in it. She feared having lost her in the gardens, and had got up after having torches lit in order to search for her, but it was futile; she had disappeared completely, and the queen had returned to bed in a frightful chagrin. When her son came in she let it burst forth.

He was so afflicted himself that he did not perceive the queen's tears. Seeing him so agitated, she said to him: "Doubtless you've come to announce something frightful to me?"

"Yes, Madame," said the prince, "for I've come to tell you that I want to die if I cannot recover my princess."

"What, my son? Do you love that unfortunate princess already?"

"What, your Camion?" said the prince. "Can you suspect me of it, Madame? It's my dear whale that has been stolen from me; it's only for her that I can't live, and it's Marmotte, cruel Marmotte, who has taken her."

"Oh, my son," said the queen, "I am much more afflicted than you, for if someone has stolen your whale, someone has also stolen Camion from me; she disappeared from her case yesterday evening."

They then told one another about their reciprocal adventures, and bewailed their common misfortune together. The king was informed of the cries and despair of the queen and the chagrin of his son. He came to the apartment where that tragic scene was unfolding, and as he had a good deal of intelligence he immediately thought of having posters put up regarding Camion, offering a large reward for anyone who brought her back. Everyone thought that expedient marvelous, and even the queen, in spite of her great dolor, was obliged to agree that one could never imagine such a singular thing without having a transcendent mind.

The posters were made and distributed, and the queen was calmed by the hope of soon having news of the little princess. For Zirphil, the loss of the princess interested him as little as her presence; he resolved to go in search of a fay of whom he had heard mention; he asked the king and queen for permission, and departed, only accompanied by a squire.

*

It was a long way from that land to the one where the fay was, but time and obstacles could not stop the amorous impatience of young Zirphil. He passed through countries and realms without number; nothing in particular happened to him, because he did not want it to; for, being as handsome as amour and as brave as his sword, adventures would have been presented to him if he had wanted to go in search of them.

Finally, after a year of traveling, he arrived at the commencement of the desert where the fay had her dwelling. He dismounted and left his squire in a little cabin with orders to wait for him and not to be impatient. He went into the desert, which was frightful by virtue of its solitude; only owls lived here, but their cries did not frighten the magnanimous soul of the prince.

One evening, he perceived in the distance a light that made him believe that he was approaching the grotto, for who else but a fay would reside in that horrible desert? He walked for a long time during the night; finally, at daybreak, he discovered the famous grotto, but a lake of fire separated him from it, and all his valor could not save him from the flames that spread out to the right and the left.

He searched for a long time for what he could do, and his courage nearly abandoned him when he saw that there was not even a bridge; despair served him better; beside himself with chagrin and amour, he decided to end his life in the lake if he could not traverse it.

He had no sooner made that strange resolution than he executed it and threw himself headlong into the flames, but only felt a mild heat, which did not inconvenience him, and passed to the other side without difficulty.

Scarcely was he out of it when a young and beautiful salamander emerged from the lake and said to him: "Prince Zirphil, if your love is as great as your courage, you ought to hope for everything from the fay Luminous; she loves you, but she wants to test you."

Zirphil made a profound reverence to the salamander in order to thank her, for she did not give him time to speak; she plunged back into the flames, and he continued on his way. He finally arrived at the base of a rock of prodigious height, which seemed to be entirely ablaze, so brilliant was it. It was a carbuncle so large that the fay was comfortably lodged inside it.

As soon as the prince approached, Luminous emerged from the rock. He prostrated himself before her; she had him get up and enter the grotto.

"Prince Zirphil," she said to him, "A power equal to mine has balanced the good fortune with which I endowed you at birth, but you ought to expect everything of my cares. However, it will require as much patience as courage to vanquish the malevolence of Marmotte; I cannot tell you anymore."

"At least, Madame," said the prince, "Do me the favor of telling me whether my beautiful whale is unfortunate, and whether I shall see her again soon."

"She is not unfortunate," said the fay, "but you can only see her after having crushed her in King Merlan's mortar."

"O Heaven!" cried the prince. "She is in his power, and I have to dread, not merely the amour that he has for her, but also the horror of crushing her with my own hands!"

"Arm yourself with strength," said the fay, "and don't hesitate to obey; all your happiness depends on it, and that of your wife."

"But she'll die if I crush her," said the prince, "and I would rather die myself..."

"Go," said the fay, "And don't argue. Every moment you lose adds to Marmotte's fury. Go to the abode of King Merlan. Tell him that you are the page I promised him, and count on my protection." Afterwards, she showed him, on a map, the route that it was necessary to follow in order to reach the abode of King Merlan; then she dismissed him, after having told him that the ring that the whale princess had given him would enable him to see everything that he had to do when the king ordered difficult things.

He set forth, and after a journey of a few days he arrived in a pastureland terminated by the sea, on the edge of which a small ship of mother-of-pearl garnished with gold was moored. He looked at his ruby and saw himself inside, boarding the ship; he went aboard, and after he had detached it, the wind pushed it out to sea.

After a few hours of navigation, the ship stopped at the foot of a castle of rock crystal built on piles. He leapt down and went into a courtyard that led to a magnificent vestibule and apartments without number, all the walls of which were rock crystal, admirably engraved, creating the most beautiful effect in the world. Men with the heads of fish of all species lived in the castle. He had no doubt that it was the dwelling of King Merlan; he quivered with anger, but he constrained himself in order to ask a turbot, who seemed to be the captain of the guard, how he could see King Merlan.

The turbot-man gave him a sign gravely to approach, and he went into the guard-room, where he saw a thousand armed men with the heads of pikes, who formed a hedge as he passed by. Finally, he reached the throne room, after having pierced an infinite crowd of fish-men. They did not make a lot of noise, for they were mute; the greater number had the heads of whitings; he saw several of them who appeared to be the most considerable, by virtue of the crowds surrounding them and the self-important manner they adopted toward others.

He reached the king's cabinet, from which he saw the council emerging, composed of twelve men with the heads of sharks. Finally, the king appeared himself; like the others, he had the head of a whiting, but he had fins on his shoulders, and from the waist downwards he was a veritable whiting. He could speak, and his attire only consisted of a sash of dorado-skin, which was quite brilliant. He had a helmet in the form of a crown, from which rose the tail of a cod, forming its plume. Four whitings were carrying him in a Japanese porcelain bucket as large as a bath-tub; it was full of sea-water; his greatest magnificence was to have it filled twice a day by the dukes and peers of his court; that employment was much sought-after.

King Merlan was very large, and looked more like a monster than anything else. When he had spoken to a few of those who had brought him petitions he perceived the prince. "Who are you, my friend?" he said to him. "By what hazard has a human come here?"

"Sire," said Zirphil, "I am the page that the fay Luminous promised you."

"I know what he is," said the king, laughing and showing his teeth, like those of a saw. "Take him to my seraglio and let him teach my crayfish to talk."

Immediately, a troop of whiting surrounded him and took him where the king had ordered. As they went past the apartments again, all the fish, even those in greatest favor, gave him abundant signs of amity. He was taken through a delightful garden, at the end of which was a charming pavilion of mother-of-pearl, with large coral branches ornamenting the walls.

The whiting favorites introduced him into a similarly-ornamented hall, the windows of which overlooked a magnificent pool. He was made to understand that it was his dwelling, and, after having shown him a small bedroom that opened in a corner of the hall, which he understood to be his, the whitings withdrew and he remained alone, quite astonished to find himself a prisoner of sorts in his rival's abode.

He was reviewing the state of his affairs when he saw the door of his room open and ten or twelve thousand crayfish, conducted by one larger than the others, came in and arranged themselves in straight lines, which almost filled his apartment. The one marching at their head climbed up on a table that was beside him and said to him:

"Prince, I know you, and you owe a great deal to my cares; but as it is rare to find gratitude in humans, I shall not tell you what I have done for you, in order not to destroy the sentiments that you have inspired in me; know, then, that these are King Merlan's crayfish, that they alone can speak in this empire, and that you have been chosen to teach them fine language, social etiquette and the means of pleasing their sovereign. You will find them intelligent, but it is necessary, every morning, that you choose ten of them to be crushed in the king's mortar, in order to make a broth."

The crayfish having stopped speaking, the prince spoke. "I did not know, Madame, that you had been good enough to take an interest in my regard; the fact that I feel gratitude for it already might help you to lose the bad idea that you have conceived of humans in general, since, on the assurance you have given me, I feel capable of being touched by it; but what worries me greatly is knowing what it is necessary to do in order to reason with the persons whose education you have been good enough to confide to me; if I were sure that they are as intelligent as you, I would have little difficulty, and I would be honored by that task, but the more they seem to me to be possible to teach, the less courage I would have to punish them for that of which they are probably not culpable; having lived with them, how will I deliver them to a torture...?"

"You are an obstinate and great talker," said the crayfish, "but we shall be able to reduce you." Then she rose up above the table and, leaping to the floor, took on the true form of Marmotte, to the life—for she was that wicked fay.

"O Heaven!" cried the prince. "So this is the person who boasts of being so interested in my days, the one who has rendered them unhappy? Oh, Luminous," he went on, "You have abandoned me..."

He had not finished speaking when Marmotte precipitated herself through the window into the reservoir and disappeared. He remained alone with the twelve thousand crayfish.

After having thought for a while about what he was going to do to teach them to live, for which they were waiting in great silence, it came to his mind that he might well find among them the beautiful and unfortunate whale, since the frightful Marmotte had ordered him to crush ten of them every morning.

Why crush them, he thought, *if not to enrage me?* "No matter," he exclaimed, getting to his feet, "Let us at least try to recognize her, in order to die of dolor before her eyes." Then he asked the crayfish whether they would be kind enough to let him search among them to see whether there might be one of his acquaintance.

"We don't know anything, Sire," said the first one to speak, "but you can seek information until it is time for us to return to the reservoir, for it's absolutely necessary for us to spend the night there."

Zirphil then began his search, but the more he searched, the less he discovered; he only remarked from a few words that he extracted from those he questioned that they were as many princesses transformed by the malevolence of Marmotte. It gave him an inconceivable chagrin to be obliged to choose ten of them for the king's broth.

414

When evening came, they made him perceive that it was necessary to return to the reservoir, and it was not without difficulty that he resolved to deprive himself of the pleasant amusement of seeking the princess. In the entire day he had only been able to speak to a hundred and fifty of them, but as he was at least sure that she was not among those, he decided to take ten from that number.

He had no sooner chosen than he got ready to carry them to the king's kitchens, but he was stopped by the most astonishing bursts of laughter that seized the victims he was about to immolate. He was so surprised by that, that he could not speak for some time; finally, he interrupted them to ask what was so pleasant about what he was about to do. They redoubled their laughter, with such noisy bursts and so wholeheartedly that he could not help mingling his laughter with theirs, in spite of the chagrin he felt.

They tried to speak, but they could not; they interrupted one another to say: "Oh, I can't do any more!" or "Oh, I'm going to die!" or "No, there's nothing so funny!" and laughing.

Finally, he arrived at the palace, laughing like them with the full force of his lungs, and when he had shown a pike-head that was in charge of the kitchen what he was holding in his hands, he was brought a green porphyry mortar garnished with gold, into which he put the crayfish and got ready to crush them. Then the bottom of the mortar opened and a brilliant flame emerged, which dazzled the prince and retreated as the bottom closed again. He could not see anything any longer, including the crayfish, which had disappeared. That astonished him, and yet caused him joy, for he had been afflicted by the thought of having to crush such joyful crayfish. The pike appeared annoyed by the adventure, and wept bitterly. The prince was as astonished by that as he had been by the laughter of the crayfish; he could not determine the reason, because the pike-head could not speak.

Greatly troubled by his adventure, he returned to his pretty apartment, where he no longer found the crayfish; they had returned to the reservoir.

The next morning, the crayfish came in without Marmotte; he searched for the princess, but did not find her again. He chose ten of the most beautiful; the same thing happened; they laughed, and the pike wept when they disappeared with the flames. For three months in succession he always saw the same thing; he did not hear any mention of the King of the Merlans, so he was only anxious about not seeing the beautiful whale.

One evening, when he was returning home from the kitchen, he was traversing the palace gardens, and as he went past a palisade that surrounded a charming arbor, in the middle of which was a little fountain, he heard talking. That astonished him; he had believed all the inhabitants of the realm to be as mute as those he had seen. He walked more slowly, and heard a voice saying: "But my princess, as long as you don't reveal yourself, your husband will never recognize you?"

"What do you want me to do?" said another voice, which he recognized as one he had heard so many times. "The cruelty of Marmotte obliges me not to make myself known without risking my life and his. The sage Luminous, who is guiding him, hides my face from him in order to conserve us both; but it's absolutely necessary that he crush me; that's an irrevocable decree."

"But why must he crush you?" said the other. "You've never wanted to tell me your story. Your confidante Citronette would have told me, if she hadn't been chosen last week for the king's broth."

"Alas," said the princess, "The poor woman has already suffered the torture that I'm awaiting; I would have liked to be able to take her place, for she's surely in the grotto now."

"But tell me," said the other voice, "since it's such a beautiful night, why you're subject to Marmotte's vengeance? I've already told you who I am, and I'm burning with impatience you know your better."

"Although it renews my dolor," said the princess, "I can't refuse to satisfy you. Also, it involves talking about Zirphil, and I deliver myself joyfully to everything that can remind me of him."

One can easily judge the pleasure that the prince felt at that fortunate moment. He slipped gently into the arbor but, as it was very dark, he could not see anything; he therefore listened intently, and this is what he heard, word for word:

"My father was the king of a country neighboring Mount Caucasus. He reigned as best he could over a people of incredible unruliness; there were perpetual revolts; the windows of the palace had often been broken by stones thrown at them. The queen, my mother, who was very intelligent, composed harangues for him to appease the seditions, but when one had succeeded one day, there was a new impetus the following day. The judges were weary of condemning people to death and the executioners of hanging them; finally, there came a point so violent that, seeing all our provinces united against us, my father decided to go into the country in order not to see such disagreeable things. He took the queen with him and left one of his ministers, who was very wise and less cowardly than my father, to govern the kingdom.

"My mother was pregnant with me, so she had difficulty arriving at the foot of Mount Caucasus, which my father had chosen as his habitation. Our malevolent subjects lit fires of joy at their departure, and the next day, they killed our minister, saying that he wanted to be ruler, and that they preferred the king. My father was not touched by their preference, and remained hidden in his little house, where I was soon born. I was named Camion, because I was very small. The king and queen, very weary of the honors that had cost them so dear, wanting to hide my birth, raised me as a shepherdess.

"After ten years, which seemed to them to be ten minutes, so content were they with their retreat, the fays that inhabited the Caucasus, indignant at the wickedness of the men who populated our realm, resolved to bring order to it.

"One day, when I was with my sheep in the meadow adjacent to our garden, I was accosted by two old shepherdesses, who begged me to give them shelter for the night. They seemed so exhausted and sad that my soul was moved by compassion. 'Come,' I said to them. 'My father, who is a pastor, will be glad to receive you.' I ran to the cabin to warn him of their arrival; he came to meet them, and received them with much generosity, as did the queen, my mother. I brought my ewes back and I drew milk from them for our guests. In the meantime, my father prepared them a nice little supper, and the queen, who, as you already know, was very intelligent, conversed with them marvelously.

"I had a little lamb, which I loved madly. My father summoned me to give it to him, so that he could put it on the spit. I was not accustomed to resist his will, so I brought it to him, but I was so afflicted by it that I went to weep next to my mother, who was so occupied in talking to the good women that she did not notice. 'What's the matter with little Camion?' asked one of them, who saw that I was in tears.

"'Alas, Madame,' I said, 'it's my father, who is going to roast my little lamb for you.'

'What!' said the one who had not yet spoken. 'It's for us that this harm is being done to pretty Camion!' Then she got up, and waved a wand, and instantly, a magnificently served table emerged from under the ground, and the two old shepherdesses became two ladies, so beautiful and so glittering with gems that I stood there, motionless. I didn't even pay attention to my little lamb, which was bounding around the room and making a thousand leaps, rejoicing the company greatly. Finally, I ran to him, after having kissed the hands of the beautiful ladies, but I was astonished to see all his wool changed to silver cannetille, and all covered in pink ribbons.

"My father and my mother were occupied in serving the fays, for you have deduced that they were two of them. They lifted up the king and queen, who had prostrated themselves.

"'King and Queen,' said the one who appeared to be the more majestic, we have known you for a long time, and your misfortunes have moved us to pity. Don't believe that grandeurs dispense one from the woes attached to human life; you must know from experience that the more elevated one's rank is, the more sensitive one is to their experience. Your patience and your virtue have put you above your misfortunes; it is time to give you the recompense. I am the fay Luminous, and I have come to ask you what might suit Your Majesties. Speak, and have no fear of putting our power to the proof. Confer together; your wishes will be granted; but above all, don't talk about Camion; her destiny is separate. The fay Marmotte, envious of all that she promises of brilliance, has obscured her for some time, but she will sense the price of her happiness more when she has known the misfortunes of life; we shall protect her by softening them, which is all we are permitted to do. Speak; afterwards we can do everything for you.'

"After that speech the fays fell silent. The queen turned toward the king in order to tell him to respond, for she was weeping on learning that I was destined to be unhappy; but my father was in no better state to talk than she was. He made pitiful cries, and I, seeing them weeping, quit my sheep in order to weep with them. The fays waited with a great impatience and in complete silence for our tears to end.

"Finally, my mother pushed my father slightly, to make him perceive that they were waiting for his response. He therefore took his handkerchief away from his face and said that, since it was decided that I would be unhappy, none of the benefits that were offered to him could be agreeable to him, and he refused the good fortune that was promised to him, since it would always be poisoned by the idea he had of what I had to dread. Seeing that the poor man was not going to say another word, the queen added that she begged the fays to take away their lives on the day when destiny made me feel its rigor, and that the only favor they demanded was that of not witnessing it.

"The good fays, moved by the extreme dolor that reigned in the royal family, spoke in whispers for a while; then Luminous, who had already spoken, said to the queen: 'Console yourself, Madame; the misfortunes by which Camion is menaced will not be so great that they cannot end happily, for as soon as the husband we have destined for her has obeyed what destiny will order him to do, she will be happy with him forever, and our sister's malignity will not be able to do anything to him or to her. It is a prince worthy of her that she shall give her, but all that we can tell you that it is absolutely necessary that you lower your daughter into the well every morning and that she bathes there for half an hour. If you observe that rule exactly, perhaps she will avoid the evils by which she is menaced; it is in her twelfth year that this destiny must be accomplished; if she reaches thirteen without feeling the effect, there will be nothing more to fear. That is all with regard to her; as for you, wish and we can grant your wishes,'

"The king and queen looked at one another, and after a short silence, the king asked to become a statue until my thirteenth year was accomplished, and the queen limited her wishes to asking that the well where I had to bathe would always be appropriate to the season. Charmed by that excess of tenderness, the fays added that the water would be scented with orange blossom, and that every time that, and as many times as, the queen threw that water over the king, he would resume his natural form, and would become a statue again when he wished. Then they took their leave of us, after having praised the king and queen for their moderation, and promised to aid them every time they had need of it, on burning a sprig of the cannetille with which my lamb was covered.

"They disappeared, and I felt chagrin for the first time in my life on seeing my father the king become a large statue of black marble. The queen dissolved in tears, and so did I, but finally, as everything ceases, I stopped crying and no longer occupied myself with anything but consoling my mother, because I felt that I was full of reason and capable of sentiments.

"The queen spent her life at the foot of the statue, and after having bathed as I had been ordered to do, I went to get milk from our ewes, which we ate to sustain ourselves, for the queen did not have the strength to want anything else, and it was only out of amity for me that she wanted to conserve a life that seemed so bitter to her.

"'Alas, my daughter,' she said to me sometimes, 'what use have our grandeur and our elevation been to us?'—for she was no longer hiding my birth from me—'would it not have been better to have been born in a lower rank, since the crown entails such great chagrins? Only virtue, my dear Camion, enables me to support them, with the aid of my tenderness for you; but there are moments when my soul seems to want to separate itself from me, and I confess that I feel relief in imagining that I might die. It is not for me that you ought to weep,' she added, 'but your father, whose dolor, even greater than mine, brought him to want almost to cease to live. Never forget, my dear daughter, the gratitude that you owe him.'

"'Alas, Madame,' I replied, 'I am incapable of ever forgetting him, and I am even less likely not to remember that you wanted to live in order to help me.'

"I was bathed every day, and my mother was very annoyed always to see the king as an inanimate statue, but she dared not recall him to life, fearing to give him the dolor of being witness to what must happen to me; the fays not having specified it, we were in mortal anxiety in that regard. The queen, especially, imagined frightful things, because her ideas, having a vast field in which to expand, set no limits on her fear. For myself, I was only slightly embarrassed by it, so true is it that youth is the only time when we enjoy the present.

"My mother said to me incessantly that she had a desire to revive the king; I had the same thought. Finally, after six months, seeing that the fays' bath had embellished me considerably and ornamented my mind, which was being formed from day to day, she resolved to satisfy it, at least, she said, to give the king the pleasure of seeing me, so she ordered me to bring her water from the well. In fact, after the bath I sent up a vase full of the marvelous water, and the statue was no sooner sprinkled with it than my father became a man. The queen threw herself at his feet to beg his pardon for having troubled his repose. He lifted her up and embraced her tenderly; peace was soon made, and she presented me to him.

"I was ashamed to tell you that he was charmed and surprised," said the voice, interrupting itself, "for how can you believe that I, the ugliest of crayfish, am a beautiful princess?"

"Of course I believe you," said the one to whom she was speaking. "I can boast of being as charming as one can be beneath this vile shell. But continue, I beg you, for I'm waiting impatiently for the end of your story."

"Well, then," said the other voice, "the king was delighted with me, gave me a thousand caresses, and asked the queen whether she had any news. 'Alas,' she said, 'who can come to give me any in this desert? Moreover, uniquely occupied in mourning your metamorphosis, I scarcely seek to inform myself about a world that is nothing to me without you.

"'Well,' said the king, 'I will give you some myself; for don't believe that I have always been asleep. The fays who watch for us have enabled me to see my subjects punished. Of my entire kingdom they have made a vast pond, and all the inhabitants are fish-people. A nephew of the fay Marmotte, whom they have established as king, persecutes them with an unequaled cruelty; he eats them for the slightest fault, but at the end of a time that is unknown to me, a prince will come who will be king in his stead, and it is in that great kingdom, which will be reestablished, that Camion will find all her happiness. That is all I know. It's not a bad way to have passed the time,' he added, laughing, 'to have known those things. The fays came to inform me every night, and I would perhaps have known more if you had left me longer, but in sum, I'm delighted to see you, and I don't know whether I'll become a statue again so soon, given the pleasure I have in being with you.'

"We spent some time very happily. The king and queen were a little sad, however, when they thought that I was approaching thirteen years of age. As the queen bathed me with great care she hoped that the prediction would not come to pass, but who can boast of going against destiny?

"One morning, when the queen had already got up and was picking flowers to decorate our cabin, because the king liked them very much, she saw an ugly beast emerge from beneath a tuberose plant, very similar to a marmot. That animal threw itself upon her and bit her nose; she fainted because of the pain the wound caused her, and after an hour my father, having not seen her return, went to search for her. Imagine his astonishment on seeing her nearly dead and covered in blood!

"He uttered frightful screams; I went to his aid and we carried the unconscious queen back and put her to bed; she did not recover consciousness for another two hours. Finally, she began to show signs of life, and we had the pleasure of seeing her, a moment later, in very good health, save for the pain of the wound, which was causing her to suffer a great deal. She asked immediately whether I had been to bathe, but we had been so occupied that I had forgotten. She was very alarmed; however, seeing that no accident had happened as yet, she was reassured, and told us about her adventure, which surprised us greatly.

"The day passed without any other chagrin; the king had taken a rifle and had searched everywhere for the accursed beast without finding it. The next day, at daybreak, the queen woke up and came to find me in order to repair the previous day's fault. She lowered me into the well as usual, but alas, O fatal and exceedingly unfortunate day, at that same instant, the sky, although serene, made a frightful thunder heard; the air lit up, and a fiery dart emerged from a blazing cloud, which fell into the well. My mother, frightened, let go of the rope that held me and I fell to the bottom, without any other harm than feeling that half my body was nothing but an enormous fish, of the kind known as a whale.

"I swam around for a while, and called to the queen with all my might. She did not reply; I was afflicted, and I was weeping bitterly, as much for her loss as my metamorphosis, when I felt an unknown power forcing me to descend to the bottom of the water. Having touched it, I entered into a crystal grotto, where I found a kind of nymph, rather ugly, so much did she resemble an oversized frog. However, she smiled at my approach and said to me: 'Camion, I am the nymph of the bottomless well; I have orders to welcome you and to make you accomplish the penitence that is destined to you for having failed to bathe. Follow me and don't argue.'

"How, alas, could I have done otherwise? I was so troubled and so desperate at finding myself dry that I did not have the strength to speak. She took me by the tail and dragged me, not without suffering, into a green marble hall that was near her grotto, and put me in a golden vat full of water, where I began to recover my spirits.

"The good nymph appeared delighted by that. 'My name is Citronette,' she said; 'I am commissioned to take care of you; you can give me any order you wish. I know the past and the present perfectly; as for the future, it is not given to me to penetrate it. So, command, and at least I shall be able to help you pass the time of your penitence without tedium.'

"I embraced the good Citronette at those words, and set about telling her the events of my life; then I asked her what had become of the king and the queen.

"She was about to reply to me when a frightful marmot as large as a human being came into the hall and chilled me with horror. It was walking on its hind legs and leaning on a golden wand, which gave it a certain grace. It approached the vat, where I would have liked to be able to drown myself, so frightened was I, and it lifted the wand and touched me with it.

"'Camion,' it said, 'you are in my power, and nothing can get you out of it but your obedience and that of the husband my sisters have destined for you. Listen to me, and lose that fear, which is not befitting to a great courage. Since your childhood I have wanted to take care of you and to marry you to my nephew, King Merlan. Luminous and two or three of my sisters had already taken possession of that right; I was annoyed by that, and I let my ill humor fall on you; unable to do anything against them, I resolved to punish you for their stubbornness, and I endowed you with being a whale for at least half your life. My sisters protested so much against the injustice that I reduced my vengeance by three and a half quarters, but I reserved for my complaisance making you marry my nephew. Luminous, who is imperious, and, unfortunately, above me, did not want to hear of that accommodation, because she had already destined you for a prince that she protects. It was therefore necessary again to cede to her opinion, in spite of my resentment. All that I was able to obtain is that the first one who delivers you from my paws will be your husband.'

"It paused. 'These are their portraits,' it said, showing me two golden lockets. 'You will know them by that, but if one of them comes to deliver you, he must give you his faith in marriage in the vat, and in order to get out of it, is necessary that he flays your whale's scales one by one; otherwise, you will always remain a fish. My nephew would not worry about that, but Luminous's protégé might find it very onerous, for he gives me the impression of being a very delicate little gentleman. Employ your cleverness, therefore, to make him flay you, and after that, you will no longer be unfortunate, if that is what it is to be a beautiful whale, very fat and well-nourished, and having water up to your neck.'

"At those words, to which I made no reply, I was very afflicted, as much by my present state as by the flaying through which I had to pass.

"Marmotte disappeared, leaving us the two picture-lockets. I was bewailing my chagrins and my situation, without thinking of looking at them, when the good and pitiful Citronette said to me: 'Come on, it's necessary not to be afflicted by evils that one can't remedy. Let's see whether I can't help you to console yourself. First of all, don't weep so much, for I have a tender heart, and I can't see your tears without having a desire to accompany them with mine. Let's dissipate them by looking at these portraits.'

"As she finished speaking, she opened the first locket and showed it to me; we both uttered the screams of Melusine on seeing a vile head of a whiting, albeit painted with all the advantage that it had been possible to give it; in spite of that, nothing so ugly had ever been seen in human memory. 'Take that object away,' I said to her. 'I can't bear the sight of it any longer. I'd rather be a whale all my life than marry the horrible whiting.'

"She didn't give me time to finish my imprecations against the monster. 'Look at this young darling,' she said. ''Oh, that one could flay us at his pleasure; we wouldn't be so distressed by it!'

"I looked quickly, to see whether what she said was true, and was convinced of it only too soon. A noble and charming physiognomy was presented to my gaze; tender and delicate eyes embellished a face full of mildness and majesty; an impression of intelligence reigned therein that completed the graces of the delightful painting; long black hair, naturally curly, gave it an air that Citronette took for nonchalance, but which I didn't scorn when I found nothing in it but charm and tenderness.

"I therefore gazed at that lovely face with a pleasure that I didn't perceive. Citronette noticed it first. 'In good faith,' she cried, 'that's the one we'll choose!'

"That folly drew me out of my reverie, and, blushing at my ecstasy, I said: 'What's the point of flattering myself? Oh, my dear Citronette, this seems to me to be another of the cruel Marmotte's tricks. She has exhausted her art in order to give me the regret of never finding a similar object in nature.'

"'What!' said Citronette. 'Reflections on this portrait already? Truly, I hadn't expected it so soon.' I blushed again at that bad joke, and became very embarrassed at having revealed too naively the effect that the beautiful painting produced on my heart.

"Citronette read my thought again. 'No,' she said, embracing me, 'don't repent of that confession; I find your good faith charming, and to console you, I'll tell you that Marmotte is not deceiving you and that there is a prince in the world who is the veritable original of that picture.'

"That assurance gave me a momentary joy, but an instant later I lost it, thinking that the prince in question would never see me, since I was in the bowels of the earth, and that Marmotte, by means of her power, would sooner enable my dwelling to be pierced by her monstrous nephew than aid a prince that she hated because he had been destined for me without her consent.

"I did not hide what I was thinking from Citronette; any pretence would have been futile, for she read the most secret of my thoughts with a surprising facility; I preferred, therefore, to honor her with them, she merited it by her attachment to me, and I found a great consolation in that; for I experienced from that day on that when one's heart is filled by an object, one is glad to be able to talk about it. In fact, I was in love from that moment on, and Citronelle, with a great deal of intelligence and clarity, rid me of the confusion and disturbance that the commencement of a grand passion imports into a soul.

"She softened my dolor by allowing me to talk about it, and gently changed the subject of the conversation, which almost always revolved around my tenderness and my chagrins. She told me that the king had been transported to the abode of King Merlan, and that the queen, at the moment when she had lost me, had become a crayfish.

"I could not understand that. 'One does not become a crayfish,' I said.

"'Do you understand any better how you have become a whale?' she said. She was right, but one is often astonished by things that happen to others, although one has the greatest subjects of astonishment oneself. My scant experience enabled that. Citronette often laughed at my innocence, and was surprised to see me so eloquent in my tenderness, for it is true that I was, on that chapter, and I found that the passion in question bears great enlightenment into the mind.

"I no longer slept; I woke the obliging Citronette a hundred times a night in order to talk to her about my prince. She had told me his name, and told me that he hunted almost every day in the forest above the place where I was buried. She proposed to me that she try to lure him into our abode, but I did not want to consent to that, although I was dying of desire for it. I was afraid that he might die for want of respiration; we were accustomed to it, and that was different. I feared that it might be too bold a step; furthermore, I was desolate at appearing to him as a whale, and I would have died if he had an aversion for me like the one that the sight of the King of the Merlans had inspired in me.

423

"Citronette reassured me by telling me that, in spite of the whale's tail, my face was charming. I believed it sometimes, but more often I was anxious about it, and after having looked at myself, I did not find myself good enough to believe that I could inspire amour in the man who had enabled me to know it so well. Because of that, my self-esteem sustained my virtue. Has anyone any other that is veritable, alas? It is very rare to find a virtue pure enough not to be founded on any such motive.

"I spent my days imagining means of seeing him and making myself visible to him, which I destroyed as soon as I had imagined them. Citronette was a great help to me at that time, for it is necessary to admit that she had an infinite intelligence and even more kindness and generosity.

"One day, when I was even sadder than usual—for amour has the property that it often bears tender souls to sadness—I saw the frightful Marmotte come in with two individuals that I did not recognize at first. I got it into my head that it was her frightful nephew that she had brought me; I uttered cries of fright. 'But when she's flayed," said the vile Marmotte, 'she won't scream any louder; see whether one is doing her any great harm!'

"'My God, my sister,' said one of the persons who had come with her, whom I recognized joyfully for those I had once seen in our hamlet; let's leave your talk of flaying and say to Camion what we have to tell her.'

"'Gladly,' said Marmotte, 'but it's on the conditions that you know.'

"The good fay, without listening to her or replying to her, then addressed herself to me, 'Camion,' she said, 'we are too distressed by your condition not to think of remedying it, in as much as you have not merited it. My sisters and I have resolved to do everything in our power to ameliorate it. This, then, is what we have imagined. You are going to be presented at the court of the prince for whom I have destined you since childhood, but, my dear child, you will not appear such as you are, and it is ordered that you return three times a week to spend the night in your vat, for until you are married...'

"'And flayed,' the vile Marmotte interjected, laughing. The good fay turned toward her, shrugging her shoulders, and resumed immediately:

"'Until you are married, you will be a whale here. The rest, we cannot tell you. You will be instructed in due course, but above all, keep your secret, for if a word escapes you that tends to reveal it, neither I nor my sisters will be able to do anything for you, and you will be delivered to my sister Marmotte.'

"'That is what I am waiting for,' said the evil fay, 'and I already see her in my power, for a secret kept by a girl is a phenomenon.'

"'That is her affair,' said Luminous—she was the one who had already spoken to me. 'At any rate, my daughter,' she said to me, 'you shall become a little enamel doll, thinking and speaking; we will conserve all your features, and I give you a week to examine whether what I am saying is agreeable to you. We will come back then, and you will tell me whether you consent to it, or whether you would prefer to wait here for the event that will bring you one of the two husbands that we have destined for you.'

"I did not have time to respond; the fays left after those words, and I remained confounded by all that I had just seen and heard. I remained with Citronette, who made me envisage that it would be a good fortune for me to be an enamel doll. I sighed when I thought that my prince would never have a liking for such a toy, but in the end, the desire to see and know him prevailed over that of pleasing him, and I decided to accept the course of action that had been proposed to me, all the more so as Zirphil—thus he had been named to me—might well be anticipated by King Merlan, and that idea made me die of dolor.

"Citronette told me that he hunted every day in the forest above me, and every day I made her take on the form of a stag, a hind or a wild boar in order to bring me news, which never failed to correspond to what my heart thought, for she depicted him to me a hundred times above the portrait of him that I had, and my imagination embellished him even further, to the extent that I was resolved to see him or die.

"I only had one more day to wait for the fays, and Citronette had gone into the forest as a wild boar in order to ward off my impatience, when I saw her return followed by the exceedingly lovable Zirphil. I cannot describe my joy and my astonishment; there are no terms adequate to express them. But what transported me above all was that the charming price seemed enchanted by me; perhaps what I felt was too strong not to aid me to deceive myself, but in sum, I believed that I saw in his eyes that he felt what he had made me know.

"Citronette, more attentive to my happiness than to respecting our ecstasy, extracted us from it by begging him to flay me or marry me. Returning to myself then, and sensing the danger of my situation, I joined in with her, and by virtue of our cries and our tears he resolved to give me his faith. I had no sooner accepted it than he disappeared, without knowing how, and I found myself in my ordinary form, lying in a good bed; there was no longer any question of being a whale, but I was still in the bowels of the earth, in the green hall, and Citronette had lost the power to emerge from it and to transform herself.

"I waited for the fays with a frightful tremor; my tenderness had been redoubled by the knowledge of its object, and I feared that my charming spouse might be caught up in the fays' vengeance, not having waited for them to be witness to my marriage. Citronette did her best to reassure me, but I could not vanquish my dolor and my fear.

"Marmotte appeared with the daylight; I did not see Luminous or her companion. She did not seem as irritated as usual; she touched me with her wand without speaking to me, and I became a charming little doll, which she put in her toothpick-case and transported herself to the abode of the queen, my husband's mother. She gave her to me, with an order to have me marry her son, or to expect all the woes that she was capable of inflicting on them. She told them that I was her goddaughter and that my name was Princess Camion.

"I did in fact, acquire a considerable amity for my mother-in-law; I found her charming, in being the mother of Zirphil, whom I adored, and my caresses obtained hers. Every night I was transported to the green hall, and I enjoyed the pleasure of spending them there with my husband, for the same power acted on him and transported him as well as me into that subterranean dwelling. I did not know why I was forbidden to tell him my secret, since I was married, but I kept it, in spite of the impatience he was in to know it.

"You will see," said the person who was speaking, sighing, "how one cannot avoid one's destiny. However," she said, interrupting herself, "it is beginning to get light, and I sense that I am utterly fatigued by being out of the water; let's resume the road to the reservoir and tomorrow, at the same time, if we aren't chosen for the broth of the unworthy King of the Merlans, we'll resume the thread of the story. Let's go."

Zirphil did not hear any more, and resumed the route to his own apartment, very afflicted by not having told the princess that he was so close to her; but the fear of augmenting her woes further by that indiscretion consoled him for not having risked it. The dolor of seeing her ready to perish at his hands, however, determined him to interrogate the crayfish again in order to discover their history.

Prince Zirphil went to bed, but it was not to sleep; he could not close his eyes all night. Having found his princess again, to see her as a crayfish ready to be sacrificed to the broth of King Merlan seemed to him to be a torture even worse than the death to which he thought she was reserved. He was sighing and agitating cruelly when a loud noise became audible in the garden; at first he could only hear it confusedly, but on listening carefully he distinguished flutes and marine conches. He got up and looked out of the window; then he saw King Merlan, accompanied by the twelve sharks that composed his council, advancing toward the pavilion.

He went to open the door promptly, and the troop came in; the king, in his tank, first had all the sea-water drawn out by the peers of the realm who were accompanying him, and after having rested for a moment and had the members of the council take their places, he addressed himself to the young man.

"Whoever you are," he said, "you have apparently resolved to make me die of hunger, for you send me a broth every day that I cannot swallow; but young man, I want to tell you that if you are in accord with enemy powers in order to poison me, you have made a bad decision; as the nephew of the fay Marmotte, I am beyond any reach, and my life is secure.

The prince, astonished to see himself suspected of such a base sentiment, was about to respond proudly, but as he raised his hand his gaze happened to fall on his ring, and he saw Luminous therein, who was putting her finger over her mouth in order to signal to him to keep quiet. He had not yet taken it into his head to consult it, so much had his dolor occupied him. He did, in fact, keep quiet, but an indignation appeared on his face that the sharks noticed; they mimed applause, which meant that they had not thought him capable of it.

"Oho!" said the king. "Since this myrmidon appears so annoyed, it's necessary to make him work before us. Let someone go to my kitchen and bring back the crayfish mortar; I want to regale the council."

Immediately, a pike-head went to fetch what the king had demanded. In the meantime, the twelve sharks took a large net, which they threw into the reservoir through the window, and brought out three or four thousand crayfish.

During the interval that the council employed in fishing and in which the pike-heard went to fetch the king's mortar, Zirphil reflected, and sensed that the most critical moment of his life was approaching, which was to decide absolutely his good or ill fortune. He armed himself with a resolution proof against anything, and, turning all his thoughts toward the fay Luminous, he begged her to be favorable to him. He looked into the ring at that moment, and saw the beautiful fay, making signs to him to use the pestle courageously. That animated him, and relieved him of some of the dolor he felt in regard to that impending cruelty.

Finally, the unfortunate mortar appeared. Zirphil approached it with a good grace and prepared dutifully to obey the king; but the same thing happened that had previously happened in the kitchen; the bottom of the mortar opened and the flame devoured them. The king and his accursed sharks were greatly amused by that spectacle, and did not delay in refilling the mortar.

Finally, only one of the four thousand remained; she was beautiful and delightfully plump. The king ordered that an attempt be made to shell her, in order to see whether he could eat her raw. She was given to Zirphil in order for him to try; he was tremulous at that new torture, but he was much more so when he saw the poor crayfish put her two paws together and, her eyes full of tears, say to him: "Alas, Zirphil, what have I done to you to want to do me so much harm?"

Moved by those words, his heart pierced with dolor, looked at her sadly. Finally, he took it upon himself to ask the king to let someone else crush her.

The king, jealous of his authority and entirely resolved, was inflamed by anger at that humble plea, and threatened Zirphil with being crushed himself if he did not shell her.

The poor prince took her back from one of the sharks, to whose hands he had confided her, and with a little knife that he was given, he approached the trembling crayfish. He looked at his ring and saw Luminous laughing, and speaking to a veiled person whose hand she was holding; he did not understand that at all, and the king, who did not give him time to reflect, shouted at him to finish it. The prince inserted the knife into the shell with so much force that the crayfish cried out in pain; he turned his gaze away from hers, and could not help weeping; in the end, he continued, but to his great astonishment, he had no sooner finished shelling than he saw in his hands the villainous Marmotte, who leapt to the ground, uttering bursts of laughter so noisy and disagreeable, while mocking Zirphil, that it prevented him from feeling ill, for he had been ready to faint.

The astonished king cried: "What! It's my aunt!"

"Truly, it's her," said the persecuting beast, "but my dear Merlan, I've come to give you some terrible news."

Merlan went pale at those words, and the council assumed an air of contentment that finished disconcerting the king and his frightful aunt.

"It's all over, my darling," Marmotte continued. "You're going to return to your damp realm, for this little dimwit you see has turned out to have a constancy proof against anything, and he has triumphed over all the ambushes I've set for him to prevent him from stealing the princess I had destined for you."

At those words, King Merlan fell into an excess of fury that cannot be described; he voiced extravagances that demonstrated clearly that he had very keen passions. Marmotte tried in vain to calm him down; neither pleas not threats did any good; he broke his tank into a thousand pieces and, remaining dry, he fainted.

Marmotte, beside herself with wrath, turned to Zirphil, who had remained a tranquil spectator to that tragic scene, and said to him: "You've won, Zirphil, by the power of a fay to whom I'm obedient, but you're not yet at the end of your troubles; you can't be happy until you've returned to my hands the case that contained the accursed Camion. Even Luminous is in accord with that, and I've obtained from her that you'll go on suffering until that time.

With those words, she loaded King Merlan on to her shoulders and hurled herself into the reservoir with the sharks, the palace and all its inhabitants. Zirphil found himself alone at the foot of a great mountain, in a country as arid as it was deserted, without finding any vestige of a habitation, nor even the great reservoir. Everything had disappeared at once.

*

The prince was even more afflicted than astonished by such an extraordinary event; he had become familiar with prodigies; he was only sensible any longer to the chagrin that the persecution of the fay Marmotte caused him.

"I can't doubt," he said, "that I've crushed my princess. Yes, I've crushed her, and I'm no happier for it. Oh, barbaric Marmotte! And you, Luminous, you left me without help, after having obeyed you at the expense of everything it might cost a heart as sensitive as mine."

His dolor and the scant repose that he had had since the previous night, which he had spent in the labyrinth, cast him into a weakness in which he would probably have perished if he had not had enough courage to desire to live.

"If I could only find the wherewithal to sustain myself," he said, "but in this horrible solitude, I won't even find a single fruit that might refresh me."

He had no sooner pronounced the final word than his ring opened, and a little table emerged laden with excellent dishes. It grew large enough in a moment to become appropriate to the person for whom it was destined. He found everything there that could flatter his taste and his eyes, so elegantly organized was the meal. In sum, nothing was lacking; even the wine was delicious. He rendered thanks for it to Luminous, for who else could have protected him so appropriately? He ate, drank, and recovered his strength

When he had finished, the table lost its form, and went back into the ring.

As it was late, he made little headway in climbing the mountain, and lay down under a wretched tree, which hardly had enough foliage to protect him from the insults of the air.

"Alas," he said, as he lay down, "that is how men are made; they forget past benefits and are only sensible to the present harm. At present I'd trade my table for a bed less hard."

A moment later he sensed that he was in a very good bed, but he could not see anything, for it seemed that the obscurity had become more intense; that was because of the good curtains that surrounded the bed, preserving him from the cold and the damp. He went to sleep after having thanked the gods and attentive Luminous again.

When he woke up, at daybreak, he found himself in a cot of yellow and silver taffeta, which was placed in the middle of a similarly-colored satin tent, and embroidered all over with bright silver letters, which formed the name *Zirphil*, and all those letters were supported by ruby whales. Everything necessary that could be imagined was in that pretty tent.

If the prince had been in a more tranquil situation he would have admired that elegant habitation, but he only looked at the whales, got dressed and emerged from the tent, which was folded up and went back into the ring, as it had emerged therefrom.

He set forth toward the top of the mountain, having no more difficulty in finding what he needed to eat or sleep, since he was certain of having either as soon as he formed the wish. He only had the anxiety of finding Luminous again, for the ring was mute on that subject, and he found himself in a land so unfamiliar and so deserted that he had no alternative but to allow himself to be guided by hazard.

After having spent several days climbing constantly without discovering anything, he arrived on the edge of a shaft carved into the rock. He sat down next to it in order to rest, and started crying out, as he was accustomed to do: "Luminous! Can I not find you, then?"

The last time he pronounced those words, he heard a voice that emerged from the shaft, which said: "If that is Zirphil, let him speak to me."

The joy that he had in hearing that voice was even less than that he felt in thinking that he recognized it. He launched himself toward the rim and said: "Yes, I'm Zirphil; but you, are you not Citronette?"

"Yes," she said, and with that, she emerged from the well and came to embrace the prince.

The pleasure that the sight of her gave him is inexpressible; he bombarded the nymph with questions about her and the princess. Eventually, after the enthusiasm of the first moment, they spoke more reasonably

"I'll tell you, then," she said, "everything you don't know, for since you crushed us, we've enjoyed a happiness that was only troubled by your absence, and I waited for you here, on the part of the fay Luminous, in order to instruct you as to what remains for you to do in order to become the possessor, without trouble and without dread, of a princess who loves you as much as you love her; but as it still requires some time for you to achieve that happiness, I'll tell you what remains for you to know of the marvelous story of your lovely wife."

Zirphil kissed Citronette's hands a thousand times, and followed her into her grotto, into which she took him, where he nearly died of pleasure and dolor when he recognized the place where he had seen the divine whale for the first time. Eventually, after sitting down and having a meal that emerged from his ring, he asked the good Citronette to take up the story where the princess had suspended it.

"As it is here," she said, "that Luminous will come to find you, you can learn everything that you want to know in the meantime, for there's no need for you to run after her. She has confided you to my care, and a lover is less impatient when one talks to him about the one he loves.

"The fay Marmotte was unaware of your marriage; she had transformed our friend into an enamel doll, believing that you would be put off by her figure. Luminous conducted that affair herself, knowing that nothing would take the princess away from you if you married her, or if you destroyed her enchantment by flaying her. You married her, and you know everything that has happened since. By night, she resumed her form, and came to lament the chagrin she had in spending the days in the pouch of your mother, the queen, for Marmotte had obtained from Luminous that the princess would suffer until you had fulfilled your destiny, which was to flay her, so angry was she to know that you had married her and that King Merlan, her nephew, could no longer become her husband.

"As she was no longer a whale, it was very difficult to have her flayed, but Marmotte, fertile in expedients, had imagined having you crush her, and had forbidden the princess to tell you anything about that, under the penalty of your life, and had promised her the greatest felicities afterwards.

"'How will he ever bring himself to crush me?' she said to me sometimes, while waiting for you. 'Oh, my dear Citronette, if it were only my life that Marmotte was threatening, I would give it to her without difficulty, in order to spare my husband the chagrins that are in preparation for him; but it is my husband's life that is threatened, the life that is so dear to me. Oh, Marmotte, barbaric Marmotte! Is it possible that you take pleasure in making me suffer so cruelly, when I have not given you any reason for it?'

"She knew the time prescribed for your separation, but she could not tell you. The last time you saw her, you know that you found her all in tears; you asked her the reason; she gave the pretext of your attention for little Camion, and made a crime of it; you appeased her feigned jealousy; but the fatal hour when Marmotte would come arrived; you were transported to your father's palace and the princess and I were changed into crayfish and put in a little rush basket that the fay put over her arm. Then, mounting a chariot pulled by two snakes, we went to the palace of King Merlan. The palace in question had once been that of the king, the father of the princess; the city, having been changed into a lake, formed the reservoir where we lived so frequently since, and all the fish-people were the unruly subjects of that good king.

"It's necessary to tell you, Sire," said Citronette, interrupting herself, "that at the moment when the princess fell to the bottom of my well, the fays that had come to help them before appeared to that unfortunate prince and the queen, his wife, in order to console them for the loss of the princess, but the unhappy couple, knowing that it was into their kingdom that Camion would be relegated, chose to come here rather than be distanced from her, in spite of what they had to dread of the ferocity of King Merlan, whose aunt had had him crowned king of the fish-people. The fays did not disguise anything from them of the destiny of the princess, and the king, her father, asked to be the guardian of the kitchens and Merlan's mortar.

"As soon as the fay had struck him with her wand, he became a pike-head, as you saw him during his function, and you ought no longer to be surprised to have always seen him weeping bitterly when you brought the crayfish in order to crush them; for, as he knew that his daughter was due to suffer that torture, he always thought that it was her that you were bringing, and that unfortunate prince did not have an instant's repose, for his daughter had nothing that could enable him to recognize her.

"As for the queen, she asked to be changed into a crayfish, in order to be with the princess; that was done.

"In our regard, on our arrival in Merlan's abode, the fay presented us to him, and ordered him to have a crayfish broth made every day. After that order, we were thrown into the reservoir. My first concern was to search for the queen, in order to soothe the chagrins of the princess slightly, but either because of the order of destiny or ineptitude on my part, it was impossible for me to find her. We spent our days afflicting ourselves while searching for her, and our best moments were those in which we recalled the circumstances of our unfortunate lives.

"You finally arrived; we were introduced to you, but it was forbidden to us to make ourselves known to you before you interrogated us, and we dared not infringe that law, irritated as we were to suffer its rigor for trivia. The princess told me that she nearly died of fright on seeing you in conversation with the cruel Marmotte; we saw you interrogating our companions with a mortal impatience, deducing easily what decision you had made, but you did not reach us soon enough. We also knew that it was necessary to be crushed, but we had learned that we would immediately reestablished in our original estate, and that the wicked Marmotte would have no further empire over us.

"On the eve of the day when you were due to begin subjecting us to that torture, we were all lamenting our destiny, and we had assembled in a cavity of our reservoir when Luminous appeared. 'Do not weep, my children,' said the amiable fay. 'I have come to inform you that you will not be exposed to suffer that which threatens you, provided that you go to your torture cheerfully, and that you do not respond to any questions that your conductor asks you. I cannot tell you anymore; I'm pressed for time; but remember what I have prescribed and you will not have to repent of it; let those to whom destiny is most cruel not lose hope, everything will be well.'

"We all thanked the fay, and we appeared before you firmly resolved to keep our affairs secret. You spoke to some, who only gave you vague replies, and when you had chosen ten of us we went back to the reservoir, where the assurance of our imminent deliverance gave us a natural gaiety that served the projects of our protectress very well. What Luminous has said in the last place gave the beautiful Camion a liberty of spirit that rendered her charming in the eyes of the queen, her mother, and to me, for the queen had finally recognized us and the three of us did not quit one another.

"The queen and I were chosen one morning; we did not have time to bid adieu to the princess; an unknown power acted upon us at that moment, and we had a state of mind so cheerful that we nearly died laughing at the pleasant things that escaped us. We arrived in the kitchens, carried by you. We had no sooner touched the bottom of the fatal mortar than Luminous came to our aid in person, and, rendering me my natural form, transported me to my ordinary dwelling. I had the consolation of seeing the queen and our companions also resume theirs, but I don't know what became of them. The fay embraced me and told me to wait for you and tell you all these things when you came to search for the princess.

"I waited for this moment with impatience, as you can believe, Sire," Citronette said to the prince, who was listening to her. "Finally, I came to sit at the entrance to my well yesterday, when Luminous appeared. 'Our children will be happy, my dear Citronette' she said to me, 'Zirphil has to return the case to Marmotte in order to complete his labors, for he has finally flayed her.

"'Oh, great queen,' I cried, are we fortunate enough no longer to have any doubt of it?'

'Yes,' she said, 'that's very true; he thought he had only flayed Marmotte, but it really was the princess, and Marmotte had hidden in the hilt of the knife that served for that species of sacrifice; at the moment when he had finished shelling the crayfish, she made the princess disappear and took her place in order to intimidate him again."

"What!" cried the prince. "It was my charming wife to whom I did so much harm? What! I had the barbarity to make her submit to such a cruel torture! Oh, Heaven, she will never forgive me, and I fully deserve that."

The unhappy Zirphil spoke so impetuously, and was so greatly afflicted, that poor Citronette was quite afflicted herself at having given him that cruel news.

"What," she said, finally, seeing him plunged in those reflections. "You didn't know?"

"No, I didn't know that," he said. "What determined me to flay that unfortunate and exceedingly charming crayfish was that I saw Luminous in my ring speaking to a veiled person, and even laughing with her; I flattered myself that that was my princess, and I thought that she had passed into the mortar like all the others. Oh, I shall never console myself for that stupidity."

"But Sire," said Citronette, "the charm depended on flaying her or crushing her, and you had not done either one; in any case, the person to whom Luminous was speaking was the queen, the mother of the princess; they were waiting for the end of the adventure, in order to seize your wife, to preserve her for you; it was necessary that it happened."

"No matter," said the prince. "If I had known, I would have pierced my heart with that frightful knife."

"But think," said Citronette, "that if you had pierced your heart, the princess would have remained in the power of your enemy and your frightful rival forever, and that it is far better to have shelled her than to have died in order to leave her unhappy."

In fact, that reasoning, taken from the truth of the matter, appeased the prince's dolor, and he consented to take a little nourishment in order to sustain himself.

They had just finished their small meal when the vault of the hall opened and Luminous appeared, sitting on a carbuncle drawn by a hundred butterflies. She got down, aided by the prince, who bathed the hem of her robe with a torrent of tears.

The fay lifted him up, and said to him: "Prince Zirphil, it is today that you are to collect the fruit of your heroic labors. Console yourself, and finally enjoy your happiness. I have vanquished the fury of Marmotte by my pleas and your courage has disarmed her. Come with me to receive your princess from her hands and mine.

"Oh, Madame," cried the prince, throwing himself at her knees, "is it not a dream that I am hearing? Can it be that my happiness is veritable?"

"Do not doubt it, Sire," said the fay. "Come to your kingdom to console your mother for the absence and death of the king, your father; your subjects are waiting for you in order to crown you."

In spite of his joy, the prince felt a grief that moderated it at the news of the death of the king, his father; but the fay, in order to extract him from his affliction, had him climb up alongside her, and permitted Citronette to put herself at their feet. Then the butterflies deployed their brilliant wings and set forth for the realm of King Zirphil.

On the way, the fay told him to open the ring, and he found inside the case that it was necessary to return to Marmotte. The king thanked the generous fay a thousand times over, and they arrived in the kingdom where they were awaited with so much impatience.

The queen, Zirphil's mother, came to welcome the fay as she descended from her chariot, and all the people, informed of the return of the prince, made a din of acclamation that extracted him from his dolor slightly. He embraced the queen tenderly and they all went up into a magnificent apartment that the queen had destined for the fay.

They had no sooner entered it than Marmotte arrived in a chariot lined with Spanish leather, drawn by eight winged white rats. She was guiding the beautiful Camion with her father and mother, the king and queen.

Luminous and the queen went toward one another and embraced; the prince went respectfully to kiss her paw, which she held out to him, laughing, and he presented her case to her. Then she permitted him to kiss his wife and she introduced him to the king and the queen, who embraced him with a thousand transports of joy.

The members of the numerous and illustrious assembly were all talking at the same time; joy reigned everywhere. Camion and her charming husband were the only ones who did not say a word, they had so many things to say; their silence had a certain touching eloquence that moved everyone; the good Citronette wept with joy as she kissed the hands of the divine princess.

Finally, Luminous took them both by the hand and advanced with them toward the queen, Zirphil's mother.

"Here, Madame," she said, "are two young lovers who are only waiting for your consent to be happy, to complete their good fortune; my sister, the king and queen here present, and I all beg you to grant it.

The queen responded to that politeness as she had to, by embracing the two spouses tenderly. "Yes, my children," she said to them, "live happily together, and suffer that in yielding my crown to you, I share with you a happiness to which I would like to have contributed."

Zirphil and the princess threw themselves at her feet, from which she lifted them up, and she embraced them again; they implored her not to abandon them, and to aid them with her advice.

Then Marmotte touched the beautiful Camion with her wand; her garments, which were already magnificent, became silver brocade, embroidered with diamonds, and her beautiful hair spread out and coiffed her so perfectly that the kings and queens confessed that she was dazzling. The case that the fay was holding changed into a crown made entirely of brilliant diamonds, so beautiful and so artfully wrought that the chamber and the entire palace received a new brightness therefrom. Marmotte placed it on the head of the princess.

The prince appeared in his turn with garments exactly matching Camion's, and from the ring that she had given him emerged an exactly similar crown.

He married her there and then, and they were proclaimed king and queen of the beautiful country.

The fays gave the royal feast, in which nothing was lacking. After having spent a week with them and heaped them with benefits, they departed again, taking the king and queen, Queen Camion's parents, back to their realm, whose inhabitants they had punished, and which they had repopulated with a new people, faithful to their masters.

As for Citronette the fays permitted her to come and spend some time with her beautiful queen, and, knowing that it was her only desire, consented that Camion would have the pleasure of seeing her whenever she wished.

The fays finally left, and no one was ever as happy as King Zirphil and Queen Camion were. They made one another's felicity; the days seemed moments to them. They had children, which rendered them even more fortunate. They lived until extreme old age, always loving one another with the same ardor and always desirous of pleasing one another. After them, their realm was divided, and after various changes, it became, under one of their descendants, the flourishing empire of the great Mogul.

Philippe de Caylus: *Princess Azerolle; Or, Excessive Constancy*

In one of the great lotteries in which the fays in which the fays draw lots for the realms they are to protect, that of Aglantiers fell to the fay Babonette. She was a good creature, too simple to know evil and too timid to disapprove of it, credulous by virtue of good will and virtuous by virtue of weakness, with no sort of intelligence, no memory, and a negligence for her person that greatly augmented the unpleasantness of her old age,

The Council of Fays applauded the luck of the draw; the realm of Aglantiers was governed by a king so sage that the title of protectress was only an honorary one; but in those days, as today, prudence was almost always the victim of events. Babonette had scarcely taken possession of her charge than the good king died of apoplexy, recommending to the fay a unique son whom he left in the cradle.

Babonette, delighted to be able to make use of her authority, had no sooner been declared regent than she quarreled with the little prince's maidservants; she dismissed the nurse because she did not know a single ghost story, and took her back after having made her swear to learn by heart all those that she told her. The king's name was changed to Doudou,[45] which was, she said, more expressive and more appropriate to win the hearts of the people.

As soon as the young king was old enough to receive ideas, Babonette thought of nothing but inspiring him with a mortal aversion for women. Otherwise, the care of his health occupied her uniquely; the fear of its deterioration made her dismiss his masters at the first sign of distaste for lessons, so the prince, at fifteen was still on his ABC; the rest of the realm was brought almost to the same condition.

The ministers easily perceived Babonette's incapacity, but, far from bringing to the young king's education the cares that might have substituted for it, they secretly applauded his ignorance. That false politics has only been abolished after long experience of its lack of success.

The prejudice that the fay had inspired in Doudou was soon manifest. As soon as he could be obeyed, he forbade women entry to his court. The annoyance resulting from the execution of that order gave birth to the phrase that old people abuse: "It wasn't like that in our day…," which was established then as a maxim.

---

[45] Doudou is French baby-talk for what is nowadays known in English as a "security blanket," or a "cuddly toy." It is derived by phonetically doubling the word *doux* [soft].

The young men became vulgar, dirty drunkards and hunters. The ministers yawned in the council, supped sadly and went to bed quarreling with their valets. The courtiers went to sleep in every corner of the antechamber; ambition scarcely had the force to wake them up.

Things were in that state when the fay Canadine arrived in the court. Curiosity, and a few duties of decorum had engaged her to visit Babonette; she was received as a fay of importance. The king, as absolute as a spoiled child, dared not refuse to see her, but the audience he gave her was brief, serious and embarrassed, and ended with two or three bows that he made as he withdrew, without looking at her.

However, Canadine was made to attract the attention of those who saw her. Her stature and her beauty were equally majestic. It is true that her features were a trifle pronounced; she could have passed for a Roman beauty; but she had so much splendor that, at thirty, she scarcely seemed to be older than twenty. Decided in her sentiments, firm in her resolutions, violent when her desires were opposed, disarmed by submission, good in principle, attentive by virtue of self-esteem, her commerce would have been charming if an unfortunate passion had not partly obscured her good qualities.

Proud of the victories she had won over her heart in scorning the amour of the greatest kings, she had not protected herself against the challenge of a child, handsome, in truth, but so sullen that a less difficult woman would scarcely have looked at him. However, the first glance decided Canadine's passion. If there are unlucky stars, there are glances that are no less cruel.

Astonished by the impression that the young king made on her, Canadine only attributed it, at first, to the kind of compassion that affects us when we see precious things profaned; she made reproaches to Babonette for the lack of care she had taken in forming a prince who, in spite of his boorishness, showed so much natural grace, and who could have been made into a prodigy with a little art.

"One can see that you're speaking as a fay of the world," Babonette replied. "I don't regret what I've done; women are the ruination of youth. In my time, a young fay wouldn't have dared to say what you say; everything's going the wrong way at present; I don't say a word, but if women were wiser, men would only be better for it. Anyway, what I say isn't to annoy you; I'd be very sorry to do that. Wouldn't you also like it if I had killed the poor child making him learn this, that and the other? It's all very well to be scholarly, but all those geometries only put stupidities in a young man's head; my Doudou is healthy, that's the main thing. When I marry him off, we'll see..."

Canadine, having no doubt that it was futile to combat such well-established prejudices, only thought about repairing the damage that they had done to the young king by proposing to improve him. Her heart, virtuous of its own accord, deceived her; an interest dearer than that of generosity was making her act.

In order to succeed in her enterprise, she set aside as far as she could the method ordinarily followed in the education of youth; her power responding to the fecundity of her imagination, there was nothing of all that furnishes objects of study or amusement to the entire world that she did not present to young Doudou in agreeable forms. Curious, like all children, his questions would have exhausted any other complaisance than that of amour, but, far from responding, as is commonly done, by evasion or by substituting one error for another, Canadine did not let any opportunity escape to explain the king the causes and effects of everything that struck his senses.

Amusements, whatever they might be, are an immediate liaison with the arts of the sciences; the prince, having the necessary dispositions was soon beyond all the educations given and received with so much fatigue. Doudou's joy at each discovery was communicated to the fay; she obtained sensual pleasure from perfecting the object of her tenderness. Only the good fortune of being loved surpasses that of being necessary to the person one loves.

The king, fully occupied by curiosity and the pleasure of satisfying it, no longer gave the fay any evidence of his general hatred of women; it was even necessary that, as his intelligence developed, confidence being established in his heart, he gradually came to the point of no longer being able to do without Canadine. However, a cold respect, and a marked inattention to her face, made it evident that he considered her to be old because she was fifteen years older than him. The chagrin that the fay felt at that profound indifference opened her eyes to the state of her heart. At first she revolted against a penchant so humiliating for her, but there was no longer time to fight it; the intelligence, graces and sentiments that she had given the prince—all her benefits, in sum—had become weapons against her.

In vain, Canadine had recourse to the pride that had enabled her to triumph so many times; her combats had the usual result. As weak as a mere mortal, she loved no less, and no longer thought of anything but rendering herself lovable, redoubling her attention, care and complaisance for the king.

Perceiving from day to day that she was not making any progress, amour suggested to her a means of winning his heart that seemed to do honor to her reason. To the same extent that the young prince showed a taste for the arts and things of pure amusement, he showed repugnance for business and politics. Canadine could not imagine a sacrifice more delicate and more useful to his interests than giving him her hand, since, by taking sole charge of affairs, nothing would prevent the king from devoting himself to his pleasures.

She went to find Babonette; after having exaggerated the necessity of marrying off her ward, she made her see all sorts of inconveniences in giving him a young woman, and told her that the realm of Aglantiers had become so dear to her since she had been resident there that she was ready to sacrifice for the good of the state the repugnance she had for marriage.

"What!" cried Babonette, transported by joy. "You'd really like to marry my dear Doudou? How good you are! Oh, virtuous people always do the right thing! The poor child will be delighted to caress you; I've told him so much about his mother, whom he has never seen, and whom he'll think he's rediscovering."

Although Canadine was hardly content with the representation, the foundation of the speech was so much to her liking that she did not doubt the success of her project any more than Babonette did.

They were both mistaken. The fay protectress ran to see the prince in the same transport of joy that had gripped her at Canadine's proposal, but no matter how she represented the advantages of such an alliance and the dangers of a refusal, the king remained unshakable in his resolution not to love any woman. He assured the fay that the good will he had shown to Canadine was of no consequence, that he had profited from the instruction she had given him, but that, fundamentally, his gratitude was quite independent of amour, that she annoyed him too frequently with a detail of sentiment that he did not understand at all, and that, in sum, if she demanded that he pay for her benefits with his person, she could withdraw whenever she liked.

Babonette, slightly disconcerted to hear her Doudou talk like a king, had to take that response to Canadine. Seeing that she maintained a profound silence, and that dolor was painted on her face, she suspected that the prince's refusal did not please her.

"You're very good," she said, "to be chagrined. If I were you I'd leave it there and wouldn't give it any further thought. That's what comes of having put foolish notions in his head; I'll wager that if you'd left him to me, he'd have married you gladly, but good minds think they know better than others; I've always heard it said that they only do stupid things."

Canadine shut herself away within herself, devouring her shame and her dolor, formed a thousand plans destroyed as soon as they were projected. Retreat appeared to her to be the most decent course of action and she was trying to affirm herself in the resolution to follow it when Babonette, which had carried on talking, said to her: "You've had a fine dream, you couldn't find a nicer husband. You're much older than he is, you'd put him to rights; he loves you, I know, what more does he want?"

"He loves me?" exclaimed Canadine, waking up as if from a profound sleep. "He loves me! Oh, I'm only too sure of his hatred."

"Oh, as for hatred, you're mistaken," said Babonette. "I know full well how I've brought him up; if it weren't for me, I'm sure he'd love you forever."

Hope is as inseparable from amour as from life; the idea of being loved, wherever it comes from, and however ill-founded it might be, bears a seductive charm into the soul, against which an unfortunate amour cannot defend itself. Canadine could not resist it; her generosity, equal to her tenderness, completed her determination not to quit the king.

He hasn't yet attained the degree of perfection to which I want to bring him, she said to herself. *He needs my care, for himself and his kingdom; would I not be guilty of all the faults he might have if I abandoned him because of an unjust impulse of my self-esteem? Since I love him, it's up to me to please him. Oh, what would be my advantages over him if my generosity did not surpass my ingratitude?*

How uplifted a decent woman is when she can find in amour the semblance of virtue!

Doudou and Canadine saw one another without explaining themselves; once the embarrassment of the first meeting was past, the king resumed his ordinary progress; he even believed that the fay had no part in Babonette's proposition, since she never mentioned it.

Canadine had too much knowledge of the heart to compromise herself by making the king the reproaches he merited; she even felt that, in order not to make him draw away from her further, it was necessary to measure prudently the hours that she spent with him. She often sacrificed the pleasure of seeing him to the fear of being importunate; but, always present by virtue of the benefits and pleasures she procured the prince, she found a more delicate sensual pleasure in multiplying them infinitely, although she did not enjoy them herself.

Following the plan of that new conduct, Canadine, who had previously accompanied the prince when he went hunting, only went with him rarely; she contented herself during his absence with preparing fêtes for his return.

One day, when the king, left to his own devices, had been separated from the rest of the hunting party while pursuing a hind too ardently, he was extremely surprised, after having penetrated a fort with a great deal of difficulty, to find himself in a kind of hall of vast extent, and to see in one of its corners a young woman under an awning of silver gauze, sitting next to an old woman who seemed to be asleep.

Doudou stopped a few paces away in order to consider that prodigy. The young woman was holding a book, but as she raised her distracted eyes from time to time, which she returned to her reading with as little application, she perceived the prince, almost at the same time as he stopped to gaze at her. Their disturbance was equal.

After a moment of attention, the young woman put her book down on her knees and began tidying her coiffure, which the wind had deranged slightly; a few flowers placed artlessly in the most beautiful hair in the world were its only ornament; a large curl was readjusted and brought back over her cleavage with a care suggestive of a desire to please rather than modesty.

For his part, the prince, after having arranged himself on his horse and giving himself as much grace as he could, took out his handkerchief, wiped his face, put on his gloves in haste, and advanced as close to the awning as possible.

He dismounted and approached the young woman with a trouble and an embarrassment that were unknown to him.

"How beautiful you are!" he said, putting one knee on the ground. "How much adoration you would merit, if you weren't a woman!"

"I'm not a woman," she replied. "My name is Azerolle.[46] The fay Severe, whom you see here, has made my castle inaccessible. But is your name not Turlupin?"

"No, Madame," replied the king, slightly disconcerted. "Princes of my blood have never borne ignoble names."

"I'm very sorry about that," replied Azerolle, lowering her eyes.

"Why?" said the prince. "My name is Doudou."

"That's of no consequence," she replied. "I see that I've been deceived."

"How?" said the prince. "Has someone talked to you about me?"

"I thought so," she replied, "and I don't understand this at all."

"Me neither," he said. "Explain yourself more clearly, I implore you."

"I'll tell you everything," the young woman continued. "Perhaps you can clear up my doubts. I've never seen anyone except the fay; she tells me that I once had a father and a mother. Do you have those, yourself?"

"Of course," the prince replied. "They were a king and a queen."

"Mine too," said Azerolle. "But tell me, since you have a father, are there many men in the world?"

"A great many," replied the king, "And almost as many women."

"Oh, that's good," said the princess. "I'm beginning to see the light."

"And I," said the prince, "understand you even less."

"It's no longer necessary, now, for you to understand me," replied Azerolle, sadly.

"What are you saying?" cried Doudou. "Every moment augments my curiosity; I feel that it isn't possible to live without being enlightened as to your fate."

"Well," said the princess, "since you want to know everything, I want to tell you everything, but on condition that you also tell me whether you're a man."

"Oh, nothing is more true," replied the prince, hotly, "but charming Azerolle, why did you doubt it?"

"Since you're a man," she interjected, "your name is Turlupin?"

"Oh, let go of your Turlupin," said the prince, impatiently. "Never mention him to me again."

"I won't talk about him anymore," said the princess, "since it distresses you; however, I would have liked to tell you that Severe is bringing me to him in order that he will marry me and make me his queen."

---

[46] Azerolle, more usually rendered Azerole, is a species of hawthorn sometimes known as the Mediterranean medlar

"What! You're going to be married!" cried Doudou.

"Yes," said Azerolle. "I've been told that he was the only man in the world; I was very glad about that, but now..."

"Go on, beautiful Azerolle, go on," said the prince, with a vivacity whose cause he could not determine. "Do you desire that the fay should change that resolution? How happy I would be..."

"Oh, no," replied the princess "Apparently, all men resemble one another, and it's all the same to me."

"Oh, that's women!" cried the prince. "I haven't been deceived; they're perfidious even before knowing perfidy."

"I believe you're quarreling with me," said Azerolle. "What have I done to you?"

"Nothing, Madame," replied the prince. "Your beauty made me forget that I ought to flee you. Your speech has returned me to myself. Adieu, Princess."

"Wait," said the princess. "I have something else to say to you."

"Oh, cruel woman!" said the prince. "You'll see whether I flee."

"Won't you come to see me when I'm a queen," she went on.

"Doubtless you'd like that," said the prince. "My unhappiness would be one more triumph for your charms."

"I don't understand what that means," replied Azerolle, mildly, "but in truth, I'd be very sorry if you were unhappy."

The princess pronounced those words in such a naïve and tender tone that they completed the destruction of the residue of prejudice that was still combating in the prince's heart.

"You don't want me to be unhappy?" he said to her. "Well, love me, then. I adore you, Azerolle; you've triumphed over the most insensible of hearts; you've made it experience the delightful sentiment that is called amour; I can't be mistaken about that. But I shall lament if you don't feel it for me! If it's in your heart, as I see it in your eyes, it will unite our souls, and my happiness..."

"Get up," said Azerolle blushing. "If the fay wakes up and hears you, I believe we'd be doomed. Flee," she added, pushing him away with one of the hands that the prince had seized and was kissing passionately. "Go away, since it's necessary for us to part."

Doudou, alarmed by the princess's first words but reassured by the tone of the last ones, knelt down, as if there were no Severe in the world.

Their sentiments were too naïve and too tender for dissimulation to have any place therein. They made mutual confessions as ingenuous as the hearts from which they departed.

Neither of them would have thought of separating had it not been for a movement on the part of the fay, which persuaded them that she was about to wake up this time. Hastily, they imagined a thousand means of seeing one another again, which appeared to them to be very easy to execute.

The prince mounted his horse and drew away, not without looking back for as long as he was able to see Azerolle. When he had lost sight of her, he remained so preoccupied that he did not emerge from his reveries until he reached the entrance to the peristyle of his palace, without knowing how he had arrived there.

It is not necessary to be a fay to perceive the slightest change in the heart of the person one loves; a more touching languor, a tender gaiety, a tranquil reverie and a softer speech all reveal a veritable amour. Canadine perceived her new misfortune a moment after the king's arrival; does not jealousy give rise to simple suspicions and cruel doubts that one wants to dispel, from which one only emerges into an even crueler certainty?

Doudou was too amorous not to respond ingenuously to the fay's first question, although it had no connection with his adventure; he blushed and immediately recounted his encounter with Azerolle. He painted her beauty, graces and naivety delightedly, but he only said what was necessary to express the sentiments that she had inspired in him; in order to doubt that, Canadine did not even have the resource of exaggeration.

That confession had a very different effect on the two fays. Babonette wept with joy: "What a stroke of luck!" she said. "The poor child, how well he said all that! It reminds me of myself. But where is this little Azerolle, so that I can go in search of her for you?" Addressing Canadine, she continued: "How happy they will be! We'll marry them. I'm sure that they'll never cease caressing one another; we'll rejoice in that." She turned to the prince and added: "Are you very much in love, then? Come here, my little sparrow, so that I can embrace you."

When the impatience of the mind is combined with that of the heart, it is very difficult to impede their effects. Carried away by jealousy, chagrin and indignation, Canadine touched the king with her wand and said, with a bitter smile: "There, Madame, put that cherished sparrow in a cage."

"Oh, you're right!" said Babonette, running to the prince, who was now a sparrow. "It's necessary to lock him up. You're a little quick, but that's not to make you any reproach; he's very pretty like this."

Noble souls do not commit any sin with impunity. Shame followed immediately after Canadine's impulse. She got up precipitately in order to go in search of the unfortunate bird and return him to his original form, but he had already escaped through an open window. Instinct combining with amour guided him at top speed into the forest where he had left Azerolle.

When he arrived there she was still arguing with the fay, in order not to quit a place where she hoped to see her lover again. The prince found so much pleasure in attributing to himself the resistance that she was opposing to Severe's orders that he did not think of being afflicted by the tears that she was shedding in abundance. He perched on her shoulder, and by means of chirping

443

he tried to express his tender gratitude to her, but the princess was too occupied with him to perceive him.

The fay, surprised and impatient at Azerolle's resistance, pulling her rudely by the arm, forced her to climb into her chariot. The king, unsteady on his feet, lost his balance because of the involuntary movement that the princess made, and was obliged to use his wings to follow her. What efforts it cost him in order to match in his flight that of the crows that bore the chariot away with an extreme rapidity! But no matter how long they last, the fatigues of amour are never felt.

After having traversed immense spaces, Severe, Azerolle and the sparrow, in convoy, finally arrived in the avenue of a castle situated on a mountain much higher than those that surrounded it, which were nevertheless the highest in the world. That place, sad in itself, had been chosen by Turlupin's father for his son's habitation in preference to many others that he might have built with the magical art in which he was very knowledgeable. In spite of his art, however, and in spite of the consideration he had acquired among the fays and the genii, his son had remained so prodigiously stupid that he had not found any place more appropriate to hide him than the inaccessible castle.

Turlupin, who was stout and restless, might have had a passable appearance without a dirtiness that neither shame not the desire to please could correct.[47] Familiar without respect, importunate without self-esteem, curious by virtue of vanity, proud by virtue of baseness, he was fond of gaiety and tenderness above all. The former was expressed by laughter as continual as it was misplaced, the latter by a gesticulation as tiresome as it was impertinent.

He was very young when his father died; his aunt, the fay Severe, had taken responsibility for his education. She soon sensed that nothing could be done with such a good-for-nothing prince, but ambition is not limited by the measure of talents. Severe, who took it for a virtue—because she knew no passion more blameworthy than amour—thought that it could not be taken too far; she therefore determined to give her nephew a kingdom. It was in consequence of that resolution that she had brought up Princess Azerolle, the heiress of a great State, in complete solitude and ignorance; because she knew that the secrets of her art were insufficient to veil Turlupin's faults, and in order to engage the princess to marry him, it had been necessary to deprive her of means of comparison, the sole arbiter of the value of things.

---

[47] This description suggests that Caylus might have had in mind when attributing this name to his character the members of a fourteenth-century religious sect who were called "turlupins" derisively; orthodox Churchmen who condemned them as heretics condemned them as dirty, indecent and promiscuous, apparently because they wore scanty clothing in order to emphasize their vow of poverty. The verb *turlupiner*, however, means to bother or pester someone.

In addition, Severe had no knowledge of the heart; she was mistaken, as many people still are today, about the power of the sacred knot of marriage, and had no doubt that the princess would love her husband as soon as it was tied.

She had noticed Azerolle's resistance that day, and the tears she had shed had caused her some anxiety, but she reassured herself as to the authority of which she had always made an infallible usage. She contented herself with ordering the princess to be cheerful, in a tone apt to fortify the least well-founded sadness.

As they approached the castle, they saw Turlupin, who was amusing himself by sweeping his courtyard. He was clad in black culottes, the lining of which could be seen through a few rips, an old dead-leaf damask indoor jacket, retained for the third time, a calico kerchief knotted around his neck, and a night-cap, the short head-piece of which left a fleece as yellow as it was dirty visible at the top. Although he was expecting the ladies he was very surprised to see them; surprise is always the first reaction of simpletons.

Turlupin's astonishment did not end this time; as soon as his eyes were assured that his aunt was arriving, he fled, crying with all his might: "Fire! Fire!" At the same time, he unleashed a salvo of canisters so prodigiously laden that the majority burst and wounded with their shards the crows that were drawing the fay's chariot. The frightened birds scattered in panic and, applying her effort unequally, fractured the chariot, which was only made of lightly woven canes. Fortunately for Azerolle, the chariot touched down at that moment. The fay, however, was unable to avoid a slight wound in the arm. Azerolle, who was lighter, did not come to any harm; she only showed the tender sparrow a leg that caused him to remember his metamorphosis with more regrets than the fatigue of the voyage had caused.

Severe and Azerolle picked themselves up as best they could, for Turlupin, who had promptly put on a coat and donned a wig powdered with the best flour in the house, in order not to lack dignity, was waiting for them on the perron shouting: "O joy! O joy! Don't be afraid..."

"That's a fine amusement!" the fay said to him, as she approached.

"Ha ha, Aunt!" he interjected, bursting into laughter. "You're not a good trumpet horse, since you're scared by noise. It doesn't matter; let's have fun."

The fear of the reply prevented Severe from responding; she contented herself with making a sign to him to give his hand to the princess. He obeyed, but going in first, he pulled her after him, pointing out the beauty of the apartments. When they had arrived in a magnificent drawing room that terminated them, he stopped, and turned to Azerolle.

"Let's go, Mademoiselle," he said, bluntly, "You know why you're here; we'll soon be familiar together; let's begin to banish ceremonies." At the same time he grabbed Azerolle's head, and would have kissed her in spite of her resistance but for the tender sparrow, which had come in at the same time as the company, and which, flying into Turlupin's face, pecked him on the cheek with all his might, while Severe, already in a bad mood because of her fall, losing all patience, slapped him on the other.

"Oh! It's you, then, Aunt, who wants to be kissed?" he said, embracing her before she had thought of defending herself. "I know how one avenges oneself for slaps given by ladies." Perceiving then that blood was running down his cheek, he looked around. "Oho!" he said, angrily, but with an affected laugh. "It's a bird that's allowed itself to be shut in. "That's funny! Someone fetch my cat; you'll see a fine game; you'll see how he swallows them. That'll amuse you, won't it, Mademoiselle!"

At that cruel threat, the sparrow flew into Azerolle's arms, hoping to find a refuge there.

Every unfortunate creature is protected by tender souls, but that protection is even surer when one requests it of those who are feeling the pains of amour; moved by an impulse more forceful that ordinary compassion, the princess asked for mercy for the bird.

Turlupin replied to her in a self-contented fashion: "Mademoiselle, you have only to pronounce it." Then he asked the fay to heal his cheek, which was done instantly. She seized that pretext to take him to one side, and make him reproaches regarding all the stupid things he had done since their arrival.

"Good, good," replied Turlupin, still laughing. "You have your reasons." Drawing closer to the princess and giving her a knowing wink, he said: "It's because she's jealous, but I'm not fooled. She wants me to bore you with compliments; in truth, they give me a headache. Here, Mademoiselle, I'm a cheerful fellow who doesn't engender melancholy. Oh, you'll love me, once we've..." He interrupted himself. "But reply to me, then!"

"No, Monsieur," replied Azerolle, without having heard what he had said.

"Ah!" he cried, laughing more forcefully. "She's playing the little sweetie! But we'll see, when I'm your husband..."

At the word *husband*, the princess, who was dreaming with all her heart about the one she would have liked to have, looked up at Turlupin, and could not hold back tears that flowed in abundance,

"Uh oh!" he said. "That's even worse. Come here, Madame Severe; I don't know what to say to people who weep."

The fay approached; but, struck by the sight of the sparrow sitting on the princess's shoulder, to which she had not previously paid any attention, she stopped, seeking to disentangle the truth of the suspicions to which the power of her art had just given birth regarding the metamorphosis of the prince.

She considered him attentively, unembarrassed by Azerolle's tears. Azerolle continued to weep, without perceiving the fay's stare. The tender bird, uniquely occupied with the dolor of his princess, was fluttering around her throat and passing his beak over her chin, without worrying about the astonishment of Turlupin, who never ceased crying: "That's admirable! One might think there was finesse in it," when Canadine and Babonette came in, making a racket that extracted all four of them from their occupations.

Canadine, who had immediately repented of having metamorphosed the prince in the first place because of the sole regret of having offended him, had no sooner perceived his flight than, reflecting on the facility that he had of re-joining Azerolle in the form of a bird, she sensed jealousy gripping her heart again with more vivacity than repentance had made had caused her to lose it.

Her dolor, in changing its motive, only became more violent. *How blind anger is!* she thought. *My vengeance has given him the means to flee me and return to my rival. Doubtless he's already with her, softening her with his inno-cent caresses; in spite of his metamorphosis they'll see one another, understand one another; amour will lend them an intelligence superior to any other power. Doubtless they're complaining about me…perhaps they hate me…me, I'm creat-ing hatred! Oh, if I merit that frightful sentiment, constancy, virtue and delicacy, are you nothing, then, but fruitless chimeras of a tender and generous heart?*

In the midst of the saddest reflections, the dangers that the prince was run-ning presented themselves to Canadine's imagination; all other interests yielded to that of preserving him. "Come on, sister," she said to Babonette, "Let's run to his aid."

"It's always well done to help the unfortunate," replied the old fay, "but where are they…? What does it matter? Let's go anyway, perhaps we'll encoun-ter them…I love you for being so good…"

Canadine consulted her books and soon discovered the prince's move-ments. She also discovered Severe's designs, which reassured her a little; but Doudou was enjoying the sight of her rival; it was necessary to separate them.

She sensed the need she had of Babonette, as much to carry out decently the project she had formed of abducting the young king as to balance out Se-vere's power by means of the authority that Babonette's great age gave her.

They both mounted into the first chariot that came to hand and five minutes later they arrived at the inaccessible castle. Canadine was so impatient to see what was happening there that, not finding the door open, she went in through the window. This time, Turlupin's stupidity had no part in his astonish-ment; an entire equipage passing through a window would have astonished many others.

Severe went to meet her sisters, whom she recognized immediately, but Canadine, without responding to her compliments, advanced precipitately to-ward the sparrow king. The caresses he was making to her rival had not escaped her first glance.

"Oh, cruel man," she cried, "the surest means to extract you from the pleasure you're taking is to render you your original form!" At the same time, she touched him with her wand, and he tender sparrow became the tender Doudou.

Azerolle's confusion suspended the pleasure she had in rediscovering her lover; she blushed and lowered her eyes with as much embarrassment as if she had been aware of the indecency of the liberties that the prince had taken.

Indignant to the last excess, Severe would have punished him for his temerity immediately if Canadine had not shoved Babonette, whispering to her: "If you don't make use of the superiority of your power, your child will perish."

That was the only fashion of moving her. "Gently!" she said to Severe. "Although it's not honest to contradict people in their home, I won't permit you to do anything against King Doudou. But to show you that it isn't by virtue of ill will that I'm opposing my power to yours, I consent that he be judged and punished, if he merits it, by the council that we'll hold, and that, submissive to our united will, we can dispose of him one after another. You have virtue, Canadine has intelligence and I have experience; we're worth our price. Let's go, my sisters, let's assemble and judge."

Although Canadine was very annoyed that Babonette had forsaken the absolute power that she had had over the prince, it was necessary to subscribe to it. Severe, no less mortified to find a power above her own, dissimulated, resolved to profit from the mistake that the fay protectress had just made, or to try to bring the council to her will. She contented herself for the present with remonstrating to the two fays that it would be indecent to leave the prince and the princess while they were occupied in determining their destinies.

"You're right," said Babonette. "What shall we do with them?"

"If you'll permit," said Severe, "I'll prevent them from talking to one another."

"Willingly," said the fay protectress, "provided that you don't do them any harm."

"Have no fear," replied Severe. At the same time, she touched the prince and the princess with her wand; they became the most beautiful white marble statues that had ever appeared. At that moment, the prince was looking at Azerolle in a fashion so tender, and seemed so penetrated by amour, that Canadine could not see him without an emotion in which unhappy tenderness and timid jealousy were mingled. Azerolle, who had finally dared to raise her eyes, still humid with the tears she had shed, toward the prince, was expressing the pleasure of seeing him again with so much naivety that the two statues gazing at one another, and the fay, almost as motionless, formed an interesting group.

Severe and Babonette extracted Canadine from her sad reverie; all three went into a neighboring room in order to hold council there, and Turlupin remained alone with the prince and the princess. Since his initial astonishment, so many others had succeeded it that his eyes were still staring and his mouth open. In that attitude, he did not weary of circling around the statues, without having understood anything of what had happened. On their return, the fays found him still in the most stupid admiration.

At first, the council had been very agitated. Babonette, stimulated by Canadine, wanted absolutely to take her prince back to his Estates. Severe claimed arrogantly that the insult rendered to her nephew, whose wife the princess was to be, demanded an exemplary punishment. Canadine represented, with all the moderation that her prudence could suggest to her, that the law only ordered the punishment of infidel women; that, unjust as it might be, it was necessary to follow it and punish Azerolle, by making her suffer a few light penalties. Severe, in refuting that proposition, commenced to mingle so much bitterness in the dispute that Canadine, fearing Babonette's weakness, proposed a compromise.

"Your principal interest," she said to Severe, "Is the marriage of your nephew with the princess. You could oblige her to marry him, but since you don't find her worthy of him so long as she has a penchant for the prince, it's necessary to try by all sorts of means to detach them from one another. Let's put them to all the proofs that might render them inconstant; they'll doubtless succumb, and in completing your project you'll satisfy your revenge. Let's commence by rendering the princess ugly, in such a fashion that Doudou will by the first to become disgusted with her."

Severe made a few difficulties, but she yielded, because she was fundamentally convinced that it was not every day that she would find queens and realms to give her nephew.

Babonette delighted to hear that no harm would be done to her prince, consented willingly to his heart being broken by the contradictions that his amour was about to make him experience. Petty souls are only aware of bodily pains and reverses of fortune.

They went back into the drawing room to carry out their project. Either out of malice or awkwardness, as she pronounced the fatal words, Severe touched both statues instead of one; as they were reanimated they both became frightfully ugly; their eyes encountered one another without recognition, but, their stature and their clothing leaving them in no further doubt of their misfortune, they both uttered a cry as they said; "Is that you I see?"

Each of them, to begin with, only suffered on the part of the object of their tenderness; their self-esteem was not involved. Severe did not leave them in that consoling error for long. She led them to a mirror and forced them to look at themselves. The two unfortunates were no sooner convinced that they were experiencing the same deformity than, putting their hands over their faces, they uttered another cry more dolorous than the first, and each fled through a different door.

Turlupin was beginning to accustom himself to prodigies; the last one only provoked a loud burst of laughter, and he said to Severe: "Oh, that's a good trick, that one! But it's nothing to laugh at, is it? For, frankly, if the princes I'll have from that ugly mug resemble her, I won't have any great pleasure in caressing them. Come on, they've gone; let's amuse ourselves; I want all my servants to get drunk this evening, in order to welcome you."

"Shut up, fool," Severe said to him.

"Thank you, Aunt," he said, putting one foot behind the other. "Mesdames," he added, "I beg your pardon for my aunt. She's always in…in…arguments. That's what makes…but what does it matter? As for me, I like to laugh. Come on, to joy, to joy!"

At the same time, a very loud band of musicians entered, playing *La Descente de Mars*.[48] Turlupin hastened to offer his hand to Canadine, asking her to dance the courante with him, "which I find," he said, "very gay and in good taste."

The fay declined.

"My word, Mesdames," he said, in a mocking tone, "you're difficult; for myself, I can't do any more; it's necessary to excuse a poor country boy."

Severe was suffering too much from the impertinence of her nephew to give him time to make any more gaffes; she proposed to the two fays that they go to the apartments that were destined for them, under the pretext that she needed to rest before supper. She conducted her nephew to his, where she was tempted to lock him in.

The prince and the princess had both fled in different directions, finding a great many open doors; the last one led them into a garden of prodigious extent. They kept walking, without knowing where they were, each so occupied with their sad adventure that they would not have stopped if hazard had not led them into a hornbeam arbor, to which the two long pathways that they had followed led. Although the night was already sufficiently dark to hide their features, there was still enough daylight to make out their faces.

"Is that you, my princess?" said the sad Doudou, turning his face away.

"Yes," replied Azerolle, hiding hers with a handkerchief.

"How unfortunate we are!" they cried.

"You are less so than me," said Azerolle, "It would take a lot for Severe to have disfigured you as much as me."

"Oh," said the prince, "what would it matter to me to be even more horrible," said the prince, "if I didn't fear appearing odious to you?"

"If you only have that anxiety," said the princess, "you have nothing to lament. Just now, while walking, I recalled your features; I still find them less disagreeable than those of the vile Turlupin."

"What!" cried the prince, falling to his knees. "You don't hate me? Perhaps you haven't looked at me properly. When you've seen me, I'll horrify you."

---

[48] "La Descente de Mars" from the opera *Thésée* (1632) by Jean-Baptiste Lully, features a striking trumpet fanfare.

"Why do you have that dread?" said Azerolle. "I don't have it, myself. Although I'm much more frightful than you, I imagine that you'll still love me, because it isn't my fault."

"What charms that confidence has for my heart!" the prince said to her, transported. "Yes, my dear Azerolle, yes, I shall adore you as long as you live; but alas, you'll be obliged to marry Turlupin; I won't survive that frightful misfortune."

"Well," said Azerolle, "Marry me quickly. Since you're a king, you can make me a queen just as well as him."

In spite of his chagrin, the prince could not help smiling at Azerolle's ingenuousness. "The proposition you're making me, Princess," he said, "is the unique object of my desires, but Severe will always oppose my happiness, as long as she hopes to oblige you to be her nephew's wife."

"Oh, I assure you that I never shall be," replied the princess, "unless I'm married without my perceiving it. I don't know how it's done, but I'll keep myself on my guard."

"They can't marry you without you knowing," said the prince. "Your consent will be the knot that binds you."

"Well, if that's the case," she replied, "I'm your wife, for I consent with all my heart to be."

"That confession delights my heart and my senses," replied the prince. "What would my happiness be, my dear Azerolle, if I were free to take advantage of it!"

"What!" said the princess, nonplussed. "You don't want to be my husband?"

"Pardon me...," said the prince, swiftly.

"No, no," she interrupted. "I can see that you fear loving me too much. Severe has told me that one loves madly, as soon as one is married. I already love you a great deal, but I'd only want to be our wife in order to love you more."

"Your words penetrate my soul with tenderness," replied the prince, squeezing one of Azerolle's hands in his. "My heart can't suffice for all the love you're giving it. Yes, my dear princess, I experience what happiness and extreme misfortune can be, united in a tender heart at the same time."

"I believe it's necessary for you not to hold my hand," said Azerolle, taking it away.

"Why?" said the prince.

"I don't know," she replied, slightly nonplussed, "but it seems to me that it's not good."

"Eh! What do you fear, my princess?" he added, moving even closer to her.

"Nothing," she replied. "Let's go. It's dark; they're doubtless looking for us. I'll be scolded."

The young king, as respectful as he was tender, dared not resist Azerolle's will. On the way, the lovable children made new vows to love one another forever. As they approached the castle, sadness spread through their hearts; it increased as the light came closer. In communicating to one another the dread they had of seeing one another again, with how many tender protestations was it not accompanied!

The three fays had been so busy, Severe with scolding Turlupin, Canadine with her dolor and Babonette with visiting every corner of the house, that no one had perceived the absence of the lovers. They did not appear until it was time to sit down at table. Prepared as they were to see them, their first glance made them shiver; for the rest of the evening they did not raise their eyes again.

The supper was sad, in spite of the long bursts of laughter that Turlupin uttered every time he looked at the prince. For a few moments, scorn aided the young king to moderate himself, but in the end he became so impatient that he would have made Turlupin pay dearly for the distress that his joy was causing him if Severe had not imposed silence on her nephew. The entire company had so little pleasure in seeing one another that they separated early.

Gradually, the fays found themselves established in the inaccessible castle, without knowing when they would leave it, since only the inconstancy of the prince or the princess could divide the interests that bound them together.

In fact, whatever was added to the ugliness of the prince and princess, all that the necessity of always being together could produce of quarrels, ennui and distaste, and although the young lovers were forbidden any other dissipation and any other pleasure save that of talking to one another, which was made into an obligation, they seemed no less fond of one another and no less eager to be together.

The knowledge with which Canadine had ornamented the mind of the young king was an infinite resource for him to sustain long conversations; in clarifying Azerolle's mind and developing her heart he rendered her a thousand times more lovable. She thought in a more refined way, without having lost her ingenuousness and without her candor diminishing; she expressed herself more gracefully. Those amiable children, entirely occupied with their sentiments, grew accustomed to their ugliness, to the point of no longer regretting their former beauty.

Only Canadine was unhappy, not because she had hoped that the prince's deformity might weaken the tenderness she had for him—in the heart of a reasonable woman, amour is independent of looks—but because her pains were much increased by the resentment that Doudou showed her whenever they met. Since the day of the first metamorphosis she had not found a moment to justify herself. The prince avoided her with as much care as she took to seek him out.

Finally hazard contrived what vigilance had not been able to achieve. One morning, when Severe had prolonged the reprimands that she made to the princess regularly every day, Canadine, on going into the assembly hall, found the prince alone there, waiting impatiently for Azerolle to emerge. She approached him with the timidity that virtue humiliated by amour inspires.

"You're avoiding me," she said, "If you'd care to listen to me..."

Scarcely had she pronounced those few words than the prince interrupted her, saying: "I know, Madame, everything that you want to say to me; this is my response. You caused my misfortunes; there is only one way to make me forget them and to regain over my amity the rights that your former generosity had acquired. I love Azerolle; you cannot doubt that; if you were as attached to me as you say, would you not have found a means to free us from the unjust power that retains us here? Render me happy with the one I love and I will forget the offense that you have done me."

"Oh, cruel man!" cried the fay. "Can I not give you my life; it would cost me far less than what you are asking? You only read your own heart; if you knew mine, far from complaining, you would take account of all that it has not done to avenge me for your outrages. But you owe me nothing," she added, with more composure. "It's me who owes you sacrifices; name any that is in my power and you will be obeyed. Only know that nothing can remove you from this place except yourself; cease to love Azerolle and you will be free."

"I would prefer the most horrible slavery to the liberty that would cost me my amour," replied the young prince. "I ask you nothing for myself; render the princess the beauty that Severe has stolen from her, and I will be satisfied."

After a moment of reflection, Canadine replied to him: "You shall see your princess again with more charms than she has ever had, Prince." Adopting a sadly ironic expression, she added: "You will see how unnecessary beauty is to please you; you will stay as you are until you have learned what it costs to love without return."

The young king did not hear the fay's last words; content with what he had obtained, he quit her abruptly and ran to discover whether his dear Azerolle had come out of Severe's room, in order to tell her the good news.

Amour outraged and fortunate amour are both reefs for virtue. Canadine, in despair, lost much of her generosity; she could not refuse a vengeance that the prince had just indicated to her himself. After having assembled Severe and Babonette, she represented to them the mistake the three of them had made in wasting time for which they were accountable to the universe; that it was futile to hope to see distaste born between two lovers who, only seeing one another, naturally would not quit one another, however horrible their faces were.

"I don't understand that at all," said Babonette. "I would have bet my key, my wand and even my hood that those two young people would have quit one another by now. But since it's still the same, my opinion is that we should marry them, as we couldn't, with all our art, match them better. That Azerolle is the best child in the world; she suits my Doudou perfectly; what prevents us from rendering them happy? For myself, I consent to it."

"What!" retired Severe, red with chagrin. "Have you forgotten the outrages that your Doudou has committed against me? Have you forgotten that I've only taken care to raise Azerolle in favor of my nephew and that I don't want to lose the fruit of so much trouble?"

"Oh, you're right," said Babonette. "Yes, yes; what should we do?"

"If you would let me dispose of the fate of the princess," replied Canadine, "I'd commence by restoring her original beauty."

"That's well imagined!" Severe put in, sarcastically.

"My God, let's do that," said Babonette. "She has more intelligence than us. Come on, I give you back my power; you're good, you love my prince, all will be well."

Severe contested as best she could the futility of the project. Canadine, after having assured her that she would not stop there, reminded her of their convention, and made her understand that her power was nothing without Babonette's and that she ought to yield gracefully to their combined wills. Severe, confounded, withdrew without replying.

Canadine did not waste a moment in taking advantage of the authority that she had just acquired. She rendered the process not only her original splendor, but added graces, charms and I know not what, rarely united in extreme beauty, in profusion. She went to present the king to his beautiful princess herself, attentive to the impression that the change would make on him. She enjoyed her vengeance as soon as the first glance.

The admiration that Azerolle's beauty caused Doudou was not so pure that a mixture of sadness could not be discovered therein, which revealed the return of self-esteem. His transports were timid, his joy was embarrassed, and the thanks he gave Canadine included a slight reproach for having done too much. For her part, the princess, whom Canadine had placed in front of a mirror, content with her beauty, which a little jealousy caused her to compare with that of the fay, also wanted to surpass her in the majesty of her stature. She stood up straighter; her bearing became nobler; she mingled a modest pride with the tenderness of her eyes, the comparison of which also satisfied her. But while she was enjoying her triumph, she bore into the heart of her lover, without being aware of it, a first affliction of chagrin, which was followed by many others.

The prince had too little knowledge of women to think that a simple emulation of beauty might steal moments from amour. Azerolle appeared to him to be too occupied with herself, and attributed the new augmentations that she added to her charms to the scorn that his ugliness inspired in her. To hide the disturbance that his reflections spread over his face, he went out abruptly, without listening to Canadine, who tried to prevent him from doing so.

Azerolle, whom vanity could not distract for long, tried to follow him, but she was stopped by Turlupin, who ran to present her with a cat, which, he said, had just fallen from the clouds. Accustomed to his platitudes, no one paid any attention to what he said. The princess liked cats, she could not forbid herself to accept that one with eagerness; it was worth a graceful bow to Turlupin and thanks by which his stupidity was disconcerted.

"Fie, Mademoiselle," he said to her. "You take things too seriously; anyway, it's yours, you can make cabbages or beets of it, it didn't cost me anything."

While Turlupin was confounded in compliments, the princess praised the beauty of her cat. It was not that there was anything singular about the color of its fur—it was black marked with white, like many others delivered to the gutters—but two large black prominent eyes, a high forehead, and ears placed by the hand of the Graces, formed a tender physiognomy, a thousand times more deductive than beauty; its mouth, small and agreeable, did not belie the mildness of its gaze; it only opened to give expression to her caresses by a delicate, fluty and methodical mewl; never teeth, nor claws. In sum, the qualities of its heart seemed to compete with the charms of its face.

Although Azerolle was enchanted to possess that marvelous animal, she did not forget that the prince had quit her in chagrin; she departed like lightning, holding the cat in her arms, caressing it on the way; she ran everywhere that she thought she might find the afflicted Doudou.

That cat entered considerably into the designs of Canadine; she remained very surprised by the little distraction that it had caused the princess.

Turlupin, without knowing why, was even more astonished by it. "But...but...but, Madame," he exclaimed, "she's taking the cat away." That sentence is conserved so exactly in the archives of the house of Turlupin that its descendants still make use of it today in cases of unexpected flight.

Meanwhile, Azerolle, after having run in vain to all the places in the garden where her lover was accustomed to walk, finally perceived him on the edge of a freshwater canal that limited one of the sides of the vast enclosure. He had his face propped up by his hands, in the attitude of a man dreaming sadly.

Azerolle slowed down as she drew closer to him; her step was so light that she arrived next to him before he perceived her. She extracted him from his reverie by giving him two or three taps with her cat's paw on his hand.

Young Doudou's mind had so little disposition to gaiety at that moment that that innocent teasing made him resentful of the cat; he pushed it away rudely, and reproached the princess for that pleasantry with so much bitterness that, astonished by such a new fashion of speaking, she thought that the animal's claws had scratched him. She made him tender apologies, but the prince, without replying to them, explained himself immediately with regard to the scorn that he thought he had remarked in her eyes.

The ingenuous Azerolle justified herself with so much candor that the reconciliation followed immediately after the explanation.

That first quarrel, however, was soon followed by a second. The king, having become anxious, could not abide the caresses that Azerolle gave the cat during a conversation whose pleasure he did not want to be shared. The princess replied to his reproaches again in a fashion to disarm him, but still without quitting the cat.

"Isn't it cruel," the prince continued, "that you prefer the most malevolent of animals to me? Azerolle, Azerolle," he added, "you would not have treated me with this repugnance when our misfortunes were common; I'm beginning to displease you; soon you'll find me frightful. I am, it's true, but is it for you to reproach me?"

While the prince was speaking, the cat—which, in addition to the annoying humor typical of its species, seemed to be impelled by a particular interest—put to use everything it could to attract the attention of young Azerolle: caresses, attitudes, gestures, everything was employed with the most seductive grace.

Unless one has a natural aversion to those animals, can one resist their provocations? The process yielded to admiration, picked up the cat, and kissed it enthusiastically, saying: "Come, pretty puss, you're too lovable."

At those words, the young king, carried away by an unprecedented impulse, snatched it abruptly from Azerolle's hands. He was about to throw it in the canal when it escaped, and became a young man, with a face such as one would take if one could choose, of a beauty equal to Azerolle's.

"Stop, Prince!" he cried to the king, who was advancing toward him with fury painted in his eyes. "When you have heard me out, you can do what prudence suggests to you." At the same time, he drew nearer, in a manner as noble as it was respectful.

He told the king that his name was Zumio,[49] and that for a long time, Canadine had rendered him the unhappiest of genii, by the scorn with which she repaid the insurmountable amour that he had for her; that his woes made him sympathetic to those of others; and that he only occupied himself with helping unfortunate lovers. Having discovered by the enlightenments of his art, not only what the prince and the princess were being made to suffer, but also the traps that were being prepared for them, he had come to offer his services, without demanding any gratitude from them, because he admitted candidly that the desire to avenge himself on Canadine had some part in his design.

The tone of honesty that the genius displayed in his speech, and the interest that he seemed to express in exaggerating the dangers that threatened the tender lovers, penetrated them with fear and confidence. They employed all the expressions that the generosity of their souls could furnish them to persuade Zumio of their gratitude and to obtain a positive promise from him not to abandon them.

---

[49] Caylus's genius was co-opted from the present story into one of the moralistic tales penned at the end of the eighteenth century by the Comtesse de Genlis, governess of the children of Philippe d'Orléans, translated into English in *Tales of the Castle* (1785). It is unlikely that the character assisted the modern adoption of the term for a kind of vibrator, in spite of his seductive conduct in feline form.

The genius assured them modestly that, his art being inferior to Severe's, he could only help them with his cares and his advice. It was therefore necessary to imagine means that might lead them to the end of their troubles. The adroit genius, while destroying all those that Doudou proposed, did not fail to praise their invention, and only received the small suggestions that Azerolle mingled with theirs from time to time with the benevolent smile that is accorded to children who say pretty but futile things.

So much deference on the part of Zumio, and so little reason for jealousy, completed gaining the confidence of the prince, to the point of making him agree that is was first necessary for the genius to pretend to be in love with Azerolle, and that if the king took no umbrage at that, he would be thought to be inconstant, which was the only way to procure their liberty.

Zumio added that his interest ought to be their guarantee of good faith, since by means of that arrangement he was working for his own happiness, because Canadine might become sensible by virtue of jealousy, not having been by virtue of amour.

He spoke of his passion in such a penetrating tone, and affected so much indifference for Azerolle, taking the precaution of warning her, in such a cold manner, that she would only be the pretext, and not at all the object, of his gallantries, that she blushed, and Doudou could not help smiling.

They separated from him in order better to conceal their intelligence. The genius went to prepare himself in order to arrive at the castle in pomp; the prince and the princess hastened to return there, in order subtly to enjoy the surprise that his arrival would cause Canadine, without forgetting to applaud themselves on the way on such a fortunate encounter.

They found Severe, Babonette and Canadine at the windows overlooking the avenue, watching Zumio's carriages, which were already beginning to file along it. They were as elegant as they were magnificent, brilliant and numerous, traveling in the most beautiful order.

The two old fays were asking questions reciprocally about the unexpected visit. Canadine, unaccustomed to pretence, carefully avoided those addressed to her; a violent passion can inspire ingenious deception, but an elevated soul sustains it poorly.

As for Turlupin, in the disturbance in which so much unfamiliar society had put him, he had run to his grain-loft, from which he cried out with all his might: "Close the gates, they'll make my courtyard dirty!"

Finally, after a prodigious number of pages, liveried servants, carts and horses, the handsome genius was seen to arrive in a varnished pink cameo caleche with harness and ornaments decorated with emeralds. Seeing the ladies at the window, he descended at the gate and came toward them with a noble, easy-going and respectful air, making graceful reverences from time to time. He was followed by brilliant young people as gallantly clad as he was.

Severe waited for him gravely in the fine drawing room, and Zumio, after having bowed to her three times, addressed a compliment to her on her nephew's impending marriage, on the part of the sovereign genius, who had charged him, he said, with the title of ambassador to her, in order to be a witness to that great alliance. Severe was so flattered by such a distinction that her face became almost cheerful. She replied to the genius with dignity; then they went into another apartment, where the conversation became general.

Zumio had so much grace, he was so handsome, and his adornment had a festival air that rendered him so brilliant, that Doudou, prepared as he was to see him, could not look at him without a certain interior tremor. More familiar to jealous hearts than easy to describe; his face became a burden to him. He dared not speak for fear of being noticed; his embarrassed gaze wandered from the genius to Azerolle, whom he found to be much too occupied with that new company.

In a few days, Zumio became necessary to everyone. He amused Babonette with tales, Severe with moral treatises, Doudou with the hope of his happiness, Azerolle with praises of her lover and Turlupin with puns. He gave fêtes; every day brought a new one. The pleasures succeeded one another so rapidly that had they left people with the liberty of thought, they would not have found time to communicate their reflections.

However, the gaiety spread over faces only consisted of demonstrations; no one was content. Canadine was suffering even more from the pretence that she had imposed on herself than her unfortunate passion.

Azerolle delivered herself to the diversions like a young person savoring them for the first time, but that was not without regretting the days when she had had no other pleasure than that of conversing with Doudou. She lent herself in good faith to Zumio's cajoleries, with no other design than advancing her lover's happiness, but the inevitable dissipation in the tumult gave her, without her being aware of it, an appearance of coquetry that tore the heart of the tender prince.

The difficulty the latter had in talking to her, the impossibility of putting a stop to the fêtes that were insupportable to him: everything drove him to despair, including the chagrin of not daring to hate his rival. As soon as Zumio perceived any discontentment on his part, he hastened to heap him with amities and protestations; then he deployed threats of abandonment so cleverly that he reduced him to begging him insistently to continue playing the same role.

It is sufficient to be unhappy, or to be honest, to be duped. Doudou was both; the artifices of the genius would have deceived the most suspicious.

For her part, Severe, in spite of the honors that flattered her ambition, was no more content than the others. Apart from the chagrin that pleasures in general caused her, she feared that Zumio's gallantries might indeed render Azerolle infidel, but in his own favor, which would produce nothing for her nephew. She took Canadine to task one day.

458

"There was no point," she said, "in giving you our power, if you didn't want to make any other usage of it except rendering Azerolle more beautiful. Instead of the efficacious help you promised me, I see nothing but gallantries that wound me and fêtes that irritate me. If you had less empire over Babonette I would soon have determined her to let my power act, and we would see as many useful punishments as we are seeing frivolous amusements."

In order to calm her, Canadine was obliged to make her party to her designs. "You have seen," she told her, "that ugliness has not altered the amour that we wanted to destroy. The distaste that the young people were supposed to acquire for one another when you obliged them to be together relentlessly had no more success; nothing remains to you to test their constancy but jealousy and infidelity. Jealousy was born in the heart of the prince the moment I embellished Azerolle, and you shall judge how right I was to summon Zumio here to serve your vengeance...

"He is," she continued, "one of the genii who resemble men most closely; he has limited his powers to deceiving women. After having deceived a large number, he found that Souveraine was lacking to his triumph; why not employ them to seduce her? He succeeded in that, but almost as soon disillusioned as she was vanquished, the firmness of her soul led her courageously to sacrifice her reputation to an exemplary vengeance.

"She convened a numerous assembly; after having had the perfidious genius dragged before it, she invited all the fays who had reproached him to add their voices to hers, in order to confound and condemn him. But she offered herself as an example in vain; she made them sense the price of the sacrifice she was making for the common, and not one of them spoke. The blushes on the faces of some, the embarrassment of others and the consternation on all the faces did not even leave the old beyond suspicion of having a good deal to say.

"'Well, my sisters,' said Souveraine, 'since a false shame, or perhaps a residue of seduction, prevents you from confounding the traitor, I'll take charge of the vengeance myself. You'll be a cat,' she told him, 'until in that form you've inspired the jealousy of a perfect lover. But your punishment would be too mild, if I limited it to so little; I want,' she added, 'that the knavery that is so natural to you, to be the instrument of your mercy or your torture. Until the end of the centuries you shall have the most decrepit face with the most violent desires, unless within six months from today you triumph over a constancy proof against anything, without pleasing, without loving and without the object that you want to seduce discovering the falsity of your character...'

"See," added Canadine, "whether I could have put the infidelity of the princess in better hands. Since the wellbeing or misfortune of Zumio is dependent on it, what success should we not expect of his skill?"

"That's all very well for Zumio," replied Severe, "but what will my nephew get out of it?"

"The conditions that Souveraine has attached to the success of his enterprise are so difficult to fulfill," replied Canadine, "that there is every appearance that before their accomplishment, the prince will have rejected a futile constancy, and you'll be left the mistress of disposing of Azerolle."

Severe contented herself with those arguments, being unable to find any better; she even forbade the princess to speak to Doudou, in order to contribute in some way to the advancement of the project; but that new contradiction only augmented the pains of the lovers without decreasing their constancy.

Azerolle incessantly made reproaches to Zumio for having engaged her in a deception that, far from being useful to them, rendered them more unfortunate. For his part, the genius reproached her so often that her pretence was too poor to deceive the fays that in the end, the credulous princess went to so much trouble to appear infidel, that her lover soon had no doubt that she was. That was not enough for Zumio to bring his enterprise to a conclusion, however; it was necessary that Azerolle betray him.

A pure and confident soul does not easily acquire ideas disadvantageous to the person she loves. Perhaps the artful genius would not have succeeded in convincing Azerolle of the infidelity of Doudou if the unfortunate prince had not seemed to accord with him to contribute to his misfortune. His jealousy had increased considerably since Severe had forbidden Azerolle to speak to him. Deprived of the relief that the jealous often find in making reproaches, and unable to suffer the dolor that was devouring him, he saw no one but Canadine who could soothe his heart by sympathizing with his pains.

If dread has made gods, needs have made amity; they are treated similarly. So long as Canadine's instruction had been necessary to the young king, he had had a sort of amity for her; fortunate amour had entirely stifled it; afflicted amour caused it to be reborn.

The silence that the fay had long imposed on her passion, and the scant interest that Doudou had taken in it, had easily made him forget that she loved him. It was, therefore to her that he addressed his plaints, with no anxiety as to the fashion in which they might be received.

The tender fay immediately felt pleasure in the prince's confidence. She flattered herself momentarily that she might find enough satisfaction in the amity that he showed her to compensate her for her amour. She even had the generosity not to augment the young king's pains be seconding, by means of a falsity of which she was capable, his suspicions of Azerolle's infidelity. The situation was too delicate to be sustained for long, however, so Canadine became even more unhappy than the lovers themselves. Her long and frequent conversations, always in private, only served to second Zumio's designs.

The genius, whom time was pressing, and who knew the hearts of the lovers too well not to dread a return if he let things drag on, imagined a deceit that succeeded. He had noticed a cabinet fitted into the wall that was adjacent to the bed where Azerolle slept. Although the door was exactly sealed, the force of his art caused it to open. He had one of the young men of his following hide there, who took an oracular tone while the princess was asleep and repeated to her several times the words: "Princess Azerolle will only recover her faithful lover by uniting herself with Zumio in the knot of marriage...."

That oracle had all the effect that the genius had promised himself.

The dread of engaging herself to Zumio, and the hope of recovering her dear Doudou, as tender as her, agitated her all night long, without her being able to decide what she ought to do. It was reserved to the genius to determine it.

It was not difficult for him to extract from the princess the confidence of her embarrassment. It was then that, affecting considerable disinterest, he feigned more dread of uniting himself with her than she had of making indissoluble engagements with him. In skillfully persuading her to give him her hand, he appeared to be making a greater sacrifice than her. The artifice was pushed so far as to demanding from her a promise, confirmed by oaths, that if the prince did not intervene at the first words of the ceremony, she would not take it amiss if he abandoned his design.

With precautions so specious, was Azerolle able to doubt his good faith? She swore more oaths than he wanted never to be his; and, their arrangements made, the genius quit her, in order to dispose Severe not to trouble the fête.

The most difficult part was done, since Severe had permitted a tone of gallantry to be established in her house more revolting for women of her sort than amour itself. It did not require much artistry on Zumio's part to make her consent that he should marry the princess in his quality as an ambassador in order to put her at that very moment into the hands of her nephew. He did not fail to let her understand that she would be immortalized in the realm of the genii by rescuing him from the vengeance of Souveraine.

It is necessary to know how ambition works in a false mind to understand the satisfaction with which Severe pressed Zumio to bring his enterprise to a conclusion.

During that conversation, Azerolle, delivered to herself, could not resist the penchant that drew her toward her lover. Seeing that she was not observed, she ran to him, but he was so irritated by the long conservation that she had just had with Zumio, to which he had been a witness, and the keen interest that she had seemed to be taking in it, that, far from receiving her with tenderness or even with reproaches, he drew away from her in order to go and join Canadine, saying to the unfortunate Azerolle: "It's too late, Madame, my decision is made; I'm quitting you forever."

A more skillful woman would easily have detected the violence of the amour in the tone of those terrible words, but the tender princess only heard the sentence of death. Convinced that she had reached the culmination of misfortune, she went out to look for the genius, and pressed him to bring forward the sole means that remained to her to attempt to bring the infidel Doudou back under her dominion.

Delighted, Zumio assured her that everything was ready for that same evening; that, in order to avoid spectators, he would give a masked ball what would occupy the youth of his retinue, always importunate in such situations.

As the hour approached, Azerolle's dread and hope took on new force. She believed, however that she could not take too many precautions to assure her liberty; she went to throw herself at Severe's feet, and only quit her after having demanded the fay's word that the ceremony that was about to take place would not engage her to Zumio. Severe gave it to her, with all the less scruple because she was deceived herself.

Reassured regarding the danger of her engagements, Azerolle was not sure of the promises of the oracle; her mortal anxieties were redoubled at every instant.

The prince, who knew nothing of what was happening, devoured by his despair, sought to soften it by imparting it to Canadine.

It would have required a great deal for the tender fay to savor tranquilly the hope that she could not forbid herself; she reproached herself bitterly for leaving Doudou in an error that rendered him so unhappy. A hundred times she was ready to reveal Zumio's artifices, but amour prevailed and she remained silent.

As for Babonette, she applauded everything, as usual.

Turlupin, leaving the care of his interests to his aunt, only thought of amusing himself. While everyone was occupied with such important matters, he had slipped, without being perceived, into the cabinet that the pretended oracle had left open; it was the place where Severe enclosed under thirty keys the magical compounds and implements necessary to great enchantments. Turlupin, delighted to be rummaging in a place that he had never had permission to enter, amused himself by composing, with everything he found there, a gallant masquerade in order to surprise the company agreeably.

Scarcely had the ball begun when the woeful Doudou went into the next room, as usual, with his friend the fay. As soon as Zumio perceived that, he made a sign to Severe and the witnesses designated for the ceremony, and presented his hand to the princess to conduct her to it. The tremulous Azerolle allowed herself to be drawn, without having the strength either to oppose it or to consent to it; a mortal pallor expressed the state of her soul better than she felt it herself.

While the apparatus for the ceremony was being arranged and the genius beside her was able to sustain her, her eyes were avidly attached to those of the prince, seeking to detect there a return of tenderness, which cost her a great sacrifice. The prince, who had obliged Canadine to reply to his questions, informed of the cause of the preparations he could see, was gazing at Azerolle, but with a fury whose effects only seemed to be suspended by the choice of victims.

Zumio, hastening the ceremony, was already mocking Souveraine in the depths of his heart. The excessively credulous Azerolle was about to renounce forever the man she loved, believing that she was drawing closer to him, when

Turlupin suddenly emerged from the cabinet, ridiculously clad, with a great torch in his hand, shouting with all his might: "I am Amour! I am Amour..."

Scarcely had the light of the magic torch struck the eyes of the tender lovers than they ran into one another's arms, crying simultaneously: "You love me! I can see it!"

Zumio, less surprised than in despair at the sudden effect of the torch, of which his art permitted him to know the virtue, tried to retain the princess, but she turned toward him indignantly. "Stop, wretch!" she said to him. "I know you: you're an evil genius."

Those words—which still find accurate applications today—were no sooner pronounced than the castle was shaken to its foundation. The air became as brilliant as the brightest daylight, and Souveraine appeared in all her majesty.

A mortal tremor seized the perfidious Zumio; Souveraine touched him with her wand. "Go, traitor," she said, "wander from country to country until the end of time, inspiring everywhere the scorn that you merit."

At the same time, his seductive face, which had contributed more than a little to his perfidies, was changed into a humiliating decrepitude, passions took possession of his heart, and he disappeared.

Souveraine then addressed Severe. "You have spent centuries," she said to her, "composing that torch in order to know and punish tender hearts; spend as many composing another that discovers false virtues. You will discover what there is in veritable ones more essential than the consequences of amour."

To Babonette, she said: "As for you, I limit your empire henceforth to taking care of my menagerie."

Looking at Canadine, she said: "For you, Madame, I can only have pity. If you want to come with me, I offer you my amity. I would be glad if it can soften the pain caused to you by a constancy so poorly rewarded."

Canadine threw herself at Souveraine's feet, after having thanked her with as much nobility as sensibility. She implored her, by all the generosity that she was testifying to her, to take away from her the privilege of immortality.

Souveraine did not refuse that entirely, but she postponed it until a time so distant that it as easily visible that she was counting on the fay discovering a cure for her heart in the meantime. But Canadine, after having lived in an obscure retreat for centuries, finally achieved the only happiness to which she aspired; she obtained permission to die, and did not take long to profit from it.

All her orders having been given, Souveraine returned King Doudou to his original beauty, and invited him to mount her chariot with Princess Azerolle, leaving Turlupin in his castle, his mind so charged with astonishments that he amused himself all his life recounting them to his valets. She took the happy lovers to the realm of Aglantiers, where she left them, after having honored with her presence the brilliant spectacle of their union.

They lived for many years, without anything diminishing their happiness or their constancy.

Carl Gustaf Tessin: *Faunillane; Or, The Yellow Child*

The Prince of Percebourse having lost his father and his mother in his youth, followed the penchant that he had for traveling. He roamed several lands, spending a great deal there, and returned to his homeland augmented in merit and diminished in money.

He lived in a country held in affection by the fays, and among the various beauties with which they had ornamented a place that pleased them, none equaled the Avenue of Ideas. The trunks of the trees were an alabaster of their natural color, the leaves emerald, and the fruits that only came once every thousand years ripened in the blink of an eye and formed diamonds, at first as big as water-melons, but which then shrank by degrees, becoming tiny in an instant, just like the foam that suddenly spreads over champagne and disappears similarly; only the Sancy of the French crown has been plucked therefrom, and that in the fullness of its decline, its comrades having disappeared before it was picked.[50]

The sun is unable to penetrate that lovely place to the extent that it is necessary to see clearly without being dazzled, and at night, five hundred and eighteen million lamps render a glare well above that of the sun; it is then that most people stroll.

Percebourse was there one day, carefully exploring all the corners and coverts of the admirable place, when he suddenly found himself in a garden filled with the largest and most marvelous fruits in the world.

First of all, near the entrance, there were two currant bushes that bore redcurrants of a prodigious size; the prince had a desire to eat one. As soon as he had bitten into it, the redcurrant opened up and a lovely woman emerged, so young that she still seemed to be a child, but leaning on a staff with a pair of spectacles on her nose.

"Well, by all the fays!" cried Percebourse. "Where have you come from, my little maid? And why do you disfigure your pretty face with those nasty spectacles?"

---

[50] The Sancy diamond, named for its one-time possessor Nicolas de Harlay, Seigneur de Sancy (1546-1629) had a very colorful history. After being borrowed by Henri II and Henri IV it was sold to James I of England, but returned to France with the exiled Stuart king James II, who sold it to Cardinal Mazarin, who bequeathed it to Louis XIV when he died. Tessin had no way of knowing that it would be plundered after the 1789 Revolution and follow a tortuous route via Russia, India and America to arrive back in the Louvre in 1978.

"Alas, Sire," replied the Queen with the Golden Scarves—for it was her— "it is for having disobeyed the One-Eyed Giant, the mortal enemy of the Enchanter Bushy-Eyebrows, my uncle, and filling myself up with redcurrants in spite of his prohibition, that I find my eyesight so weak that, if it were necessary to sew my chemises myself, I'd go naked for want of being able to thread a needle."

"That's quite an appetite you had," said the prince, smiling. "But why does a child who ought to be jumping and turning somersaults need that nasty crutch?"

"Alas, Sire," replied the child, "it's that vile giant again who endowed me with it. Piqued by his prohibition of a paltry redcurrant, I ran afterwards to powder his beard gray and show that I laughed at his orders and rules. He took my intentions badly, and by sneezing, damaged my knee-joints so badly that my weakness hasn't permitted me to walk without a stick since."

"That's a hard-hearted colossus. But why were you stuffed into that redcurrant?" asked Percebourse.

"Alas, Sire," replied the Queen with the Golden Scarves, "it's for having had a kingdom full of gardens and gardeners without ever planting anything there but cabbages and currants. But what do all these details matter to you? You appear to me to be full of other cares; I only want to limp back home to spin gold in order to maintain my poor subjects."

"Go, my charmer," said the prince, obligingly, kissing her little hand with a force that made her squeal loudly. "Go eat cherries, peaches and melons, and don't amuse yourselves with your boxes of powder; go have pavilions built, order flower-beds, fountains and orchards; in a word, as in a thousand, go obey and please the giant, for fear that he might crush you."

The queen made a very gracious reverence, and went her own way, while the prince, without pausing for long over the extraordinary nature of that adventure, reached out to pick another redcurrant, choosing a smaller one in order not to risk biting into an imprisoned queen.

Scarcely had he touched it than it split, and he saw two small white hands emerge, the fingers interlaced, twiddling the two thumbs around one another at an incredible speed.

"Oho!" he said. "I haven't seen anything similar in my travels." And as the hands approached his nose very closely, he wafted them away with the back of his hand, as one tries to waft away a puff of smoke; but the two hands persisted and accelerated their movement.

"Little hands, which don't belong to anyone," he said, becoming impatient again, "although you're nice and plump, people like me don't like anyone playing with their nose. At least go to join your body, in order that I can see whether it's pretty enough to permit you such a liberty, for I've seen beautiful arms with hideous faces."

The hands did not say a word, but, as if offended by such a suspicion, their rapidity became incomprehensible—which did not prevent the prince from remarking that the left one lacked a finger. As he was quick, he caught them, wrapped them in a strawberry leaf and put it in his pocket.

"Am I not going to eat a wretched redcurrant" he said, as he picked another one. This one, borne to his mouth, split like the others, and a plump little finger appeared, the color of snow, proportioned like the most beautiful finger in the world; its movement was to flick in a precipitate but measured fashion, which disturbed Percebourse's well-powdered wig so forcefully that, without further ado, he seized the finger rapidly and shut it in his toothpick-case. Then, drawing away from the fatal currant bush, he went forward, thinking about the Queen of Scarves, the two mutinous hands and the flicking finger.

He perceived an apricot tree bearing fruits so large that it was impossible to eat one without slicing it. He picked one, took out his knife, sat down under the tree, laid out a white handkerchief and started to slice the apricot.

"Hey! Hey!" cried a head, bounding over the grass.

What became of the prince at that sight! It was a perfect female head, with long black curly hair; two large eyes, similarly dark but not curly; eyebrows like jet arched like rainbows, fashioned so that no poor little hair surpassed another; a small turned-up nose; and a vermilion mouth so small that it would have been necessary to slice the apricot into thirty thousand morsels in order to enable it to taste one. But that head was always tilted toward the right shoulder, and no matter how the prince tried to straighten it, it always fell over, with a meditative expression that augmented its charms and interested him in its favor.

"Beautiful bust or wig-head," said the prince, anxiously, "where is your body?"

"Look in the trunk of the tree," replied the tilted head, looking at him with a gaze that burned his heart so deeply that it spread an odor of charred flesh throughout the garden.

"Alas," he exclaimed, "how can I cleave that tree, having neither an ax nor a saw?" He stuck his knife into it, but his knife shattered like glass; he scratched it with his fingernails, and, having ripped them all out he took out the two hands that he had put in his pocket and started scratching again, so forcefully that the nail of the right thumb stayed there. He wrapped it very quickly in black taffeta, and was in despair at having spoiled the beautiful hand without having made any progress in his task or being able to reach the beautiful body.

He was about to abandon a labor that seemed futile when his good genius suddenly inspired him to approach the eyes of the tilted head to the root of the tree. It caught fire so suddenly and so violently that his greatest anxiety was that it would consume the body as well. What was his joy when he saw it leap through the flames! The body was so proportionate, so well made, that all it lacked to be a model was two hands and a head.

He picked up the one that was on the ground, which fit it marvelously. He took the finger out of the case, which joined the hand, and the two hands the two arms, to form the most beautiful woman in the world, with a tilted head, and who only ceased twiddling her thumbs long enough to give her finger time to flick the roots of her hair—which, as we have said, was black.

"Admirable or divine goddess, fay, queen or princess, what put you there?" said the prince, swooning.

"The slaps I gave the giant," said the charming stranger.

They were about to take the conversation further, and doubtless to declare the most urgent things, when they were interrupted by the hissing of a thousand snakes, which were drawing a chariot composed of chopped hearts traversed by darts. A woman with a wrathful expression was in that horrible vehicle; her dress was black, streaked with bright flames; the snakes that she had instead of hair were tied up with a dead-leaf-colored ribbon, and behind her there was a Fury who was curling her snaky locks with a hot iron, which made the crawling population hiss in a manner as terrible as it was singular.

"I am the fay Envious," she cried, as soon as she was within range to be heard, "the Queen of the Land of Desires. What do you want, prince, for having liberated the most useful of my works, and a princess who causes envy and chagrin to Greek and Roman beauties?"

"I desire the princess," he said.

"Take her, the fay interrupted, "on condition that the daughter to whom she will give birth a year from now is put under my protection and confided to my care; and I swear by my snakes, by my darts, by my fire, my corroded hearts and my tresses, that I will render her so perfect that she will be no less envied than her mother."

The prince and the princess lowered their eyes, the prince with joy and gratitude, and the princess by virtue of modesty and decency, at hearing herself named as a maker of daughters when she had not yet consented to marriage. But the fays know everything, so that one knew that the marriage would take place, that a daughter would be born of it, and that she would have her under her protection, so she disappeared without even waiting for their consent.

"Well," said the prince, as soon as Envious had disappeared, "your story, Madame?"

"Alas," said the princess—for enchanted princesses are rich in *alas*es, so this one said *alas*—"I am Pensive, dissimulative and curious..."

"Pensive, dissimulative and curious!" repeated the prince, shaking his head three times. "Hmm! If we weren't already married before the fay...but it doesn't matter. Go on, if you please, and begin with your name, as everyone else begins."

"My name is Princess Pensive," she continued, "and I shall receive an inheritance of faerie when my grandmother, the fay Matador, dies, for in our family there has always been a fay, and that power usually skips the daughter to pass to the granddaughter..."

"By the way," said the prince, "it appears to me, beautiful princess, that it's necessary to conclude our marriage, and afterwards, you'll have plenty of time to tell me all these things, which already reek of the marvelous and the admirable. It's sufficient, for the present, for me to know that I'm marrying a lovely and well born princess."

Pensive, who knew society too well to show any urgency, but who was nevertheless not sorry to change estate, which came back to her characteristics of dissimulation and curiosity, gave her hand to Percebourse, who led her out of the garden into the Avenue of Ideas, and from the Avenue of Ideas to the Temple, and from the Temple to the bed.

The possession, far from diminishing the charm and felicity of that union, augmented them, which was a manifest proof of the protection of the fay and gave desire to the happiest of husbands.

The prince, solely occupied with his satisfaction, had passed six months without remembering the story when, eventually, at midday one fine morning— for Pensive's mornings only commenced at midday—he begged her to finish it.

"Sire," she said, this time without the *alas*, "I am Pensive, dissimulative and curious..."

"By our daughter to come," cried Percebourse, "you've told me that, and I know it. Go on."

"I've always liked going for walks," she continued. "One day when I was taking that pleasure, I encountered the One-eyed Giant on a river bank. I was about to run away on seeing him when he grabbed my dress and stopped me. 'I'll bet my beard and my height,' he said to me, 'that you're thinking about some absent individual who has rendered homage to you, and who doesn't displease you.'

"I didn't think that question merited a reply, and I kept quiet. 'You're pensive, my beauty,' he added, 'you're thinking about a defeat.'

"That reproach irritated me, and earned the giant a slap, for I'm prompt Prince, just so you know," she said, raising her voice.

"And I'm quick, Princess, just so you're not unaware of it," Percebourse replied, taking what she had just said as a threat.

Pensive, calming down, took up the thread of her discourse.

"'If you had a tender and reasonable heart,' said the giant, 'one could talk business with you.'

"'Me, a tender heart, Sire!' I said, 'I've never been in love, and I don't intend ever to fall in love.'

"'You're dissimulative,' the monster interrupted. That impoliteness earned him a second slap, but without being disconcerted, and not feeling, I believe, any great pain, he cried: 'I have a step-brother. Oh, little brute, if only you knew him!'

"'And what is he like?' I said.

"'You're curious,' he replied.

"That misplaced curiosity guided my hand to his cheek again, this time with a force such that the giant, who had seemed immovable after the first two slaps, went as red as Gobelins scarlet and, sneezing, because a part of his enchantments were at the tip of his nose, he separated my finger from my hand, my hands from my arms and my head from my neck, and shut each part in the place where you found them. 'Stay there, slapper,' he said 'until a young prince comes into the garden, pensive with regard to a princess, dissimulative with regard to the choice of his chagrins, and curious to taste these fruits; for, as reverie, dissimulation and curiosity have put you there, only reverie, dissimulation and curiosity can get you out.'

"You know the rest, Sire, having succeeded in accordance with my desires and fulfilled my wishes."

Percebourse did not stop short, and was able to see that, if the princess really loved him, he loved the princess.

At the predicted time, Pensive gave birth to a girl whom she called Faunillane, after the Isle of Fauns, which belonged to her father, but as she has worn a golden robe lined with black ever since, she is more commonly known as the yellow child.

Scarcely had she opened her eyes to the light of day than a mite was seen to enter the room where she was, which soon became an ant, and then a spider, and then a cockchafer, and then a silkworm, and then a lizard, and then a frog, and then a toad, and then a viper, and then a grass snake, and then a rattlesnake, and then a crocodile, and then a winged dragon carrying the fay Envious on its back.

"Where's the child?" she asked.

"Here she is," said the princess, who did not know what it was to break a promise.

Envious disappeared with her prey and put her in an apartment hollowed out in a single diamond. To nourish her she gave her two white balls to suck, which rendered her so beautiful, gracious, perfect and lovable that there was no talk of anything but her beauty and the good fortune of the man who would be able to possess her. Her mildness aided her greatly in making herself desired, and it is said in the journal of her life that she only ever cried or wept at the end of eighteen months, when those balls were metamorphosed into grouse wings, chicken thighs and cocks' crests.

Near the place where Faunillane spent her early years thus was the famous Isle of Woods, where a Temple had been built of a structure more Gothic and venerable than new and magnificent. It contained the ashes of a long race of our kings, prodigies of their centuries and the love of their subjects. Next to that Temple dwelt Princess White Dove, who found on her bed one night a little boy as beautiful as the daylight. Her ambition told her that it was the son of Jupiter, but her reason said no, and even the public claimed that her reason was right.

As no one could imagine where the prodigy came from, while awaiting a favorable revelation he was confided to the care of the fay Tease, called thus not because of her teasing, which had nothing extraordinary about it, but because of an ogre named Bull's-Eye, whom she married, who was hairy and played the lute admirably well. She had known Princess Pensive for a long time, so well that she had made her a present of her portrait to ornament the hall where the ogre played at the head of his musicians. She also carried a sketch of her face made in haste, with a crushed nose, and was linked in amity with the enchanter Bushy-Eyebrows, who had a reputation for great power and little credit.

The Prince of Elbows, as the foundling was named, was raised with admirable care regarding external appearance, but in such a school his interior was scarcely purified, with the result that the innocence of his nature and the malice of his guardians chose him as the battlefield on which a hundred conflicts a day took place, under the conduct of Luxury, Pleasures and Sensuality.

It seemed that his happiness lacked nothing but being linked forever to Princess Faunillane, so the enchanter worked to that end so forcefully, and by means of the composition of a liquor so infernal, that his wife, named Fatty with the Triple Chin, was suffocated by it.

For her part, the fay Envious, who knew how the destiny of the princess would suffer from it, put everything to work to prevent such an ill-matched marriage, and as her power alone was insufficient for that, she went to find the fay Spigot, who joined forces with her; together they plotted the doom of Tease and Bushy-Eyebrows.

Spigot, full of courage, went to find them in the form of a young hunter and engaged them to come into a tent erected in an agreeable wood, filled with game. As soon as they were inside, the tent changed into the fay's Steel Palace, and, by means of her grimoire, she imprisoned that enemy couple in a glass filled with a liquid the color of capillary syrup,[51] placed on the sill of a window, the crystal panes of which were misted by the exhalations of the liquid.

That prison appeared to be eternal, and might have been, but for a visit that Princess Pensive made to Spigot. As soon as the bottled pair saw her they started dancing the passepied with such rapidity that the glass fell over, which attracted the gaze and animated the natural curiosity of the princess, who opened the jar and put her nose inside in order to see such a marvel at closer range.

Scarcely had the enchanter and the fay sensed the approach of liberty than they took advantage of it, and since that time they have desolated the universe more than ever.

---

[51] "Capillary syrup" was a supposedly-medicinal compound made by boiling maidenhair fem, *Adiantum capillus-veneris*, with sugar.

"My beautiful little Prudent, who don't know what you're doing," said Spigot, "you merit being put in that liquid, with your impertinent curiosity."

Pensive, who agreed in her heart that she had merited that reproach, withdrew shamefacedly, imploring the fay not to abandon her, and not to permit the marriage of the Yellow Child and the Prince of Elbows.

"Good," said the irritated fay, "you merit being changed into a pigeon and delivered to the power of your father."

At that point, Envious came in, accompanied by Prince Percebourse.

"Not the glass and the liquid!" she cried. "No, fay, friend, you mustn't do her any harm." Then, turning to the prince, she added: "I know that you've lost considerable treasures in foreign lands, and your daughter will only be given to a prince who will try to discover them, will succeed in doing so, and will bring them back, in order that your estate will know a perfect envy."

As soon as that edict was published, all the young princes started running like lunatics, some to the Paris Opéra, others to the Mercantile Palace, others to the public games, others to the homes of traitors, others to friends who borrowed money, others to the homes of a thousand beauties, and yet others who had no idea where Percebourse had been, started digging in the earth and searching it, to see where his wealth was buried.

All those treasure-hunters were accompanied by a little dog named Joke, who knew all the mysteries of Percebourse and Pensive.

Their return is awaited, in order to learn to whom Faunillane, who is becoming more lovable and more charming every day, is destined. Meanwhile, one cannot doubt the happiness of her fate under the protection of such a powerful and redoubtable fay.

Jeanne-Marie Leprince de Beaumont: *Prince Fatal and Prince Fortunate*

There was once a queen who had two little boys as beautiful as the day. A fay, who was a good friend of the queen, had been asked to be the godmother of those princes and to make them some gift.

"I'll endow the elder," she said, "with all sorts of misfortunes until the age of twenty-five, and I'll call him Fatal."

At those words the queen uttered loud cries and implored the fay to change the gift.

"You don't know what you're asking," she said to the queen. "If he isn't unfortunate, he'll be malevolent."

The queen dared not say any more, but she begged the fay to let her choose a gift for her second son.

"Perhaps you'll choose wrongly," said the fay, "but no matter; I'll grant him whatever you ask me for him."

"I want him to succeed in everything he wants to do," said the queen. "That's the means of making him perfect."

"You might be mistaken," said the fay, "so I'll only make him that gift until the age of twenty-five."

Nurses were given to the two little princes, but on the third day the nurse of the elder prince caught a fever; he was given another, who broke her leg in a fall; a third lost her milk as soon as Prince Fatal began to suckle; and, the rumor having run around that the prince brought bad luck to his nurses, no one any longer wanted to nurse him, or even go near him. The poor child, who was hungry, did not excite pity in anyone however.

A vulgar peasant woman who had a large number of children that she had great difficulty feeding said that she would take care of him if they gave her a large sum of money; as the king and queen did not like Prince Fatal, they gave the nurse what she wanted and told her to take him to her village.

By contrast, the second prince, who had been named Fortunate, came along marvelously. His papa and mama loved him madly, and did not even think about the elder of the two.

The malevolent woman to whom Fatal had been given had no sooner taken him home than she took away all the fine linen in which he was wrapped to give it to one of her own sons, who was the same age as him. Having wrapped the poor prince in a wretched shirt, she took him into a wood, where there were a lot of wild beasts, and put him in a hole with three lion cubs in order that he would be eaten. However, the mother of the lion cubs did not harm him; on the contrary, she suckled him, which rendered him so strong that after six months, he was running around on his own.

Meanwhile, the nurse's son whom she passed off as the prince, died. The king and queen were glad to be rid of him.

Fatal remained in the wood for two years, and a nobleman of the court, who was hunting, was astonished to find him in the midst of beasts. He took pity on him, took him to his house, and, having learned that a child was wanted to keep Fortunate company, he presented Fatal to the queen.

Fortunate was given a master to teach him to read, but the master was commanded not to make him cry. The young prince, having heard that, cried every time he was given a book, with the result that at the age of five, he did not know his letters, whereas Fatal could read perfectly and already knew how to write. In order to frighten the prince, the master was ordered to whip Fatal every time Fortunate failed in his duty; thus, Fatal could apply himself to being good, but it did not prevent him from being beaten. Besides which, Fortunate was so willful and so malevolent that he always mistreated his brother, whom he did not know. If he were given an apple or a toy, Fortunate snatched it from his hands; he made him shut up when he wanted to talk, and obliged him to talk when he wanted to be quiet. In brief, he was a little martyr, on whom no one took pity.

They lived thus until they were ten years old, and the queen was very surprised by her son's ignorance.

"The fay deceived me," she said. "I thought my son would be the most knowledgeable of all princes, since I wished that he would succeed in everything he attempted."

She consulted the fay on that matter, who said to her: "Madame, it was necessary for you to wish that your son had good will rather than talents. He only wants to be very naughty, and he succeeds in that, as you can see." After having said that to the queen, she turned her back on her.

The poor princess returned to her palace, greatly afflicted. She wanted to scold Fortunate, in order to oblige him to do better, but instead of promising her to correct himself, he said that if he were chagrined, he would let himself die of hunger. Then the queen, very frightened, took him on her knees, kissed him, gave him sugared almonds, and told him that he need not study for a week as long as he ate as usual.

Meanwhile, Prince Fatal was a prodigy of science and mildness. He was so accustomed to being contradicted that he was not at all willful, and only devoted himself to anticipating Fortunate's caprices. But the malevolent child, who was enraged to see that his companion was cleverer than himself, could not bear him, and his tutors, in order to please their young master, beat him continually.

In the end, the malevolent child told the queen that he did not want to see Fatal any longer, and that he would not eat unless he was thrown out of the palace.

Fatal was put out on the street, therefore, and as everyone was afraid of displeasing the prince, nobody wanted to take him in. He spent the night under a tree, dying of cold—for it was winter—and having nothing for his supper but a piece of bread that had been given to him out of charity.

The following morning, he said to himself: *I can't continue doing nothing; I'll work for my living until I'm old enough to go to war. I remember having read in history books that simple soldiers have become great captains. Perhaps I'll have the same good fortune, if I'm an honest man. I have no father or mother, but God is the father of orphans; he gave me a lioness for a nurse; he won't abandon me.*

After having said that, Fatal got up, said his prayer—for he never missed praying to God in the morning, and when he prayed he had his eyes lowered, his hands joined and he did not turn his head from side to side.

A peasant who was passing by and who saw Fatal praying to God with all his heart said to himself: *I'm sure that boy will be an honest fellow; I have a yen to take him to guard my sheep. God will bless me because of him.*

The peasant waited for Fatal to finish his prayer and said to him: "Would you like to come and guard my sheep, my young friend? I'll nourish you and take care of you."

"I'd like that," said Fatal, "and I'll do my best to serve you well."

The peasant was a prosperous farmer who had a lot of servants, who often stole from him; his wife and children also robbed him. When they saw Fatal they were very content. "He's a child," they said. "He'll do whatever we want."

One day, the wife said to him. "My friend, my husband is a miser who never gives me any money. Let me take a sheep, and you can say that a wolf has carried it off."

"Madame," Fatal replied. "I'd like with all my heart to be of service to you, but I'd rather die than tell a lie or be a thief."

"You're nothing but a fool," the woman said to him. "Nobody would know that you've done it."

"God would know, Madame," Fatal replied. "He sees everything that we do, and punishes liars and those who steal."

When the farmer's wife heard that she threw herself upon him, hit him and tore out his hair. Fatal wept, and the farmer, having heard him, asked his wife why she was beating the child.

"Truly," she said, "he's a glutton. I saw him this morning eating a pot of cream that I wanted to take to market."

"That's bad, being a glutton," said the peasant, and immediately called one of his servants and commanded him to whip Fatal. The poor child protested in vain that he had not eaten the cream; his mistress was believed rather than him.

After that, he set forth with his sheep, and the farmer's wife said to him: "Well, do you want to give me a sheep now?"

"I'm very sorry," said Fatal. "You can do what you want to me, but you won't make me lie."

The malevolent creature, in order to avenge herself, engaged all the other domestics to maltreat Fatal. He stayed out in the country night and day, and instead of giving him something to eat, like the other servants, she only sent him bread and water. When he returned she accused him of all the evil done in the house.

He spent a year with that farmer, and although he slept on the ground, and was very poorly nourished, he became so strong that people thought he was fifteen when he was only thirteen. In addition, he became so patient that he was no longer chagrined when he was scolded inappropriately.

One day, when he was at the farmhouse, he heard it said that a neighboring king was fighting a great war. He asked his master for leave and went on foot to that prince's kingdom in order to be a soldier. He enlisted with a captain who was a great lord, but who resembled a street-porter, he was so brutal. He swore, he beat his soldiers and he stole half the money that the king gave him to feed and clothe them. Under that malevolent captain Fatal was even more unfortunate than with the farmer. He had enlisted for ten years, and although he saw the greater number of his comrades desert, he did not want to follow their example, for he said: *I've received money to serve for ten years; it would be stealing from the king if I broke my word.*

Although the captain was an evil man, and he mistreated Fatal like all the others, he could not help holding him in esteem, because he saw that he always did his duty. He gave him money to carry out his commissions, and Fatal had the key to his room when he went on campaign or dined with his friends. The captain did not like reading but he had a large bookshelf in order to make people who came to his house think that he was intelligent—for in that country it was thought that an officer who did not read history would never be anything but a fool or an ignoramus. When Fatal had done his duty, instead of drinking and gambling with his comrades, he shut himself away in the captain's room and tried to learn his métier by reading the lives of great men; and he became capable of commanding an army.

He had already been a soldier for seven years when he went to war. His captain took six soldiers with him to go to visit a small wood, and when he was in the wood, the soldiers said in low voices: "It's necessary to kill this wicked man who has us caned and steals our bread."

Fatal told them that it was necessary not to commit such an evil deed, but instead of listening to him, they said that they would kill him with the captain, and all five drew their swords. Fatal set himself beside his captain, and fought with so much valor that he killed four of the soldiers himself.

His captain, seeing that he owed his life to him, begged his pardon for all the harm he had done him, and when he told the king what had happened, Fatal was made a captain and the king gave him a good pension.

Well, the soldiers would not have wanted to kill Fatal, for he loved them like his children, and, far from stealing what belonged to them, he gave them his own money when they did their duty. He took care of them when they were wounded and never reprimanded them because he was in a bad mood.

Meanwhile, there was a great battle, and when the commander of the army was killed, all the officers and soldiers fled; but Fatal shouted loudly that he would rather die with his weapon in his hand than flee like a coward. His own soldiers cried that they would not abandon him, and their good example having made the others afraid, they rallied around Fatal and fought so well that they took the son of the enemy king prisoner.

The king was very content when he knew that he had won the battle, and told Fatal that he would make him the general of all his armies. Then he introduced him to the queen and his daughter the princess, who gave him their hands to kiss. When Fatal saw the princess he was immobilized. She was so beautiful that he became madly amorous, and it was then that he became very unhappy, for he thought that a man like him was not made to marry a great princess.

He resolved, therefore, to conceal his amour carefully, and he suffered the greatest torments every day; but it was even worse when he learned that Fortunate, having seen a portrait of the princess, whose name was Gracious, had become amorous and had sent ambassadors to ask for her in marriage.

Fatal thought he would die of chagrin; but Princess Gracious, who knew that Fortunate was a cowardly and malevolent prince, begged her father so forcefully not to force her to marry him that the ambassador was told that the princess did not want to marry yet.

Fortunate, who had never been contradicted, became furious when the response of the princess was reported to him, and his father, who could not refuse him anything, declared war on Gracious's father—who was not greatly embarrassed by that, for he said: "As long as I have Fatal at the head of my army, I have no fear of being beaten." He therefore sent for his general and told him to prepare to make war.

Fatal, however, threw himself at his feet and told him that he had been born in the kingdom of Fortunate's father, and could not fight against his king. Gracious's father became very angry, and told Fatal that he would put him to death if he refused to obey him, but that, on the contrary, he would give him his daughter in marriage if he defeated Fortunate.

Poor Fatal, who loved Gracious madly, was very tempted, but in the end, he resolved to do his duty, without saying anything to the king; he quit the court and abandoned all his riches.

Meanwhile, Fortunate put himself at the head of his army in order to go to war, but after four days he fell ill with fatigue, for he was very delicate, never having done any exercise. Heat, cold and everything made him ill. However, the ambassador who wanted to pay his court to Fortunate told him that he had seen the little boy that he had thrown out of the palace at the court of Gracious's father and that it was said that the latter had promised him his daughter.

At that news Fortunate became extremely angry; as soon as he was cured he went to dethrone Gracious's father, and promised a large sum of money to anyone who brought him Fatal. Fortunate won great victories, although he did not fight himself because he was afraid of being killed. Finally, he laid siege to his enemy's capital city and resolved to attack it. On the eve of that day, Fatal was brought to him, bound in heavy chains, for a large number of people had set out to search for him.

Fortunate, delighted to be able to avenge himself, resolved that before the attack he would have Fatal's head cut off within view of his enemies. That same day he gave a great feast to his officers because he was celebrating his birthday, having just completed twenty-five years.

The soldiers who were in the city, having learned that Fatal had been captured and that his head was to be cut off in an hour, resolved to perish or save him, for they remembered the good that he had done them while he was their general. They therefore asked the king for permission to make a sortie in order to fight—and this time, they were victorious. Fortunate's gift had ceased. As he was trying to flee, he was killed.

The victorious soldiers ran to remove Fatal's chains, and at the same moment two chariots brilliant with light appeared in the air. The fay was in one of the chariots, and Fatal's father and mother in the other, but asleep. They only woke up when the chariots touched the ground, and were very astonished to find themselves in the middle of an army.

Then the fay addressed the queen and, introducing Fatal to her, said: "Madame recognize in this hero your elder son; the misfortunes that he has experienced have corrected the faults of his character, which were violent and reckless. Fortunate, on the contrary, who was born with good inclinations, has been utterly spoiled by flattery, and God has not permitted him to live any longer, because he was becoming more malevolent every day. He has just been killed, but, to console you for his death, know that he was on the point of dethroning his father, because he was tired of not being king."

The king and queen were very astonished, and they embraced Fatal wholeheartedly, of whom they had heard very advantageous mention. Princess Gracious and her father learned about Fatal's adventure with joy; he married Gracious, with whom he lived for a long time in perfect concord, because they were united by virtue.

Charles Duclos: *Acajou and Zirphile*

Intellect is not always worth as much as one assumes, amour is a good teacher, and providence does well what it does; that is the moral of this tale—it is as well to inform the reader of that, for fear that he might misunderstand it. Limited minds never suspect the intention of an author and those that are too vivid exaggerate it, but neither of them like reflecting; that is why I mention the matter.

There was once, in a land situated between the realm of the Acajous and that of Minutia, a race of maleficent genii who were the shame of their species and the bane of humankind. Heaven was touched by the prayers made against that accursed race; the majority perished tragically, none remained but the genius Podagrambo and the fay Harpagine, but it seemed that those last two were the inheritors of all the malevolence of their ancestors.

They were both unintelligent; the quality of genius or fay only gives power, and malevolence is more often associated with stupidity that with intelligence. Podagrambo, although a very noble, very highly-placed and very powerful lord, was still very stupid. Harpagine was reputed to have more intelligence because she was more malevolent—the two qualities are still confused today—although that proves that she had very little; that is because she was annoying, although malicious. As for the genius, he was wicked enough only to desire evil and imbecilic enough that if anyone had done him a favor he would not have perceived it. He had a gigantic stature, with all possible ill grace. Harpagine was even more frightful: tall, stiff and dark; her hair resembled serpents, and when she transformed herself it was usually into a spider, a bat or an insect.

Those two monsters had no less presumption. Harpagine prided herself on her charms and Podagrambo his good fortune; they had a small, elegantly furnished house, in which one could see ugly Chinese figurines, Martin varnishes,[52] chaises longues and cushions; it was there that they went to annoy one another; they finally threatened the public with marrying, in order to perpetuate their names. Posteromania is the common eccentricity of the great; they love their posterity but do not like their children at all. The proposition of the genius and the fay was received as a declaration of war.

The great Council of Faerie thought the affair sufficiently important to warrant a general assembly. The matter was exposed, agitated and discussed; there was a great deal of talk and deliberation, but something was nevertheless

---

[52] "Martin varnish," named for its French popularizer, who imported the idea from the Far East in the early eighteenth century, involved the addition of powdered gold or bronze to the varnish in order to give it a metallic sheen.

resolved. It was decided that Podagrambo and Harpagine could never marry unless they made themselves loved; that sentence seemed to condemn both to celibacy; or, if they were able to become lovable, it would be necessary for them to change character, and that was all that was desired.

Immediately, they searched their Colombat[53] for some house they could honor with their choice; but it was not sufficient to find a party, it was necessary that they make themselves loved; they understood that they would never succeed in that without a singular artifice. However blind self-esteem may be, one soon discovers one's faults when interest becomes involved.

Harpagine, more inventive than the genius, said to him something like this: "My plan is to take children so young that they don't have any ideas as yet. We'll bring them up ourselves; they'll never see anyone else, and we'll form their hearts to our liking; the prejudices of childhood are almost invincible. My party," she added, "is already chosen. The King of the Acajous only has one son, who is about two years old; I'll ask for his education to be confided to me. He wouldn't dare refuse me; he'd fear my resentment, and one does more for those one fears than those one esteems. I'll do the same for you with regard to the first little princess that is born."

Podagambro approved of a plan so well-conceived and the fay departed on her great mustached dragon; she arrived at the home of the King of the Acajous and made her request, which the poor prince dared not refuse.

Delighted to have the little Prince Acajou in her hands, Harpagine left again, and thought of nothing thereafter but carrying out her project. With a stroke of her wand she built him an enchanted palace, which I beg the readers to imagine according to their taste, and of which I will spare them the description for fear of boring them. What I am obliged to tell them, however, because they are not obliged to divine it, is that Harpagine, is designing the garden of the palace to serve as a promenade for the little prince, attached a talisman to it, which prevented him from leaving it unless he fell in love; and as she was the only woman he could see, she did not doubt that her sex alone would take the place of beauty and that the desires of adolescence would give birth to amour in Acajou's heart.

An accident that Harpagine had not foreseen undermined her design from the outset and obliged her to amend her plan. Acajou had received at birth the gift of beauty, he was to be the best looking prince of his time; that flattered the fay's hopes marvelously, who knew in addition that the first fruits of the most lovable young men belong by right to the old, but what caused her chagrin was that the child had also been endowed with all the qualities of intelligence. Harpagine sensed that they would only make him more difficult to seduce. She

---

[53] One of several popular Almanacs issued annually in France was published in Paris by the Veuve Colombat.

resolved immediately to correct by art what her pupil had received from nature and to spoil his intelligence, being unable to deprive him of it.

She went into her laboratory, where she composed her drugs; the most efficacious words and the most powerful charms were employed; she composed two bowls of magic sugar; in one there were pastilles whose virtue was to inspire bad taste and falsify the intellect; the other contained bonbons of presumption and stubbornness; the person who ate them always judged falsely and seasoned mistakenly, sustained his sentiment obstinately and gave himself to everything ridiculous—with the result that the malign fay had every reason to hope that if the prince ate them, he would feel a passion for her all the more powerful because it would be more extravagant.

She went immediately to give the bonbons to the child, but as she engaged him by her caresses to eat some, she tried to adopt a jovial expression, which caused her to make such a frightful grimace that the child was scared and threw the bowls in her face. A so-called reasonable person would have been easier to seduce, but enlightened nature gives those who have not yet delivered themselves to reason a surer instinct, which warns them of what is contrary to them.

The bonbons of presumption were those that the fay regretted the least; she had no doubt that Acajou's birth would always give him enough, but she could never get him to swallow any of them. She gave them to a traveler as a precious curiosity, adding to them the virtue of multiplying themselves. The man who received them brought them to Europe, where they had a brilliant success. Everyone wanted to have them; they were sent as presents; everyone carried them in a pocket in little boxes; they were offered as gallantries, and that custom is still conserved today. They do not all have the same virtue, but the old ones are not completely lost.

Meanwhile, Harpagine imagined giving Prince Acajou such a bad education that it would be more effective than all the bonbons in the world.

The news spread then that the Queen of Minutia was about to have a child, and all the fays were invited to witness the birth. Harpagine went along with the others. The queen gave birth to a girl who was, as one might suppose, a miracle of beauty, who was named Zirphile. Harpagine was counting on asking the queen to confide her education to her, but the fay Ninette had already anticipated her, and was charged with bringing up the princess.

Ninette was the declared protectress of the realm of Minutia. She was no more than two and a half feet tall, but her small figure brought together all the charm and grace imaginable. She could only be reproached for an extreme vivacity; it seemed that her mind was too restricted in such a small body; always thinking and always in action, her penetration often carried her beyond objects and prevented her from discerning more precisely those she could not reach. Her piercing sight and lively step were the reflection of her mental qualities.

In order to remedy that excess of vivacity, which fools strove to imitate, and which they called hare-brained in order to console themselves for not succeeding, the Council of the Fays had made Ninette a present of a pair of spectacles and an enchanted crutch.

The virtue of the spectacles was to weaken the eyesight and temper the vivacity of the intelligence in relation to the soul and the body. That was the first invention of spectacles; they have since been employed for an entirely opposite purpose; that is how everything is abused. What proves, however, how harmful spectacles are to the intelligence is seeing how aged supervisors are deceived every day by inexperienced young lovers, which can only be blamed on spectacles. As for the crutch, it served to render the stride more reliable by slowing it down.

Ninette only made use of the fays' presents when it was a matter of conducting a delicate affair; she was, in any case, the best creature one could see: an open soul, a tender heart and a scatterbrained mind rendered her an adorable woman.

The fays who witnessed the birth of the princess thought of endowing her, as was customary, and, being true women, were commencing with gifts of beauty, grace and all the external seductions, when Harpagine, whose malice was more enlightened than the benevolence of the others, said, muttering between her teeth: "Yes, yes, you'll have all that, but you'll never have anything but a stupid beauty, I'll answer for that, for I endow you with the most complete stupidity."

Having spoken, she left. The fays did not take long to perceive their negligence. But Ninette, having put on her spectacles, said that she would substitute by means of education for what the child lacked in the matter of intelligence. The other fays added that in order to remedy in part the harm that they could not destroy totally, the imbecility of the princess would cease as soon as she fell in love. A woman who only has need of that remedy is not completely without resource.

Having taken Zirphile in her arms, Ninette transported her to her palace in spite of the traps of the wicked fay.

On the other hand, Harpagine was no longer occupied with anything but giving her pupil the worst education she could imagine, in order to stifle his intelligence by bad cultivation. As she hoped that stupidity would render all the cares that were taken on Zirphile futile, she ordered the governors of the little prince only to talk to him about ghosts, phantoms and the Great Beast, and to read him tales of fays in order to full his head with a thousand nonsensical ideas. We have conserved in our day, out of stupidity, what the fay invented out of malice.

When the prince was a little older, the fay summoned masters from all directions, and as, in making mischief, she never settled for the mediocre, she changed all the objects of those masters. She invited a famous philosopher, the Descartes or Newton of his era, to teach the prince to ride a horse and use weapons. She charged a musician, a dancing master and a lyric poet with teaching him logic. The others were distributed in accordance with the same pattern, and they made much less difficulty because they were all particularly smitten with what was not their profession. How many people there are who encourage the belief that the same care has been taken of their education!

With so many precautions, Harpagine did not doubt the success of her project. However, in spite of the lessons of all his masters, Acajou succeeded in all his exercises; he did not acquire, in truth, any useful knowledge, but errors did not obtain any purchase on his mind. A fortunate compensation! After good lessons, the most instructive are ridiculous ones, and those of Acajou's masters put him on guard against their precepts.

He became as handsome as Amour; he was made for painting; all his graces developed. Harpagine pretended that all that was growing for her; it is necessary to let her pretend, and see what happens.
*

While Harpagine was striving with all her might to make an idiot of Acajou, the fay Ninette was losing her own mind trying to give one to Zirphile. The little fay's court assembled all the amiable people there were in the realm of Minutia. On the days when she received them in her apartment nothing was more brilliant than the conversation.

There was no discourse in which there was only common sense; there was a torrent of sallies; everyone questioned; no one responded accurately and everyone understood marvelously, or did not understand at all, which comes to the same thing for brilliant minds; exaggeration was the favorite figure and very much in fashion; without having keen sentiments, without being occupied with useful objects, they always talked the language. People were "furious" about a change in the weather; a ribbon or a pompom was "the only thing in the world they loved;" between the shades of a color they found "a world of difference;" there was nothing by which they were not "overwhelmed" or "confounded."

In sum, they exhausted excessive expressions on trivia, with the result that if, by chance, they came to experience violent passions, they could not make themselves understood and were reduced to remaining silent, which gave rise to the proverb that great passions are mute.

Ninette did not doubt that the education Zirphile received in her court would eventually triumph over her stupidity, but the charm was very powerful. Zirphile became more beautiful every day, and the most stupid child that one could ever see. She dreamed instead of thinking and only opened her mouth to say something silly. Although men are not hard to please in the matter of a pretty girl, and always find that she speaks like an angel, they could only praise her beauty. The poor child, always ashamed, received their eulogies as a favor and responded to them that it was a great honor. That was not what they wanted, however, and they laughed at her naivety and sought to seduce her innocence.

It is necessary to know a little about vice to fear its traps. Zirphile was candor itself, and candor is no safeguard for virtue, but Ninette watched over her dear pupil carefully. She put her among her maids of honor, where there were often vacant places; the majority left before their time was finished; there was no corps in the court more difficult to recruit.

Zirphile was not spoiled by the example; it was in vain that the young courtiers gathered around her. Too great a desire to appear lovable prevented them from being so. Zirphile was untouched by their homage; all their discourse seemed to her to be insipid or fatuous. In addition, men are governed by their senses before knowing their heart, but the majority of women need to love and are rarely seduced by pleasures if they are not led astray by example. At any rate, no accident befell Zirphile because, for safety's sake, she did not allow any man to approach too closely for her honor, or even certain women too closely for her innocence.

While she lived thus at Ninette's court, Acajou was becoming bored in Harpagine's home. He was already fifteen; his intelligence only served to inform him that he was not made for living with all that surrounded him. He began to sense the nascent desires of nature, which, without having any determined object, sought one everywhere. He had already perceived that he had a heart, of which the senses were only the interpreter. He experienced the melancholy that one could place in the rank of the pleasures, although it makes one desire more intense ones. He sighed after someone who could dissipate that disturbance, but sought solitude nevertheless. He withdrew to the most distant regions of the park; it was there that, in seeking to clarify his ideas, he sometimes made a rather stupid figure.

Harpagine, who knew Acajou's trouble, flattered herself that she would soon be the remedy for it; but she saw with chagrin that all the caresses she tried to give him only served to revolt him and put him in a bad mood. Offered caresses rarely succeed, and it is even rarer that they are offered when they merit being sought.

Harpagine was in despair. The council of fays had pronounced that he would only remain in her hands until he was seventeen, after which she would not have any power over him.

The Kings of the Acajous and Minutia were waiting for that happy moment impatiently, in order to unite their kingdoms by the marriage of their children. The genius had no sooner learned about that project than he swore that it would not come to fruition. He prepared a superb equipage and went to Ninette's court. He was received with the species of politeness that one has for all powerful people, which does not oblige any esteem.

In order not to waste time with superfluous compliments, he declared his sentiments—which is to say, the desires she inspired in him—to Zirphile right away. The little princess, who had not learned to dissimulate, did not let him languish, and declared naively all the repugnance she felt for him. He was quite astonished by that, but instead of being put off, he attempted to touch her heart in order to obtain her hand. He thus tormented himself in search of all the means of pleasing. Unfortunately, the more one searches for them, the fewer one finds.

He tried to imitate the agreeable men of the court, but everything that did not render him merely ridiculous made him appear more sullen. There are ridiculous things that do not affect all sorts of faces, and even a few compatible with grace, but Podagrambo did not shine in that regard; the more he tried to play the fop, the more he proved that he was only a fool.

Finally—for I do not like long stories—after having wearied the court with his idiocies and fatigued Zirphile even more with his insipidities, he was no further forward than on the first day. He was considered the most tedious genius that had ever been seen; that was a discourse repeated from the apartments all the way to the outbuildings.

Podagrambo suspected that he was the joke of the court; that was not by virtue of his penetration, but an eccentricity common among fools is to think more highly of themselves while believing that others are speaking ill of them. In his chagrin, he returned home in order to meditate some spectacular vengeance and to discuss with Harpagine means of abducting the princess.

Ninette, having anticipated the enterprises that might be formed against her dear Zirphile, had given her a scarf, the charm of which was such that it wearer need have no fear of any violence.

Meanwhile, the innocent Acajou could not emerge from the melancholy that was consuming him, and Zirphile was harassed by the same trouble. They often went for solitary walks, and when hazard conducted each of them separately to the palisade that separated Ninette's and Harpagine's gardens—for as I have said, or should have said, they were neighbors—they felt drawn by an unknown force and halted by a secret charm; each of them reflected separately on the pleasure they savored in that place, the most neglected in the park; they returned to it every day, and night had difficulty tearing them away from it.

One day, when the prince was plunged in his meditations next to that palisade, he let out a sigh. The young princess who was on the other side, in the same state, heard it. She was moved by it; she concentrated all her attention; she listened.

Acajou sighed again. Zirphile, who had never understood what anyone said to her, understood that sigh with an admirable penetration; she responded immediately with a similar sigh.

The two lovers—for they were lovers, from that moment on—understood one another reciprocally. The language of the heart is universal; it only requires sensibility to understand it and to speak it. Amour sent at that instant a flaming arrow into their hearts and a ray of light into their minds.

After having heard one another, the young lovers sought to see one another, in order to understand one another better. Curiosity is the fruit of the first knowledge. They advanced; they searched; they parted the branches; they saw one another. Gods, what transports! Their age, the vivacity of their desires, the tumult of their ideas, the fire that animated their senses, and perhaps even their ignorance, are necessary to understand their situation.

They remained motionless for some time; they were gripped by the tremor that the novelty of pleasure bears into new senses. They touched one another; they maintained silence. However, they let a few poorly articulated words escape. Soon, they were talking with vivacity; they asked one another a thousand questions; they did not make any accurate responses, but they were satisfied with what they said and found themselves enlightened regarding their doubts. They understood, at least, that they desired one another without knowing one another, that they had found what they were looking for.

Acajou, who had only ever seen Harpagine, found himself transported into a new world; and Zirphile who had never paid the slightest attention to the men of the court, thought she was seeing a new being. Acajou kissed Zirphile's hand. The poor child, who did not believe that she was according a favor, even less committing a sin, let him do it. Acajou, whose intentions were too good for him to imagine that caresses could offend anyone, redoubled his, and Zirphile returned them naively; having not the slightest idea of vice, she could not have any of modesty.

They sat down on the grass; it was there that they embraced. They clasped one another narrowly. Zirphile delivered herself to all the transports of her lover; she received him in her arms. Acajou raised his hands to his dear Zirphile's nascent breasts; he pressed his mouth to hers; their souls flew to their lips; they were confounded; they were plunged into a divine intoxication; they floated in pleasures and were borne away by a torrent of delights; their desires were inflamed and they did not understand how they could be so happy and yet desire more. They enjoyed all the beauties that they saw and did not imagine that there were hidden ones on which the final phase of happiness depended. It seems to me, however, that they did not profit badly from a first lesson.

Those amiable children were so intoxicated by their felicity that they forgot all Nature and gave no thought to separating. But as they were much later than usual in returning from their walk, Harpagine and Ninette came to look for them, and each of them called to her ward from her own side. Our lovers were frightened by their voices, and, separating regretfully, they feared that their union might be troubled if it were suspected. Amour is confident in its desires and timid in its pleasures.

The image of Zirphile that was engraved in the depths of Acajou's heart enabled him to see Harpagine more horrible than ever. As for Zirphile, although she was obliged to suspend the pleasure of seeing Acajou, what she had just savored gave a new shine to her beauty and spread an air of satisfaction throughout her person. Pleasure embellishes and amour brightens.

Nothing equals the surprise that Zirphile's intelligence caused the entire court; that same evening in Ninette's apartment someone made one of those bad jokes so familiar to mediocre individuals who think they have some superiority over others a little more stupid; poor Zirphile was often the object of them; she replied this time with so much accuracy and finesse, and so little bitterness, that the bad jokers—who were women—were astonished by the sagacity of her replies and humiliated by the manner in which she made them; the men were charmed, and applauded.

Ninette wept with joy and the women blushed with chagrin. Until then they had been able, albeit with difficulty, to pardon Zirphile for her beauty because of her stupidity, but there was no longer any means of doing that; they had no other resource but malevolence. That last quality, in causing hatred, often creates respect, but the little princess was too well-born to make use of that vulgar means.

Our two young lovers had found Amour's first lesson too good not to return to his school. What a joy it is to be instructed by pleasures!

To begin with, lovers, like thieves, take superfluous precautions; by degrees they neglect them; they forget the necessary ones too, and are caught. That is exactly what happened to our imprudent young couple, and it was the genius who surprised them. Fools only live on the faults of the intelligent. One evening, he saw the young lovers retiring; he was beside himself with rage, but as he had a maxim of never doing anything without asking for advice, although he carried on regardless afterwards, he resolved to consult Harpagine.

On learning the news, the malevolent fay conceived the most violent chagrin. The genius told her that there was no other means of avenging herself than abducting the princess. Although the fay was as furious as him, she preferred to get rid of her rival rather than seeing her in the same place as her lover; she therefore concealed her anxiety and told the genius that it was necessary for him to take charge of that endeavor, flattering herself that he would never have the intelligence to succeed in it.

The next morning Podagrambo hid behind a tree near the palisade where the lovers came in search of one another. Acajou's masters had orders to prolong their lessons so that he could not reach the rendezvous before the princess.

Acajou, so mild in character, showed ill humor for the first time; even temper does not subsist with passion. While he was becoming impatient, the tender Zirphile came to the palisade; she was anxious on not finding her lover there; he had the habit of preceding her. She looked everywhere, and finally dared to enter Harpagine's park and passed close to the genius. At the sight of him, fear seized her and she tried to flee, but it was with so little precaution that her scarf remained hooked on a branch. Instantly, the genius seized her by the dress.

"Aha!" he said. "You come here in search of a marmoset, innocent beauty, and it's for him that you spurn me!"

Poor Zirphile, seeing herself betrayed by fear itself, which had caused her to lose her scarf, had recourse to dissimulation. Before having loved she would not have been so clever. A first adventure, which inspires conceit in a young man, renders the falsity necessary to women; one sex is obliged to blush at what makes the glory of the other.

Although Zirphile was candor itself, she attempted to deceive the genius. "I am astonished," she said, "that you impute to amour a pure effect of my curiosity, which is what made me enter this place. I am no less surprised that you make use of violence, you who can expect everything of your birth, and even more of your amour."

The genius was mollified somewhat by that flattering speech, but although the princess was advising him to hope for everything of his merit, and he was quite convinced of it, he did not want to let her escape.

"If your heart is so sensible for me," he said, "You should not make difficulties about coming to my palace. All these petty concerns of vulgar lovers are frivolous formalities that only delay pleasure without rendering it more intense."

"Well," Zirphile replied, "I'm ready to go with you, and to prove my sincerity, return my scarf to me, so that no evidence will remain here of my escape and your violence."

The genius thought he might swoon with pleasure and admiration for Zirphile's presence of mind.

"Oh, certainly!" he cried. "It's necessary to confess that amour gives women intelligence, for I would never have thought of that, and would have gone away like a fool."

Immediately, he detached the scarf and handed it to the princess, kissing her hand. But she, no longer having anything to fear, pushed him away scornfully.

"Go away, traitor," she said, "or fear the wrath of the fays; that scarf is the pledge of their protection for me."

As she finished speaking she drew away, leaving the genius confounded, arrested by a force to which his own power was obliged to cede. He could only admire Zirphile's presence of mind more than he had before.

That reflection was doubtless not the one that occupied him most. After having remained motionless for some time, he went back to find Harpagine, confused and desperate, and told her by what charm his power had been rendered futile.

Although the fay learned with chagrin the virtue of the enchanted scarf, she was somewhat consoled by the failure of the enterprise of the genius. She hid the different interest that she took in it, however, and, as consolers are never more eloquent than when they are afflicted themselves, she calmed him down by promising to destroy the enchantment of the scarf and render him master of the princess.

The fay was unaware of the misfortune that menaced her. While she was deliberating with the genius as to the means of reestablishing their power, Acajou ran to the palisade. After waiting for some time for Zirphile, impatience made him enter Ninette's park, and, torn between fear and desire, he gradually progressed as far as the palace.

The news of his arrival soon spread there. Ninette came to meet him, followed by her entire court. Acajou advanced respectfully toward the little fay and kissed the hem of her dress. As soon as he and Zirphile saw one another they ran to one another, and the presence of the entre court did not prevent them from giving one another the most vivid evidence of the pleasure they had in seeing one another again.

Zirphile recounted naively the danger she had run; the prince had become even dearer to her in consequence. The more women have risked, the readier they are to sacrifice more. Ninette, naturally indulgent, did not pause to examine whether there might have been anything irregular in the conduct of the young lovers; it was sufficient that fortune had arranged everything for the best.

Having learned about the flight of Acajou, Harpagine entered into the most horrible anger, and came to demand his return, but, fortunately for him, he had reached his seventeenth year that very day and the fays' decree freed him then from the power of Harpagine. She conceived so much rage in consequence that she lost her amour for him, which had only ever been a sentiment foreign to her heart, and, no longer meditating anything but projects of vengeance, she left in order to invite the fay Envious to form an alliance with her.

The celebrations that followed Acajou's arrival did not permit anyone to occupy themselves with Harpagine's resentment.

The men who had tried to please Zirphile lost all their pretentions on seeing Acajou. The women never wearied of admiring his beauty, and they all became secret rivals of his lover. Acajou was so full of his amour that he did not even perceive the enticements of which he was the object. They came from all directions, but when it was admitted that the hearts of the two lovers were closed to any other sentiment than their own amour, it was generally decided that Zirphile had become even more stupid since she had fallen in love than she had been before; that Acajou's beauty was devoid of physiognomy and had nothing piquant about it; that their amour was as ridiculous was it as new to the court; and that it did not constitute a society.

People paid no further attention to them, therefore, and they were so occupied with one another that they did not perceive the desertion of the court any more than they had perceived its urgency. Ninette, who had previously protected Zirphile's conduct with so much care against the temerity of the court fops, left her with Acajou without anxiety; she believed that true love is always respectful, and that the more a lover desires the less he dares to attempt.

The maxim is delicate, but I do not believe it to be absolutely reliable; however, it was not belied in this instance.

They were only waiting for the Kings of Acajou and Minutia in order to celebrate the marriage; their ambassadors had arrived and had already settled everything; the liveries were made; the garments were being finished; they only lacked a pompom; the latest fashions had been ordered from Paris, from Chez Chapt, modeled on dolls of the same size as Ninette. In brief, everything essential was ready; it only remained to negotiate matters regarding the laws of the two states and the interest of the peoples.

The two lovers did not quit one another for an instant. Often, in order to escape the tumult of the court, they spent days in the most remote boscage of the park. They gave one another a thousand innocent caresses; they continually said the trivial things so interesting to lovers, which are repeated incessantly without ever being exhausted, and which are always new.

One day, while they were enjoying one of those delightful conversations, the heat obliged Zirphile to take off her scarf in order to talk with more liberty. Harpagine, who had rendered herself invisible in order to surprise them, appeared to their eyes escorted by the fay Envious, mounted on a chariot drawn by snakes and surrounded by a prodigious quantity of hearts pierced by arrows; they were as many talismans representing all those who rendered homage to envy, and the arrows were the image of the merit that caused the greatest torture to the envious.

Harpagine immediately struck Zirphile with her wand and carried her away in the midst of a cloud at the very moment when Acajou was kissing her hand.

The unfortunate prince prostrated himself before the fay, begging her only to make the weight of her vengeance fall on him and to spare the princess. He said everything that love and generosity inspired, in vain. The cruel fay looked at him with blazing eyes.

"Do you dare to hope for any mercy?" she said. "My heart is no longer sensible to anything but hatred. I want to exercise my vengeance at a single stroke on you and your lover; she will pass into the hands of your rival, who is odious to her."

With those words, the chariot flew away, and left Acajou plunged in the utmost despair.

Ninette was soon instructed by her art of faerie of what had happened, but the misfortune of people who know everything is that they never foresee anything. She came to look for the prince. He was beside Zirphile's scarf, which he was moistening with his tears. The little fay neglected nothing to console him, without being able to make herself heard. After having taken him back to the palace almost in spite of himself, she shut him in her cabinet, put on her spectacles and consulted her large books in order to discover what action she could take in that misfortune.

The court reasoned variously; some talked about it a great deal but scarcely cared about it; others, without saying anything, took more interest in it. The women, above all, were untouched by the loss of Zirphile; several flattered themselves that they might console the prince.

They were still in the first phase of court news, in which everyone talks without knowing anything, recounting the circumstances while waiting to know the facts, and so much is said about so little, when they saw Ninette appear, who announced with vivacity the Zirphile could easily be extracted from the hands of the genius. Everyone hastened to discover what means would be employed.

"Listen to me," said the little fay. "I've just discovered that all the power of Podagrambo and Harpagine depends on an enchanted vase that they possess in a secret place in their castle; it's guarded by a subaltern genius who is transformed into a Chartreuse cat. It's unnecessary to employ great efforts to take possession of it; it's sufficient for the adventure to be undertaken by a woman of irreproachable honor, something that ought not to be rare at the court. She will not find any obstacle, but for any other person to attempt the adventure would be futile."

"That's a fortunate discovery!" said a fop. "I'm most eager to compliment Prince Acajou."

"Shut up," said the fay. "If it required a reasonable man, no one would choose you."

"I'm not joking," relied the young fop, in an ironic tone. "I really dread that a competition in virtue here that might degenerate into a civil war."

"I've anticipated that inconvenience," retorted Ninette, "So I want lots to be drawn in order to prevent any reason for jealousy."

The tickets were made immediately, and the name that appeared was that of Amine. That was a young woman who was pretty rather than beautiful, lively, scatterbrained and exceedingly coquettish, free in speech, circumspect in conduct, continually making enticements and always afflicted by a troop of young men.

Hearing herself proclaimed, Amine was neither prouder nor more embarrassed than usual, but a certain murmur went up that did not seem to be a very definite applause. Ninette took that as a bad augury for success; that is why she nominated Zobeide to accompany Amine, because two virtues are better than one. Zobeide was a little older and more beautiful than her companion; she was in addition a prodigy of virtue and slander; it was even claimed that she was so severe in her sagacity as to have the right to tear apart all the other women pitilessly. A fine privilege of virtue!

At any rate, the two of them departed, and went, following their instructions, to a small building separate from Harpagine's palace. Amine, still lively, marched in the lead. They did not find any obstacle; they went through several doors that opened of their own accord. They finally reached a chamber where they perceived a vase on a marble table, the form of which was not commendable; it closely resembled a chamber pot. I am sorry not to have a nobler term or image. They would never have imagined that it was the treasure for which they were searching if Ninette had not described it.

If the form of the vase was vulgar, its virtue was admirable; it rendered oracles, and reasoned about everything like a philosopher; it was then a great eulogy to be compared to one for reasoning.

Amine and Zobeide also found the cat that had been mentioned to them; they tried to stroke it, but it scratched Zobeide, although it allowed Amine to caress it, gave her the velvet paw, arched its spine and fluffed up its tail in the most elegant fashion.

Amine, charmed by such a fortune beginning, took the vase and was already lifting it up when Zobeide tried to touch it with her hand. Immediately, a thick smoke emerged from it, which filled the room. A frightful noise was heard. Fear gripped Amine; she dropped the vase on the table from which she had taken it, and the genius appeared instantly with Harpagine. They seized Amine and Zobeide and only spared their lives in order to lock them up in a dark tower.

Ninette was soon informed, as usual, of the failure of the enterprise; she sought the reason and learned from the whole court that Amine was as sage as she was coquettish, whereas Zobeide savored the pleasures of a secret commerce with an obscure lover while she fatigued everyone by the display of her false virtue.

Ninette immediately declared that, the vase having cracked when Amine had dropped it on the table, the power of the genius, without being completely destroyed, had at least been weakened by that accident.

Acajou, no longer listening to anything but his despair, made a vow, in order to avenge himself on the genius's enchanted pot, to destroy all the chamber pots that he encountered, and from that moment on he executed his oath on all those he found in the palace. There was a frightful disorder; the scandal was so great that Ninette tried to make him listen to reason with regard to so many innocent vases, but she was never able to calm him down.

In that embarrassment she had recourse to the Council of Fays. The affair seemed very important, and it was decided that, the power of the genius being weakened, he could no longer keep all of Zirphile's person; that, without losing her life, her head would be separated from her body and transported to the Land of Ideas until it was reunited with her body by the person who could reach that land and disenchant her.

Ninette proposed that it would be more appropriate to leave the head than the body in the power of the genius, for fear that he might make her fall in love with him while she had lost her head, and marry her immediately. The fays paid attention to that difficulty, and ordered that the body would be permanently wrapped in a living flame that would not allow anyone to approach it except the master of the head.

The fays' sentence was carried out as soon as it was pronounced. The genius wanted to attempt the adventure, without ever being able to approach the Land of Ideas. The mad can easily reach it, but the stupid can never land there. As for Acajou, who was madly in love, he had no difficulty in getting there.

491

The Land of Ideas is very singular, and the form of its government does not resemble any other. There are no subjects; everyone there is a king and reigns as sovereign over the entire State without usurping anything from the others, whose power is no less absolute. Among so many kings, jealousy is unknown; they merely wear their crowns in a different fashion. Their ambition is to offer it to everyone and to want to divide it; that is how they make conquests.

The limits of so many realms contained within a single one are not fixed; everyone extends or narrows them according to his caprice.

Acajou recognized that he was in the realm of Ideas by the multitude of heads that he encountered in his passage; they hastened toward him and all spoke to him at the same time in all sorts of languages and in different tones. He searched for the head of Zirphile but could not see it.

Sometimes he encountered heads that, having resisted misfortune, had been lost in prosperity, some by fortune, others by dignities. He found the heads of wastrels, a multitude of misers, and a quantity lost in war, the heads of authors lost by virtue of success, others by failure, several by appearances of success, and a host by envy and chagrin at the success of their rivals. Acajou found an infinite number of heads lost incognito, which he never wanted to name and I do not want to guess. There were many heads of philosophers, mystics, orators, chemists, etc. He saw many lost by caprice, by putting on airs, by indiscretion, and, in turn, by libertinage and superstition. Some excited his compassion; he drew apart from others as importunate, and trampled underfoot all those that envy had doomed.

In order to find Zirphile, Acajou searched for heads that were said to have been lost for amour, but when he examined them closely he only found the heads of coquettes or those jealous without amour. Fatigued by so much research, in despair because of his lack of success, stunned by all the stupidities he heard, the prince retired into a clump of trees in order to get away from the multitude of crazy heads by which he was assailed. He lay down on the grass and started reflecting on his misfortune.

As he looked around he saw a few trees laden with fruits. He was so exhausted that he had a yen to eat a pear. He picked it, but scarcely had he put his knife to it than a head emerged from it, which he recognized as that of his dear Zirphile. Nothing can express the astonishment and pleasure of the prince. He got up in haste in order to embrace such a dear head, when it moved away a few paces and placed itself on a rose-bush in order to make a body of sorts.

"Stop, Prince," she said to him. "Remain tranquil, and listen to me. All the efforts you make to grasp me will be futile. I would throw myself into your arms if destiny permitted it, but as I am enchanted, I can only be picked up by hands that are also enchanted. Alas, I sigh after my body, and I don't know whether it is still worthy of me; it is still in the hands of the genius and I dare not think about that without shuddering; my head spins."

"Reassure yourself," said Acajou. "The fays, touched by your misfortunes, have taken your body under their protection."

"How you tranquilize me!" said Zirphile. "In any case, dear prince, you know that all my tenderness is for you, and you would be too generous to reproach me for a misfortune of which I am innocent."

"That is well said," replied the delicate Acajou, "but inform me promptly where I can find the enchanted hands you mentioned to me."

"You will find them," said Zirphile, "in the park where they are fluttering; they are those of fay Nonchalante, who was deprived of them because she did not know what do with them. I'll tell you the story. There was once..."

"Oh, damn it," Acajou interrupted, impatiently, "I don't have time to listen to tales; as long as I have the hands I don't care about their story. I'll go to look for them right away."

"Go," said the princess, "and deliver me from the cruel enchantment in which I'm languishing. You might have noticed that all the lost heads that are in this abode only seek to show themselves, without blushing at their estate; there's only me who is obliged to hide myself in fruits; as I'm the only head lost by amour, I'm an object of scorn for the others..."

The head continued to talk but the prince had already gone. He had realized that the princess, since she was no longer anything but a head, had become rather fond of talking.

He had not taken a hundred steps through the park when he encountered the enchanted hands, which were fluttering in the air. He tried to approach them in order to catch them, but as soon as he tried to touch them he received flicks, which appeared, to begin with, to be very insolent. However, as his happiness depended on grasping them, he employed all his skill in trying to catch the fatal hands. Every time he thought he had them they escaped him, giving him a slap, or knocking his hat to the ground. The more ardor he put into pursuing them, the more they fled him.

That pursuit went on so long that poor Acajou was completely out of breath. He stopped for a moment, and, finding himself next to a trellis he plucked a cluster of grapes in order to refresh himself. Scarcely had he tasted one, however, than he felt an extraordinary revolution within him. His mind's vivacity was augmented and his heart became more tranquil. His imagination was increasingly inflamed; all the objects therein were painted with fire, passing with rapidity and effacing one another, in such a fashion that, not having the time to compare them, he was absolutely incapable of judging them.

In a word, he went mad.

The fruits of that garden, by virtue of an intimate rapport with the heads that inhabited it, had the virtue of causing the loss of reason, but, unfortunately, they had no effect on intellect. Acajou found himself, in an instant, the most mentally active and most insane of princes

The first effect of such a sudden change was the cooling of the heart. Acajou lost all his amour. Veritable amour can only subsist with reason. Instead of the tender and respectful urgency that he had previously had for Zirphile, he only conserved a slight memory of her. He did not even feel compassion for the misfortune of the princess. The fact of having lost her head appeared to him to be a hilarious thing. It is often from that point of view that a mind devoid of judgment envisages the misfortune of others.

Conceit succeeded modesty in Acajou's mind, and replaced very amply with pretentions the real merit that he had lost.

"I must have been quite mad to run after a head," he cried, "when I could turn those of all the women of the court of Minutia. Let's go; it's necessary to fulfill my destiny, which is to be generally loved and admired without engaging my liberty."

Having said that, he left.

Seeing Acajou arrive, Ninette ran to meet him and asked him about the fate of Zirphile. The prince told her that she was only a head, which could not be grasped; that all his cares had been futile, that he had made his decision; and that constancy without happiness was the virtue of a fool.

He proffered a quantity of other fine maxims, which soon enabled Ninette to understand that the prince's character had changed considerably, but that he had an infinite amount of wit. In the beginning, she was sorry that he had not bought the princess back; however, as the present object always prevails over the absent one in lively minds, she consoled herself for the loss of Zirphile by means of the pleasure of seeing Acajou again.

The entire court hastened around him, more out of curiosity than interest. They expected only to find a sage and modest prince, who would give them, as usual, all the ridiculous things imaginable, but they soon conceived a more advantageous idea of him. The conversation became lively and brilliant.

The attentive reader will doubtless recall that the fay's spectacles served to shorten the sight; she had taken them off in order to see the prince arrive from further away, and as she had not put them back on, she formulated arguments at the limit of vision.

Acajou did not stop talking; he said in a moment a thousand extravagant things that delighted the entire court with admiration and rendered all the women mad for him. They listened avidly, and cried: "Oh, how witty he is!" In the end, they gave him so many eulogies that he was obliged to blush, even by conceit. It seemed that the greatest good fortune that could happen to a prince was to lose his reason; all those who encountered him complimented him on it, and the others wrote it down.

Acajou no longer having any amour, became the declared lover of all the women, the fury of good fortunes combining easily with madness. He began with a fairly pretty woman, a free spirit liberated from prejudices, who made the reputation of all the young men since she had lost her own. As it was not necessary to have her to be scornful of her, and sufficient to have had her to be disgusted with her, he quit her two days later. He took another with a charming face, a tender heart and a mild character, who only needed, in order to merit being loved, to receive fewer lovers.

Acajou disdained fixing her, and soon gave her several rivals. He was only occupied in extending the list, and they all hastened to be inscribed there, only having found him lovable since he had been incapable of love.

After having had a large enough number of celebrated women to put to his credit, he resolved to seduce a few uniquely to make them lose the reputation for virtue that they had. If he learned that there was a woman loved tenderly by a cherished husband she immediately became the object of his cares, and such was the latitude that the title of fashionable man inspires that he succeeded in everything in which he should have failed.

The affairs that the prince had at court did not prevent him from descending into the bourgeoisie, where his successes were even more rapid because those who submitted thought they were associating themselves with women in society in sharing their stupidities. Even the men, instead of hating him, envied him and sought him out, admiring him without esteeming him.

Although those who employ their time very badly are those who have the least remaining, the prince had plenty of empty moments by virtue of the lightness with which he treated his good fortune. In any case, fashion required one sometimes to appear bored. He therefore sought a new dissipation in intellectualism, which was then in fashion. It is true that, in order to avoid a certain pedantry that study often gives, the secret had been found of being a scholar without studying. Every woman had her geometer or her intellectual, as she had once had her spaniel.

Acajou, following that plan, gave himself body and soul to all the areas of science and literature. He talked physics and geometry. He made metaphysical dissertations, verses, tales, comedies and operas. The prince excited general admiration. It was claimed that professional authors could not come close to him. Everyone knows that that is only men "of a certain fashion," who have what is called "class," that are superior to the genius of the world and quite "without pretention."

Nothing was comparable to Acajou's lot; a collection of his witty sayings was published, which became everyone's favorite reading; it was entitled *Perfect Persiflage*—a very useful work at court, appropriate to render a young man brilliant and insupportable.

In the end, Acajou fund himself fatigued by his own success; he had never put anything but pleasure in place of amour; posing had succeeded pleasure, and distaste had almost the effect of reason and rendered life insupportable; an honest man would be unfortunate to be condemned to it. Without becoming more reasonable, he became sad. In any case, the property of intellect alone is to excite admiration at first and then to weary its own admirers. The majority of the women who had had the ambition to please him began to blush at finding themselves on an exceedingly numerous list, and disfavored him; he was even accused of being wicked, under the pretext that he made up songs and jokes that mocked his best friends and held up everyone to ridicule. However, he had no evil intention; he only wanted to divert himself by amusing others; but people are always unjust.

Ninette, not understanding how her dear Acajou could cease to be fashionable, put on her spectacles in order to judge the matter without prejudice, and after having examined it thoroughly, recognized that he did indeed have a great deal of wit, but that he was no less mad for that. She engaged him to recount everything that he had done in the realm of Ideas.

Acajou, not knowing where she wanted to get to, gave her a very detailed account, because he loved talking about himself. When he reached the cluster of grapes that he had eaten, Ninette cried: "Ah! I'm no longer astonished that you have so much intellect!"

"Oh, why?" said Acajou.

"It's because you have no common sense," the fay replied.

"A fine conclusion!" said Acajou.

"I know," said Ninette, "that you have too much intellect to be easy to convince, especially when someone talks reason to you, but that's because you've lost yours. The fruits of the realm of Ideas are a deadly poison to it. Fortunately, we have the remedy; I have a trellis whose virtue is to cause the loss of intellect; it's only known to me. I sometimes give the grapes to members of my court who have too vivid an imagination; I want you to taste some."

"I can see people here who have certainly eaten them to excess," replied Acajou, "but I swear to you that I'm not tempted to make use of them. Look elsewhere for the secret of becoming reasonable and that of losing intellect."

"There's no surer one," the fay interjected, "and you're no longer in a state to sacrifice any."

With that, Ninette said a great many flattering things to the prince. She knew that the intellect allows itself to be seduced by self-esteem more readily than persuaded by reason."

Acajou, however, in spite of all Ninette's eloquence, was mad enough not to want to lose intellect; that had to be the work of amour.

The young prince had never savored true pleasures, because his desires had always been anticipated; his whims only clung to the novelty of objects, and vivacity uses them up so quickly. He had fallen into a languor, from which caprice extracted him occasionally, only to plunge him back into it again. The amour of which Zirphile had made him feel the initial effects reawakened as soon as the intoxication of the senses had dissipated and vanity was no longer nourished. He sensed a void in his heart that only amour could fill. The misfortune of those who have loved is to find nothing that can replace amour.

Acajou confided his situation to Ninette and begged her to enable him to see Zirphile again, since he would also lose his intellect if he were deprived of her any longer. The fay then took her crutch and led Acajou into a garden that only she knew. That place was garnished with trees laden with the most beautiful fruits in the world, each of which had a particular virtue.

Some caused the loss of the passion for gambling, which is so deadly; others the passion for contradiction, so inconvenient in society; these the passion for domination, so insupportable; those the passion for affairs, so useful to those who possess it and so exhausting to others; and several others, including the satirical spirit, so amusing and so detested, and its even more dangerous opposite, the spirit of complaisance and flattery. One does not see those excellent fruits in our desserts. It is a great pity that that excellent garden is not open to all evil spirits; they would come back more amiable, without being any more stupid than they were before. First I would send there…,

[*A sheaf of pages is missing here more considerable than the rest of the work; any readers who regret that can substitute names, beginning with their own.*]

Having made Acajou approach the trellis whose grapes caused the loss of the spirit of presumption, posing and conceit, Ninette ordered him to pick a cluster. Then, having put on her spectacles, and taking Zirphile's scarf, she said: "Prince, take this scarf; where you go into the Land of Ideas you will only have to wave it in the air, holding it at one end. The enchanted hands that you pursued in vain will come to seize it, and you will be able to catch them. You will then be able to take possession of the head of the princess. When you need to eat or drink you have only to take a few grapes; they will be sufficient for you. Also give some to Zirphile, in order to calm the vapors that must have altered her head somewhat; without that precaution you'll find her so different from herself that, after having been inconstant by virtue of madness, you might well become so by virtue of reason. When you have the head we shall soon be in possession of the body by the attraction that affects women whose head carries away the body. It's appropriate, before your departure, that you eat some of these grapes."

Acajou hesitated slightly, but, animated by the desire to see Zirphile again, and perhaps believing that his intellect was proof against anything, he put a few grapes in his mouth. The effect was sudden; it seemed that he had previously been enveloped by a cloud that had just dissipated and that a veil had been lifted from before his eyes. Objects all appeared different to him. He blushed instantly, and no longer dared speak except to express his gratitude to the fay.

When he went back into the palace he found a collection of his works on his table; he wanted to scan it, in order to verify his condition. He could not imagine then that he had been stupid enough to write them; he yawned on reading his romances and his comedies, and that same evening he hissed one of his operas.

Having wearied the court with his extravagances, and annoying it again by virtue of the return of his reason, Acajou departed the next day before dawn and returned to the Land of Ideas, guided as promptly by amour as he had been by madness.

He found the same objects that he had encountered the first time and followed Ninette's advice exactly. With the aid of the scarf he rendered himself the master of the enchanted hands. He immediately went in search of Zirphile's head, and to that effect he opened a prodigious quantity of pears without finding it. From there he passed on to peaches and melons, and was making a frightful devastation of fruits when he heard a loud burst of laughter. He looked to see where it was coming from and perceived the head of the princess, which, instead of coming to him, mocked his research and his urgency.

As amour is weakened by absence and madness spreads by contagion, Zirphile's head had lost much of the vivacity of its passion and was beginning to adapt to the new country that it inhabited. Acajou sighed, but, remembering the marvelous grapes, of which he had a cluster, he threw a few of them to the head of the princess, which swallowed them, while bantering.

Her blindness was immediately dissipated. She flew toward the enchanted hands, with which the prince received her. Nothing can express the transports by which he was seized. He let the hands go where they wished, and no longer occupied himself with anything but the precious head of his dear Zirphile. He covered it with kisses, which she could not avoid.

She was completely red with modesty, although, in the state in which she found herself, her lover's caresses could not have very dangerous consequences. In any case, it is not always necessary to listen to the plaints of modesty; that which is born of amour easily pardons the transports that it is obliged to forbid.

Acajou wrapped the princess's head in her scarf and resumed the road to Ninette's palace. Night having surprised him, a terrible storm blew up, which obliged the prince to seek shelter. As one can imagine, it was not for him. Lovers fear nothing, but he wanted to put Zirphile under cover, in addition to which he feared bumping the princess's head or his own against some tree.

In that embarrassment he perceived a light in the distance toward which he directed his footsteps. After having walked, at the risk of breaking the dearest head—which is to say, that of the princess—he arrived at the foot of a pavilion that terminated a garden; he knocked on the door.

A moment later he saw an old woman appear who was holding a candle in her hand, and who asked him, grumbling, who he was and what he wanted. Acajou did not want to identify himself in a condition so unworthy of his rank. He hesitated momentarily over the quality he ought to adopt, and as he had a head full of his principal misfortunes and all the pottery he had broken at one time, he replied, without really knowing what he was saying, that he was a poor man who repaired broken faience and that he was asking for shelter for the night.

At those words the old woman's face softened slightly. "Come in," she said, "be welcome. You can render me a service; I have a cracked chamber pot that you can repair."

The old woman immediately went to fetch that precious item of furniture and put it in Acajou's hands in order that he could get to work. The prince, as ashamed of the profession that he had just adopted as of the first usage that he had to make of it, took the old woman's pot. Then, recalling the terrible oath he had made never to spare any chamber pot until he had disenchanted the princess, he was uncertain for some time between the dread of perjury and that of violating hospitality.

Scruple finally prevailed, and he threw the pot against the wall, breaking it into a thousand pieces.

I do not know whether the reader, indignant at Acajou's lack of politeness, will be astonished by what followed, or whether, by virtue of a singular sagacity, he has already anticipated it. At any rate, those who do not have much penetration will be very glad to learn that the chamber pot in question was the fatal vase to which the power of the genius and the fay was attached, and the custody of which they had confided to the old witch. Scarcely had he broken it than there was a sound like thunder, and frightful howling. The castle was destroyed; the palace collapsed. The genius and the fay, delivered to their impotent rage, fled into the desert, where they perished miserably.

Acajou, without being moved by all that upheaval, marched toward the terrible place where the body of the princess was enchanted. The flames that defended it divided as he approached, and, at the moment when he presented the head to it, the body advanced to meet it and was reunited with it.

The fay Ninette appeared instantly, followed by her entire court; her first thought was to deliver the unfortunate. The fluttering hands were disenchanted and returned to the fay Nonchalante, on condition that she was laborious. She devoted herself absolutely to toil, and invented the art of tying knots.

Amine and Zobeide were taken out of prison. From that time on Amine had the privilege of doing anything without anyone having anything to say about it; apparently, she was sensate enough to take advantage of it. As for Zobeide, she doubtless continued to live as usual, but ceased to spread slander.

Ninette, after having given her first cares to the unfortunate, was only occupied thereafter with the marriage of the two lovers. It was celebrated with all possible magnificence. They lived happily and had a large number of children, all of whom were prodigies of intelligence, because they were born with an extreme penchant for amour.

THE DECADENCE OF THE FAYS 1751-1788

Author Unknown: Cornichon and Toupette

Advertisement

A manuscript in characters unknown to me fell into my hands a year ago, I ran to the libraries; my consultations were futile. I consulted scholars of ancient languages, equally fruitlessly. I imagined that it was magic. I am not a sorcerer; the fashionability of that passed a long time ago in France. What an embarrassment! Far from being discouraged, however, my curiosity was only more piqued.

"At least let's see the Cabalists," I said. I paled for six months over Paracelsus, Cornelius Agrippa, Raymond Lull, Albertus Magnus and the rest. If those authors did not provide me with complete enlightenment, at least they put me on the track. I found established there the existence of powers of the air, fays, genii, gnomes, sylphs, etc., and a relation of those intelligences with the Cabalists, the motive for which must, I judged, reside in the signs that they used. The acquaintance of a few Rosicrucians spared me a great deal of labor. I had myself initiated, but I was reduced to my own studies.

By dint of observing those signs and the letters of my manuscript, I thought that I was able to discern a few distant connections. I knew that the science of numbers is a principal branch of that of the Cabalist; I had recourse to the most profound algebra, and I eventually succeeded in discovering the unknown term. All the clouds that covered my work were dissipated, and I soon found myself in a state to compile a Cabalitico-Fayic Dictionary, with the aid of which I perceived that I possessed a precious fragment of the history of the fays.

The author, who appears to be contemporary, did not have it in mind to enlighten posterity as to the nature and the functions of fays, and the climes that they inhabited; that is a pity for the Republic of Letters. Faerie is a genre that is gaining favor every day; details of all those matters would have removed many doubts and enriched a foundation that produces so many fine tales.

I could dispense with talking about my translation; I am sheltered from the criticisms of confrontation; I want to say, however, that it is not literal. Fayicism in French would be more disagreeable than Germanism, or any other ism, for which translators are sometimes reproached. The facts, however, and everything that can be rendered into our language without torture are conserved there faithfully. I have been tempted, it is true, to suppress the greater part of a fragment that serves as an introduction to the book; that is the disaster of the islanders. That appears to me to be a little serious for a work that could be treated as a bagatelle, but I made the reflection that the fate of these puerile tales, with which children are amused, does not affect the entire horoscope of my book, which unites all the characteristics that one can reasonably demand for the confidence of a history, and that fragment also contains rather curious things, of which I dare not retrench any.

I confess that I have not been so reserved with regard to a large number of minor events detailed with a care as affected as it is futile, repetitions and reflections that a child might have made; I have excised all that, but I have taken care to note it in the relevant places. Although it is true that, while often suppressing the reflections of my author, I have permitted myself a few, that is because I thought them much better than his. That a translator can take the liberty of inserting a few of his own thoughts within those of his author is a small retribution for faithful, rather tedious labor, which it would be unjust to refuse him.

One might perhaps be astonished not to see in a work of this importance, either an index, or a privilege, or even a list of errata; that is because the urgency one has in producing a book of which one has a good opinion does not leave time to compile and index; I might provide one in subsequent editions, and even a list of errata, which will be all the better because one could then add one of afterthoughts. With regard to the privilege, there are so many good books that are published without one, that one is content with an approval; but it is so ample that, out of modesty, it has not been judged appropriate to print it. It will suffice to say that it relates principally to the words "the end."

That, I believe, is all I have to say about this work, and perhaps it will be too much, but I beg you to consider that it is necessary for an advertisement to advertise.

There was once a land a very long way from here, and in that land there was a spring that rejuvenated old people and aged young ones. That marvel was the work of the fay Dindonnette, also known as the Fay of the Island, and sometimes as the Fay of the Spring; she was a former protectress of the people of the country. That fay, the best creature in the world, but the most ill-advised, considering that youth almost always aspires to a more advanced age, while old people, on the contrary, incessantly praise and regret their youth, thought that she might procure their common happiness by procuring the accomplishment of both wishes.

If she had been acquainted with the works of Monsieur Pope,[54] she would have learned there that all is well; or if, at least, she had made her design public, perhaps someone would have been found with sufficient common sense to point out the inconveniences to her; but, having no suspicion of any, she wanted to add to that benefit the pleasure of surprise.

It was during the night that the sole source of fresh water in that land, which was small and surrounded by an immense sea, acquired by means of her power the quality that I have just said, to a degree in conformity with her zeal—which is to say, excessive. She did not fail, early in the morning, to go and station herself in a place near the spring, which was in the center of the city, in order to enjoy, without being perceived, the spectacle of the first metamorphoses that would occur there.

It did not take long to convince her that her intentions were fulfilled even beyond her hopes. Infants visibly acquired the stature and vigor of adolescents, and decrepit old people exchanged their caducity for the weakness and imbecility of early childhood. She believed that she had extracted them from the power of death. The joy that she felt did not permit her to follow any longer the design she had had of remaining unknown; recognition is such a legitimate price of benefits that she could no longer refuse the delicate pleasure of enjoying that which she thought she merited. She declared to all the people that such an astonishing marvel had assembled around the spring that it was owed to her.

It is not easy to represent the joy of those who gained from that exchange, the dread and disturbance of the others, and the general surprise of everyone. But the facility that the former had to spread out in all directions, or to let their common delight burst forth by coming together, caused it to prevail over the plaints of the latter, reduced by the weakness of the state into which they entered to moaning in isolation. The result was that the bulk of the nation, believing themselves to be fortunate, never ceased blessing the good fay Dindonnette, who had enabled them suddenly to find themselves in the state, or very nearly, in which everyone had desired to remain for life.

However, the effects of the enchanted water became ever more obvious as the use of it continued. Such rapid progress gave everyone fear for the future. It was not without suspicion that they approached the spring; they gave way easily to the most eager. Those who thought they still lacked the charms of the most beautiful youth were there at dawn.

They would have been fortunate if they had been able to fix themselves, but every drop of water that they swallowed thereafter, acting in accordance

---

[54] The reference is to Alexander Pope's "An Essay on Man" (1733-34), which attempts to "vindicate the ways of God to Man," arguing that God's work—the Universe—is perfect, and that its apparent imperfections are due to the limitations of human intellectual capacity. Voltaire's characterization of Pangloss in *Candide* (1759) might well have had Pope in mind as well as Gottfried Leibniz.

with the irrevocable supernatural laws that had been given to it by the fay, soon made them surpass the imperceptible limits of the pleasant state that they had desired with so much ardor. Those who had been extracted from the infirmities of old age were seen, with astonishment, transported into infancy, and the prospect of an imminent caducity drove the young to despair.

The fay was alarmed herself, but it was too late; like gods, fays cannot destroy their work.

What was the desolation of that miserable people when the veil of a false joy had been lifted by the experience of a few days! They saw the full extent of their misfortune. Everyone set about digging wells in all the places they thought appropriate to it, but in vain. The bosom of the earth only offered in those climes masses of stone or arid sands. To increase the misfortune, the rainy season, the duration of which is brief and fixed, had just passed, and would not return for nine or ten months. People took advantage of the nocturnal dew, which was abundant, but far inferior to their needs, as well as animal milk and all the liquids that fruits and plants could produce when their juices were expressed.

The sea opposed invincible obstacles everywhere to the aid that a nation instructed in the art of navigation might have been able to obtain from elsewhere. The poor folk did not have the idea of a ship; content with the small portion of land that was their lot, they did not know that there was any elsewhere; or, if they suspected it, the one that they inhabited having thus far furnished all the things necessary to life, they had not envisaged anything beyond that could tempt their desires and which merited troubling the peaceful way of life that made their happiness.

In that extremity, a few, seduced by the hope of attaining more fortunate climes, dared to trust their strength in order to swim across vast seas. Their sudden loss, perceived from the shore, deterred the others. Several, seeing themselves constrained to draw the imbecility of infancy or the caducity of old age from the spring, avoided that cruel alternative by a voluntary death. A small number, more attached to their duties and the objects of their inclination, consecrated to the service of others the residue of vigor that they still enjoyed, until they were relegated themselves to the two extremities of life, and, equally incapable of procuring their needs, they were enveloped in the common doom.

It is true that the water did not contain any positively mortal cause, but the thread of the days of those who were obliged to drink it was nevertheless cut; the spindle merely turned more rapidly, bringing back the same individual several times over though the various ages, which had previously only been seen once in the course of human life. But such a prompt passage from one state to the other brought an indescribable disturbance to society. One arrived there without having had the leisure to prepare for it; nor were others, occupied with themselves, able to anticipate it and to dispose for every age what was necessary to its usage, and to constitute for every person his estate, his rank and his profession.

In order to regulate the general economy of the state and that of particular families it would have required the new ideas that such a great change can produce. It was necessary to put the views of the legislator in proportion with the sudden revolutions to which the life of the people had just been subject. What a task! Could the plan of a sage government, the belated work of the experience of several centuries, be born in such sad circumstances?

If those whose experience and reflections had acquired reliable notions of the things that form the bonds of society and ensure its consistency had been able to conserve them in the various states through which they passed so rapidly, everything would have evened out. No one would have been surprised to see a weak infant, provided with the enlightenment that he had once acquired, directing the difficult toil of a robust laborer who had not yet seen two harvests; and in the Senate, the advice of a man who had already given evidence of his merit and his talents would have imposed itself on young old men in spite of the mask of infancy. But that was not the way it was; every age was followed by its natural advantages and inconveniences; imbecility was the prerogative of both extremes, and the progress or decline of reason depended, as among us, on the state of the organs.

The man who fell into infancy on emerging from old age did not carry with him any memory of his past knowledge. A new world was offered to his astonished sight, and the apprenticeship that it was necessary for him to make in order to be useful to himself and to others was always forestalled by the fatal term in which decrepitude diminishes the exercise of reason, at the same time as it suspends or forbids the usage of corporeal faculties—hence the entire privation of any education, which entails that of the idea of the common good and the means of finding one's own. Sentiment was only an obscure instinct, which reason only enlightened for brief intervals, and only served to render those who enjoyed it more miserable, by revealing greater woes to them without allowing them to perceive the slightest remedy.

That situation, utterly deplorable as it was, might still have allowed those who experienced it to subsist physically for some time, but other misfortunes combined with it as a necessary consequence of the first. The child who is born finds an aid in the bosom of his mother that assures his life; the language of cries is always understood by maternal love. On the contrary, the old people did not find anyone to sustain their decline into infancy; the law had not substituted outside aid for the difference there is between maternal and filial love, since there was no law; it was only a small number of those wretches who found in their children cares capable of postponing their doom momentarily.

An even deadlier blow collaborated in the destruction of that unfortunate people. The fatal water operating more powerfully on those who drank it immediately, the growth of children in the maternal womb had almost its usual duration, and the term of childbirth usually surprised those unfortunates in a state of old age or infancy, which cost the lives of both.

In sum, the combination of so many fatal causes destroyed that people in a matter of months, and the desolate Dindonnette, their protectress—or, rather, their murderer—having not been able to render them any other service than the duties of the sepulcher, quit that place of horror never to return.

A few centuries after those events, the fay Selnozoura[55] who usually made a tour of the world twice a week, on medical advice, for a change of air and to find some relief for the restlessness in the limbs that tormented her, stopped off on the Island of the Spring. She never directed her route via the same places; that small part of the world was unknown to her. The beauty of the climate engaged her to explore it.

Cornichon and Toupette were accompanying her. The latter had been given to her at the most tender age by the genius Kristopo,[56] her uncle by marriage and her neighbor, who had taken her off the hands of poor and incapable parents and given her an education. Cornichon had been bought some time afterwards from a slave merchant; his family was unknown but he appeared to be a little older than Toupette, who was now fourteen years of age.

Their early childhood had made the amusement of the fay, who loved the children dearly, and the affection she had for them increased as age developed a thousand lovable qualities in them. None of Toupette's escaped Cornichon, who rendered her a sincere homage. Toupette mingled with a marvelous sagacity all of Cornichon's merit, and was too amiable not to love him madly; when Amour makes such good use of his power, he is sure of general applause. The fay gave him all of hers; the innocent expression of the sentiments of their hearts, which was given free expression in her presence, amused her.

Her design was to marry them eventually, but the status of wife might have rendered Toupette less appropriate to traveling, and the obligation of sometimes

---

[55] Author's note: "In the original language, this name contains the idea of grit and also that of agitation. The former was doubtless caused by the fay's character; the other, which appears contrary to it, was apparently combined with it by reason of her continual travels. It is noticeable that ancient names are appropriate to the qualities and occupations of the people to whom they were given." Naturally, the author does not bother to explain that, in familiar French terminology, Cornichon refers to a stupid person and Toupette to an impudent one. nor does he point out other *double entendres*, arising from the fact that Cornichon is derived from *corne* [horn] and that a *toupette* is a tuft, although that etymology eventually become relevant to his plot

[56] Author's note: "In spite of the care that I have given to it, I have not been able to find any significance in this name relative to character. Kristopo was a good genius all round; perhaps there was nothing remarkable about him." The name could not, of course, be derived from the Greek cris- [separate, or decide] and topos [place]

separating from her for long intervals, so she had contented herself with flattering them with their union without marking a precise time for it. That hope ameliorated the ennui of the ambulant life they led, and the fay diminished its fatigue by means of the power of her art.

She made use of a kind of little ship, which carried them through the air nine hundred and fifty times more rapidly than ours carry us over water. Her stables were full of extremely fast hippogriffs of great beauty, and the clouds that were at her orders would have furnished her with comfortable vehicles if she had wanted to make use of them, but she usually only made use of supernatural means in cases where art and industry could not do anything. The profound knowledge that she had of mechanics had given her the idea of the vehicle in question, and she made use of it with pleasure.

It was, as I have said, a small ship, whose port was on the platform of the highest tower in her palace. When she wanted to set sail, the vessel was released on a slide in the same manner as a ship is launched on to water. Then a large number of balloons attached around it sustained it in the air; she placed herself at a tiller that could be maneuvered with one hand, and the other operated a kind of keyboard, the keys of which corresponded to the various maneuvers of the sails and disposed them in a manner suitable to receive the wind that departed from a huge bellows operated by Toupette and Cornichon. It was fabricated in a manner to augment the impulsion of the air prodigiously, and yet to be handled with as much facility as winding a watch.

It was by that means that she traveled immense distances in such a short time, rising up into the clouds or skimming, so to speak, the surface of the sea. When she landed, a dragon that remained in the depths of the hull during the journey took up a position on the deck in order to guard the ship; once back aboard, when she wanted to rise up into the air, a trigger that she touched released springs embedded along the keel of the vessel, which, by their common effort, made it leap high enough to be sustained by the column of air established beneath it, and simultaneously enabled the bellows to act upon the sails and carry it even higher. In the same way, a bird rising into the air only employs the movement of its wings after having detached itself by means of a leap proportionate to its weight.

She usually communicated to her traveling companions the admirable subtlety that hid her from the most piercing eyes; it was only rarely that, slowing her progress, she consented to be perceived. A few of the most agreeable countries and favorite nations enjoy that advantage from time to time. One can imagine how our young people would feel about that: to see the entire world and not to be seen by anyone is to lose half the pleasure.

Anyway, as I have said, struck by the beauty of the place, Selnozoura descended to the Isle of the Spring. She was surprised to find the countryside deserted, but her astonishment increased when, having entered the city, she found all its houses uninhabited, without any vestige of war or conflagration to which the cause of such a misfortune could be attributed. She wanted to discover it by means of her art.

While she was carrying out the operations for that on her own, Toupette and Cornichon wandered through the desolate city. The fatal spring, near to which hazard conducted them, offered them clear and fresh water. They were thirsty; they drank from it.

The art of faerie had just instructed Selnozoura of what she wanted to know. She hastened to rejoin her children—that was what her tenderness called them. At that moment, having slaked their thirst, they were considering the architecture of the spring.

"Oh, be careful not to drink that deadly poison," she shouted at them from a distance. "You'd be doomed!"

"What?" said Toupette. "What you call poison is the most delicious water I've ever drunk in my life, and Cornichon thinks the same."

"Oh, wretches," she said, "you've drunk some! Oh, you had to stray away from me!"

Then she told them about the destiny of the unfortunate islanders.

"You're going to experience a similar fate, my poor children," she added. "The power of fays operates when they wish for new marvels, but it doesn't go as far as destroying the work of another fay. You're soon going to pass into the state of the most decrepit old age. At least I can lessen its penalties by my efforts, and protect you from death, sustaining your misery by means of all the cares that the others lacked, but the charm is already operating. Cornichon's stature appears to be increasing, and a more masculine physiognomy is taking the place of his features."

While the fay was speaking, Cornichon, who was looking at Toupette, thought he was making similar discoveries in her regard. Far from his ideas leading to the sad consequences that could be drawn from the adventure, however, that present state filled him with joy. The fay had the custom of opposing to the desire he incessantly voiced to marry her with, among other reasons, the obstacle of their great youth; a moment had just removed that difficulty. He did not delay making use of that with regard to Selnozoura.

"Cease, divine fay," he said, "to complain of our fate. If the two termini of our lives must, as you say, follow one another closely, let us hasten to seize the brief interval that separates them in order to unite us. What does it matter that our old age is anticipated, if our happiness is too?"

At that speech Toupette found the profound sadness into which she had plunged diminishing. Her gaze, which she had just directed, while blushing, at Cornichon, settled on the fay, and marked the anxiety that her sentiments were in.

Selnozoura had sensed all the force of Cornichon's reasoning, and had been touched by the manner in which he had expressed them. "Yes, my children," she said, "you will be content. But this deadly place, the cause of your misfortunes, is inappropriate to celebrate the nuptials that my amity wants to render celebrated for you. Let us return to Bagota"—that was her ordinary place of her residence. "My entire court will be eager to contribute to your present amusements, and the hundred subaltern genii who are at my orders will be incessantly occupied thereafter in banishing the cares associated with old age."

The lovers would have preferred promptitude to splendor in the accomplishment of their wishes, but the experience they had of the rapidity of their journeys assured them that they would be in Bagota in a matter of hours, even though they were more than four thousand five hundred leagues away. They did not insist, and they departed.

On the way, Toupette begged the fay to maintain silence regarding the adventure of the spring; there was no need to become the topic of all conversations in advance, and give that purchase to the malignity of a hundred young women who only saw her nascent charms and her favor in the fay's eyes with jealousy. The fay promised that, and declared on arrival the marriage of the young lovers, which she fixed for the following night. They received compliments in consequence, and even endured speeches.

The advantageous change that had taken place in their persons in such a short time was easily remarked, and surprised everyone, but as no one divined its cause, it served to establish the proverb that travel forms young people. And with that, a thousand young persons of both sexes thought about seeking to obtain the two places that they foresaw that the marriage was about to make available.

In the meantime, the genius Kristopo arrived in Bagota. He was accustomed to making a few visits of amity to his nice from time to time, and she was glad that he had chosen the one when the establishment of Toupette would show him the value she placed on his presents.

Kristopo was surprised by the progress that the young woman had made, as much in terms of intelligence as grace. In his previous trips to Bagota, the child had amused him and occupied him. He began to be afflicted by Cornichon's good fortune; the idea of marrying Toupette himself came to mind. His passion, which was increasing with every passing moment, left very few for reflections on the disproportion between his age of three thousand years with Toupette's fourteen.

It was soon a firm decision, and there was no time to lose; she was about to pass into the power of Cornichon. He immediately went, therefore, to make his niece party to his intentions. He did not believe for an instant that his relative could hesitate over the preference that he was requesting. Imagine his astonishment when, after having employed, very gently, perfectly sensate representations, made in Kristopo's own interest, that he would soon repent of such an alliance. Selnozoura concluded with a formal refusal, which she then sustained with vivacity, against all the persistence that he renewed incessantly.

508

Finally seeing their futility, the genius appeared to yield to the fay's arguments, but he was only more confirmed in his initial design, and, taking advantage of the access to Toupette that he had, and a moment when she was alone, he carried her away via the chimney of her apartment a few moments before the one that was to accomplish her union with Cornichon, who was already waiting in the temple and complaining of her slowness.

As soon as he arrived in Ratibouf, the capital of his estates and his ordinary residence, Kristopo neglected nothing to justify with her the irregularity of his procedure, the blame for which he put on the fay. He had omitted nothing in order to obtain her consent; he had only endured a refusal that he had had no reason to expect; his passion was extreme, however, and time was pressing. Her marriage with Cornichon was preparing a misfortune for her all the more frightful because it would have no limits other than the duration of life, which was unknown. In those circumstances, was it natural that he should sacrifice himself to Selnozoura's caprice? And ought she even to have decided, without his participation, the fate of a child that she had from him? Toupette, therefore, instead of being afflicted, ought to give the greatest approval to his conduct and bless the moment that had just removed her from the tyranny of the fay and broken a marriage unworthy of her, in order to elevate her to the supreme honors that she was about to share with him.

Far from appreciating those reasons, Toupette was not even in a state to listen to them. Kristopo thought they would have more success when she had recovered from her initial astonishment, and ceased to importune her for several days.

Meanwhile, several ambassadors came successively on the part of the fay demanding Toupette's return, in the most pressing but the most futile manner. Even the threat of a cruel war did not shake the genius, who, far from changing his mind, often renewed his entreaties with regard to his captive, with as little result.

He thought that the authority of her parents might have more weight with her than arguments. He proposed to send for them. She consented to that, more in order to rid herself of his odious pursuits for while than in the design of subscribing to their will, which she foresaw would be in conformity with that of the genius. She only demanded of him that he suspend his solicitations until their arrival.

The courier who was dispatched to them found them both ill. They told him that their consent to such an honorable union could be presumed; that Kristopo's generosity toward their daughter would dispense him from the ordinary step if they alone could dispose of her; but that, since he had judged their consent necessary, they begged him also to obtain that of Selnozoura, without which they never regulated any matter of importance in their family, because of the infinite obligations that they had to the fay, and which, she being his relative and his friend, he would have no difficulty in obtaining.

The good people were unaware of the quarrel that had developed between Kristopo and Selnozoura; they were very surprised to learn from the messenger that their daughter's resistance could only be vanquished by their presence, but they asked for time to recover from their illness. The courier waited in vain for their cure; the malady only got worse. Anticipating the anxiety of his master, he asked them, in default of their presence, for their written consent, which they gave before a notary, to take effect as soon as it was ratified by Selnozoura, which they believed to be not in doubt.

The genius did not doubt that the document in question would be victorious; he ran to communicate it to Toupette, carefully refraining from mentioning the clause regarding Selnozoura's consent, which was not expressed therein. Her tears soon undeceived him; she begged him to defer the execution of his designs until her parents' recovery put them in a state to attend the wedding; the sight of them would augment her joy, if the reflections that she made in the meantime overcame her repugnance for the marriage, or would sustain her courage and at least serve as a consolation, if her heart still refused to accord with her duty.

Toupette would not have obtained that further delay from the passion of the genius if the alteration he remarked in her features had not persuaded him that her health was interested in it. In fact, the enchanted water, combined with chagrin, was beginning to produce a very considerable change in her. He believed her to be ill, and on her refusal to see any physicians, he occupied himself at least with diverting her by means of the variety of the fêtes that he prepared for her.

She wanted a change of air, and obtained permission for that. Not doubting that his presence was importunate to her, Kristopo had the generosity to leave her alone in the countryside.

I have said that Selnozoura had made the genius the most bitter complaints for the insult he had made her in the person of Toupette, and that those complaints had been followed by threats to extract a reckoning by way of arms. Cornichon, who sensed the importance there was for him and for Toupette in her prompt return, never ceased to press the fay to hasten the execution of her threats.

The interests of her dignity, combined with that of the poor lovers, determined her to march numerous troops to the frontier of Kristopo's estates; for his part, he prepared a defense proportionate to the excess of his passion for Toupette. They both commanded numerous and affectionate peoples, and, not content with their own forces, they had interested the neighboring powers in their quarrel by means of alliances. Their difference divided the fay nation.

The embarrassments inseparable from such a situation disrupted the voyages that Selnozoura was accustomed to make, which had no longer had the same charms for, her in any case, since her separation from Toupette. A change of air was, however, absolutely necessary to her, and the physicians did not relent on that article. What she imagined in order to procure it without her affairs suffering in consequence is curious enough to warrant reporting.

Every day she dispatched a large number of sylphs charged with empty containers, which they went to fill, in accordance with the choice she made, sometimes in one country and sometimes in another, with the air that was breathed there. As soon as they returned, all the air that her apartment contained was extracted carefully by means of pneumatic machines, and the new air was immediately substituted for it.

That was very ingenious, but what was even more remarkable is that the fay and all those who were allowed to enter her apartment took on the different mentalities every day of the peoples whose air they breathed. And although the interval of twenty-four hours was not sufficient to convince anyone that those differences extended into the utmost depths of the character, at least it indicated that a longer usage of the same air would infallibly produce that effect.

There were some days when that effect was more sensible, in proportion to the distinction of the character of the nation from which the air had been extracted. That of France, for example, although it ordinarily arrived in smaller quantities because it evaporates easily, nevertheless made itself noticeable, especially when it was taken from the capital.

At any rate, the verity of that singular fact was so fully recognized that the courtiers never failed to find themselves every morning at the Bureau where the couriers deposited their containers while waiting for daylight to reach the fay's apartment, in order to be informed of the country from which they were coming, and to regulate their daily conduct in consequence. There is every appearance that that is the origin of the phrase "the air of the bureau."[57]

Now, it happened one day that young sylphs charged with going in search of the new air started larking about along the route; they threw containers at one another's heads, they played with them like balloons and indulged in abundant other mischief that gradually loosened the fastenings sealing the vessels, and even punctured the containers in several places, in such a way that the air that was initially trapped there gradually escaped. As it was immediately replaced, however, by that introduced through the opposite openings, the sylphs did not notice any voids and continued their route without suspicion.

It was only after they had arrived that they perceived the accident, but as it was too late to remedy it and they were too timid to make the confession, they kept the secret and contented themselves with blocking the openings in the containers as best they could until the time came to take them to the fay's apartment and to distribute it: no longer, as before, a unique air, but a composite of the air

---

[57] The French expression *prendre l'air du bureau* [take the air of the office] is used to mean seeking information as to what is happening in a workplace during a period of absence, or, more generally, spying.

of almost all the nations of the world that they had traversed in their most recent journey.

Because the place that had been indicated to them that day was almost at the antipodes of Bagota, the day in question was marked by actions so full of sagacity on the fay's part, and so far from the extremes to which the usage of the unique air of certain countries had sometimes taken her, that she perceived it herself, and asked for the same air the following day. Then the sylphs made no difficulty about confessing their adventure.

That served to enlighten the fay, and to inform her that there is good everywhere; that the very excesses tempered one another; and that, in sum, from the collaboration of a host of the most opposed qualities, a median quality results that is good. Fixed in that opinion, she only wanted to use a composite air, and that is what is known as a good atmosphere.

I cannot help making a reflection here that would not have escaped my author if he had lived in our day, which is that this passage is so fundamentally in conformity with the opinion established in a few chapters of the book of *The Spirit of the Law* that one could suspect its author of plagiarism if one believed him to be versed in the history of the fays—but there is little likelihood of that.[58]

The fay had succeeded in procuring a suitable atmosphere, the restlessness in her legs still remained. A machine that set them in movement, and procured the necessary exercise without requiring her to leave her apartment, produced that effect. My author describes that machine, which is very similar to Abbé de Saint-Pierre's *trémoussoir*.[59]

---

[58] *L'Esprit des Lois* [The Spirit of the Law] (1748), one of the masterpieces of eighteenth-century political philosophy, is by the Baron de Montesquieu, although it was originally published anonymously, like most illicit texts. Montesquieu sometimes made use of fanciful tales in his writings, although Charles Mayer was stretching a point when he included him in annotated list of authors of *contes de fées* in volume 37 of his *Cabinet des fées*.

[59] Charles-Irénée Castel, abbé de Saint-Pierre (1658-1743) was an unorthodox *philosophe* now most famous for his *Projet de paix perpétuelle* [Plan for Perpetual Peace] (1713; abridged version 1729), which proposed the foundation of an international organization similar in many ways to the United Nations. He was a participant in Madame de Lambert's salon, along with François Fénelon and the coterie of female writers who invented *contes de fées*. He was notoriously expelled from the Académie française for criticizing Louis XIV, and in 1724 he was a founder-member of the Club d'Entresol, a discussion group of which Montesquieu was also a leading member; it was shut down by Louis XV in 1731. He invented his *trémoussoir*—a vibrating armchair (the word means "flutterer")—in order to agitate his muscles while he worked, so that he could keep fit in spite of his sedentary lifestyle.

Thus, the arts do not always have an epoch as recent as the one that is assigned to them. They often only emerge from the bosom of forgetfulness. The Chinese knew about gunpowder several centuries before the birth of those reputed in Europe to have invented it. But my reflections are straying from my subject and it is time to return to it.

Kristopo had given the command of his armies to a general of recognized capability, and those of the fay were under the command of Cornichon. The great interest that he had in the war had caused the judgment that no one was more capable than he of impelling operations with ardor. Already he was disposed to emerge from the retreat to which his chagrin had confined him since the abduction of Toupette, in which he was only visible to the fay. He went to obtain her final orders, and to promise to satisfy simultaneously, by means of a signal victory, amour, glory and vengeance.

Meanwhile, what was happening in Ratibouf distanced the genius even further from peaceful sentiments. Toupette's mother and father had finally arrived; Kristopo immediately took them to the country house where their daughter was. Imagine their surprise when, instead of the young and charming person they had expected to find, they only saw a woman, of pleasant appearance, in truth, but whose faded features only hinted at their former beauty.

In vain, the sweet names of *father* and *mother* were in her mouth, in vain she made them the most tender caresses; it was impossible for them to recognize as their daughter a person whose age surpassed theirs. For his part, Kristopo, offended by what he took to be a derision, having summoned all those who had been appointed to the service or the guard of Toupette, demanded of them angrily where she was, and who the person might be who dared to play such an indecent scene in his presence.

They replied to him that since Toupette had been in the house she had not shown herself to anyone, that she had only left her apartment—which they only had permission to enter while she was out walking—wearing a veil. It was then that she was taken, in accordance with his orders, what was necessary to her nourishment, which she ate alone. They had not had any occasion to see her, and had contented themselves with serving her carefully and guarding her with exactitude, and they had done their duty with a great deal of zeal and attention. They were as surprised as he was by what they saw, but they were firmly convinced that the person who was before their eyes was the same one that had been confided to them.

The simplicity of those responses was uniform, and the astonishment of those who made them dissipated the suspicions that the genius had conceived regarding their fidelity. He turned them on the fay, whose work that metamorphosis seemed to him to be, in order to avenge herself for the abduction of Toupette.

He was confirmed in that idea by a conversation he had with Toupette, which related to particularities of her childhood of which no one else could be informed. Then he fortified himself in the resolution of the war, no longer on a defensive footing, but accompanied by all the vigor and diligence necessary to anticipate on the fay's territory the hostilities that she was disposing to make on his. He flattered himself that he would soon constrain her by the effort of his arms to undo the magic by which he supposed that she had covered Toupette's charms. And, leaving her in her retreat with her parents, he ran to hasten the execution of his designs.

Selnozoura had not yet been informed of what had happened in Ratibouf; she had fully expected the surprise of the genius, but she was offended when she learned about his insulting imputation that she was the author of the metamorphosis. That dull and indirect manner of avenging herself was too distant from the elevation of her sentiments not to wound her sensibly. That circumstance aggravated her old resentments further; she delivered herself entirely to ideas of a striking vengeance. How the blood was going to flow!

However, her friends and the wisest heads of her Council, considering the disproportion there was between the cause of the war and the calamities that it was about to bring in its train, hazarded remonstrations on that subject. The amity with which she honored Toupette doubtless ought to have substituted for what was lacking on the side of birth and fortune and ought to have served her as an inviolable safeguard against anything whatsoever; but who was unaware of the aberrations to which a violent amour can cast a soul? The deference and past regard of the genius, her relative, which had not been belied for several centuries, proved well enough that he was no longer free at the fatal moment when he had been borne to such an extraordinary violence. Furthermore, the enchantment of the spring—for that fact was beginning to leak out in Bagota—in acting so promptly on Toupette, had forestalled the effects of the passion of the genius for her; nothing remained to him but the shame of such a blameworthy action.

These considerations were also sustained by the ministers of the powers allied to the fay, who only saw themselves engaged with regret in a war in which they had no direct interest. One of those princes—it was Zeprady, Prince of Mirliphipolia—offered his mediation. Although he had engagements with Selnozoura, former liaisons with the genius permitted a favorable opportunity to the negotiation for which he wanted to take responsibility to reach an accommodation.

The fay was fundamentally very reasonable; she understood that the advantages of war never compensate exactly for the woes that follow them, but, too proud to take the first step herself, she accepted Zeprady's proposal joyfully, and even consented to dissipate entirely the suspicions of the genius regarding the cause of Toupette's premature aging. That prince was informed in the greatest detail of the adventure of the Isle of the Spring, the state of which the definite condition of the two lovers rendered mystery futile henceforth. She demanded, however, appropriate reparations on the part of Kristopo, whose violence had evidently violated human rights and the respect due to sovereigns.

Zeprady therefore departed, furnished with the necessary passports, to go to the court of Ratibouf. One the way he saw Cornichon, who, entirely occupied with his vengeance, was only thinking of inspiring the same sentiments in the army of which he had just taken command. The order that Zeprady handed him on the part of the queen to suspend all hostile action until his return initially penetrated him with the sharpest dolor, but the hope of seeing Toupette again, which peace rendered far more certain than the events of a doubtful war, brought him back to milder sentiments, and even persuaded him to go to Ratibouf in order to be a decisive witness for the genius of the fay's good faith and the verity of the surprising adventure; he asked the prince to obtain permission for him to do that.

On arrival at the frontier of the genius's territory, Zeprady found troops assembled there ready to form a numerous army. He obtained from the general commanding them a promise that he would not press his march until he had received further orders, and, continuing to follow his own with diligence, he soon arrived in Ratibouf.

The genius could not avoid recognizing himself as the author of the war that was about to flare up. The passion that had been the sole cause of it had ceased for lack of an object. Toupette, in the state she was in, no longer interested anything but pity. In such circumstances, it is usual that natural equity resumes it rights; he lent an ear to the overtures for peace that Zeprady made him. He insisted on the verity of the offense that he believed that the fay had committed in casting Toupette into the state she was in, in order to render her possession useless to him, and demanded that he be disabused in that regard, as if the verity of that supposition did not leave the insult made to the fay by the abduction of Toupette in subsistence.

Zeprady, seeing that his negotiation would only encounter that obstacle, which was easy for him to remove, did not take the trouble to destroy the prejudice of the genius by means of the maxims of law of which he could have made use, and hastened to say that he could furnish him with an irreproachable witness; that Cornichon was only waiting for passports to come to the court and convince him that what had happened to Toupette had no relevance to the present quarrel.

The genius consented to see him; he arrived, and the story he told of the adventure of the island, which he could not help mingling with his tears, drew some from the genius; however, he still demanded his confrontation with Toupette, and sent for her.

What a surprise for her, and what various sentiments agitated her by turns when she learned that she was going to see Cornichon again! Joy doubtless occupied all her heart at first, but how short its duration was! The most sensible humiliation soon took its place, and the certainty that she had that her lover was no better treated, far from giving her confidence, brought her chagrin all the way to despair. She succumbed to it for a few moments, and it was only with great difficulty that she was persuaded to climb into the carriage.

Cornichon's disturbance was scarcely less when it was announced that Toupette was approaching. Apparently more convinced, however, that their amour was of a higher order, and independent of the graces of appearance and youth, he promised himself an infinite and mutual joy from their conversation, and that sentiment left little room for regret for the losses they had both suffered.

In fact it was evident at the moment of recognition that Cornichon's amour was of a stronger caliber, so to speak; that it was more deprived of personal interest and more united with the beloved object; and Toupette, on the contrary, allowed to show in the effusion of tenderness that she could not refuse to Cornichon, reservations that uncovered all the wounds of her self-esteem.

Everything that the people of the court most versed in the metaphysics of the heart saw assured them that that was in conformity with the rules and experience. The physicists who were present also justified those various movements in their fashion, and all of them agreed that the scene was worthy of the best sentimental drama.

The genius, no longer able to refuse the evidence that he had already accorded to the enlightenments of reason, stripped of the clouds of passion, withdrew without saying anything, but disposed to be reconciled with the fay and to employ all sorts of means to make her forget his wrongdoing.

The lovers, having been the object of the importunate curiosity of the witnesses for some time, and having endured questions that were equally indiscreet and inappropriate, were finally left to themselves.

"Oh, Toupette, my dear Toupette," said Cornichon, then, "It's you that I see again. Let the memory of our past woes be put behind us forever."

"Of our past woes, you say!" cried Toupette, dolorously. "But what can destroy the cruel impression of our present woes, and dispel from our thoughts the frightful perspective of those to come—or rather, which are hurtling toward us so rapidly? What, Cornichon, are you insensible to that? You do not love me if my misfortunes do not penetrate to the depths of your heart."

"How unjust you are to doubt it," said Cornichon. "I feel them a thousand times more than my own—or rather, confounding your condition with my own, as our hearts are confounded, I would be overwhelmed by the double weight of misfortune if I did not enjoy..."

"Oh, what enjoyment?" interrupted Toupette. "What can we enjoy at present that can compensate us or what has been taken away from us? For, in sum, don't flatter yourself: the fatal water has already had the effect on you of more than half a century, and doubtless it has treated me no better."

"I confess," replied Cornichon, "that in recalling those nascent graces, the duration of which our common accident has so cruelly hastened the progress, I find you different today, but there are graces for all ages, and you, my dear Toupette, have those of the sexagenarian age. Yes, if our eyes had not lost the extreme vivacity that distinguished them, your faded complexion would reproach them for a gleam that they alone would have conserved. A few wrinkles that I perceive on your forehead justify the reasons that your cheeks have for flattening and descending, and your breasts, in withering, fall with much more decency. It's thus that all your features, aging in intelligence, do not cease to conserve between them a harmony that proves incontestably that you have been beautiful."

"Cruel man!" Toupette interrupted, sharply. "My breasts have withered, and it's you who tell me that?"

"But Toupette," said Cornichon, "don't you remember what scant value you once seemed to place on the fragile advantages of beauty? Was my heart not the unique object of all the wishes of yours?"

"Yes, Cornichon," she said, apparently a little calmer, "of course I remember; but can I not fear some diminution in your tenderness for me, when such monstrous changes have taken place in my face? For after all, we rely a great deal on external appearances; they are what strike the senses, and what power the senses have over our hearts, alas! Who will love me, if you cease to love me?"

"That anxiety is superfluous, my dear Toupette," replied Cornichon. "It relates to an impossibility; but even supposing it were possible, could the desire of strangers ever replace mine in your estimation? You cannot even imagine it. You can see that you're forming phantoms in order to combat them."

"I can see," said Toupette, "that you take me for a visionary; it's very hard, at the culmination of disgrace, to see one's reason attacked as well."

"Oh, Toupette," he said, "how unjust you are. What, while my discourse, drawn from the purest springs of philosophy, only has your repose for an object, you can give it such an insulting meaning! But suffer that I support my arguments with a celebrated example. Are you unaware of the story of Baucis and Philemon, those two tender spouses who conserved without any alteration, into extreme old age, all the sentiments of the most perfect amour? Fortunate couple! They experienced with delight that the chains of marriage, and even the infirmities of old age, are very light when amour sustains their weight."

"A fine comparison, in truth," said Toupette, with chagrin, "a beautiful comparison. Baucis, in the course of a long life, had received thousands of times from Philemon the most sensible proofs of tenderness, while I...but seriously, either don't make comparisons or find more accurate resemblances. That one doesn't do honor to your intelligence, or at least wrongs your memory; one might think that you had prepared a new proof for my patience, by stringing together the most singular, the most extraordinary words. How unfortunate I am!"

That conversation was not taking a mild tone when the Prince of Mirliphipolia came to tell them that the genius, full of regret for what had happened, was in the sentiments most appropriate to satisfy the fay; that he had asked him to return promptly to find her, in order to assure her of it, and to ask for passports for the ministers destined to go to Bagota as soon as possible, in order to subscribe to the conditions of a peace, of which he left her entirely the mistress; and that he would go to ratify them himself as soon as he could do so with security and decency. He had been charged with saying to Cornichon that he was the master of departing with him, and taking Toupette. The genius could not resolve to see them as yet, after causing them so much pain, but he hoped to render his presence more supportable to them in the future, and that he would explain himself more clearly when he was in Bagota.

"Prepare yourselves, then," added the Prince of Mirliphipolia, "by means of a little repose, to depart with me tomorrow, as soon as daylight begins to appear. I'll leave you now."

Cornichon and Toupette, anticipated the hour of their departure considerably; their misfortunes had deprived them for a long time of the sweetness of a long slumber, and the situation in which they found themselves was not conducive to sleep; they met up before dawn.

Joy was dominant in Cornichon's heart; Toupette was dejected. The pleasure of her liberty was poisoned by the idea of the usage that she was going to make of it. "Was not my prison preferable," she cried, "to the humiliation that awaits me in Bagota, where, instead of the charms that attracted the homage of men and the envy of women, I can now only offer subjects of scorn, or at least pity, for the former and a prideful triumph for the malignity of the latter?"

Cornichon tried to dissipate her chagrin by means of arguments similar to those he had used the day before; they were no better received. He persisted; Toupette had the vapors; he was embarrassed by that, but, still attached to the reasoning that the candor and ingenuity of his amour suggested to him, he only repeated them and did not vary them. The vapors were augmented; he was frightened that reason had no purchase on that malady, it being his only resource.

Finally, with the aid of smelling salts, Toupette recovered a passable tranquility, and the reflections that they both made on the mysterious promises that the genius had made them via the prince furnished them with a series of conjectures that, without producing anything certain, nevertheless occupied them agreeably enough until Bagota, where they arrived the same day.

It was late; Toupette was glad about that, she was far from desiring to see many people. The fay had retired, but having learned that the prince had arrived, she did not want to put off until the following day hearing his report, succinctly at least, on the success of his mission.

After having thanked him and put off until the next day a more extensive narration of his negotiations, she could not dispense with seeing Toupette, and even less with shedding tears for her fate. She consented to the plea that the unhappy lovers made her to keep a retreat in their apartments appropriate to their situation, and only to be visible to her.

The following days having been employed in the examination of the conditions of the peace, their ratification and the expedition of orders for the lieutenant of the troops, attention then turned to preparations for the celebration that would follow their publication.

In accordance with his promises, the genius did not fail to come to Bagota. His satisfactions were complete; he neglected nothing to recover the amity of the fay. Everyone experienced the most vivid joy, except for the lovers, delivered to dolor and only distracted therefrom in the moments when the charitable fay wanted to slip away from her occupations in order to go to their apartments.

Although the promises of the genius had flattered their hope for a time, they reproached themselves afterwards for their credulity. Several days after his arrival, he had not even enquired about them.

In his regard, they said to themselves, *we are in the most profound forgetfulness We serve on his part for a vain and impotent pity. Alas, not even the consolation of imagining that we are susceptible to it remains to us.*

Those sad thoughts were occupying them one morning—it was the day destined for the publication of the peace treaty—when they perceived the fay, accompanied by the genius, each followed by their court, advancing toward the place where they had the custom of meeting during the day. That visit surprised them; the occupations and trappings of that great day did not seem to permit the fay her usual attentions for them; the presence of the genius and his retinue surprised them even more. In fact, Selnozoura had prepared them not to see her that day, but the genius had implored her with such insistence to take him to see the unfortunate couple that the fay, who had emerged from her palace in order to see for herself the preparations for the fête that was to solemnize the day, was constrained to postpone that care, and could not refuse to satisfy an urgency that appeared mysterious in the circumstances.

When they drew near to the apartment where Cornichon and Toupette were, the former hastened to go to meet the illustrious company, while Toupette sought to hide her confusion in the darkest party of the room. Cornichon's strength did not respond to his urgency; he stumbled at the feet of the fay, and sustained a black eye.

The alarm that caused Toupette overcame the reluctance she had to show herself; she ran to him, utterly bewildered, but her debilitated feet tripped over Cornichon's legs as he was still sprawled on the ground, and she fell upon him rudely. Her mouth having encountered the forehead of the injured man, it cost her three teeth that had been meditating escaping from her mouth for some time.

That accident drew tears from the fay. She could not help saying to the genius that it had been imprudent to come and surprise the poor couple in that way. He responded with a confidence that enabled the fay to think that he had discovered a means of compensating them; she did not reply.

A few courtiers had difficulty hiding their joy. Cornichon and Toupette were favorites; several of them had experienced that at the expense of their self-esteem. Their imminent decrepitude ought, in truth, soon to distance those objects of jealousy. Decrepit favorites are rarely seen, and accidents like the one that had just occurred hastened the moment of their retreat, and they saw all the indications of that with pleasure.

When they had been helped, Selnozoura proposed to the genius that they be left to take repose.

"It will not be in vain, Madame," he replied, "that I have engaged you to come here; a visit of consolation could have taken place in moments less crowded than today's. I chose it expressly in order to give more splendor to the reparation that I owe you for the violence that I exercised on a person who is dear to you, and more merit to the relief that I want to procure for the woes of these lovers.

"As soon as I was cured of the suspicions I had," he continued, "that the aging of Toupette was only an illusory effect of your chagrin against me, the sensible regret that I had of my procedure caused me to seek means of repairing it that would be sufficient for you and useful to the unfortunates whose union I had so unjustly prevented. The story that the Prince of Mirliphipolia had told me of the circumstances of their adventure had convinced me. It is true that I could do nothing by myself to change their fundamental situation, which was the work of a fay, but I thought at least that good advice can sometimes take the place of a service. What I have to say might substitute in some manner for what I can do; this is it.

"You might remember, Madame, that at the last Estates General of Faerie, which were held before the Tribunal of Destinies to examine the works of each Intelligence, those of the Fay of the Spring were found so constantly full of good will that no one doubted that they were a naïve expression of her character. The harm that she was sometimes able to produce was attributed to an error on her part rather than the effect of a malign intention, and it was judged that, although it was contrary to the dignity of Faerie to allow any trace of the works of intelligences to subsist, it was nonetheless in conformity with the laws of justice to dispense a fay of seeing the entire execution of disastrous things that would only have given rise to scorn. It was therefore decided that without drawing consequences for others whose views were not so honest, the Fay of the Spring would have the liberty to diminish by half the harm that she had done in the aforesaid circumstances.

"She would then have made usage of that mercy in favor of some of the inhabitants of the isle, if death, which had anticipated that decree, had recog-

520

nized any power superior to its own. How fortunate it would have been if she had at least destroyed the spring and precipitated the fatal waters at their source into the gulfs of the sea; she did not think of it, but, still disposed to do good for its own sake, she will doubtless seize the opportunity even more enthusiastically, if it is presented to her under the title of justice.

"I will take charge, therefore, of informing her that her presence is needed here, and although, as I have said, it is not permitted to her to repair in totality the harm she had done, at least she will be able to return one of these two lovers to the state in which they would presently be without this cruel adventure. It is up to you, Madame, to choose which of the two will enjoy that favor."

The last words spoken by the genius, which surprised the fay greatly, threw her into an irresolution that banished from her heart the joy that the first had commenced spreading there. The two lovers had an equal part in her affection; how could she resolve to pronounce to one of the two that he or she would continue to be the sad victim of a perpetual vicissitude, while the other would return to all the advantages of his or her age?

While she was making those reflections, the rest of the assembly was divided. "How," said the men, "can a fay as jealous of the brilliance of her court hesitate for a moment to render its most precious ornament to it by the rejuvenation of Toupette? Are beauty and grace so common here that she can neglect the opportunity to see them assembled in that charming person?"

"It is highly unlikely," said the women, on the contrary, "that it is uncertainty that is closing Selnozoura mouth's regarding her choice; it is already made. Only the presence of the two persons who interest her so strongly prevents her from declaring it. It would be cruel to make it in the presence of Toupette; the delay cannot be interpreted otherwise. How, in fact, could the fay sacrifice to the temporary charms of the face of a little girl, the important services that she has a right to expect from a man like Cornichon, as many at the head of the army as in the Council? We have just seen the zeal with which he ran to expose himself to the hazards of a cruel war, in order to avenge the glory of the fay, and his premature intelligence announces that he will be no less appropriate to ministerial politics."

However, the fay's uncertainty not permitting her to make a choice, she took time to think about it, saying that it was necessary not to occupy herself that day with anything but the fêtes ad games that a fortunate peace warranted. She left the lovers, but she could not help saying in a low voice to her uncle that his discourse had prepared her for a more complete satisfaction; that furthermore, he had not put into it anything of his own, the advice regarding the Fay of the Spring could have been discovered without him; that she expected less common services from a genius like him; and that she hoped of his amity that he would think of something for which one could have a personal obligation.

With that, they arrived in the main square, where they applauded the preparations that had been made in order to give to the publication of the peace treaty and the renewal of alliance between the two States all the accompaniments of grandeur and magnificence that an event so advantageous to the two nations demanded.

Let us leave the fay, the genius and the court occupied with that grand ceremony, and go to find Toupette and Cornichon inside their apartment.

"Finally, my dear Toupette," he said, delightedly, as soon as they were free, "I am able to give you the most decisive proof of my amour for you, since you will see it disengaged from all the exterior circumstances that customarily sustain vulgar amours. Yes, while, reentering into all the advantages of my age, I shall be the object of the desires of the loveliest women of the court, I will only be seen to be sensible to the pleasure of sacrificing them for you.

"It will be at time when I am most convinced of the return of the graces with which I was once flattered that I shall take pleasure in making a striking homage to the wrinkles and infirmities of your old age. What attention, what tender cares will I not have for you? What a pure joy will you not experience yourself in recognizing then that the illusion of beauty counts for nothing in the homage that I will render you; it will only relate to your virtues, to the most beautiful soul in the world!"

"What!" Toupette interrupted, brusquely. "It's you who count on enjoying exclusively the favor with which the genius had just flattered us, while I remain...? I know," she continued, emotionally, "that the gifts of reason and virtue are preferable to the fragile advantages of a seductive beauty; that the conquests procured by the former have a more solid glory than those of the latter; I know, finally, that a woman of merit is preferable in the eyes of reason to a pretty woman who is only that. But why not do me the honor of believing me capable of uniting that common advantage? Why, if your role would be more glorious, do you not even take the trouble to enquire as to whether I might have the ambition to pretend to it?

"Oh, Cornichon," she said, shedding tears, "what humiliation you make me experience! No, you don't merit the sentiments that I have for you; but the good fay is too equitable to share your opinion; I reproach myself for the pain it has caused me; it was as premature as your joy."

As she finished speaking she went into a neighboring cabinet abruptly, closing the door behind her. The entreaties that Cornichon made her for a long time to come back would have been futile if the time when the fay was accustomed to come to see them, which was approaching, had not determined her to emerge from her retreat, after having recovered from her disturbance somewhat, firmly resolved to make every effort to destroy Cornichon's project.

"Forget, my dear Toupette," he said, as soon as she returned, "the design that alarmed you; the delicacy of my passion had inspired it; yours is wounded by it; let us not talk about it anymore. Let us refuse, by virtue of a common scorn, an advantage that is not one for us, and which causes, on the contrary, such a diversity in our opinions. Let is submit to our original destiny, all the more willingly because it will match throughout the course of our life the different seasons through which we must pass.

"Our ages being almost similar, we shall experience the same winters and we shall see the same springs; the inconveniences that were capable of destroying an entire people who did not foresee them, and from which no one was exempt, will disappear here, where they will be foreseen and repaired successively by the cares of the best of fays. And if the bizarre nature of our fate forbids us to hope for a fortunate posterity from our union, the season of amours, as frequent for us as for the innocent birds, will have all of their ardor, and will only be distinguished by the purity of our flames."

That expedient of Cornichon's might have diminished somewhat the difficulty that Toupette envisaged in being the only one clad in all the charms of youth; doubtless she ought to have approved of it—but when one is prejudiced by an idea as agreeable as the one contained in the declaration of the genius and one applies oneself to profiting from it, it is difficult to let go of it, especially when one flatters oneself with seeing it realized. Far from applauding that opinion, therefore, she only occupied herself with casting ridicule on the terms in which it was conceived.

"Good God," she said, "what fine phrases! It's a pity that one can perceive all the travail that it cost you. Innocent birds, ardors, flames distinguished by their purity. How pretty! But wait; I'm obliged to tell you, my poor Cornichon, that the madrigal tone that is familiar to you does not suit our situation at all, and if you only have such things to say, be good enough to dispense me from listening to them."

Cornichon did not think it appropriate to continue a conversation that had engendered no much bitterness. They both commenced a mute scene, which was interrupted shortly by the arrival of Selnozoura, who, fatigued by the duration of the fête, had slipped away from it briefly and come to respire in her children's apartment.

She had anticipated a part of what had happened between them; the situation in which she found them made her understand that she was not mistaken. Toupette hastened to explain to her all the reasons she pretended to have for complaint against Cornichon. The author of these memoirs does not hesitate to list them, but as they are almost the same things that we have just reported, I shall spare the reader the repetition and content myself with saying that, in the hope of finding in association with the genius and the Fay of the Spring some means of improving their condition and perhaps extending to both of them the favor that was destined for one alone, Selnozoura excused herself from deciding their fate then, as they pressed her insistently to do. She founded her refusal on the futility there would be in announcing in advance a choice that would only take effect with the arrival of Dindonnette, who was the only one permitted to modify her work.

It was necessary, therefore, to be patient until the arrival of that fay, who made them wait for several days. I shall not say how they were employed; the reader's imagination will easily depict the fireworks, the balls, the carousels and all the other amusements that ought to celebrate the return of union to two people who had always enjoyed a constant peace and amity; it is only necessary to give each of those things the degree of perfection that is lacking among us, but which was doubtless not lacking among the fays.

Finally, Dindonnette arrived; she combined with the best intentions in the world a similar irresolution with regard to the decision she ought to make, which is usual when the murky vision of a limited mind can only discover inconvenience in a plan, without being enlightened regarding its advantages. One seeks the good with all one's heart, but gropingly, and often finds oneself so close to the bad that it is dangerous to make a false step. One knows that, one fears being criticized, and one makes the worst decision of all: that of not making any. That was exactly Dindonnette's situation.

All those who were interested in the lovers had successively taken possession of her. The fay Selnozoura, with an extreme delicacy regarding her reputation, fearing that a preference she gave to Cornichon would be interpreted maliciously, had fixed all her favor on Toupette. The genius, who feared acquiring new irons and was still shuddering at the catastrophic effects that his passion had been ready to cause, declared himself in favor of Cornichon. The divided court also gave Dindonnette various advice, founded on arguments that seemed to her to be of equal weight, and put her beyond a state to make any resolution. However, she had not been able to help indicating the day when she would make up her mind.

When it drew near, she finally settled on an inclination that she thought appropriate to satisfy everyone, because it gave everyone a part of what they wanted. Charmed by that marvelous idea, she abridged the delay that she had requested and wanted the lovers to appear before her immediately. She urged the fay and the genius to assemble the court and the people, in order to render more numerous the applause that she had no doubt that her plan would merit.

As soon as Toupette and Cornichon had arrived and everyone assembled in the great hall of the palace, the doors of which were left open, Dindonnette, having obtained silence, spoke as follows:

"Fortunate is the person who can repair the harm she has done; even more fortunate is the person who has not done any." That sentence not suffering any contradiction, she continued: "Far from enjoying the latter advantage, even the former is not accorded to me." Addressing Cornichon, she said: "I could render your beautiful youth, and," she said to Toupette, "I could also reestablish yours. I shall do both, and I shall do neither."

One can imagine the agitation that these words caused the lovers, particularly Toupette, but they only caused curiosity in the assembly, whose members did not understand them. A slight murmur rose up; then people reflected that fays ought not to talk like other people, and they shut up in order to hear what came next.

"No," Dindonnette continued, "I will not have the cruelty of abandoning one of you to the horrors of decrepitude, while I enable the other to reenter into all the rights of a flourishing youth. And since I cannot render them entirely to both of you at once, you shall at least each participate in it partially. I want half of your body to resume the vigor and graces of youth, while the other half will continue to experience the decadence to which the whole was destined. It is up to you to choose which part of you is dearer to you and ought to submit to that fortunate metamorphosis: whether it will operate by means of a perpendicular line, separating the body along its entire length, or whether a horizontal line traced at the waist will be the common term of those two states, and in the latter case, to which of the two halves thus distinguished, the superior or the inferior, youth will be attached."

It was then that all the seriousness in which people naturally found themselves was overturned. A thousand bursts of immoderate laughter were unleashed at once; no one, except for the two lovers and Dindonnette, who were astounded, could resist it. Even Selnozoura, who felt obliged to restrain herself in order to restrain others, could not hold back at the excessive ridiculousness of such an idea.

Finally, after a few moments, she got a grip on herself, and those who believed that they ought to resume a decent air of gravity commenced to render it to others. Thereafter, Dindonnette recovered slightly.

Selnozoura thought then that she was obliged to offer an opinion that would terminate such a comical scene. "I believe," she said to Dindonnette, "that your benevolent intention and the extent of your power would be no less fulfilled if, instead of assembling such opposite states in a single individual, you enabled them to enjoy alternately the advantages and disgusts attached to old age and the prime of life, for a time of which you ought to fix the duration, just as you ought to choose which of the two will be rejuvenated first."

"That's marvelous," she said, "and in truth, that was my first idea; one should always stick to one's first impulse. I thought inappropriately, on the word of certain people who do not understand anything, that it was necessary to correct it by reflection, and see how one is deceived: would you believe that that happens to me every day? But I'm disabused. Now, to which of the two should we return youth first?"

Cornichon, ever ready to sacrifice his interests to Toupette's, hastened to fix her choice by begging her to let it fall on her.

"I am too sure of Toupette's heart," he said, "to fear that that change would rob me of the smallest fraction of it, and since she has that little whim, it's necessary, Madame, if you please, to satisfy it."

What joy did she not express at that moment? What gratitude did she not testify to her lover? Protestations of the most tender concerns, as was only just, were commencing to form a discourse full of pathos on her part, when Dindonnette, charmed no longer to have to exercise a liberty that fatigued her, hastened to touch her with her wand. Immediately, Toupette, like a snake shedding its old skin, found herself stripped of her wrinkles, and allowed to be seen in their place the features of a perfect beauty and the stature of a nymph.

The two fays and the genius were overjoyed, the men were charmed, the women confounded in their pretentions, and everyone was dazzled. Cornichon's surprise, although he was prepared for that event, was so great that he fell over, crying with all his might: "Help me, my dear Toupette." But the latter's joy scarcely left her enough presence of mind to give her liberators a part of the evidence of gratitude that she owed them, and Cornichon would have been at risk of not recovering his feet so soon if Selnozoura, who had been the first to perceive his fall, had not taken care to have him lifted up.

Then Toupette ran to him, slightly confused by having been deaf to his voice. She assured him that she would repair that distraction the next time he fell, and as the fay, who wanted to take her away, was calling to her, she promised Cornichon as she quit him to render him a faithful account of all the pleasures that the change was about to procure for her.

Selnozoura returned to her apartment via uncovered galleries, in order to let the people who had not been able to find room in the hall to see such a singular marvel, to which they gave a thousand blessings.

She had no sooner arrived than the genius approached her in order to bid her adieu.

"What, then, is the reason for such a precipitate departure?" she said. "Won't you flatter me with a longer sojourn?"

She was about to continue to express her astonishment when he interrupted her, saying: "Am I not unfortunate enough, Madame to have broken the ties that attach me to you by so many titles once? Do you want me to risk failing you again, and rendering myself utterly unforgivable? Is this not the same object whose charms cast me into the greatest aberrations? Alas, far from having lost their power over my heart, I sense only too clearly that, if they were capable of overturning my reason while they were only nascent, the degree of perfection that they have acquired will render them even more redoubtable. Suffer, then, Madame, that a longer sojourn with you be postponed until the time when, Cornichon enjoying the favors of destiny in his turn, I shall be able to see Toupette without danger."

"But in that regard," exclaimed Dindonnette, "we've forgotten to fix the epoch in which Toupette must cede her condition of youth to Cornichon. The poor fellow! Alas, I believe that there's no longer time. How stupid I am. But truly, no, there's no longer time; that condition ought to have been announced before Toupette was touched by the wand. Oh, fatal wand! But you, Madame," she added, addressing Selnozoura, "should have warned me."

Dindonnette's forgetfulness had not escaped Selnozoura, but the same motives of delicacy that had prevented her from appearing to be too interested in Cornichon had retained her again in that occasion; she had not dared to warn Dindonnette about her neglect.

"Your operations, Madame," she said to her, "were so prompt that I did not have time to enable you to perceive what was lacking therein. No, undoubtedly, our laws being formal in that regard, the conditions of a work of faerie cannot be substituted after the touch of the wand, which puts an inviolable seal on it. Cornichon can only expect the change of his state due to the enchanted water, which, in the decrepitude he is in, cannot fail to arrive soon; so the projected union can be concluded, and Toupette will fulfill successively in his regard the functions of wife, nurse and governess."

"How sorry I am," said Dindonnette, "that I cannot witness that wedding; I have infinite affairs at home, whereas, if had thought of it I would have marked a term to Toupette's metamorphosis short enough to enable me to attend the marriage—a week, for example; I couldn't spend any longer here."

"But Madame," said Selnozoura, "that would have made their condition worse instead of making it better, the enchanted water having much longer periods. Then again, what means are there of uniting people who trade conditions so frequently?"

"I agree," Dindonnette replied, "that the period of a week is a little short, and I hadn't thought about it. Let's not talk about it anymore, since it's no longer relevant; but as for the marriage, I sustain the possibility of it in the circumstances in question, and in the state of complete infancy. I know what I'm talking about; I'll explain myself: at the anticipated moment of the metamorphosis, they would be brought together, as is practiced between people who want to marry. When the moment came, Toupette, who would feel her strength abandoning her, would be retained by Cornichon, who would feel his own increasing proportionately and his stature straightening, and would recovering the free use of his tongue in order to pronounce the necessary words; they would then seize that moment of parity, and you would see married people! Oh, how pleasant that would have been!"

As it was evident that the good fay had resolved only to say and do absurd things, they dispensed with replying to her. Selnozoura gave all her attention to the genius, who, persisting in his resolution not to see Toupette any longer, took his leave of her and refused absolutely the offer she made, in order to retain him, to send that young person to one of her country houses for as long as it pleased him to remain in Bagota.

"You do not have enough obligation to me, Madame," he said, "to make that sacrifice; it is for me to depart and to remain far away from your court for as long as the common laws of human nature conserve for Toupette the charms that are so deadly to me; but I depart penetrated by the sentiments that you might desire of a good friend and relative, who will always regret having ceased to be one and will only occupy myself with giving you evidence of it."

Having said that, he launched himself into the air, where he was sustained all the way to his palace by two sylphs who held him by his ears; that was the mode of travel he found most convenient—everyone has his own taste.

When a day so very full had passed, Toupette, on turning to her apartment, found Cornichon, who was waiting for her with the utmost impatience. Before quitting her, Selnozoura had not failed to recommend silence to her in Cornichon's regard as to Dindonnette's forgetfulness, which excluded him forever from the favor that Toupette alone would enjoy. There was no need for that; the sight of her delighted him so much that he forgot himself entirely. The pleasure he had driven out of his mind the thought that he might have been seen with an equal pleasure; he would not have traded one for the other.

"How beautiful you are, my dear Toupette," he said.

"It's true, she said, "that people have found me sufficiently so, and I'm not sorry that you share the common opinion in that regard; but how are you after your recent fall?"

"What kindness," he said, moving a little closer to her. "That's your usual amity, I'm sure of it. But beautiful Toupette, I won't limit to that sentiment my pretentions to your heart..."

"What?" she said, moving away. "You have more extensive pretentions? Oh, you have too much intelligence for that!"

At that moment, one of the genius guards commissioned to make a round of the palace every evening in order to maintain the order there that the fay had established, made audible at the door of Toupette's apartment the sound of his halberd, which served as a signal for retreat. Toupette informed Cornichon of that, and they terminated a conversation that was about to become embarrassing for both of them.

As he quit Toupette, Cornichon could not help saying to her that she was very exact. She excused herself on the basis of the day's fatigue, and they separated.

The following day and those that followed, until Dindonnette's departure, were employed in giving her less noisy, and hence more sociable, amusements than those with which she had found Selnozoura's court occupied on her arrival. Hunting, fishing, walking and several other pleasures particular to the fay species, were alternately brought into play; my author gives an exact description of them, which I believe I can pass over, at the risk of the reproach that translators often run of having truncated their author.

Finally, Dindonnette, after having asked for and given a thousand various items of advice on politics, finance, war and pompoms, and having sufficiently wearied everyone, departed, as she had promised.

Returned to herself then, Selnozoura did not forget, among the domestic cares to which she delivered herself, the consolation of Cornichon. She found him in the dispositions of indifference as to his fate in which we represented him just now, provided that he could enjoy the sight of Toupette. She believed that he was in a state to hear that it was, in fact, the only pleasure that was reserved to him, because of the stupidity of the Fay of the Island. Toupette, who was present, had new proofs in that occasion of the violence of his passion, which was entirely detached from his own interest.

Time passed, however, and while Toupette spent it with all the pleasure imaginable, a deluge of infirmities overwhelmed Cornichon; nothing remained to him of humanity but a heart that Toupette alone still animated, and thoughts that were incessantly directed toward her.

She was good and compassionate, it is true, but in the end, those most estimable of all virtues, which give activity to the aid of which one can expect some utility for those who receive it, become idle and as if stifled when their practice is evidently fruitless. That was the situation in which Toupette found herself with regard to Cornichon; the unfortunate fellow perceived it, and, the chagrin he felt collaborating with his infirmities, he fell into the final state of old age—by which I mean infancy.

Let us quit Selnozoura's court momentarily in order to pass to that of the genius. The affairs and amusements to which he devoted himself alternately, more in the design of distracting himself from his passion than by taste or necessity, did not produce the effect for which he hoped. Relentlessly occupied with an unfortunate amour, he could not enjoy any repose; all his art was useless to him; he thought of seeking elsewhere what it could not furnish him.

Genii have in regard to Destiny an access that is refused to mortals; he resolved to consult it. I shall not make the description of the palace of that supreme divinity, or the manner in which audiences are given there. It is sufficient to say that in the one that Kristopo obtained, he received the response that *it was only up to him to recover his tranquility in one of his horns.*

"My horns!" he cried, very surprised. "I know that the bold imagination of humans sometimes represents us in the most bizarre forms and those most distant from the truth, but..."

Destiny does not like replies; the triple veil that covers the redoubtable throne at the height from which its oracles are rendered was suddenly lowered, and Kristopo was reduced to seeking the meaning of that one in his own enlightenment. That did not furnish anything satisfactory. He wanted to consult that of his Council, and he assembled it as soon as he returned.

Of all the advice he received there, none struck him more than that of an old man who was the last to speak.

"You know, Sire," he said, "that when intelligences like yourself want to favor humankind with their precious caresses, the fruits of that temporary union do not fail to bear at birth few marks of the nobility of their origin; subject otherwise to all the infirmities of humans, it is not just that they are made in all regards like them. The particular signs of your illustrious house in that case are, for males, an almost imperceptible horn, just as a little tuft of black feathers distinguishes those who emerge female. Do you not have, Sire, any memory of having given rise to that mark?"

"It's true," replied the genius, "that some fifteen years ago, finding myself very thirsty while out hunting in an arid land, a young shepherdess of great beauty offered to guide me to a spring that she knew. That small service excited my gratitude; nine months later she gave birth to a son, but the memory of that event only increased my embarrassment by virtue of the consequences it had. I consulted my art with regard to the fate of that child and the relation it might have to mine, and discovered that he was destined to cause me violent chagrins by virtue of the competition he would have with me. The violent measures that the jealousy of the throne inspire in me all too often horrified me, but I thought that it was at least prudent to relegate that obstacle to my tranquility far away from me. I had him given to a slave merchant who was transporting several of them to another hemisphere, not doubting that such a great distance would put eternal boundaries between us. How, then, can I find that child, when I don't even know whether he's alive? And even if I could, what relation could that discovery have to my passion for Toupette?"

"If I had in hand," said the old man, "a power as great as the one that resides in you, Sire, I flatter myself that my research would not be in vain. But without having recourse yet to the supernatural means that are open to you, first consult the mother of the child, if she still exists; maternal tenderness is industrious and clear-sighted; one might obtain enlightenment from her, or at least a few clues."

The woman in question had retired to her hamlet, more sensible to the separation from her son than all the ease she might have enjoyed at the court. Someone went to fetch her. Firstly, the genius asked her whether her son did, in fact, have the horn that the old man had mentioned, which she confirmed. He then employed mildness and menaces by turns for a long time in order to determine the fearful woman to tell him what she knew about the child.

Finally, she admitted that, unable to resolve herself to be separated from him, she had followed the slave merchant for a long time when he left Ratibouf, that she had even resolved to give herself to him and travel all over the world rather than abandon her son, but that, touched by her tears, he had consented to sell him in the first city they came to, in order to conserve the hope for her of being informed of his fate, and even the means of seeing him sometimes; but that was on the express condition that she said nothing about it, for fear that he might attract the wrath of the genius, whom he had promised only to dispose of the boy three thousand leagues away from Ratibouf.

They were then in the territory of Selnozoura, and on arriving in the capital the following day, the merchant had sold her son to a lady of the fay's court, who had been struck by his beauty, and who made a present of him to her sovereign. The merchant had continued his route next day, and she, after having remained in Bagota for a few days incognito, partly consoled by knowing that her child was so well placed, instead of returning to the court, which abode no longer had any charms for her, she had fixed her residence in her cottage. From there she had gone to Bagota several times in order to have news of her dear son and to enjoy the pleasure, always incognito, of sometimes seeing him, but a horrible enchantment had finally taken him away forever from a place that could no longer offer her anything but a subject for tears.

"What is that subject, then" asked the genius.

"Alas, Sire," the poor woman replied, "at the age that you know he ought to have, he resembles a man a hundred years old, and perhaps at the present moment he had ceased to live."

All the circumstances of this story, in combination, left the genius no room to doubt that Cornichon was his son. He was glad about that. "This discovery does seem, it is true," he said, "to have some connection with Destiny's oracle. I have rediscovered one of my horns, but I don't yet see what relationship it can have to my tranquility."

"Sire," said the old man, "that first part of the oracle, grasped, is a feeble glimmer that ought to lead you to the light. The oracle, in saying that it only depends on you to discover the tranquility that you have lost, supposes on your part the collaboration of a few efforts, labors, or perhaps even sacrifices."

"Yes," said the genius, after having meditated a little, "yes Barmakaijou"—that was the wise old man's name—"your conjectures are accurate; sacrifices are doubtless necessary, and very sensible ones; but I shall not be reproached for having, for want of courage, raised obstacles to the edict of Destiny. Judge that by the resolution I have made, and to which I want to make you party.

"You know that my recent services have been of such importance for all the Supreme State of Faerie, that they have filled the measure to which favors of the first order are attached, in accordance with our customs. I was able, therefore, not long ago, to claim in my favor a fortunate uncertainty as to the object of my request, suspended thus far, and I postponed its determination until the time of our next general assembly.[60]

"My choice is made; it will neither be the Great Slipper, nor the unworthy privilege of only shaving the half of my beard that forms my prayers; I shall not be seen to solicit from my peers with such ordinary entreaties the right to wipe

---

[60] Author's note: "This is one of the articles on which one might have desired a few clarifications on the part of the author; one can only infer that, all the nations, being in accord on the general principle that it is desirable to recompense merit and services, only differed regarding the choice of the rewards proposed to them."

my nose with my foot.[61] The rejuvenation of Cornichon, the annihilation of the bizarre law of which he is the victim; that is what ought to acquit the Republic toward me, as the sacrifice of my passion for Toupette in favor of my son will acquit me toward my niece."

That resolution was applauded, and the action appeared magnanimous. Kristopo, in separating from his Council, commanded a profound secrecy regarding the affair, as he did to Cornichon's mother, who was weeping with joy as she had just wept with sorrow.

A few punctilious readers might perhaps say that this incident is pillaged from Seleucus, father of Antiochus;[62] the value of that criticism depends on the times when the two events happened, which is a point of chronology whose discussion is not my subject.

The time of the General Assembly of Faerie was imminent; as soon as it arrived, the genius transported himself there. Selnozoura had also gone there. Imagine her surprise when, in the audience that was granted to Kristopo to make the exposition of his services and the requests that they merited, she heard that they were limited to the rejuvenation of Cornichon. Was it on the part of a rival that one ought to expect such an extraordinary mark of disinterest? But she was even more astonished when, on leaving the audience, the genius approached her and requested Toupette for Cornichon, in the capacity of his father.

Such a generous procedure completed effacing from the fay's heart all the nasty impression that the previous conduct of the genius might have left there. A mutual confidence succeeded it. The genius told Selnozoura about everything that he had done since his departure from Bagota, Destiny's oracle, and the result of his Council; the description of such sage conduct received further applause on his part. They departed urgently for Bagota, where Kristopo wanted to go in order to hasten Cornichon's happiness.

"I shall take charge, Madame," he said to the fay, "of obtaining the consent of Toupette's parents."

"That will not be difficult," she replied. "It's necessary to confess to you that those who pass for such have only lent themselves to the necessity of hiding the origin of that young person, which is much more illustrious. Cornichon will not be making a misalliance, since Toupette is the fruit of the complaisance that

---

[61] Author's note: "I am tempted to believe that there is a misprint in the text here, in view of the impossibility of this action, but genii are very extraordinary things." This is a joke; the French colloquialism "*il ne se mouche pas du pied*" [he doesn't wipe his nose with his foot] refers to someone who does things in grand style.

[62] Seleucus I Nicator, who took over most of the Alexandrian Empire in the third century B.C. after the death of Alexander the Great, allegedly permitted his son Antiochus to marry his stepmother, Stratonice, after being persuaded that Antiochus was in danger of dying of lovesickness.

one of our companions felt obliged to have for a young mortal who pleased her greatly; she did not think it appropriate to make her childbirth public; those sorts of adventures are not always well received. She confided her secret to me, and as soon as she had brought the child into the light, I took charge of her. You had occasion to see her in the hands of the pretended parent to whom I had given her in your estates; you can judge in consequence how capable she was of profiting from an education superior to the one those poor folk could have given her; they abandoned her to you with joy when you told them that you had the design of placing her with me, and I received her from you as a stranger. You know the rest.

"If that is so," said the genius, "Toupette ought to bear a few marks of her origin."

"Yes," said the fay, "a little cluster of black feathers placed above her left breast distinguishes her without disfiguring her; that is why she was given the name Toupette, just as I gave that of Cornichon to your son because of the little horn that I discovered in his hair, of which it imitates the color so well that one might mistake it for a curl. The similar accident that heightens the whiteness of Toupette's breast has been mistaken thus far for an advantageous adornment. The absolute power over her given to me by her mother, who is a friend of mine, responds for her consent, but the laws of secrecy forbid me from revealing her to you; that is all I can tell you."

"Good, my niece," said the genius. "It's enough; at least I know in consequence that Toupette is my relative; that mark is precisely the one particular to fays of our house who desire to have contraband goods. I only love my daughter-in-law more for that, and my happiness would be complete if I could think that you were her mother."

"My uncle is always joking," the fay replied, blushing slightly. Then she changed the subject; they agreed that they would keep the secret of Cornichon's fate until the moment of his union with Toupette, which would be the epoch of his rejuvenation.

As soon as they arrived in Bagota the fay told Toupette that she had finally made the resolution to marry her, that the ceremony would only be deferred until the following day, and that she was to dispose herself for it.

"Your kindness, Madame, would answer to me for my happiness in the choice that you have made for me, if Cornichon's misfortune did not mingle regrets with an event that ordinarily only causes joy. If the unfortunate fellow enjoyed an estate similar to mine, I would not be reduced to asking you who the husband is that you have destined for me."

"Be tranquil as to your fate," the fay said, "but you will only be informed of that at the moment of your marriage."

Toupette withdrew in silence. Part of the night was employed by her in divining that future husband; a host of amiable men were presented to her imagination but her free heart did not settle her ideas on anyone; weary of thinking about it she abandoned herself to her destiny with sufficient tranquility.

Rumor of Toupette's marriage and the mystery that Selnozoura was making of the choice of her husband assembled in the fay's apartment, early the next day, all those who might pretend to it by virtue of various entitlements. The altar was already decorated and a crowd of people filled the temple, while the fay still maintained silence. Having entered, and not seeing Cornichon there, she commanded someone to fetch him.

""Madame," said Toupette then, "please spare that poor fellow the sight of a ceremony that is bound to fill him with dolor, if he is still susceptible to it, and to which his presence would only bring a sort of ridicule if he is not."

"I would like," said the fay, "not to raise the matter in this situation of a liberty that I criticize in you, and content myself with telling you that he will not be out of place."

Toupette made no reply. Cornichon was brought; the sight of the numerous assembly only excited in him an infantile laughter, and everyone was astonished that a fay so sage was acting out of character in that way.

When everything was arranged and the aspirants arranged in a semicircle were avidly seeking the fay's gaze, she said to Toupette: "Approach. And you," she added, addressing those supporting Cornichon, "place him beside her. This, my daughter," she said, "is a husband of whose tenderness, virtues and misfortunes you are aware; as many entitlements enough to render him dear to you; accomplish the decrees of Destiny in giving your hand to him without hesitation."

"Oh, Madame!" cried Toupette, seized by surprise and taking a backward step. "Yes, doubtless he has my compassion, but is that not all that one can give to the state he is in at present? Is it necessary…?"

The fay's gaze made her understand that all remonstration was vain. She took Cornichon's hand. The genius then touched all three of them with his wand.

"Enjoy, my son," he said, "the grace of Destiny, and know, simultaneously, your wife and your father."

It is not easy to describe the effect that the surprise produced on the spectators of that marvel. The hopes of the confounded aspirants, and the joy of a thousand women to whom that event rendered a lover about to escape them, cast an infinite variety into the scene; but in the dependency that all those people were in on the principal subject formed by the two spouses, they only appeared as accessories, as if lost in a vague background. It was from Toupette and Cornichon that all the light by which it was illuminated departed: all that beauty can borrow from amour, and all that amour itself borrows from joy, was found combined so advantageously in the two lovers that it is impossible to give an accurate idea of it.

That is how my author expresses it, and it is necessary to believe it; he would not have lost such a beautiful opportunity to go into detail.

After the ceremony the spouses were escorted back to the palace by the fay and the genius, in the midst of the acclamations of an innumerable crowd.

Fêtes that ceded nothing in magnificence to those that had celebrated the return of peace filled the first days of the union of Toupette and Cornichon. The genius witnessed that with the liberty of mind that had been promised to him by Destiny, and only returned to his estates after having extracted a promise from the fay that the spouses would make occasional visits to his court.

They passed thus, in the continuation of their life, days that no adversity troubled, and to which a numerous posterity added a further degree of happiness.

Here our author, at the end of the career that he had proposed, seems to request of the reader the prize that he believes to be due to him. The merit of a translator does not give him the same rights; I do not request any, fortunate if the approval that I have procured in this work is not mingled with a few suspicions as to its utility; there are no genuinely useful works except those that have truth for an object, and all of this is perhaps not true.

Attributed to Marie-Antoinette Fagnan: *Minet-Bleu and Louvette*

Intelligence without looks is very little, beauty without intelligence is even less. The fay Louvette, as everyone knows—everyone, that is who has some knowledge of the court of the fays—was, for five days a week, a very small person of frightful ugliness; for the other two days she had a majestic stature and a ravishing beauty. It is not to lose everything only to have two good days a week, when one can make the most of them, but one inconvenience rendered that advantage useless, which is that in changing her face she changed her soul, character and sentiments.

On the five days of ugliness she was tender, good, gentle, passionate and as amiable as one can be with a repulsive exterior and a face that displeases. She employed those five days of ugliness in obliging people, flattering them and seeking to please; she spared no effort to find a genius, an enchanter or a mere mortal capable of attaching himself to what is called true and solid merit, that of the heart and the sentiments; she made attempts with regard to everyone, but nothing succeeded for her. However, if the good little fay made so many enticements and advances, it was not because she was a coquette—it is as well to be informed of that, because there was a slight resemblance—but because it was written that she would only recover her original form, which had been very attractive, when she had made herself loved veritably in her ugliness. That sentence was traced in the book of destiny, of which everyone knows the name although no one has ever read it.

One might suspect, however, how she had attracted that disgrace; it was by disdaining the sighs and scorning the prayers of a detestable, maleficent, ugly enchanter more powerful that her; those are events so ordinary that one has no need to spell them out, but if you do not state them there is always some blocked mind that cannot divine anything, and will charge you with a crime.

Louvette had, as has been said, two days of a ravishing beauty; she united in that short interval all the graces that can attract and please the eyes; if she had been mistress of conserving the same sentiments, which did not produce anything in her ugliness, she would have captivated and charmed the world; she would not have found a heart made to resist her. But in becoming beautiful she became stupid, proud, disdainful, and unbearable; her arrogance, her scorn, her lack of sentiment and taste—in brief, her attitude—drove away those that her face had attracted; it was sufficient to talk to her and listen to her immediately to lose that opinion and the natural desire to find a beautiful person accomplished. Beauty alone commences by placing it in the hearts of all men, but it needs something more to sustain it there, and in Louvette, everything concurred in banishing it therefrom.

She could not instruct either those who adored her when she was beautiful or those whom he would have like to persuade to love her when she was ugly that she was the same person in those two different forms; that was one of the conditions of her metamorphosis and the return to her original state. It was thought at court that there were two Louvettes, one beautiful and one ugly. It was at the court of the fays that all this happened; I don't know if I have said that, but, as it needs to be said, it is as well to say it here as elsewhere. The court is a country, in which people sometimes see everything and in which, also, they sometimes do not pay attention to anything, with the result that it was a long time before anyone noticed that the two Louvettes never appeared simultaneously.

Meanwhile the little fay had the chagrin, for five days a week, of being the joke and the reject of the same lovers who had, for the other two days, a disposition to adore her that she rendered futile by her manners, and by her lack of taste and return for them. The situation was rather sad, so Louvette was, indeed, very sad, and even more so on the days of beauty that those of ugliness—which proves that it is better to be ugly with intelligence and sentiments than to be beautiful while lacking everything else.

Such was her condition when destiny offered her a person as ill-treated as herself, and for the same reasons. He was a young prince; that is expectable; what is not expectable is that his name was Minet-bleu, which came not only from the singular blue color of his eyes, but also the garment of changing blue taffeta that he wore all summer long, and which he had first brought into fashion, suddenly taken up by all the agreeable men of the court, including the musicians and other talented individuals. He had originally been one of the Adonises over whom all the women agreed in going mad, without quite knowing why.

When those universals, those men of the day, appear, the old fays are not the last to run to them; they are so badly received by those messieurs that they certainly ought to correct them, but does one correct faults that one loves? The fay who experienced the rigors of the handsome Minet-bleu, punished him for it immediately; there are debts of honor for which an outraged fay never asks for an instant's credit. She treated him as the enchanter had treated Louvette; perhaps the two malevolent individuals knew one another; perhaps they had tipped one another the wink. The only difference was that Minet-bleu was only endowed with a repulsive ugliness, accompanied by all the merit of the heart and charms of the mind, for two days a week, and conserved for the other five his original beauty, deprived of everything that could make something of it: devoid of soul, intelligence, taste and sentiments, as indifferent and cold as a automaton, he only looked in order to see, and talked in order to talk, without ever giving the impression of thinking or feeling.

Minet-bleu's two days of ugliness and sensibility were precisely the same ones when Louvette was beautiful and indifferent; and the five days when she was ugly and sensitive were the same ones when the prince enjoyed all the charms of his cold and inanimate face. It was in the latter condition that he had to make himself loved in order to get out of it. He was even condemned to inspire a veritable passion in a woman of merit, in which he was even more maltreated than the fay, who could make herself loved in her ugliness, because it is more difficult to please when one is incapable of loving than when one does not have a lovable face.

The conformity of the two adventures of Louvette and Minet-bleu produced the effect that it naturally would produce. The prince, in his two days of ugliness, fell madly in love with Louvette, who was then in her two days of beauty; he was received with all the outrage and scorn of which she was capable; but once those two days were over, the prince exacted his revenge; poor Louvette reentered her time of complete ugliness, while the handsome Minet-bleu recovered his ice and scorn with his lovely face. The fay wasted in her turn with regard to him the gazes and sighs that seemed to render her even uglier. That is the privilege of confirmed ugliness; everything harms and augments it, principally the very things that make beauty better.

However, the prince's court was soon deserted. The coquettes who had initially been amused by his pretty face and the prudes who had been dazzled by it, wearied of his impolite and excessively consistent coldness; only Louvette, who had no choice, remained attached to him.

Men are more incorrigible than women; their self-esteem is more blinkered and more tenacious; with the consequence that, although they made no more progress with the fay when she was beautiful than the women made with the prince in his beauty, they took longer to take it as read. Scarcely had two lovers retired, repelled by that insupportable beauty, than new ones appeared, ready to augur better of their talents and their merit. Because of that, Louvette, in her ugliness, enjoyed with regard to her lover an advantage and a pleasure that he did not have in her regard when she was in her beauty. That pleasure consisted of almost always being alone in the company of the one she loved, and not having a rival to witness the indifference of which she was the object; that was not a small consolation. Although that indifference did not diminish, at least it did not appear to increase; that was another consolation. Everything that nourishes hope is the wealth and the most genuine charm of amour.

Minet-bleu, on the other hand, was the butt of the insults and scorn of his beauty; in the presence of his rivals he was always the most maltreated. What torment! Fortunately, he had so much intelligence that he took less harm from all that ill-treatment that another, but did he suffer any less for that?

That stormy court was often renewed; Minet-bleu was its doyen; no outrage had been able to repel or banish him. At first, no one paid any heed to that, but after a long time it was noticed, and gave rise to gibes. He held firm. His constancy seemed prodigious; women made a few reflections about it; they resolved in consequence to have pity on him and to try for that reason to forget his face, even if they had to give him audience with closed eyes. It was understood that he must be something extraordinary; the fashion set in, and in no time at all there was a woman of good appearance who made it a serious affair to steal that lover from "the insupportable beauty"—for Louvette, in her two days of beauty, was more commonly known by that name than any other.

History does to say whether the prince responded in the fashion that was hoped to all the generosity with which everyone wanted to heap him at once. Louvette, who found him detestable in his assiduities, found him even more so in his absences, and punished him equally for both; everything was good in order to torment him.

It is appropriate to remark in passing that, when once an ape becomes fashionable, he has the talent of sustaining it better than another; the taste that one acquires becomes a fury in no time.

A certain fay, known as Confidante, found that she was the only one at court who had not yet had a private conversation with Minet-bleu. Confidante was at least as beautiful as Louvette, but she was even more insensible, with the result that in favor of her recognized insensibility, the other fays forgave her for her beauty; although it was a bad quality for a confidante, they trusted her nevertheless; none had yet been trapped by it; she had the best heart and the best mind of any fay at the court. At the end of the day, she could not be reproached for more than two or three indiscretions and as many caprices. Characters as even-tempered as that are very rare, so hers enabled her to be generally liked by all her companions. She knew, therefore, everything that they knew regarding the merit of the ugly Minet-bleu; she knew so much that the curiosity that is the daughter and mother of all the woes that arrive down here, came to give her the bad advice to steal the prince from all his conquests.

Of all the tyrants that dabble in governing the head of a beauty, curiosity is the most absolute, although there are others more powerful; when it speaks, all the others shut up to listen and hasten to serve it. The fay Confidante had frequent opportunities to speak to Minet-bleu; she was charged in his regard with all the trivia and all the little secrets of her companions. As soon as she had made her decision, she made her charge—which is to say that she spoke on her own account and let it be divined that she wanted the prince to listen. He had acquired more experience in one month of good fortune than one acquires in ten years of study, with the consequence that he divined more than anyone wished, which is known as divining accurately.

Those who are on a level plane in what is called character might perhaps wonder how Confidante, being so insensible, could suddenly become so different, and so passionate for an ape. But have I said that she loved him? Not at all. She was curious, and nothing more. Curiosity resembles everything, but is nothing; it resembles love, hatred and all the passions; it can take on their appearance, just as it can quit it.

Confidante did not enjoy the confidence and error of her companions for long; they all agreed in detesting her and speaking ill of her. They joined forces in order to steal Minet-bleu from her, and that theft was no longer treated as an affair of taste but of honor, politics and vengeance. They applied themselves to it very seriously, therefore, and Confidante, whose curiosity might not have retained her with the little wretch for more than twenty-four hours, found herself engaged by pique, self-esteem, and the necessity of putting up a good defense.

Her enemies regarded the insupportable beauty, who was Louvette, as the person who ought to avenge them; the prince's passion for her was well-known; they therefore worked to inspire in that fay, not curiosity, nor amour for Minet-bleu, but aversion and jealousy for her rival.

Anyone who thinks that jealousy cannot be born without amour is badly mistaken. It can come from aversion for a rival, pride, self-esteem, or the desire for a preference that one does not want to employ, without being able to resolve to see another profiting from it. That was the species of jealousy that the fays stimulated in Louvette's heart. It did not take long for them to produce it; one woman alone can do the impossible in that genre working upon another; it is easy to imagine what many fays working together can achieve.

Louvette, guided by their advice, soon hated her rival as perfectly as anyone could desire. She did not love Minet-bleu yet, but she had a keen appetite to render Confidante and him very miserable. She made a pleasure and a study out of doing both of them bloody turns and employing against them what are known as the ruses of war.

She interrupted all their conversations and rendezvous. Sometimes she affected airs of languor and passion, which gave birth to hopes in the heart of the prince; at other times she exerted herself to thwart the interest of her rival. At times when Minet-bleu could have been with Confidante, she occupied him; she appeared to want to listen to him, and to commence to love him; at times when she had no fear of that rival, or when Minet-bleu hoped for the recompense for the sacrifices she had demanded of him, she treated him with a despairing harshness.

At any rate, she saw him for longer; once the project of vengeance began, she was with him more often, and alone with him more often. I do not know whether anyone can divine what happened. This is it: that whole game of jealousy and vengeance produced on her the same effect that curiosity had produced on Confidante; in believing that she was only imitating jealousy and passion, she became all the more so because she had initially had a contrary design. It is thus that Amour plays with our projects; that is how all his games end up.

As soon as Louvette began to perceive her illness she began to take care to hide it—a futile effort, which only produces further betrayal. Fortunately, Minet-bleu loved her too much to perceive his good fortune as promptly as he would have done if he had not been loved as much. That change produced another: gradually, the prince's ugliness began to diminish.

That metamorphosis happened so slowly that it was almost imperceptible for the others, but it made great strides in the heart and eyes of Louvette. Every time she saw him, she found him more lovable, and that was exactly what he needed to become even more so.

The fays soon suspected that nascent amour; they had gradually avenged themselves on Confidante; they had counted on also avenging themselves on the prince, in view of what they knew of the character of Louvette—as if Amour does not make characters entirely anew when necessary!

The ugliness of the prince, which was already no longer ugliness, since it had to cease and cease by virtue of amour, was succeeded for five days, as you know, by Louvette's ugliness, which, until then, had appeared to increase rather than diminishing; but a fortunate hazard came to her aid.

The handsome Minet-bleu, parading his indifference and his charms in a nearby wood, was attacked by a gang of brigands. As can be imagined, he defended himself with a great deal of valor, wounded the most aggressive and dissipated the rest, but he came back with his left hand pierced by an arrow. The wound was slight, but the arrow was poisoned—which is of the utmost consequence, when one is not immortal. The surgeon who examined the wound said what he thought with all the discretion appropriate to such a case; however, he allowed it to be glimpsed that there was no other remedy than finding someone promptly whose mouth could draw the venom out of the wound by extracting blood. He added that there was a danger in that for whoever attempted it.

Scarcely had he finished speaking than Louvette, dissolving in tears, took possession of her lover's hand; she applied her lips to the wound, and whatever effort he made to withdraw his hand, she would not let go until she had drawn out all the poison by extracting all the blood with which it might be mingled.

The prince, more moved and more troubled by Louvette's action than by his injury and the danger he had been in, looked at her without having the strength to speak to her or to hold back his tears. Has there ever been ugliness in which there is soul, sentiment and veritable tenderness? No, of course not; so Louvette, in that state, appeared very beautiful to her lover—and was, in fact. When we perform a beautiful action, we do not have our ordinary appearance; we have the appearance and the features appropriate to the action.

Esteem, pity and gratitude entered at that moment into the soul of the prince, never to emerge again. He saw Louvette with entirely different eyes, and from that moment on she was no longer the same. A fortunate error is that which occasions a reality!

She lost her deformity and resumed her original charms, and as she recovered them, he became increasingly attached, with the result that in no time at all, she became the most beautiful of fays and he the most tender of princes. He also became the most handsome in his two critical days, as the insupportable beauty lost that name to become amiable and tender.

Things were taken on either part to such a degree of perfection that they recognized one another as being the same persons who had caused so many woes in their double form. Everyone else recognized them too, saying that they had suspected it, although no one had actually thought of it.

It was that point that destiny wanted them to reach before uniting them. As that was the only thing that remained to do, and both of them wanted it sincerely, no obstacle was raised to it. The Queen of the Fays performed the ceremony, and ordered fêtes that were among the most brilliant, according to connoisseurs. Louvette communicated immortality to her lover, in accordance with the privilege of faerie. He made very good use of it, and at the moment when I am writing this, they are still as happy as on the first day.

Marianne-Agnès Falques: *Durboulour; Or, The Benevolent Lioness*

There was once a king who was a great servant of God and his Prophet; he was the father of three sons, whose mothers, whom he loved very much, gave birth to them on the same day. The more he was the master of placing the crown on one of their heads, the more he wanted to know which of them was the most worthy of it, and would render his subjects happy. He resolved, therefore, to test them, and said to them: "The one who is the most courageous and the most robust, and who can render the best account of his travels, can be assured of having preference and being my successor. Then he ordered them to go hunting, in order for them to commence applying themselves.

Each of them chose a horse from the stables, took provisions, and set forth. Their names were Gulbidar, Scandarbi and Durboulour. They hunted without having found anything, and returned very sadly to their father's palace, consoled after a fashion by seeing their common misfortune.

Durboulour remained behind for a few moments in order to examine something bright that he perceived in the sky, albeit very high. It was a feather that descended spinning, and which cast a great light. As soon as it reached the ground he picked it up, with all the care it merited; it was made of gold garnished with diamonds and precious stones. Beautiful as it was, it was only a feather, and a hunter would have been ashamed to boast about such a hunt, so he did not mention it to his brothers, much less to the king, his father.

That prince embraced his children and consoled them, saying that the poor success of their hunt proved that it was necessary to arm themselves with patience in the world, and that events did not always respond either to desire or will. Then he told them to go to bed.

Meanwhile, Durboulour found the means to place the beautiful feather in a secret place in the palace, where only the king ordinarily went. By night the latter perceived a bright light through the door; he did not doubt that a fire had started in his apartment; he ran there, and recognized with surprise the effect of the beautiful feather, the examination and the property of which charmed him. No one but one of his sons could have entered that place, so he sent for them and said: "My sons, to which of you do I owe the most beautiful of feathers?"

Scandarbi and Gulbidar cried simultaneously: "It's to me."

The king turned to Durboulour. "You aren't saying anything?"

"What do you expect me to say, Sire? It's only a feather, and the two of them are disputing it. But ask them how it is made, and Your Majesty will soon see whether the truth is in their mouth. That's the means of recognizing which of them has been fortunate enough to render that feeble homage to Your Majesty."

The competitors for a kingdom do not usually love one another, and that affair, of which Durboulour had all the honor, united the hatred of his two brothers against him. The king had no suspicion of it, and paternal love made him excuse those who had done wrong.

A few days later he said to them: "I've reflected a good deal, my children; this feather presents an object of a voyage worthy of princes like you. It's necessary to bring me the marvelous bird that bears these feathers. Depart, take the money you will need, but each depart alone. The one who brings me the beautiful bird will be my successor."

They set forth, and when they had ridden for a fortnight they found a great forest, at the entrance to which they saw a superb white marble fountain; it was facing three roads, and bore inscriptions that indicated the nature of each of the roads in question: *The man that goes to the right burns; the man that goes to the left drowns; the man who takes the middle course never returns.* They were embarrassed by that reading.

Scandarbi and Gulbidar were of the opinion to go elsewhere, but Durboulour said that he was resolved to make the proof of the three roads alone. After much argument they agreed to draw lots, but his brothers cheated Durboulour and made the road from which no one returned fall to him. They agreed the time when they would meet up again and promised that they would wait by the fountain for a determined time, in order to return to their father together.

Scandarbi found water in the route that he followed, but he did not risk drowning. Gulbidar did in fact, find fire in the one that had fallen to him, but as it was very hot he did not think that it was a good idea to approach it. They returned promptly to the fountain, therefore; they bought tents and settled down under the finest shade, savored the fresh air and spent the days in delights, content to have one competitor fewer, for the verity that they had found in the inscriptions convinced them that Durboulour would not be able to escape the danger to which he had exposed himself. They hunted for their pleasure, but in truth, they scarcely launched any arrows except at birds.

"Who knows," they said, "whether we might be fortunate enough to find the one we're seeking, and which the king has the folly of desiring. What tells us that it's there rather than here?" But that is not the way that one pursues virtue and makes a celebrated name for oneself. Hazard rarely presents difficult things.

Meanwhile, Durboulour, resolved not to neglect anything to belie the inscription, and at least to sell his life dearly, was less sorry to perish in thinking about the hatred of his brothers, which presented the prospect of an unhappy life if he did not merit the generosity of his father. He therefore wanted, at any price, to obtain it by rendering himself worthy of it.

After riding for some time, occupied with those ideas, he perceived a lioness ahead of him, the physiognomy of which was beautiful and majestic.

They looked at one another for some time, and then the lioness said: "Have you no fear, young man, in following such a dangerous road?"

"Far from being afraid," the prince replied, "everything ought to tremble before me."

"That's very proud," she said, "But I won't answer for your not having another opinion in a little while. If you take another few steps you'll be devoured, and I feel sorry for you; your physiognomy and your courage interest me. Believe me, return whence you came, for you'll find in these parts a huge snake that devours everything."

"Anyone who allows himself to be eaten," said the prince.

"I swear to you," said the lioness, "that I'm no more timid than anyone else, and that it has eaten all the lions I've made. I had two in my last litter, which are already grown and give rise to the finest hopes; I keep them carefully hidden, but I live in continual fear."

"I hope to tranquilize you soon," said the prince.

"You reassure me slightly," said the lioness, "but I dare not guide you to the place where you will find the monster."

Eventually, the prince's words having inspired the confidence that true courage always gives, she called her children and told them to look after and take good care of Durboulour's horse. To him she said: "Mount me, if you please; I cover more ground in an hour than the best horse in twenty-four. Don't be astonished by my movements or the diligence with which I carry you through the woods and mountains."

In fact, she stopped shortly thereafter and said to the prince: "You'll find the monster in that little valley a short distance away. Go look at it, you who fear nothing; I'll wait for you here."

The prince set forth, and did not take long to encounter the monster—or rather, to see it coming toward him. Durboulour was not astonished, and cut off its head; but another one grew, just as strong. The same thing happened several times; the combat was beginning to become unequal, but the prince decided to strike a blow at the tail; it was so terrible that it separated it from the body. Then it fell, its strength failing, and the prince found himself master of the terrain.

He got his breath back, cut the tongues out of all the heads, even those that were still in the body, and made a parcel of them, which he carried away. He came to find the lioness, who was so delighted that she said: "Dispose of me and I'll do anything you wish; I'll carry you wherever you want to go."

"Madame," the prince said to her, "permit me to mount you, and that I take you first of all to see the state in which I put your enemy.

They found it dead, in great putrefaction, but the lioness, in order to satisfy a desire for vengeance quite natural in females, gave it a few bites with her teeth and scratches with her claws. They quit that place of horror in order to go and take some rest near a spring that the lioness knew; she renewed her assurances of attachment to the prince so eagerly that he told her his story and the motive for which he had undertaken his journey.

After shaking her head several times during his story, the lioness said: "The marvelous bird is a long way from here, if I can believe what I've heard said about it. Your horse wouldn't take you there in twenty years, but I've told you that I'm at your orders. I'm going to take you to see a fay, a friend of mine, whose dwelling is more than thirty days' journey from here by ordinary means of transport. She might be able to give you more reliable information about what you're seeking. Come on, mount me; I'll take you at a rapid pace, traveling day and night. Hold on tight and don't sleep any more than I do."

After several days the lioness stopped and said to the prince: "You see that tree on that little arid mountain? That's where the fay I mentioned to you makes her abode. Go to her house, salute her and say to her: 'Good day and good evening, beautiful and great lady, admired and beloved by all those who know her.' That isn't true, but she'll be flattered by it, and you'll see that she'll receive you kindly."

What the lioness had said happened. The fay found the young prince as beautiful as a sun, and was touched by his compliment and the polite boldness that he testified to her.

"I hate all men," she told him. "I do them as much harm as possible, but I want to give you pleasure; perhaps it will cause others pain. In any case, it requires a great interest to have determined you to come into this desert, where no man has ever appeared."

The prince confided his designs and his adventures to her. The fay was astonished that he had defeated the monster of the forest.

"Here are its tongues, Madame," he said.

The fay admired his modesty and mildness, for virtues also touch the wicked; she could not even help saying: "The dear child! What risks he has run! Come let me embrace you; you merit people taking an interest in you, my good friend. Oh, if I were younger…the misfortune of being old is that it's necessary to be sage. Listen; I don't know exactly where the bird you're asking about is, but I have an older sister who can tell you. Take this box of mastic to her on my behalf; she'll know what that means. She lives on the fifth mountain after this one."

The prince thanked her, took his leave of her and went to find the lioness, to whom he rendered an account of his visit. The lioness immediately put him on her back, and, traversing all the mountains while the prince counted them carefully, they arrived at the home of the second fay.

Durboulour was very well received by her, but she told him that she was very sorry not to be able to instruct him

"Don't worry," she said, "my other sister, even older than I am, can give you news of it." She told him where she lived, and gave him half the box of mastic to give to her.

The lioness, still meek and grateful, undertook that journey as cheerfully and as promptly as the others. The last fay lived in an old ruined castle. The prince went into it, and the fay looked at him with an expression to make anyone tremble, but he did not. She softened at the sight of the mastic and the pleasure the prince gave her by virtue of the grace with which he spoke to her and talked to her about her sisters.

When it came to questions regarding the marvelous bird, however, she said: "I have absolutely no idea where it lives, and, in consequence, where you might find it." Seeing how that discourse afflicted the prince, however, she added: "Don't worry; my son knows; he'll be back soon, and I'll engage him to instruct you and prevent him from devouring you, for he's an ogre by taste and temperament; it's a fault I've never been able to correct in him."

A few moments later the son arrived. The fay had the prince hide, and the ogre said, as they all do: "I smell fresh flesh."

"You're right, my son," said the fay, "but it's a man recommended to me by your aunts, and I beg you to inform him of the place where he can find the marvelous bird; he's come a long way."

"Since you and my aunts are interested in him," the ogre said. "I want to be of service to him."

The prince appeared and approached, proudly but nobly, and the ogre, who had never shown or been shown any politeness, was so flattered to receive some that he said to the prince: "I want to oblige you; in addition, I'm at war with those to whom the bird belongs. This is what I advise you to do in order to take possession of it. Go straight through the verdant valley that you can see down there, and then pass nineteen mountains; go up to the summit of the nineteenth and you'll see the shining garden of the palace in which the bird is contained, in a cage worthy of it. Don't allow yourself to be dazzled by anything you see or distracted by anything you hear.

"When you've arrived at the door of the place where the thing you desire is confined, you'll find a broad staircase that descends underground. It has nineteen steps; only go down eighteen and you'll be able to see whether the bird's guardians are asleep or awake. Those guardians are eighteen giants condemned to conserve the garden, the bird and the cage against all those who come, like you, to take possession of it, but they don't have the power to climb the nineteenth step. If you find them awake, turn back; if they're asleep, take the bird very quickly, and leave the same way."

The fay thanked her son for his kindness and his good advice, but she said to Durboulour: "That's only advice; I can give you something more essential. Take my ring of princely metal; kiss it as soon as you find yourself in a difficult situation; it will help you, either by means of the ideas it gives your enemies or the expedients it presents to you. Go, my son; come back this way, and don't forget to bring back my ring, if you can escape all the dangers you're about to run."

After having thanked them and bid them adieu, the prince followed the ogre's advice. He traversed the garden; after having found the staircase and seen the giants asleep, he took the bird and the cage, and was half way across the garden, when the trees there, from which the prince had almost emerged, spoke to him on seeing him go past. The most beautiful was their spokesman. "What! You're taking away our bird! At least take a few leaves and fruits in order to conserve that masterpiece of nature and art, that marvel of marvels."

Those trees were gold and silver, the leaves emerald and the fruits diamonds, rubies and pearls, Durboulour could not help admiring them, and although he had been told in the fay's house—and the lioness had repeated it to him a hundred times on the way—not to respond to anyone and not to take anything from the garden, the prince did not think he was risking anything in collecting one of those branches laden with flowers and fruits, in order to shelter the beautiful bird from the insults of time during the journey.

He had no sooner broken one than the tree started shouting; "Help Help! He's cutting our branches!" The other trees repeated the same plaints. Those cries woke the giants and gave them the power to emerge from the subterrain built in gold and large diamonds and come to the aid of the trees.

They seized the prince, who had no doubt that he was doomed, but he did not forget to kiss the princely metal ring; it alone could extract him from such great danger.

A council was held, and the giants, struck by the courage and resolution that the prince had shown thus far, agreed that it was necessary to let him live, on condition that he went in search for the saber of the Sufi Salomon for them, which they could not acquire by themselves, and which was necessary for them to obtain their liberty.

They put that proposition to the prince, who promised them to go in search of it, even if it was in Hell. They indicated the mountain to him in the hollow core of which it was guarded by a blind giant who was condemned to grind gold in a huge mill. That saber had great virtues, and any king who possessed it would be able to regard himself as the master of the world.

The prince set forth to execute that great design and came to find the lioness, whose great reproaches he endured. She told him that if he no longer had any desire to be king and to succeed his father, she had a great desire to return home in order to be in the bosom of her family. She calmed down, however and told him that if he failed in anything that had been prescribed for him in future, she would abandon him without taking the trouble to enquire as to how he would be able to return home.

The prince promised her everything, and begged her insistently to take him to the place indicated to him. She consented to do that, and set forth with her customary diligence.

They arrived at a huge cavern excavated in a mountain of multicolored marble. He approached it quietly, and saw the giant, who was asleep—or rather, pretending to be asleep. He also saw the saber suspended from a large golden nail above his head. He took it, but as he was leaving the cavern the giant seized him, for the blind have very keen hearing

"Aha!" he said. "You can't escape me."

The prince kissed his ring, and said: "Don't hold me so tightly."

The giant relaxed his grip and said: "Before I decide how to kill you, I want you to tell me what your design was in taking the saber confided to me. I also want to know who told you where to find my retreat."

The prince, who could not tell a lie, told him truthfully everything that had happened to him.

"Is all that true?" said the giant

"I can't assure you anymore," said Durboulour, "but if you want a witness, I'll go to fetch the lioness who bought me."

"Call her," he said, "but I'll keep hold of you."

It was necessary to endure that mistrust. The lioness came, very vexed by everything she saw. The prince said to the giant: "I haven't had time to warn her; let her tell you what she knows about my adventures."

The lioness gave an account in conformity with what he had just said.

"I'm utterly sick of being blind," said the giant. "My brethren give me the desire to imitate them and trust you; you have courage and skill, for you needed a lot in nearly carrying away the blade. There's one means of returning my sight; if you can succeed in that, I swear that I'll render you master of the saber."

The prince and the lioness promised to attempt anything.

"Well," said the blind giant, "I'll give you your life; I'll do more, I'll let you go; on condition that you bring me the chemise of Matchin-Paticha, the daughter of a great king, whose estates are thirty days' journey from here."

The prince engaged himself by oath to bring it to him and left, very annoyed by the further enterprise that he was obliged to undertake and very afflicted by the fatigue that he was about to cause his good friend the lioness. He assured her very strongly that the blind giant had been much wilier than him.

"I can see that," said the lioness, "but I have an obligation to you that I shall never forget. Mount up, mount up, and let's make this further expedition quickly."

They arrived, without knowing their way, on the bank of a very wide river. Seeing that he could not pass over it, Durboulour kissed his ring. Immediately, a ship appeared in which everything was gold, including the slightest equipment, except for the heads of the nails, which were brilliant diamonds.

After having admired the superb machine, the prince boarded it, and did not find anyone there. He examined everything carefully and read an inscription attached to the main-mast; it told him that by turning the lever below the inscription to the right, the vessel would go wherever he wanted.

"What!" he said. "Take me to the palace of Matchin-Paticha right away!"

And right away, the ship set sail.

The astonished prince continued reading and saw that by turning the lever to the left and saying: "Let the ship return to the place from which it set forth," it would immediately turn back. Those words, accompanied by a gesture, made the vessel return to its original location.

The prince found that conveyance very comfortable, and came to render an account to the lioness of what he had seen.

"Depart, Prince," she said to him, "and conduct yourself in a fashion to be able to take possession of the chemise you're seeking. In the meantime, I'm going to rest, and you'll find me here."

The prince embraced her, boarded the ship, turned the lever, set forth more rapidly than the wind, and found himself facing the king's palace.

The ship's cannons saluted of their own accord; the flag, a gold and silver oriflamme embroidered with pearls and gems, was deployed. The king, the queen and the princess ran to the windows of the palace; the entire port resounded with cries of joy and admiration.

The king descended to the shore himself in order to see such a marvelous thing at closer range. Durboulour distinguished him easily by means of the honors that were rendered to him. He disembarked, and proved to him that he knew how to behave with crowned heads.

"Where have you come from?" the king asked. "Where are you going?"

"I'm the son of a king," said the prince, "I'm traveling in the interests of the family, and I'd like to see the great Tchin-Matchin, father of the beautiful Paticha."

The king embraced him and invited him to come to his palace. The prince accepted that honor and thanked him for the guard that he offered to put around his ship during his absence. "It guards itself," he told him. "One can't board it without a ticket, and I can't receive more than one person at a time there."

That discourse was confirmed by what happened to a few curious individuals or marauders; they wanted all the more to board the ship because they perceived that no one was guarding it, but after having received the equivalent of a hundred blows with a rod, they were thrown into the water with such great vivacity that some of them perished there.

The queen and the princess received the prince equally well; his politeness, and above all, curiosity, eventually determined the king to visit the beautiful ship, in spite of the danger that the courtiers found in leaving his sacred person exposed to the will of a stranger; but he was brave.

The prince went aboard for a few moments beforehand, under the pretext of receiving him, but in fact to cover up the inscription on the main-mast and to hide the lever. The king was charmed and surprised by everything he saw. The queen and a few viziers were equally well received, but always alone.

550

Finally, what the prince had anticipated arrived; the princess had so much desire to see the marvel that the king, who loved her, could not refuse her that satisfaction. He was reassured by so many examples that she was finally given that permission, on condition, however, that in order to preserve the delicacy of the court and the decency of her estate as a marriageable daughter and princess, Durboulour allowed her to explore the ship on her own, and that he would always remain in view of everyone next to the main-mast.

The princess was no sooner aboard the ship than the prince turned the lever and departed with the greatest rapidity, in the midst of the cries and regrets of the people and the court.

The prince was with the lioness in a trice. They were delighted to see one another again. He embraced her, and presented the princess to her. The princess was slightly alarmed by the presentation, but the mildness, the politeness and the behavior of the lioness soon reassured her. She had them both climb on to her back, and she returned to the marble cavern where the blind giant lived.

When they had arrived, the prince asked the princess very politely to give him her chemise.

"In verity, Monsieur, that proposition is never made; I would never consent to it."

"Don't think," said the prince, "that I can dispense with it; I swear to you that I only came in search of you for that. I would give you my life; you ought to give me your chemise."

"But what about my rank? What about modesty? What about decency?"

"Your rank is not offended, for no one can know what happens in this desert; with regard to your modesty, I ought to preserve it; I'll go away; Madame"—he indicated the lioness—"will help you to undress."

He did, in fact, retire. The lioness persuaded her to put on her garments without a chemise; she consented to that, all the more so because it was a matter of the interests of the prince, and she was beginning to fall in love with him.

When the giant heard someone approaching he asked: "Is that the desired chemise?"

"Yes," said the prince, "But you're too cunning for me. Put your hands behind your back, let me tie them; you can smell the chemise and you'll see by its odor that it can't belong to anyone else."

The giant obeyed. What would one not do in order to recover one's sight?

"Ah, that's it!" he said. "I know the fine odor of roses and plantain. How obliged I am to you, my dear friend! Give it to me so that I can rub my eyes with it."

But the prince had already taken a step back and said from a distance: "Fair exchange. The chemise is well worth the saber. Take your saber with your teeth, being it to me and I'll put the chemise under your arm."

"Oh, the blind are very unfortunate!" said the giant. "They bear all the expense of confidence."

Everything was executed in accordance with the prince's proposition, although the giant would dearly have liked to keep both; Durboulour, once he was master of the saber, was astride the lioness in a moment, with the princess behind him.

Durboulour was obliged to propose to the beautiful Paticha, however, to take her home.

"What!" she said. "Take me back to my father without a chemise! Oh, Prince," she added, "that wouldn't be becoming to you or to me." That was a pretext to hide the desire that she had to go with him. In fact, when one has given one's chemise, liking and attachment are well proven.

When they had arrived at the brilliant palace, the prince only went down the eighteen steps, and showed the giants who were guarding the marvelous bird the saber of the Sufi Salomon. They prostrated themselves at the sight of it, and handed over the cage and the bird scrupulously, which the prince took away without looking back. He heard all the trees in the garden uttering cries of joy, and saying: "Saber, great saber, beautiful saber, by the virtue of the saber we're going to recover our original state."[63]

The prince, the princess and the bird returned to the lioness, who was, in truth, a benevolent animal, whose manners were charming. She took them very swiftly to the house of the old fay, the mother of the ogre. The Prince presented Paticha to her, returned her ring, testified his gratitude to her, and returned with the lioness to the place where she made her ordinary dwelling.

She found her children in good health; she shed tears of joy, for they had been very good and had behaved in accordance with the advice they had received in their infancy from such a good mother. She found them grown and embellished; she caressed them all the more because they had taken very good care of the horse; they had taken it to the best pasturage, where they had guarded it with all possible care. In sum, Durboulour found it as fat as a dervish,

After the most tender adieux, and reiterated embraces, the prince and the princess separated from the lioness, not without tender protestations of gratitude and amity. The prince visited her several times in the course of his life, and he bore lions in his standards in order to render such a solid and essential friend illustrious.

The prince's horse did not carry them as comfortable or as swiftly as their good friend. Durboulour was often obliged to go on foot and lead it by the bridle, but they finally arrived at the white marble fountain just as his two brothers were about to leave.

---

[63] Author's note: "All Oriental books are full of the prodigies of Solomon's sword and ring, so no one ought to be surprised by this event."

They were as sorry as they were astonished to see Durboulour again, but they did not give him any evidence of it; on the contrary, they heaped him with amities and questions, to which he replied with the frankness of a worthy man.

They took the road to the parental home together, but the two brothers agreed between themselves that, Durboulour being the only obstacle to their good fortune, it was necessary to render themselves masters of the marvelous bird and the beautiful Paticha.

"Since he has told us his adventures, we can do it," they said, "and, in sum, the one who doesn't succeed the king can marry a princess, heiress to a great kingdom."

Those ideas occupied them, and they resolved to execute them at the first opportunity. It did not take long for them to find one.

Durboulour was dying of thirst; the caravan well had neither a pulley nor a rope; travelers ordinarily carried them with them. Scandarbi and Gulbidar had them, but they refused them to their brother; they only offered to give him a hand to descend into the well. Thirst sometimes causes the most enlightened man to lose intelligence. He accepted their offer, and when he was at the bottom they were preparing to fill it with stones when they thought they heard a caravan approaching, for crime blurs the senses.

They drew away promptly, abandoning their unfortunate brother and threatening to kill the beautiful Paticha if she continued her tears and groans. Not content with that ill-treatment, they told her that if she dared to mention Durboulour, and if she contradicted anything they said, she was assured of dying.

Full of hope, and no longer seeing any obstacle to their project, they arrived at the court of the king, their father, who embraced them and asked them for news of Durboulour. But they told him that, always having been reckless, he had wanted to take the road from which no one returned and had doubtless perished, since they had waited for him at the white marble fountain for a lot longer than they has agreed.

"But Sire, here is the marvelous bird. It's true that neither of us can boast of having made its conquest alone, for if one of us killed the snake, the other had the courage to obtain the saber of Solomon and to carry away Princess Paticha, who will be able to console him for the loss of your estates, assuming that the marriage is to your liking,"

The king, ever prudent, said that he would consult his Council, and occupied himself with the marvelous bird, which he admired all the more the more he gazed at it; but that did not prevent him from preparing a house for the princess and treating her in a manner appropriate to her rank, particularly in giving her numerous chemises.

Meanwhile, the unfortunate Durboulour was in despair in the well. To have surmounted so many difficulties, to have succeeded in his projects, to have carried away a princess who was worth all treasures, to be loved by her, and to lose everything in a moment by virtue of such a cruel perfidy, of which his brothers were the authors, no longer having the ring of princely metal, was to experience all misfortunes at the moment of coming into port; and although his courage sustained him, he spent a very bad night.

But he had always been lucky, and he was again. Firstly, he found a stone on which he could sit down. The next day, a caravan did, in fact, arrive, and everyone knows that they stop at every well. He asked for help; it was given to him with ropes, and he was pulled out.

He was recognized as the son of the king, for the caravan was composed of subjects returning to the capital. He was given the best horse and all the help they could offer him. In the end, he arrived the following day, when the king was at table with other two princes.

They were a little confused on seeing him appear, but the rumor caused by the arrival of Durboulour, who was believed to be lost, served to hide their trouble.

The king had Durboulour advance and embraced him, saying: "You have need of consolation, my poor child; your voyage has not been fortunate.

"Oh, Sire, I do not see the beautiful Paticha."

"You'll see her soon and in good health," replied the king.

"My voyage has been fortunate, then," the prince went on, with vivacity. "You must have been given the marvelous bird."

"It's in my cabinet," said the king, "and I owe it to the valor and cares of your brothers."

"Oh, Sire," said Durboulour, "how hard it is to be obliged to accuse persons so close and who were so dear to me of such great crimes!"

"What tale are you telling?" said Scandarbi, insolently. "Do you want to cast suspicion on our conduct?"

"I don't want anything," said Durboulour, "But you have apparently killed the great snake?"

"Undoubtedly," he said.

"How many times did the head grow again?"

"Five times," he said.

"And how many remained?"

"Four," replied the brother.

"That isn't true, for here are the tongues of the eleven that I cut off, or that I left in the body."

The king, who knew very well the tongue of a snake—a knowledge that all kings need to have—examined them and said: "He's right; they're the snake's."

"Good," said Scandarbi. "When I killed the beast, I didn't bother with them."

"But Sire," said Durboulour, addressing the king, "it's apparently Gulbidar who carried off the beautiful Paticha?"

"I told the king that," he said.

Then, putting himself on his knees before his father, Durboulour begged him to summon her and interrogate her himself.

The beauty arrived, delighted to see Durboulour. She threw her arms around him, in spite of the modesty that still reigned in her person. She related everything that had happened, agreed with pleasure that she had sacrificed her chemise, and did not disguise the barbarity with which Scandarbi and Gulbidar had treated Durboulour by leaving him in the well, where the entire caravan certified that they had found him.

The king made the two princes leave the table and sent them to prison under strong guard. "Come, my children," he said to Durboulour and Paticha, "take the places of which courage and virtue have rendered you so worthy of filling. The realm is legitimately yours," he said to Durboulour. "The difficulties, the dangers and the success have acquired it for you veritably. It seems to me that more fortunate still is the amour given to you by a princess worthy of all prayers, but it requires the consent of the king, her father."

Ambassadors were sent forth immediately; they came back with those of Tchin-Matchin, charged with full powers, and the marriage was celebrated.

Gulbidar and Scandarbi could not sustain the good fortune of their brother and died of languor and chagrin. Old age carried away the king a short time later, and Durboulour was happy on the throne with the beautiful Paticha.

Courage brings everything to a conclusion.

Nicolas Bricaire de Dixmerie: *Lindor and Delie*

A certain enchanter and a certain fay had loved one another for such a long time that they began to hate one another. Both of them, however, wanted to appear as if they still loved the other, because they were afraid of one another. Their power was almost equal, their character entirely opposite; that was what had caused one to be nicknamed the fay Anger and the other the enchanter Pacific.

One was extreme in everything, loving and hating recklessly, protecting and persecuting with the same ardor, doing good, doing harm and repenting by turns—in a word, the best and worst of all women. The other, to all the good qualities of the first, only added a small number of faults. He had the power to do harm, but only used it moderately, virtue was henceforth as rare as that of obliging. He was, one might say, one of those people who do good by inclination and permit evil when pushed to the limit.

He permitted himself that in a quarrel that he and the fay Anger had against the fay Docile and the enchanter Quarrelsome, another couple as ill-assorted as them. Quarrelsome and Docile had succumbed; they were subjected to the most bizarre metamorphosis, but it was due to finish some day, and that of Anger and Pacific to succeed it. The latter found in that common peril one more reason to remain together, and, perhaps, one less to remain lovers.

They were walking together one day and becoming irritated with one another without daring to say so, so they said almost nothing. They paid more attention to the conversation of a young man and a young woman who did not seem disposed either to irritation or to silence. Amour and sincerity presided over their conversation; they talked about their tenderness and their happiness, and talked about it so eloquently that they rendered their eavesdroppers jealous.

"That's what we've said more than once," said the enchanter to the fay, coldly.

"That was a long time ago," she said, in the same tone. As she said that she stared at the young man, who seemed to her to be well worth the trouble—which was true.

For his part, the enchanter examined Delie—that was the name of the young woman—whom Nature had created charming and whom Amour embellished further.

How happy they are! the two witnesses to their felicity thought, separately. Already, and still separately, they were thinking of raising an obstacle to that.

It was the fay who explained herself first, but without explaining too much. "Admit," she said to the enchanter, "that that spectacle amuses you. It only depends on you not to be deprived of it so soon. Let's oblige these young people to remain with us, until they become boring."

That advice was avidly received. They acted in concert, and had recourse to the power of enchantment and faerie. Less than that was required to draw two lovers uniquely occupied with one another away from their ordinary route. Both thought they were going home, but they found themselves in a magnificent palace surrounded by vast and superb gardens. Their surprise was great, and their dread even greater, because they feared being separated; but before then, their captors wanted to enjoy their embarrassment.

"Where are we?" said Delie to Lindor. "How were we able to go astray like this?"

"I don't know," he said. "While walking, I only saw Delie, and as long as it was permitted to me to see her, I only perceived her."

The enchanter and the fay had listened to that conversation without allowing themselves to be seen. They judged it appropriate to appear, and redoubled the young couple's astonishment.

"Who are you?" the fay asked Lindor.

"I'm Delie's lover," Lindor replied

"What is your fortune?"

"Delie's amour."

"But in sum, what are your views, your ambition?"

"Always to be loved by Delie."

The enchanter asked almost the same questions of Delie, who gave him very nearly the same replies.

Night fell; the two lovers were separated almost without having had the time to perceive it. Delie was taken to an apartment that, in certain centuries and certain countries, could have made her forget more than one Lindor, but Lindor was always present to his dear Delie; she did not see anything of what surrounded her—or, rather, she saw nothing that was not frightening.

"Where's Lindor?" she cried. "What is he doing? What is he thinking?" It was to the walls that she addressed those questions, and it suddenly seemed that the walls replied to her; she heard these lines sung:

Have no fear for your lover,
Have no fear for yourself;
Delie, another lover loves you,
And will love you constantly.
He can do anything by his supreme art,
Except to silence his torment;
But in spite of that extreme amour,
Have no fear for your lover,
Have no fear for yourself.

Delie, simple as she was, did not believe either the music or the words. She divined that a rival could only be a rival—which is to say, an enemy. She trembled for Lindor, who was only trembling for her.

Both, however, were equally well treated; their wishes were anticipated on every point, except for the one that touched them uniquely: the charm of seeing and speaking to one another.

The enchanter wanted to judge the effect that his music had produced on his young captive. In that he was following the example of the fay, whom he knew to be with Lindor; and no lover ever felt as much joy in being deceived, or as much in taking his revenge. He employed all his eloquence in reassuring Delie, but did not reassure her.

The fay dared more, which only means that she went into greater detail. She flattered Lindor with the most fortunate future. "Have no fear and hope for everything," she said to him. Those few words meant many things, but a fay is permitted to say anything.

For his part, Lindor only talked about Delie; she alone could make him feel the happiness about which the fay spoke to him...

"She alone?" said the latter, with chagrin.

"Yes, Madame," affirmed the young man, rhapsodically. "I dare not, nor do I want to, believe that any other could replace her."

"What does it matter, provided that she is replaced well?"

"Oh, Madame," Lindor replied, naively, "can Delie ever be replaced?"

That response finished irritating the fay. She quit Lindor, to whom that conversation gave food for thought. He shivered at the danger his mistress was in. He had reason. When a rival, in order to avenge herself, only has to want it, it is almost certain that she will want it. However, the fay did not want it yet; she hoped to seduce or dazzle an inexperienced young man easily; she had no doubt that the enchanter would have the same intentions in regard to Delie, and the same success in his intentions. That was what the fay wanted to clarify with him, without allowing herself to be penetrated, for their power did not extend as far as reciprocal divination, a faculty that could become dangerous between two long-time lovers.

"What shall we do with the children?" the fay asked the enchanter the next day.

"Whatever you like," the latter replied. "I believe that one can't do anything more agreeable to them than to reunite the,"

"I would have liked to enjoy their embarrassment a little longer," said Anger.

"We'll come back to that," said Pacific. "For the present, let's enjoy their satisfaction." Personally, he wanted to enjoy the fay's embarrassment, and to procure Delie, whom he hoped to win, a moment of joy.

Who could depict the naïve transports of the lovers? The enchanter and the fay observed them in silence, and observed one another at the same time. But the silence was not maintained for long; the fay was the first to break it, so much was Lindor's joy causing her impatience. As for the enchanter, he suffered and kept quiet.

"Admit," Anger said to him, "that that couple are not very circumspect."

"They're all the happier for it," replied Pacific.

"They scarcely perceive that we're examining them."

"That's because they have something better to see."

"What activity that Lindor puts into his discourse. Will his protestations never end?"

"He's at an age when one thinks oneself able to promise everything and deliver everything."

"In truth, this is taking indulgence too far, What! Suffering that he kisses Delie's hand thirty times?"

"It's a lot, I agree, but..."

"But can't you see her offering him the other one?"

"You're right," said Pacific, a trifle emotional. "To deprive herself thus of both hands is too much..."

"Meanwhile, there they are, drawing away to approach those bushes..."

"Stop! Stop!" the enchanter shouted at them. The tone in which he pronounced those words caused the fay to judge that he was taking no less interest in the actions of the young couple than she was. She followed his example and dissimulated.

They approached Lindor and Delie, who avoided them. It was then the fay who spoke first, and it was to Delie that she affected to speak.

"You must have been told to flee certain occasions," she said to her.

"What occasions?" asked Delie, naively.

"Those which might lead to certain liberties."

"What do you call liberties?" asked Delie, again.

"Those for example, that you're about to permit."

"What! Just that?"

"What more would be necessary?"

"I don't know."

So much the better, the enchanter said to himself. "A little less severity," he whispered to the fay.

"Have no fear," she replied, smiling. Then, continuing to question Delie, she added: "What is your father?"

"That I don't know," replied Delie.

"What is your mother?"

"I don't know that either."

"What hand raised you, then?"

"I don't know; I've never seen it."

"In sum, what was the first object to strike your gaze?"

"Lindor."

The enchanter asked the same question of Lindor, and he replied: "Delie."

"Heavens!" the enchanter and the fay cried, then. But they recovered from their disturbance and continued questioning Lindor.

"I don't know who I am," he told them, "or to whom I was born. A tower in which I lived alone was my unique dwelling for a long time. A being that I never saw, but which I heard, provided for all my needs. It taught me to speak without telling me whether I would ever be able to speak to anyone, nor whether anyone similar to me existed. I spent my early years thus, without knowing what years were. When I was twelve, nothing had irritated me yet; I did not appear to have lacked anything. By the time I was fifteen, everything irritated me and it seemed that I was lacking everything. I felt deprived of the only thing that could make my happiness, without knowing of what that happiness consisted, or what might contribute to it."

"What were your ideas then?" asked the fay, in an interested tone.

"Madame," Lindor said, embarrassed by the question, "I only had very confused ones, but they developed as soon as I perceived Delie..."

"Go one with your story," they fay interjected, swiftly.

Lindor obeyed. "Every day," he went on, "my prison became more unbearable to me; I did not know, however, that there were other inhabited places. The moment finally came when I was no longer ignorant. I suddenly felt my tower shake, and I saw the vault split; everything collapsed. I fell with the debris myself, but without suffering any injury, and finally found myself freed from my prison by the fall. The daylight, which I had never seen, dazzled me at first; I had difficulty distinguishing objects. But what object stuck my first gaze? A young beauty about to perish, forcibly attached to a wall that I saw about to crush her."

"A beauty?"

"Oh, Madame, it was Delie!"

That exclamation did not please the fay at all, whom the story affected in a singular fashion. It was the same for the enchanter.

Lindor went on: "To see Delie, to admire her, to feel sorry for her, to fly to her rescue were, for me, the work of an instant. I snatched her from the peril that menaced her; I carried her away in my arms. Oh, Madame, what a delightful moment for me!"

What an annoying story, Anger said to herself.

"When I had contemplated Delie at my ease," Lindor added, "I looked around, and saw nothing but ruins. At that moment, a young man with an interesting face appeared. 'Have no fear,' he said to us. 'I am the genius Beneficent, the same one who broke your irons. The perils that threatened you until this moment were the causes of your imprisonment. Be free henceforth, and love one another as much as those to whom you owe the light of day hate you.'

"'What! Do we owe it to the same individuals?' I asked him, anxiously.

"'No,' Beneficent replied. 'But the Council of Genii obliged the fay who was Delie's mother to marry the enchanter who was Lindor's father. They hoped by that means to put an end to their disputes; there is no better proof that the sagest arbiters can be mistaken. At any rate, the couple has been subject for some time to the most bizarre destiny, and it is to you alone that the advantage of putting an end to it is reserved.'

"'Oh! What is it necessary to do?' we asked, eagerly.

"'The favorable moment has not yet come,' said the genius, 'but it will...'"

"I shall be able to prevent it," said the fay in a low voice. Then she made a sign to the enchanter, and Delie and Lindor were separated again.

"We're very stupid, in spite of all our magical science," the enchanter said to the fay. "But for the hazard that rendered us masters of these young people, perhaps we would soon have suffered the fate of Docile and Quarrelsome, our enemies and our victims. Everything tells us that Delie and Lindor are their children; they have escaped the perils that menaced them, and their reunion is preparing inevitable ones for us."

"Well," said the fay, "it's necessary to prevent them from being reunited, from seeing one another, and above all from loving one another; for Amour is too ingenious, too fertile in expedients."

"The surest way is to enable them to love someone else," added Pacific.

"Let's try the surest way," said the fay.

"Let's try," said the enchanter, eagerly.

They soon judged that the attempt in question would go badly if they did not use artifice. Such an expedient was sure to please them, and often pleases people who are neither enchanters nor fays.

So, the jealous couple deliberated. After a few uncertainties, from which the best composed councils are not exempt, they had recourse to illusions. The fay borrowed the face of Delie, the enchanter that of Lindor; but they lacked what the art of magic cannot give them—I mean the sympathetic virtue by means of which Delie and Lindor were incessantly attracted to one another. The genius Beneficent had endowed them with it without informing them, and without them even perceiving it, so readily did their hearts lend themselves to it. Hence, without that secret agent, any resemblance with them became fruitless.

It is easy to imagine the sadness into which Delie and Lindor were plunged they found no less bizarrerie than injustice in the conduct of their tyrants; they had no hope of ever seeing one another again. What a state for two loving hearts, who believed that they would love one another forever!

Already, one night had gone by; already, the day that had succeeded it was in its decline; and Delie was still weeping. She refused herself repose and disdained the aliments that the enchanter offered her. "It's in order to live," she said, "that one nourishes oneself, and I ought not to live any longer, since it's necessary to renounce Lindor."

At that same instant, she believes that she hears her lover cry to her: "Live for Lindor, who loves you and is returned to you!" A door opens, and Delie does, indeed, believe that she sees him. She utters a cry of joy, and wants to fly to meet him, but an unknown power stops her. The cry of joy is succeeded by a cry of dolor and surprise. Twice Delie wants to extend her arms to the person she believes to be Lindor, and twice that interior force opposes it. Distraught, beside herself, unable any longer to resist the antipathy that astonishes her and masters her, she tries to flee; she only sees the pretended Lindor at her feet with a horror mingled with despair.

The latter judged from then on that his stratagem would not have the success that he had promised himself. One can deceive the eyes, but in amour the heart is not as easily abused. He did not lose all hope, however. "What!" he said to Delie. "It's you who are fleeing me? It's to Delie that Lindor appears odious?" At the same time, he tried to take the hand that Delie had offered the previous day with such good grace to the veritable Lindor; but Delie pulled it away, shivering: a further motive for regret for her; her sighs and sobs were suffocating her.

"Oh, Lindor!" she cried, finally. "Oh, dear Lindor, pity me. How unhappy I am! Lindor, I no longer love you!"

"Heavens!" cried the enchanter, once again taking the hand that Delie withdraws again, still weeping. "It's over, then? What will become of the unfortunate Lindor, if you abandon him?"

"Eh! What will become of me, if Lindor abandons me," said the afflicted Delie. "His name alone penetrates my soul. However, it's only too true that your presence chills me…oh, Lindor, dear Lindor, is it possible that I can no longer love you"

As she finished speaking, Delie wept harder and harder, making greater efforts at the same time to draw away.

The enchanter had the science but not the malevolence of his peers. He was patient, a very rare virtue in anyone who can dispense with having it. He did not want to overwhelm the charming and naïve Delie any longer.

"I'll deliver you of my presence, which is inconveniencing you," he said. "Perhaps another time will be more favorable. Perhaps you'll remember that your Lindor was dear to you and he will become dear to you again."

With that the enchanter did, in fact, leave, Delie tried to follow him, but recoiled after taking two steps. She wanted to call to him, but her voice died on her lips; her entire body remained motionless, annihilated, petrified.

An almost similar scene unfolded between the fay and Lindor. The latter, interned like Delie, was occupied in groaning like her and for her. Suddenly, he saw the doors of his prison open as if of their own accord. He escaped, and searched with his eyes for the place in the palace in which Delie might be imprisoned. Without her, liberty, and life itself, were very little. From the palace, which he explored in vain, he passed into the gardens: there he paraded his gaze again, piercing the most profound pathways at a glance and not perceiving anything.

Finally, he cast his gaze a few paces away from him, and saw—or thought he saw—Delie lying on a bed of grass, delivered to a peaceful slumber.

"Heavens, it's her!" exclaimed Lindor. "Can my heart no longer divine her? Ought it not have brought me to her feet immediately? Why am I not yet there? Am I afraid of troubling her slumber? Amour and joy excuse everything; let them be my only guides…but what is this lukewarm sensation? Where are the transports that Delie is always able to inspire in me? Is it no longer her? Am I no longer myself? They're her features, her charms, what other power could unite them? I can hear her dreaming, and it's my name that she's repeating. She's calling me, but I dare not fly into her arms…what am I saying? Far from flying there, I'm ready to flee!"

Such were the combats that Lindor experienced. They annoyed the fay, who, as you will have presumed, was not asleep. She appeared to wake up, fixed her gaze upon Lindor, and advanced toward him precipitately. What was her surprise on seeing that with every step forward she took, Lindor took one backward! He was no less surprised than the person he was fleeing.

"Dear Lindor," she said, "our troubles are over; the enchanter and the fay consent to our happiness; they will no longer raise any obstacles to it. We can love one another, we can say so; we're free, and masters of this place."

Thus spoke the fay as she advanced, and Lindor continued to recoil. She stopped, and Lindor did the same.

"Oh, Delie," he cried, "where are we? What a frightful change! Can it be that I experience for you the same indifference and the same aversion as for the fay?"

Insolent boy! said the latter to herself.

"Yes," he went on, "An invincible ascendancy is driving me away from you; but it's doubtless unnatural; it's an effect of the art of our persecutors. Oh, Delie, what place have we come to inhabit? What a place, where one changes thus, where one can change for Delie! How I hate our tyrants, since they have taken away from me the ability to love you."

The fay's anger was at its peak. She advanced a few paces, and fortunately, Lindor continued to back away. The fay had forgotten the role of Delie in order to resume her own, but in the end, she conserved the one she had taken first, the surest means of making Lindor despair. "Go, traitor," she said to him. "Go take your vain excuses elsewhere; they cannot impose on me. Amour is independent of magic; it subjugates it to his power. Go, flee, renounce Delie forever, as she is renouncing you forever."

With those words, she drew way, and Lindor, in despair, could neither call her back nor follow her.

The enchanter and the fay found one another, and held a new council. Anger shouted loudly; Pacific tried to calm her down.

"We can no longer hope for anything from metamorphosis," he said to her. "A secret instinct, stronger than all our magic, prevents those children from being mistaken. In any case, I pity their situation..."

"Have pity on yourself," replied the fay, utterly furious. "What kind of enchanter pities those who resist him? You're unworthy to occupy such a rank!"

"Admit," he said, in the most placid tone possible, "that this desire to dominate has made us commit more than one stupidity."

"What pettiness to recognize them!" added the fay.

"But, for example, this bizarre metamorphosis of Docile and Quarrelsome, what does it tell you?"

"That they are two humiliated enemies."

"But you know how imperious and impetuous the latter was."

"He was right, and as for us, it doesn't matter; he'll remain what he is."

"I admit that I feel sorry for Docile, a fay so gentle and so patient."

"She was wrong to be; she sustained her rights poorly, and it was by derision that I metamorphosed her into an eagle."

"But if that double metamorphosis ends, ours..."

"That's what it's necessary to prevent."

"But what if Delie and Lindor really are destined to put an end to it?"

"It's for that reason that it's necessary to keep them here. Quarrelsome, in the state in which we've put him, won't be able to get in here, and doesn't matter to me if Docile can."

The enchanter made a few further objections, and combined them with reasons so sage and so moderate that he drove the fay to distraction.

Nevertheless, she seemed to calm down—which is to say, she made a little less noise.

"Well," she said to the magician, "let's use another illusion. It's very little for you to have borrowed the face of Lindor and me that of Delie; I want them to appear to be us to one another's eyes."

"But what if they continue to love one another under that new exterior?" said the enchanter.

"So much the better," said the fay. "We'll be avenged and they'll be punished, for you can presume that we won't lose sight of them."

The enchanter tried to employ other arguments, but Anger got carried away, and Pacific agreed to everything.

As for Lindor, he continued to wander like a furious madman in the gardens of the palace. He contemplated with despair the bed of grass where he believed that he had seen Delie, whom he believed to be outraged by his disdain.

"What! It's her that I fled!" he cried, beside himself. "It's her that I'm renouncing forever! I've been able to stop loving her! I've been able to merit her hatred! What frightful ascendancy is dominating me?"

As he pronounced those words, he raised his eyes to the heavens and saw a huge eagle flying overhead. The eagle was holding a sword in its claws, which it dropped at Lindor's feet.

"Thank the gods!" said the afflicted lover. "Here's a remedy for my woes..."

"Stop!" cried a voice that he did not recognize. "The moment to make use of it has not yet arrived; be courageous still, but be so appropriately."

Lindor had all the respect for that oracle that one has for things that one does not understand. He seized the sword, and waited for the moment to make use of it.

A further proof awaited Delie and him, however. The two magicians had agreed to furnish them with the means to encounter one another.

Delie perceived that she could leave her apartment, where she had believed that she was narrowly confined. She went into the gardens again where she had seen her dear Lindor before, and where she hoped to see him again and repair her involuntary coldness. He was, in fact, there. The sympathetic instinct that guided them soon brought them together.

They both shivered when they perceived one another, but neither of them recognized the other.

It's the fay, thought Lindor.

It's the enchanter, thought Delie.

"Oh, let's flee!" they exclaimed, separately; but while saying those words, they advanced further toward one another.

They were soon within range to speak to one another, still without recognizing one another. The emotion that they experienced astonished them and afflicted them.

Is it really true, Lindor said to himself, *that I have been able to flee from Delie and that my penchant is drawing me toward the fay? Is it really her that is causing me this impression, so sharp, so tender, so worthy of Delie, whom I outraged? What perfidy! What a transformation!*

Delie was making herself the same reproaches, combined with the same reflections, feeling and thinking like Lindor. The situation of the two lovers could not have been more critical or more violent.

The enchanter and the fay were enjoying it without being seen; for them it was a triumph of sorts, but one of those triumphs at which one cannot help blushing, so the enchanter reproached himself for it; as for the fay, she did not reproach herself for anything. Could it be a misfortune for Lindor to believe that he loved her? As for Delie, she thought that she had a little more to lament in believing that she loved the enchanter.

The young couple had made futile attempts to speak to one another indifferently. Lindor yielded to his ascendancy; he was at the knees of the pretended fay; he spoke to her tenderly, and she listened to him. He was holding one of her hands, which she did not think of pulling away.

"It is, however, my hand that he believes himself to be holding," said the fay to the enchanter. "It's at my knees that he believes himself to be."

"Agreed," said the magician, "but at the same time, it's me whom Delie believes she can see at her knees; it's to me that her hand is abandoned."

That observation did not please the fay at all. She advanced, and Lindor still thought that he perceived Delie in her. He got up precipitately, ashamed.

The enchanter had appeared at the same time, and Delie had similarly mistaken him for Lindor. What confusion and dolor took possession of her soul!

What completed the deception and desolated the young couple is that in Delie's eyes the fay had not changed her face and it was the same for the enchanter with regard to Lindor.

"What!" said the latter, furiously. "It's not enough to deceive Delie, it's necessary to render her witness to my infidelity!"

"Alas," said Delie in her turn, "What will the unfortunate Lindor think? I've fled him, and he sees his rival at my knees, his rival that I tolerate there. Oh, let's die..."

"I can't stand it any longer," said the enchanter to the fay. "That poor child is going to faint."

"Oh, let her, let her," said Anger. "She knows what she's doing; but fortunately, we're here."

As for Lindor, he was ready to turn the sword that the eagle had given him against himself.

Suddenly, he saw the same eagle hovering above him, holding a monstrous snake in its claws. The enchanter and the fay uttered a cry and remained motionless. The eagle swooped down, and dropped the snake at the feet of Delie, whom Lindor still believed to be the fay. She tried to run away.

"What!" he said. "A fay afraid of snakes! No matter; I can't love her but I ought to defend her." As he spoke, he fell upon the reptile, and with a single sweep, he severed its head. But what was his surprise to see the same snake become a man and clasp him in his arms, crying: "Oh, my son! Your generosity will be recompensed. Recognize your father, recognize Delie; let Delie recognize you. We shall all be avenged."

In fact, when Quarrelsome—for it was him—had resumed his form, Pacific had lost his; he was wandering in the garden in that of a sheep. But the fay had not yet been subjected to any metamorphosis; she still conserved the face of Delie in Lindor's eyes, while the true Delie still appeared to be the fay, while he only offered to her gaze the features of the enchanter: a further subject of dolor for the young lovers, for whom the saddest ordeals seemed to be reserved.

The fay Anger brought them to a climax; she wanted to complete despairing her rival. "Look at that eagle," she said to her. "That's your mother. She'll retain that form in the eyes of the entire world, and you'll retain mine and I yours in Lindor's eyes."

"What!" cried Delie, shuddering. "My mother will conserve the form of an eagle, and I that of the fay, and the fay mine? Oh, give me that sword..."

Delie seized it, and was about to stab herself; all Lindor's diligence could not prevent her from wounding herself slightly in the hand. A few drops of blood fell therefrom. Immediately, the fay Anger flew away in the form of an owl, and the eagle became a woman again, worthy by her beauty of being Delie's mother.

But Delie herself had not yet recovered her own charms in Lindor's eyes, and Lindor still offered the features of the enchanter to the eyes of his mistress.

"The poor child!" said the owl, perched in a tree. "It was me that he thought he was defending, though; it's a pity that he's condemned to keep the features of the enchanter."

For his part, the sheep said: "It's very sad for Delie to have traded faces with the fay."

"The fay Anger was a good woman, though," said the enchanter Quarrelsome in his turn.

"In truth, I regret the enchanter Pacific," the fay Docile added, privately.

As for Delie and Lindor, they did not say anything; gazing at one another, they loved one another in spite of their unfamiliar faces, and felt that they would love one another even more under their natural forms.

Both of them, however, uttered a cry of joy at the sight of the genius Beneficent.

"Console yourselves," he said to them. "I haven't lost sight of you." Immediately, addressing himself to the fays and the enchanters, he added: "All four of you appear to me to be embarrassed; admit that one often risks that when one has all power except that of repairing stupidities. It's to put an end to yours that I'm descending among you today, but let's commence with these young people who have been their victims, without ever having been their accomplices. Let Delie," he continued, "cease to resemble the fay..."

"Ah! So much the better!" exclaimed the sheep.

"Let Lindor," Beneficent added, "quit the features of the enchanter..."

"Ah! So much the better!" cried the owl.

"Let Pacific," the genius went on, "resume his form, not to quit it again..."

"Ah! So much the better!" exclaimed Lindor.

"Let Anger quit the form of an owl to resume her own permanently...

"Ah! So much the better!" cried Delie.

"That's not all," Beneficent went on, "Let Pacific be united with Docile, and Quarrelsome with Anger.

"Ah! So much the better!" cried Anger, Quarrelsome, Docile and Pacific, all at the same time.

They wanted to thank the genius but he had already disappeared. The two magician couples promised one another to take advantage of his advice. They had done one another enough harm reciprocally to banish all rancor between them, but the only truly happy ones were Delie and Lindor. They had never oppressed anyone, and they were in love.

Jean-Jacques Rousseau: *Queen Fantasque*

"There was once a king who loved his people..."
"This is beginning like a tale of fays," the Druid interrupted.
"It is one," replied Jalamir.

So, there was a king who loved his people, and in consequence, was adored by them. He had made every effort to find ministers as well-intentioned as himself, but, having finally recognized the folly of such research, he had made the decision to do by himself all the things that he wanted to preserve from their maleficent activity. As he was very stubborn in the bizarre project of rendering his subjects happy, he acted in consequence, and such unusual conduct made him ineffably ridiculous to the aristocracy. The people blessed him, but in the court he was considered to be a madman. Except for that he did not lack merit; so he was named Phoenix.

If that prince was extraordinary, he had a wife who was less so. Lively, irresponsible, capricious, foolish in the head, sage in the heart, nice by temperament, nasty by caprice: there, in a few words, is the portrait of the queen. Her name was Fantasque: a celebrated name that she had received from her ancestors in the female line, and the honor of which she sustained worthily. That person, so illustrious and so reasonable, was the charm and the torture of her dear husband, for he also loved her very sincerely, perhaps because of the facility she had in tormenting him.

In spite of the reciprocal amour that reigned between them, they spent several years without being able to obtain any fruit of their union. The king was penetrated by chagrin by that, and the queen suffered an impatience whose effects the good prince was not the only one to feel. She held it against everyone that she had no children, and there was no courtier whom she did not ask thoughtlessly for some secret in order to have one, and whom she did not render responsible for its lack of success.

The physicians were not forgotten, for the queen had an uncommon docility in their regard, and they did not prescribe a single drug that she did not have prepared very carefully, in order to have the pleasure of throwing it in their faces the moment it failed to take effect.

The dervishes had their turn; it was necessary to have recourse to novenas, prayers, and above all to offerings, and woe betide the servants of Temples to which Her Majesty went in pilgrimage; she rummaged everywhere, and under the pretext of going to breathe a purified air she never failed to turn the monks' cells upside-down. She also wore their relics and decked herself out alternately in all their different equipages. Sometimes it was a white cord, sometimes a leather belt, sometimes a hood, sometimes a scapular. There was no sort of monastic masquerade that her devotion did not adopt, and as she had an alert appearance that rendered her charming in all her disguises, she did not quit any without having taken care to have herself painted in it.

Finally, by virtue of devotions so well executed and medicines so sagely employed, Heaven and earth granted the queen's wishes; she became pregnant at the moment when she was beginning to despair of it. I leave the joy of the king and the people to be divined; as for her own, as in all her passions, it went as far as extravagance; in her transports she broke everything; she embraced all those she encountered indifferently—men, women, courtiers and valets—and to find oneself in her passage was to risk being stifled. She did not know, she said, any delight similar to that of having a child, to whom she could apply the whip entirely at her ease in her moments of ill-humor.

As the queen's pregnancy had been awaited in vain for a long time, it passed for one of those extraordinary events of which everyone wanted to have the honor. The physicians attributed it to their drugs, the monks to their relics, the people to their prayers and the king to his amour. Everyone was interested in the child that was to be born, as if it were their own, and everyone made sincere wishes for the fortunate birth of a prince, for they all wanted one, and the people, the aristocracy and the king united their desires on that point.

The queen took it amiss that everyone wanted to prescribe to her to whom she ought to give birth, and declared that she intended to have a girl, adding that it appeared rather singular to her that anyone dared to dispute the right to dispose of an item of property that belonged incontestably to her alone.

Phoenix tried in vain to make her listen to reason; she told him frankly that it was none of his business, and shut herself in her cabinet in order to sulk—a cherished occupation to which she routinely devoted six months of the year. I say six months, but not consecutively; that would have been as much repose for her husband; it was taken instead at intervals appropriate to cause him chagrin.

The king understood very well that the caprices of the mother do not determine the sex of a child, but he was in despair that she was giving the spectacle of her opposition to the entire court. He would have sacrificed anything in the world for universal esteem to have justified the love that he had for her, and the fuss that he made, inappropriately, and this occasion was not the only folly that the ridiculous hope of rendering his wife reasonable had made him commit.

No longer knowing to what saint to pray, he had recourse to the fay Discreet, his friend and the protectress of his realm. The fay advised him to adopt the policy of mildness—which is to say, to apologize to the queen. "The sole objective of all women's fantasies," she told him, "is to disorientate masculine arrogance slightly and accustom men to the obedience appropriate to them. The best means you have of curing your wife's extravagances is to be extravagant with her. As soon as you cease to constrain her caprices, be assured that she will cease to have any, and will only wait to become sage until you have been rendered completely mad. Take things with a good grace, then, and try to give in on this occasion in order to obtain everything you want on another."

The king believed the fay, and in order to conform to her advice in the queen's circle he made the decision to tell her quietly that he was sorry that he had contested with her so inappropriately, and that he would try to compensate her in future, by his complaisance, for the ill-humor in which he appeared to have put her by his discourse and by arguing impolitely against her.

Fantasque, who feared that Phoenix's mildness might cover her alone with all the ridicule of the affair, hastened to respond to him that beneath that ironic apology she saw even more pride than in the preceding disputes, but that, since the wrongs of a husband do not authorize those of a wife, she would yield on this occasion, as she had always done.

"My prince and my husband," she added, loudly, "orders me to give birth to a son, and I know my duty too well to fail to obey him. I am not unaware that when His Majesty honors me with marks of his tenderness, it is less for love of me than that of his people, whose interests occupy him scarcely less by night than by day. I ought to imitate such a noble disinterest, and I will request from the Divan an instructive memoir regarding the number and sex of children befitting the royal family: a memoir important to the good of the State, on which every queen ought to learn to regulate her conduct during the night."

That fine soliloquy was heard by the entire circle with a great deal of attention, and I leave it to you to estimate how many bursts of laughter were rather maladroitly stifled. "Ah!" said the king, sadly, as he left, shrugging his shoulders. "I can see clearly that when one has a mad wife one cannot avoid being a fool."

The fay Discreet, whose sex and name sometimes contrasted humorously in her character, found that quarrel so enjoyable that she resolved to amuse herself thoroughly. She told the king publicly that she had consulted the comets that predict the birth of princes, and that she could guarantee that the child to be born would be a boy, but she assured the queen secretly that she would have a girl.

That advice suddenly rendered Fantasque as reasonable as she had previously been capricious. It was with an infinite mildness and complaisance that she took all possible measures to desolate the king and the entre court. She hastened to have the most superb layette made, affecting to render it so appropriate to a boy that it became ridiculous for a girl; it was necessary that the design in question change several fashions, but all that cost her nothing. She had a beautiful necklace of that order prepared, brilliant with stones, and insisted that the king appoint the young prince's governor and tutor in advance.

As soon as she was sure of having a girl she talked about nothing but her son, and did not omit any of the futile precautions that might enable those which ought to have been taken to be neglected. She laughed in bursts when imagining the astonished and stupid expressions of the noblemen and magistrates who were to honor her childbirth with their presence.

"I seem to see," she said to the fay," on the one hand, our venerable Chancellor putting on his spectacles in order to verify the sex of the child, and on the other, His Sacred Majesty lowering his eyes and stammering: 'I thought...but the fay told me...it's not my fault, Messieurs,' and other equally witty apothegms collected by the scholars of the court and soon relayed all the way to the farthest reaches of India."

She pictured with malign pleasure the disorder and confusion into which the marvelous event would throw the entire assembly. She imagined in advance the disputes and the agitation of all the ladies of the palace to protest, adjust and conciliate at that unexpected moment the rights of their important responsibilities, and all the court astir for a bonnet.

It was also for that occasion that she invented the decent and spiritual custom of having the new-born prince harangued by magistrates in robes.

Phoenix tried to suggest to her that it was to debase the magistracy for no reason and to cast an extravagant comicality over all court ceremonial to go in grand apparel to display to Phoebus a little brat before he could understand, or at least respond.

"So much the better!" said the queen, briskly. "So much the better for your son! Will he not be very fortunate if all the stupid things they have to say to him are exhausted before he can understand them; would you like to save for him until the age of reason speeches liable to render him mad? For God's sake, let them harangue him at their ease while we can be sure that he doesn't understand anything and has less ennui in consequence. You ought to know that one doesn't always get away so cheaply."

It was necessary to do it, and on the express order of His Majesty, the Presidents of the Senate and the Academies began to compose, study, cross out, and riffle through their Vaumorière[64] and their Demosthenes in order to learn to speak to an embryo.

Finally, the critical moment arrived. The queen felt the first labor pains with transports of joy that are rarely observed on such occasions. She complained with such a good grace and wept so cheerfully that one might have thought that the greatest of her pleasures was giving birth.

Immediately, there was a frightful rumor throughout the palace. Some ran to find the king, others the princes, others the ministers, others the senate and the greatest number went to roll their barrel, as Diogenes always had, in order to look busy. In the haste to assemble so many necessary people, the last person anyone thought about was the obstetrician, and the king, who was beside himself with anxiety, having mistakenly asked for a midwife, that inadvertence excited immoderate laughter among the ladies of the palace, making the childbirth the most hilarious of which anyone had ever heard mention.

---

[64] Pierre d'Ortigue de Vaumorière (1610-1693), author of the oft-reprinted *L'Art de plaire dans la conversation* [The Art of Pleasing in Conversation] (1692).

Although Fantasque had kept the fay's secret as best she could, it had nevertheless leaked out to the women of her household, and they had guarded it so carefully themselves that the rumor took three days to spread throughout the city, with the result that, for a long time, the king had been the only person who did not know it. Everyone was therefore very attentive to the scene that was in preparation; public interest furnishing a pretext to all the curious to amuse themselves at the expense of the royal family, they made a fête out of watching the countenances of Their Majesties and seeing how, with two contradictory promises, they fay could get herself out of the affair and conserve her credit.

"Oh, Milord," Jalamir said to the Druid, interrupting himself, "agree that it is my prerogative to make you impatient, within the regulations. For you sense clearly that this is the moment for digressions, portraits, and the multitude of beautiful things that every intelligent author never fails to employ appropriately at the most interesting point, in order to amuse his readers!"

"How, by God," said the Druid, "do you imagine that that there are enough idiots to read all that intelligence? Learn that one always has enough to skip it, and that in spite of Monsieur the Author, one has soon covered his display of the pages of his book. And do you, who are playing the quibbler here, think that your words are worth more than the intelligence of others, and that to avoid the imputation of a stupidity it's sufficient to say that it's your prerogative to do it? Truly, it isn't worth saying it in order to prove it. And unfortunately, I don't have the resource of turning the pages."

"Console yourself," said Jalamir mildly, "others will turn them for you, if this is ever written down. However, consider that, with the whole court assembled in the queen's chamber, it's the finest opportunity I shall ever have to depict so many illustrious eccentrics for you, and perhaps the only one that you will ever have to know then."

"May God hear you," retorted the Druid, in jest. "I shall know them only too well by their actions, so make them act if your story has need of them and don't tell me about them if it doesn't. I don't want any other portraits than the facts."

"Since there's no means," said Jalamir, "of enlivening my story with a little metaphysics, I'll stupidly pick up the thread, but telling tales for the sake of telling tales is tedious; you don't know how many good things you're going to miss! Help me, I beg you, to find my place, for the essential has carried me away to the extent that I no longer know where I was up to in the tale."

"To the queen," said the Druid, impatiently, "that you have had so much trouble bringing to childbed, and with whom you've been holding me in suspense for an hour."

"Uh oh!" said Jalamir. "Do you think that the children of kings are laid like a thrush's eggs? You're going to see whether it wasn't worth the trouble of perorating."

So, the queen, after many cries and much laughter, finally extracted the curious from anxiety and the fay from intrigue by giving birth to a girl and a boy more beautiful than the moon and the sun, who resembled one another so strongly that people had difficulty telling them apart. That was because in their infancy they were dressed alike.

In that moment so desired, the king, emerging from majesty to render himself to nature, made extravagances that at any other time he would have left to the queen, and the pleasure of having children rendered him so childish himself that he ran on to his balcony and shouted at the top of his voice: "My friends, all of you rejoice; to me a son has just been born, to you a father, and to my wife a daughter."

The queen, who found herself at such a fête for the first time in her life, did not perceive all the work that she had done, and the fay, who knew her capricious spirit, contented her, in conformity with what she desired, by first announcing to her a daughter. The queen had her brought to her, and what surprised the spectators greatly was that, although she embraced her tenderly, in truth, she had tears in her eyes and an expression of sadness that was ill matched with the one she had previously had.

I have already said that she loved her husband sincerely; she had been touched by anxiety and moved by what she had read in his eyes during her suffering. She had made, at a time singularly chosen, admittedly, reflections on the cruelty there was in desolating such a good husband, and when her daughter was presented to her she only thought about the regret that the king would have in not having a son.

Discreet, whom the intelligence of her sex and the gift of faerie enabled to read hearts easily, immediately penetrated what was happening in the queen's, and no longer having any reason to hide the truth, she had the young prince brought.

The queen, having recovered from her surprise, found the expedient so hilarious that she uttered bursts of laughter dangerous in the state she was in. She fainted. They had a great deal of difficulty bringing her round, and if the fay had not answered for her life, the sharpest dolor would have succeeded the transports of joy in the heart of the king and the faces of the courtiers.

But what was most singular about the whole adventure was that the sincere regret that the queen had for tormenting her husband caused her to be gripped by a more intense affection for the young prince than for his sister, while the king—who, for his part, adored the queen—marked a similar preference for the daughter that she had desired. The indirect caresses that those two unique spouses gave one another thus soon became a very marked fondness, and the queen could no more do without her son than the king could his daughter.

That double event gave a great pleasure to all the people, and reassured them at least for a time with regard to the fear of lacking masters. The strong minds who had mocked the fay's promises were mocked in their turn; but they did not admit themselves beaten, saying they did not even accord to the fay the infallibility of the deception, nor to her predictions the virtue of rendering impossible the things she announced. Others, founded on the predilection that was beginning to declare itself, pushed impudence so far as to sustain that in giving the queen a son and the king a daughter, the event had completely belied the prophecy.

While everything was disposed for the pomp of the baptism of the two newborns, and human pride prepared to shine humbly at the altars of the gods...

"One moment," the Druid interjected. "You're confusing me in a terrible fashion. Tell me, I beg you, in what place we are. To begin with, to render the queen pregnant, you paraded her among relics and monks. After that you suddenly passed on to India. Now you're talking to me about baptisms, and then the altars of the gods. By the great Thalamis, I no longer know whether, in the ceremony you're preparing we're going to worship Jupiter, the holy Virgin or Mahomet. It's not that it matters much to me, as a Druid, whether the two babies are baptized or circumcised, but it's still necessary to observe the costume, and not to expose me to mistaking a bishop for the Mufti and a missal for the Koran."

"The great misfortune," Jalamir said to him, "of being as subtle as you, is being easily mistaken. May God preserve from evil all the prelates who have seraglios and mistake the Latin of the breviary for Arabic; may God give peace to all the honest lunatics who follow the intolerance of the prophet of Mecca, ever ready to massacre the human race sanctimoniously for the greater good of the Creator. But you ought to remember that we're in a land of fays, in which no one is sent to Hell for the good of his soul, in which no one regards the foreskin of a man as grounds for damning or salving him, and in which the miter and the green turban cover sacred heads equally, to serve as signals to the eyes of sages and ornaments to those of fools. I know full well that the laws of geography, which regulate all the religions of the world, want the two newborns to be Muslims, but only the males are circumcised, and I need my twins both to be administered, so find it good that I baptize them."

"Do it, do it," said the Druid. "That, faith of a priest, is the best motivated choice I've ever heard in my life."

The queen, who took pleasure in overturning all etiquette, wanted to get up after six days and go out on the seventh, under the pretext that she felt quite well. In fact, she was nursing her children: an odious example of which all the women represented the consequences to her very forcefully. But Fantasque, who feared the ravages of spoiled milk, sustained that there was no time more wasted for the pleasure of life than that which comes after death, that the breast of a dead woman withers no less than that of a nurse, adding in the tone of a duenna that there is no cleavage so beautiful in the eyes of a husband than that of a mother nursing her children.

That intervention of husbands in concerns that regard them so scantly made the ladies laugh abundantly, and the queen, who was too pretty to be one with impunity, appeared from then on, in spite of her caprices, almost as ridiculous as her husband, whom they called derisively the Bourgeois of Vaugirard.

"I can see you coming," the Druid said immediately. "You want to give me, insensibly, the role of Schah-Baham[65] and make me ask where there is also a Vaugirard in India, like a Madrid in the Bois de Boulogne, an Opera in Paris and a Philosopher at court. But continue your rhapsody and don't extend any more traps for me, for, not being married or a Sultan, it's not worth the trouble of being an idiot."

Jalamir continued without replying to the Druid.

Finally, everything being ready, the day arrived for opening the gates of Heaven to the two newborns. The fay went to the palace early in the morning and declared to the august spouses that she was going to give each of their children a present worthy of their birth and her power.

"I want," she said, "before the magic water removes them from my protection, to enrich them with my gifts, and give them names more efficacious than those of all the flat-feet in the Calendar, since they will express the perfections that I shall be careful to give them at the same time; but as you ought to know better than I do the qualities that suit the happiness of your family and your people, choose them yourself, and thus exert one single act of will over each of your two children, which twenty years of education rarely achieve in youth, and reason no longer contrives at an advanced age."

Immediately, there was a great altercation between the two spouses. The queen wanted to regulate the character of her entire family to her whim alone, while the good prince, who sensed all the importance of such a choice, did not care to abandon it to the caprice of a wife whose follies he adored without sharing them. Phoenix wanted the children to become reasonable people one day; Fantasque preferred to have pretty children, and provided that they shone at the age of six, she did not care much whether they might be stupid at thirty. The fay strove in vain to bring Their Majesties into accord; soon the character of the newborns was no longer anything but a pretext for dispute, and it was not a question of being right, but of reckoning with one another.

Finally, Discreet thought of a means of settling everything without putting anyone in the wrong, which was that each of them would dispose as they pleased with the child of their own sex.

---

[65] Schah-Baham is a character in the notorious libertine fantasy *Le Sopha, conte moral* (1737) by Crébillon *fils*.

The king approved of an expedient that provided the essential by shielding the heir presumptive of the crown from the bizarre wishes of the queen; and, seeing the two children on the knees of their governess, he hastened to take possession of the prince, not without gazing at his sister with an expression of commiseration. But Fantasque, all the more mutinous because she had less reason to be, ran like a madwoman to the young princess and took her in her arms.

"You've united everything in order to exasperate me," she said, "but in order that the king's caprices should turn in spite of him to the profit of one of his children, I declare that I demand for the one I have the exact opposite of what he demands for the other. Choose now," she said to the king, with an air of triumph, "And since you find so many charms in directing everything, decide with a single word the fate of your entire family."

The fay and the king tried in vain to dissuade her from a resolution that put the prince in a strange embarrassment; she did not ever want to let go, and said that she congratulated herself greatly on an expedient that would cause to reflect upon her daughter all the merit that the king was unable to give his son.

"Oh," said that prince, exceeded by chagrin, "you've never had anything but aversion for our daughter, and you're proving it in the most important occasion of her life. But," he added, in a fit of anger of which he was not the master, "in order for her to be perfect in spite of you, I demand that this child resemble you."

"So much the better for you and for him," retorted the queen, hotly, "but I'll be avenged and your daughter will resemble you."

Scarcely had those words been uttered on either part with an unequaled impetuosity that the king, in despair at his recklessness, would have liked to take them back, but it was done, and the two children were endowed without return with the characteristics demanded.

The boy received the name of Prince Caprice and the girl was called Princess Reason, a bizarre name that she made so illustrious that no woman has dared to wear it since. Thus, the future heir to the throne was endowed with all the perfections of a pretty woman, and his sister the princess was destined one day to possess all the virtues of an honest man and the qualities of a good king: a division that did not appear to be the best intended, but on which there was no going back.

The joke was that the mutual amour of the two spouses acted at that instant with all the force that is always rendered, but often too late, on essential occasions. Predilection not ceasing to act, each of them found that the child that ought to resemble them had the poorer share, and thought less of congratulating themselves than of complaining.

The king took his daughter in his arms and hugged her tenderly. "Alas," he said to her, "what use will your mother's beauty without her talent to make the most of it? You'll be too reasonable to turn anyone's head!"

Fantasque, more circumspect about her own verities, did not say all she thought about the sagacity of the future king, but it was easy to suspect, by the sad manner in which she caressed him that in the depths of her heart she had a high opinion of her share.

Meanwhile, the king, gazing at her with a sort of confusion, made her a few reproaches with regard to what had happened. "I sense my errors," he said, "but they are your work. Our children might have had much more value than us; you are the cause of the fact that they will only resemble us."

"At least," she said, immediately, throwing her arms around her husband's neck, "I'm sure that they will love one another as much as is possible."

Touched by the tenderness in that sally, Phoenix consoled himself with the reflection that he had so often had occasion to make, that in fact, the natural goodness of a sensible heart suffices to repair everything.

"I can divine all the rest so well," said the Druid to Jalamir, interrupting him, "that I can finish the tale for you. Prince Caprice will turn everyone's head and will be too much the imitator of his mother not to be their torment. He will turn the kingdom upside down trying to reform it. To render his subjects happy he will put them in despair, always blaming others for his own mistakes, unjust for having been imprudent, regret for his faults will cause him to commit new ones. As sagacity will never guide him, the good that he would like to do will augment the harm that he will actually have done. In a word, although, fundamentally, he is good, sensitive and generous, his very virtues will be prejudicial to him, and his stupidity alone, combined with all his power, will make him more hated than a reasoned malevolence would have done.

"On the other hand, your Princess Reason, a new heroine of the land of the fays, will become a prodigy of wisdom and prudence, and without having adorers will make herself so adored by the people, that everyone will wish to be governed by her; her good conduct, advantageous to everyone and to herself, will only do harm because her brother will incessantly oppose obstacles to her virtues, to which public prejudice will attribute all the faults that she does not have, even though it does not have them itself.

"There will be question of inverting the order of succession to the throne in order to make the fool's bauble subservient to the distaff, and fortune to reason. The Doctors will expose with emphasis the consequences of such an example, and will prove that it is better that people blindly obey the madmen that hazard has given them than to choose reasonable leaders for themselves; that although a madman is forbidden to govern his own property, it is good to leave him the supreme disposition of our property and our lives; that the most insensate of men is preferable to the wisest of women, and that if the male or the first-born is an ape of a wolf, it is necessarily good politics that a heroine or an angel born after him should obey his will.

"Objections and replies will follow on the part of the seditious, in which God knows how your sophistic eloquence will burn. For I know you, it is above all in speaking ill of what is that your bile is exhaled voluptuously, and your bitter frankness seems to rejoice in the wickedness of man because of the pleasure that it obtains from reproaching them."

"My God, Father Druid, how you go on," said Jalamir, very surprised. "What a flood of words! Where the Devil do you get such fine tirades? You'll never preach as well in the sacred wood, although you'll never speaker truer. If I let you go, you'd soon change a tale of fays into a treaty on politics, and it would be found every day in the cabinets of the Princes Bluebeard or Donkeyskin instead of Machiavelli. But don't go to so much trouble to divine the end of my tale. To show you that denouements are not lacking when necessary, I'll expedite one briefly that isn't as scholarly as yours, but is perhaps as natural and surely more unexpected."

You know, then, that the two twin children were, as I've remarked, very similar in their features and dressed in the same way. The king, believing that he was holding his son, was holding his daughter in his arms at the moment of the influence, and the queen, deceived by her husband's choice, having mistaken her son for her daughter, the fay took advantage of that error to endow the two children in the manner that suited them best. Caprice was therefore the name of the princess, and Reason that of the prince, her brother, and in spite of the eccentricities of the queen, everything was found in the natural order.

Having succeeded to the throne after his father's death, Reason did a great deal of good with very little fuss; seeking to fulfill his duties rather than to acquire a reputation, he did not make war on foreigners or do violence to his subjects, and received more blessings than eulogies. All the projects formed under the previous reign were executed under his, and, in passing from the domination of the father to that of the son, the twice fortunate people believed that they had not changed master.

Princess Caprice, after having caused multitudes of tender and admirable lovers to lose their lives or their reason, was finally married to a neighboring king, whom she preferred because he had the longest moustache and leapt best at hopscotch.

As for Fantasque, she died of an indigestion of grouse-legs in a stew, which she wanted to eat before going to the bed where the king was getting bored waiting for her, one night when, by dint of enticements, she had engaged him to come and sleep with her.

Marie-Jeanne Riccoboni: *The Blind Man*

A civil war had divided the gnomes and rendered them unhappy when the queen of the genii, attentive to maintaining harmony among all the beings submissive to her power, appointed Nirsa, the prettiest of the fays who formed her court, to become their arbiter, to terminate their differences and to give them, along with peace, all the benefits of which it is the source.

The charming Nirsa descended to the center of the earth, appeased the troubles of the gnomes, dissipated the factions that existed, and, satisfied to have rendered them tranquility by reestablishing their original unity, she quit them and resumed the route to the brilliant abode where the queen of the fays resided.

As she rose up again toward the ethereal vault, Nirsa was dreaming in her chariot; the doves who were carrying it away with rapidity, dazzled by the glare of the sun, of which they had lost sight for several days, did not fly as high as usual, and gradually drew nearer to the earth. Nirsa chanced to lower her gaze, and found herself above an agreeable and solitary grove of trees. Two individuals of different sex, sitting at the foot of a sycamore, appeared to be penetrated by a sharp dolor; they were mingling their tears, and it was easy to see that the same subject was obliging them to shed them.

The fay felt touched by compassion; as she thought that the finest prerogative of a great power is to grant mercies and give birth to joy in all hearts, she steered the flight of her doves earthwards; while they conducted her there, gently, she fixed her gaze on a metallic stone, on which every object that she desired to see was immediately engraved, Instantly, the story of those young lovers was traced before her eyes.

Nadine, the daughter of a priest of Vishnu, had been brought up with Zulmis, whose parents, consecrated to that god, also served him. On the faith of an oracle, their marriage was planned; they were permitted to see one another and to talk to one another incessantly; the liberty of always being together accustomed their hearts to the sweetness of amour, Nadine, adored by Zulmis, loved him passionately. For two years they had been hoping for the return of Alibeck, a sage revered in the country; he had undertaken a journey in order to find them a marvelous water; that water would have destroyed the obstacles that opposed their happiness. Alibeck was no more, but no one knew that, and Nadine and Zulmis were still waiting for him.

Nadine's lover, endowed with all the virtues and all the charms that render a person lovable, had never seen the sun; a thick veil hid it from him. His eyes, closed since birth, could not perceive Nadine's charms; his soul was attached to hers by stronger bonds than those woven by beauty; her mildness, her generosi-

580

ty, the evenness of her humor and the nobility of her sentiments subjugated him to a heart formed to appreciate the qualities of his own.

Nadine's mother, initiated into the mysteries of Zoroaster, by virtue of a superstition born of ideas natural to magi, regarded the blindness of Zulmis as a mark of reprobation. "The Sun enlightens all those he loves," she said. "Doubtless he hates Zulmis; let Zulmis appease his anger; let him see, or let him renounce the hand of Nadine."

An oracle, consulted a long time ago, assured that Zulmis would see the light before the end of his twentieth year; the sage Alibeck, who had promised to penetrate the spring of Zetma in order to draw the miraculous water therefrom, had not returned; that day, the last of such a cherished hope, was rendering them unhappy forever; in an hour, Zulmis would complete his twentieth year; his eyes would not open; the priests of Vishnu were about to separate them cruelly, to disunite their hands and lacerate their hearts, to force them to say to one another: "I disengage you from your oaths." While awaiting that fatal moment, Zulmis and Nadine were weeping and moaning, and swearing to adore one another forever.

Nirsa had no need for further instruction; emerging from her chariot, she wished to take the form of Alibeck, and found herself metamorphosed into a venerable old man.

In whatever form it pleased Nirsa to show herself to humans, she always conserved the advantages attached to the nobility of her being. Her soul, superior to that of mortals, enlightened her and guided her incessantly; just as a masked individual, standing before a mirror, although struck by an image different from their own, does not lose the idea of their own features, the fay, in a strange form, spoke and acted like the object whose appearance she had taken, without ever forgetting that she was Nirsa.

She advanced at a slow and majestic pace toward the place to which the desire to oblige attracted her. As soon as Nadine perceived her, she uttered a cry of joy and ran to meet her.

"O sage, cherished by Heaven!" she said. "O Alibeck, is it you that I see? Have you come to fulfill our desires, to grant our prayers? Have you brought us the divine specific? Are you going to render us happy? Oh, how many tears your long absence has cost us! Another moment, and I would have lost Zulmis forever!"

As she spoke she led the fay to her lover. Nirsa contemplated him with pleasure; the flowers of the first youth appeared in his complexion in the most vivid colors; his stature was tall, graceful and light, his features regular and delicate; long chestnut-colored hair, naturally curly, fell over his shoulders. The name of Alibeck, the hope that he conceived in his arrival, spread over his cheeks the splendor of a new rose. Nirsa would have declared him the most beautiful of the children of Adam if Nadine's charms had not suspended her judgment.

The fay sat down between them on a bed of grass, calmed their fears, reassured their as-yet-uncertain hearts, replied to their questions and promised to render them happy.

"A part of your wishes," she said, "will be accomplished before the end of the day; the obstacles that oppose your wishes will disappear at my voice; you shall be united. However, amiable Nadine, if I am to fulfill your desires, you must expose them with sincerity; consult your veritable interests carefully; without opening the eyes of Zulmis, I can link the two of you with a soft chain. Is it his hand or the end of his blindness that you are asking of me? If the blindness ceases, will you not be losing something?"

"Eh! What can I lose?" said Nadine, astonished.

"More than you think," said Nirsa. "Zulmis deprived of the light will always love you; the qualities that have given birth to his love will maintain it incessantly; your husband will be your lover; you will grow old in the eyes of others, but you will conserve an eternal youth for Zulmis. Your years will go by in a peaceful repose, Zulmis will owe you all his pleasures, his happiness will depend on you alone, and when the Author of Nature recalls you to his celestial abode, you will arrive there without having experienced the cruel pains caused by jealous impulses, the abandonment of an ingrate or the regret of loving an inconstant."

"And Zulmis?" said Nadine. "If he remains deprived of light, will he be happier for it?"

"No," the fay continued. "In possessing you he will enjoy a great wealth, but he will never know its full extent; he will not contemplate charms the sight of which would augment his pleasure continually; none of Nadine's smiles will ever bear the intoxication of sentiment into his soul; he will not know that Nadine is beautiful, but he will always love her, and Nadine will be perfectly happy."

"She will be perfectly happy!" cried Zulmis. "Oh, that is everything for me; I don't know what I might lose by remaining in obscurity, but sage Alibeck, obtain the hand of Nadine for me and I will have no regrets; if I always hear the melodious sound of that cherished voice, if I touch Nadine's hand; if she squeezes mine gently; if she loves me, if she tells me so, and repeats it to me a thousand times in a moment, all my wishes will be granted. Are there other gods? Even greater ones? Oh, if there are, Zulmis cannot comprehend them, and does not desire to know them."

"But can you not enable him to see the light and render him constant?" said Nadine, sighing.

"Do you believe," said Nirsa, "that the science of a mortal can surpass the power of Heaven? Do you not know the extreme lightness of that sex? As soon as your lover's eyes survey so many objects capable of charming his gaze, how can you hope that he will fix them on one alone? Is the immensity of this universe sufficient to the anxious desires and audacious wishes of men? Some have been seen who, dissatisfied with the beauties offered to their eyes, have wanted to force the intelligences of the air to descend to earth in order to give them new pleasures."

"Alas," sad Nadine, "if I request that Zulmis remains in his estate, my amour and my complaisance will be his only happiness, he will only feel them, he will not know any others. Oh, if an unkind fate deprived him of me, what would his consolation be? I would take away, with his regrets, the sad certainty of leaving him in eternal dolor. Dear Zulmis, the interested concern of conserving your tenderness for myself would render me cruel in your regard. I would be depriving you of all the goods you might savor. I would be depriving you of the sight of the sky, that of creatures, water, woods, flowers, the marvels of nature, the brilliant stars, the glitter of which charms and astonishes us. No, oh no, powerful Alibeck, open Zulmis's eyes, let him see, let him admire, let him enjoy the objects that might perhaps take him away from me. It doesn't matter; render him happy. Let him be happy, and let him cease to love me, if his inconstancy can add to his felicity."

"No, Alibeck, no," cried Zulmis, "let me never see the light of day! Let me be deprived of it forever, if its light would render Nadine less dear to me!"

Nirsa, touched by those tender sentiments, took the hands of Nadine and Zulmis, and united them. "Charming couple," she said to them, always love one another in the same way. Take me to the parents who want to separate you; let us go to the temple of Vishnu, and you shall know the power of Alibeck."

All three of them went to a parvis of the temple. Nadine's relatives and those of Zulmis were assembled there, about to send for the young lovers in order to disunite them. The sight of Alibeck filled them with surprise and joy; hope animated Zulmis's friends, and the expectation of an event moved all hearts. The priests prepared in the silence to follow the orders of the sage. The fay received their respects, and, placing Zulmis on an elevated seat, she passed a precious stone over his eyes three times; then, speaking in a loud voice she pronounced these words:

"If the Supreme Being has not condemned you forever to this sad obscurity, let the veil fall from your eyes and enjoy henceforth the contemplation of his works."

Zulmis's eyelids were then seen to part; they were gradually raised, and his eyes opened. A cry of surprise, uttered by him, announced the prodigy that the fay had just brought about. She ordered everyone to leave the place where Zulmis was, and, offering herself alone to his first gaze, she spoke to him; but astonishment rendered him insensible, mute and motionless; he dared not deliver himself to his joy; he feared being seduced by an agreeable dream, and trembled that a sad awakening might cause his happiness to vanish.

"Zulmis," said Nirsa, "if the light of day wounds you, close your eyes for a while; you will open them again and distinguish more easily the objects by which you are surrounded."

Dazzled but enchanted, Zulmis cried: "Never, oh, never, will I close them voluntarily, these eyes so long deprived of the brilliant spectacle that strikes them."

His mother, unable to retain the rapid movements of her heart, ran to him and clasped him to her bosom. "On, my son! Oh, bounty of Heaven! Oh, Alibeck! Oh happy day!" she repeated.

"What do I hear?" said Zulmis, embracing her ardently. "It's my mother; it's the person whose helpful hand guided me in the obscurity, whose attentive complaisance researched my desires all the way to the depths of my heart; her voice has come to penetrate it; let her features interest me; let my stirred sensed perceive them for the first time; let them inspire me with respect, veneration and gratitude! Oh, my mother, my tender mother! Render me even happier, show me Nadine, give me Nadine. O sage Alibeck, deign to teach me to distinguish my dear Nadine!"

Tears of joy were flowing from the eyes of Zulmis's charming mistress. She was about to advance, but a sign from Nirsa retained her.

At the rumor of Alibeck's return a numerous crowd had hastened to run to the temple; the fay made the young priestesses approach who were eager to see Zulmis; he found himself surrounded by them. Nadine mingled with them, anxious, troubled and agitated; an impulse that she had not felt before made her remark the adornment of her companions, and regret never having occupied herself with her own.

The timid and uncertain gaze of Zulmis searched for Nadine, scanning so many varied attractions; his heart dreaded making a mistake; his eyes finally stopped on his lovable mistress; he wanted her to be Nadine; considering all those young beauties, he fixed his eyes on Nadine for a second time, sighed, and pointed her out to Alibeck. "Oh," he said, "will I be inconstant? Will a new object seduce me? If this is not Nadine, I am ingrate and unfortunate."

Those words penetrated the depths of Nadine's heart. "What, Zulmis, my dear Zulmis," she said, "Would you cease to love me?"

"Oh, that's the sound of her voice," cried Zulmis, "it's her, it's Nadine, it's the divinity of my soul; all the marvels of Nature, of which I had no idea, are assembled in that charming face. Oh, Alibeck, deprive me, if you wish, of the sight of the world entire, but augment, redouble in me the faculty of seeing, of admiring, of adoring my dear Nadine."

Cries of joy rose up all around the tender lovers; they were girdled with a chain of flowers; they advanced toward the altar, where the high priest united them forever. Zulmis, sure of possessing Nadine, turned toward all those who were congratulating him.

"O sweetness! O pleasure! O enchantment!" he repeated. "Oh, my friends, are you as happy as me when on meeting one another, you say: 'I'm glad to see you.'?"

While Nadine and Zulmis were attracting all gazes, Nirsa quit the form of Alibeck. As soon as she was perceived under her own, admiration succeeded surprise; the women bowed profoundly, the men prostrated themselves at her feet.

"Inhabitants of this peaceful place," said the fay, "the virtues of these lovers are recompensed; they will love one another always, and the angel of death will transport them together into the sublime regions where a new life commences. You, who share their joy, always remember the passage of Nirsa through your lands."

Then she disappeared; at a gesture she made, the sylphs erected a superb palace near the temple for Zulmis and Nadine, and immense treasures were brought there. All those who were present at that marvelous event saw the most ardent of their wishes granted, and Nirsa, the charming Nirsa, rose up again to the brilliant abode of the fays with the sweet satisfaction of having made people happy.

Nicolas-Edmé Restif de la Bretonne: *Sireneh*

There was once a fay who was as malevolent as she was beautiful, although those two qualities, beauty and malevolence, seem contradictory. Pucellomaneh had had her of Merovech,[66] initially a muleteer and then leader of one of the Frankish tribe that devastated and conquered the Gauls.

Now, such was the rule imposed by Perforimoth the Black that Pucellomaneh could not constrain the inclinations of her daughters. Little Sireneh was therefore entirely willful, not listening to any of her governesses, for the reason that she was superior to mortals by virtue of her mother.

When she had grown up—which is to say, when she was fifteen, Pucellomaneh asked her, as she had done her eight older sisters, Semiramis, Eurydice, Sappho, Olimpias, Phryné, Cleopatra, Berenice and Zenobia, that she should choose, in order to be happy in future, between three things that she proposed to her: firstly, to marry a sylph, who would regard her as beneath him, because she was only a demi-fay; secondly, to consecrate herself to the worship of the great Ether, the source of all the fire that exists in the universe, and by that means, to elevate herself to the rank of perfect fay, either becoming the purifier of everything mortal there was within her; or thirdly, to spend her life in sensual pleasures, which would lose her that which she had of the fay in order to render her entirely a woman, but with the advantage that she would be able to take, and make others take, any form she wished, as soon as they had eaten something in her home or participated in her favors.

Sireneh reflected momentarily, and as she had a reason much more highly developed, although she used it badly, she settled on the third choice—which made the fay sigh, for she believed that her daughter had a bad character. But as I said before, such is the law among the Fays, Sylphs and Kings, that when they have reached the age of reason, each can choose their way of life; fortunate is the one who chooses well!

The fay could only employ exhortations, much as a Queen Regent does in handing back the reins of government to her son the King; he can do as he likes.

---

[66] Merovech was the legendary founder of the Merovingian dynasty of Frankish kinds, after whom they were supposedly named. History says nothing about him, but legend dropped vague hints about his being the descendant of a sea-god, which lends him a vague connection with Sireneh via her name, the mythical sirens being daughters of the river-god Achelous, and to the story of Circe, whose mother was supposedly an Oceanid.

"Daughter," Pucellomaneh said to the young Princess, "the choice you have just made will not render you happy! On the contrary, you're preparing cruel punishments for yourself."

"I'll support them," replied the demi-fay. "but I want a life that has keen pleasures, or I prefer death."

"You can only die after having lived; that's the difference that your birth puts between you and mortals by both parents. The latter can die whenever they want; you, on the contrary, by conducting yourself sagely, might be immortal; by leading an excessive life you'll live for a hundred years at the most, and you'll have all the symptoms of old age at eighty."

"A hundred years!" exclaimed Sireneh. "That's more than I would have asked for. Come on, I want to exercise my rights right away."

"Oh, my daughter," cried the fay, "I'm being cruelly punished for the involuntary fault I committed on seeking out your father! Reflect again. I love you tenderly, and to prove it to you, I'll change this desert island made by the two branches of the Shannon into a superb palace." Ceasing to speak, the fay lifted her arms, and at a sign made by a long golden wand that she always carried, ten thousand genii appeared and as many common fays, who built a superb palace on Urilove Island, surrounded it with magnificent quays, planted trees of every species there, with the trunk, foliage and fruit, and thus formed delightful gardens in a trice, the trees of which would not suffer transplantation.

The palace was furnished voluptuously and the fay instructed an old peasant fay to keep the grain-lofts, pantries and cellars of the palace perpetually full of provisions, and to fill two cabinets, one with gold and silver and the other with diamonds and pearls. All of that was completed in three days, during which Pucellomaneh left Sireneh to her own devices.

On the third day the mother-fay reappeared. "You can see how much I love you, my dear daughter," she said to Sireneh, "by all that I've done for you. Change your plan of life while you still can; I have experience and I assure you that the first two proposals I made you will render you as happy as one another, while the third will be fatal for you."

"I've chosen," replied Sireneh, rather harshly, "and I won't change my mind."

The mother-fay sighed and went away; Destiny did not permit her to insist any further. Pucellomaneh was even forced to leave two very ugly dwarfs and two hideous female dwarfs with her daughter, in order to follow her orders.

As soon as Sireneh found herself free, she was only embarrassed by the choice of pleasures; she was ignorant of them all. In order to instruct herself, she consulted her two female dwarfs.

Luxuriette,[67] the uglier one, replied: "Milady, we'll teach you, my sister Friandine and I, one for one thing and one for another, and when you want to

---

[67] *Luxure*, in French, means "lust." *Friandise* means "gluttony."

have your orders carried out outside, my brother Debauchin will go anywhere; if you want to amuse yourself in the interior of the palace, with things that require the arm of a man, my other brother Crapulophile is devoted to your will. Speak—or order me to suggest ideas for your amusement to you."

Sireneh smiled. At first she had only considered the two female dwarfs Luxuriette and Friandine, with repugnance, and the two male dwarfs Debauchin and Crapulophile with horror, but that speech reconciled her perfectly with the four monsters. She even saw them with pleasure assembling around her and presided over the council they held regarding the best means of amusement.

Luxuriette opened the session.

"You're young, you're beautiful, you inspire desires, but it's necessary that everything relates to you. You're too wise to think about having children, who will torment you one day and make you grow old. If you have any nevertheless, it's necessary to expose them, to let anyone who wants them take responsibility for them. You must obtain the submission of the men who have pleased you, and if the servile instrument of your pleasures displeases you, you must annihilate him, in order to savor the pleasure of change incessantly. You must avoid amour but if, by chance, that passion enters into your heart, it will be necessary temporarily to give me a fraction of your power, which consists of metamorphosing men into animals."

"I'll give it to you," said Sireneh.

"Do you swear on your faerie?"

"I swear on my faerie that I will cede to Luxuriette half of my power of metamorphosing men into brutes, to use as she wishes."

"That's sufficient. As soon as I see you smitten, I'll immediately turn your lover into an animal so hideous that you'll soon be free. I also have, by myself, the power to show nakedly the most secret thoughts of every human being, and I'll take advantage of that for your profit. What pleasures you're going to savor!

"And when Milady is weary of them," said Friandine, "she'll hand her over to me. I'll prepare her the most delicate dishes; I'll assemble in her cellars the most exquisite wines in the world and the finest liqueurs; she'll savor the pleasure of good cheer, then that of drunkenness; then...I'll hand her back to my sister, who will put her back in the arms of voluptuousness."

"You speak as if you can do everything!" exclaimed Debauchin. "Who will bring you the handsome men? Who has been assembling those wines, liqueurs and delicate dishes here for a long time?"

"Me, it's me," Crapulophile put in, "who will give them seasoning; it's via me that you'll enjoy, without wearying, lust and gluttony, drunkenness and debauchery, delightful crapulousness! It's me who served Sardanapalus, Chilperic, Mustapha and many others; it's me who rendered them happy. They've been criticized, but they enjoyed themselves. All the other advantages of mortals are mere smoke."

"I abandon myself to your zeal," Sireneh replied. "Don't leave me the time to desire, for desire makes me impatient."

The four monsters smiled, and went to their posts—but Luxuriette's was beside Sireneh.

Her first concern was to give the demi-fay adornment, something so provocative and at the same time so well-adapted to her genre of beauty that no one would be able to see her without feeling the keenest desires. She set her at the window of her palace, which overlooked the highway from the famous city of Rome to the famous city of Dublin, in order that she would be seen by all the Princes, all the knights and all the handsome men traveling from either of those two great cities to the other.

A handsome cavalier was just passing, with his bow in his hand and his arrows in his quiver, gracefully attached behind his back. Sireneh looked at him very attentively.

"Shall I invite him in to refresh himself, Milady," said Luxuriette.

"No, no," said Sireneh, sighing slightly. "I dare not."

"What! You're timid with regard to a man! You, Fay! Think, then, how far you are above him."

Those words reassured Sireneh; she made a sign to the cavalier, whom the monster's *psst* had caused to raise his eyes. He stopped, surprised, and as if in ecstasy, for the trees that surrounded Urilove Island had hidden they fay's palace from him until that moment, and he was seeing it for the first time. As the arm of the Shannon by the side of the road was very narrow, the cavalier saw all of Sireneh's beauty; she alone existed; without her he would have admired the palace greatly, but he scarcely paid any attention to it.

"Princess, or Fay," he shouted, "tell me how it is that this island, previously deserted, has been changed into a delightful garden and covered with a palace worthy of Worden? How, above all, does it contain such a touching beauty?"

Luxuriette, who had retired behind the Princess, showed herself immediately and replied to him: "Young cavalier, turn the bridle of your horse and go to the west of the isle; there you'll find a superb drawbridge made of cedar, ebony and campeachy; a dwarf who guards it will lower it as soon as you have pronounced the two words *Foudre-Love*.[68] Go, and don't forget them."

The cavalier could see all that there was of the marvelous, but he was too valiant to be frightened; he was unaware that when one has to combat sensuality, it is in the manner of the Parthians and the Massagetae, while fleeing. He went back to the west of the isle, and as he turned he perceived the dwarf guarding the bridge, who was amusing himself playing with a donkey and a pig, his two favorite animals.

---

[68] The "magic words" are given thus in the original, deliberately adjoining the French word for "thunderbolt" or "lightning" with the English term, and leaving no further doubt as to the intended significance of the island's name.

As soon as Debauchin saw the cavalier, he put on a gracious expression in spite of his ugliness and shouted to him: "Young stranger, what renders you so bold as to approach this bridge confided to my guard? For know that I am the guardian of this delightful isle, named Urilove Island, inhabited by the Miracle of Beauty, young Princess Sireneh, whom her mother, Queen Pucellomaneh, has imprisoned here in order to guarantee the virtue of the young virgin from the attacks of man."

The cavalier, angry at the dwarf's audacity, shouted to him: "Lower the potences,[69] in order that I can enter the island and the palace."

"No!" said the dwarf, laughing. "There are two powerful words, which alone can open the passage to you. Pronounce them, and these beams will fall on to their supports."

Then the cavalier recalled the two words the Luxuriette had spoken. "Foudre-Love!" he cried.

At those powerful words, the donkey started braying and the pig squealed, to which their females replied, and the drawbridge descended gravely, offering the cavalier a comfortable, solid and spacious passage. He entered the isle feverishly; immediately, the two bridges were raised again and their chains were lodged in iron crampons.

The cavalier dismounted. The dwarf showed him a stable, equipped with everything necessary. Debauchin unsaddled the charger himself and his brother Crapulophile, who had arrived, took responsibility for guiding the cavalier into the palace.

Finghall—that was the cavalier's name—followed the second dwarf, who first took him to the kitchen, where the dwarf Friandine was.

"It's necessary to refresh yourself," the male and female dwarfs said to him. "You'll appear more advantageously before the Princess."

"No, no," said Finghall, "I'm in too much haste to see her."

"You can only talk to her after you've taken your boots off, put on new underwear and a superb coat that we're going to give you."

"I want to appear as I am!" cried Finghall, swearing.

Crapulophile and Friandine smiled and said: "It's necessary to oblige you, but at least take a glass of this fine wine, whose gleam surpasses rubies; she how it shines! It comes from France, and the King of the land doesn't drink a better one."

"I only want a glass of beer or honeyed liquor," replied the cavalier.

He was served honeyed liquor in a goblet made of a single ruby, which had the same appearance as the wine. Finghall put it to his lips in order to taste it; he

---

[69] In French this word can mean "crosspieces," but it can also mean "gallows." Its English meaning, the quality of being potent, adds a further layer of sexual symbolism that might or might not have been intended by Restif.

found it too delicious and rejected it without swallowing it. He got up immediately and told the dwarf to take him to the young Princess.

"We'll summon the one who ought to introduce you," said the two dwarfs. Immediately, they whistled, but with so much accord that their whistles rendered the most harmonious sounds.

Luxuriette appeared. "Ah, it's you," she said, recognizing the cavalier. "Is he refreshed?"

"No, he didn't want to taste anything."

"You can appear before the Princess nevertheless," said Luxuriette. "Come." And to her two comrades, she said: "You can prepare a delightful snack; I believe the gentleman is too courteous to refuse to take part in it with the Princess."

She took Finghall to Sireneh, who received him blushing.

The cavalier was amazed by the charms of the ravishing Beauty, but an idea occurred to him: *Perhaps she's an ugly old woman who has only put on a deceptive appearance...* And that idea cooled him down.

He remembered that he had from the fay Wrwcwcw, the protectress of his family, a secret to destroy charms. He made use of it immediately.

"Pardon me, Milady," he said to the Princess, "but would you come on to this terrace?"

Luxuriette, who had read his thought, made a sign to her mistress to go out into the daylight. Then the cavalier took a magic glass from his pocket, which had the power of reassembling the sun's rays and dissolving the charm surrounding a decrepit old lady—but Sireneh only appeared even younger.

"Oh, Milady," cried Finghall, "how beautiful you are!"

Sireneh smiled, blushing, which embellished her further. She had had such tender sentiments for the cavalier at first that she had said to Luxuriette: "If this one wants to love me, I sense that my heart will be fixed on him; I'll ask my mother for him as a husband and bring joy to his heart." Finghall's conduct however, the motives of which she had penetrated, indisposed her toward him and made her want to avenge herself.

As she was unaccustomed to it, she was not able to disguise the movement of her eyes well enough for the cavalier not to see something harsh there. He was suspicious, and remembered another admirable secret, which he had from his mother, who had it from the fay Wrwcwcw; it consisted of an operation that resembled somewhat the art of drawing. One took a pencil; one looked at a young and pretty woman; one sketched all the lines without filling them in, without shading them, and one had her face stripped of flesh, as it would be at eighty or a hundred years of age.

Finghall asked for a pencil and vellum. Luxuriette, who needed to see him operate in order to read his thoughts, gave him what he requested. He drew the beautiful fay; the attention he gave to that work cooled his heart again, which became tranquil, and when he had finished he kept his eyes fixed upon it.

Luxuriette, surprised by all that she saw, said to her mistress, in the language of the fays, which mortals cannot hear: "*Sacamadeh; tolosebeh; souramih; sosquédémah!*"—which is to say: "This man is protected by some powerful fay; in order to subjugate him, a powerful amour is necessary, such as you felt at first." In the language of the fays, as you can see, each word expresses an entire idea.

In staring at the sketch that he had just made, Finghall really saw Sireneh as she would be at a hundred years of age; the talisman that operated by the power of the fay Wrwcwcw, showed her aquiline nose entering her mouth; her vivid eyes extinct and red; her rosy cheeks taking on the color of a lizard's belly; her reed-like waist encircled; her square back rounded; her slim legs bent; her supple and delicate feet covered in calluses and wrinkled.

The knight made a gesture of disgust. "Adieu," he said, without looking at Sireneh. "I have urgent business, which doesn't permit me to give my time to *girls*. My friend Rathemor is waiting for me help against his enemies, and I'm reproaching myself for the time lost."[70]

He went out immediately, without Sireneh having had any power over him, and he went to get his horse. He heard whinnying on an esplanade of grass that was on that was at the western tip of the island. He called: "Come, my dear Northailade" Come to your master." The horse was accustomed to obeying his voice, but it did not come.

Annoyed, Finghall advanced in the direction from which he had heard his horse's whinnying. He saw a beautiful mare, which was delivering itself to the pleasures for which Friga inspires the desire. He ran to his charger, cracking his whip so loudly that the entire island echoed it, but what was his astonishment and dolor when, approaching, he only found a donkey! The mare kicked twice and drew away.

Finghall tried to dissipate the charm that was disguising his horse, but his efforts were futile. Northailade started braying and fled into a clump of trees, farting.

The desolate Prince looked for the dwarf, in order to chastise him for his negligence in guarding his horse, but he searched everywhere without finding him.

The drawbridge was lowered; Finghall passed over it, and as soon as he had set foot on the ground the two chains were raised. Then he saw the dwarf Crapulophile descending from the tall tree in which he had been hiding, who shouted to him: "If you'd eaten and drank before presenting yourself to the Prin-

---

[70] Like Finghall (Fingal) and Dermid, Rathemor (Rathmore) is an adaptation of a name taken from James Macpherson's fragmentary fake epic *Ossian*, translated into French in 1777 By Pierre Letourneur. Substantial chunks of Letourneur's translation are paraphrased in the frame story in which the present story is contained.

cess, none of that would have happened to you. Adieu, handsome gentleman; you'll never enter this isle again."

Finghall went away on foot, therefore, very annoyed by his adventure. When he was opposite the window at which he had first perceived Sireneh, he only saw Luxuriette, to whom he complained about the loss of his horse.

She burst out laughing and replied to him: "Come and take him back. It's a trick of the dwarf; I'll return your horse to you, on condition that you taste the snack that has been prepared for you..."

At the same time, she opened a window, whose panels extended from one bank to the other, and showed him the meal, set out. Finghall was tempted, but a secret voice told him that it was better to lose his horse and continue his route to the next village, where he could obtain another, such as he might find it. He therefore walked for about two hours and finally arrived at a village called Rocelib, where he asked about the palace on Urilove Island, the Princess who lived there, etc. No one appeared to know anything about it.

Was it an illusion? he wondered. *But it's only too real that I've lost my beautiful horse Northailade!*

He sent two peasants, who were joined by twenty others, to ascertain the truth, while he looked for a horse, which he could have saddled while he ate dinner.

The Rocelibans ran with all their might; they soon arrived at Urilove Island and were strangely surprised to see the delightful gardens, a superb palace, a drawbridge and, at the windows, a beautiful Princess, two female dwarfs and two male dwarfs. There was also a mare with a donkey, which she was leading by the halter and which she was kicking, a pig, and another donkey, which appeared at the portal of the drawbridge. After examining everything, they went to make their report, which caused such great astonishment throughout the canton that people never ceased to come to see those marvels, rumor of which reached the ears of the Prince of the land, named Dermid.

As for the brave Finghall, seeing that he had not been mistaken, he chose a good horse and continued his route until he had arrived in the Estates of his friend Rathemor.

As soon as Prince Dermid was informed of the existence of the marvelous palace of Urilove Island and the beauty of the Princess, he formed the resolution of going there in disguise, to see everything for himself.

He soon arrived at Urilove Island; his surprise was extreme on seeing the superb palace and the magnificent gardens, but it increased even further when, having arrived opposite Sireneh's windows, he perceived the beautiful princess, who smiled at him. He was alone at that moment; on his orders, his retinue had remained behind a clump of trees that hid it from sight.

He responded to the Beauty's smile with an obliging salute. Immediately, Luxuriette called to him: "Handsome cavalier, go down a little further, following the course of the river; at the western tip of the isle you'll find a drawbridge guarded by a dwarf. Pronounce the word *Foudre-Love* and the two beams will be instantly lowered on to their supports, and you can come and refresh yourself in this delightful abode."

Dermid spurred his horse and arrived at the drawbridge in a trice.

"Open up!" he shouted to the dwarf, who was playing with his donkey and his pig.

Debauchin did not seem to hear him.

"*Foudre-Love!* Open up, then!" shouted the Prince.

Immediately, the drawbridge came down of its own accord and the Prince entered the island—but the two beams rose up again and closed the passage to the Prince's retinue.

Without being astonished, he said to the dwarf: "Take me to the Princess that I saw at her window, for I can only perceive tortuous paths through the bushes and I don't know which route to follow.

"Lord," the dwarf replied, "I'll hand you over to my brother, who will take you to my elder sister, who will introduce you without delay to my younger sister, who will take you to the Princess. But you seem to me to be very weary; I have an excellent French wine here—would you like to taste it?"

At the same time he poured the Beaune into a ruby cup.[71]

The Prince was thirsty; he drank it in one draught. The dwarf sniggered joyfully and conducted Dermid to Crapulophile. On the way, a sweet odor was exhaled by a flowery bouquet garnished with violets, lilies-of-the-valley, lilies, tuberoses and red, white, yellow and mottled roses.

"That odor is delicious," the Prince said to his guide.

"That's nothing, Lord; you're going to smell one a hundred times more agreeable when you approach Princess Sireneh, my mistress."

The dwarf had scarcely finished speaking when Dermid's sense of smell was agreeably struck by the perfume of the delicious dishes that Friandine was preparing.

"Come closer, handsome cavalier," said the female dwarf, "and taste the sauces I'm making. See these delicious dishes! They'll be served to you as soon as you've saluted the beautiful Sireneh, my mistress."

As she finished, she presented the Prince with a mouthful of what she was preparing, with poultry, game and fish. Dermid took a few mouthfuls and found the taste of the dishes exquisite.

Meanwhile, Luxuriette came forward. She took the cavalier by the hand, and as soon as she had touched him, he felt a devouring fire flowing through his veins. He pressed her to take him to the young beauty that he had seen at the window. The female dwarf introduced him into a voluptuous and magnificent

---

[71] Beaune is a well-known *appellation*, but Restif probably has a *double entendre* in mind; *beau-âne* would mean "fine donkey."

room, at the back of which he perceived Sireneh, sprawling limply on a big bed. Full of ardor, Dermid ran to her, and knelt down.

"I adore you, Celestial Beauty," he said to her, "And I shall grant all your wishes. Speak, dispose of my fate!"

"Handsome cavalier," the perfidious Sireneh replied, "I am young and naïve; I do not understand the language of gallantry; however...what you say...flatters my ears agreeably..."

At these words, insidious and true at the same time, Dermid stood up, transported; he pressed the fatal Beauty in his arms; he could not command his desires...

But it was too late. Sireneh could not succumb with a mortal until he had resisted other attacks. She looked at the Prince with a disdainful smile. "Moderate that audacious haste. May I know who my vanquisher is, and if he is worthy of me?"

"Beautiful Princess, or rather, young Fay," replied the feeble Dermid, "You do not have to blush at your lover. I am the King of Ultonia and I descend in a direct line, at the sixth generation, from the great O'Boruma, of whom an Oracle predicted that his posterity would one day unite all Evinland under his laws.

"I know from my mother," Sireneh replied, "that the Boruma family, sons of Kemiredi, which will one day be named the O'Brinne or O'Brien family, will be covered with glory and honors; but, King as you are, and whatever your nobility, you have fallen into my nets and I can dispose of your fate."

In the meantime, she picked up a Japanese porcelain cup full of water, which she threw in his face.

Dermid immediately fell on to all fours, and started to bray when he tried to speak.

Such was the first trial of Sireneh's power. The two female dwarfs and the two male dwarfs burst out laughing. Sireneh was delighted herself with the power to do evil. Debauchin put a bridle on the new donkey and Luxuriette climbed on top of it, made it run, trot, walk and perform all kinds of maneuvers—which amused the Princess greatly.

Afterwards, they took the donkey to the stable, where Debauchin's was lodged, along with his pig, as well as Finghall's horse, now a donkey—and the metamorphoses of those two new colleagues were so similar that it was necessary to put a mark on the newcomer in order to be able to recognize it. Luxuriette thought that mark ought to be a *salière*,[72] and gave the unfortunate

---

[72] This is a complex play on words; *salière* normally means salt-cellar nowadays, but it can also mean a kind of groove or hollow—modern dictionaries offer the example of a groove above a horse's eye, but one eighteenth-century dictionary cites "the hollow that thin women have at the height of the breast." Presumably in illustration of the latter meaning, the original text puts a long s in

Dermid the name of Insiposubolaneh, which, in the language of the fays, means "he has lost the salt of his wisdom."

Meanwhile, the men following the Prince asked to enter the island. Sireneh, still timid, was reluctant to receive fifty men, as many guards as pikemen, but Luxuriette made her understand that she had nothing to fear.

Debauchin lowered the drawbridge and the entire troop entered, asking for their master. The dwarf porter put them in the hands of Crapulophile, who offered them wine and liqueurs. They threw themselves upon them, for they were thirsty, and drank until they were completely drunk.

In that state, there was no need for Sireneh to metamorphose the drunkards herself; it was the work of the inebriation alone. They went to sleep as men and woke up as pigs.

Sireneh and the four dwarfs wanted to give themselves the pleasure of witnessing the awakening of the new herd of pigs. It was delightful! While they were asleep, Crapulophile had stripped them absolutely naked. When they woke up, believing themselves to be still human, they tried to rub their eyes and looked for their clothes. Not finding any, they tried to speak, and grunted. Then, looking at one another and seeing themselves surrounded by pigs, each of them tried to pick up a stick in order to chase away the sordid animals—but they no longer had fingers; one of two pointed horny growths enveloped the thumb and index-finger, and the other the remaining three fingers. Surprised, they looked at one another, the hair on their backs bristling with horror; they all started grunting in unison, so horribly that the entire island resounded with it and the frightened birds flew away.

After Sireneh, Luxuriette, Friandine, Debauchin and Crapulophile had laughed at the scene, holding their sides, Sireneh ordered that Insiposubolaneh be brought to her. On seeing him, all the new pigs formed a circle around him. Large tears fell from the donkey's eyes; he tried to speak, but it was an explosive braying, to which all the pigs replied with deafening grunts.

Sireneh, disgusted to have such guests, had the drawbridge lowered, and Debauchin, aided by his brother Crapulophile, both armed with whips, chased the entire herd off the island, as well as all their horses, metamorphosed into hares.

Scarcely had the band touched the land where Sireneh no longer reigned than all of them stood up on their feet and became human again, but they were all so fatigued by their position—especially the Prince, whom Luxuriette had made to gallop—that they could not move. They looked at one another with a sort of imbecility. Finally, they recovered a little reason. Dermid was put back on his horse; his guards climbed on to theirs as best they could, and they re-

---

brackets after the word, while the translation offered of the name in the language of the fays attributed to the new donkey echoes the connection with "salt," bearing in mind "Attic salt," or wit.

turned to Killnackrenan Castle, where they recovered from their fatigue—but their memories never came back entirely.

Meanwhile, Sireneh, who had become more malevolent by the exercise of malevolence, renewed her cruel amusements every day. Sometimes they were simple travelers that she drew into her abode and then metamorphosed into various animals, according to her caprice. Sometimes she attracted to her island common men and women; she left the former to Luxuriette and Friandine, and delivered the latter to Debauchin and Crapulophile—after which, she metamorphosed them, sometimes into billy-goats and nanny-goats, sometimes into boars and sows, and sometimes into dogs and bitches. In that new situation she kept them for a few weeks in order to amuse herself with their antics, especially with their manner of making love; when she wearied of them she had the drawbridge lowered, expelled them from the island, and had the cruel pleasure of seeing their stupid astonishment at their change of state.

Several more years went by, during which Sireneh delivered herself unreservedly to the cruel deportments. Meanwhile, Dermid had a son, a young man of the greatest promise, as courageous as Finghall and as virtuous, but a lover of peace and all modest virtues. He had attained the age of twenty when his father said to him one day:

"It seems to me—although the idea is like a dream—that I once had the most extraordinary adventure on an island formed by a river similar to the Shannon. At the window of a palace I saw an accomplished Beauty. A female dwarf, it seems to me, made a sign to me; a drawbridge came down and I entered the island. I was served delicious dishes; I tasted all the delights of Friga. It seems to me that I walked thereafter on all fours…but I only have a confused memory of all that; perhaps it was only a dream. All that I can recall is that the island must be outside my Estates; it's either on a river on the continent or, at least, in the kingdom of Lagenia, Mommonia or Connacy.

"That day, I had come out of Dunnaghall by the Fermanagh gate; I marched for a long time and went astray. Take the same road, my son, march straight but at hazard; perhaps you'll come upon it, as I did; then we'll know the truth about a matter that has troubled me for a long time.

Fitz-Dermid, excited by his father's discourse, only delayed his departure for the time necessary to make preparations for his journey. He took with him the elite of the youth of Ultonia, and on the appointed day, he emerged from Dunnaghall by the Fermanagh gate.

The Prince and his troop marched for a long time, and reached the Shannon. They went along it and passed through Limerick. Finally, in the fourth day, they went astray without being able to recognize where they were. The countryside appeared to them to be uncultivated, offering nothing but the image of a frightful desert. While they were very anxious, they heard a cock crowing at midday. They directed their steps in that direction.

Shortly thereafter, they heard a peacock screeching to the north. They did not know what to think, and stopped. A horse whinnied in the east; a moment later, an ox bellowed to the west.

While the Prince and his troop were astonished to find themselves surrounded by habitations that they had not seen, the cock crowed, the peacock screeched, the horse whinnied and the ox bellowed all at the same time, without discontinuity. The Prince took his troop southwards, and soon they saw a great river through the trees, which they mistook at first for the sea. On emerging from the wood, however, they saw both its banks; in the middle there was a large island, at the eastern tip of which stood a superb palace; all the rest seemed to be an enchanted garden.

"That's the abode of the dangerous fay!" exclaimed the young Prince. "Remember, all of you, that Finghall escaped from her hands, and mastered her by refusing everything that was offered to him on the island, but that his horse, having taken something, was metamorphosed into a donkey. Arm yourselves with courage, not for combat—one is only attacked here by gluttony and lust—but to overcome our appetites. Let those who think that they will not have the strength to refuse a good meal, an agreeable liqueur or the caresses of a pretty woman not enter that island!"

The young Prince added: "Look at that host of animals of all species with which it is populated! They were once men and women, whom the cruel fay has plunged into brutality. Dread such a cruel fate and constrain yourselves; for if you drink a single glass of beer in that place, eat a single mouthful or take a single kiss, you will be in the power of the cruel Sireneh, all of whose pleasure consists of doing evil."

After that speech, the young Prince spurred his horse in the direction of the palace. As soon as she had perceived him in the distance, Sireneh had posted herself at the window, and when she was within the range of sight she smiled at him and made obliging signs. The young Prince responded, saluting her courteously.

Then Luxuriette spoke. "Young and handsome cavalier," she said, "you and your brilliant troop must be tired; this isle abounds in refreshments of every sort. Go down to the western tip; you'll find a drawbridge there, which will be lowered to let you pass as soon as you have pronounced the words *Foudre-Love*." As she finished speaking, she withdrew, and drew Sireneh away, in order that the cavalier would not reply.

Fitz-Dermid descended along the river and reached the drawbridge. He perceived Debauchin, who was amusing himself with some newly-metamorphosed leverets, who were licking his hands and face while caressing him.

"Dwarf, lower the drawbridge," the Prince called to him.

Debauchin did not seem to hear him, and continued playing with his leverets, uttering bursts of laughter so loud and so piercing that the Prince was deafened by them.

Fitz-Dermid was reluctant to pronounce the words that the female dwarf had given him, and the idea occurred to him to take the island by storm. He assembled his troop; faggots were cut from the nearby hedges and they tried to fill in the ditch.

Debauchin smiled. "Insensates," he shouted, "who believe that they can take pleasure by force! You're mistaken. It's by means of laughter and games that one attacks the beautiful Sireneh; her lance only inflicts gentle wounds; her quiver is only full of arrows that tickle as they wound, and instead of blood they cause sensual tears to be shed."

At those words, although they were pronounced by a deformed dwarf, the entire troop stopped working; but as they had already thrown a great many faggots, the courageous Prince wanted to see whether he might be able to cross the ditch. He looked at it, but to his surprise, each of the faggots had been changed into an iron spike, the sharp and menacing points of which offered nothing to the reckless but pain and death.

Fitz-Dermid understood that he could not combat a supernatural power with human arms. Encouraged by the example of Finghall, he pronounced the two talismanic words that would give him passage into the isle. Immediately, the beams lowered and Debauchin hastened to come and offer his services to the Prince as well as all his retinue. With one hand he presented him with a delicate cloth to wipe away the sweat that was covering his face, and with the other a glass of ruby liquid that had an odor of ambrosia.

Fitz-Dermid rejected the fine cloth, pushed away the fatal cup with his other hand and told the dwarf to conduct him to Sireneh.

"My brother will introduce you into the palace," replied the dwarf, smiling. He hastened to hand Fitz-Dermid over to Crapulophile, who made every effort to engage him to take some refreshment. The young Prince refused, and, turning to his retinue, he exhorted all of them not to accept anything. The majority, however, burned by thirst, had already succumbed; Debauchin was moving among them in order to engage them to drink or eat.

Crapulophile handed Fitz-Dermid over to Friandine, who tempted the young Prince's sense of smell with the perfume of the most delicate dishes. Instructed by his father's misfortune, however, and by the courageous resistance of Finghall, he overcame the fire of the lust-of-taste. He was the only one who had that empire over himself; Friandine finished seducing all those whom Debauchin and Crapulophile had tempted unsuccessfully.

Meanwhile, Luxuriette had come running, and, seeing her sister occupied with the Ultonians who had followed the Prince, she took Fitz-Dermid to Sireneh.

The fay, who had secretly witnessed the Prince's courage and the attack, of a kind previously unseen, that he had just mounted on the drawbridge, employed all the skill of her seductive art. She took a few steps toward him when he appeared at the entrance to the room.

"Young hero," she said to him, "you have overcome me. No one, before you, has dared to seek to take this isle by right of conquest; it was a glory reserved for you. I recognize that I am vanquished and surrender to you, the master; command here as sovereign; my power will cease throughout the time that you dwell here. Such is the law to which I am submitted by my destiny that I owe conquest of the hero who, braving my charms, has attempted to reach me weapon in hand."

As she finished speaking she looked at the Prince languidly, and swooned into his arms, her upper body half-naked.

Fitz-Dermid shivered involuntarily; the beauty of Sireneh, and her soft and suppliant expression, stirred a tender compassion in his entrails. But great hearts have resources unknown to the vulgar; what ought to have diminished his courage reanimated it.

It is virtue that raises me above her and will defeat me, he thought. *Let us follow virtue, which preserves from enslavement.*

He pushed Sireneh away gently, looked at her without emotion, and went out to call to his companions—but how great was his pain when, having reached the middle of the palace courtyard, he no longer saw anything but pigs, dogs, donkeys, rams and deer. He called the Ultonian Lords by name. Immediately, two pigs, six donkeys, four large dogs, three rams and two deer approached, shedding tears.

"Oh, my comrades, my friends!" exclaimed the young Prince. "Is it like this that I shall take you back to your homeland? Rid yourselves of the monsters you're dreaming that you are! You're men, and it's only a deceptive bark that covers you!"

Sireneh followed the Prince. "Their cure depends on you," she told him.

"Yes, it depends on me," said Fitz-Dermid—and, seizing the fay by the hand, he said to her: "I'm taking you with me to the King, my father, and you'll remain imprisoned until you have returned my companions to their natural form."

Sireneh smiled; then, raising her wand, she struck the air three times.

Immediately, a violent wind rose up, which uprooted trees and caused rivers to flow back toward their source. All the animals, seized by panic, sought to flee; Fitz-Dermid feared that they might throw themselves in the river and drown there. He seized Sireneh by her beautiful hair and threatened to run her through with his sword if she did not stop the storm. The fay fell to her knees, her breasts uncovered, and gazed at the Prince with an expression capable of disarming the strongest courage. However, Fitz-Dermid was still threatening her, his sword raised, when he felt its tip seized. All the animals uttered a shrill cry and lay down on their bellies.

Fitz-Dermid turned his head and saw a tall woman, still beautiful, in a chariot suspended in mid-air by four flying dragons.

"Prince," said Pucellomaneh—for it was her—"you have overcome my daughter, she is yours; she is losing her power as a fay at this moment; she is becoming a mere mortal; but she will have this palace, this island and the kingdom of Connacy for a dowry. Marry her; I will answer for her affection. She will love you tenderly and will give you handsome Princes who will bear your name gloriously. I shall remain the protectress of your family and I shall watch over its wellbeing; if any Princess thereof is sterile, I shall remedy it with my power."

"Milady," replied the young Prince, "I have a father, who is my King. Let us go to find him, and if he consents, I'll marry your daughter."

Immediately, the fay Pucellomaneh touched the animals with her wand, and they all resumed human form. They left the island then with Fitz-Dermid, who returned to his father, the King.

The old King of Ultonia consented to the marriage of his son with the fay's daughter. The marriage took place on Urilove Island, but the celebrations were held at Tuam, the capital of Connacy, and then at Dunnaghall. It is since that time that the fay Pucellomaneh protects the house of Connacy, of which Queen Dadameh of Mommonia is the issue, and she watches in particular over its perpetual conservation, the greatest Princes of Evinland having emerged from that house.

PART III: AFTER THE REVOLUTION

VOICES IN THE WILDERNESS 1790-1870

Pierre-Alexis Ponson du Terrail: *The Fay: A Christmas Story*

In my grandfather's château...

Don't believe, my young friends, that my ancestor was a great lord. He was a poor soldier, esteemed by everyone because he was brave, and whom I loved myself, with veneration and respect, because he was good. His château was old and poor, like him; its decoration was sparse, and its cracked walls were somewhat reminiscent of the threadbare cloaks full of holes in which Spanish beggars—the proudest and noblest in the world—drape themselves so arrogantly.

Fortunately, God, who always reestablishes equilibrium, had hidden some of those holes beneath the festoons of a climbing vine and green ivy; he had encircled it with a meadow, through which a babbling brook ran, had given it the blue sky for a roof and the mountains of the Alps for a majestic horizon.

In my grandfather's château there was a vast hall, in which a large fire blazed in winter. In the corner of that hearth, sitting in old leather armchairs with gilded nails, an old man and a child were to be found every evening. The old man had a young mind, an excellent memory and a facile verve; he told fine stories of times past, full of noble actions, great heroic deeds, and humble traits of virtue.

The child listened with profound gratitude.

That old man was my grandfather; that child was me.

The evening usually extended from seven to ten o'clock.

At ten o'clock, my grandfather asked for his cane and his candlestick, and went to bed.

I sometimes stayed by the fireside for another half-hour, dreaming, as one does at twelve, with my eyes fixed on the bizarre pictures formed by the blaze, which underwent incessant metamorphoses, sometimes into a palace and often into cottages, occasionally throwing forth little a blue flame that I imagined to be a good fay, impertinent and smiling, whose indecisive and wild reflection would take delight in throwing a fantastic gleam upon the old tapestries with discolored characters that extended over the walls.

One evening, my young friends—it was Christmas Eve—it was exceedingly cold, I can assure you; snow covered the meadow, the wind was moaning in the chimneys and making the fir-trees shiver, and my grandfather, who had many old wounds and rheumatism, had asked that his big bed with serge curtains be warmed.

There was a clock in the big hall. The clock had chimed eleven, and yet I was still beside the fire, all alone, dreaming delightfully and building many castles in Spain—for I had in my hand three tawny yellow shiny disks, whose tremulous gleam I considered in the firelight with an indescribable joy, because they were three gold coins.

My grandfather had just given them to me, saying: "Last year, at this time, I gave you toys; this year I prefer to let you make your own choice. You can go to town tomorrow with Pierre and buy whatever you want. Think hard."

My grandfather doubtless had a hidden motive in doing that.

I was, therefore, reflecting, and like the good La Fontaine's milkmaid, I was hesitating between buying a farm and acquiring a palace...all for sixty francs!

At first I settled on a rifle: a real rifle with which I could shoot rabbits in the warrens and water-fowl in the ditches; then I thought that I had one of those already, and wondered whether I would do better to opt for fishing equipment and furnish myself with hooks, lines and nets.

Then again, from nets I passed on to a boat: a beautiful new boat, painted green and yellow, which would surely do marvelous service in the river that passed five hundred meters from the château.

Then, finally—and I certainly should have begun with that—I remembered on display a library of beautiful books bound in gilt-trimmed morocco, containing a host of things much more beautiful than their binding.

The rifle, the nets and the boat struggled hard for a minute against that fourth and more serious fantasy, but, in the end, the books won, and my choice would have been definitively made, if...

If I had not suddenly seen one of the logs in the fire throw out a little blue flame.

That flame grew, little by little, soon lighting up the entire hearth, and then the room.

I closed my eyes, dazzled, and when I opened them again, the flame had disappeared—but in its place, before me, I saw a beautiful young woman, the sight of whom drew a cry of admiration from me.

If you want to imagine her exactly, my friends, look at your older sister, your sister of fifteen or sixteen, whose eyes are thoughtful and whose mouth is slightly earnest; or, better still, imagine the portrait of your mother, painted at eighteen, who doubtless already had a presentiment of the petty chagrins and anxieties that you would cause her, and whose forehead was beginning to be veiled by a pensive melancholy, when her lips still had a fresh and open smile— the naïve and joyful smile of youth.

She had blonde hair, large blue eyes, thoughtful and very soft, little pink and diaphanous hands, which one would gladly have kissed, respectfully, for an entire day. She was dressed in white, like the angels of paradise, and her head bore a crown of cornflowers and daisies that perfumed the air around her.

She came toward me, smiling, scarcely touching the parquet with her tiny feet, and placed her white hand on my shoulder.

"I'm the Christmas Fay," she said to me, "and I bring children toys much more beautiful than those they can buy."

I looked at her in astonishment.

"Because I'm a fay," she went on, "I'm able to know everything. I saw your hesitation, and I came to advise you. Would you like to come with me?"

"Oh, yes!" I said, enthusiastically.

"We're going to midnight mass. Come on."

I picked up my mantle and cap, and I followed her. We went through the corridors without making a sound, and arrived at the front door, which opened without creaking, and Lord Ebony, the big black dog that mounted guard by night let us pass without a murmur.

As I have said, there was already a thick mantle of snow on the ground; the trees were so heavily laden with it that they resembled the forests of crystallized sugar that confectioners display on New Year's Day. It was no longer cold, though, because the Fay seemed to spread a gentle warmth around her, and the wind, doubtless at the sight of her, eased and took refuge in the dark forests that serve as its shelter on fine days.

The snow gradually hardened beneath our footsteps, and the moon lit our route.

The village was half a league away, but we were going at a rapid pace and we soon reached the first houses—humble cottages covered with thatch, built with dry stones cemented with clay, sheltering poor laborers who scarcely earned enough during the summer to have bread to eat in the winter.

"It's not yet time for mass," the little Christmas Fay said to me, still holding me by the hand. "Let's go into Père Jean's house for a little while; I can see light through the worm-eaten planks of his door."

Père Jean was an old soldier who had served under my grandfather and who only had one leg. He was poor and had nothing to live on but his trade and the work done by his daughter, a beautiful virtuous girl full of courage, whom God had sent him, like Oedipus' Antigone or Fingal's Malvina, to shore up his old age with her sturdy youth.

Père Jean wove baskets with rushes from the river and reseated the crude chairs of the village. His daughter worked in the fields.

We went into the cabin, the fay being invisible to its inhabitants, of course. The fay was only manifest to me.

Père Jean was lying down, moaning dolorously. Winter was a harsh season for him; the stump of his leg made him suffer horribly; his wounds often reopened, and it was often impossible for him to work for entire months.

That day was the twentieth that Père Jean had spent in his bed.

"Look, and think hard," the Fay breathed in my ear.

I did, indeed, look—and I saw that there was nothing on the table but a pot of frozen water instead of wine, nothing in the fireplace but meager twigs, nothing in the bread-bin but a small quantity of black bread. I still had my three gold coins in my hand. I considered them furtively by the light of the hearth; I saw an effigy of Napoléon shining on one, and I put it in the hand of the old soldier, who wept effusively and called me his son.

"Come on," said the Christmas Fay, drawing me away.

We went out. It was still not yet time for mass, and near the church there was another cottage, similarly lit.

"Knock and go in," the Fay said to me.

The cottage belonged to a widow named Marthe, a poor woman whose husband, a chamois-hunter, had been killed in a ravine the preceding year, leaving her with five children, a tiny field and a house that now seemed large and empty.

The village laborers, taking pity on the widow's distress, had agreed to take turns cultivating her field, but the year had been bad, the potatoes had failed and the hemp was poor.

Marthe was sitting by her meager fire, surrounded by her young children, who had put on their poor Sunday clothes in order to attend the birth of the infant Jesus. In the meantime, they were devouring a black wheat galette, and the dear children of the good Lord offered some to me—and as, when they came to the château, they shared my games and my bread and jam, I accepted my share of their coarse cake.

"They won't have any Christmas toys," the little Fay whispered to me very softly.

I opened my hand and considered my second gold coin. It bore the imprint of King Louis XVI—Louis XVI, who had initially been called Louis the Desired before being given the name of the Martyr King. I remembered the many acts of noble charity about which my grandfather, who had had the honor of being among the officers of his household, had told me during our winter evenings...and I let my Louis XVI fall into the apron worn by Rose, the youngest of the widow's children.

"Come to the church," the Fay set to me.

"I still have one gold coin," I murmured.

"Come nevertheless," she said, with a smile.

We went into the church, where all of the candles were burning, and where the altar was dressed with its finest and whitest cloth. Instead of letting me sit down on the old seigneurial bench where I usually sat, the Fay took me to the sacristy, where the curé was getting ready to put on the gilded chasuble that was used on solemn occasions.

He was a good old priest who put the gospel into practice, the providence of the poor, the father of orphans, the mainstay of widows, the consoler of all. He had baptized me, taught me the first pages of the catechism and given me my first instruction in Latin.

"Ask him," the Fay whispered to me, "why, on Christmas Eve, he has a worn soutane."

I went to him.

"My good Monsieur le Curé," I said to him, "didn't my good father give you a little money last month, telling you that it was for a new soutane?"

"Yes, my friend," the pastor replied, naively, "but the next day, Marguerite Dubois—you know, little Marguerite—married Pierre the shepherd. Well, my child, Marguerite had no dress new enough to be married in, and I thought that, old as it was, my soutane might perhaps last until next Easter."

For the third time I opened my hand and examined my third and last gold coin. It bore the effigy of King Charles X.

A few days earlier, I had seen grandfather go pale on reading an issue of the *Quotidienne*, and then shed hot and silent tears as he let it fall to the ground. And when I asked him, in alarm, why he was weeping, he had replied: "I'm weeping for my old king, who has just died in exile."

Charles X had died on foreign soil.

"Monsieur le Curé," I said, then, taking on a coaxing voice, "you know that every year, on Saint Charles's Day, Papa had the custom of coming to mass in his best suit. This year, we shall have a mass for the dead instead of a celebration mass, and Papa would be very displeased if you celebrated that funeral ceremony in an old soutane. Here's twenty francs that I'll lend you; if that's not enough, I'll ask my mother for some money, and you can give it back to me later, when your poor folk have everything they need."

The old priest took me in his arms and said to me, emotionally; "May God bless you, my child, as I bless you myself."

I turned around, very proudly, to search with my gaze for the kindly eye of the little Christmas Fay...but the Fay had disappeared.

Sophie Rostopchine de Ségur: *The Little Gray Mouse*

I. The Little House

There was a widower named Prudent who lived with his daughter. His wife had died some time after the birth of the girl, whose name was Rosalie.

Rosalie's father was fortunate; he lived in a large house that he owned; the house was surrounded by a vast garden in which Rosalie could wander as much as she wanted.

She was brought up with tenderness and mildness, but her father was habituated to an obedience without reply. He forbade her to address unnecessary questions to him and to insist on knowing what he did not want to tell her. He succeeded, by means of care and surveillance in almost uprooting within her a fault that is unfortunately all too common, curiosity.

Rosalie never went out of the park, which was surrounded by high walls. She never saw anyone except for her father; there was no domestic in the house; everything seemed to be done by itself. Rosalie always had what she needed, whether it was garments, books, needlework or toys. Her father brought her up himself, and Rosalie, although she was nearly fifteen years old, was not bored and did not think that she could live otherwise, surrounded by people.

In the depths of the park there was a little house with no windows, which only had one door, always closed. Rosalie's father went into it every day and always carried the key on his person. Rosalie knew that it was a shed for enclosing the garden tools; she had never thought of talking about it.

One day, when she was looking for a watering-can for her flowers, she said to her father: "Father, please give me the key to the little house in the garden."

"What do you want with that key, Rosalie?"

"I need a watering-can. I assume that I'll find one in the little house."

"No, Rosalie, there's no watering-can in there."

Prudent's voice was so changed in pronouncing those words that Rosalie looked at him, and was surprised to see that he was pale and that sweat was inundating his brow.

"What's the matter, Father?" said Rosalie, frightened.

"Nothing, my child, nothing."

"It was asking for the key that upset you, Father. What is there in that house that frightens you so much?"

"Rosalie, you don't know what you're saying. Go and look for your watering-can in the greenhouse."

"But Father, what is there in the little house?"

"Nothing that can interest you, Rosalie."

"But why do you go there every day without ever allowing me to accompany you?"

"Rosalie, you know that I don't like questions, and that curiosity is a nasty fault."

Rosalie did not say anything else, but she remained pensive. That little house, to which she had never given a thought, was causing friction in her head.

What can there be inside it? she wondered. *How pale my father went when I asked to go into it! He thought, then, that I'd be running some danger by going into it. But why does he go into it himself every day? It's doubtless to take something to eat to the ferocious beast he has locked up in there. But if he had a ferocious beast I'd hear it roaring or agitating in its prison, and no sound is ever heard in that cabin; so it isn't a beast! Anyway, it would devour my father while he's in there...unless it's tied up. But if it's tied up, there's no danger for me either. What can it be...? A prisoner! But my father is good; he wouldn't want to deprive some poor innocent of air and liberty. It's absolutely necessary that I unravel this mystery...what can I do? If I could get the key off my father, just for half an hour...perhaps he'll forget it one day...*

She was extracted from those reflections by her father, who was calling for her with an altered voice.

"Here I am, father; I'm coming in."

She did indeed go in, and examined her father, whose pale and distraught face indicated an intense agitation. Even more intrigued, she resolved to feign cheerfulness and carelessness in order to make her father feel secure, and thus to contrive to take possession of the key, to which he might not give any thought if Rosalie did not appear to be thinking about it herself.

They went to table; Prudent did not eat much, and was silent and sad, in spite of his efforts to appear cheerful. Rosalie showed such gaiety and insouciance that her father ended up recovering his customary tranquility.

Rosalie was to be fifteen in three weeks; her father had promised her an agreeable surprise for her birthday. A few days went by; there was only a fortnight to wait.

One morning, Prudent said to Rosalie: "My dear child, I'm obliged to go out for an hour. It's for your fifteenth birthday that I have to go. Wait for me in the house, and believe me, Rosalie, don't give in to curiosity. In a fortnight you'll know what you want so much to know, for I've read your thoughts; I know what's preoccupying you. Adieu, my daughter; refrain from curiosity."

Prudent embraced his daughter tenderly and drew away as if he were reluctant to leave her. When he had gone, Rosalie ran to her father's room, and was overjoyed to see the key, forgotten on the table. She seized it and ran to the end of the park. Having arrived at the little house she remembered her father's words.

Refrain from curiosity. She hesitated, and was on the point of taking the key back without having looked into the little house when she heard a faint groan emerged from it. She stuck her ear against the door and heard a faint voice singing softly:

I'm a prisoner,
And alone on the earth.
Soon I ought to die,
Of never getting out of here.

There's no more doubt about it, she said to herself. *It's an unfortunate creature my father keeps locked up.*

Knocking gently on the door, she said: "Who are you and what can I do for you?"

"Open the door for me, Rosalie; please open the door."

"But why are you a prisoner? Have you not committed some crime?"

"Alas, no, Rosalie; it's an enchanter who is retaining me here. Save me, and I'll testify my gratitude to you by telling you who I am."

Rosalie no longer hesitated; her curiosity prevailed over her obedience. She put the key in the lock, but her hand trembled and she could not open it. She was about to give up when the little voice continued:

"Rosalie, I can tell you many things that will interest you. Your father isn't what he appears to be."

At those words, Rosalie made a last effort; the key turned and the door opened.

II. The Fay Detestable

Rosalie looked avidly; the little house was dark; she could not see anything. She heard the little voice, which said:

"Thank you, Rosalie, it's to you that I owe my deliverance."

The voice seemed to be coming from the ground. She looked, and perceived two little shining eyes in a corner, that were looking at her with malice.

"My ruse has succeeded, Rosalie, to make you give in to your curiosity. If I hadn't sung and spoken, you'd have gone back, and I'd have been doomed. Now you've freed me, you and your father are in my power."

Without understanding the extent of the misfortune that she had caused by her disobedience, Rosalie divined that it was a dangerous enemy that her father had held captive, and she wanted to retreat and close the door.

"Halt there, Rosalie. It's no longer in your power to retain me in this odious prison, from which I'd never have got out if you'd waited the fifteen years."

At the same moment the little house disappeared; only the key remained in the consternated Rosalie's hand. Then she saw a little gray mouse nearby, which was looking at her with its little sparkling eyes, and which started to laugh in a little discordant voice.

"Hee hee hee! What a frightened expression you have, Rosalie. In truth, you amuse me enormously. How kind you are to be so curious! For nearly fifteen years I've been locked in that frightful prison, unable to do any harm to your father, whom I hate, and to you, whom I detest because you're his daughter."

"Who are you, then, malevolent mouse?"

"I'm the enemy of your family, my dear. My name is the fay Detestable, and I wear my name well, I assure you; everyone detests me, and I detest everyone. I'll follow you everywhere, Rosalie."

"Leave me alone, wretch! A mouse isn't greatly to be feared, and I'll find a means of getting rid of you."

"We'll see about that my dear. I'll attach myself to your footsteps wherever you go."

Rosalie ran toward the house; every time she turned round she saw the mouse galloping after her, laughing in a mocking fashion. Having arrived in the house she tried to crush the mouse in the door, but the door remained open in spite of Rosalie's efforts, and the mouse remained on the threshold.

"Wait, nasty beast!" cried Rosalie, beside herself with anger and fear. She seized a broom and was about to land a violent blow on the mouse, when the broom burst into flames and burned her hands. She threw it on the floor and pushed it with her foot into the fireplace so that the floorboards did not catch fire. Then, seizing a cauldron that was simmering on the fire she threw it over the mouse; but the boiling water became good fresh milk. The mouse started drinking it, saying: "How kind you are, Rosalie. Not content with having freed me, you're giving me an excellent breakfast.

Poor Rosalie started to weep bitterly; she did not know what would become of her, when she heard her father coming back.

"Father!" she said. "My father! Oh, Mouse, for pity's sake, go away. Don't let my father see you!"

"I won't go away, but I'll hide behind your heels until your father learns about your disobedience."

Scarcely had the mouse hidden behind Rosalie than Prudent came in. He looked at Rosalie, whose embarrassed expression and pallor betrayed her fear.

"Rosalie," said Prudent, in a tremulous voice, "I've forgotten the key to the little house. Have you found it?"

"Here it is, Father," said Rosalie, presenting it to him and becoming very red.

"What's this spilled cream?"

"It was the cat, Father."

"The cat? The cat brought a cauldron into the middle of the room to spill it?"

"No, Father; I was carrying it, and I spilled it." Rosalie spoke in a low voice, and dared not look at her father.

"Get the broom, Rosalie, to sweep away that cream."

"There is no broom any longer, Father."

"No broom! There was one when I went out."

"I burned it, Father, by mistake, in...in..."

She stooped. Her father, who was staring at her, darted an anxious glance around the room, sighed, and headed slowly for the little house in the park.

Rosalie collapsed into a chair, sobbing. The mouse did not budge. A few moments later, Prudent came back in precipitately, his face distraught with fear.

"Rosalie, wretched child, what have you done? You've yielded to your fatal curiosity and freed our cruelest enemy."

"Forgive me, Father, forgive me," cried Rosalie, throwing herself at his feet. "I didn't know the harm I was doing."

"That's what always happens when one disobeys, Rosalie; one thinks one's only doing a little harm and one ends up doing a great deal to oneself and others."

"But Father, what is that mouse, then, which causes you such great fear? If it has so much power, how were you able to keep it prisoner, and why can't you lock it up again?"

"That mouse, my daughter, is a wicked and powerful fay; I am the genius Prudent, and since you've freed my enemy, I can reveal to you what I had to keep hidden from you until the age of fifteen years.

"I am, as I say, the genius Prudent; your mother was only a simple mortal, but her virtues and her beauty touched the Queen of the Fays as well as the King of the Genii, and they permitted me to marry her. I gave great fêtes for my marriage; unfortunately, I neglected to invite the fay Detestable, who, already irritated by seeing me marry a princess after my refusal to marry one of her daughters, swore an implacable hatred against me, as well as my wife and children.

"I wasn't frightened by her threats, because I had a power almost equal to hers and the Queen of the Fays loved me dearly. Several times, my enchantments thwarted the effects of Detestable's hatred. A few hours after your birth, however, your mother felt very sharp pains, which I couldn't soothe; I went away for a moment in order to invoke the help of the Queen of the Fays; when I came back, your mother no longer existed, the evil fay had taken advantage of my absence to cause her death, and she was about to endow you with all the vices and all possible woes; fortunately, my return paralyzed her malevolence. I stopped her at the moment when she had just endowed you with a curiosity that would be your downfall and put you entirely in her dependency at the age of fifteen.

"By means of my power, combined with that of the Queen of the Fays, I counterbalanced that fatal influence, and we determined that you would not fall into her power at the age of fifteen unless you succumbed to your curiosity three times in grave circumstances. At the same time, the Queen of the Fays, in order to punish Detestable, changed her into a mouse and imprisoned her in the little house, and declared that she would be unable to get out unless you, Rosalie, opened the door voluntarily; that she would not recover her true form unless you succumbed three times to curiosity before the age of fifteen; and finally, that if you resisted that deadly penchant at least once, you would be freed forever, as well as me, from Detestable's power. I only obtained those favors with great difficulty, Rosalie by promising that I would share your fate and that, like you, I would become Detestable's slave if you yielded to your curiosity three times. I promised myself to bring you up in such a manner as to destroy that fatal defect within you, which could cause you so much misfortune.

"It's for that reason that I kept you within this enclosure, and didn't permit you to see any of your fellows, not even domestics. I procured you by means of my power everything that you might desire, and I was already applauding myself for having succeeded so well—in three weeks you would be fifteen, and would be delivered forever from the odious yoke of Detestable—when you asked me for the key to which you seemed never to have given a thought.

"I couldn't hide the dolorous impression that request made on me; my disturbance excited your curiosity; in spite of your gaiety and your artificial insouciance, I penetrated your thought, and imagine my dolor when the Queen of the Fays ordered me to render your temptation possible and resistance meritorious by leaving my key within reach at least once. I had to leave that fatal key, and facilitate by my absence the means of succumbing.

"Imagine, Rosalie, what I suffered during the hour that I had to leave you alone, and when I saw your embarrassment and redness on my return, which indicated to me only too well that you had not had the courage to resist. I had to hide everything from you, and not tell you about your birth and the dangers you had to run before you were fifteen, under pain of falling into the power of Detestable.

"And now, Rosalie, all is not lost. You can still redeem your fault by resisting your fatal penchant for a fortnight. You were to be united at fifteen with a charming prince, one of our relatives, Prince Gracious. That union is still possible. Oh, Rosalie, my dear child, out of pity for yourself, if not for me, have courage and resist."

Rosalie had remained at her father's knees, her face hidden in her hands and weeping bitterly; at those last words she recovered a little courage and, embracing him tenderly, she said: "Yes, Father, I swear to you, I'll repair my fault. Don't leave me, Father, and I'll seek in your company the courage that I might lack if I were deprived of your sage and paternal surveillance."

"Oh, Rosalie, it's no longer in my power to stay with you; I'm under the power of my enemy; she doubtless won't permit me to remain in order to forearm you against the traps that her malevolence will set for you. I'm astonished not to have seen her yet, for the spectacle of my affliction would be a pleasure for her."

"I'm close to you, at your daughter's feet," said the gray mouse, in its shrill little voice, showing itself to the unfortunate genius. "I was amused by the story of what I've already made you suffer, and that's why I didn't show myself sooner. Say adieu to your dear Rosalie; I'm taking her with me, and I forbid you to follow her."

As she spoke she grasped the hem of Rosalie's dress with her sharp little teeth in order to drag her away with her. Rosalie uttered piercing cries and clung to her father, but an irresistible force drew her away. The unfortunate genius seized a stick and raised it over the mouse, but before he had time to bring it down the mouse put its little paw on the foot of the genius, who remained motionless, resembling a statue.

Rosalie embraced her father's knees and begged the mouse for mercy, but the mouse, uttering its shrill diabolical little laughter said: "Come on, come on, my dear, it isn't here that you'll find the wherewithal to succumb twice more to your little defect; we're going to travel the world together, and I'll enable you to see a lot of countries in a fortnight."

The mouse was still pulling Rosalie, whose arms, wrapped around her father, were resisting the extraordinary force that her enemy was employing. Then the mouse uttered a little discordant cry, and suddenly the whole house was in flames. Rosalie had enough presence of mind to reflect that by letting herself burn she would lose the power to save her father, who would remain eternally in the power of the fay Detestable, whereas by conserving her own life she would also conserve her chances of saving him.

"Adieu, Father!" she cried. "*Au revoir* in a fortnight! Your Rosalie will save you, after having doomed you."

And she ran away, in order not to be devoured by the flames.

She ran for some time, not knowing where she was going. She continued thus for several hours; finally, exhausted by fatigue and half-dead from hunger, she risked approaching a good woman who was sitting on her doorstep.

"Madame," she said, "would you be kind enough to give me shelter? I'm dying of hunger and fatigue; permit me to spend the night in your house."

"How does a beautiful young woman like you find herself on the high road, and what is that beast accompanying you, which looks like a little demon?"

Rosalie turned round and saw the gray mouse, which was looking at her with a mocking expression,

She tried to chase it away, but the mouse refused obstinately to go. The old woman, seeing that struggle, shook her head and said: "Go on your way, Beauty; I don't lodge the devil and his protégés in my house."

Rosalie continued on her way, weeping, and everywhere that she presented herself, people refused to receive her with her mouse, which never quit her. She went into a forest, where she found a stream, fortunately, to slake her thirst, and fruits and hazelnuts in abundance. She drank, ate and sat down near a tree, thinking anxiously about her father and what might become of him in a fortnight. While reflecting, in order not to see the accursed gray mouse, Rosalie closed her eyes; fatigue and the obscurity brought slumber and she fell profoundly asleep.

III. Prince Gracious

While Rosalie was asleep, Prince Gracious was hunting in the wood by torchlight; the deer, hotly pursued by the dogs, came to huddle fearfully near the bush where Rosalie was asleep. The pack and the hunters launched themselves after the deer, but the dogs suddenly ceased barking and grouped silently around Rosalie. The prince dismounted in order to start the hounds hunting again. He was very surprised to perceive a beautiful young woman sleeping peacefully in the forest.

He looked around and did not see anyone; she was alone, abandoned. On examining her more closely he saw the traces of the tears she had shed, and which were still escaping from her closed eyes. Rosalie was simply dressed, but in a silken fabric that denoted more than ease; her pretty white hands, her pink fingernails, her beautiful chestnut hair, carefully put up with a golden comb, her elegant footwear and a necklace of fine pearls indicated an elevated rank.

She did not wake up, in spite of the hoofbeats of the horses, the baying of the hounds and the tumult of a numerous gathering of men. The prince, amazed, could not weary of gazing at Rosalie; none of the members of the court knew her. Anxious about that obstinate slumber, Gracious took her hand gently. Rosalie slept on; the prince shook her hand lightly, but without being able to wake her.

"I can't abandon this unfortunate child," he said to his officers, "who might perhaps have gone astray by design, the victim of some odious malevolence. But how can we carry her away unconscious?"

"Prince," said his chief huntsman, Hubert, "can we not make a stretcher of branches and carry her thus to some nearby hostelry while Your Highness continues the hunt?"

"Your idea is good, Hubert. Have a stretcher made on which we can deposit her, but it's not a hostelry to which you'll carry her, it's to my own palace. This young person must be of noble birth; she's as beautiful as an angel. I want to make sure myself that she receives the care to which she has a right."

Hubert and the officers had soon arranged a stretcher, over which the prince laid his own cloak; then, approaching Rosalie, who was still asleep, he lifted her gently in his arms and placed her on the cloak. At that moment, Rosalie seemed to be dreaming. She smiled and murmured, in a low voice: "My father, my father...! Saved, forever...! The Queen of the Fays...Prince Gracious...I can see him...how handsome he is!"

614

The prince, surprised to hear his name pronounced, no longer doubted that Rosalie was a princess under the yoke of some enchantment. He had the stretcher-bearers walk slowly in order that the movement would not wake Rosalie; he remained at her side all the time.

They arrived at Gracious's palace; he gave orders for the queen's apartment to be prepared, and, not wanting anyone else to touch Rosalie, he carried her all the way to her room himself, where he deposited her on a bed, recommending the women who were to serve her to inform him as soon as she awoke.

Rosalie slept until the next day; it was broad daylight when she woke up. She looked round in surprise. The wicked mouse was not nearby; it had disappeared.

Am I delivered from the malevolent fay Detestable? she wondered, joyfully. *Am I in the home of some fay more powerful than her?*

She went to the window; she saw men-at-arms, and officers wearing brilliant uniforms. More and more surprised, she was about to call to one of the men, whom she believed to be as many genii and enchanters, when she heard footsteps. She turned round and saw Prince Gracious, dressed in a rich and elegant hunting costume, who was before her, gazing at her with admiration. Rosalie recognized the prince of her dream immediately, and exclaimed involuntarily: "Prince Gracious!"

"You know me, Madame?" said the prince, astonished. "How, if you have recognized me, have I been able to forget your name and your features?"

"I have only seen you in a dream, Prince," Rosalie replied, blushing. "As for my name, you can't know it, since I only knew my father's yesterday."

"And what is that name, Madame, that has been hidden from you for such a long time?"

Rosalie told him then everything that she had learned from her father. She confessed to him naively her culpable curiosity and the fatal consequences that had followed it.

"Judge my dolor, Prince, when I was obliged to quit my father in order to save myself from the flames that the evil fay had lit, and when, rejected everywhere because of the gray mouse, I found myself exposed to die of cold and hunger. But soon, a heavy slumber full of dreams took possession of me, and I have no idea how I come to be here, and whether it is in your house that I find myself."

Gracious told her how he had found her asleep in the forest, and the words of her dream that he had heard, and he added: "What your father did not tell you, Rosalie, is that the Queen of the Fays, our relative, had decided that you would be my wife when you were fifteen; that is doubtless what inspired me with the desire to go hunting by torchlight, in order that I could find you in the forest where you were lost. Since you will be fifteen in a few days, Rosalie, deign to consider my palace as yours; able in advance to command here as queen. Soon, your father will be returned to you, and we will be able to go to celebrate our marriage."

Rosalie thanked her young and handsome cousin warmly. She went into her dressing-room, where she found women waiting for her with a wide choice of dresses and coiffures. Rosalie, who had never been occupied with her toilette, put on the first dress that was offered to her, which was pink gauze garnished with lace, and a lace bonnet with pink pads. The tresses of her beautiful chestnut hair were lifted up to form a crown.

When she was ready, the prince came to fetch her to escort her to the mid-day meal. Rosalie ate like a person who had not dined the previous day.

After the meal, the prince took her into the garden; he showed her the greenhouses, which were magnificent; at the end of one of the greenhouses there was a small rotunda garnished with selected flowers; in the middle was a crate that seemed to contain a tree, but a stitched cloth covered it entirely; all that could be seen through the fabric were a few points shining with an extraordinary gleam.

IV. The Tree in the Rotunda

Rosalie admired all the flowers greatly. She thought that the prince was about to lift or tear the cloth of the mysterious tree, but he made as if to leave the greenhouse without having mentioned it to Rosalie.

"What is the tree that is so well wrapped up, prince?" Rosalie asked.

"That's the wedding present that I destine for you," said the prince, gaily, "but you ought not to see it before you're fifteen."

"But what is it that shines so brightly beneath the cloth?" Rosalie persisted.

"You'll know in a few days, Rosalie. I flatter myself that my present won't be an ordinary gift."

"And I can't see it beforehand?"

"No, Rosalie; the Queen of the Fays has forbidden me to show it to you before you're my wife, under pain of great misfortunes. I dare to hope that you love me enough to contain your curiosity for a few days."

Those last words made Rosalie tremble, in reminding her of the gray mouse and the misfortunes that menaced her, as well as her father, if she yielded to the temptation that had doubtless been sent to her by her enemy, the fay Detestable. She did not say any more, therefore, about the mysterious cloth, and continued her walk with the prince.

The whole day passed agreeably. The prince introduced her to the ladies of his court, and told them all that they were to respect in Princess Rosalie the wife that had been chosen for him by the Queen of the Fays. Rosalie was very amiable to everyone, and everyone rejoiced in the idea of having such a charming queen.

The next day and the following days were spent in fêtes, hunts and prome- nades. The prince and Rosalie saw Rosalie's birthday, which was also to be their wedding day, approaching with joy, the prince, because he loved his cousin ten- derly, and Rosalie because she loved the prince, because she wanted very much to see her father again and also because she wanted ardently to see what the crate in the rotunda contained. She thought about it incessantly; at night she dreamed about it and in the moments when she was alone she had extreme diffi- culty in not going to the greenhouses in order to try to discover the mystery.

Finally, the last day of the wait arrived; the next day, Rosalie would be fif- teen. The prince was very occupied with the preparations for his wedding, to which all the good fays of his acquaintance, and the Queen of the Fays, were to witness.

Rosalie found herself alone in the morning; she went for a walk, and, while reflecting on the happiness of the next day, she headed mechanically toward the rotunda. She went into it, pensive and smiling, and found herself facing the cloth that covered the treasure.

It's tomorrow, she thought, *that I shall finally know what that cloth con- ceals. If I wanted to, I could easily know today, for I can see a few little open- ings into which I could easily introduce my fingers...and by pulling it up slight- ly...in fact, what is it that I'd know? I could put the cloth back after taking a peek...since it's going to be mine tomorrow, I can surely cast a glance at it to- day...*

She looked around, did not see anyone, and forgetting entirely, in her ex- treme desire to satisfy her curiosity, the generosity of the prince and the dangers that threatened her if she yielded to the temptation, she put her fingers through one of the holes, and pulled lightly. The cloth tore from top to bottom with a noise like thunder, and offered to Rosalie's astonished eyes a tree whose stem was coral and its leaves emeralds; the fruits that covered the tree were precious stones of all colors: diamonds, pearls, rubies, sapphires, opals, topazes, etc., as large as the fruits they represented, and with such a gleam that Rosalie was daz- zled by it.

Scarcely had she envisaged that unparalleled tree, however, than a louder noise than the first extracted her from her ecstasy. She felt herself lifted up and transported to a plain, from which she saw the prince's palace collapse. Frightful cries emerged from the ruins of the palace, and soon Rosalie saw the prince emerge from the rubble himself, bloody and clad in rags.

He advanced toward her and said, sadly: "Rosalie, ingrate Rosalie, see the state to which you have reduced me, and all my court. After what you have just done, I have no doubt that you will yield a third time to your curiosity, that you will consummate my misfortune, that of your father, and your own. Adieu, Rosalie, adieu! May repentance expiate your ingratitude toward an unfortunate prince who loved you, and only wanted your happiness!"

As he spoke he drew away slowly. Rosalie had dropped to her knees, inundated by tears. She called to him, but he disappeared from her sight without even turning round to contemplate her despair. She was about to faint when she heard the discordant little laughter of the gray mouse, which was in front of her.

"Thank me, then, Rosalie, for having aided you so well. It's me who sent you by night those beautiful dreams of the mysterious cloth; it's me who gnawed through the cloth to facilitate the means of looking at it. Without that last ruse I really think that you might have been lost to me, as well as your father and Prince Gracious. But one more little peccadillo, my dear, and you'll be mine forever."

And the mouse, in its infernal joy, started dancing around Rosalie; its words, malevolent as they were, did not excite Rosalie's anger.

It's my fault, she said to herself. *Without my fatal curiosity, without my culpable ingratitude, the gray mouse wouldn't have succeeded in making me commit such an unworthy action. I ought to expiate my dolor by my patience and my firm determination to resist the third proof, however difficult it might be. In any case, I only have a few hours to wait, and as my dear prince said, his happiness, my father's and my own depend on me.*

Rosalie did not budge, therefore. The gray mouse employed all possible means to make her walk, but Rosalie persisted in remaining where she was, facing the ruins of the palace.

V. The Casket

The whole day passed thus. Rosalie suffered cruelly from thirst.

Ought I not to suffer even more, she said to herself, *in order to punish me for what I have made my father and my cousin suffer? I'll wait here for my fifteenth year to elapse.*

Night was beginning to fall when an old woman who was passing by approached her and said: "My beautiful child, would you do me the favor of keeping this casket for me, which is very heavy to carry, while I go to see a relative nearby?"

"Willingly, Madame," said Rosalie, who was very obliging.

The old woman handed her he casket, saying: "Thank you, my beautiful child. I won't be absent for long. Don't look inside the casket, for it contains things…things such as you have never seen…and such as you will never see. Don't put it down too rudely, for it has a fragile shell and a rude shock might break it…and then you'd see its contents. And no one must see what there is inside."

She departed as she finished speaking. Rosalie put the casket down beside her, gently, and reflected on all the events that had happened. Night fell entirely; the old woman did not come back.

Rosalie looked down at the casket, and saw with surprise that it was illuminating the ground around it.

What is it, she thought, *that is shining inside that casket?*

She turned it around in all directions, but nothing could explain that extraordinary glow to her. She placed it on the ground again and thought: *What does it matter to me what the casket contains? It's not mine; it belongs to the good old woman who confided it to me. I don't want to think about it any longer, for fear of being tempted to open it.*

In fact, she did not look at it any longer, and tried not to think about it. She closed her eyes, resolved to wait thus for the return of the daylight.

Then I'll be fifteen years old; I'll see my father and Gracious again, and I won't have anything more to fear from the malevolent fay.

"Rosalie, Rosalie," said the little voice of the mouse, precipitately. "Here I am, close by. I'm no longer your enemy, and to prove it, if you wish, I'll enable you to see what is in the casket."

Rosalie did not reply.

"Rosalie, didn't you hear what I'm proposing to you? I'm your friend, believe me, please."

No response.

Then the gray mouse, which had no time to lose, launched itself upon the casket and set about gnawing the lid.

"Monster!" cried Rosalie, seizing the casket and clasping it to her bosom. "If you have the misfortune to touch this casket, I'll wring your neck instantly!"

The mouse darted a diabolical glare at Rosalie, but dared not brave her anger. While it sought a means of exciting Rosalie's curiosity, a clock chimed midnight.

At the same moment, the mouse uttered a lugubrious cry, and said to Rosalie: "Rosalie, the hour of your birth has sounded now; you're fifteen years old; you have nothing more to fear from me. Henceforth, you're out of my reach, as well as your odious father and your frightful prince, and I'm condemned to keep my ignoble form of a mouse until I can succeed in making a young woman as beautiful and well born as you fall into my traps. Adieu, Rosalie; you can open the casket now."

As she finished speaking, the gray mouse disappeared. Rosalie, suspicious of her enemy's words, did not want to follow her final advice, and resolved to keep the casket intact until daybreak.

Scarcely had she made that resolution than an owl that was flying overhead dropped a stone on to the casket, which shattered into a thousand pieces. Rosalie uttered a cry of terror.

At the same moment she saw the Queen of the Fays before her, who said to her: "Come, Rosalie; you have finally triumphed over the cruel enemy of your family; I'm going to return you to your father; but before then, eat and drink."

And the fay presented her with a fruit, of which a single mouthful sated Rosalie's hunger and slaked her thirst. Immediately, a chariot harnessed to two dragons appeared near the fay, who climbed into it and helped Rosalie to join her.

Having recovered from her surprise, Rosalie thanked the fay warmly for her protection and asked her whether she was going to see her father and Prince Gracious.

"You father is waiting for you in the prince's palace."

"But Madame, I thought that the prince's palace was destroyed and he was wounded and reduced to poverty."

"That was only an illusion to give you more horror of your curiosity, Rosalie, and to prevent you from succumbing to it for a third time. You'll find the prince's palace as it was before you tore the cloth covering the precious tree that he destined for you."

As they fay finished speaking, the chariot stopped next to the perron of the palace. Rosalie's father and the prince were waiting there with all the court. Rosalie threw herself to her father's arms and those of the prince, who did not seem to remember her fault of the day before.

Everything was ready for the marriage ceremony, which was celebrated immediately. All the fays participated in the fêtes that lasted for several days. Rosalie's father lived with his children. Rosalie was cured forever of her curiosity; she was loved tenderly by Prince Gracious, whom she loved all her life. They had beautiful children, and they gave them powerful fays for godmothers, in order to protect them against wicked fays and evil genii.

Édouard Laboulaye: *The Castle of Life*

I

A few years ago, finding myself in Capri, the most charming of the islands in the Gulf of Naples on one of those beautiful autumn days that are full of calm and light, I had a desire to go in a boat to Paestum, stopping at Amalfi and Salerno. It was easy to do; there were fishermen on the beach who were returning to the mainland and asked for nothing better than to take a foreigner with them.

On boarding the boat I found four mariners with a friendly manner, muscular arms and sun-bronzed faces, and, in their midst, a little girl eight or ten years old, with a strong and sturdy figure, a pink face and dark and lively eyes, who alternately commanded or begged the crew, with the majesty of an Italian woman or the grace of a child. She was the owner's daughter; I could not doubt that, by virtue of the proud smile she gave me as I entered the boat.

Once at sea, with everyone at his oar, as I found myself alone on the boat with nothing to do, I took the child on my knees in order to chat to her and hear from her dainty lips the Neapolitan dialect that sounds so sweetly in the ear.

"Talk to her, Excellency," the owner cried to me, triumphantly. "Small as she is, she's already as knowledgeable as a canoness. If you want, she'll tell you the story of the King of Starza Longa, who married his daughter to a snake, or that of Vardiello, whose stupidity procured him a fortune. Would you prefer that of the enchanted hind, or the ogre who gave Antuono de Maregliano the staff that did its duty, or the Castle of Life…?"

"Go for the Castle of Life!" I cried, in order to interrupt a list of tales as numerous as the beads of a rosary."

"Nunziata, my child," said the fisherman, in a solemn tone, "tell His Excellency the story of the Castle of Life, as your mother has told it to you so many times. And you," he added, addressing the oarsmen, "try not to strike the water so hard, in order that we can hear."

It was thus that, for more than an hour, the boat glided soundlessly over the motionless waves, and a mild October sun turned the mountains crimson and made the sea scintillate, all five of us, attentive and silent, listened to the child who talked to us about faerie in the midst of an enchanted nature.

II

Once, in Salerno, commenced Nunziata gravely, there was a good old woman, a fisher by profession, whose only wealth and support was a boy about twelve years old, her grandson, a poor orphan whose father had drowned one stormy day and whose mother had died of chagrin. Gracious—that was the child's name—only loved his grandmother in the world; he went with her every morning before dawn to collect shellfish or to haul the nets on to the shore, while waiting for him to be strong enough to go fishing himself and brave the waves that had killed his parents. He was so handsome, so well made and so becoming that as soon as he went into the town with his basket of fish on his head, everyone ran after him; he had sold his stock even before arriving at the market.

Unfortunately, the grandmother was very old; she only had one tooth left in the middle of her mouth, her head was unsteady and her eyes were so red that she could no longer see. Every morning she had more difficulty getting up than she had the day before, and she felt that she could not go on any longer. So, every evening, before Gracious wrapped himself in his blankets in order to sleep on the ground, she gave him good advice for the time when he would be alone. She told him which fisherman it was necessary to see and which ones it was necessary to avoid; how, by always being mild and hard-working, prudent and resolute, he would make his way in the world and end up having his boat and his nets.

The poor boy scarcely listened to all that wisdom. As soon as the old woman took that serious tone he cried: "Grandmother, grandmother, don't leave me. I have arms, I'm strong; I'll soon be able to work for two; but if, on coming back from the sea, I don't find you in the house, how do you expect me to live?" And he kissed her, weeping.

"My child," the old woman said to him one day, "I won't leave you as alone as you fear; after me, you'll have two protectors that more than one prince would envy you. A long time ago I obliged two great ladies, who won't forget when the time comes to call them, which will be soon."

"Who are these ladies?" asked Gracious, who had only ever seen fishermen's wives in the cabin.

"They're two fays," replied his grandmother. "Two great fays: the Fay of the Waters and the Fay of the Woods. Listen to me carefully, my child; there's a secret that it's necessary for me to confide to you; a secret that you must keep, as I have, and which will make your fortune and your happiness.

"Ten years ago, in the same year that your father died and your mother also left us. I went out at daybreak to surprise the crabs sleeping in the sand; I was leaning over the ground, hidden by a rock, when I saw a halcyon that was floating gently toward the beach. That's a sacred bird that it's always necessary to protect, so I let it land and didn't budge, for fear of frightening it. At the same time, I saw a beautiful green snake emerge from a fissure in the mountain and slither over the sand, which stretched out its great coils in order to approach the bird.

"When they were close to one another, without either of them seeming surprised by the encounter, the snake wrapped itself around the halcyon's neck, as if it were embracing it tenderly. They remained enlaced like that for a few minutes, and then they separated abruptly, the snake to go back into the stone and the bird to plunge into the waves, which carried it away.

"Very astonished by what I'd seen, I came back the next day at the same time. The halcyon also arrived on the sand at the same time, and the snake came out of its retreat. They were fays, there was no doubt about it; perhaps enchanted fays to whom I could render a service. But what should I do? To show myself might displease them and put me in danger; it was better to wait for a favorable opportunity, which hazard would doubtless provide.

"For a month I lay in ambush, watching the same spectacle every morning. One morning, I perceived a big black cat, which arrived at the meeting place first and hid behind the rock, almost within arm's reach. The black cat could only be an enchanter, according to what I'd learned in my childhood. I promised myself to keep an eye on it. And, in fact, scarcely had the halcyon and the snake embraced that the cat braced itself, swelled up and launched itself at the innocents. I threw myself on the brigand in my turn, which already had its victims in its murderous claws. I seized it, in spite of all its convulsions, although it bloodied my hands; and pitilessly, knowing who I was dealing with, I drew the knife that I used to open water chestnuts and I cut off the monster's head, feet and tail, awaiting with confidence the success of my devotion.

"I didn't have to wait for long; as soon as I'd thrown the body of the beast in the sea, I saw two beautiful ladies before me, one crowned with white feathers and the other with a snakeskin scarf; they were, as I've already said, the Fay of the Waters and the Fay of the Woods. Enchanted by a wretched genius who had surprised their secret, it had been necessary for them to remain a halcyon and a snake until a generous hand liberated them; it's to me that they owe their liberty and power.

"'Ask us for whatever you wish,' they said. 'Your wishes will be granted immediately.'

"I reflected that I was old and had suffered enough in life not to begin again, while for you, my child, a day would come when nothing would be too good for your desire, when you would want to be rich, noble, a general, a marquis, or perhaps a prince. *On that day*, I said to myself, *I'll be able to give him everything; a single moment of such happiness will, repay me for eight years of pain and misery*. I therefore thanked the fays and begged them to reserve their good will for the moment when I needed it.

"The Fay of the Waters took a little feather from her crown and the Fay of the Woods detached a scale from her snakeskin. 'Good woman,' they said to me, 'when you want us, place this feather and this scale in a vase of pure water, and call us, forming a wish at the same time; even if we're at the ends of the earth, you'll see us before you in an instant, ready to pay today's debt.'

"I lowered my head as a sign of gratitude; when I raised it again, everything had vanished; there were even no more scratches or blood on my arms; I might have thought that a dream had deceived me if I hadn't had in my hand the snake's scale and the halcyon's feather."

"And where are those treasures, Grandmother?" Gracious said.

"My child," the old woman replied. "I've hidden them carefully, not wanting to show them to you until you were a man and in a state to make use of them; but since death is going to separate us, the moment has come to give you those precious talismans. You'll find at the back of the hut a wooden chest covered in rags. In that chest is a little cardboard box wrapped in oakum; open that box and you'll find the scale and the feather carefully wrapped in cotton. Be careful not to break them; treat them with respect; I'll tell you what remains to be done."

Gracious brought the box to the poor woman, who could no longer get out of bed; she took the two objects out herself.

"Now," she said to her grandson, handing them to him. "Put a plate full of water in the middle of the room. Put the scale and the feather in the middle of the water, and then make a wish. Ask for fortune, nobility, intelligence, power, anything you like, my child; only, as I sense that I'm dying, kiss me, my child, before expressing that wish, which will separate us forever, and receive my blessing one last time. It will be one talisman more to bring you good luck."

To the old woman's surprise, however, Gracious did not come either to kiss her or to ask for her blessing. Quickly he put the plate full of water in the middle of the room, threw the feather and the scale into the middle of the plate, and cried from the depths of his heart: "I want my grandmother to live forever; appear, Fay of the Waters! I want my grandmother to live forever; appear, Fay of the Woods!"

Then the water started seething and seething; the plate became a great basin that the walls of the cottage could scarcely contain, and Gracious saw two beautiful young women emerge from the depths of the basin, whom he immediately recognized, by their wands, as fays. One had a crown of holly leaves mingled with red berries, with pendant diamond earrings cut to resemble acorns; she was clad in a robe as green as an olive leaf, and above it she had a striped pelt that was knotted like a sash over her right shoulder. She was the Fay of the Woods. As for the Fay of the Waters, she had a coiffure of reeds with a white robe entirely bordered by grebe-feathers, and a blue scarf that lifted up over her head at times, inflating like the sail of a ship. Great ladies as they were, they both smiled as they looked at Gracious, who had taken refuge in his grandmother's arms, trembling with fear and admiration.

"Here we are, my child," said the Fay of the Waters, who spoke for them, being the older. "We heard what you said. The wish you formed does you honor, but although we can aid you in the project you've conceived, you alone can carry it out. We can prolong your grandmother's existence for a while, but in order for her to live forever it's necessary for you to go to the Castle of Life, four long days' journey from here in the direction of Sicily. That's where the Fountain of

Immortality is. If you can accomplish each of the four stages without turning aside from your route and if, when you arrive at the castle, you can answer the three questions addressed to you by an invisible voice, you'll find what you desire there; but my child, think hard before making that decision, for there's more than one danger on the route. If you miss attaining the goal of your day's journey even once, not only won't you obtain what you wish, but you'll never get out of that land, from which no one has ever returned."

"I'll depart, Madame," Gracious replied.

"But you're very young, my child," said the Fay of the Woods, "And you don't even know the way."

"It doesn't matter," said Gracious. "You won't abandon me, beautiful ladies, and to save my grandmother I'll go to the ends of the earth."

"Wait," said the Fay of the Woods; and, detaching the lead from a broken window, she put it in the palm of her hand.

The lead began to melt and boil, without the fay seeming to be inconvenienced by the heat; then she threw the metal into the hearth, which was fixed there in a thousand varied forms.

"What do you see in all that?" the fay said to Gracious.

"Madame," he replied, after having looked attentively, "it seems to me that I can see a spaniel dog with a long tail and big ears."

"Call it," said the fay.

Immediately, barking was heard, and from the middle of the metal a black and flame-colored dog emerged, which started gamboling and leaping around Gracious.

"This will be your companion," said the fay. "You can call him Faithful. He can show you the way, but I warn you that it's up to you to lead him and not form him to lead you. If you make him obey, he'll serve you, but if you obey him, he'll doom you."

"And me," said the Fay of the Waters. "Should I give you something, my dear Gracious?"

Looking around, the lady saw a piece of paper on the ground, which she pushed into the hearth with her dainty foot. The paper caught fire; when the flame had died down, thousands of little sparks were seen running after one another like nuns going to chapel on Christmas Eve with candles in their hands. The fay followed all those sparks with a curious gaze; when the last one was almost extinct, she blew on the piece of paper. Suddenly, the little cry of a bird was heard; a frightened swallow emerged, which went to collide with all the corners of the room, and ended up collapsing on Gracious's shoulder.

"She will be your companion," said the Fay of the Waters. "You can call her Pensive. She can show you the way, but I warn you that it's up to you to lead her and not for her to lead you. If you make her obey, she'll serve you, but if you obey her, she'll doom you.

"Stir those black ashes," added the good Fay of the Waters. "Perhaps you'll find something there."

Gracious obeyed; from beneath the ashes of the piece of paper he picked up a rock crystal bottle that shone like a diamond.

"It's in that," the fay told him, "that it's necessary to collect the water of immortality; it would break any container made by human hands."

Beside the bottle Gracious found a dagger with a triangular blade. It was quite different from his father's stiletto, which he had been forbidden to touch; with that weapon, one could stand up to the proudest enemy.

"You shan't be more generous than me, sister," said the other fay, and, taking a straw from the only chair that there was in the house, she blew on it. The straw immediately swelled up, and in less time than it takes to say it, it formed an admirable carbine encrusted with nacre and gold. A second straw produced an ammunition belt, which Gracious put around his body, and which fit him marvelously. One might have thought he was a prince going hunting. He was so handsome that his godmother wept with joy and affection.

The two fays disappeared.

Gracious kissed the old woman, ordering her to wait for him, and he got down on his knees in order to ask for her blessing. The grandmother gave him a fine sermon to recommend him to be patient, just, charitable and above all never to depart from the straight path. "Not for me," added the old woman, "who accepts death gladly and who regrets the wish you made, but for you, my child, in order that you come back. I don't want to die without you closing my eyes."

It was late. Gracious lay down on the ground, too agitated, he thought, to go to sleep; but slumber soon surprised him. He slept all night, while the poor grandmother gazed at the face of her dear child, illuminated by the vacillating glow of the lamp, and could not weary of admiring him, and sighing.

III

Early in the morning, when dawn had scarcely broken, the swallow started chirping and Faithful tugging the blanket.

"Let's go, Master, let's go," said the two companions, in their own language, which Gracious understood, by virtue of the fays' gift. "The sea is already whitening the beach, the birds are singing, the flies buzzing, the flowers opening to the sun. Let's go; it's time."

Gracious kissed his old friend one last time and took the road that leads to Paestum. Pensive flew from right to left chasing flies; Faithful caressed his young master or ran on ahead of him.

They were not yet two leagues from the town when Gracious saw Faithful chasing ants; they were marching in regular columns, dragging their provisions with them.

"Where are you going?" Gracious asked them.

"To the Castle of Life," they replied.

A little further on, Pensive encountered cicadas, who were also setting forth on a journey with bees and butterflies. They were all going to the Castle of Life in order to drink at the Fountain of Immortality. They walked on together, as people following the same route do. Pensive introduced Gracious to a young butterfly, which chatted pleasantly. Amity comes quickly in youth. After an hour, the two companions were inseparable.

Going straight ahead is not to the taste of butterflies, so Gracious's friend incessantly got lost in the grass. Gracious, whose life had not been free and who had never seen so many flowers and so much sunlight, followed all the butterfly's zigzags, no longer worrying about the day's journey that it was necessary to finish. After a few leagues however, his new friend felt tired.

"Let's not go any further," he said to Gracious. "See how beautiful this nature is! How good these flowers smell! How these fields are embalmed! Let's stay here; this is where life is."

"Let's go on," said Faithful. "The day is long and we're only at the beginning."

"Let's go on," said Pensive. "The sky is pure, the horizon infinite; let's keep going forward."

Gracious, recovering himself, made sage arguments to the butterfly, which was still fluttering from right to left, but in vain.

"What does it matter to me?" said the insect. "Yesterday I was a caterpillar; this evening I won't be anything; I want to enjoy today." And it settled on a wide-open Paestum rose.

Its perfume was so strong that the butterfly was choked by it. Gracious tried in vain to recall it to life, and after having wept for it, he stuck it to his hat with a pin, like a cockade.

Toward midday it was the turn of the cicadas to stop.

"Let's sing," they said. "The heat is going to overwhelm us if we struggle against the ardor of the day. It's so good to live in sweet repose! Come on, Gracious, we'll cheer you up, and you can sing with us."

"Let's listen to them," said Pensive. "They sing so well."

But Faithful did not want to stop. He had fire in his veins; he yapped so long and hard that Gracious forgot the cicadas in order to run after the importunate dog.

When evening came, Gracious encountered a honey-bee laden with pollen.

"Where are you going?" he said to her.

"I'm going home," said the bee. "I don't want to quit my hive."

"What!" said Gracious, "Laborious as you are, you're going to be like the cicada and renounce your share of immortality?"

"You castle is too far away," the bee replied. "I don't have your ambition. My daily work is sufficient for me, and I don't understand your voyages. For me, work is life."

Gracious was a little sorry to have lost so many traveling companions on the first day, but on thinking about the ease with which he had covered the first stage his heart was full of joy; he stroked Faithful, trapped the flies that Pensive brought him in his hand, and went to sleep full of hope, dreaming about his grandmother and the two fays.

IV

The next day, Pensive woke her young master at dawn.

"Let's go," she said. "The sea is already whitening the beach, the birds are singing, the flies buzzing, the flowers opening to the sun. Let's go; it's time."

"One moment," said Faithful. "The stage isn't long; we'll see the temples of Paestum before midday, where we have to stop this evening."

"The ants are already en route," said Pensive. "The road is more difficult than yesterday and the weather sultrier. Let's go."

Gracious had seen his grandmother smiling at him in a dream, so he set forth with an ardor keener than the day before. The day was splendid; to the right was the sea, pushing its blue-tinted waves gently and rolling them over the sand murmurously; to the left, in the distance, were mountains edged with pink; in the plain there was long grass dotted with flowers, and a path planted with aloes, jujubes and acanthias; facing him was a cloudless horizon. Rapturous with pleasure and hope, Gracious thought he was already at the end of the voyage. Faithful bounded into the fields and put frightened grouse to flight. Pensive lost herself in the sky, playing with the light.

Suddenly, in the midst of reeds, Gracious perceived a beautiful goat-kid looking at him with languid eyes, as if it were appealing to him. The child approached. The kid bounded, but without drawing far away. Three times it recommenced the same maneuver, as if it wanted to tease Gracious.

"Let's follow it," said Faithful. "I'll cut it off; we'll soon capture it."

"Where's Pensive?" said the child.

"What does it matter, Master?" replied Faithful. "It'll only take a moment. Trust me; I was born for hunting; the kid is ours."

Gracious did not need to be asked twice; when Faithful made a detour he ran after the kid, which only stopped between the trees and bounded away as the hunter's hand reached for it.

"Courage, Master!" cried Faithful, leaping out of ambush; but with a head-butt, the kid launched the dog into the air and fled more rapidly than the wind.

Gracious launched himself in pursuit; Faithful, his eyes and mouth ablaze, ran and yapped furiously; they crossed ditches, furrows and branches without anything stopping their audacity. The tiring kid lost ground; Gracious redoubled his ardor. He was already extending his hand to seize his prey when the ground suddenly gave way beneath his feet and he fell with his companion into a trap that had been covered with leaves.

He had not recovered from his fall when the kid approached the edge and shouted to them: "You're betrayed. I'm the wife of the king of the wolves, who will eat both of you." So saying, she disappeared.

"Master," said Faithful, "the fay was right to recommend that you didn't follow me. We've been stupid and it's me who has doomed you."

"At least we'll defend our lives," said Gracious. And, taking his carbine, he loaded it with two cartridges, in order to await the king of the wolves.

Calmer then, he examined the deep ditch into which he had fallen. It was too high for him to get out of it, so it was in the hole that he had to await death. Faithful understood his master's gaze.

"Master," he said, if you take me in your arms and throw me with all your might, perhaps I can reach the edge. Once outside, I can help you."

Gracious had no great hope. Three times he tried to throw Faithful up; three times the animal fell back. Finally, at the fourth attempt, the dog grabbed hold of a few roots, and aided himself so well with his teeth and paws that he got out of the tomb. Immediately, he pushed cut branches into the ditch, which he had found on the edge.

"Master," he said, "fix these branches in the earth and make a ladder. Hurry up!" he added. "Hurry up! I can hear the king of the wolves howling."

Gracious was adroit and agile. Anger doubled his strength; in less than a moment he was outside. There, he made sure of the dagger in his belt, changed the percussion-cap in his carbine, placed himself behind a tree and waited for the enemy.

Suddenly, he heard a frightful cry; a horrible beast with fangs as large as a boar's tusks, ran at him with enormous bounds. Gracious took aim with an anxious hand and fired. The shot struck home. The wolf spun around, howling, but it resumed its charge immediately.

"Hurry up and reload your carbine, Master!" cried Faithful, hurling himself courageously into the monster's face and gripping its neck with his sharp teeth.

The wolf only had to shake its head in order to throw the poor dog to the ground; it could have swallowed him in a single mouthful, and Faithful would have slid down its throat, leaving an ear behind. It was Gracious's turn to save his companion. He advanced boldly and fired his second cartridge, aiming for the shoulder. The wolf fell, but getting up with a supreme effort, it threw itself upon the hunter, who fell over beneath it. Receiving that terrible impact, Gracious thought that he was doomed, but without losing courage and summoning the good fays to his aid, he drew his dagger and plunged it into the animal's heart, As it was about to devour its enemy, its limbs suddenly stiffened, and it died.

Covered in blood and saliva, Gracious got up tremulously and sat down on a fallen tree. Faithful dragged himself over to him without daring to caress him, for he sensed how guilty he was.

"Master," he said, "What's going to become of us? Night's approaching, and we're so far from Paestum!"

"It's necessary to depart," cried the child, and he got up; but he was so weak that he was obliged to sit down again.

A burning thirst was devouring him. He had a fever; everything around him was spinning. Then, thinking about his grandmother, he started to weep. To have forgotten such beautiful promises so soon and to die in the land from which no one returns, and all for the lovely eyes of a kid! What remorse poor Gracious had! How sadly it was finishing, that day so well commenced!

Soon, sinister howling was heard; it was the brothers of the king of the wolves, which were running to his aid. Gracious embraced Faithful, who was his only friend; he forgave him for an imprudence for which they were both about to pay with their lives. Then he slid a bullet into his carbine, said his prayer to the good fays, recommended his grandmother to them, and prepared to die.

"Gracious! Gracious! Where are you?" cried a little voice, which could only be that of Pensive.

And the swallow arrived, fluttering, to alight on her master's head.

"Courage!" she said. "The wolves are still some way off. There's a spring nearby to slake your thirst and stem the blood-flow from your wounds, and I can see a hidden path in the vegetation that can take us to Paestum."

Gracious and Faithful dragged themselves all the way to the stream, trembling with dread and hope. Then they took the covered path, somewhat reanimated by Pensive's chirping. The sun had set; they walked in the dark for hours, and when the moon rose they were out of danger. A difficult and dangerous route remained, only to have more ardor in the morning: marshes to traverse, ditches to cross, thickets in which faces and hands would be torn; but, thinking that if he could repair his fault and save his grandmother, Gracious had a heart so light that his strength increased at every step, along with his hope.

Finally, after a thousand fatigues, they arrived in Paestum as the stars were about to mark midnight.

Gracious threw himself down on a step of the temple of Neptune, and after having thanked Pensive, he went to sleep, with Faithful at his feet, bruised, bloody and silent.

V

His slumber did not last long. Gracious was on his feet before daybreak, which kept him waiting. On going down the steps of the temple he saw the ants, which had built a heap of sand and were burying the seeds of the new crop there. The entire republic was in motion. Each ant was going and coming, speaking to its neighbor, receiving or giving orders; some were dragging wisps of straw, others carrying tiny slivers of wood, transporting dead flies or heaping up provisions; it was an entire establishment for the winter.

"What!" said Gracious to the ants. "Aren't you going to the Castle of Life any longer? Are you renouncing immortality?"

"We've worked enough," replied one of the workers. "The time of the harvest has arrived. The road is long, the future uncertain, and we're rich. It's insane to count of tomorrow; the wise person makes the most of the present moment; when one has accumulated honestly, the true philosophy is to enjoy it."

Faithful thought that the ant was right, but as he no longer dared give advice, he contented himself with shaking his lead as they left. Pensive, on the contrary, said that the ant was nothing but an egotist, and that if enjoying life was all there was, the butterfly was wiser than her. At the same time, livelier than ever, Pensive flew at top speed in order to scout the way ahead.

Gracious marched in silence. Ashamed of the follies of the previous day, although he regretted the kid slightly, he promised himself that on the third day nothing would deflect him from his route. Faithful, his ear torn, followed his young master, limping, seemingly no less thoughtful than him.

At about midday they looked for a favorable place to rest briefly. The weather was not as it had been the previous day; it seemed that the locale and the season had changed. The route took them through fields recently scythed for the second time, and beautiful vines charged with grapes. It was bordered by tall fig-trees covered in fruits, in which thousands of insects were buzzing. There were gilded mists on the horizon; the air was mild and warm; everything invited a repast.

In the most beautiful of meadows, next to a stream that distributed freshness far and wide, in the shade of plane trees and ash trees, Gracious perceived a herd of buffalo ruminating. Lying limply on the ground, they formed a circle around an old bull that seemed to be their chief and king. Gracious approached civilly and was received politely. A nod of the head invited him to sit down; he was shown large jars full of cheese and milk. The traveler admired the calm and gravity of the placid and powerful animals. One might have thought them as many Roman senators on their curule chairs. The golden rings that they wore through their noses added to the majesty of their aspect.

Gracious, who felt calmer and more composed than the previous day, could not help thinking that it would be good to live in the bosom of that peace and that abundance; if happiness was anywhere, it was doubtless there that it was necessary to seek it.

Faithful shared his master's opinion. It was the time when the quail were migrating to Africa; the ground was covered with weary birds, which were recovering their strength before traversing the sea. Faithful only had to bend down to carry out a princely hunt; sated by game, he lay down at Gracious's feet and started to snore.

When the buffalo had finished ruminating, Gracious, who had feared being indiscreet until then, engaged in conversation with the bull, which displayed a cultivated mind and had long experience.

"Are you the masters of this rich domain?" he asked.

"No," replied the old buffalo. "We belong, like everything else, to the fay Crapaudine, the Queen of the Vermilion Towers, the richest of all the fays."

"What does she demand of you?"

"Nothing except to wear this gold ring in the nose and to pay her a rent of milk," replied the bull. "At the very most, to give her one of our children from time to time to regale her guests. At that price, we enjoy our abundance in perfect security, so we have no one to envy on earth; there is no one happier than we are."

"Have you never heard mention of the Castle of Life and the Fountain of Immortality?" said Gracious, timidly. Without knowing why, he blushed as he asked the question.

"In our fathers' day," said the bull, "there were a few ancients who still talked about those chimeras; wiser than our ancestors, we know today that there is no other happiness than ruminating and sleeping."

Gracious got up sadly in order to set forth again, and asked what the square red towers were that he could see in the distance.

"Those are the Vermilion Towers," replied the bull. "They close the road. You'll have to pass through Crapaudine's castle in order to continue on your way. You'll see the fay, my young friend; she'll offer you hospitality and fortune. Believe me, do as your predecessors have done; all of them have accepted the benefits of our mistress, they've all found it good to renounce their dreams in order to live happily."

"And what became of them?" Gracious asked.

"They've become buffaloes like us," the bull replied, tranquilly. Not having finished his siesta, he lowered his head and went to sleep.

Gracious shivered and woke Faithful, who got up, grumbling. He called Pensive, but Pensive did not respond; she was chatting with a spider which had extended a great web between two branches of an ash-tree; it was glistening in the sunlight and was full of flies.

"Why that long journey?" the spider said to the swallow. "What's the point of changing climates and expecting to obtain your life in the sun from time or a master? Look at me; I don't depend on anyone and draw everything from myself. I'm my own mistress; I enjoy my art and my genius; I draw the world to me; nothing can trouble either my calculations or a happiness that I only owe to myself."

Three times Gracious called Pensive, who did not hear him; she was in admiration before her new friend. At every moment a dazed fly threw itself into her web, and every time, the spider, an attentive hostess, offered the new prey to her astonished companion, when a sudden gust of wind blew, so light that the swallow's feathers were not even ruffled. Pensive looked for the spider; the web was thrown to the winds, and the poor little creature was hanging by one foot to its last thread when a bird carried it away in passing.

Having resumed marching, they arrived at Crapaudine's palace. Gracious was introduced with great ceremony by two fine greyhounds caparisoned in crimson and wearing broad collars sparkling with rubies. After having traversed a large number of rooms filled with paintings, statues, gold fabrics and silks, and caskets overflowing with money and jewels, Gracious and his companions entered a round temple that was Crapaudine's drawing room. The walls were lapis, the vault of azure enamel was supported by twelve fluted columns of solid gold, which bore capitals of acanthus leaves in white enamel edged with gold.

In a large velvet armchair there was a toad as large as a rabbit; that was the goddess of the place. Draped in a large scarlet mantle bordered with bright spangles, the amiable Crapaudine had a ruby diadem on her head the gleam of which animated her fat cheeks slightly, streaked with yellow and green. As soon as she perceived Gracious, she extended four fingers covered with rings toward him. The poor boy was obliged, out of respect, to bend over and carry them to his lips.

"My friend," said the fay, in a hoarse voice that she tried in vain to soften, "I've been waiting for you; I wouldn't want to be less generous to you than my sisters have been. In coming this far you've seen a small part of my riches. This palace, with its paintings, its statues, its coffers full of gold, these immense domains, these innumerable herds, all this is yours if you wish; it only depends on you to be the richest and happiest of men."

"What is it necessary to do for that?" asked Gracious, emotionally.

"Less than nothing," replied the fay. "Cut me into five pieces and eat me up. That isn't such a frightful thing," she added, with a smile, and, looking at Gracious with eyes even redder than usual, Crapaudine started drooling agreeably.

"Can one at last season you?" Pensive said, who could not look at the fay's beautiful gardens without envy.

"No," said Crapaudine, "it's necessary to eat me entirely raw; but one can stroll in my palace, look at and touch all my treasures and tell oneself that by giving me that proof of devotion, one can have it all."

"A little courage, Master," sighed Faithful, in an imploring voice. "We'd be so comfortable here!"

Pensive did not say anything, but her silence was a confession. As for Gracious, who was thinking about the buffaloes and the golden ring, he did not trust the fay. Crapaudine divined that.

"Don't think," she said, "that I want to deceive you, my dear Gracious. In offering you all that I possess, I'm also asking for a service for which I want to recompense you worthily. When you've accomplished the task that I'm proposing to you, I'll become a young woman as beautiful as Venus; if not, my toad's feet and hands will remain to me. That's very little, when one is rich. Ten princes, twenty marquises and thirty counts have begged me to marry them just as I am; when I'm a woman, it's you to whom I'll give my preference; we'll enjoy my immense fortune together. Don't blush at your poverty; you have a treasure on your person that's worth as much as all of mine; it's the bottle that my sister has given you." And she extended her viscous fingers to seize the talisman.

"Never!" cried Gracious, recoiling. "Never! I don't want either repose or a fortune; I want to get out of here and go to the Castle of Life."

"You'll never get out, wretch!" cried the fay, furiously.

Immediately, the temple disappeared; a circle of flames surrounded Gracious, and an invisible clock began to chime midnight.

At the first stroke, the traveler shivered; at the second, without hesitation, he threw himself into the midst of the flames. Was not dying for his grandmother the sole means for Gracious to testify to his repentance and his love?

VII

To Gracious's surprise, the fire drew aside without touching him; he suddenly found himself in a new country with his two companions beside him.

That land was no longer Italy; it was a Russia, it was the end of the earth, Gracious was lost on a mountain covered in snow. Around him he saw nothing but huge trees covered in frost, which were dripping water from all their branches. A damp and penetrating fog chilled him to the bone. The sodden earth gave way beneath his feet; to complete his misery, it was necessary to descend a steep slope at the bottom of which a torrent ran that broke noisily against the rocks.

Gracious drew his dagger and cut a tree branch in order to sustain his uncertain steps. Faithful, his tail between his legs, was yapping feebly. Pensive did not quit her master's shoulder; her bristling feathers were covered with little icicles. The poor animal was half-dead, but she encouraged Gracious and did not complain.

When, after infinite difficulty, they arrived at the foot of the mountain, Gracious found a river covered in enormous blocks of ice that were colliding with one another and spinning in the current. It was necessary to cross that river, without a bridge, without a boat, and without help.

"Master," said Faithful, "I can't go any further. Cursed be the fay who put me in your service and extracted me from the void!"

Having said that, he lay down on the ground, and did not move again. Gracious tried in vain to render him courage, and called him his companion and his friend. All that the poor dog was able to do was to respond one last time to his master's caresses by wagging his tail and licking his hands. Then his limbs stiffened and he expired.

Gracious loaded Faithful on to his back in order to carry him to the Castle of Life, and climbed resolutely on to a block of ice, still followed by Pensive.

With his staff he pushed that frail raft into the middle of the current, which carried him away with a frightful rapidity.

"Master," said Pensive, "can you hear the sound of the sea? We're going to the abyss, which will devour us! Give me one last caress and adieu!"

"No," said Gracious. "Why would the fays have deceived me? Perhaps the shore is nearby; perhaps, above the clouds, there's the sun. Rise, rise, good Pensive; perhaps, beyond the fog, you'll find light and you'll see the Castle of Life."

Pensive spread her half-frozen wings and rose up courageously in the midst of the cold and mist. Gracious followed the sound of her wings for an instant; then silence fell, while the block of ice continued its furious course through the night.

Gracious waited for a long time, but finally, when he sensed that he was alone, hope abandoned him; he lay down to await death on the vacillating block of ice. Sometimes, a livid flash of lightning traversed the cloud; horrible thunderclaps were heard; one might have thought it the end of the world and time.

Suddenly, in his despair and abandonment, Gracious heard the cry of the swallow; Pensive fell at his feet.

"Master, Master, you were right!" she said. "I've seen the shore; the aurora is up above. Courage!"

Having said that, she opened her wings convulsively and remained motionless, and lifeless.

Gracious, who had got up with a start, put the poor bird that had sacrificed herself for him over his heart, and with a superhuman ardor, he drove the block of ice forward in order to find salvation or doom.

Suddenly, he recognized the sound of the sea, racing and rumbling. He fell to his knees and closed his eyes, awaiting death.

A wave as high as a mountain collapsed on his head, and threw him, unconscious, on to the shore on which no one had set foot before him.

VIII

When Gracious recovered his senses there was no longer any ice, nor cloud, nor darkness. He had run aground on the sand in a pleasant country, where the trees were bathing in a pure light. Facing him was a beautiful castle from which a lively spring was escaping, which threw itself bubbling into a blue, calm, sea as transparent as the sky.

Gracious looked around. He was alone, alone with the remains of his two friends, which the waves had carried to the shore. Fatigued by so much suffering and emotions, he dragged himself to the stream and, leaning over the water in order to refresh his desiccated lips, he recoiled in fear. It was not his own face that he had seen in the water; it was that of an old man with white hair, who resembled him.

He turned round. There was no one behind him...

He approached the spring again; he saw the old man again—or rather, he could not doubt, the old man was him.

"Great fays!" he cried, "I understand; it was my life that you wanted for my grandmother's; I accept the sacrifice with joy."

And without worrying any more about his old age and his wrinkles, he plunged is head into the water and drank, avidly.

When he got up again, he was astonished to see himself as he had been on the day when he had quit the paternal house: younger, his hair blacker, and his eyes shinier than ever. He picked up his hat, which had fallen next to the spring, and on which a drop of water had chanced to fall. O surprise! The butterfly that he had attached there flapped its wings and tried to fly away.

Gracious ran to the beach in order to pick up Faithful and Pensive. He plunged them into the beneficent spring. Pensive escaped, uttering a cry of joy, and went to lose herself in the eaves of the castle. Faithful, shaking the water off his ears, ran to the palace stables, from which magnificent guard dogs emerged, which, instead of leaping after the newcomer, celebrated his arrival and welcomed him like an old friend. It was the Fountain of Immortality that Gracious had finally found; or, rather, it was the spring that escaped from it, a spring already much enfeebled, which gave two or three hundred years of life at the most to those who drank from it—but nothing prevented them from doing it again.

Gracious filled his bottle with that beneficent water and approached the palace. His heart was beating forcefully, for one last ordeal still remained to him; so close to succeeding, one fears failure even more. He went up the steps of the perron; everything was closed and silent; there was no one there to receive the traveler. When he reached the last step, ready to knock on the door, a voice, more soft than severe, stopped him.

"Have you loved?" said the visible voice.

"Yes," Gracious replied. "I have loved my grandmother more than anything in the world."

The door opened, in such a fashion that a hand could have passed through it.

"Have you suffered for the one you loved?" said the voice.

"I've suffered," said Gracious, "doubtless a great deal by my own fault, but a little for the person I wanted to save."

The door opened half way; the child perceived an infinite perspective: woods, waters, a sky more beautiful than anything he had ever dreamed.

"Have you always done your duty?" the voice went on, in a harsher tone.

"Alas, no," Gracious replied, falling to his knees, "but when I have failed in it, I have been punished by my remorse even more than by the rude proofs I have traversed. Forgive me, and if I have not yet expiated all my faults, punish me as I merit, but save the one I love; preserve my grandmother for me."

Then the door opened its two battens, without Gracious seeing anyone. Intoxicated by joy, he entered a courtyard surrounded by arcades garnished with foliage. In the center was a jet of water that emerged from a clump of flowers more beautiful, larger and more odorous than those of the earth. Next to the source there was a woman clad in white, of noble bearing, who did not seem to be more than forty years old. She walked toward Gracious and welcomed him with a smile so soft that the child felt touched to the depths of the heart, and tears came to his eyes.

"Don't you recognize me?" the lady said to Gracious.

"Grandmother, is that you?" he cried. "How do you come to be in the Castle of Life?"

"My child," she said, hugging him to her bosom, "the person who brought me here is a fay more powerful than the Fays of the Waters and the Woods. I shall not return to Salerno again; I shall receive here the recompense for the little good that I have done, while savoring a happiness that time will not dry up."

"What about me, Grandmother?" Gracious cried. "What will become of me? After having seen you here, how can I go back there to suffer in solitude?"

"Dear son," she replied, "one can no longer live on earth when one has glimpsed the celestial delights of this dwelling. You have lived, my good Gracious; life has nothing more to teach you. More fortunate than me, you have traversed in four years the desert where I languished for eighty; henceforth, nothing can separate us any longer."

The door closed again.

Since then, no one has ever heard any mention of Gracious or his grandmother. It is in vain that the King of Naples a search mounted in Calabria for the palace and the enchanted spring; they have never been found again on earth. But if we understood the language of the stars, if we sensed what they say to us every evening in putting their gentle radiance over us, we would have learned a long time ago where the Castle of Life and the Fountain of Immortality are.

IX

Nunziata had finished her story while I was still listening; I admired those eyes, which were shining with a naïve faith in the marvels that her mother had related to her. I followed the gestures of the little hands, which seemed to be painting people and things.

"Well, Excellency," the fisherman shouted to me, "you're not saying anything? The marchesina has charmed you as she has charmed so many others. That's not just a story either; we can show you Gracious's house in Salerno."

"That's all right, *patron*," I replied, slightly ashamed at being amused by such fables. "The child narrates agreeably, and to thank her for it, as soon as we land, I'd like to buy her an ivory chaplet with big silver beads."

She blushed with pleasure. I kissed her, which made her blush even more, while her father gazed at me, and turned eyes shining with joy toward his companions.

637

"Tomorrow," he said, "tomorrow, if you wish, she'll tell you an even more beautiful story, which will make you laugh and weep."

The next day, we went from Amalfi to Salerno, and Nunziata...

But that is a secret, which I shall keep for next year, if the tale of Gracious has not bored the reader too much.

Charles Baudelaire: *The Gifts of the Fays*

There was a great assembly of the fays, in order to proceed with the distribution of gifts among all the new-born children who had arrived in life during the last twenty-four hours.

All those ancient and capricious sisters of Destiny, all those bizarre mothers of joy and dolor, were very various: some had a somber and sullen appearance, others a playful and mischievous air; some were young and had always been young, others were old, and had always been old.

All the fathers who believed in the fays had come, each carrying his new-born in his arms.

The Gifts, the Faculties, the good Luck and the invincible Circumstances were accumulated alongside the tribunal, like prizes on a display-stand in an award ceremony. What was particular to this occasion is that the gifts were not the recompense for an effort but, on the contrary, favors accorded to those who had not yet lived, favors able to determine their destiny and to become the source of their woe as well as their happiness.

The poor fays were very busy, for the crowd of solicitors was huge, and the intermediary world, placed between humans and the gods is submissive, like us, to the terrible law of Time and its infinite posterity, the Days, the Hours, the Minutes and the Seconds.

In truth, they were as bewildered as ministers on a day of audiences, or the administrators of the Mont-de-Pieté when a national holiday licenses gratuitous distributions. I believe that they even glanced at the hands of the clock from time to time with as much impatience as human judges who, having been sitting since the morning, cannot help dreaming about dinner, the family and their cherished slippers. If there is a measure of precipitation and hazard in supernatural justice, we ought not to be astonished if it is likewise in human justice. We would, in any case, be unjust judges ourselves.

So there were a few blunders committed that day, which might have been considered bizarre if prudence rather than caprice had been the eternal distinctive characteristic of fays.

Thus, the power of attracting fortune magnetically was awarded to the unique heir of a very rich family who, not being endowed with any sense of charity, nor any covetousness for the most visible wealth of life, was subsequently to find himself prodigiously embarrassed by his millions.

Thus, the love of the Beautiful and poetic potency were given to the son of a somber vagabond, a quarryman by profession, who could not, in any fashion, aid the faculties nor relieve the needs of his deplorable offspring.

I have forgotten to tell you that the distribution, in these solemn cases, is without appeal, and that no gift can be refused.

All the fays had risen to their feet, believing their chore to be accomplished, for no gift any longer remained, no largesse to throw to all that human fry, when a worthy man—a poor petty tradesman, I believe—stood up and, seizing with his hand the robe of multicolored vapors worn by the nearest fay, cried: "Hey, Madame, you've forgotten us! There's still my little boy! I can't have come for nothing."

The fay might have been embarrassed, for nothing any longer remained. However, she remembered just in time a law that is well known but rarely applied in the supernatural world inhabited by those impalpable deities friendly to humans and often constrained to adapt to their passions, such as fays, gnomes, salamanders, sylphides, sylphs, nixies, and undines of both sexes: I mean the law that concedes to fays in a case similar to the one in question—which is to say, that of the exhaustion of lots—the faculty of giving another one, supplementary and exceptional, always provided that she has sufficient imagination to create it immediately.

The good fay replied, therefore, with an aplomb worthy of her rank: "I give your son…I give him…the gift of pleasing!"

"But pleasing how? Pleasing…? Pleasing why?" demanded the petty shopkeeper, stubbornly, who was doubtless one of those argumentative individuals, so common, who are incapable of elevating themselves as far as the logic of the Absurd.

"Because! Because!" replied the fay, angrily, turning her back on him; and, rejoining the procession of her companions, she said to them: "How do you like that arrogant little Frenchman, who wants to understand everything, and who, having obtained for his son the best lot of all, dares to interrogate and contest the incontestable?"

THE AFTERGLOW 1871-1914

Catulle Mendès: *The Last Fay*

One day, in a caleche made of a cob-nut shell and harnessed to four lady-birds, the fay Oriane[73]—who was no larger than the nail of a little finger—was returning to the forest of Broceliande, where she had the custom of living with her peers. She was coming back from the baptism of three robins, which had been celebrated in the hollow of a wall overgrown with wisteria; the fête had been very pleasant in the nest under the leaves; the pretty cries of the new-born birds moving their pink wings, almost devoid of down, had permitted the hope that the fay's godchildren would be excellent singers one day.

Oriane was, therefore, in a very good mood, and as joy makes one benevolent, she rendered services along the road to all the people and things she encountered, stuffing clusters of mulberries into the baskets of children going to school, blowing, in order to help them blossom, on eglantine buds, and putting oats out of the reach of dewdrops, for fear that mites might drown in them while passing through them. Two peasant lovers were embracing in a field where the green wheat scarcely came up to their ankles; she made the sheaves grow and ripen so that no one could see their kisses from the road. And as, in doing the good that joy counsels one to do, one becomes even more joyful, the fay Oriane was, at that point, so full of pleasure that, if she had not feared tipping the carriage over, she would have started to dance in the nutshell.

Soon, however, it was no longer the time to be content. Alas, what had happened? She had been quite sure of following the correct route, but there, where the forest of Broceliande had stirred in the breeze the enchanted mysteries

---

[73] The name Oriane was most familiar in France as the name of the heroine of *Amadis de Gaule*, the enormously popular French translation of the Iberian imitation of French romance *Amadis de Gaula*, where she is named Oriana; she is not an enchantress, although Urgande (Urganda), borrowed from the same text, is. The enchantress Mendès has in mind is the fay who raises the enchanter Maugis in the romances *Les Quatre fils Aymon* and *Renaud de Montauban*, whose name is more often rendered as Oriande, although it is also given as Oriane in one of Jean Lorrain's *contes*.

of its profound verdures, there was no longer anything but a vast plain, with scattered buildings, beneath a sky soiled by black smoke.

"What has become of you, green and gilded clearing where one danced by starlight, thickets of roses, bushes blooming with thorns, grottoes where slumber smiled on golden moss, in the perfumes and music, and you, subterranean palaces with walls of crystal, which a thousand chandeliers of living gems illuminate on days of celebration? What has become of you, Urgande, Urgèle, Alcine, Viviane and Holda the pagan,[74] and Melusine the charmer, and you Melandre, Ariel, and you too, Mab and Titania?"

"It's in vain that you will call them, poor Oriane," said a lizard that paused in its flight between the stones. "Humans have flooded in great number over your dear solitudes; in order that houses could be built, in order to open a passage for frightful machines breathing vapors and flames, they have felled the trees, burned the rose-thickets and thorn-bushes, filled your mysterious crystal palaces with the stones of your grottoes, and all the fays have succumbed in the disasters, beneath the collapses. I saw Habonde,[75] who was about to escape, die with a little scream under the foot of a passer-by, like a cricket one crushes."

On hearing that, Oriane began weeping bitterly over the fate of her dear companions, and over her own destiny too; for truly, it was a very melancholy thing to be the only fay left in the world.

What would she do? Where would she hide? Who would defend her against the fury of wicked humans?

The first idea that occurred to her was to flee, no longer to be in that sad place where her sisters had perished. But she could not travel by carriage, as was her custom; the four ladybirds, which she had always treated so well, having heard what the lizard said, had just taken flight, with the ingratitude of all winged creatures. That was a hard blow for the unhappy Oriane, all the more so because there was nothing she detested more than walking. She resigned herself to it, however, and set forth, taking small steps, amid grass that was taller than she was.

---

[74] *Holde la païenne* [Holda the pagan] is a character from German folklore, Frau Holle or Holda, featured in the Brothers Grimms' *märchen*. The epithet is added because Jakob Grimm claimed that the character had formerly been a Teutonic goddess, relegated to a lower status in folklore following the Christianization of the German lands. That notion is referenced more explicitly when the borrowed fay is cited again, as *Madame Holde* [Madame Holda] in "Prince Lys and the Wave of Snow."

[75] Dame Habonde, who appears in the Medieval allegory *Roman de la Rose*, is probably a derivative of the Roman goddess Abundantia, a personification of prosperity. The name is rendered as Abonde in other *contes* by Mendès, including "Prince Lys and the Wave of Snow."

She had resolved to go to the home of the robins of the wall overgrown with wisteria; the mother and father of her godchildren would not fail to give her a good welcome; their nest would be a refuge, at least until autumn.

One does not go as quickly with tiny limbs, as in a cob-nut shell drawn by the good God's flying creatures. Three long days went by before she perceived the overgrown wall; you can imagine how weary she was. But she would finally be able to rest.

"It's me," she said, as she approached, "it's me, the fay godmother; come take me, good birds, on your wings and carry me to your abode of moss."

No response; not even a little robin head emerging from the leaves to see who was there. And on widening her eyes, Oriane saw that someone had attached to the wall, in the place where the nest was, a piece of white faience, traversed by the wire of a telegraph line.

As she was going away, not knowing what would become of her, she saw a woman who was carrying in her arms a basket full of wheat and pushing the door of a barn in order to go in.

"Oh, Madame," she said, "if you keep me with you and protect me, you won't have reason to repent of it; fays, like goblins, understand better than anyone how to sort out the good grain from the nasty rye-grass and winnow it, even without a basket. Truly, you would have a very useful servant in me, who would save you a good deal of trouble."

The woman did not hear, or pretended not to hear; she pushed the door completely and threw the contents of her basket under the cylinders of a machine that winnowed the wheat without there being any need for goblins of fays.

A little further on, on the bank of a river, Oriane encountered men who were standing still around enormous bales, and there was a ship near the bank. She thought that the men did not know how to embark their merchandise.

"Oh, Messieurs," she said, "if you keep me with you and protect me, you won't have reason to repent of it. I'll summon robust gnomes to your aid, who can leap even with burdens on their shoulders; they'll soon have transported all these heavy things. Truly, you would have a very useful servant in me, who would save you a great deal of trouble."

They did not hear her, or pretended not to hear her; a huge iron hook was lowered, plunging into one of the bales, and after a half-turn in mid-air, the later settled gently on the deck of the ship, without the involvement of any gnome.

As the day wore on, the little fay saw two men through the open door of a tavern who were playing cards, leaning over a table; because of the increasing obscurity, it was becoming very difficult for them to make out the figures and the colors.

"Oh, Messieurs," she said, "if you keep me with you and protect me, you won't have reason to repent of it. I can summon to this room all the glow-worms that light up on the edges of woods; before long you'll be able to see clearly enough to continue your game with all possible pleasure. Truly, you would have a very useful servant in me, who would save you a great deal of trouble."

The gamblers did not hear her, or pretended not to hear her; one of them made a sign, and three great jets of light sprang out of three iron spikes toward the ceiling, illuminating the whole inn, much better than three thousand glow-worms could have done.

Then Oriane could not help weeping, understanding that men and women had become too knowledgeable to have any need of a little fay.

But the next day, she began to hope again. That was because of a young woman who was dreaming, leaning on her window-sill, while watching swallows in flight.

It's certain, Oriane thought, *that the people of this world have invented many extraordinary things, but in the triumph of their science and their power, that can't have renounced the eternal and sweet pleasure of amour. I've been very foolish not to have thought of that sooner.*

And, speaking to the young woman at the window, the last fay said:

"Mademoiselle, I know a young man in a distant country more beautiful than the day, whom, without your ever having seen him, you love tenderly. He isn't the son of a king or the son of a rich man, but blond curls give him a crown of gold and he holds infinite treasures of tenderness for you in his heart. If you consent, I can bring him to you before very long, and you'll be, thanks to him, the happiest person who has ever existed."

"That's a fine promise you're making me there," said the young woman, astonished.

"I'll keep it, I assure you."

"But what are you asking of me in exchange for such a service?"

"Oh, almost nothing," said the fay. "Let me curl up—I'll make myself even smaller than I am now in order not to inconvenience you—in one of the dimples that a smile puts at the corner of your mouth."

"As you please! It's a bargain."

The young woman has scarcely finished than Oriane, no large than an almost-invisible pearl, was already nestling in the pretty pink nest. Oh, how comfortable she was there! How nice it would be, always.

Now, she no longer regretted that humans had devastated the forest of Broceliande; and immediately—for she was too content to neglect to keep her word—she brought the young man more beautiful than the day from the distant country. He appeared in the room, crowned with golden curls, and knelt down before his beloved, with infinite treasures of tenderness in his heart.

But at that moment, a very ugly, aged individual appeared, with gummed-up eyes and a slack lip; he was carrying, in an open casket, a million in precious stones. The young woman ran to him, embraced him, and kissed him so passionately on the mouth that poor little Oriane died, asphyxiated, in the dimple of her smile.

Jean Lorrain: *Melusine Enchanted*

So sweetly she intoxicated gazes,
Resplendent with a purity so divine
That her people expelled her from her city.
The beautiful Melusine;
Because of her eyes, the color of aquamarine,
The roseate fires of her breast
And her beautiful red hair
Scattered over her long neck.

For a long time, far from the towns
That surrounded the ramparts,
Through the forest wandered
The beautiful Melusine;
Fearful and weeping, her brocade dress
Torn on the hawthorn thickets
And her bare feet bloodied in the thin grass
Of the clearings where roe deer grazed.

She reached the lands of enchantment thus
In the golden heaths green with holly,
And there her blue eyes saw that the wolves
Were following her in a troop
And the errant clouds and the moon,
And even the long-eared owls
Stopped in the heavens when she
Paused in the russet fields...

Raymondin de Lusignan woke up.

The little wood of ash-trees where he had gone to sleep was weeping softly in the rain, and on the mist-drowned horizon, the heathlands extended as far as the eye could see. The singing voice had fallen silent, and as far as his gaze could reach, there was silence and solitude.

For how many hours had he been sleeping in that arbor in the wild wood, and what had become of the members of his retinue? A great disturbance stirred within him, and he felt his arms and sides curiously, his temples moist with sweat, unknowingly glad of the rain.

So sweetly she intoxicated gazes,
Resplendent with a purity so divine
That her people expelled her from her city.
The beautiful Melusine...

The song pursued him, and, his fingers having encountered the ivory horn hanging from his belt, he now remembered having traversed the heath in bright sunlight, under the glare of midday. A strange torpor, an irresistible pressure, had gripped him, and he had yielded to it, since he found himself sitting here, seven hours later, in the dusk, his head bare under the downpour and his heart obsessed by a name that he had never heard before.

Melusine! Melusine! That name, so sweet that it seemed to caress the lips like lips, and intoxicate thought like a philter...

He was, however, quite alone; there was no one in the ten leagues of gorse and fleeting heather, gray in the rain, extending to the hills that closed the horizon, but the song was still buzzing in his ears, the song and the musical voice that was singing it.

At that moment, with an abrupt flutter of wings, a rook flew over his head, and Lusignan then remembered a little old woman, ragged and wrinkled, encountered gathering dry branches from the mossy feet of the ash-trees, at the moment that he had entered the wood.

An old crone at midday, a rook at dusk!

Lusignan, a great hunter of wolves and killer of wild boar, knew exactly how to recite in Latin an *Ave* and a *Pater*; he pronounced them at that moment, suspecting in his long sleep some entrapment of the fays. Do legends not make them dance by night in the violently scented air of the heather and the gorse, as in the moonlit mists of ponds?

And, having signed himself three times, the Comte got to his feet, shook the residual rain from his crimson cloak with a shrug of the shoulders, and, taking his bearings from the last gleams of the setting sun, strode straight ahead through the heather in the direction of his burg.

"And the jealous fays have changed her into a serpent; her imperious beauty, which charmed the birds in the sky and the errant beasts in the woods, frightens the solitudes today.

"Transformed into a monstrous hydra, she sleeps all day in the sun, coiled up in the russet grass of the heath; by night she crawls sadly over the pebbles of dry stream-beds silvered by the moonlight, and her regretful hissing awakens echoes from ravine to ravine.

"Where is that? Far away and close at hand, here and there, in the land of the fays, who watch over their prisoner invisibly, in the golden heaths, made verdant by the holly, which you have traversed a hundred times without suspecting the malign ladies laughing in the brushwood, sitting around you in a circle.

"In the land of the fays, where the ensorcelled hydra has been waiting for a hundred years for the bold knight who, gripping her head in both hands, will dare to kiss her viscous lips, where death resides.

"The jealous fays have changed her into a serpent; her imperious beauty, which charmed the birds in the sky and the errant beasts in the woods, frightens the solitudes today.

"Only the lips of a man can break the enchantment, but for the promised hero, the hydra is still waiting. When, in the russet heather, overwhelmed by the heat, will the lethargic serpent rear up on her tail, hissing, to be gripped around the neck by her liberator? When will the virgin, finally liberated, spring forth, as naked as a pearl and as white as foam, from the scales of the monster?

"The charm is in the beauty that slumbers, captive in the squamous and noisy sheath of the hydra; deliverance is in the kiss of the hero with a soul sufficiently tempered to drink the poison and confront death.

"To him the power and numerous lineage, to him fortune and renown; he will found a heroic and princely house."

And the voice died away, as if stifled by the thickness of the wall. Raymondin, who was asleep, his arms crossed over his breast, in the big oak bed blazoned with his arms, raised himself up on his elbow, moist with sweat. That voice of dream had not pronounced a name, and yet a conviction gripped him that the song was speaking of Melusine, Melusine still and Melusine forever. He pricked up his ears and, thinking that he could hear voices whispering under the window, he got up, ran barefoot over the tiles to the narrow casement overlooking the open country, and opened the frame. Outside, dawn had scarcely broken: a wan, cold dawn of the end of October, a shroud of mist floating over the valley, reminiscent of a sea of vapors, with a few hilltops emerging here and there, half-shadowed.

And Lusignan, having leaned out, perceived a kind of beggar standing in the mist, at the foot of the seigneurial keep, with his beard and hair braided like that of bohemians. With copper loops in his ears, draped in a mantle of broad-striped fabric, he was leaning on a staff and, his eyes sparkling under bushy eyebrows, he was muttering, his mouth fill of confused words, and seemed by his gestures to be negotiating with soldiers that he, Lusignan, could not see, but assumed to be the guards at the postern.

Lusignan called out and ordered that the old man should be brought to him straight away. His squire came back almost immediately, head bowed; he had not seen anyone at the foot of the keep. Monseigneur must have been the victim of some dream; the sentinel on duty at the postern of the burg had not seen anyone at all since the previous evening.

Chagrined, Raymondin returned to the window. The equivocal beggar with the braided beard was no longer there; a vision of the early morning, he had vanished into the mist.

It was then that the mild lord fell into a profound melancholy.

From that day on, everything that had interested him before—the handling of arms, shooting with the bow, jousting with the lance, and even the pleasures of the hunt, whether hunting with falcons in the meadows or beating the profound forests for deer and wild boars, everything that had once been the joy of his life, suddenly ceased to occupy him.

He wandered all day long, depressed and dismal, through the countryside, inattentive to the footfalls of his mare, letting her wander at random through the brushwood and the crops, more like a phantom riding, in expiation, some beast of dream than an honest and loyal knight.

In the evenings he returned, harassed, and sat down without unsealing his lips at the seigneurial table, where he no longer listened to the chaplain's *Benedictus*. On Sundays, he scarcely went to church. He was no longer able either to kneel, or to sit down, and his friends no longer recognized him. He became thin, haggard and pale, and let his hair and beard grow; they spilled out beneath his helmet, dusty and bushy. By night, he got up with a start, to stride, in the wind and the rain, along the round-path of the ramparts. One might have thought that he was listening to voices, and the sentinels feared seeing him pass close by at midnight, muttering confused words. In the vicinity, the opinion was affirmed that bohemians had cast a spell on him.

A year from then, on a sultry day in August, as he was coming back at dusk from one of the distant aimless excursions with which he now consumed his life, his mare, whose bridle he had allowed to rest on her neck, as usual, made an abrupt somersault, which woke him from his torpor. He stood up in the saddle and opened his eyes wide.

A few paces in front of him, in the vast bare plain, three women—or, rather, three female forms—were agitating, seemingly dancing around a great fire of dry grass. With the look of old beggar-women clad in singularly luminous rags, they were shaking thin bare arms frenetically above the flames, and with burst of wild laughter, which were not so much audible as divined by the contortions of their bodies, they were whirling in the smoke, as if transparent, even brighter than the atmosphere of the bright summer's day, the color of amber against the inflamed redness of the evening.

They pronounced his name three times, and evaporated in the air—and Lusignan thought about the little old lady in the ash-wood, and then the bohemian beggar glimpsed at dawn at the postern of the burg.

But who was the third? For he had certainly recognized the other two, but what he did not recognize and was frightened not to be able to recognize, was the locality into which his mare had brought him. Those undulations of the terrain, those meager trees at ground level and that chain of mountains on the horizon were unknown to him.

A great sadness gripped him in that hostile solitude. He was no longer in the immense plain of a little while before; he had before him an uncultivated and ravined heath, florid with dwarf thistles and tall flowering mallows, with the debris of a temple scattered here and there, and stumps of columns strewing the terrain. And although there was not a breath of wind in the air, the faded rosy mallows and the hostile thistles quivered sadly under a red and green sky: the red of blood and the green of wounds.

He urged his mount forward but this time, his mare refused to obey, and Lusignan, having leaned forward to see the obstacle, perceived the serpent at her feet.

Gold-speckled green in hue, which became blue underneath, the hydra was asleep, coiled up on a bed of dry laves; its triangular and fabulously small head was agape, showing in its black maw a triple row of sharp teeth, and six heavy necklaces of precious stones embraced it at intervals, to indicate that it was of royal birth. Its head reposed on a large crimson lily, and Lusignan, having dismounted and attached his mare to a nearby cypress, approached it stealthily.

Abruptly, he seized the serpent by the head, and lifted it with all the strength of his arms to the level of his lips, and, in spite of his disgust, applied his mouth to the mouth of the monster.

Suddenly awakened, with a shrill hiss, the hydra had coiled itself furiously around the gentle lord. It had enlaced the man, and was crushing his ribs with all the weight of its rings; it held his feet tight with its tail, and froze his abdomen with the cold of its scales.

And under the frightful embrace, and the forked tongue that darted forth menacingly, the oppressed warrior fainted; and, frozen, drank with avid lips the drool and venom of the monster. He drank them three times.

Then, through the solitude, the high mallows rustled madly, and the thistles ignited with a metallic gleam. With a long, long cry, the liberated virgin had surged naked from the hideous envelope and thrown her arms around the neck of her conqueror; then, suddenly, she had lowered her eyes, her large eyes the color of shadow, and became entirely pink, roseate from the toenails of her naked feet to the fresh eglantine of her breasts.

Melusine was ashamed, seeing that she had no garment.

Lusignan then threw his warrior's mantle over the splendid nudity of the virgin and, kissing her pouting lips, sat her on the rump behind him. The mare whinnied, and, vibrant with desire, his heart inundated with delight, the proud lord carried his blushing prey away through the pink heather of the landscape that had become familiar once again.

In the brushwood, the voices of the fays sang: "To Lusignan power and a numerous lineage! To Lusignan a warrior and royal house!"

The sun, completely set, had disappeared from the horizon, but one last oblique ray illuminated, like a golden dot, the russet hair of Melusine, going on the rump behind her master to found the race of the Lusignans.

Catulle Mendès: *Prince Lys and the Wave of Snow*

I do not have a clear memory of whether I have taken the tale I am about to tell from the legend of Saint Armentarius, where mention is made, as early as the year 1300, of a Provençal fay named Esterelle—the same one, no doubt, who put all the gifts of poetry and charm into the cradle of our dear Paul Arène[76]—or whether it has stuck in my memory for having once read Olaüs Magnus, who was a very savant historian of fades and formosas, of which, in his day, there was a great multitude in Sweden.[77] It might also be the case that I had invented the story.

Imagination or memory, I cannot help being moved, not only by compassion for Prince Lys but by a personal sadness, and you will be moved in the same way, for is not his adventure still our adventure too? But for us, it does not end so happily...

Here is the tale:

There was once, in kingdom in the North, all white with snow and all luminous with frost, a young prince who was known as Prince Lys because he was whiter than the purest of the country's snows, and also because he had in the face the impression of a strangely candid soul. Although he had attained twenty years of age with the first snowflakes of last winter, he did not want to hear any mention whatsoever of marriage. It served no purpose to show him the portraits of the most beautiful princesses of the earth; he did not deign to cast his eyes upon them, to the great chagrin of the king and the queen, whose only child he was, and who were naturally very desirous of seeing their lineage continued.

The ladies and damsels of the court were also in the greatest melancholy for, more handsome than it is possible to say—as handsome as young Esplandian was when he appeared in white armor of Oriane's island—he had no

---

[76] The Provençal poet Paul Arène (1843-1896) published "Deux légendes de la mer," which mentions the fays Esterelle and Morgane in the literary supplement of *L'Écho de Paris*, of which Mendès was the editor, on 13 March 1892.

[77] *Historia de Gentibus Septentrionalibus* [A Description of the Northern People (1555; French version 1561) by the Swedish Catholic clergyman Olaüs Magnus was a patriotic work that is the source text of much information about Scandinavian folklore, including stories of sea-nymphs, although he does not use the exotic terms *fade* and *formose* [formosa], here recruited by Mendès to refer to supernatural creatures. *Fade* appears in the English romance of *Gawain and the Green Knight*, apparently as an English equivalent of *fée*. *Formose* is derived from the Latin, meaning "beautiful"

less coldness toward them than toward the daughters of foreign sovereigns. If by chance, at some fête he passed between the double row of marquises and countesses, he hastened as much as he could, not without an air of disdain, or, when etiquette obliged him to walk less rapidly, he kept his eyes lowered toward the carpet, as if to avoid seeing the shoulders and cleavages of so many beautiful women in low-cut dresses.

The most common opinion was that Prince Lys was the victim of an enchantment. Yes, a spell must have been cast upon him. But who had done that? On the day of his first smile in his royal cradle, his parents, as was the custom in those days in that country, had not failed to invite all the most powerful fays. Urgèle had come in her robe the color of jasmine spangled with silver, so that she seemed to be wearing a fragment of the Milky Way; Abonde had come, clad in golden convolvulus, with a bee tintinnabulating in every flower; and Mélusine, who, for having been a serpent, leaves behind the fugitive gleams of narrow and supple garments; and Titania, very small, all around whom flew ribbons of pearl and chrysolith, and whose train was carried by a fat man with an ass's head braying amorously, as comically as possible.

The last to come, but not the least radiant, was one who does not always deign to come to the celebration of royal births, Madame Holda, a little less pouty for having been made into a goddess, but so marvelously beautiful, and, in addition to her lunar or auroral satin robe, allowing the sight of a breast more miraculously sublime that the one that made the old men marvel when the Argienne appeared on the rampart with a lily in her hand. Madame Holda was particularly amiable toward the newborn prince; as he was waking up from his first slumber, she took him in her arms, and cradled him momentarily over that adorable breast...[78]

Truly, the child who had had such powerful and radiant godmothers ought not to have had to fear either enchantments or spells,

However, the young prince because increasingly antisocial. He did not want even the portraits of princesses to be shown to him; he no longer consented to appear at court. As soon as no one was looking, he escaped from the palace, and his sole joy was to wander all alone in the whiteness of the Northern country.

Prince Lys often remained motionless for entire hours, his gaze and his arms raised toward some snowy mountain, whose summit, in the evening, was gilded by a star, or, in the morning, tinted roseate by the dawn—and slowly, tears ran from his eyes toward the ecstatic smile of his mouth. Then he resumed

---

[78] Argiennes (female inhabitants of Argos) were said in some Classical documents to have special privileges with regard to the temple of Hera; the specific reference here is to a poem by Mendès, "Ballade de l'amant fidèle" which invokes the appearance of one with a symbolic lily in hand to frighten white-haired old men.

his route, the road of Dreams, which goes no one knows where; and he staggered as he walked, like a man carrying an excessively heavy burden.

At other times, in some path scintillating with frost, he picked one of the flowers, so white, that are known as snowdrops, and he kissed it for a long, long time with bewildered lips...

But then he shook his head, dropped the flower, and sighed profoundly, his head between his hands.

Sometimes, too, with untrodden snow taken from the slope of a hill, he tried to make between his hands a roundness of splendor and candor, but he doubtless did not find it splendid enough or candid enough, for he let the snow fall from his fingers, and sobbed desperately...

One day, he went much further than usual. He had traversed plains and climbed mountains and, from the height of a rock, he saw the sea in the distance, bristling with icebergs, where the iridescent daylight was dazzling, and much closer, so soft, so purely profound, slowly fading away in delectable swellings, the sea that had once given birth to Venus, now named Holda, the goddess become a fay, as beautiful and mysterious as itself.

But the waves, in that country, because of the reflection of the snows, which add further whiteness to the whiteness of the foam, swell more delectably than toward any other shore. And Prince Lys experienced a joy unknown until that day, the never-realized presentiment of which had caused him, after cruel hopes, so many torturing disappointments...

One wave, in particular, enchanted and attracted him, rising so exquisitely, so round, so smooth, so white so reminiscent of...he knew not what.

And, his arms forward, he slid deliciously toward the wave, the wave similar to Madame Holda's breast...

Frédéric Boutet: *The Valley Named Solitude*

I shall give you
The magic opal and the gold ring
And what is worth more than glory or fortune,
My robe woven with moonlight.
Leconte de Lisle, "*The Elves.*"

A summer night, warm and moonlit.

The valley is slumbering in Solitude. And in the primitive majesty, the hills, covered with woods, hold up their immemorial peaks to the heavens.

To the west, a torrent surges from an elevated gorge, tumbling down the mountain-side. Framed by hanging draperies of ivy, singing with its harmonious voice, the stream runs over the shiny rocks and rebounds in crystal spray and vaporous foam. Masses of vegetation emerge and, seemingly floating in the middle of the water, mingle there in long filaments, which descend all the way to the lake bathing the foot of the hill.

The lake is sparkling with silver, thanks to the indolent waves softly agitating the rushes and water-lilies girdling the waves. Toward the middle, pale lacustrian plants extend their corollas, in soft or violent hues, and their fleshy leaves. The banks are fresh grass speckled with asphodels. Large trees shade the base of the mountain,

The most beautiful flowers grow in multitudes in the valley, where woods of myrtle and ebony mingle with holm-oaks, whose old mossy trunks welcome virgin vines, honeysuckle, jasmine and wild roses. Great white rocks loom up in the clearings, along with grass banks that are reminiscent of altars or tombs. No animate being appears to inhabit the valley.

The full moon, bathing the valley with its magical light, adds a romantic prestige to everything. On their obscure slopes, the high hills conceal mysteries and apparitions; white vapors visit the profound and woods and linger in the shadows cut out on the water; at a distance, the flowers seem as far away as the nebulous stars, swaying the harmony of their embalmed heads; the reeds stirring in the silvery undulation of the lake seem to be listening to distant voices responding to the voice of the cascade, which is expanding into the silence and vibrating languorously.

And in the enchanted purity, Night reigns over the Solitude.

Now, two human creatures appear, emerging from the wood: a man and a woman. They are young, walking side by side, wearing cotton tunics.

Beneath her black hair, covered by a white veil, the woman's face seems possessed of a passionate, troubling and triumphant beauty. With her large blue eyes she contemplates the valley, and sometimes glances at her companion, who remains taciturn.

Both move toward the lake. They stop by the cascade, on the grassy bank where the waves die indolently at their feet.

After a moment, the man, extending his arm, calls three times to the Fay whose name is Solitude, or Chimera, but whom no one knows.

And the face of the Fay rises from the lake. She looms up in the midst of the flowers, in the middle of the waters, which seem to form transparent draperies, as light as rays of moonlight, streaming with iridescent pearls, dressing her with long pleats. Heavy tresses, glaucous and amber, fall over her shoulders. Her eyes, luminous and changing, are like the sky or the sea. Her smiling mouth is melancholy. Above her forehead, large droplets form a crown, scintillating like diamonds, while others form a necklace at her throat and bracelets round her bare arms. And the beauty of the Fay spreads invincible charms, and there seems to be an indefinable allusion within her to the beauty of the young woman who is contemplating her, standing on the banks where asphodels flower.

The man's eyes are lowered, and he stands there silent and tremulous. Finally, his voice rises up, hesitantly, in the harmonious music of the cascade.

"Solitude," he says, "Chimera, Unreality, whatever your name is, whom I have loved uniquely in the past, I am abandoning you because I want to give myself, with no return, to the woman beside me—to this woman, love for whom has arisen before my disgust for the real world to make me adore everything real in her person. She has entrapped me with light bonds stronger than any chain. Her smile is now my life, her body is my universe, and I am the slave of her eyes.

"Adieu, you who are the multiple, adorable and deceitful soul of the valley named Solitude! Adieu. My hours will no longer be your hours. Charms stronger than yours have enchanted me, for living lips have educated me in love..."

He falls silent.

The Fay cries: "You want to leave me, then, for a woman! Have you lost the memory of dreams in which I have cradled you for so many nights, the immense joys that you have known in me and the marvels I have created for your pleasure? With me, you have possessed all things by means of thought, and is that not the true possession? Have I not given you all splendors and all voluptuousness? We have built magical palaces in the sumptuous domains of our caprice. In the gardens of our fantasies we have extended rivers and lakes beneath the setting sun, magic mirrors through which our visions have passed. We have made the most beautiful flowers grow, more perfumed than the flowers of the earth, and the breeze has engendered heady religious effluvia and unforgettable harmonies in the embalmed branches.

"Our dreams have sailed over seas of amethyst, emerald and topaz, beneath skies of unknown purity, beneath clouds as pompous as fêtes. We have, for ourselves alone, brought all centuries, all civilizations and all barbarisms, to life again. Every city and every nation of times past and present has offered itself to us, without ever causing us to know disillusionment, since its decor reproduces our very dreams.

"You have known all glories and all triumphs. You have been an invincible conqueror, made peoples tremble with the hoof-beats of your horse. You have been a philosopher and a scholar; masters of science throughout the world have bowed down before your genius. You have been an artist whose divine works were adored by generations. You have possessed perfect beauty allied with irresistible force and universal intelligence!

What women have I refused you? Empresses celebrated for their charm, the priestesses of every cult, the most famous courtesans, all women, in their various beauty, have been delivered in turn to you with passion, with terror and with pride, in accordance with your caprice. You have descended the tenebrous roads of vice, horror and blood. You have known corruption, theft, murder and sacrilege. You have known the proud abasement of supreme debauches and the delights of cowardly ferocities. You have enjoyed tears that you have caused to flow. You have enjoyed supplications and impotent rages, broken by your will!

"Have you not lived all lives, savored the bitterness and charm of all joys and all misfortunes, all strengths and all weaknesses? Have you not possessed all human things completely, and have you not raised your proud desire toward things that are not of the earth, toward unknown paradises, supreme delights?

"Come back—you do not know what earthly loves are, in which sensuality engenders dolor and death!

"Come back, come back—I have the secret of every dream, the key to every door, and my kiss is immortal..."

Thus speaks the Fay—but the rival voice of the living woman rises up and replies to her: "No, you're not immortal, and you're not anything at all. In you there's nothing true, and the joys you invoke are not your own. You see them in the distance and cannot attain them...as water flees the thirst of the damned. In vain you try to entice them, in vain you strive in exhausting struggle; your imposture cannot deceive entirely, and your voice is false, to which you provide the reply yourself...

"A man cannot believe you, he cannot love you; you have prostituted, in your impotence, the very identity of his desire, to which you have given birth without satisfying it, of which you are the reflection without ever being the image.

"You are within him, and too much within him. He lacks in you the unforeseen that is present in others, which is the personal soul of a living creature whose will, taste and desire, acting out of free choice, gives the pride and joy of having been chosen.

"You are an automatic figure, whose mechanism always acts in the same way. Like the actor of an overly familiar play, you know the intrigue before it is knotted, and the vain simulacrum of the anticipated denouement, only suggesting the joy that it would give if everything were sincere. And your kisses give themselves to the void, and your arms open to embrace a fugitive shadow...

"That is the Paradise you promise to your lovers. It is by means of that bait of lies that you want to vanquish me, who is soul and flesh—who possesses, for the enjoyment of pensive tenderness, the enigmatic profundity of my eyes, the mysterious softness of my passionate words and the expression of love that extends over my beauty, like the caress of a spring evening over a garden; who possesses, for sensual pleasure, the irresistible attractions of my naked flesh, the transport of my embrace and the intoxication of my kiss...

"I am the dream and the reality; I am the divine flower that is uniquely capable of intoxicating the body and the mind! I am the One who is stronger than the World! And all joys without me are nothing, and all misfortunes with me are nothing. A single one of my loving glances can send the bitterest dolor to sleep, and render all pride and enjoyment to my lover, in disdain for those who are not loved.

"When a man drowns his eyes in mine, he forgets earth and heaven; when my lips are on his lips, he faints, scorning everything else; when voluptuousness turns him upside-down on my quivering breast, from which perfumes of love rise, I am his triumph and his God!

"Don't try to fight me; I abandon to you those of whom cruel destiny has made objects of horror, disgust and pity, and who only have your exaltations to deceive the desires of their flesh that real kisses will never calm. They are granted to you in advance and no one will compete with you for them, but my lover, in his youth and beauty, is not destined to that puerile pursuit of an ungraspable mirage. He was created for sincere embraces, for living caresses, for all the seductions of human passion! I love him and he loves me, and for our marvelous amours the days and nights unfurl their enchanted future..."

She has seized her lover's hand, and gazes proudly at the Fay named Solitude or Chimera, but who is unknown. Now the poignant voice of the Fay rises up again, to the accompaniment of the rhythmic resonance of the water.

"Oh," she said, "your reproach is unjust! The soul of a man cannot be content with the world; it always seeks the impossible here. Borne by my wings, with me, the Chimera, it launches toward the great sky, where its dreams search madly for their incarnation...

"A man soars into the sky with me, his Chimera...and if he is able to give himself to me completely, I envelop him with unparalleled joys. If he does not ask himself whether he is dreaming or not, the dream will not deceive him and will give his mind unequaled voluptuousness, and even give him voluptuousness in the flesh. However, the majority cannot; they want to attach me to the earth and search around them for the realization of that which cannot be realized.

656

"It is the cruel dementia of this man that wants to abandon me; that is his damnation, for what he loves in you, poor creature whose attractions will wither tomorrow, what he loves unconsciously in you, is me: the Fay named Chimera. With his dreams, his hopes and his sense of beauty he has woven a magical cloak of seduction and harmony, which he has thrown over you. As he has made up the appearances of your body cosmetically, with his illusions, he has fashioned another soul for you, a companion of his own soul. He has created you in the image of his desire, and has so much desire that you should be thus that he truly believes that you are...

"What he loves in you is the reflection of his dreams of me! You are the road guiding him toward the goal, you are the opium that procures intoxication, but you are not the goal and you are not the intoxication; you are merely the mask of the phantom he adores, which he embraces recklessly upon your lips, to which he addresses his passionate plaints and all the delirious ardors of his soul: the redoubtable phantom that makes you shiver when you see its shadow passing in your lover's eyes; the phantom that, on earth, is known as the Ideal.

"O Ideal, eternal enemy, eternal benefactor, it is for you that the prodigious efforts are accomplished of solitary martyrs, the destined suffers of torment whose Hell and redemption you are. It is because of you that the happiness attained is poisoned by disillusionment and the worst dolors are soothed. It is because of you that there are supplicant triumphs and agonies full of ecstasy, for you are glory and misfortune, and the true God!

"Be careful, O Daughter of Men, for I tell you this: it is the Ideal that your lover always thinks that he has found in you, and will find until the moment he sees you for what you are: an imperfect human creature a thousand times inferior to his dream. Then he will weep all the tears of dolor and shame, and you will suffer a distress more atrocious than any other, for he will scorn you, and that will be unjust...

"And in the reality that you possess, the horizons of the dream will be effaced forever, definitively, and you will be condemned to veritable life, to the horror of monotonous days of bitterness and hatred, to the intolerable unhappiness of having lost faith in the Chimera...and that is the unavoidable Future."

The young woman, leaning toward her lover, smiles, and, plunging her eyes into his, intoxicates him with her breath, which has the scent of jasmine, murmurs: "Come, my love, it's the nuptial hour; the night is enchanted and I am mad with love. Come—our first kiss will give us the Ideal

They both quit the bank where the waves died near the asphodels, going toward the woods of flowering myrtles, toward voluptuousness, toward real life...

They walk, enlaced together, madly in love, without seeing the tenacious shadows that attach themselves to their heels: the shadows named Disillusionment, Lassitude and Disgust; those named Jealousy, Deception and Hatred; and without seeing, in front of them, seizing each of their seconds in order to make it the prey of the past, the hideous Old Age that oppresses, ever more cruelly, and the fear of Death.

And the Fay named Solitude, named Chimera, but who is unknown, remains in the middle of the waters, weeping crystal tears, raising her bare, writhing arms toward the heavens, as if to implore or curse the enchanted Moon.

Anatole France: *The Story of the Duchesse de Cicogne and Monsieur de Boulingrin, Who Slept For a Hundred Years in the Company of the Beauty in the Dormant Wood*

I

The history of the Beauty in the Dormant Wood is well known; there are excellent versions of it in verse and prose. I shall not attempt to tell it again; but, having had the communication of several memoirs of the period that have remained unpublished, I have found anecdotes relative to King Cloche and Queen Satine, whose daughter slept for a hundred years, as well as various members of the court who shared the slumber of the princess. I propose to communicate to the public what appears to me to be the most interesting of these revelations.

After several years of marriage, Queen Satine gave her husband, the king, a daughter who received the names Paule-Marie-Aurore. The baptismal celebrations were arranged by the Duc des Hoisons, the grand master of ceremonies, in accordance with a formula that dated back to the Emperor Honorius, and in which nothing could be deciphered, so mildewed was it, and gnawed by rats.

There were still fays in those times, and those who were titled came to court. Seven of them were asked to be godmothers: Queen Titania; Queen Mab; the sage Viviane, educated by Merlin in the art of enchantments; Melusine, whose story Jean d'Arras wrote and who became a snake every Saturday—but the baptism was held on a Sunday; Urgèle; the white Anna de Bretagne; and Mourgue, who brought Ogier the Dane into the land of Avalon.

They appeared at the château in robes the color of time, of the sun, of the moon, and nymphs, all sparkling with diamonds and pearls. As each one took her place at the table, an old fay by the name of Alcuine was seen to enter, who had not been invited.

"Don't be annoyed, Madame," the king said to her, "by not being among the persons invited to this celebration; you were thought to be enchanted or dead."

Fays doubtless died, since they grew old. They all ended up by dying, and everyone knows that Melusine became a scullion in Hell. By an effect of enchantment, they could be imprisoned in a magic circle, in a tree, in a bush, in a stone, or changed into a statue, a hind, a dove, a stool, a ring or a slipper. In reality, however, it was not because she was thought to be enchanted or dead that the fay Alcuine had not been invited; it was because her presence at the banquet had been judged contrary to etiquette. Madame de Maintenon was once able to say without the slightest exaggeration, that "there are no austerities in convents as stern as those to which etiquette subjects the noble." In conformity with the royal will of his sovereign, the Duc des Hoisons, the grand master of ceremonies, had refused to invite the fay Alcuine, who lacked a quarter of nobility necessary to be admitted to the court. To the ministers of the state who protested that it was of great importance to assuage that powerful and vindictive fay, of whom a dangerous enemy was made by excluding her from celebrations, the king had replied peremptorily that he would not invite her since she had no birth.

That monarch, even more unfortunate than his predecessors, was a slave to etiquette. His obstinacy in subordinating the greatest interests and the most pressing duties to the slightest duties of an obsolete ceremonial had caused the monarchy grave damage on more than one occasion and caused the realm to run redoubtable perils. Of all those perils and all that damage, those to which Cloche exposed his house by refusing to bend etiquette in favor of a fay without birth, but illustrious and redoubtable, were neither the most difficult to foresee not the most urgent to avoid.

Old Alcuine, enraged by the scorn she had endured, gave Princess Aurore a deadly gift. At fifteen years of age, as beautiful as the daylight, that royal child was to die of a fatal wound caused by a spindle, an innocent weapon in the hands of mortal women but terrible when the three spinning Sisters twist and wind around it the thread of our destinies and the fibers of our hearts.

The seven fay godmothers were able to soften Alcuine's edict but not abolish it, and the fate of the princess was thus determined: "Aurore will pierce her hand with a spindle; she will not die, but she will fall into a slumber of a hundred years, from which the son of a king will come to awaken her."

II

Currite ducentes subtermina, currite, fusi
Catullus[79]

With regard to the sentence that struck the princess in her cradle, the king and the queen interrogated anxiously all persons of knowledge and good sense, including Monsieur Gerberoy, the permanent secretary of The Academy of Sciences and Doctor Gastinet, the queen's obstetrician.

"Can one sleep for a hundred years, Monsieur Gerberoy?" asked Satine.

"Madame," the academician replied, "We have examples of more or less long slumbers, of which I will cite a few to Your Majesty. Epimenides of Cnossos was born of the amours of a mortal and a nymph. While still a child, he was

---

[79] The quotation is an oft-repeated refrain in a section of a poem representing the predictions of the three Fates regarding the wedding of Thetis and Peleus. An approximate translation would be "Run on, draw the thread; run on, spindles."

sent by Dosiades, his father, to guard the flocks on the mountain. When the ardors of midday scorched the earth, he lay down in a dark and cool grotto and went to sleep for fifty-seven years. He studied the virtue of plants and died at a hundred and fifty-four, according to some, two hundred and eighty-nine, according to others.

"The story of the seven sleepers of Ephesus is reported by Theodorus and Rufinus in a document sealed by two silver seals. Here are the principal facts, rapidly exposed. In the year 250 A.D., seven officers of the Emperor Decius who had embraced the Christian religion, having distributed their possessions to the poor, took refuge on Mount Celion, and all seven went to sleep in a cavern. Under the reign of Theodosius II, the bishop of Ephesus, they were found to be as bright as roses. They had slept there for a hundred and forty-four years.

"Frederick Barbarossa is still asleep. In a crypt under the ruins of a castle, in the middle of a dense forest, he is sitting at a table of which his beard makes the tour seven times. He will wake up to chase away the crowd that croak around the mountain.

"Those, Madame, are the greatest sleepers of whom history has conserved the memory."

"They're exceptions," replied the queen. You, Monsieur Gastonet, who practice medicine, have you seen people sleep for a hundred years?"

"Madame," replied the obstetrician, "I have never exactly seen it, and do not expect ever to see it, but I have observed curious cases of lethargy that I can, if she desires, bring to the acquaintance of Your Majesty. Ten years ago, a demoiselle Jeanne Caillou, received at the Hôtel-Dieu, slept there for six consecutive years. I have observed myself the young woman Léonide Montauciel, who went to sleep on Easter day of year 61 only to awake on Easter day of the following year."[80]

Monsieur Gastinet," asked the king, "Can the point of a spindle inflict a wound that causes someone to sleep for a hundred years?"

"It isn't probable, Sire," replied Monsieur Gastinet, "but in the domain of pathology, we can never say anything, with assurance: *this can happen, that cannot happen.*"

"One can cite Brunhild," said Monsieur Gerberoy, "Who, pricked by a thorn, fell asleep and was awoken by Sigurd."

"There is also Guenillon," said Madame la Duchesse de Cicogne, the queen's first lady-in-waiting."

And she sang:

He sent me to the wood
To pick hazelnuts.

---

[80] Although the legendary sleepers cited are all drawn from actual sources, these examples seem to have been invented.

The wood was too high,
The beauty too small.

The wood was too high,
The beauty too small.
She stuck in her hand
A very green thorn.

She stuck in her hand
A very green thorn.
At the pain in her finger
The beauty fell asleep...[81]

"What are you thinking, Cicogne?" said the queen. "You're singing!"

"Pardon me, Your Majesty," the duchesse replied. "It's to ward off the spell."

The king had an edict published by which he forbade anyone to spin with a spindle or to have spindles about their person, on pain of death. Everyone obeyed. It was still said in the country that "the spindle must follow the mattock," but that was out of habit. The spindle had had its day.

III

Like all great statesmen, the Prime Minister who governed the monarchy under the feeble King Cloche, Monsieur de La Rochecoupée, respected popular beliefs, Caesar was pontiff maximus, Napoléon had himself blessed by the Pope; Monsieur de La Rochecoupée recognized the power of the fays. He was not a skeptic, he was not incredulous. He did not argue the falsity of the oracle of the seven godmothers, but, not being able to do anything about it, he did not worry about it. It was his character not to worry about evils unless he was able to remedy them.

In any case, the announced event was not imminent, according to all appearances. Monsieur de La Rochecoupée had the views of a Statesmen, and Statesmen never see beyond the present moment. I am speaking of the most perspicacious and the most penetrating. In any case to suppose that the king's daughter would one day fall asleep for a century, was, in his eyes, only a family matter, since the Salic law excluded women from the throne. He had, as he put

---

[81] These lines are adapted from a much longer song published in Jérôme Bujeaud's *Chants et chansons populaires des provinces de l'ouest* (1866), which were widely reprinted thereafter and seemingly first linked to the Perrault tale on which the present story is based by Frédéric Dillaye in 1880, although whether or not the song predates Perrault is a matter of conjecture.

it, other cats to skin. Bankruptcy was there, hideous bankruptcy, threatening to consume the wealth and the honor of the nation. Famine was rife in the realm and millions of poor people were eating plaster instead of bread. That year the Opéra Ball was very brilliant, and the masks more beautiful than usual.

The peasants, the artisans, the shopkeepers and the daughters of the theater were deeply afflicted by the fatal malediction that Alcuine had put on the innocent princess. By contrast, the aristocrats of the court and the princes of the royal blood showed themselves to be quite indifferent. And there were businessmen and men of science everywhere who did not believe in the fays' sentence for the reason that they did not believe in fays.

One of those was Monsieur de Boulingrin, the Secretary of State for Finance. Those who asked him how he could not believe in them, since he had seen them, did not know how far skepticism can go in a rational mind. Nourished on Lucretius, imbued with the doctrines of Epicurus and Gassendi, he often made Monsieur de La Rochecoupée impatient by means of the display of a cold atheism.

"If not for yourself, be a believer for the public," the Prime Minister said to him. "But in truth, there are moments when I ask myself, my dear Boulingrin, which of us is the more credulous with regard to the fays. I never think about them and you're always talking about them."

Monsieur de Boulingrin was in love with Madame la Duchesse de Cicogne, the wife of the ambassador in Vienna and the queen's first lady-in-waiting, who belonged to the highest aristocracy in the realm, a woman of intelligence, slightly stiff and slightly stingy, who lost her income, her lands and her shirt at pharaoh.[82] She had a certain generosity toward Monsieur de Boulingrin, and did not refuse him a commerce to which she was not borne by temperament, but which she deemed appropriate to her rank and useful to her interests. Their liaison was formed with an artistry that revealed her good taste and the elegance of prevailing mores; the liaison was admitted, stripped by its admission of any base hypocrisy, and showing itself at the same time to be so reserved that even the most severe saw nothing in it to criticize.

During the time that the duchesse spent in her estates every year, Monsieur de Boulingrin lodged in an old dovecot separated from his lover's château by a sunken road that ran alongside a pond where the frogs launched their assiduous cries from the rushes by night.

One evening, while the last reflections of the sunlight were tinting the stagnant water the color of blood, the Secretary of State for Finance saw three young fays at the crossroads dancing in a round and singing:

---

[82] The card game "pharaoh" is more often called faro in America, where it became very popular in the nineteenth century.

Three girls in a meadow
My heart steals,
My heart steals,
My heart steals at your whim.[83]

They enclosed him in their round, and agitated their slender and light forms around him rapidly. In the twilight, their faces were obscure and limpid; their hair shone like fire follets.

They repeated

Three girls in a meadow

so often that, stunned and ready to fall, he asked for mercy.

Then the most beautiful, opening the round, said: "My sisters, give leave to Monsieur de Boulingrin, who is going to the château to kiss his beauty."

He passed on without recognizing the fays, mistresses of his destiny, and a few paces further on, he encountered three old beggar-women who were walking curbed over their staffs, their faces resembling three apples cooked in the ashes. Bones covered with more dirt than flesh stuck out of their rags. Their bare feet extended immeasurably in fleshless toes, similar to the vertebrae of an ox-tail.

As soon as they perceived him they smiled at him and blew him kisses; they stopped him as he went past, calling him their darling, their beloved, their dear heart, covering him with caresses that he could not escape, for, at the first movement that he made to flee, they sank the sharp talons that terminated their hands into his flesh.

"How handsome he is! How pretty he is!" they sighed.

With a long frenzy, they solicit him to love them. Then, seeing that they are not reanimating his senses, frozen by honor, they heap him with abuse, strike him with redoubled blows of their crutches, knock him to the ground, trample him underfoot, and when he is crushed, broken and pounded, lame in every limb, the youngest one, who is at least eighty, crouches over him, tucks up her skirt and sprinkles him with a noxious liquid. He is three-quarters suffocated by it, and immediately, the other two, replacing the first, inundate the unfortunate gentleman with an equally stinking fluid. Finally, all three draw away, saluting him with a "Bonsoir, my Endymion! Au revoir, my Adonis! Adieu, handsome Narcissus!" and leave him in a faint.

When he recovered consciousness, a nearby toad, making fluty sounds delightedly and a cloud of mosquitoes were dancing in the moonlight. He got up, with great difficulty, and resumed his route.

---

[83] This song originates from "Angélique" a short story by Gérard de Nerval published in *Les Filles de feu* (1854).

Once again, Monsieur de Boulingrin had failed to recognize the fays, the mistresses of destiny.

The Duchesse de Cicogne was waiting for him impatiently.

"You're very late, my friend."

He replied to her, while kissing her fingers, that she was very kind to reproach him, and he apologized for the fact that he was suffering somewhat.

"Boulingrin," she said, "sit down here."

And she confided to him that she would gladly consent to receive from his royal treasury a gift of two thousand écus, appropriate to correct the insults of fate in her regard, pharaoh having been terribly contrary to her for six months.

On the advice that the matter was urgent, Bouligrin immediately wrote to Monsieur de La Rochecoupée to ask him for the necessary sum of money.

"La Rochecoupée will be glad to obtain it for you," he said. "He's obliging, and takes pleasure in serving his friends. I will add that one recognizes in him more talents than one ordinarily sees in the favorites of princes. He has taste and business intelligence, but he lacks philosophy. He believes in fays, on the evidence of his senses."

"Boulingrin," said the duchesse, "you stink of cat's piss."

IV

Seventeen years, to the day, had gone by since the fays' sentence. The dauphine was as beautiful as a star. The king and queen were staying, along with the court, at the country residence of Les Eaux-Perdues.[84] Have I any need to relate what happened then? Everyone knows that Princess Aurore, roaming the château one day, went as far as a tower where, alone in an attic, an old woman was threading her distaff. She had not heard of the prohibitions that the king had made of spinning with a spindle.

"What are you doing there, my good woman?" asked the princess.

"I'm spinning, my lovely child," replied the old woman, who did not know her.

"Oh, that's nice!" said the dauphine. "How do you do it? Give it to me. I want to see if I can do it as well."

She had no sooner taken the spindle than she pierced her hand with it and fell unconscious.[85]

King Cloche, informed that the fays' sentence had been carried out, had the sleeping princess put in a blue room, on an azure bed embroidered with silver.

---

[84] *Perdu les eaux* is the French expression parallel to the English reference to a pregnant woman's waters having broken.

[85] The author inserts a specific reference here to Perrault's *Contes*, from which he is quoting literally.

Agitated and consternated, the courtiers readied tears, practiced sighs and composed a dolor. Intrigues were formed on all sides; it was announced that the king was dismissing the ministers. Black calumnies were brooding. It was said that the Duc de La Rochecoupée had concocted a philter to put the dauphine to sleep, and that Monsieur de Boulingrin was his accomplice.

The Duchesse de Cicogne climbed up the little stairway to the abode of her old friend, whom she found in a nightcap, smiling, for he was reading *La Fiancée du roi de Garbe.*[86]

Cicogne told him the news, and how the dauphine was in a lethargy on a blue satin bed. The Secretary of State listened attentively.

"You're not thinking, I hope, my dear friend, that there's the slightest faerie in this?" he said; for he did not believe in fays, even though three of them, ancient and venerable, had stunned him with their amour and their crutches and soaked him to the skin with a noxious liquid in order to prove their existence to him. It is a fault of the experimental method, employed by those ladies, that an experiment addresses the senses, the evidence of which can always be refuted.

"It's certainly a matter of fays!" cried Cicogne. "Madame la Dauphine's accidents might do the greatest harm to you and me. People won't fail to attribute it to the incompetence of ministers, and perhaps their malevolence. Does one know how far the malevolence will go? You're already being accused of parsimony. If you believe the rumors, you've refused, on my interested advice, to pay the guards of the unfortunate young princess. More than that, there's talk of black magic and bewitchment. It's necessary to confront the storm. Show yourself, or you're doomed."

"Calumny," said Boulingrin, "is the scourge of the world; it has killed the greatest men. Anyone who serves his king honestly must be prepared to pay tribute to the monster that crawls and flies."

"Boulingrin," said Cicogne, "get dressed."

And she snatched off his nightcap, which she threw under the bed.

A moment later they were in the antechamber of the apartment where Aurore was asleep, sitting on a bench, waiting to be introduced.

Now, at the news that the sentence of destiny had been accomplished, the fay Viviane, the godmother of the princess, rendered in great haste to Les Eaux-Perdues, and, in order to compose a court for her goddaughter on the day when she would wake up, she touched everyone that was in the château with her wand: "governesses, maids of honor, chambermaids, gentlemen, officers, butlers, cooks, scullions, errand-boys, doormen, pages, footmen; she also touched all the horses in the stables, with the grooms, the mastiffs of the farmyard and

---

[86] *La Fiancée du roi de Gerbe* one of the most licentious of Jean de La Fontaine's "*contes*" in verse, first published in 1666. It would have been familiar to Anatole France, who might also have seen the 1864 comic opera by Daniel Auber based on the poem.

little Pouffe, the princess's little dog, which was next to her on her bed. Even the skewers that were over the fire, full of grouse and pheasants, went to sleep."[87]

Meanwhile, Cicogne and Boulingrin were waiting on their bench, side by side.

"Boulingrin," the duchesse whispered in her old friend's ear, "doesn't this affair seem shady to you? Don't you suspect a conspiracy of the king's brothers to lead the poor fellow to abdicate? Everyone knows that he's a good father. They might want to cast him into despair?"

"That's possible," replied the Secretary of State. "In any case, "there isn't the slightest faerie in this affair. Only worthy country-women believe in those tales of Melusine."

"Shut up, Boulingrin," said the duchesse. "There's nothing as odious as skeptics. They're impertinent people who mock our simplicity. I hate strong minds; I believe that it's necessary to believe—but I suspect a somber conspiracy here..."

As Cicogne pronounced those words, the fay Viviane touched them both with her wand, and put them to sleep like all the rest.

V

"There grew in a quarter of an hour, all around the park, such a great quantity of trees, large and small, brambles and thorns, interlaced with one another, that no beast or human could get through them; with the result that nothing could any longer be seen but the tops of the towers of the château, and then only from a long way away."[88]

Once, twice, three times, fifty, sixty, eighty, ninety and a hundred times Urania closed the ring of time, and the beauty with her court, including Boulingrin, beside his duchesse on the antechamber bench, were still asleep.

Whether one regards time as a mode of the unique substance, whether one defines it as one of the forms of the sensitive self or an abstract state of the immediate exteriority, or whether one makes it purely a law, a relationship resulting from the course of real things, we can affirm that a century is a certain interval of time.

VI

Everyone knows the end of the enchantment, and how, after a hundred terrestrial cycles, a prince favored by the fays traversed the enchanted wood and penetrated as far as the bed where the princess was asleep. He was a German princeling who had a nice moustache and orbicular hips, and with whom, as

---

[87] The author inserts another specific reference to Perrault.

[88] Again the author gives a reference to Perrault.

soon as she was awake, she fell, or rather got up, in love, and whom she followed to his petty principality with such precipitation that she did not even address a single word to the people of her household who had slept with her for a hundred years.

Her first lady-in-waiting was touched by that, and exclaimed, with admiration: "I recognize the blood of my kings."

Boulingrin awoke alongside the Duchesse de Cicogne at the same time as the dauphine and her entire household.

As he rubbed his eyes, his good friend said to him: "Boulingrin, you've been asleep."

"No I haven't," he replied. "No, Madame."

He was sincere. Having slept dreamlessly, he did not perceive that he had been asleep.

"I've slept so little," he said, "that I can repeat to you what you just said a second ago."

"Well, what did I just say?"

"You said: 'I suspect a somber conspiracy.'"

The entire little court was dismissed as soon as its members awoke; everyone had to provide their own means of refection and travel.

Boulingrin and Cicogne hired from the château's steward a seventeenth-century rattletrap hitched to a nag that had already been very old when it had fallen asleep for a century, and had themselves taken to the railway station of Les Eaux-Perdues, where they caught a train that took them to the capital of the realm in two hours. They were very surprised by everything they saw and everything they heard. After a quarter of an hour, however, they had exhausted their astonishment, and nothing any longer caused them to marvel.

They did not interest anyone. People understood absolutely nothing of their story. They did not excite any curiosity, for our minds do not attach themselves either to anything that is too clear or anything that is too obscure for them. Boulingrin, as one can imagine, could not explain what had happened to him at all, but when the duchesse told him that all of it was not natural, he replied:

"Dear friend, permit me to tell you that your physics is very poor. There is nothing that is not natural."

No relative remained to them, nor any friends, nor possessions. They were unable to find the location of their dwelling. With the little money they had on them, they bought a guitar and sang in the streets.

They earned by that means enough to eat. Cicogne gambled at manille by night, in the taverns, all the sous that had been thrown to them during the day, and in the meantime, Boulingrin, in front of a salad bowl of warm wine, explained to the drinkers that it is absurd to believe in fays.

OTHER WORKS OF FRENCH FANTASY
AVAILABLE FROM BLACK COAT PRESS

www.ingramcontent.com/pod-product-compliance
Lightning Source LLC
Chambersburg PA
CBHW032030120726
47901CB00001BA/11